*T*he night air was warm and soft. When Wren awakened, her first thought was of Caleb. For an instant she thought she had only dreamed that he had come to her, loved her. She realized that she was alone, her naked body covered by his shirt.

A splash from the stream attracted her attention; a plume of white shot up as Caleb threw the water over his body. Wren was mesmerized by the sight of him. She rose, casting aside his shirt, and waded into the stream, oblivious of the chill, knowing only that she had to be near him, to feel his arms encircle her once again. . . .

By Fern Michaels
(published by The Random House Publishing Group)

ALL SHE CAN BE
CINDERS TO SATIN
DESPERATE MEASURES
FOR ALL THEIR LIVES
FREE SPIRIT
SEASONS OF HER LIFE
SERENDIPITY
TENDER WARRIOR
TO HAVE AND TO HOLD
TO TASTE THE WINE
VALENTINA
VIXEN IN VELVET

The Captive series
CAPTIVE PASSIONS
CAPTIVE EMBRACES
CAPTIVE SPLENDORS
CAPTIVE INNOCENCE
CAPTIVE SECRETS

The Texas series
TEXAS HEAT
TEXAS RICH
TEXAS FURY
TEXAS SUNRISE

The Sins series
SINS OF OMISSION
SINS OF THE FLESH

CAPTIVE SPLENDORS
&
CAPTIVE SECRETS

TWO NOVELS

FERN MICHAELS

BALLANTINE BOOKS • NEW YORK

2006 Ballantine Books Mass Market Edition

Captive Splendors copyright © 1980 by Fern Michaels Inc.
Captive Secrets copyright © 1991 by Fern Michaels Inc.

All rights reserved.

Published in the United States by Ballantine Books, an imprint of The Random House Publishing Group, a division of Random House, Inc., New York.

BALLANTINE and colophon are registered trademarks of Random House, Inc.

ISBN 0-345-49568-3

Printed in the United States of America

www.ballantinebooks.com

OPM 9 8 7 6 5 4 3 2 1

CAPTIVE SPLENDORS

Prologue

Soft sounds emanated from the center of the large four-poster bed which dominated the geranium-silk-draped room. Impatiently tossing back the bedcovers and exposing their naked bodies to the chill air which even the fire in the grate could not dispel, Caleb van der Rhys rolled over onto his back and brought her with him. In the fire's glow Celeste read his features, seeing there his unadulterated lust and thrilling to the gleam of dominance in his night-dark eyes.

Grasping her hips firmly, he lowered her body onto his, watching the display of emotions cross her face. Her fingers tore into the furring of soft hair on his chest and stroked the tight cords of muscles banded across his ribs. His hair was tousled and dark against the pillow and his eyes bore through her, seeming to command her senses, greedily enjoying the pleasure he was giving her. His strong, lean thighs accepted the burden of her weight; his hands caressed her breasts, then strayed to where their bodies merged, becoming one.

From below, the throb of music could be heard, and the familiar clinking of taproom glasses blended with laughter. As her passions mounted, Celeste lost

1

her awareness of the sounds in Madame du Toit's bordello. The man beneath her was all-consuming.

She felt his eyes burning into her, watching for the approach of her ecstasy. Low moans of desire escaped from deep in her throat, her pulses raced, and a thin sheen of moisture veiled her skin. Suddenly she felt herself tumble backward against the mattress; he followed her movement, burying himself deep within her. And still his eyes watched her, triumphant now, realizing the power he held over her senses, fulfilling her passions while he slaked his own.

In the two years Captain van der Rhys could be counted among Celeste's clientele, she had always found herself looking forward to his next visit. Lusty and powerful, he was a magnificent lover, showing many sides to his expertise. Even now, as she watched him dress, she realized the power he exuded, the heady, masculine strength and potent domination he held over women.

Demanding, forceful, yet with a boyish charm which most women found irresistible, Caleb sat on the edge of the bed and pulled on his soft knee-high boots.

"If you like," she whispered, her voice a soft, contented purr, "I could meet you outside Madame du Toit's."

He smiled, seeming to weigh her words. "Meet me where, my sweet? My ship is my home. Ships' captains don't usually keep apartments in port."

"Marseilles is a very big port," she pouted. "You come here often. I could keep the apartment for you, see to things . . ."

He threw back his head and laughed, the sound filling the room. "Could you, now? Celeste, don't ruin the evening. I've told you before, I have no need for an apartment and less need for a woman to keep it for me. Isn't it enough that the time I do spend in France I spend here with you?" To soften her disappointment, he leaned over and buried his face in her breasts.

2

"No! It is not enough! Once again I will be the laughingstock among the other girls. I am the only woman you seek out here at Madame du Toit's, and yet you care so little for me that you do not keep me for yourself." Her lower lip jutted out in a display of pique, and her finely arched brows came together over the bridge of her upturned nose. "I think perhaps you have other women."

"Certainly I have other women!" he answered good-naturedly. "Just as you have other men!"

"But that is my business!" she retorted, throwing back the covers and kneeling beside him, wrapping her scented arms around his neck in gentle persuasion. "How would I live otherwise? I am sick of Madame du Toit's. Why is it you never bring me out to your ship? I could stay with you, be there whenever you wanted me, instead of only for a few hours at night."

Her petulance was beginning to grate on him. He reached for his waistcoat and pulled it on with a fury. "I've told you I never bring women out to my ship."

"Yes, yes, something about it being a sacred shrine where your father and stepmother realized their love for one another. Bah! I never thought you could be accused of being sentimental!"

Once again Caleb regretted ever having told Celeste about the history of his ship, the *Sea Siren*. He owed his foolishness to the liquor he had consumed and perhaps to a barely admitted loneliness. Instantly he knew he would never again return to Madame du Toit's. Celeste had begun to bore him with her strident demands and pleas.

As if realizing she had pressed too far, Celeste became immediately contrite. She drew herself against him, her lips near his ear, whispering that she would never plague him about his ship again.

His hands found her wealth of golden hair and pulled it viciously until she was once again lying back on the pillows. His mouth came crashing down upon hers, his breath hot and wine-scented. Her pulses throbbed rhythmically, her fingers tore at his clothing, her hips arched in offering. His lips trailed a familiar path from her mouth to her breasts; his hands possessed her, igniting fires she had thought were quenched.

A slow, sly smile tugged at the corner of her mouth and her long, slanted eyes gleamed with conquest. He forgave her; he always would. In time she would manipulate him, make him see he couldn't live without her. She wanted him, needed him; in all her experience she had never known another man like him. His touch could fire her passions, his lips could conquer her desires. A slow curl of heat warmed her like a summer sun, and she knew she wanted him, again, and again . . .

When she had reached a dizzying height, Caleb tossed her away from him, leaving her hanging over an empty abyss. "That's right, Celeste, you'll never plague me again."

His boots were almost soundless on the carpet as he strode to the door and banged it shut behind him.

Chapter One

Tyler Payne Sinclair strode down the wide gallery which winged out over the main staircase and entrance hall of his London town house. As he glanced at the impressive row of family portraits lining the wall, he again realized how difficult it was for him to comprehend that, since his father's death, he had inherited the title of Baron and taken his father's place in Parliament. All the dire threats put forth by his parents to disinherit him if he should ever marry his distant cousin, Camilla Langdon, had not come to fruition. When Camilla's jackanapes father had finally met his end at the hand of Sirena van der Rhys, the elder Sinclairs had experienced a change of heart. Or so they had told themselves and Tyler, explaining that Camilla, once free of Stephan Langdon's evil influence, had been found to be a girl of exquisite taste and a loving nature. It had never been spoken aloud that they would sooner have cut off their arms than alienate themselves from their only son.

Tyler's dark eyes became thoughtful as a squeal of girlish laughter rang in his ears. He would sorely miss Wren when she left with Sirena and Regan, who were expected in London within a fortnight. Now that Camilla had at last come into her own with approaching motherhood and little else filled her thoughts, he would be lost without Wren's exuberance for life and her flattering dependency on him.

How alike the beautiful Sirena and Wren were, yet how unalike. He supposed he should resign himself to the fact that he would always worry about her in the manner of an older brother. He could never seem to gain the detachment toward her that even the role of a substitute stepfather would designate during these years in which Wren had come under his care. He sighed heavily. It was time for Wren to return to the Spice Islands with Sirena and Regan and find her place in life, whatever that might be. Just as long as it didn't include that dandy, Malcolm Weatherly.

God! How was he to explain that fop to Sirena? He shuddered as he pictured how those emerald eyes would spew fire when she was told that her little Wren was bent on marrying that rapscallion as soon as he could properly ask for her hand. A grudging smile split Tyler's handsome face. If Malcolm Weatherly managed to escape Sirena's fury, he would find he still had Regan to deal with. Tyler imagined he himself should be chagrined to consider that Regan might be able to gain control of a situation where he had not, but he soothed his spirit with the thought that Regan had not lived under Wren's charm and winning ways for these past three yeears.

Tyler had found it impossible to deny Wren anything, and Camilla had found herself in the same predicament, especially where it concerned Mr. Weatherly's courtly attentions. In fact, Camilla's fondness for Wren was surprising on all accounts. Tyler smiled again as he thought of his pretty blond wife. Camilla had come a long, long way from that pretty, empty-headed young girl he had known and loved in spite of her selfish, self-serving behavior. She had grown into a loving, tender woman, and Wren, as well

6

as he, was grateful for her cloak of maternal regard. The only area where Camilla was disapproving of Wren lay in the young girl's friendship with the Puritan, Sara Stoneham. But even in that Camilla was being protective and defensive of her little family. The Puritans were speaking out dangerously against the King's control of the Church of England, and there were even rumblings of civil war.

As a member of Parliament, Tyler knew Camilla's fears were not unfounded, but he refused to allow his own concern to color his feelings toward Wren's young friend. Sara Stoneham was a lovely girl from a notable family, one he had known for years. If her religious preference was different from his, it mattered little to Tyler. Besides, how could he, in all conscience, have turned Sara out into the street when she had come here, at Wren's invitation, to await the arrival of her parents in London?

Tyler quickened his step toward the elaborately carved door of Wren's apartment to bid the girls good night. He had lifted his hand to knock when the sound of their voices penetrated the thick panel.

"Wren! In the name of all that's holy, I didn't think you were ever coming back! What could you have been thinking of? Sneaking off with Malcolm and staying out so late! What if the Baron or the Baroness popped in to say good night? What would I have told them?"

Wren spun around the room, her blue and mauve striped silk skirt ballooning away from her slim legs like a brightly colored parasol. She hugged her arms close to herself, an expression of rapture softening her features. "Ooh, Sara, don't spoil this for me. You're always so disapproving every time I'm with Malcolm. Not tonight. Please?" Wren's eyes glowed softly in the light of the lamp, her thick lashes casting feathery shadows on her smooth cheeks.

Sara noticed the huskiness in Wren's voice and that

7

her hair was disarrayed and wispy tendrils curled toward her ivory brow. There was no mistaking that look of voluptuous satisfaction which pouted her kiss-bruised lips, nor the languid, sensuous expression in her eyes. Sara was familiar with these outward signs of lovemaking. She had seen them branded on her own features after slipping out of school for a spring night's rendezvous. And, like Wren, but unknown to her, she, too, had spent breathless hours in Malcolm Weatherly's arms. She knew how the touch of Malcolm's hands on her flesh could transport her to worlds never before imagined . . . how his lips could plead and then tease until she was half mad with wanting him, with wanting to give herself to him. Then, suddenly, it had ended. The secret notes had stopped arriving; when she had slipped out of the dormitory at night, hoping to meet him, she had waited until the chill, damp, early-morning air had penetrated her clothing, causing her to shudder from the cold and from the deeper, more painful quiver of love lost.

After several weeks of pining for Malcolm and experiencing rapidly dropping grades, Sara had heard it rumored that Wren van der Rhys was keeping trysts with a handsome stranger. Her suspicions aroused, Sara had managed to befriend Wren and learned that indeed it was Malcolm Weatherly who tempted the innocent, young Wren to brave the dark and perilous rose trellis for a few moments in his arms. It was torture being here with Wren and knowing she was Malcolm's new love, but Sara was beyond helping herself. In some undefinable way, being close to Wren was like being near Malcolm.

"You don't like Malcolm, do you, Sara?" Wren said quietly, touching her friend's sleeve. "I know you've gone along with my little deceptions, but underneath you disapprove, don't you?"

Sara turned so that Wren couldn't see her face. She wanted to lash out, to scratch Wren's beautiful face, to force her to face the truth. Poor silly little Wren. Couldn't she see that Malcolm was more interested in her family's wealth than he was in her? Sara wished she had the courage to tell Wren that Malcolm had loved *her*, Sara, until he had discovered that the Stonehams had lost favor with the Crown over some loose remarks about the King's failure to call together a session of Parliament. Times were uneasy for Puritans, to say the least. A swift seizure of properties, and the Stonehams were on the verge of bankruptcy. But to reveal this to Wren would mean a certain end to their relationship and to her vicarious closeness to Malcolm. Sara's only satisfaction lay in the fact that Malcolm didn't love Wren. It was just a scheming, self-serving game he was playing. Sara knew she should hate Malcolm Weatherly, and she'd even experienced twinges of guilt because she was keeping the truth from Wren, but she couldn't hate him. She loved Malcolm Weatherly more than she had ever loved another person in her entire life. I must love him, she told herself; otherwise what kind of person am I, to have allowed him to do the things he has done to me?

A sly smile tugged at the corners of Sara's generous mouth when she remembered the nights alone in Malcolm's arms, the things she had done, the things she had permitted Malcolm to do to her. No one in the world knew what they had shared, and Malcolm certainly wouldn't tell.

"Sara, answer me," Wren persisted. "Why don't you like Malcolm?"

"Wren, it's not that I don't like him. It's just that . . . how will you explain Malcolm to your . . . to Sirena and Regan?"

"Why can't you ever bring yourself to refer to Sirena and Regan as my parents? They are, you know. They're the only parents I've ever had, and they consider me their very own daughter," Wren an-

9

nounced defiantly, her amber eyes lighting from within.

"Not in the true sense of the word, Wren," Sara said falteringly. She recognized that light in Wren's eyes, and it only meant an ensuing argument for the unfortunate person who dared to cross swords with her. Sara swallowed and pressed onward. "One of these days you're going to realize that Sirena doesn't belong on a pedestal and that she's a human being like the rest of us mortals. And you must stop thinking about the infamous sea witch—you're always talking about her and making her your idol. For shame, Wren! Here you are, contemplating marriage with old Mally, and it's time to leave such fantasies behind. Now that you've finished school and are ready to meet society, you must put all that nonsense behind you. Do you understand what I'm saying?"

Sara faced Wren and saw that her ploy had been successful. Once again she had put doubts in Wren's mind about the relationship between herself and her parents. She was quick to see that the seeds she had sown weeks ago as to Wren's rightful use of the van der Rhys name had taken root and had begun to flower. Besides, this well-worn path of conversation was a perfect distraction for Wren's too-personal questions concerning Sara's opinion of Malcolm.

Outside the door, Tyler massaged his temples. He hadn't meant to eavesdrop, but hearing that Wren had slipped out of the house for a clandestine meeting with Weatherly had stunned him. He hadn't realized things had progressed so far. Now he found himself anticipating Wren's answer. Sara was correct. Wren had been living in a make-believe world, and her fantasies were the prime reason she had fallen prey to Malcolm Weatherly's charm. The stories about the Sea Siren, infamous piratess, told to Wren when she was a child, were meant to be just that. Stories. Fairy tales for a child to dream about, not a basis on which Wren should build her life.

"Sara Stoneham! There is a person, a real person, who was the Sea Siren! I really don't care if you believe me or not, but you're wrong—she doesn't occupy all my thoughts, and I know you think I'm trying to pattern my life after her, but I'm not! There could never be another Sea Siren." A wistful note crept into Wren's voice. "The Siren was the most beautiful creature who ever rode the seas. Long, flowing hair, eyes the color of emeralds and skin like spun honey. She was a master of fencing, and there wasn't a man who could best her. I could never hope to compete with her, either in looks or in actions. My eyes are the wrong color and my skin is too pale. And I'm too short, much too short. And try as I might, I'll never equal her skill with the rapier."

"See? Listen to yourself! Do you hear you compare yourself to that sea witch in such an unfavorable light?" Sara grasped Wren's wrist and dragged her over to the pier glass. "Look at yourself! Look!" Reluctantly, Wren lifted her eyes to the glass. "Now, tell me that what you see there is not more beautiful than any fantasy about a female pirate! Tell me that just the sight of you doesn't turn all men's eyes. I've been to the Royal Exchange with you, Wren. I've seen the effect you have on the masculine sex. Didn't Rolland Chalmers send you love notes that nearly singed the fingertips? What did he say to you? That your hair was a cloud of dark night and your eyes were golden embers and your skin—"

"Stop it, Sara!" Wren wrenched herself away. "I never said I was ugly!" she protested.

"True. But you compare yourself to this sea witch and it eats at you. Admit it, Wren. Why can't you put these thoughts behind you? Take a word of advice from an old friend. You'd better concentrate on the problem at hand. Prepare yourself for what your guardians are going to do when they find out about Malcolm. Somehow I can't see the van der Rhyses

11

giving your their blessings over old Mally, not after what you told me about them."

"They'd better give it, otherwise I'll run away," Wren declared recklessly.

It was time to intervene, Tyler decided. Privacy be damned. He knocked and opened the door at the same time. "It's late, young ladies, and you need your beauty sleep. Or so my wife has been telling me all these years." He looked from one girl to the other. Sara was tall and slender, like a yellow tea rose, he told himself. And Wren was like a tapered candle flame. Right now her eyes were like banked fires, ready to flare into flame if the conversation were allowed to continue. The girl had an ungovernable temper where it concerned Sirena and the Sea Siren.

Sara laughed, tossed her white-gold curls and quickly embraced Wren. "Baron Sinclair is right, Wren. We get along so well and we're best friends. Let's not spoil it now. Besides," she added coquettishly, "Baron Sinclair has been so kind in allowing me to spend these few days with you before my parents arrive, I must insist that I am on his side."

"I didn't realize we were taking sides," Wren snapped as she wriggled out of Sara's embrace. "Tyler is right, though. We do need our beauty sleep—at least I do. Malcom is taking me to the country tomorrow and I want to look my best. Don't frown so, Tyler," she said as she threw her arms about him. "Sirena will love Malcolm just as I do, and believe me when I tell you she won't hold it against you that I've been permitted to see him. She's going to love him, you'll see."

"Somehow, little one, I can't share your optimism."

"You're behaving like the new father you soon will be," Wren teased, yet there was a ring of steel in her voice that could set Tyler's teeth rattling. He knew in his gut that Sirena would take one look at the modish Malcolm Weatherly and rip out her rapier and cut him

12

to pieces. Also, Sirena would blame him from start to finish for the relationship between Wren and Weatherly. Sirena van der Rhys never did things in half. No, he would receive full blame, and if she didn't cut him down, then Regan would. Wren was the apple of Regan's eye, and no dandy was going to snap up his little girl. Perhaps they would take mercy on Tyler when he told them he was about to become a father. He blanched as he imagined Sirena's face after she heard the news. How well he knew her. She would say, "Congratulations," and then cut him down. She had style, he must admit. Camilla would be forced to intervene on his behalf, and he would take the coward's way out. God, how could he have been so foolish to let Wren get herself tangled up with Weatherly? How could he have foreseen that a mild flirtation would blossom into an engagement? Why didn't he insist, right now, that she make a quick end of Weatherly? Because the girl could wrap him around her little finger—it was that simple. Women had always been his weakness. Jehovah! He hoped Camilla gave birth to a boy; otherwise he wouldn't have a chance of living to forty. He had to get himself in hand; he couldn't let the girls see how upset he was. He forced a smile to his lips, quickly pecked both of them on the cheek and exited the room, his stomach crawling with fear. Sirena would cut him down in his prime.

Sara's hyacinth eyes were watchful as she and Wren prepared for bed. "Are you really going to take a drive with Mally tomorrow?"

"Sara Ann Stoneham, stop calling Malcolm *Mally.* Yes, I'm going for a carriage ride with the man I'm going to marry. Not another word, Sara Ann," Wren shouted as she dived under the covers, her amber eyes peeping out from behind the satin-edged quilt.

"Very well," Sara acquiesced. "As your infamous Sea Siren would say, 'It's your neck!'"

13

Chapter Two

The hour was late, the night dark and silent as the hackney carrying Sirena and Regan van der Rhys made its way through the winding, narrow streets devoid of people and noise. *As dark and silent as my thoughts,* Sirena mused as she peered through the dirty panes of the carriage. The hack was taking the route from the docks to Tyler Sinclair's house, the same route she had taken with Frau Holtz nearly nine years ago when she had come in search of Regan. Bitter memories stained the joy at seeing Wren again. Whenever she thought about the time she had been forced to live in England, she knew a hatred almost as strong as that which she still harbored for the memory of Stephan Langdon. Pressing her shoulder securely on Regan's as he rolled against her in sleep, she felt a small knot of something akin to fear weave its way around her stomach. How did Regan feel about returning to England? Returning not only to England, but to the house of his former wife. What would the flowerlike Camilla be like now that she was married to Tyler? By now, with the lapse of time, childlike Camilla would be a woman fully grown, complete with a woman's wiles. Would she tease and flirt with Regan,

and what would be Regan's reaction? Sirena sighed.
She wouldn't find out this evening, that was for certain. Dawn would soon be approaching. The Sinclair
household would be asleep and unprepared for guests.
Surely Tyler wouldn't mind that she and Regan were
arriving a week ahead of schedule. Nothing annoyed
Tyler.

A smile tugged at the corners of her mouth as she
recalled their days in Newgate Prison. In truth, that
experience was probably the only thing that had ever
annoyed good old Tyler. And if the truth were told,
he had probably enjoyed every minute of it.

Sirena sighed again, wearily. That had been so long
ago. Another time, another life. Unconsciously, she
reached out to touch Regan, to reassure herself that he
was still there. How wonderful he felt, so hard and
firm. And how vulnerable he looked in sleep. Her
bottle-green eyes lighted up momentarily as she realized that Regan was not in the least vulnerable. Well,
perhaps in one area, where Wren was concerned. How
eager he was to see the girl, to wrap her in his arms
and make the sounds all fathers make when they look
at their beloved daughters. Even though Regan and
Sirena had adopted Wren, they couldn't have loved her
more if she had truly been theirs. Was this because
they had produced four strapping boys who one day
would be like Regan and Caleb? Sirena often wished
she had given Regan a daughter of his own. No
matter, Wren was their daughter, and that was enough.
She carried the van der Rhys name, and Sirena was
her mother and Regan was her father. And little Wren
had five brothers who loved her dearly. Especially
Caleb.

The hackney came to an abrupt halt and Regan
was jostled from his comfortable position against her
shoulder. "Good God, Sirena, are we finally here?"

Sirena patted his arm. "Now, Regan, remember
your promise to me. You won't demand that Wren be

awakened. Morning is soon enough. As a matter of fact, it would be wise to insist that neither Camilla nor Tyler be awakened. Your promise, Regan."

Regan grinned. "I must have been drunk when I agreed to such a promise, sweetheart."

"Not drunk, darling, just in a rather compromising position."

"One of these days I'll manage to be one step ahead of you, Sea Witch," he said fondly.

"I miss the children and I want to return to Java as quickly as possible. That was part of the promise."

"You're jealous of Camilla. I've felt it ever since we approached English waters," Regan teased.

"You're a bull, Regan, and I'm not jealous. If she makes one false move in your direction, it's *your* eyes I'll scratch out!"

Regan shuddered. She would do it, too. She might be the mother of four strapping boys and the stepmother of two other children, but she could best him in any way she chose and he knew it, not that he would ever admit it to her. Even now, after all these years, she was still as slim and fast as she had been when he first met her. Little did she know that he was aware that she still practiced daily with her rapier. One day he had by chance overheard her telling Frau Holtz that it was the only way to keep fit. As usual, she was right, he grimaced as his hands found their way to his midsection. Too much good food and rum would ruin the best of men. Not that he overindulged, but it was so easy to throw caution to the winds when a man was happy and contented. Regan was more happy and contented than he had ever been in his life, and now that Wren would be going back to Java with them, his cup would run over. The only thing missing was Caleb. If Cal would only see fit to make his home with them in Java, he swore to all the Gods in Heaven that he would never sin again. What more could a man ask?

"Do try to be quiet, Regan. We don't want to awaken the entire household."

"My dear, I will walk on tiptoe, as though I were walking on eggs. You need to have no fear of my awakening your dear friend Tyler."

"You're baiting me, Regan. Morning is only a few hours away, and sleep is what you need."

"If you're trying to tell me I'm getting old and feeble, you can bite your tongue, young woman. I can still outshine that Sinclair, and well you know it. I'll tell you one thing: I'm not looking forward to seeing either him or Camilla. I gave you my word that we would leave as soon as it was decently possible. I'll keep my word. No noise, I'll sleep in your arms, and you'll wake me at the first early light. I want to see what manner of young lady our Wren has become."

Giggling like two small children, Regan and Sirena followed an aging servant up the curving staircase.

"Reminds me of the time I spent three days in Clarice's brothel." Regan grinned as he pinched Sirena on the thigh.

"If you think I'm going to ask you to tell me about *that* little escapade, dear husband, you're wrong. I'll take it up with you tomorrow," she said, her eyes glinting dangerously.

"A slip of the tongue, sweetheart. You know how boastful I am at times. It was Dykstra who spent three days there. I merely stopped by to see how business was doing."

"You kept that—that—*establishment* in business all by yourself. Don't blame Captain Dykstra," Sirena hissed.

"Well, I do feel a certain responsibility for him. After all, I did take him there, and Clarice . . . what she did . . . actually . . . You're right, we'll discuss it tomorrow. Suddenly I feel so tired I can barely keep my eyes open."

"If I were you, I'd sleep with them open the rest of the night," Sirena warned ominously.

The moment the door closed behind the servant, Regan gathered Sirena in his arms and kissed her passionately. God, how he loved her. He had baited her on purpose just to see her respond with anger. It was his way of proving to himself that she still loved him. He had to see her anger to know for certain that their love had not banked, that it could be rekindled in a moment with a few choice words. Right or wrong, he had to do it, and Sirena understood and played the game right along with him. God, how he loved her. Even more now than on the day he had married her for the second time.

Tyler Sinclair descended the stairs with the same worried expression on his face as he had worn when he had finally drifted off to sleep. He felt his stomach churn as the housekeeper told him that the van der Rhyses had arrived unexpectedly during the night and insisted that the Baron and the Baroness remain undisturbed.

"Is the Baroness ready for breakfast?" the housekeeper asked.

"The Baroness is feeling under the weather this morning. Have one of the maids bring her some mint tea and a sweet roll in about an hour. She will be down for luncheon with our guests."

Good Lord, what am I going to say to Sirena? he wondered as he seated himself at the breakfast table. Perhaps he was worrying about nothing. Both of them might really like Malcolm Weatherly. No one likes Malcolm Weatherly except Wren, he answered himself. Camilla had said that Malcolm could pass muster in a dark room, but this was the bright light of day, and both Sirena and Regan were clear-eyed and as sharp as axes.

Tyler bit into a sweet roll and chewed with a vengeance. Two more rolls and two more cups of coffee laced with rum—or was it three cups of rum laced with coffee?—and he was ready to meet any and all challengers, providing they didn't carry a rapier or a cutlass. Damn it, he was feeling the edges of drunkenness and it was still breakfast time. To be cut down in his prime! "Never mind the coffee, just give me the bottle," he demanded of the cook.

"But, Baron Sinclair, your kippers are ready, and Cook prepared them especially for you."

"Kip, kip, kip," Tyler hiccuped drunkenly. "The child is nothing more than a little kipper, that's what she is."

"Do my eyes deceive me, or are you drunk?" Sirena's melodious voice called out from the doorway. "Two hours past dawn and you're in your cups." Camilla must be up to some of her old tricks to make Tyler resort to spirits so early in the morning, Sirena mused. Tyler was no sot; at least he had never been one before. On the other hand, being married to Camilla should be reason enough to turn to drink. Hadn't Regan tipped the bottle more than usual during his short-lived marriage to that fair petal of flowerhood? A wide smile broke across Sirena's face as she patted a perspiring Tyler on his head. "I can forgive you anything, Tyler, since you've been so generous to give our Wren a home and take care of her."

Tyler extended a shaking hand to grasp Regan's and finally conceded failure when he couldn't establish contact.

"You resemble a fish out of water, Sinclair," Regan said, his eyes narrowed in suspicion. No self-respecting man drank at dawn, or what passed for dawn in this damnable country. Camilla was undoubtedly leading Tyler a merry chase. Suddenly Regan grinned as the thought struck him that, but for the grace of God, he could be walking in Sinclair's

19

boots. Mercifully there was a God, and every day he thanked Him for his good fortune.

Tyler thought the van der Rhyses a striking pair. Regan looked as fit and agile as a man twenty years his junior. Only a slight salting of gray at the temples hinted that it was almost nine years since Tyler had last seen him. He noted happily that Sirena had been treated well by the passage of time. A vague aura of maturity about her belied the sparkle in her extraordinary green eyes, and she wore her hair in a more sedate style, rather than loose and flowing. But her figure was still trim and girlish. Tyler had a vision of Sirena as she had looked aboard her ship, her long, tawny legs revealed by tatter-edged breeches cut up to her curvaceous hips, the salt spray glistening on her skin, her dark hair free to blow in the wind. He knew that beneath her wide skirts and decorous manner still lived the beautiful Sea Siren.

"Tell me, Tyler, how is your business thriving?" Sirena asked.

Tyler flinched. Damn her, she knew something was troubling him, and she hadn't changed a bit. She knew it had something to do with Wren; he could feel it in his bones and see it in her sea-green eyes. There was nothing for him to do but tell both of them the straight of it. With any luck, they would listen with open minds and hear him through. Mentally he squared his shoulders and stood up, his back to the seated couple. He fixed his gaze out the window, on a tree swaying in the early-morning breeze, and watched a sparrow take wing.

Sirena and Regan exchanged glances and waited patiently for him to speak.

"You were never one of my favorite people, van der Rhys," Tyler began, "but you, Sirena, were always like a sister to me. I agreed to look out for Wren and act as her guardian while she was here at the academy. I've done the best I could, but you,

Sirena, filled her head with so many tales of the Sea Siren and all that rubbish that there was little I could do when it came to things of that nature. She's devious, something I found very hard to accept. Camilla tells me that all young girls are impressionable and devious; she calls it women's wiles. What I'm trying to say to you is that Wren fancies she is in love with and wants to marry a man named Malcolm Weatherly. She plans to have him ask for her hand. The young man is a dandy, a fop of the worst sort."

"What's this tale you're peddling, Sinclair?" Regan demanded, leaping from his chair. His intentions were clear to Sirena, who reached out for his arm.

"Regan, hear him out," she pleaded.

"Thank you, Sirena," Tyler said quietly, grateful for her interference. All signs of inebriation gone, he proceeded to tell them what he knew. "You see, I was unaware of this affair until very recently, and then I learned about it quite by accident. From what I've been able to gather, Wren met this Weatherly while at the academy. She was shopping in town when she happened to make his acquaintance. She continued to see him without the knowledge of her teachers or the headmistress. This is what I meant about her being devious, or wily, if you prefer. Now that I have the straight of it, I can tell you the whole story. After the nightly bed check made by the dormitory housemother, Wren would slip out and meet Weatherly somewhere on the grounds. It seems that one night the headmistress couldn't sleep and decided to go to the library for a book. It was there that she discovered the two lovers in what she termed a 'shocking embrace.' The headmistress then questioned Wren, who had the good sense to tell the truth. In turn, the matter was brought to my attention with the request to remove Wren from her classes. She came here with a friend of hers, Sara Stoneham, who was a party to the affair. Sara would let Wren back into the dormitory at night after the lovers' tryst. Her parents are due to arrive in London within the next few days to take her home. I'm afraid they're quite shocked by the whole matter. They're Puritans," he added, as if that explained everything.

"Your Wren is a very determined young lady," he went on, "and we've had to allow Weatherly admittance to see her. If we didn't, Wren announced that she would run off with him. What would you have had me do, Sirena? Right or wrong, I thought it best to keep her here till you arrived and took matters in your own . . . capable hands. God only knows what would become of her if she ran off with that fop. That's it," he concluded, turning about, a high flush on his cheeks.

"Damn your eyes, Sinclair!" Regan roared. "I trust you with my daughter and look what happens! One small favor, that was all we asked, and you couldn't handle it! It's a damn good thing you aren't a parent!"

Tyler's eyes were tortured. "I know," he said morosely, "but now I find that in a few short months I will be. All I can say is I'm sorry for this other news."

Sirena leaned back in her chair, her eyes thoughtful. "It's not your fault, Tyler. I see how it happened, and you're right. Wren is an impressionable child— at least she was when she left us. I had hoped she would outgrow that quality as time passed. And it wasn't only I who filled her with tales of the Sea Siren. Frau Holtz allowed the child to cut her teeth on the tales of my derring-do. I place no blame on your shoulders, old friend, nor does Regan. Right now he's a trifle upset, but when he has time to think on the matter, he'll realize you are not responsible. We're at fault. It was a mistake to have sent her here at such an early age. She needed more guidance, more parental love. No, it is Regan and I who are to blame. What we have to do is to look at the matter calmly

22

and arrive at some sort of solution. We cannot alienate Wren; we love her too much. A talk with the man of her choice will be in order, of course. Also a talk with her friend's parents. It is well that we arrived early to put all these matters straight, don't you agree, Regan?" Sirena touched him lightly on the hand.

Her light touch and calm voice worked their soothing magic on the irate Dutchman.

Regan's tone was brisk when he addressed Tyler. "A drink, Sinclair, to show that neither my wife nor I hold you responsible. We both know that Wren is capable of being wily. She's manipulated me on more than one occasion, and she was still a child at the time. I'm afraid that when it comes to women, we men are at their mercy."

"That's damn white of you, van der Rhys," Tyler said in a relieved tone. "If we put our heads together and really talk this out, we should be able to come up with a solution. She can't be permitted to marry that ass. If we start from there, we'll think of something. For now, why don't we enjoy our kippers?"

While Sirena and Regan breakfasted, Wren was getting dressed, her eyes wary as she watched Sara go about her morning ablutions. Sooner or later the articulate Sara would start to chastise her. The sooner she got on with it, the sooner she would be finished. Why did everyone think he or she had to expound on her affairs? The only one who seemed to be on her side was Camilla. Camilla said there was nothing more beautiful than young love. Camilla should know. Hadn't she loved Tyler from the time she was sixteen years old?

"Are you ready, Sara?" Wren asked quietly.

"Yes, and I'm famished. I hope Cook has prepared something extra special this morning."

Evidently the voluble Sara wasn't going to say anything. Wren shrugged. Maybe Sara had finally realized that Wren wasn't going to pay any attention to her vicious comments about Malcolm. What could a straight-laced Puritan know about love anyway?

The two girls descended the wide, circular staircase, which was thickly carpeted in a deep burgundy and muffled their footsteps. Suddenly Wren put a finger to her lips to warn the other girl to be quiet. She frowned. The voices she heard sounded like Regan's and Sirena's. It couldn't be! They weren't due for another week . . . It was! With a sound akin to a war whoop, she raced down the remaining stairs, leaving a wide-eyed Sara behind. Catapulting into the dining room, she threw herself into Sirena's arms and hugged her with all her might. Satisfied that the living, breathing Sirena was no mirage, she extricated herself and turned to Regan.

His anguish of moments ago forgotten, Regan felt his face split into a grin as he clasped the laughing, happy girl to him.

Sirena watched the display of emotion between the two and felt sentimental tears smear her eyes.

"When did you get here? Why didn't you wake me? How long can you stay? Did Tyler tell you about Sara? It's so good to see you! I'm so happy," Wren squealed delightedly. "Look, here is my friend Sara. Come." She beckoned to the girl standing in the doorway.

The introductions completed and the girls seated with plates of food in front of them, Regan leaned back and lighted one of his cheroots, apologizing for smoking at the table. He wanted his cigar, and he didn't want to go into Tyler's library for fear he would miss something.

It was Sirena who took the initiative and spoke first. "Well, little one, it seems that Tyler's duties are coming to an end. Are you ready to return to the Spice Islands and make your home with us again? We've missed you."

"Darling Sirena, do we have to discuss that now? I'm so happy just seeing the two of you that I don't want to talk about anything *except* the two of you. Tell me, how are the boys, and have you heard from Caleb?" If Wren noticed the tightness around Regan's mouth, she gave no sign as she filled her mouth with kippers.

"You won't recognize the boys," he said. "They've grown so, I barely recognize them myself. Each is as fair as a staff of wheat, but with their mother's green eyes. Caleb is still shipping cargo for the Dutch East India Company and making a thriving show for his efforts. We have no complaints other than we've all missed our little girl and want her home with us so we can be a family again."

Now, say it now, Wren, Sirena pleaded silently. Don't make it harder for Regan, for if you do, he may never forgive you. Be honest, little one. Do it now; say what has to be said now. Surely you must know that Tyler has told us of your plans.

Wren carefully avoided Sirena's eyes. "You've told me of everyone but Frau Holtz and Jacobus. How are they? How I've missed the Frau," Wren sighed, smiling at Regan.

"You know that the Frau married Jacobus and made an honest man of the old sea salt. They're both well and send their regards and can barely contain themselves till your arrival."

Say it, Sirena continued to beg silently. Wren continued to ignore her mother's silent thoughts.

It was obvious that Sara was embarrassed for her friend. She placed her napkin on the table and directed a pleading look at Tyler. Interpreting her gaze correctly, he rose and held out his hand. "If you'll excuse us, I promised to show Sara a book I purchased yesterday. She wants it as a gift for her father."

Regan rose politely, and Sirena smiled at the departing girl. Wren was on her own, it appeared and would get no help from her friend, which was as it should be.

Silence. Each was waiting for the other to say something. The girl should know that Regan could outwait a tropical storm. Much squirming and downcast eyes did nothing for his disposition. He waited. Sirena waited. Wren swallowed hard and looked squarely at Regan. "I'm sure that Tyler has told you . . ."

"Sirena and I would prefer that you tell us," Regan said quietly. "Both of us are disappointed that you didn't see fit to write of your coming plans."

"A letter wouldn't have reached you in time," Wren cried miserably. "I know that you both must be disappointed, but sometimes these things happen. A woman meets a man and they fall in love. Isn't that what happened between you and Sirena? I can't help how I feel. I didn't want it to happen, but it did. I'm certain you'll both like Malcolm and that he will like you. He loves me dearly, and I think he will make me a fine husband. With your approval, of course," she added hastily.

Sirena sat back and let Regan do the talking. He was so much better at handling Wren than she was. "First of all, young lady, Sirena and I were not boy and girl; we were man and woman. You're but a child compared with Sirena at your age. We sent you here for an education, not to have you fall head over heels for the first dandy who pays you any mind. The world is full of men like Malcolm Weatherly. We had hoped that an education would help you acquire a little judgment. Now we learn the headmistress expelled not only you but also your friend. Tell me, Wren, was it showing good judgment when you involved another in your escapades? Think of how Sara's parents must feel. By helping you, her friend, she earned a black mark against her reputation. It was thoughtless of you. A woman wouldn't do something so foolish, and that's why Sirena and I question your emotions concerning Malcolm Weatherly. It seems that you have more growing up to do. If your swain is bent on asking me for your hand, I am afraid I must deny it."

Wren's eyes narrowed and then flamed. "Sirena was one year older than I when she married you," she said coolly. "And, Regan, you're not my father, so if you do deny my hand to Malcolm, I'll run off with him."

If she had shot him a blow to the heart, she couldn't have wounded Regan more. Sirena wanted to reach out and slap the defiant pout on Wren's mouth. How could she have spoken in that way?

"Regan is the only father you've ever known. How dare you speak to him in such a manner! Apologize this instant!" Sirena demanded furiously.

"And you're not my mother!" Wren cried suddenly as the enormity of what she had said struck her. Never one to back off, she lashed out again. "I never asked you to pick me up off the street. I never asked you for anything. I worked for you and Frau Holtz. I did my share and wanted to do more, but you wouldn't let me. I never wanted to come here and go to that fancy school. You forced me to! I pleaded with you, begged you, and all either of you could say was that it was for my own good. Now you tell me it isn't. Don't I deserve the right to be happy? How can you deny me the one thing I'm asking of you? The one thing I'm asking in all the years you've cared for me. Tell me, Sirena. Can you tell me, Regan?" she all but shouted. "No, I see you can't!" Tears streaming down her cheeks, she ran from the room and made for the front door, almost upsetting a maid carrying a heavy tray.

Sirena's own eyes were as moist as Regan's as they rose to look out the window at Wren's retreating back. Sirena tugged at Regan's arm. "She didn't mean it, I'm sure she didn't. Girls say things they don't mean when they're upset. Right now she thinks she's in love. We have to be patient and let her know we understand, that we pray things will work out for the best. We can't allow ourselves to become angry and say things we don't mean. We're the adults, and we must act like parents. Please don't be hurt, Regan. I couldn't bear it."

Regan gathered her in his arms. "As usual, you're right. We'll do our best to make the right decisions for Wren." His voice faltered.

Tyler, drawn by the commotion, bounded into the room. His heart felt as if it would break when he saw the expressions on Regan's and Sirena's faces. He was powerless to offer words of encouragement; instead, he offered another cup of coffee.

Sirena's eyes went to Regan's granite face, then to Tyler's helpless-looking countenance, and from there to the shimmering silver and crystal on the breakfast table. She knew she should say something to make Regan's sorrow lift. Wren in love! Beautiful, child-like little Wren in love! Impossible! And, according to Tyler, with a bounder, no less!

Her long, slender fingers toyed with an ornate silver spoon as her mind raced. Womanly instinct warned her to be silent, but how could she bear the stricken look on Regan's face? He was wounded to the quick. She was not fooled; in her heart she knew he had harbored a secret hope, a desire actually, that Wren and Caleb would one day find each other. Gossamer dreams. Yet she, too, had hoped for the same thing.

Tyler broke the silence, his voice measured and quiet. "Time. Perhaps time is the answer. When she goes back to Java with you, things will mend."

"Tell me, Tyler, how does one mend a broken heart?" Sirena asked coolly. Regan's eyes remained inscrutable.

"Absence makes the heart . . ."

"Grow fonder," Sirena finished the sentence.

"In her own way Wren is as spirited as Sirena,"

Regan declared. "If she fancies herself in love, no amount of talking or cajoling is going to change anything. We have to come up with some sort of . . . plan to make her see this oaf for what he is. Between the three of us, we should be able to think of something. What does Camilla have to say about all this?" Regan demanded of Tyler.

"In all honesty, I don't know, and I haven't had the heart to concern her with the problem. Wait till you see her, Sirena. She's come a far way from the girl you once knew." Tyler's eyes shone as his face split into a proud grin. "However, not to digress. When Camilla's pregnancy became apparent to Weatherly, it was obvious that he was uncomfortable in her presence. In fact, the way his eyes avoided her, it was almost as though he were loath to look at her. At one point I found myself itching to punch his face to a bloody pulp. The only thing that held me back was my affection for Wren. But I tell you, I sensed he thought Camilla an obscenity and he didn't want to sully himself by being in the same room with her. I'm not being dramatic. I observed this for myself. Camilla, on the other hand, blithely happy because of our coming child, was oblivious to his reaction. Her only comment was that Weatherly seemed to behave decidedly coolly to her."

Regan's spine stiffened as he heard Sirena inhale an almost imperceptible breath. He didn't fail to see the narrowing of her bottle-green eyes. If there was one thing that could stir Sirena into action, it was an attack on motherhood. How any man could regard pregnancy as a disfigurement was totally beyond Regan. To him Sirena had never looked more beautiful than when she had carried their children. Even near the end of each term, when she had been heavy and ungainly, the serenity and glow from within had given her the aura of a madonna. Regan's eyes met Sirena's across the table, and he wasn't surprised when he saw hers light like shards of emeralds and burn with warmth. How well they understood each other.

Tyler saw the look that passed between them, and suddenly he felt himself an intruder. Clearing his throat in embarrassment, he pushed his chair back from the table. "There are matters which are clamoring for my attention. Stay and enjoy your breakfast. Perhaps, Regan, you'd like to take Sirena for a walk through the gardens. We try to keep it the way my mother used to. Though she did much of the work herself, Camilla and I rely upon the gardeners."

Sirena smiled. "Tyler, you mustn't feel as though Regan and I require entertaining. Naturally, we can't impose ourselves on you. Besides, we have quite a lot of thinking to do about Wren. We'll excuse you, Tyler. Won't we, Regan?" she asked her husband, kicking him under the table to prompt his response.

Regan wanted to groan aloud from the pressure of her shoe against his shin, but he forced himself to smile. "Of course we will, Sinclair. And you must erase that look of concern from your face. Wren is our daughter, and we'll do the best we can for her. Sirena and I appreciate all you've done for the girl these past three years. We're only sorry that she's caused you and Camilla any worry. We'll take up the reins now and only hope we can do as well as you have."

Sirena beamed approval. She couldn't have said it better. Regan's shins were tender of late, and poor Tyler looked so tortured. Things would work out; she would see to it. And if Weatherly pressed matters for the worse, she would simply cut him down and that would be the end of it. Then Regan's world would be right side up again. No one was going to make Regan look as he had moments after Wren's outburst. And that included her own children. She resolved to do all in her power to prevent that look from ever crossing

30

his face again. Regan belonged to her. No one, save herself, would ever hold the power to make him suffer. She smiled, her face radiant as she gazed deeply into Regan's eyes, hers full of promise and his full of trust.

Their stroll through the baronial garden was aimless, Sirena touching a blossom here and there, basking in Regan's nearness. "There's something I've been wanting to tell you, Regan," she said. "Actually, it's a surprise I've been saving for the right moment. Perhaps it will erase that pained expression from your eyes, and the only person who can do that right now is Caleb. He's here, Regan! He's been here and waiting for us for over a fortnight. He had a cargo to be delivered to England, and he promised to wait for us. Now, tell me I've made you happy with my little surprise!"

Regan grinned. "Of course it makes me happy, but I was saving the same surprise for you. Farrington wrote me that Cal would be stopping to check on his investments, and I was saving his appearance for just the right moment." He gathered her in his arms. "Already I know the way your mind is working. Caleb will arrive on the scene, sweep our little Wren off her feet, and everyone will live happily ever after. Cal may have other plans, sweetheart. I know, I know," he said as she began to protest, "that Cal would do anything you asked, and he probably will do as you want, but remember that you are holding two lives in your hands. You can manipulate to a point; then you must back off and let Heaven take over. Only too well do I recall your words the last time Wren and Caleb were together. You said she was Caleb's destiny. I felt that, too, but Cal is a man now, not a boy."

"And Wren is a young woman now. A beautiful young woman who can turn a man's head with a toss of her curls," Sirena murmured. "She is his destiny. I

31

feel it here," she said, placing her hand over Regan's heart. "At times Heaven needs a gentle nudge."

"I couldn't agree more," Regan laughed.

"Then it's settled. We'll turn Wren over to Caleb and see how matters progress. And if for some reason things don't go the way we want, we'll draw straws to see which of us cuts down that bounder Weatherly." Sirena giggled girlishly.

"I'll say one thing for you, Sirena van der Rhys. Living with you has never, ever been dull," Regan whispered, drawing her close and lifting her off the ground. He kissed her soundly and set her down firmly, his arm around her slim shoulders.

Sirena laughed. "Come, kind sir, we have some planning to do in regard to young Wren and Caleb."

Chapter Three

A cigar clamped between square white teeth, dark eyes smoldering, Caleb van der Rhys strode the deck of the decrepit gambling ship while murderous thoughts raced through his mind. Thank God he had never consented to Lord Farrington's opening the hull of his beloved *Rana* and making her a permanent fixture on the wharf. It would have broken his heart to find her in such total disrepair. And Sirena! What would Sirena have said to find her *Rana*, the ship he had renamed *Sea Siren* after her, little better than a garbage scow? The last time Caleb had been aboard the gambling folly in which he and Farrington were partners, business had been thriving. Carpeted rooms and gleaming wood and brass had accented the gambling tables in the main lounge. Private staterooms, furnished impeccably with satins and brocades, had catered to gentlemen and their club members. At one time the folly had been the most popular casino in England. And now ... now this!

Slowly and deliberately, his sun-bronzed hand removed the cigar from between his teeth. His dark eyes became cool and calculating as he stared down the dapper Lord Farrington. "While the cat's away, the mouse will play. There'd better be a good answer as to why this establishment is in such sorry condition. Tell me, what lady or gentleman would set foot on this rotting barge? What happened to the money I sent you for improvements? Where did it go? Who frequents this den of iniquity besides longshoremen and cutthroats? Let's take a look at the profit-and-loss statements. Or is it all loss and no profits? Speak up, Farrington! Did that same cat take your tongue? Ah," Caleb said softly, "I see it has." Again the cigar found its way between his gleaming teeth, and he talked around it. "Five minutes, Farrington, and then over the side you go. You'll barely make a splash. The books?" he demanded coldly.

Farrington jumped at the lash of Caleb's temper. His hands twitched nervously as he played with the cuffs of his meticulously laundered shirt. "Cal, my boy," he began hesitantly, pausing to clear his throat, "what you see here is a man fallen on hard times. Money is tight; even the gentry are careful with their sterling. It's all I can do to keep body and soul together," he whined. "True, profits are slim at best. I'm in debt over my head, and there's little to be done

33

for it. If the clientele of this establishment has—er—fallen to the good folk who earn their bread on the wharf, it is merely a sign of the times."

"Cut your flowery speeches," Caleb growled. "Remember, I know you too well."

At Caleb's stony look, Farrington changed his tactics. "After you left England, I couldn't make a go of it. Well, you know, the women came for a night's diversion because of you and your charm," he simpered. "The men came because the ladies prodded, and because they saw in you something they themselves were lacking. Unfortunately, I was a very poor substitute. Oh, in the beginning I lied and said you were away on business, hoping they wouldn't become wise. But that was a foolish mistake on my part. I should have been looking for a replacement to carry on for you. Alas, my heart wasn't in it." Farrington glanced covertly at Caleb, who was close to fuming. He continued rapidly, his eyes carefully watching Caleb's fist for fear it would come crashing down into his face. "It's your fault, Caleb. You left me to fend for myself. Quite a lot to expect of an old man. A tired, old man at that. This was the best I could do. I have a few pounds squirreled away, and if you're in need, I can let you have it." His tone became pleading, his eyes begging as he braved another look at Caleb.

Caleb moved along the deck, his booted foot prodding at loose planks. He felt disgust as his dark eyes raked the ship in her sorry state of disrepair. He felt responsible for the old reprobate following him. He swiveled, his body light and lithe. "Two thousand pounds and that's it. I don't give a damn if you have to do the carpentry work yourself. Hire as many men as you need, and I'll give you exactly one fortnight to get this scow in shape. I'll take care of the printing and have the handbills distributed. You'll have a gala the likes of which you've never seen before. And," he went on ominously, "if my share of this business doesn't improve almost immediately, I'll keep good on my promise. Skinny old men make barely a splash in the cold water of the Thames."

Aubrey Farrington straightened his back and stared at Caleb. "I'll do it, Cal. I'm sick and tired of being a weasel. A man needs his self-respect. You have my word. I do thank you for being so generous. I won't fail you."

"It's a wise man who heeds the first warning," Caleb acknowledged, lighting another cigar. "I'll be back in a few days to see how things are progressing," he tossed over his shoulder as he strode from the deck.

Envy, pure and simple, coursed through the old man's veins. Ah, to be young again and to look like Caleb van der Rhys. His old eyes narrowed as he watched Caleb stroll down the wharf, the eyes of the scurves on his back. He knew if one of them made a move, Caleb would have him by the throat and begging for mercy. There was no more of the boy in Caleb. He was a man and had come into his own. Farrington would have sold his soul at that moment if the devil could promise to turn him into another Caleb van der Rhys. Sold it cheerfully, with no regrets.

Caleb climbed lightly into the hired hack and gave the driver directions to Tyler Sinclair's home on Pall Mall, near Charing Cross Road. He estimated that the drive through London at midday would take more than an hour, and he looked longingly at the Rooster's Tail Pub, where he could be enjoying a cool ale instead of a hot, dusty ride. He sighed, knowing there was no hope for it; he had to contact Tyler for news of Sirena and Regan's arrival.

The route to Tyler's home took him along Thames Street, which ran parallel to the wharves along the river. He pulled at his collar with irritation and wished he were still at sea aboard his *Sea Siren*. Having kept true to a promise she had made him long ago, Sirena had put her ship, the *Rana,* into Caleb's care. Because of his regard for her and for an adventure they had both shared, he had renamed the ship the *Sea Siren.*

Caleb's attention was centered on the view through the grimy windows of the hack. It was always the same, never better, only a little worse now. This was the London of the people. The groomed, tree-lined streets near Charing Cross and Hyde Park were the London of the privileged. These narrow streets and byways and tall buildings leaning heavily on one another, where the shadows seemed darker than anywhere else in the world, represented the people's city.

And yet, for all its ugliness, there was a beauty here, too. London was a polyglot of the ages, old and battered and touched with evil; still, it brimmed with color and a decadent glory. Here was the heart of the city, not behind those beautiful brick edifices of the rich. Here the city teemed with life. The streets were crowded with porters struggling to carry their heavy loads of merchandise as they cried dire curses at any who dared to detain their progress. Merchants and vendors pushed their carts through the narrow alleys, calling out their wares to housewives who swarmed to make their purchases.

Church steeples stabbed the gray sky, which was thick with smoke from the chimneys and rife with the stench from the soap stewers, and through which only the strongest sunlight could penetrate. And each steeple boasted its own melodious bell but only added to the cacophony.

The very center of an Englishman's life was the numerous taprooms and pubs, which were recognized by swinging signs painted in gaudy colors and identified, by those who could not read, by their caricatures of yellow bulls, crimson roosters, goggle-eyed owls and various shields and, most of all, by tankards of ale.

Having seen these sights all too often and feeling stifled by them, Caleb settled back in the hack and thought ahead to his visit with Tyler and Camilla. While Caleb's business in London was infrequent, he did manage to see Tyler on occasion, but never Camilla. Tyler had always met him at his offices on New Queen Street or aboard the *Sea Siren* or at a convenient taproom. It had been years since Caleb had set eyes on Camilla, and he wondered if those years had been kind to her. Each time he was in his company, he had asked Tyler how Camilla fared, always expressing his interest with friendly courtesy, never with any obvious familiarity. He didn't know how knowledgeable Tyler was about his and Camilla's affair while she had been married to Regan, and he didn't wish to dredge up old laundry and leave Camilla to pay the bill with her husband.

Caleb pulled at his collar again. He didn't like having these old memories crop up. He remembered all too well the way he had agonized over his betrayal of Regan with his stepmother. And yet he hadn't been able to help himself. He remembered the way his heart had hammered in his chest and his hand had itched to run his fingers through Camilla's soft golden curls. His involvement with Camilla had tortured him, had stung his conscience to the point where he couldn't face his father. He had felt sick with himself, but there had been no help for it. He had fallen in love with Camilla. She had been so young, so sweet, so tender. And when he had taken her in his arms, despite the prick of his conscience, and she had whispered over and over, "Caleb, I need you, I need you," and offered her lips, he had taken them greedily, feeling her fragile weight in his arms. He had been overcome with emotions of love and desire and protectiveness. And when he had carried her to his bed and she had pulled him down beside her, the scent of her skin and the soft swell of her breasts had exorcised the feelings of deception and betrayal against his father. Camilla had been in his arms and cried that she needed him, and he had closed his mind to any voice of conscience which had told him it was wrong.

Caleb shook himself from his reverie. He assured himself that he was only thinking of Camilla now because he was certain to see her again. It had all washed out in the end, and he was thankful Regan had never needed to know that his own son had cuckolded him. All had worked out for the best. Camilla had found her love in Tyler, and Regan had returned to his one true passion, Sirena.

Assured that the past was well behind him and that he was now in control of his own destiny, Caleb cockily quirked an eyebrow. He was a man now, no longer the boy he had been who had fallen under Camilla's charms. He could certainly take care of himself no matter how urgently Camilla might express her desire for him and her entreaties that they become more than friends. No, this time he would be in full control of himself, even if that meant disappointing Camilla. He had no doubt whatsoever that Camilla would wish to resume their past relationship. After all, she had been married to Tyler Sinclair for almost nine years, and, knowing Camilla, he assumed she had become bored with her role as Tyler's wife.

Humming a tuneless melody, Caleb settled back in the seat and contemplated the steps he would take to keep the ardent Camilla at bay.

Malcolm Weatherly smoothed his richly embroidered dark blue waistcoat and watched with a practiced eye as the groom readied the phaeton for his drive with the shy little bird called Wren. I could do worse, Malcolm thought as he fastidiously brushed a speck of lint from his cuff. After all, Wren was a van der Rhys, and it was well known that her father was one of the wealthiest men in the trades of the Dutch East India Company. Marrying Wren would serve to advance his own station in life, a station, he was loath to admit, that had sorely descended to just above the poverty level.

Wren van der Rhys. Weatherly sneered. An awkward name at best. In no way did it suit the vital, amber-eyed maiden he was intent on making his own. A handsome dowry would certainly be forthcoming—if her father did not take it upon himself to look too closely into Malcolm's credentials.

If the van der Rhyses doted upon their daughter as he had been led to believe, there should be no problem. He shrugged his slim shoulders and glanced down at his boots. He would have to have them resoled very soon. He must remember to keep his feet planted firmly on the ground to avoid discovery of the newsprint which peeked out of the h'penny-size hole in the leather. Style, breeding and class distinction were all-important and if it were not for his wastrel uncle, he wouldn't be in these dire straits.

Malcolm had just returned from a visit to his banker, and the news was worse than he had expected. At his current rate of expenditures, he had only three more months left to him in London. At the end of that time his bills would have caught up with him and his landlady would be tossing him out for unpaid rent—lock, stock and barrel. Yes, Wren would do very nicely indeed for added insurance against that calamity ever happening. And to think he had almost tied himself to Sara Stoneham! The very thought of it terrorized him. Malcolm had assumed that Sara's family was still wealthy and influential. Instead, he had learned, and just in the nick of time, too, that because of the Stonehams' religious views and rash statements against the Crown, their properties were, one by one, being stripped from them. A nice kettle of fish *that* would have been, being saddled with an ex-heiress who was a Puritan to boot!

Wren was another matter entirely. How fortunate it was that he had made acquaintance with her, and so soon after Sara! Luckily, Sara was a wise girl who seemed to know when to keep her mouth shut. Malcolm grinned as he thought of the nights he had made love to Sara, and her passionate responses. That alone was enough to keep her quiet. A wise girl didn't boast that she was no longer a virgin. What Malcolm couldn't quite understand though, was the relationship between Sara and Wren. He shrugged. There was no accounting for women.

He reached into his breast pocket and withdrew a silver snuffbox. Turning it over in his palm, he gazed at his reflection in the polished metal. He never used snuff, considering it a nasty habit which spoiled one's shirt fronts with grains of yellow tobacco. But the box had become an affectation he used to cater to his vanity. It was unseemly for a man to carry a mirror, and the box did just as nicely. He smiled at his reflection, proud of his sterling good looks, his smooth skin and strong chin and bright, intelligent eyes. Women had always turned to stare at him, and he reveled in their attentions. Perhaps his inheritance had been badly handled and stolen from him, but nothing, not even time, would ever steal his handsomeness. He had only to remember his father, whom he resembled. Age had improved his good looks, touching his dark, wavy hair with a feathering of gray at the temples, that added a distinguished air to his boyish charm. And Malcolm was careful with his diet, maintaining the slimness and grace of a dancer. Wren hadn't stood a chance against his charms once he had put them into use. Any more than had Lady Elizabeth Rice, favorite paramour of King Charles. Malcolm laughed aloud. Wonderful, power-hungry, greedy Elizabeth, so ripe for an escapade with an ardent young man who was wise enough to keep their affair to himself rather than boasting about it to add to his own prestige.

It wasn't difficult to understand why King Charles, for all his self-righteous proclamations on the sanctity of marriage, preferred Lady Elizabeth to his dark and homely queen, Henrietta Maria. Lady Elizabeth was as fiery-natured as her flaming hair, and, most important of all, she was discreet, a necessity for a long regime as the King's favorite.

Malcolm had made her acquaintance quite by accident, almost in the same way he had met Wren. Lady Elizabeth had been taking the air in Hyde Park, and he had been so entranced with her beauty that he had boldly initiated a conversation. From there the flirtation had taken wing; when Elizabeth had invited Malcolm to a quiet dinner at her modest apartments on Drury Lane, he had quickly and eagerly accepted. They had been together several times before Malcolm had discovered that the King enjoyed sleeping beneath the same bed linens and between those same alabaster thighs.

Malcolm had thought he had succeeded in keeping his financial difficulties from Elizabeth, but only a few nights ago did he realize this was far from the truth. At first he had feared she would put an end to their affair, but to his surprise she had watched him warily through her azure-blue eyes and told him about a certain collar being fashioned for the King to wear on the anniversary of his son's birthday celebration. Bit by bit, Elizabeth had apprised Malcolm of the situation, carefully avoiding mentioning the name of the goldsmith who was creating the sensational collar. And sensational it would be, according to Elizabeth's description. "Worth a King's ransom," she had declared.

At first Malcolm hadn't understood why she was telling him about it. Finally it had dawned on him that Elizabeth was offering him information that suggested the collar was within reach of someone enterprising enough to relieve the goldsmith of it before its delivery to the King. She had been more than willing to part with the scheme, for a fair share of the profits, of course. Tucking the gleaming snuffbox into his breast pocket, Malcolm nearly chortled out loud. Either way he couldn't lose, so long as he wasn't caught snatching the collar red-handed. If the robbery went off well, as he hoped it would, he wouldn't have to saddle himself with a wife for whom he cared nothing otherwise, failing all else and if the jeweled collar were beyond reach, he would acquire for himself a lovely, rich wife.

Seeing that his hired phaeton was approaching the drive to Baron Sinclair's home, he straightened his cravat and slipped a peppermint into his mouth to sweeten his breath. He stepped lightly from the carriage just as a hackney cab came up the drive and stopped behind him. Malcolm turned, expecting to see Baron and Baroness Sinclair. Instead, a tall, powerfully built man with hair the color of polished mahogany and a complexion like newly minted copper exited the cab, a fragment of a cigar clamped between his teeth. Malcolm watched curiously as the man hooked his thumbs into his vest pockets and looked about, his dark eyes sharply appraising.

Removing the cigar from his mouth, Caleb tossed it into the shrubbery and advanced toward the front door. Malcolm, surprised by the stranger's proprietary air, quickly fell into step behind him. They both reached for the bell pull at the same time, and there was a moment of embarrassed hesitation as they measured each other.

"It seems we are bound for the same place," Malcolm said haughtily. "If you please, sir," he added, pushing his way in front of Caleb and grasping the bell pull firmly.

Caleb took an immediate dislike to the dandy, and his quick eye did not fail to notice that Malcolm's cuff had been ineptly mended.

"Are you expected, sir?" Malcolm asked arrogantly.

"I am," Caleb replied simply, his dislike for the man growing.

"I, too, have an appointment. I frequent the Baron's

home rather regularly, and I'm sorry to say I've never made your acquaintance. Allow me to introduce myself. Malcolm Weatherly," he announced, extending his hand.

"Caleb van der Rhys," Caleb stated, making no move to return the gesture.

Malcolm blinked. Van der Rhys! Surely this man was too young to be Wren's father. He tried to determine if Caleb had recognized his name. He knew only that in appearance he ran a sorry second to van der Rhys. Standing next to this sun-bronzed giant made him feel as though he'd been dipped in milk and hung out to dry.

Caleb seemed completely uninterested in Malcolm. If Tyler counted this dandy among his friends, that was his business. Then, of course, perhaps this Weatherly was a friend of Camilla's. Caleb grinned, his square white teeth gleaming in his tanned face. Perhaps Camilla hadn't changed after all.

Weatherly wondered what the man's private joke was. It seemed to amuse him considerably. He glanced down at Caleb's boots and felt a twinge of envy. Caleb's feet were encased in the finest leather boots Malcolm had ever seen. They were moroccan, from the looks of them, and polished to a high gleam. Van der Rhys was as impeccably dressed as he. But the other man carried himself so effortlessly, with a casual air of superiority that only money could provide. Undoubtedly a woman's man, he thought sourly, yet with a hidden power and a self-assurance that were enviable. In the split second before the maid opened the door, Malcolm decided he would never want to face Caleb van der Rhys in a life-or-death confrontation.

The moment Sally, the dimpled maid, opened the wide oak doors, Caleb grinned and winked at the flustered girl, his manner easy and assured. As if he belonged, Weatherly thought, grimacing.

"Follow me," Sally giggled as she all but ran ahead of the two men, her cheeks flushed and her hands trembling slightly because of the sun god who had entered the house. She skidded to a stop and held open the doors to the morning room for Caleb and Malcolm to enter. "Who shall I say is calling?" she asked Caleb, not even bothering to glance in Malcolm's direction. She *knew* whom he was here to see. Lord love a duck, wait till Miss Wren hooked her eyes on *this* one! Wait till the rest of the staff hooked their eyes, too. All the downstairs maids would be peeking and giggling for weeks, herself included.

"Caleb van der Rhys to see the Baroness." Caleb smiled winningly. He enjoyed the flustered look the little maid wore. He knew the effect he had on women, and it secretly amused him. Until they started playing the little games women play, and then it annoyed him. In that one respect he was most like Regan. He wanted a woman who would be a match for himself and would be honest. He wasn't interested in any weeping and wailing or coy deceptions. A little fire and spirit always made for a worthy encounter.

"Sir," Sally, the maid, said, curtsying low, "the Baroness is indisposed and won't be down till luncheon. Would you care to leave your card, or would you like to see Miss Wren?"

Caleb threw back his head and laughed, making Sally sigh in near ecstasy. "Next to the Baroness, Miss Wren is just the person I'd like to meet. Tell her Caleb is here and to move as fast as her legs will carry her to my arms." He laughed again as the maid cast a puzzled glance at Malcolm and ran from the room.

Wait till the girls in the kitchen hear about this! she told herself. Lordy, I'll be the center of attention for weeks. Morry, the houseboy, will be so impressed with me, he might even ask me for a walk after supper!

Forgetting her training in her excitement, Sally knocked loudly on Wren's door and opened it at the same time. "Miss Wren, Miss Wren, you're to come quick! There's a gentleman downstairs in the morning room. A gentleman to end all gentlemen! Wait till you see him. Lordy, he's the handsomest man my eyes have ever seen! Come," she said, holding out her hand in a girlish fashion.

Wren's lashes drooped. Malcolm was early. She wasn't ready for a confrontation between Regan and him. She would have to plead a headache and hope for the best. How could she face Malcolm now, after the hateful things she had said to Sirena and Regan? Malcolm was so sensitive to her moods that he would immediately know something was wrong. "Tell Mr. Weatherly I've a horrid headache and I'm resting. Give him my apologies and ask him to return at tea-time," Wren begged. "And say that I'm sorry I won't be able to take that drive with him today."

"No, no, Miss Wren," Sally cried in agitation. "His name is Caleb van der Rhys, and he said if he couldn't see the Baroness, then he wanted to see you. Miss Wren, he looks . . . he looks like a—a god," she whispered. "I quite forgot myself in his presence and almost swooned at his feet." As an afterthought, she added impishly, "Your other gentleman friend is in the morning room with him."

Wren's heart fluttered and she felt faint. Caleb! Caleb was downstairs waiting to see her! Caleb was in the morning room with Malcolm! "Damnation!" she muttered under her breath.

The maid frowned. "Miss Wren, for shame. Young ladies never say such words."

"This lady does," Wren said through clenched teeth. "Very well, I'll go down and see my two . . . gentlemen callers." She tossed her dark hair, pinched her cheeks for added color and wiped at her incredibly long lashes with the back of her hand. Why hadn't someone told her Caleb was in England? That was the least Sirena and Regan could have done. They knew how fond she was of Caleb. It must be some sort of trick on their part. Sirena, Regan said, was as tricky as a fox. And for both men to arrive at the same moment was more than a coincidence. "Damnation!" she said aloud, her eyes defying Sally to make any comment. The little maid remained mute, happy that she would get still another glimpse of the sun-darkened giant in the morning room. How she wished she were quality folk with a gentleman caller the likes of Caleb van der Rhys!

"I'm ready, Sally," Wren said, smoothing the skirt of her rose morning gown. One light flick of her fingers to her hair and one last deep breath. Her shoulders squared imperceptibly as she approached the morning room. Sally opened the doors and Wren stepped through. Her amber eyes went immediately to Caleb and she wanted to faint. She forced a smile and, as the good teachers had taught her, walked to the center of the room, both arms extended appealingly in welcome.

Caleb, caught up in Malcolm's boring discussion of London weather, was stunned at her entrance. Merciful God, Sirena was right. What a beauty! Where was the little girl he had known so long ago back in Java? His heart hammered in his chest as he scooped Wren into his arms, ignoring an outraged Malcolm Weatherly.

Tears glistened in the girl's amber eyes as Caleb held her away from him for a moment. "You're all grown up now," he murmured, his voice full of awe. "Who would have believed the little girl who had run barefoot on the wharves could end up like this?" He pointed to her elegant morning gown, then lowered his voice to a bare whisper. "I don't think I care to call you my sister any longer." His dark eyes teased her. "Little sisters should never look as you do."

The amber eyes smoldered momentarily and then became banked fires waiting for another time to be rekindled. Casually, Wren removed herself from Caleb's arms and turned to acknowledge Malcolm Weatherly. "Malcolm, this is my . . . this is my . . . brother Caleb."

"We've met," Malcolm said curtly. Wren had never looked at him in quite the way she looked at van der Rhys, and, supposedly, *he* was her intended. He had never seen a sister look at a brother in just that way, nor had he seen a brother so overcome by a sister's beauty. A small worm of fear crawled around his stomach and then settled down to rest at Wren's next words.

"I'm so glad you arrived early, Malcolm. Sirena and Regan are here; they arrived during the night and are quite eager to meet you. Everything has been arranged for luncheon, when the Baroness will come down to join us. Until then, why don't you and Caleb take a walk through the garden? I'll join you both shortly." She placed a gentle hand on his arm.

"That doesn't sound like one of your better ideas," Caleb said with a grimace. "Now, if you had said, 'Let's remove our shoes and romp through that lush carpet of grass . . . together,' I would be the first one into the garden. However, I guess it's you and me, Weatherly, for a stroll." He turned and grinned wickedly, sending Wren's heart into a quick pounding. "Patience, as you know, is not one of my better qualities."

Wren laughed, the first genuine laugh she had uttered in months. "I remember. If things go well, perhaps we can romp through that meadow of green before you leave for home."

Caleb's dark eyes lightened at her words as he followed Malcolm from the room.

Outside in the spacious marble foyer, Wren leaned against the wall and took several deep breaths. Of all the damn days for Caleb to arrive. "Damn, damn, damn," she cried as she ran through the hall and up the curving stairway.

47

Chapter Four

Unaware of the drama unfolding below, Baroness Camilla Langdon Sinclair slid out from her ruffled, canopied bed and stretched luxuriously, cupped her hands around her protruding stomach and sighed happily. Soon she would be a mother. If someone had told her she would ever welcome this state in her life, she would have laughed. Tyler was so happy, and the way he doted on young Wren was how he would dote on their own child. Even more so. Dear, sweet, wonderful Tyler, who loved her and understood her. Tyler was wonderful. Life was wonderful. The sun was shining and she was glad to be alive. The child growing inside her was the fruit of her and Tyler's deep love. Nothing would ever destroy that love; she wouldn't allow it.

With the help of her maid, she bathed and dressed in a becoming gown of soft gold, cleverly designed to conceal her condition. As if she wanted to hide it. Why had she listened to that prudish seamstress who had said it was unseemly for a "lady-in-waiting" to reveal her condition? *Reveal* it! God! She wanted to *flaunt* it! To shout about it from the rooftops! And all the while to sport her burgeoning belly and milk-heavy breasts in a declaration of womanhood fulfilled. She wanted the whole world to know she was expecting a baby. She would walk with her shoulders thrown back and belly thrust forward in full evidence. She wanted Sirena and Regan to know how happy she was.

Camilla tilted her head and listened. How quiet the house was. By now, with the newly arrived guests, the house should be ringing with Wren's happy laughter and Regan's boisterous good humor. On the other hand, as Tyler had worried, things might not go well once Wren informed them of her intentions. Well, she, for one, wasn't going to worry about it. Nothing was going to spoil her good mood. After all, Wren was already eighteen years old. And hadn't she, Camilla, been secretly married at the same age?

Camilla Sinclair had been little more than sixteen when she had first laid eyes on Tyler Sinclair. Her father, Stephan Langdon, had been distantly related to the late Baron, Tyler's father, through marriage. It had been a sun-kissed summer when she had traveled to Knightsbridge with Stephan to spend a few weeks at the Sinclairs' summer home. It had been no secret to her that Stephan was considered the black sheep of the family and was barely tolerated by the Baroness while the kindly Baron believed in letting bygones be bygones and had warmly welcomed them into his home.

During that glorious summer she and Tyler had fallen madly and impetuously in love, much to Stephan's greedy pleasure and the Baroness's dismay. Even repeated warnings to Tyler that his mother would disinherit him if he continued his dalliance with Camilla had not dampened his ardor. They were in love; that was all that mattered, and later, when it had seemed that the Baroness would have her way and they would be separated, Camilla and Tyler had run off to be married.

At first Stephan Langdon had been overjoyed with the alliance between his only child and the wealthy Sinclair son. But when Tyler had decided to reveal his secret marriage to his parents, Stephan had reconsidered. "Don't do it," he had said. And Tyler, young and still several years away from the time when he would inherit a large part of the Sinclair estate, had heeded his words.

Tyler had thought that it was *his* skin Stephan had been bent on saving. It hadn't taken him long to realize that Stephan Langdon had known the Sinclairs were intractable and that Tyler would most certainly be disinherited, leaving Langdon not only with the burden of a daughter but also with that of an impoverished son-in-law. Tyler would have been disinherited and ostracized, and, along with him, Stephan would have found himself an outcast. He had known the Sinclairs would have avenged themselves on him for his part in the romance and banished him from their society.

The main reason Langdon had been acceptable to his peers was because he had had the Baron's endorsement. Without that, and because of his sullied reputation, he would have been cast like a leper from the fashionable drawing rooms he so coveted.

Innocently, and with Camilla's consent, Tyler had agreed to keep their marriage secret. It had been understood that when he reached his majority, he would lay claim to Camilla. But Stephan had not been able to wait five more years to ease his financial predicaments. When Regan van der Rhys had arrived in London and word of his extraordinary wealth had spread, Stephan had adroitly placed his daughter in conspicuous proximity to the Dutchman. Circumstances, which had been unknown to either Stephan or Camilla at the time, had led to her marriage to Regan.

She had been a girl then, Camilla now reasoned, a

foolish, self-centered girl who had easily been led by her calculating, conniving father. The only honesty she had ever displayed had been her love for Tyler. Everything and everyone else had been a farce. Even in another man's arms—Regan's, Caleb's, little matter whose—it had always been Tyler. Tyler, who knew her for herself, her virtues as well as her faults, especially her faults. Tyler knew them all and loved her in spite of them.

Camilla smiled a self-satisfied smile and patted her swelling abdomen. It had taken quite a few years to become pregnant with this child, but now she had all a woman could ask for. A husband, a child about to be born, and the freedom to be herself and reach out for what she wanted.

While Camilla preened and pampered herself, Wren was pulling one day dress after another from the tall clothespress. This one was disregarded because it wasn't her most becoming color. That one because it didn't suit her mood.

Her eyes spewing amber sparks, she caught a glimpse of herself in the pier glass at the far end of the room. A flush rode high on her ivory cheeks, making her eyes sparkle and snap like a flame and contrasting with the unruly spill of her dark hair. Malcolm Weatherly had never brought her such excitement as had Caleb's arrival. Although infinitely handsome in his own right, Malcolm looked pale beside Caleb.

Now, why did I think that? she questioned herself. Malcolm was one of the most handsome men she had ever seen. And if the way he turned women's heads was any measure of her opinion, she couldn't be more correct. Malcolm had the good looks of an aristocrat blended perfectly with the charm of a rakehell. Women couldn't resist him. His black, crisply curling hair, which tumbled casually over his broad forehead and accented his sleepy-lidded, laughing eyes, gave him a boyish air. And with his sensuous smile and lithe, graceful build, it was little wonder women found him attractive. And not just young women like herself. Older women, too, more sophisticated women, seemed fascinated by him. His grooming was impeccable and his demeanor beyond reproach. Malcolm carried himself with an almost studied affectation, while Caleb just . . . Caleb just moved, effortlessly, with the natural grace of an athlete. Beside Caleb, Malcolm's carriage appeared almost mechanical.

How uncharitable I'm being, Wren scolded herself. Malcolm loved her and she loved him. Hadn't she thrown caution to the winds and practically alienated Sirena and Regan? This was no time to start having doubts about her feelings for Malcolm. Her own impulsive words of anger rang in her ears, and the vision of Regan's pained features swam before her, making the flush on her cheeks burn like fire. *I meant every word I said*, she defended herself to the mirror. *Sirena and Regan have lived their lives, are still living it, and I will do the same, with or without their approval.* She jabbed her finger toward the mirror for emphasis and turned with renewed vigor to rummage through the clothespress. She finally settled for a shimmering apricot silk which enhanced her high coloring and set off her flaming eyes to perfection.

"Wren, Wren, I've just come from the garden, and you won't believe whom I saw there!" Sara cried as she closed the door behind her, her blue eyes alight with excitement. "Malcolm and another man, a man to end all men, the kind of man we used to whisper about at the academy. Magnificent! Absolutely magnificent!" She swooned girlishly. "Wren, I swear he makes Malcolm look like a farmer." Unmindful of the cross expression on Wren's face, she burbled on. "I must ask Tyler to introduce him to me. We would go so well together, for he has hair as dark as shadows and skin like bronze. Magnificent! With my fairness, we would compliment each other perfectly!" With a carefully hidden slyness, Sara observed Wren's reaction to her words. She knew if she threw Wren at this stranger, the girl would balk and become more enamored of Malcolm than ever before. But perhaps if she pretended an interest in this man herself, Wren might be persuaded to forget Malcolm and leave him to Sara.

Wren swiveled around and grasped Sara by the arm, her amber eyes shooting sparks. Her mouth set in a grim, tight line, she hissed, "That's my brother you're speaking about, and no, you wouldn't compliment each other. Caleb is a man, not a boy, and you're only a silly, foolish schoolgirl. And if you ever call Malcolm a farmer again, I'll—I'll pull out all your hair! Do you hear me, Sara Stoneham?"

"Mercy sakes, Wren, what's gotten into you? I was only teasing you. You're upset because Sirena and Regan are here, and now all your bad deeds are coming home to roost. Maybe you're what Mother used to call a bad seed," Sara declared loftily.

"Damn your eyes, Sara, I'm not a bad seed and well you know it!"

"Of course not, little bird, ladies always speak profanity. Damn your eyes, indeed! If my mother ever heard you speak like that, she'd forbid me to associate with you. As it is, this will probably be the last you'll see of me once my parents come to save me from your bad influence. It *was* because of you I was expelled from school, wasn't it? And since you've become so sensitive about your brother, as you call him, I'll just wager my pearl comb against your silver bracelet that I can have him falling over his own feet for me within an hour!" Sara turned to hide her smile from Wren. Her ploy just might work. It had been no mere sisterly defense of a brother that had made Wren get her back up. And was she mistaken, or was Wren's defense of Malcolm something of an afterthought?

53

"Don't make me laugh, Sara. Caleb would never find himself smitten with a child like you. And a wager it is. An hour from the time you meet him."

"Wonderful. I'll flirt outrageously. The way you and I used to practice at school. Remember you said I had the longest lashes and would have men falling at my feet the day I made my debut into society?"

"I remember," Wren said through clenched teeth. Why did she have this terrible sinking feeling in the pit of her stomach? Sara was a wonderful friend, who had made living away from home bearable. And here she was, treating Sara like an unwanted piece of baggage. Caleb could do worse, she sniffed. "I'm sorry, Sara. You're my best friend and I shouldn't treat you so shabbily. Please don't be angry with me," she entreated, her tone softening in apology as she touched Sara lightly on the shoulder.

"I'm not angry," Sara said, her smile wide and gentle. "I just don't think Malcolm is the man of your dreams. Caleb, now, seems like a lusty, seafaring man, the kind your infamous Sea Siren would have gone after. He's not your real brother, Wren," she remarked distinctly, to make sure her friend understood what she was saying.

Wren's heart thumped. She herself had thought the same thing the moment she had set eyes on Caleb. He looked just like Regan, except for his dark hair and eyes. Sara was right. Caleb was the kind of man the Sea Siren would want for a lover. Wren sighed. Malcolm was the man she wanted. He was the man she wanted to marry.

"Caleb is a philanderer, Sara. He loves women. All women. I think his sole mission in life is to see how many young virgins he can bed before he takes a wife, if he should ever decide to take a wife, that is. I'm certain he's left a trail of swooning women from one port to the next. Caleb is not the marrying kind, and

I want to get married and have children. With Malcolm," she added coolly, her youthful expression composed.

Sara's stomach churned at Wren's words. Not if I can help it, my friend, she thought viciously. She had to do something, anything, to make Malcolm aware of the mistake he was embarking on. Perhaps her first idea was best. She had seen the way Caleb had looked at her in the garden. And hadn't Wren said he was interested in women? It wouldn't hurt to turn her wiles on him and see what effect that had on Malcolm. If Malcolm realized a man such as Caleb van der Rhys was interested in her, he would give up his mad idea of marrying Wren. Sweet, innocent, puritanical Wren. No, that was wrong. She, Sara, was the Puritan. A fallen Puritan. Yes, she would flirt with Caleb, and she would do it as soon as they sat down at the luncheon table.

"Are you ready, Sara? You know how fussy Camilla can be when her meals are late. If we delay any longer, we'll be the last into the dining room, and I want to be the one to introduce Malcolm to Sirena and Regan."

"I'm ready now," Sara said, patting a stray lock of hair into place. She looked every bit as beautiful as Wren, with her delicate good looks and in her pale blue, clinging gown. She would endeavor to stand next to the dashing Caleb so that Malcolm could see how well they looked together. Just like honey and cream, she thought, and smiled secretly.

Regan took one look at Malcolm Weatherly and almost exploded in anger. Sirena laid a gentle hand on his arm to quiet him as she, too, appraised the dandy through narrowed eyes. Then her glance shifted to the tall, dark giant of a man who entered the room. "Caleb!" she cried, rushing to him and throwing her arms

55

about him. "How wonderful to see you!" Suddenly she found herself being lifted from the floor and swung around in a circle.

Caleb laughed. "You're more beautiful than ever, Sirena." He set her down gently, his arm protectively cradling her shoulders as he extended his free arm to his father. "It's good to see you, Father. You look as if the burdens of parenthood haven't been too taxing. Tell me, how are my four brothers?"

"Hale and hearty and looking forward to the day they see you again. When are you coming back to Java? Where are you bound now?" Regan asked, clapping his son on the back.

"Wherever the sea takes me. The affairs of the Dutch East India Company are in capable hands. I told them not to expect me for at least a year."

A momentary twinge tugged at Regan. The boy was free to do what he wanted whenever he wanted to. His own carefree days were long behind him. He felt Sirena grow still beside him. How well she knew him. She, too, had sensed his brief, restless urge. He smiled down into her eyes, all thoughts of envy and freedom forgotten. She was all the pleasure he would ever need.

"So," Regan said jovially to his oldest son, "you haven't cut a wide enough swath with the gentle sex, is that it?"

"From Java to Sumatra," Caleb laughed. "I thought I would take a chance and see what America has to offer."

"They have wild Indians in America," Sirena remarked fearfully.

"And do you think my son is no match for an Indian? For shame, Sirena," Regan chided.

"It might be advisable if you laid back your rapier and took up the bow and arrow. I don't think the women of the world will take to a baldheaded Dutchman." Sirena smiled fondly at Caleb.

Malcolm Weatherly stood on the sidelines, a smile pasted on his face. He thought everyone was displaying incredibly bad manners. Wren's parents hadn't even acknowledged him. The Baroness, despite her bloated condition, had not seen fit to welcome either him or her guests, and Wren was conspicuously absent. And this overgrown clod of a Dutchman was getting all the attention he himself should be getting as Wren's intended. He noticed Caleb's attire, and he admitted to himself that the man's easy elegance annoyed him. No matter how hard he tried, no matter what his tailor did, he would never look like the giant standing in the middle of the room. He watched as father and son lit cigars without offering him one. How long, he wondered, could he keep this ridiculous smile on his face? Peasants, the lot of them! He needed a drink. If these bumpkins could smoke cigars in Baroness Sinclair's parlor, then he could have a drink.

Seeing Malcolm's movement to the liquor cabinet, Sirena turned and smiled winningly, her emerald eyes glowing. "You must excuse our bad manners." Her voice was low, musical—almost seductive, Malcolm thought as his eyes widened in interest. "We haven't seen our son in a long time, and it's just that we're happy to be together again under the same roof. I'm sure you understand and will forgive us. Pour me a glass of wine," she said boldly. "And then let us sit here and have a chat. By the way, I'm Sirena van der Rhys, and the fair-haired man is my husband, Regan, and, of course, you're Malcolm Weatherly. Wren spoke of you this morning." Sirena nodded sweetly as she accepted the glass of wine and downed it in one swallow, to Malcolm's acute discomfort. She wanted to tell him to fill her glass again, because she would need the dulling effect of the wine to get through this luncheon. What a fop he was, she thought with distaste. Oh, Wren, how could you?

"Would you care for another glass of wine?" Malcolm asked quietly. She must be a sot, he thought maliciously.

"If you insist," Sirena said, holding out the goblet. "Fill it to the brim."

To the brim! Malcolm's mind raced. If she drinks, what does van der Rhys do? he wondered as he handed the glass to her, careful not to spill any of the burnished liquid.

Sirena allowed her soft hand to come in contact with Malcolm's long, slender fingers. She glared directly into his eyes and then coyly lowered her lashes. If he was the fool she thought he was, he would take this as a hidden invitation to a deepening friendship, or worse. She preferred not to put a name to whatever he might think it was. She sipped at the wine, the glass held provocatively in her hands as she met his eyes repeatedly.

Regan gave Caleb a gentle nudge. "Another five minutes with Sirena, and the dandy will forget why he's here. A wager, Cal?"

"I may have not learned too much, Father, but I did learn that it's only a fool who would lay odds against Sirena." Both men threw back their heads, the slim cigars clamped between strong white teeth, and laughed uproariously.

Startled, Sirena turned to look at the two men she loved most in her life. She gasped, and then a warm, delicious feeling spread through her entire body. They were hers, Regan by marriage and Caleb by an invisible bond established between them long ago. They belonged to her, for now and forever. The delicious aura stayed with her till Regan and Caleb glanced at her again, each giving her a sly wink. They knew what she was doing with Malcolm, and both of them approved.

This is a woman, Malcolm thought wildly. And I'm

man enough to handle any woman. Women always fell at his feet, begging for his favors. Even Lady Elizabeth Rice, who could count a king among her lovers, was so smitten with him that she had confided the secret of the King's jeweled collar. But Sirena would never beg for favors, nor would she grant any. This woman would never fall at a man's feet, his or anyone else's. Sirena was a woman worthy of a man's challenge.

"What are you thinking, Malcolm?" Sirena purred, her eyes boldly meeting his.

"I was thinking that now I know where Wren acquired her beauty and grace." He smiled broadly, moving a step closer so that he could delight in the delicate, elusive scent of her perfume.

Sirena lowered her eyes to hide their dangerous glitter. Wren had her beauty, indeed! Was it possible that Malcolm didn't know Wren wasn't her and Regan's daughter? As she sipped her wine, Sirena speculated. If Malcolm was a bounder, and from every indication, along with Tyler's word, he was, then he must think he was wooing an heiress. She wondered if his feelings for Wren would be as ardent if he knew that the van der Rhyses were under no obligation to bestow a dowry on Wren or otherwise include her in any inheritance. What would his reaction be if she told him?

Sirena glanced over at Caleb again and was surprised to note that his attention was directed on the doorway behind her instead of on Regan, who was exuberantly describing the "civilization" taking place on Java since Cal had last been there. Curiously, Sirena turned and saw that Tyler had entered the drawing room with Camilla on his arm. She turned back to Caleb, whose expression was something bordering between astonishment and disappointment at Camilla's obvious pregnancy. So, Sirena thought, the young pup half expected that Camilla would be waiting for him to return to her after all these years. Think again, Cal. Camilla has other things on her mind.

Smiling, Sirena made the first move toward Camilla and clasped her in a fond embrace. The old wounds because of Regan had long since healed between them, and Camilla's acceptance of Wren into her household had firmed their friendship. "You're more lovely than ever," Sirena said warmly. "Approaching motherhood certainly becomes you. Doesn't it, Regan?" She turned to her husband, who she knew was waiting to see how she would greet his ex-wife before committing himself to any display of emotion.

Looking at Camilla, Regan was hard pressed to believe he had once been married to her so many years ago. She still looked barely more than the nineteen years of age she had been when they had first met. Yellow-haired and with violet eyes whose look of innocence belied her actual experience, Camilla was still as fetching a woman as he had ever seen, aside from Sirena, of course. He was quick to note the expression on Caleb's face, and it occurred to him to wonder again if there had ever been anything between Camilla and his son. Regan sighed. That was long ago, and he really didn't want to know. However, he couldn't have blamed Caleb for his interest in Camilla. She had been and still was as graceful and winsome as a spring daffodil.

Regan stepped forward and put his arms around Camilla, kissing her soundly on the cheek. "Sirena is right, little one. You've never been lovelier."

Tyler beamed with pride over his wife and inwardly felt greatly relieved that the van der Rhyses seemed to hold no ill will against her, which could have put a strain on his friendship for them. He knew all about Camilla's past, her duping Regan into marriage with her, her affair with Caleb, and none of it meant anything to him. He knew, without a doubt, that he had always been Camilla's one true love.

Only Malcolm stood back from the chatter and bandied compliments. When he did allow his eyes to travel to Camilla, he was careful to avoid looking at her swollen midsection. His lip curled in spite of himself as he mused that pregnant women who displayed themselves in public were as appealing as sows with suckling piglets. He noticed that he had come under Sirena's green gaze and occupied himself with the contents of his wineglass. He hoped she wasn't capable of reading his mind.

Sirena's one glance at Malcolm told her all she needed to know. She had seen that same contempt for women on another man's face, a man she had married to spite Regan. Stephan Langdon, Camilla's father, had died at the point of her own sword for his contempt of women, and her hand now itched for the weight of a rapier to put an end to Malcolm Weatherly. She knew, beyond a doubt, that she would never allow a marriage between him and Wren to take place. If she had had any doubts before, they were all behind her now. Wren, too, had suffered at Stephan's hands, and Sirena wondered why she couldn't see the sadistic similarities between the two men.

As though bidden by her thoughts, Wren and Sara entered the drawing room. Without a glance in Sirena's direction, and ignoring Malcolm completely, Wren moved toward Regan, the silk of her apricot gown rustling softly. Sirena glanced at Caleb, who seemed to have forgotten his disappointment over Camilla and not even to have noticed Sara, whose white-blond hair and pearly complexion was set off by the delicate blue shading of her gown. Caleb's attention was centered on Wren, who by now was firmly within Regan's embrace. Sirena softened toward the daughter of her heart when she saw the barely disguised look of pain leave Regan's eyes.

Malcolm carefully avoided Sara's searching gaze.

He never knew how she had managed to become friends with Wren so soon after he had refused to accede to her pleas to meet her whenever she could slip out of the academy. How fortunate that he had discovered her father's falling from grace with the Crown and his near bankruptcy. Imagine, if he had saddled himself with Sara before he had learned the truth about her family's finances! It was impossible for him to fathom why she had befriended Wren when she knew he had thrown her over for the amber-eyed girl. It really didn't matter to him that Sara was Wren's friend as long as she kept quiet about having been his lover. Malcolm smiled, a churlish lifting of the lip that showed strong white teeth. Sara would never spill that sack of beans; the damage to her reputation would be irreparable. He even doubted that Wren would believe Sara, no matter how convincing her tale might be.

While Camilla drew Sirena aside to exchange news, and Tyler and Regan began to discuss business agreements concerning the handling of certain estates, Wren and Sara gathered about Caleb, leaving Malcolm to entertain himself. Malcolm had never encountered such an inhospitable group of people. He wasn't in the habit of being ignored, especially if there were women present. And what of Sara, so blatantly flirting with the younger van der Rhys? Even Wren seemed to have forgotten his existence as she hung on Caleb's every word. If he hadn't known that Wren was Caleb's sister, he might even become jealous.

Sirena glanced over Camilla's shoulder at Malcolm Weatherly. She didn't fail to notice his chagrin at being excluded from the little celebration. One might think that if he really loved Wren, he would be jealous of the attention she was giving Caleb. Then the truth dawned on Sirena. Weatherly didn't know Wren *wasn't* Caleb's half sister. He couldn't know; otherwise he would feel threatened by Caleb's presence. She almost laughed aloud until it occurred to her that Malcolm thought *she* was old enough to be Wren's mother. Sirena sniffed and threw her head back in a haughty gesture of indignation. Malcolm Weatherly would have a healthy shock coming to him when he discovered that Wren was not the wealthy heiress he thought she was.

Chapter Five

Lunch had been a gay and lively affair, and much to Wren's relief, there had been no mention of her outrage at breakfast. In fact, it appeared as though Malcolm was winning her family over in his own quiet way. Sirena, at least, seemed to hold him in high regard, judging from the way she had directed her attention to him time and time again.

Sara had been totally captivated by Caleb's stories of his adventures in the service of the Dutch East India Company, and Wren had to admit a twinge of resentment over Sara's flirtation with him. But she really couldn't blame her friend; Caleb was charming and extremely handsome. Then again, any envy she might have experienced had been assuaged by Caleb's eyes constantly falling on her, and she hoped Malcolm had noticed Caleb's attentiveness. It pleased her to think Malcolm might be jealous. Then she realized that

Malcolm believed Caleb was her brother and had no grounds for jealousy. That belief was something Wren intended to correct at the first possible opportunity. Malcolm's jealousy was an exciting thought, but first he had to know her true relationship with the van der Rhyses. Perhaps she could get him alone after dinner tonight. She was disappointed that she hadn't been able to go for a drive with him, as she had promised, but the luncheon festivities had lingered far too long into the afternoon. Besides, a few minutes ago Sirena had invited her to go down to the wharves so that Caleb could show his family how he had careened the *Sea Siren,* and she had jumped at the chance. Even in Java, when Caleb had brought the *Sea Siren* into port on his infrequent visits, she had loved to see the warm glow in Sirena's and Regan's eyes whenever they inspected the vessel, and the way they touched each other when they thought no one was looking. The *Sea Siren* was the ship on which Sirena and Regan had first discovered their love for one another, and just the sight of her brought back tender memories for them.

Tying the ribbons of her bonnet beneath her chin, Wren turned from the pier glass to face Sara. "Are you certain you wouldn't like to come along with us? I know Sirena and Regan wouldn't mind."

"No, you go along. I've a terrible headache," Sara whimpered. She was lounging on the high bed.

"Shall I have someone bring you a headache powder or cool cloths?" Wren inquired, moving over to the bed to touch Sara's head. "You do feel warm. Shall I have Camilla send for the doctor?" A note of concern rang in Wren's voice, and worry narrowed her eyes. She had never known Sara to be ill.

"No, no, I'll be fine," Sara assured her. "You go on and have a nice afternoon. Food just doesn't seem to agree with me these days. It's nothing to worry about."

"You do look a little green about the edges," Wren teased. "Are you sure I can't do anything for you?"

Sara groaned and rolled over onto her stomach. "If you don't get away from me with that scent you use, I'll be sick all over the bed! Now go!"

After Wren had closed the door behind her, Sara tried to lie very still. What was wrong with her? She'd never been sick a day in her life. Lately she had had this queasy feeling every day before breakfast and sometimes after lunch. But she had always recovered before dinner. Through her misery she reasoned that the emotional upheaval of Malcolm's rejection and the worry over her parents' financial difficulties, not to mention those concerning her brother's criticism of the King, were causing the butterflies in her stomach. And if those reasons weren't enough, there was always the horror of facing her parents' wrath when they arrived in London.

Sara awakened to a noisy commotion in the main hall below. Greetings wafted upward, and the sound of an autocratic, booming voice brought her fully alert. Her father! There was no other voice as forceful as Jason Stoneham's, except, perhaps, that of his son, Bascom.

Sara's blue eyes snapped open wide, and she quickly rose from the bed. Suddenly the room began to reel about her so violently that she had to sit down again. Her stomach rolled once more, and she dreaded the thought of going downstairs and facing her parents. She considered lying back on the bed and pretending to be asleep.

From the sound of Jason's voice booming up the stairs, it seemed the decision was to be taken out of her hands. "Sara! Where are you! Answer me this minute!"

Then Margaret Stoneham's lighter voice joined his. "Jason! Jason! You'll wake the whole house! We were told the Baroness was napping! Jason!"

"Hush, Margaret! I intend to see my daughter immediately! Sara! Sara, where are you?"

"In here, Father," Sara managed to choke as she braced herself for the confrontation. The door to her room banged open, and through the doorway stepped Jason Stoneham. For a moment Sara almost didn't recognize him. Gone were the meticulously tailored clothes which gave such authority to his deep-chested, slightly portly figure, and in their place were the black frock coat and high-crested hat which had become the popular garb of those of the Puritan sect. Stoneham had even chosen to relinquish the broad white collar that at least offered relief to the somber costume. He removed his hat, placed it carefully on a chair and then came to stand wordlessly in front of his daughter, his hands planted firmly on his hips and a cold glare in his eyes.

"How do you do, Father?" Sara managed to speak. "Well, I trust?"

"Well enough for a man who's learned his own daughter is little less than a trollop!" he boomed at Sara's cowering figure. "How could you shame me this way? I've just come from the academy, where I heard for myself your implication in one of the tawdriest affairs I've ever been told of. The headmistress apprised me of the entire situation, and I've never been so ashamed in my life. To think that a child of mine would involve herself in a—in a—tryst! I can only wonder how long it would have been before *you* had this van der Rhys girl standing watch while *you* slipped away in the dark with some simple-minded idiot who had nothing but lust on his mind!"

"Malcolm is not a simple-minded idiot!" Sara shouted, the words out of her mouth before she knew what she was saying. "I—I mean, I did what I did to help a friend. Wren is going to marry Mr. Weatherly, so you see there was nothing evil about it."

Jason was astounded by her outburst. Neither she

nor his wife had ever spoken to him that way. "See here, daughter, remember to whom you are talking—"

"Sara! Sara!" A breathless Margaret Stoneham rushed into the room, still holding her skirts above her ankles from the climb up the stairs.

"Mother! What have you done to yourself!" Sara's mouth dropped open. Margaret Stoneham had always prided herself on her fashionable dress and carefully coiffed hair. Now she looked like an old woman. Her hair was pulled back from her face, revealing streaks of gray beneath the brim of her white cap. The silks and satins she had always worn had been traded for a coarse gown of the deepest black that was relieved only by a white collar and cuffs.

"She has done nothing more than uplift her spirit to the Lord by leaving foolish trappings behind and dedicating her life to Him," Jason expounded. "Something you could have done rather than involving yourself in a scandal, young woman. Well, all that will be behind you when you adopt the dress of our sect. Fripperies are the devil's work, turning young people's heads away from the true Word."

Sara shook her head in disbelief. Her parents had followed the Puritan doctrines for years now, but they had never carried them to extremes. Only Bascom, with his wild eyes and unhealthy gauntness, had worn the somber black costume. "When did all this come about? Surely you haven't gone to such lengths because of what I did at school!"

"Certainly not. Your mother and I have been shown the true path to our eternal rewards. Our dress signifies that we are devoting our lives to the Redeemer."

"You mean ever since you've been condemned by the Crown for upholding Bascom's preachings and because you're close to financial ruin, you can't afford to wear anything else!" Sara stormed hotly, defying her father's masterful gaze. "Mother, where are your lovely clothes, and what have you done to your hair?"

A wistful expression passed over Margaret's face, but when she realized she was under her husband's angry scrutiny, she blanched and said soothingly, "Come, now, Sara, it's not so bad. It's the way to salvation, you know. You'll soon get used to wearing our dress. If nothing else, it solves the problem of what to wear each day."

"I'll soon get— No! Never! I'll never go about looking like a black crow! Not when I've a clothespress full of silks and satins. I've worshipped with you and Father, I've listened to Bascom's preachings, but I will never wear that—that—that!" She pointed at her mother's gown and shuddered.

"You will do as I say, daughter. Margaret, have that servant girl bring up the satchel you packed for Sara. And have a footman sent to remove her things from the clothespress. My daughter will believe as I do, and her behavior will be in keeping with the sister of the leader of our congregation."

"I refuse, Father. I won't wear that nun's habit! I'd sooner go about naked than look like—"

Jason interrupted his daughter's blasphemy with a smart slap on her cheek.

Shocked, Sara gasped and held her hand to her face, too outraged even to cry.

"You will do as I say, Sara," Jason intoned threateningly as he loomed above her. "I have accepted the Baron's hospitality under the condition that I won't have you spend another night in the same apartment with that hellion Wren van der Rhys. You will move your belongings immediately, and they will be few, to your mother's room, where we can keep a watch over you."

Sara gulped back the tears which were choking her. Helplessly she watched her mother open the satchel containing a plain black gown and stiff muslin petticoats.

When Wren returned from the wharf with Regan, Sirena and Caleb, she bounded up the stairs to the apartment she shared with Sara. She wanted to change into something especially beautiful for dinner tonight; then perhaps Malcolm would look at her the way Regan had looked at Sirena aboard the *Sea Siren*. Their past was so romantic, so adventurous, so passionate. Somehow she could imagine Caleb looking at a woman the way his father looked at Sirena, with such love and smoldering hunger, but she couldn't imagine Malcolm doing the same. Maybe she had been foolish to insist that they wait until they were married before consummating their love. Chills danced up Wren's spine when she thought of Malcolm's ardent lovemaking and his protests when she begged him to stop.

"Sara, Sara," she called excitedly as she threw open the door to their sitting room, only to find the upstairs maid in place of Sara.

"Miss Sara's down the hall in Mrs. Stoneham's room," the woman explained.

"Oh, has she already dressed for dinner?" Wren asked, disappointed that she would have to wait until later to tell Sara about her afternoon.

"You might say she's as ready as she'll ever be," the maid answered mysteriously. "Miss Sara will be staying in the same room with her mother," she added.

"With her mother? Won't that be crowding it a little?" Wren's curiosity was piqued. Then she remembered that Sara hadn't been feeling well earlier. "I suppose Mrs. Stoneham wants Sara close by in case she becomes unwell again. Now, do you think you can prepare a bath for me? I've only an hour to dress for dinner. While I'm bathing, you can press my magenta satin gown. I want to look especially nice tonight."

Everyone was gathered in the drawing room, waiting for dinner to be announced. Everyone but Sara.

Wren was concerned for her friend and wanted to ask the Stonehams if Sara was feeling better, but Mr. Stoneham kept throwing her such black looks that she lost her nerve. After the introductions had been made, Wren tried to explain Sara's innocence to the Stonehams, but she was quickly silenced by a scathing look and a curt remark. Caleb came to her rescue and led her to the far side of the room to tell her something about the natives of Brazil, where he had taken his last shipment.

Even Malcolm seemed to fall under Jason Stoneham's loathing, and if Sirena hadn't gone to his rescue, there was no telling how fierce Jason might have become. Only Camilla seemed happily oblivious to the turmoil about her.

Suddenly Sara was standing in the doorway, her eyes downcast and red-rimmed from crying. Wren gasped in spite of herself when she saw what Sara was wearing. The funereal black contrasted dramatically with her skin, making it appear ghostly. Her silky, white-blond hair was drawn into a severe knot at the back of her head, and a white cap perched on top of her head.

Everyone in the room was stunned into silence. Jason stepped over to his daughter and took her arm. "How lovely you are, Sara. So pure and chaste."

Sara could not answer; she kept her eyes downcast, unable to face anyone. She wished Malcolm were not there to see her this way, and when she finally mustered the courage to look at him, all she could see in his eyes was blatant disapproval.

Wren sympathized with her friend. No one, nothing, could ever persuade her to dress herself like a Puritan if she lived to be one hundred.

Sara tiptoed out of her mother's room and closed the door on Margaret's light snores. Hastily buttoning her hated black Puritan's gown over her nightdress, she listened for a moment before moving toward the back stairs, which led down to the kitchen. Thankfully, it was the Stonehams' habit to retire early, and after a rather long session of Jason Stoneham's praying for his daughter's salvation, they had finally settled down for the night.

Jason had held true to his word and had all of Sara's clothes removed. Even her dressing gowns were considered devil's attire and had been taken from her. Now all she had to wear over her nightgown was the black dress.

She brushed her long, silky hair off her face and prayed that Malcolm had not left yet. She prayed even more fervently that her mother would not awaken and alert her father that their daughter was missing. From the front of the house she could hear good-byes being said. Caleb was leaving, and Camilla was complaining to Tyler that she was really quite weary. After a few moments, when she felt it was safe, Sara stole through the back door, into the kitchen garden and over to where the carriages were parked. The last one in line was Malcolm's hired phaeton, the driver fast asleep on his perch. Silently she pried open the door and climbed in. She didn't release her breath until she was safely hidden on the floor between the seats.

After what seemed an eternity, she felt a stirring atop the phaeton when the driver snapped to attention at Malcolm's approach. Her heart was beating so fast she thought it would explode through her breast. At least she would be alone with Malcolm. Within her stirred the faint hope that he would take pity on her and whisk her away. She didn't know how she could face life without being near him, seeing him, hearing his gentle laugh and waiting for the occasional touch of his hand.

The darkness of her gown concealed her in the shadows, and she waited until Malcolm had entered the coach and the driver had pulled away before she revealed her presence. "Malcolm, Malcolm . . ."

He turned his head, his blue-black hair shining in the moonlight. "Sara . . . ! What are you doing here?" he asked, incredulous at her boldness. "What if your father should find out? A fine mess it would be for me to explain to the van der Rhyses why you're with me!"

"Malcolm, Malcolm, please. I had to see you. It may be for the last time! My parents are taking me away somewhere, and they won't tell me where. Malcolm, please," she begged, crawling forward on her knees and placing her hand on his arm.

"Can't you see I'm done with you, Sara? Why won't you leave me be? I'll never understand your sordid attachment to Wren when you knew I had asked her to marry me . . ."

Sara rose and sat beside him. His eyes flashed with fury and she silenced him with her lips. He tried to pull himself away from her, to release her arms from about his neck, but she pressed closer, burdening him with her slender body.

Suddenly his struggles ceased and his lips were clinging to hers. "Sara, Sara, you little fool," he whispered, drawing her closer and burying his face between her breasts. Her flesh tingled where his fingers touched her, and her lips sought his again and again.

The buttons of her gown were quickly undone, and with the ease of familiarity, Malcolm pulled the black garment over her head, leaving Sara in her thin nightdress. The phaeton rocked through the streets, the driver oblivious to what was occurring in the cab beneath him. Sara's hair veiled her nakedness as Malcolm pulled the nightdress down over her shoulders and bared her firm, round breasts. She shivered with uncontrollable desire as her arms closed about him, bringing him down on top of her, relishing the feel of his lithe body pressed against hers.

He whispered her name over and over, filling her with a delight she had never known before. This was Malcolm kissing her, caressing her, penetrating her very soul. This was her love.

His mouth grazed her flesh with a practiced art, his fingers tantalized her skin, his breath was hot upon her cheek and she could feel his muscular back beneath her hands. Surging yearnings locked them together as they rode the dizzy heights and approached the crest. Sara cried out, "Love me, Malcolm, love me!"

She never wanted to leave his embrace. Her heart sang with joy as she rested against him, their passions abated.

"Sara, you must get dressed now. I must get you back to the Baron's home before your absence is discovered."

"No, Malcolm, don't make me go back there. I love you! I know you love me!" she implored, tears spilling from her eyes.

"Don't cry!" Malcolm admonished. "Why must you always cry?"

"How can you be so cruel? I've given myself to you, Malcolm, and you took whatever I had to offer. How can you think of casting me away like trash?" she sniffed.

"Trash is trash, Sara. When something is no longer needed, it becomes either treasure or trash. You, my passionate little Puritan, are no treasure." Malcolm smiled, his lips drawn into a sneer. "This is the last I'll see of you, Sara, unless, of course, you attend my wedding. But perhaps your father will have something to say about that. He seems to consider Wren a bad influence on you." Malcolm laughed aloud, the sound so derisive to Sara that she clamped her hands over her ears to block it out.

The phaeton took the return trip to the Sinclair home while Sara begged and argued and pleaded with Malcolm. But in the end she was left standing at the edge of the drive, near the stables, reluctant to go upstairs for fear her racking sobs would awaken her parents.

Chapter Six

As he had been asked to do, Caleb had come to Tyler's house for an early breakfast with Regan in order to discuss the latest events within the Dutch East India Company, for whom they were both representatives. Caleb sensed that it wasn't business which had inspired Regan to summon him for this quiet breakfast, nor was it a desire for a renewal of their relationship. Regan had something very definite on his mind, and he would take his own good time to reveal it. Whatever it was, Caleb didn't think he was going to like it.

On and on, late into the morning, Regan spoke of the Company, his home on Java, the four young sons who were impatiently awaiting their parents' return. He and Caleb caught up on news of common acquaintances and spoke of the looming civil war in England. Still Regan eluded the point of this meeting with his eldest son.

At last, when the maids kept interrupting them to clear off the table so they could prepare it for luncheon, Regan beckoned Caleb into the library. He poured himself and Caleb a healthy measure of rum and settled into an oversized leather chair. "What do you think of the young man Wren has chosen to spend the rest of her life with, Cal?"

No answer was necessary. Caleb curled his lip and drank deeply from his glass.

Regan laughed. "I thought as much. Sirena and I share your astute opinion, but Wren is another matter. She's positively smitten with him."

"Worse luck for her," Caleb muttered. "Surely you and Sirena aren't going to allow this marriage?"

"Wren is headstrong, as you know. Regardless of Sirena's and my protests, she'll do as she pleases. Sirena is quite distressed." Regan watched for Caleb's reaction on hearing of Sirena's concern. The lad was always sensitive to his stepmother and usually sympathetic to her feelings.

"What do you plan to do?"

"Nothing. What can we do? To forbid her to see him would only make him a more romantic figure in her eyes. Wren has to want to break this off on her own. She's always been sheltered. First with Sirena and myself, living on Java, where, you must admit, society isn't nearly as dazzling as it is here in London; and secondly, at the academy. I think our little Wren has fallen for the first man who has paid her court."

"A likely assumption," Caleb agreed. "You still haven't told me what you plan to do about it."

"What Wren needs," Regan continued, ignoring Caleb's remark, "is to know that she is desirable, beautiful and wanted by men other than this Weatherly."

Caleb raised his brows. "I would say you haven't enough time for that. From what I understand, Wren wants to be married before you and Sirena leave for Java."

"Exactly! And I can't tell you how happy I am that you agree with me. It's settled, then. *You* will be the man to show her that Weatherly isn't the only one who finds her attractive. Wonderful! Sirena will be delighted to hear you've brought yourself into our little scheme."

Caleb nearly choked on his rum. "I haven't agreed to anything! Do you mean to tell me that you and Sirena want me to pay court to Wren so she'll forget about Weatherly?"

"Exactly!" Regan repeated. "It's comforting to know you understand."

"You wily old fox!" Caleb exclaimed. "I never said I would do anything of the kind! Wren's a wonderful girl, a beautiful girl, but she's hardly my kind of woman. I doubt that I could bring it off, Father. And even if I did, then what? I would be the scoundrel who broke her heart."

"Oh, so you admit you could turn her head and take her mind off Weatherly?"

Caleb smiled. "Of course. Don't you know whose son I am? Say, did I ever tell you about that little tavern wench with the unusual appetites whom I happened upon in Cádiz?"

Regan leaned forward in his chair, a proud smile on his face. For the next hour they shared intimate details of the women they had loved and left behind.

Swirling the dark rum in his glass, Regan seemed intent on the burnished liquid when he casually remarked, "So, Cal, all the success you speak of with the fairer sex—it's mostly with tavern wenches and admitted prostitutes, right?"

Caleb raised an inquiring brow and smiled crookedly. "I think it's safe to say that those women are accepted authorities on the matter of what constitutes a man."

"Hmmm. I suppose you could say that; however, that's their business. Let me put it this way: you wouldn't take the word of a horse trader who was interested in your money for his nag, would you?"

"If you're saying that prostitutes always tell their customers what they want to hear because that's the way of business . . ."

"Exactly," Regan said softly, watching Caleb's indignation rise.

"You know perfectly well that women of breeding aren't allowed to associate with seamen, Regan . . . or have you been married so long you don't remember?" Caleb baited.

"I remember . . . I remember," Regan laughed. "And a catastrophe that is. Even when a girl is betrothed, there is always someone peeking over her shoulder and standing guard, not allowing a moment's intimacy. A catastrophe," Regan repeated, shaking his head.

"Come, now! A catastrophe? You're exaggerating. It's just the way things are. Every family wants to protect its daughter from bounders."

"Are you saying you're a bounder, son?" Regan raised his eyebrows and observed his son critically.

"Hell, I hope not. But I haven't had much traffic with the kind of girl I eventually hope to marry. I can't quite see myself with a tavern wench."

"No, I wouldn't imagine so. You've always wanted someone like Sirena, if I remember correctly, from when you were this high." Regan held his hand at waist level.

Caleb laughed uneasily. What was his father aiming at? Had he discovered that Camilla and he had carried on a love affair behind his back?

"What I'm saying, Caleb, is that I know you through and through. You regard marriage seriously. You'd want your wife to be your mistress as well. And you'd be right there. Nothing could be better than for a husband and wife to love each other totally, sharing their bodies as well as their souls, without the slightest hint of reticence. False modesty has been the death of many a marriage. Yet if you persist in your present attitude, you would certainly spoil any chance you have for such a marriage." Regan stared into his glass, his thoughts flying to Wren. How he would hate to think of her locked into a marriage with an unfeeling, self-serving bastard who thought only of his own satisfaction. How much happier Wren would be if she were loved by a man whose main concern was bringing her to a full realization of her passions. He thought of Sirena, his woman, beautiful, self-possessed and without inhibitions when she was with the man she loved.

Caleb laughed again, uneasily. This was by far the most difficult conversation he had ever had with Regan. "First you speak of whores and then you talk about making mistresses out of wives. In that case, what is the difference between a legitimate spouse and a woman who sells her favors?"

"The difference, my son, is between passion and venality. It is the line between inspirations of desire and planned behavior, the wide breach between tenderness and love and promiscuousness."

"God, Father, you really do take me for a bounder, a jackanapes, a whoremonger!" Caleb said hotly, the fine hairs at the back of his neck bristling. "If any other man talked to me in such a way—"

"It's because I care for you," Regan interrupted. "You haven't had the most normal upbringing. Not in the least. You've spent your life among men, aboard ship or in the seaports of the world. Not exactly the kinds of places where a man could learn to appreciate women. All I'm saying is that when the time comes for you to marry, in all likelihood it won't be to one of the doxies on the wharf. She'll be a girl carefully nurtured and watched over by her family. And in that case, her initiation into love will come from her husband, and he must take full responsibility."

Caleb ran a hand through his dark hair. "All right, Father, it seems as though you're not going to let me off without this little talk about the birds and the bees. But you're years late with it. I'll play your little game and listen to what you have to say. You were telling me about a man's responsibility for turning a sheltered, innocent girl into a passionate, responsive wife. What does that responsibility entail?"

"For one thing, a man must understand he is not an animal in a state of rut with only one purpose in mind —to satisfy himself by raping the woman." Regan's voice lowered, and a deep note of sorrow entered his next words. "You saw what rape did to Sirena and how she suffered."

"Father, whatever you may be thinking, I am not a rapist," Caleb said defensively. "I saw what happened to Sirena, I was there, yes. I'll never forget it. I don't consider myself like those scurves who—"

"Don't be so hotheaded. However you look at it, if a woman isn't ready for you, taking her is tantamount to rape. Can you imagine what it's like to be an inexperienced young girl in her first encounter with sex? The nudity of a man, the hugeness of his sex? And to be ridden? I am fully aware that it isn't always horrible to every young woman. I'm speaking of the sensitive, intelligent girl. A girl like Wren, for instance."

"I'll ask again. What responsibility does a man take?"

"Patience. Knowing how to enjoy the awakening of a woman's spirit and passions. Learning how to arouse her and lead her into the mysteries of the flesh. Even if a woman isn't a virgin, if she's been badly used, can you conceive of how frightful it would be to be taken without tenderness? Compare that fear with the delight of a woman overflowing with love for the man hungering for his body, yearning for his caresses."

"And suppose a man finds himself strapped to a woman who is incapable of this sublime passion even after every consideration and patience has been shown her?" Caleb wondered, watching for Regan's reaction.

"Then either she's a goose or the man is a bounder. And since you tell me you're not a bounder, Cal, be careful not to turn the woman you marry into a goose."

Caleb laughed again, this time uproariously, leaving behind the embarrassment he had felt earlier.

Just then the door opened and Sirena appeared. "What's going on in here between you two?" she asked, moving over to Regan, her taffeta petticoats rustling with each step she took. A puzzled expression crossed her face. "Caleb, what in the world is so funny?"

Bringing his laughter under control, Caleb managed to choke, "Nothing, Sirena. Regan was just telling me about goose herding. One more thing, Regan. Where did you learn all this?" His white teeth gleamed in a broad smile.

Regan put his arm about Sirena's waist and kissed her lightly on the cheek. "Everything I told you, son, comes from the best authority. Now, why don't you get your tail out of here so I can learn more about the subject?" he suggested in a husky voice as he gathered Sirena into his arms. "And, Caleb, close the door behind you."

Caleb sat in the garden, a feeling of doom dampening his normally outgoing personality. Why in the world had he promised Regan he would do as he had been asked? Now he wouldn't be his own man until he had resolved this problem with Wren and Malcolm. She was no one's fool. What had made Regan think she would fall for such an age-old trick? Man's vanity, Caleb told himself. He smirked slightly. It was true; he had always been successful with women, and he could have the pick of the litter, so to speak. And speaking of picking, he knew he could have little Miss Stoneham in his bed within the hour if he had a mind to. Just the thought of all her pink and whiteness sent a warm, pleasant flush through his body. She reminded him of someone, but who was it? A delicate flower ready to be plucked. He threw back his head and laughed. He'd bet his whole cargo that she had already been plucked by experienced hands, and quite soundly, too.

Some of the tension between his shoulders eased with his laughter. He needed a woman. It was that simple. But there wasn't anything he could do about it now. He had to put the first part of his father's plan into motion. Poor Wren. He would sweep her off her feet, and then what would happen to her? God forbid he would then be saddled with her. Regan hadn't said what he should do if that happened. It never occurred to Caleb that the young woman would find him anything but dashing and irresistible.

Out of the corner of his eye he saw Wren approach the garden, unaware of his presence. How in the devil had Regan managed this? Caleb wondered.

Wren continued her walk, her eyes cast downward at the flagstones, completely oblivious of Caleb. When he spoke, she raised startled eyes and flushed a deep crimson. "Hello, Caleb," she murmured, her voice a bare whisper.

"I didn't think anyone but me would be out this early," Caleb said, getting up from the iron bench and taking her slim hand in his. How unhappy she looked. Damnation, if she loved the fop, why couldn't Regan and Sirena allow her her happiness? Why did they have to interfere?

"This is my favorite time of day," Wren replied, smiling slightly. "I love to see the dew on the grass and feel it between my toes. Look," she cried girlishly, "I don't have my slippers on."

Caleb smiled in spite of himself. "I won't give away your secret. Sit down and let's have a talk. Yesterday was so hectic that we didn't get a chance to say much to each other. You've grown into a remarkable young lady, Wren. You're quite beautiful." He studied her features intently, lingering over her amber eyes and light ivory complexion. Her luxurious dark hair was tied back neatly and he fought the urge to free the pins and run his hands through the thick, silky strands.

"If you can admit I'm a woman, then why can't Sirena and Regan? I'm old enough to choose the man I want to marry." Her eyes and voice were very intense. Caleb's mouth tightened, and he chose his words carefully. "Perhaps it's because they never had a daughter of their own, and they want what is best for you. Once a parent, always a parent. Both Sirena and Regan have taken parenthood very seriously. I myself still talk over plans and decisions with my father. They're older and wiser than both of us. Try to be charitable and fair with them."

Flames shot from her amber eyes. "I should have known you would be on their side. You don't like Malcolm, admit it!"

"The one thing I would never do is take sides," Caleb lied. Damn you, Father, his mind shouted. "And as for my liking or disliking Malcolm, I hardly know the man. If you love him, then that's all I care about. Just be sure you *do* love him and that it's not something else you feel for him."

"And what might that be?"

Caleb decided to shock her. "Lust," he said curtly.

Wren heard the word, jumped up, and then drew back her arm and lashed out, striking him a stinging blow across the cheek. "Lust!" she shrieked. "That's all you or your father ever think about, isn't it? Malcolm is different. What happened to love? Oh, no, with you it's got to be lust. You're dead inside, aren't

82

you, Caleb? You have no feelings, just animal urges that have to be satisfied at the expense of some woman. Animal!"

Taken by surprise with the force of the slap, Caleb stood up and reached for her arm before she could render another attack. He pulled her to him and stared into her eyes. "Don't ever do that again. If you do, I'll forget that I'm a gentleman and give you what for." Wren stared back defiantly, her lips trembling.

Caleb felt a warm flush creep up his thighs, and his heart beat a little faster at her nearness. The sweet scent in her hair was light and tantalizing. He wanted to still the trembling of her quivering lips, to see the thick, sooty lashes close over her flaming eyes and know that he was the man who could make her sigh in delight as she nestled in his arms. She felt something, too. He could sense it in her slim body as she tried to remove herself from his tight embrace. He released her suddenly, applying Caleb's Law: Always leave them wanting more, anticipating what might have been.

His eyes became hooded, barely concealing a decidedly mocking gleam. "There are women, and then there are women. The day I decide that you're a woman, I'll let you know. Run back to your nursery and put on your slippers before Sirena and Regan see you. Grown-up ladies do not wander about barefoot in a gentleman's presence, brother or not."

Wren was infuriated at his derision of her. Childish! Not a woman! She looked almost comical as she swung her arm to strike out. Caleb, anticipating her move, stepped neatly back, and the force of her swing caused her to lose balance, sending her sprawling onto the dew-soaked grass. Caleb made no move to help her to her feet but remained standing, a smile on his face. He shook his head to show her she was indeed not a woman.

Blind with rage and humiliation, Wren reached

out and clutched at his ankle with both hands. Before he knew what had happened, he found himself sprawled next to her on the wet grass. "Pig!" she screeched. "You're no brother of mine! You're nothing but a disgusting animal!"

"Is that so? Let me show you what a disgusting animal I am," he growled, grabbing her by the shoulders and drawing her to him. His mouth came down slowly, his eyes staring deeply into hers. His lips were gentle yet demanding as his arms tightened imperceptibly across her shaking shoulders. His fingers found the pins in her hair and deftly undid them; then her long, flowing hair veiled them both as their lips clung together, neither of them wishing to relinquish the moment.

Some small warning device triggered Caleb's conscience. He had to remember where he was and what he was doing. He was doing his father a favor by kissing Wren and letting her know another man found her desirable. I have to remember that, he told himself as his lips became more demanding, his hands caressing the length of her young body. Why is Regan worried? he wondered inanely as Wren returned his ardor. Somewhere in the deep recess of his mind he heard a soft moan of desire and knew he had won. His lips moved gently and he looked down into her glazed eyes. They were both wrong, Regan and he. Wren was no girl. She was a woman.

His own eyes were dulled with the ecstasy of the kiss, his body relaxed in a warm glow, so that he barely felt Wren move till she was straddling him, her arms pinning his hands to the ground. Struggling with her skirts, she brought up her knee and jabbed him full in the groin. When he wrenched free of her, she doubled her hand into a fist and hit him square on the jaw while he sought to still the spasms in his midsection. "I said you were a pig and I meant it. You're a disgusting animal. You know I plan to marry Malcolm and you try to seduce me. Animal!" she hissed as she drew back for another blow to his face. Through pain-filled eyes Caleb found himself powerless to avoid it. He took the well-aimed stroke right between the eyes and rocked backward, his knees drawn up to his chest with his arms wrapped protectively around them.

"Damn you!" he cursed hoarsely.

"The next time you think to make a fool of me, Caleb van der Rhys, think again." Then she laughed, a light, lilting sound that was somehow devoid of humor. It sent Caleb into a near frenzy. God, how he remembered! Sirena had always laughed like that when she had met the challenge of an enemy and won!

"You can lie here and suffer till the cows come home," Wren said through clenched teeth.

Caleb watched her through a haze of distress as she picked up her skirts and daintily tripped her way back to the house. "Damn you," he called weakly as a fresh roll of pain coursed through him. He tried to struggle to his knees, only to fall backward again; his sun-darkened face whitened and he gasped in agony. His head throbbed in rhythm with the spasms in his lower regions. Christ, how could Regan have asked him for this "one small favor," and where in hell had Wren learned to fight like a longshoreman?

It was Sara who found him when she came out to the garden for one last stroll in the London sunshine before leaving with her family. She would have liked to walk through the streets and stamp the sights and sounds of the city on her memory forever, but the thought of appearing in public in the black, drab costume the Stonehams insisted she wear had dampened her resolve. Somehow she knew in her heart she would never see London again. Or Malcolm either. To have had him see her wearing the somber garb of the Puritan sect had cut bitterly into her heart.

Fanatics! That was what Malcolm thought of the followers of Cranmer and Calvin. Zealots! Sara gulped down her bitterness but couldn't swallow it whole. She had no choice but to obey her parents, for now at least. Beset by these unhappy thoughts, she nearly tripped over the figure doubled up on the lawn. She dropped to her knees, her blue eyes brimming with tears, not for the man at her feet, but for herself.

Caleb rolled to one side and opened an eye. Through the swirling red mist which clouded his vision he saw a black, wraithlike figure that seemed to float and come to rest near him. Damnation, he must be dying and the vultures were landing near him for the kill! Damn her soul to Hell and curse that wicked laugh of hers! Just like Sirena's laugh from those long-ago days at sea!

This couldn't be happening to him, not to Caleb van der Rhys. Things like this might happen to other men, but never to him.

"Lie still," the vulture's voice whispered. "I'll go back to the house for help."

With all the strength he could muster, Caleb once again struggled to his knees and held out a shaking arm for Sara to grasp. "No," he croaked, "don't go back to the house. I'll be all right in a few minutes."

Sara helped him to a sitting position and sat back on her heels, her hands folded neatly in her lap. These van der Rhyses were an odd lot. Whoever would have thought a man like Wren's brother would be subject to fits? As she waited for Caleb to get his wits together, her own misery surfaced again. Now what was she going to do?

In just the space of a few hours her whole life had been turned topsy-turvy. After throwing herself at Malcolm and having hope reborn in her heart, they had made wonderful, ecstatic love. And when she was certain that he had put his foolishness with Wren aside and realized that love was more important than marrying into a rich family, he had wrecked her dreams. He had told her in no uncertain terms that they wouldn't be seeing each other again, except perhaps at his wedding to Wren. He had actually held her in his arms and told her that their affair had been a delightful distraction but absolutely over. He was going to marry Wren. And then, most cutting of all, when she had threatened to reveal their affair to Wren, he had laughed. Laughed! He had told her if she wanted to ruin her good name, that was perfectly all right with him, but that it would be foolish on her part and all for nothing. And when she had said she would tell Regan van der Rhys what a bounder Malcolm was, he had claimed that, after all, a man would most certainly understand another man's weakness when a fetching young girl threw herself at him. And besides, a man never bought a cow when the milk was free.

To make matters worse, when she had tried to tell Wren about her and Malcolm's affair, Wren had laughed and laughed until tears rolled down her cheeks. Malcolm, *her* Malcolm, would never look at another woman! Malcolm had little use for Puritans and zealots. And then Wren had spoken in a charitable tone and assured Sara that one day she would find a love such as Wren and Malcolm shared. Malcolm was so wonderful, Wren had said with a smile, to have seen through the wiles of another woman and remain faithful. Malcolm had proved to her the kind of man he was. A good man, a fine man, and a man whom Wren loved.

Lastly, and possibly most humiliating of all, Caleb van der Rhys hadn't seen fit to return any of Sara's flirtations at lunch yesterday. All he had been capable of doing was to stare at Wren, his dark, thickly lashed eyes lighting whenever she had spoken to him.

Sara watched Caleb now with a detached interest as the white blotches on his face ebbed slightly and his breathing became more normal. With her own future so indefinite, she found it impossible to spare a moment's sympathy for his suffering. The only thing she was certain of was that her parents weren't returning home to Surrey, but they wouldn't tell her where she was being taken. Something was wrong. She had never seen her father so agitated, nor her mother so frightened. Whatever was wrong, Tyler Sinclair was somehow involved. Late into the night the Stonehams had been sequestered in his library. At today's early breakfast her mother looked as though she hadn't slept a wink, and her father was curt, almost rude. The most puzzling thing of all was that her father's mood seemed to have nothing to do with her escapade at the academy.

"I think I can stand now," Caleb said, clutching her hand as he rose to his feet. His face blanched with the effort and then regained its natural color.

Sara forced her mind to the present and spoke softly, almost whispering. "Do you have these spells often?"

"Spells?" Caleb muttered through clenched teeth. He combed a strong hand through his dark hair as he tried to comprehend her meaning. Spells! "Only when I walk in gardens before noon," he said, trying to force some sort of smile to his lips.

"I see," Sara replied primly. "Perhaps you should see a physician or take an herbal tea. Can you manage the walk back to the house?"

Fits! Spells! The pain had subsided and Caleb felt better by the minute. He held out his hand to Sara and smiled winningly. "It's been my cross to carry, lo these many years. They just come upon me. It's particularly bad when I'm with a woman. Invariably they take it the wrong way and think my fits are a result of their charms."

Sara's blue eyes narrowed. "You're as stupid and silly as your sister," she snapped, then walked off, knowing that the man behind her had somehow made a fool of her.

At the mention of Wren, Caleb's eyes darkened and he stumbled. No woman had the right to do what she had done to him. He'd wring her skinny neck if it was the last thing he did.

Regan van der Rhys had seen Wren run from the garden, her gown clutched in her hands, her bare feet soundless on the terrace. He had continued to watch, a frown on his face, as she had thrust open the doors and raced through them and up the curving stairs. "God damn it!" he had shouted to no one in particular. What could have gone wrong? "If you botched this up, Caleb, I'll . . . I'll . . . Damn it!"

He sat on the terrace for a long time before he saw Caleb stagger up the wide walkway. He said nothing as his son collapsed next to him on the iron bench, his eyes dulled, his mouth a grim, tight line.

"Don't ever ask me to do you any more favors, Father. Physically, I can't afford you."

Regan suppressed a grin. "So she got the best of you. Shame on you. How could you have allowed it to happen?"

"The same way you allowed Sirena to knee you. I was caught unawares," Caleb said hoarsely. "You can just forget your little plan. I'll have no more part in it. Let Sirena handle it. If you had let her do what she wanted in the beginning, I wouldn't be suffering like this. When are you going to learn that Sirena's the one with the answers?" His tone was bitter as he cast an accusing look at his father.

"Sometimes I forget," Regan replied sadly. "I really thought Wren would be smitten with you. You look just as I did at your age, and women found me irresistible. I had to fight them off with a stick." Regan laughed. "It's not true, like father like son."

"If I had had a stick I would have been better off," Caleb gasped as a twinging ache washed over him.

Regan's eyes held an amused glint. "You'll live through it. I did."

"Thank you, Father, for your words of wisdom, but you'll forgive me if they don't give me much comfort at the moment."

"A hot soak in a tub, a little rest, and you'll be as good as new in a month or so," Regan teased.

Caleb's eyes widened. "A month!"

"Maybe two. It's hard to tell. I wasn't there to see or feel the force of the . . . the impact. It would be best if you set your sights on six weeks, and then if you recover ahead of time, it will be like an extra reward. You'll live, Caleb. Let this be your first lesson. You need eyes in the back of your head when it comes to women. You can't ever let them best you in anything, for if you do, they have you right where they want you, in the crook of their little finger, and you'll be dancing attendance for the rest of your life. You're the master, remember that. It's up to you to tame the woman, not the other way around."

"I can't say I exactly admire your philosophy, knowing your past and how Sirena has had you dancing attendance all these years."

"Ah, you're so young, you don't understand. It just appears that way to you. I *allowed* her to do what she did, *that's* the difference. Of course she doesn't know that, and we'll just keep it our little secret. You have to fool women, lull them into what seems like a false sense of security. For a man of the world, you have much to learn," Regan concluded calmly as he lighted a cigar and leaned back, his manner amused and arrogant.

"Just remember what I said, Father. No more favors. As far as I'm concerned, Wren can do as she pleases. You've heard the phrase 'ill wind'? Well, your little Wren is an ill wind, and don't forget I'm the one who warned you." Caleb rose and made his way from the terrace without a backward glance at his father.

Not for all the nutmegs in Java would Regan have admitted that Caleb was right. He would leave it up to Sirena to take matters in hand. Who could blame him for trying? Poor Caleb. Well, his son would never fall into that trap again. At least he had learned something. The experience had not been a total loss.

Sara Stoneham stood in the dim alcove next to Tyler Sinclair's study, an intense look on her face. Another secret meeting between her father and Tyler? What could it mean? What was going on? She had to find out. Careful lest someone see her, she sidled over to the heavy double doors and pressed her ear against them, hoping against hope that she would hear something that would give her a clue to what was going on.

The voices were faint, almost unintelligible, but she didn't move, knowing that sooner or later her father would raise his voice.

"Time is of the essence, Baron. You promised you would help us, and now you want to go back on your word!" Suddenly, as if remembering his station compared with that of Tyler, Jason Stoneham softened his tone. "I'm afraid I'll have to insist my money be refunded. Immediately. Unfortunately, I cannot wait for money owed me the way I was once able to. Our circumstances have been—er—reduced, to say the least." Stoneham's face bore the pitiable lines of defeat. "Excuse me. I wouldn't ever have spoken to you in such a manner," he apologized, "but my son, Bascom, and his wife have been hiding at a lodging house near the wharves for over a fortnight. Margaret is beside herself with worry and anguish because she doesn't know what's to become of us. Damnation, man! You gave us your word that by noon tomorrow we would all be on our way to the American colonies!" Jason stormed, unable to hold back his fear and discouragement.

Sara, outside the door, could almost see Tyler bristle at her father's tone.

"Listen to me, Jason. The delay, for want of a better word, is not of my doing. There are hundreds, no, thousands of people of your sect seeking passage to the colonies. Unfortunately, for Puritans like your family who are also considered enemies of the Crown, the problem is increased a thousandfold. You, Jason, are not the only man of your religious persuasion who has lost everything he owned. As a matter of fact, I would think it safe to say that the Stonehams are faring much better than most."

"Bah! Easy enough for someone like yourself to say. You don't know what it's like to be hounded and pursued after being stripped of nearly everything you've worked a lifetime to attain." Jason's mouth turned down in a bitter line.

"No, perhaps I don't," soothed Tyler. "But I warned you. I told you to put a stop to your son's constant preaching against the Crown. But you refused to heed my advice. Bascom was a holy man, you insisted. He was appointed by God to speak out for the people. For God's sake, man! We've been friends for as long as I can remember. You were an associate in my father's law practice. Do you think I would cheat you out of a few miserable pounds?"

Jason hung his head in shame. "No, no, of course I don't. It's just that the hounds of Hell are on my trail, and I don't want to see the destruction of my family. Bascom was hasty, unwise, but nevertheless, he is the leader of our congregation. I tell you, Tyler, the change that's been wrought in him is so astounding it can only be called a miracle. Oh, I know you doubt it when he claims to have heavenly visitations. But what else can account for the fact that once he was a wastrel and now he burns with the light of salvation?"

Tyler reached out and laid a comforting hand on Jason's shoulder. "I have no right to disbelieve him. It is enough for me that you believe. I only regret that Bascom was so imprudent as to speak out publicly against the King, and in so doing, he has brought the black name of treason upon your family. However true it may be that King Charles boasts of his 'divine right' to serve as king and upholds his intolerance of the religious reformer, along with his refusal to call together legal sessions of Parliament, Bascom's preachings have wreaked destruction on all of you."

"What's done is done," Jason said weakly. "The fact remains that if I am to save my family and any small measure of my savings, we must leave England now!"

"And everything is being done to insure just that," Tyler assured him. "Already your land holdings have been sold and the money transferred to you. It should be a tidy enough sum to guarantee a pleasant life in the colonies."

"Bah! I had to sell out to the scurrilous Farrington for one-tenth of the true value," Stoneham said disgustedly.

"True. But it is one-tenth more than you would have had if the Crown had been quicker and had confiscated your holdings. As for the price, Farrington takes measurable risks also, and he paid the same as you could have gotten from another broker."

"I never thought I'd see the day when the likes of Farrington would make a fortune from respectable Englishmen," Stoneham moaned. "Once the titles have had a chance to clear, the man stands to reap great wealth by selling the properties at the market price."

"Jason, it's senseless to expound on this. What's done is done, as you said. The important thing right now is to get you and your family out of England."

"Well, what are you doing about it? I came to you for help—I begged you! And now here we sit, cooling our heels, and every moment the King's hounds are closing in on us!"

"Get hold of yourself, man! You sound as if they were on our front step. The Stonehams are not the only fugitives from the Crown. There are hundreds like you, for one reason or another."

"Mark my words, Sinclair. Soon, very soon, Cromwell will force an end to these persecutions. And when that time comes, my family and I will be the first aboard a ship returning to England."

There was a catch in Stoneham's voice that brought a choking response in Tyler's throat. Stoneham was a loyal Englishman, and the thought of leaving his country must be terribly painful to him. Tyler would have liked to pound his fists into Bascom's face and beat the man senseless. Not that he had much sense to begin with. Had it not been for his fanatical exhortations against the King, Stoneham and his family could have lived out their lives quietly and maintained their religious beliefs without interference. He supposed there was no fervor like that of a reformed sinner, which Bascom certainly was. The man actually had an insane look about him, and all Tyler could feel was pity for Stoneham, who, in his joy at Bascom's deliverance, would follow him blindly, all the while believing that his son had been found worthy of heavenly visitations from Christ Himself.

"To get back to the matter at hand," Tyler said with authority. "I explained to you that seeing to your passage would be a risky business. Farrington is also the man who was to arrange that passage. You would be among a group of others emigrating to the colonies. However, Farrington finds himself in bad straits. He's under suspicion and has been watched for the entire fortnight Bascom and his wife have been lodged near the wharves. Contact between them at this time would be foolhardy. I hate to keep reminding you, but you are fugitives from the Crown, unlike so many other

94

Puritans sailing for America. Would you endanger those good people by having the suspicion of conspiracy cast on them?" Tyler waited a moment for the impact of his words to sink in before he resumed speaking. "This delay is only a momentary setback. Good Lord, I don't know why I became involved in this at all. Whatever my sentiments about King Charles, I never wanted to put myself and my own family in jeopardy. For the time being, I've set you up in the same lodging house that your son is in. It is part of a public tavern, as you know, and your presence will not be conspicuous. Farrington will pay for all expenses incurred. What more can I do?"

"I realize I've imposed on our old association, Tyler, and I'm sorry if I've put your family in jeopardy. I'm half out of my mind with worry." Stoneham's voice lowered. "Can you give me any idea how long this will take? When can we sail? A fortnight?" he asked hopefully.

"The best I can say for now is, as soon as Farrington finds himself a new ship's captain. He's got a line on a privateer, he tells me, but there seems to be a holdup. Farrington's reputation depends on his choice of captains and vessels. You wouldn't want to risk a crossing on a leaky old tub at the hands of some drunken fool. Farrington's choice is crucial, and I, for one, wouldn't want to be standing in his shoes. Make up your mind that it's his way or none. The lot of us could end up spending the rest of our lives in Newgate. One experience with Newgate in a lifetime is all I'll ever need."

"We'll repair to the inn where Bascom is staying," Stoneham murmured.

"Jason, you know I would gladly offer you the use of my home, but there is Camilla and our coming child to consider."

"I understand, Tyler, and I would make the same choice if I were in your place. If I don't see you again before we sail . . ." His voice grew husky and he found it impossible to continue speaking. Instead, he extended his hand to Tyler, who put his arms around him and pounded him soundly on the back.

"Write to me when you're situated in America. Camilla and I might just make a journey there someday. And, Jason, between you and me, I hope the day comes soon when you can return to England. If that means we must first have a civil war between Cromwell and the Crown, then so be it."

Outside the library door, Sara blanched. America! The colonies! Indians! Before the door had opened, she raced quickly down the hall and up the stairs to her room. She had to think. She had to make a plan. America was on the other side of the world, and if she sailed with her parents, she would never see Malcolm again.

Flinging herself on the high bed, Sara sobbed uncontrollably. "I hate them all!" she wept. "I hate my father for his radical ways, and I hate my mother for her sanctimonious ways; most of all, I hate Bascom for opening his treasonous mouth and for his so-called heavenly visitations!"

Sirena stood looking out into the blackness, the night breezes blowing gently against the sheer draperies. The lamp beside her outlined her slim body through the gossamer silk of her peach dressing gown. Her dark hair tumbled down her back in charming disarray, and the air was scented with her perfume.

Regan gazed at his wife and remembered another time, long ago, when he had first seen her, outlined by the light from a window. Sirena, although no longer the girl she had been then, was somehow more beautiful, more lovely and exciting, and he knew, by some masculine instinct, that within her beat the heart of that determined, mystical, eighteen-year-old girl he had first seen.

Sirena turned, sensing his presence. Her eyes clouded with questions, but a smile parted her lips. Regan came to stand beside her and took her in his arms. She sighed with pleasure and nestled against his chest, taking delight in his arms wrapped tightly about her.

"What's the problem, sweetheart? Still brooding about Wren?" Regan asked, his lips brushing against her ear.

"At what point does a mother stop worrying about her children? Of course I'm concerned about her. Malcolm Weatherly is not the man for our daughter. Tyler's right, he's a bounder. Even without Tyler's word on it, I would have known that immediately."

"Ah, yes, your feminine intuition," Regan murmured.

Sirena turned in his arms and looked up at him. "Regan, I'm serious! Don't tell me you want to see Wren spend the rest of her life at that dandy's hands."

"No, sweetheart, I don't. But what's to be done for it? We can't tie her to her bed until she comes to her senses. And, knowing Wren, she'd deeply resent any interference by us. That girl can be as headstrong as you are."

"You'd better smile when you say that," Sirena teased, threatening him with a clenched hand.

Regan laughed merrily. "Don't deny it. She took her lessons well from you."

"Bragging or complaining?"

"Bragging, definitely bragging," he laughed.

"Well, pretty compliments don't solve our problem. What's to be done?" Concern clouded Sirena's eyes again, and she turned her head away.

Regan sighed. "I guess I'd better come up with something. I can't have you frowning and creating wrinkles across that pretty face."

"Wrinkles!" Sirena cried. "Where?" She rushed over to the pier glass and scrutinized her face.

Regan laughed again, loudly and raucously. "Still vain, eh, pet?"

"Oh, you—you scoundrel!" Her fingers found the hairbrush and Regan artfully dodged the hurled object. Lowering his head, he charged right for her, grabbed her around the waist and tumbled both of them to the soft carpet. His lips found hers and sealed them in an ardent kiss, successfully stifling her protests.

After a moment Regan drew away and looked down at her. "You win, sweetheart. If you want to talk about this situation with Wren, I'm listening."

Sirena smiled. How well this man knew her, and how she loved him. He knew she had to set her feet on a course that would resolve the problem before she could come to him, free and abandoned.

Regan got to his feet and helped her up, holding her for a moment. "Only hurry and work this out in your mind, Sirena. A man can't be expected to wait forever."

Patting him fondly on the cheek, Sirena whispered, "Do you know how much I love you, Regan? You know me so well and love me in spite of myself." She moved away from him and seated herself on a chair that was farthest from the bed. "Tell me what you think of this Weatherly, Regan."

Regan paced, as he always did when he was thinking. "I quite agree with Tyler's opinion. He's a bounder. And from what Tyler has told me, Weatherly is down on his luck. There's not much to be said for his financial status. Which could lead a worried father to suppose that Wren's main attraction for him is money."

"Agreed," Sirena said firmly. "Not that Wren couldn't have any man she wanted. She's certainly beautiful and intelligent, but Weatherly is the first man she's ever become romantic about. We can't allow her to make a mistake she'll have to live with the rest of her life. Regan, can't you go directly to Malcolm and tell him we don't approve of this match and that if Wren insists upon it, we will be forced to disinherit her?"

Regan pondered for a moment, his agate-blue eyes narrowed in thought. "No, Sirena, that wouldn't work. We've already exhibited how dear Wren is to both of us. He'd know that whatever might happen, we could never bear to have Wren live in want of anything we could provide. Naturally, if he were married to her, our beneficence would also fall on him. Any other ideas?"

"We could offer him a sum of money, a large sum. If what Tyler says about his finances is true, he just might jump for it."

"Don't you see that wouldn't work either? We'd be holding ourselves up for blackmail. Yes, Weatherly would take the initial offer, but then he'd bleed us dry while he was contriving little ways to court Wren secretly. Even if Weatherly found himself another woman, he'd still haunt us. And what if Wren were to discover we had paid him off? We'd lose her, Sirena."

When Regan halted his pacing to look at his wife, he was surprised to see Sirena's chin set in a curve of stubborn determination and her eyes flashing green fire. "What is it? You've thought of something, you little witch! Now, give over and tell me what it is!" he demanded.

"It's so simple! It's been right under our noses all the time!" Sirena laughed gaily. "Regan, did you notice the attention Malcolm was paying me this evening?"

"Notice! I noticed, all right! And I don't mind telling you I was keeping a watchful eye. I knew your game, Sirena, but I wasn't certain of his. One false move on his part, and I would have slit his gullet!"

"There, you see! That's the answer!" She went over to the desk, seated herself and withdrew a sheet of stationery from the top drawer. Her pen poised over the paper, she bit her bottom lip and began to write.

"What's that?" Regan asked. "What are you up to?"

"Thank you, darling. You've just given us the answer to Wren's problem with Weatherly. It's safe to say that the only thing more valuable to Malcolm than his fancy clothes and his money is his life. Regan, darling, you are going to threaten Malcolm."

"Threaten to kill him? Sirena, it will never work! Every father threatens murder in some way or another to the man who takes his daughter away from him. Few ever carry out the threat, and Malcolm knows it!"

"Ah, yes. That is true with a daughter. It is quite different with a wife. I've heard of many men who've met their end because they were too attentive to another man's wife. Certainly Malcolm knows of several cases himself. And you, Regan, can be most ferocious when necessary."

Regan thought for a moment and then laughed. "I can see your point. Why, if I ever thought that Weatherly—or any other man, for that matter—were to steal you away from me, he would find destiny at the end of my sword."

"Exactly. All I have to do is write this little note to Malcolm, inviting him to visit me tomorrow. The scene will be set, and you, darling, will find our young dandy in a compromising situation. I'm certain I can rely on you to take it from there."

"With pleasure." Regan made a courtly bow. "Now, hurry and finish that damn note, and I'll have a footman deliver it immediately. It's a fool's idea, but it just might work."

Sirena applied pen to paper, blotted the note and then handed it to Regan. His eyes narrowed.

"Sirena, we're taking a chance here, and, like all schemes, it could backfire on us." At Sirena's questioning look, Regan continued. "We'll have to be very careful. Wren must never know what we've done. She'd hate us, Sirena, but most of all, she'd hate you."

Sirena's eyes became distant. How could she ever bear having Wren hate her? But she knew Regan spoke the truth. "That is a chance I have to take, Regan. I would rather have Wren hate me than leave her to the wiles of a scoundrel." The moment was tense, the air charged with unasked questions. Regan knew Sirena had calculated the odds and decided to live with whatever the outcome would be. Her lips formed a smile, but there were uncharted depths in her eyes. "Regan, give the note to a footman and hurry back," she said softly. "I need you to hold me."

Chapter Seven

As Sirena stepped into the garden, the light breezes caught the ends of her hair and blew them softly against her cheeks. Her face turned to the sun, she bit into her lower lip to keep it from trembling. The scene she was about to play with Malcolm strummed at her nerve endings. She hoped Tyler hadn't noticed her fidgeting at breakfast and the way she had kept asking him the time. Malcolm should be arriving at any moment, and it was only with the help of the heavens themselves that Wren had an appointment with her dressmaker that morning. Otherwise Tyler would have had to be brought into the little plot so that he could keep Wren away from the garden.

Sirena smoothed the folds of her sea-green gown. If she was going to play the part of a seductress, she had decided to look like one. The material matched her eyes perfectly, and she had applied a touch of Spanish paper to her lips and cheeks to heighten her coloring. Trying to find humor in a situation she herself had created, she smiled and hoped she wasn't out of practice. Flirting and seduction were arts that were never lost to a woman. She waved a lace-edged handkerchief in the air; the linen had been liberally doused with scent. Poor Malcolm, she sighed with a touch more confidence. He would hardly be a match for her wiles. Later, much later, years from now, Wren would thank her. If Wren ever found out, God forbid.

Sirena settled herself on a bench near a bed of roses, a long legal paper clutched in one hand. Slowly, sensuously, she swung her foot to and fro, careful that her slim ankle and trim slipper peeked from beneath the hem of her gown. Men liked a show of ankle, and Weatherly would be no exception.

She cast a critical eye at the sun and knew that Malcolm would arrive within minutes. A promise to continue their discussion of the night before in an "intimate setting" was all she had needed to offer him to be certain he would fall prey to the plan.

When she heard his footsteps on the flagstones, she made no move to indicate she knew he was near, but bent her head over the legal paper she had snatched from Tyler's desk at the last minute.

"Mrs. van der Rhys," Malcolm said, bowing low and touching his lips to her hand in a too-familiar and ardent manner. His eyes, however, focused on the legal document in her lap; papers of that nature always represented money in one form or another. It was just possible she was working with Sinclair on the arrangements for Wren's dowry. Commendable, he said to himself, liking Sirena more by the minute.

"Malcolm," Sirena cooed, "how prompt you are. An excellent virtue. A sign of a dependable man. And you Englishmen certainly do have a flair when it comes to dressing. You must give me the name of your tailor, and I'll have Regan stop by and order some new clothes before we leave for Java." She touched the fabric of Malcolm's frock coat, letting her long, slender fingers trail lightly over his chest. "You are simply dashing." Sirena smiled and appraised the man beside her. She could understand Wren's infatuation with him. Any woman might find herself likewise smitten. His dark hair was crisp and curled softly on his well-shaped head, a rakish lock spilling boyishly onto his forehead. His features were handsome, almost pretty, but his strong, square chin lent authority to his face. He had a habit of lowering his chin and looking up through long, spiky lashes, the kind young children have after they've been crying. Only Weatherly's mouth gave a hint to the man within. Well-defined but narrow lips, which Sirena knew could curl with cruelty, were studiously curved into a smile showing gleaming, strong teeth. And beneath the stylish clothes was a sinewy, long-limbed body hardened by years of riding and athletics. Malcolm Weatherly was a vain man, and this trait would provide the key to his undoing.

Malcolm was flattered and his heart beat a little faster at her light—was it also teasing?—touch. "How is your headache this morning?"

"Oh, it's gone," Sirena said airily. "The trick to getting rid of a headache from the night before is to have a glass of wine before you get out of bed the next morning. Actually, Regan is the one who told me about drinking wine on rising. He said something to the effect that sounded like 'a little bit of the hair of the dog that bit you.'" She laughed at the befuddled look on Malcolm's face. "Sometimes Regan can be very crass. Pay it no mind; a gentleman like yourself would never say anything like that, I'm sure."

"Perhaps with another man, but never to a lady or within her hearing," Malcolm simpered.

"Now, Malcolm, there's a little something I want to discuss with you, and I do hope you will give me your word that what we say now will be just between the two of us." Sirena's voice was low and throaty.

"Dear lady, you have my word," Malcolm whispered, his eyes wide and his hands trembling at his sides.

"Now that you've met my husband and stepson, I'm sure you can see they're not . . . not quite like other men. They don't have the flair, the style, that you English have. They're more—how can I say it and not sound disloyal?" Sirena pretended to frown. "Earthy," she declared happily. "Yes, they're earthy. They don't understand young love and romance and things like that, whereas I, being a woman, do. I want you to know that no matter what they say, no matter what they do, I'm on your side." She leaned forward so that her breasts almost spilled from the low-cut gown. "I think that you are the perfect choice for our little Wren." Her slender hand reached up and touched Malcolm's cheek, and she purposely widened her eyes, a look of innocence on her face. "I feel it here," she said, taking his hand and placing it on her bosom, "that you will take care of her and we won't have to concern ourselves with her well-being. I just feel it here," she repeated dramatically, pressing his hand against the soft swell of her breasts.

"And you're right," Malcolm agreed as he tried to loosen his collar. "You can trust me with her life— with your life, too," he babbled, his eyes becoming moist.

Sirena's breath quickened at the hot look in Malcolm's eyes. Fool! her mind shouted. Where is Regan? How long can I keep up this playacting? Regan had promised that he would give her ten minutes alone with Malcolm. Surely it was long past that now.

Her ears picked up the sound of a footfall at the end of the path. At last, Regan! Sirena made her move. Her eyes became heavy-lidded as she licked at her lips, making them wet and inviting. "Come here, closer," she whispered throatily. "I have something I want to say to you, something for your ears alone." She bent forward slightly, one breast almost entirely exposed as Malcolm fought to keep his eyes on her seductive face.

"You can trust me, Sirena, with whatever it is you have to say," he whispered back, quivering at what he knew he shouldn't be seeing.

Sirena was careful not to move. "I wish," she breathed heavily, "that I were the one you were in love with, not Wren. There, I've said it and I'm not ashamed!" She heard Malcolm utter a loud groan and found his head buried in her bosom. "Darling, you feel the same way, I can tell," she murmured, gasping for breath. She clutched his head to her as he burrowed deeper into the soft flesh between her breasts. "I knew you cared for me last evening when you offered me the wine. Stay here forever," she pretended to moan.

"Forever and forever," Malcolm echoed hoarsely, his hands feverishly attacking the beautiful woman's curves.

Sirena's mind raced. Hurry, Regan! Now! Now! The warm wetness of Malcolm's mouth revulsed her. If ever she had any doubt of Malcolm's love for Wren, his actions now were proof of the bounder he was. The footsteps came closer. Hurry, Regan, hurry!

"Of all the despicable tricks!" Wren's voice rang through the garden. "How could you?" she screamed at Sirena. "Aren't you ever satisfied? Isn't Regan enough for you? How could you do this to me, of all people? Whore!" Wren's face was drained of all color, her eyes dull and hard. "I'll never forgive you for this, Sirena. Never!"

Sirena was dumbfounded. Where was Regan? Why wasn't Wren at the dressmaker's? Malcolm was flustered and looking like a plucked peacock. And here was Wren, blaming her, Sirena, not this simpering oaf who was trying to maneuver himself away from Wren's ire. Sirena was being blamed for Malcolm's perfidy. She had to do something, say something to make Wren understand it had been only a ploy to save her from Malcolm. "Wren . . . you don't understand, I wasn't—"

"I don't want to hear a word you have to say. My eyes told me all I needed to know. You have to be the center of attraction. You need men, all men, to throw themselves at your feet and adore you. Regan, Caleb, the boys, they're not enough! No, now you've set your wiles on Malcolm, on my man! Well, it won't work, Sirena, because I know Malcolm loves me! He'll always love me. *Me!* Do you hear me, Sirena? And what's more, I never want to see you again." Wren choked. "I . . . don't . . . *we* don't need you, do we, Malcolm? We don't need anything from her. Not her blessing on our marriage . . . not her money . . . not anything!"

Malcolm's mouth fell open in amazement. This wasn't exactly what he had had in mind when he had begun courting Wren van der Rhys.

"You don't mean that, Wren," Sirena pleaded. "You're my daughter, my child; sometimes I think you are more mine than the children I carried within me . . ."

Wren turned her head away, refusing to face Sirena, feeling betrayed by her. Her heart was near breaking. She wanted to throw herself into Sirena's arms, wanted to listen to any explanation Sirena might offer, yet she couldn't bring herself to do that. If she listened to Sirena, it would mean that Malcolm had betrayed her, and that was the one thing certain to destroy her.

Malcolm gazed in amazement at the two women. What were they saying? What had Sirena meant when she said that Wren was more her child than the children she had carried? Wasn't Wren Sirena's child? "Wren, speak to your father . . ."

Wren turned to face him, her amber eyes sparked with rage. "Regan is no more my father than Sirena is my mother. I only have you, Malcolm," she said with a sudden softness in her voice. "I need you. You must take me away from here—now! Please!"

Speechless, Malcolm followed Wren's lead as she took his arm and pulled him away.

Sirena sensed a presence near her and looked up into Regan's agonized eyes. "We did all we could, Sirena," he said, "and it looks as though we made a botch of it. Wren came home early and must have slipped through the gate near the stables. I was just about to make my grand entrance when she discovered you here."

Wordlessly, Sirena held out her arm and Regan drew her close. "What will we do now, Regan? We've lost her. We've lost our daughter," she murmured through stiff lips, choking back the tears.

"We'll find her again, sweetheart, you'll see."

"But she's leaving, going off with Malcolm."

"No, she won't. I'll bet on it. I heard everything. She told him she wasn't really our child. I doubt he'll have any use for her now that she's decided to quit herself of us. She'll come back, you'll see. Caleb will bring her back."

But Sirena was not to be consoled, and the tears that coursed down her cheeks burned her skin.

Outside the garden, Wren waited with Malcolm for the groom to bring his phaeton around. "I'll gather my things and meet you at your apartment," she said softly, still holding back racking sobs. "I imagine it will take no more than a few hours. Hold me, Malcolm, hold me!" she cried, hurling herself into his arms. "I've never spoken to Sirena that way. I've always loved her, always been sure of her love for me. I . . . I don't blame you, Malcolm. Sirena is beautiful, and she threw herself at you."

"I wouldn't do that if I were you, Wren," he said coldly, his tone so stiff and detached that Wren pulled away and looked up at him with bewilderment. "I mean I don't want you to come to my apartment. You've ruined everything with your silly schoolgirl mentality. I'm afraid I have no further use for you, Wren."

"Use for me? Malcolm, what are you saying?" Her voice quivered and her hands trembled. "I love you, Malcolm. I'll always love you."

"Don't say that. Can't you understand? I've enough to do with feeding myself. I can't support you, too. I haven't a farthing to my name, thanks to my wastrel uncle. I've barely enough to keep body and soul together, let alone pay my tailor's bill. Within days my creditors will be hounding me again. I can't afford you, Wren."

"We'll do something. We'll survive. I'll find some work, and you can do so many things—"

"Stop it, Wren. Get it through your head that I can't afford you. Here's my carriage." Barely waiting for the vehicle to come to a stop, Malcolm sprinted inside. "I'm sorry it worked out this way, Wren, but you've only yourself to blame."

"I'll come to you, Malcolm, I will! I'll do anything for you, work my fingers to the bone—"

"Don't, Wren. Don't make this any uglier than it is. Don't come to me. Stay away from me. I can't afford you." Banging the side of the coach with his fist, he shouted at the driver to go faster. Wren was left alone on the drive, tears streaming down her cheeks, a look of confused astonishment in her golden eyes.

Without a backward glance at the girl he had wanted to marry, Malcolm gave his driver instructions to the home of Lady Elizabeth Rice. Now, more than ever, he was interested in listening to what she had to say about the jeweled collar the King was having made for his son's birthday. Now, more than ever, he needed what revenue he could gain from the sale of those jewels. Providing, of course, that he would be successful in acquiring them. Settling back on the leather upholstery, he mentally reviewed a list of all the markets and fences on which he could unload the collar for the top price. The name of Lord Farrington kept cropping up. The Prince's birthday was still two weeks away, which would give Malcolm two days at the very most to relieve the goldsmith of his art work. The first thing he had to do was to contact Farrington. But that would be after he had spoken to Lady Elizabeth. He anticipated her smooth, white limbs welcoming him into an embrace and felt a veil of moisture gather on his upper lip. Sirena van der Rhys had set his blood on fire, and it would take the ministrations of the sensuous redhead to quench his thirst.

The tension in the Sinclair home was unbearable. Wren stayed closeted in her room, refusing to come out even for meals. Sirena snapped and snarled at anyone foolhardy enough to approach her. Regan paced Tyler's study, thinking and shaking his head. He had tried to speak to Wren and been refused entry to her room. Tyler seemed preoccupied with something he refused to share with anyone. Caleb had come to dinner and left early after a long, silent meal. Only Camilla seemed oblivious to the tension in her home. Her thoughts were fixed on her coming child, and that was her only interest now.

Sirena came downstairs after lunch the next day with orders for errands to be made. On her way to the kitchen she passed Camilla in the sitting room, busily stitching what looked like a baby blanket. "The least you can do is say something," Sirena snapped. "Don't you know what's going on in your own home? Haven't you tried to speak to Wren and find out what she's thinking? And the baby hasn't been born who needs seventeen blankets. Don't you ever do anything else?"

Camilla raised her pansy eyes, her needle poised in midair. "Whatever are you talking about, Sirena? Is something wrong with Wren? I mean, is she ill? I already know that you two are having a squabble of some kind. And you're wrong, Sirena, this is the nineteenth blanket I've stitched. England can be quite cold and damp in the winter, and a mother can never have too many blankets."

"Spare me your wisdom, Camilla," Sirena answered curtly as she headed for the kitchen.

Regan had overheard the conversation between Sirena and Camilla and almost found himself ready to make excuses for Sirena's short temper. Wisely, he turned and went in the other direction. He had enough trouble with the women in his family as it was, and he didn't care to have Sirena's rage directed toward him, which was exactly what would happen if she ever discovered him apologizing for her behavior.

Upstairs, Wren paced, wringing her hands and dashing away the tears that continually formed in her eyes. Malcolm. Poor, sweet Malcolm. Pretending he didn't love her to spare her from a life of hardship. Didn't he know she loved him more than life itself and that she would rise above anything just to be with him, to be his wife? Sweet, noble Malcolm. The past two days had been a haze of heartache and tears, and looking ahead to never seeing him again was unbearable beyond belief. It was not to be comprehended. He was her love, her life. His cruelty had been a pose, an act, and he had been driven to it by his love for her. Her love for him became overpowering, and she threw herself on the high bedstead and sobbed into her pillow. "I won't let you do this, Malcolm. I won't let you keep us apart because you think I'm not strong enough to face poverty. I'd face death itself if I could be by your side." With all the aching urgencies of young love, Wren yearned for Malcolm until she thought her heart would break. The nights she had spent in his arms, feeling his lips against hers, hearing him whisper how much he loved her, needed her, rushed back to her. She decried her silly schoolgirl fantasies about walking down the aisle to meet her husband as a virgin. Now she wished she had succumbed to Malcolm, had allowed him to make love to her; then nothing on earth could keep them apart. They would have made themselves one forever.

Suddenly, with a will and a determination she hadn't known she possessed, Wren stumbled from the bed and pushed a chair up to the clothespress. She climbed on the chair, reached for her portmanteau and pulled it down to the floor. Breathing heavily, she flung open the clothespress and searched through her wardrobe, her fingers seeking the most modest gowns she owned, automatically discarding the opulent silks and satins which had always been her vanity. A working girl couldn't wear elaborate clothing, and if she was going to help Malcolm support them, she would take only the most utilitarian items she owned.

The small trunk was heavier than the few belongings stuffed into it, and she had little difficulty carrying it. She was on her way to Malcolm, and she would make him happy, she was certain of that. If Malcolm loved her only half as much as she loved him, their marriage would be made in heaven.

Wren didn't look back, for she feared she would falter. Regan and Sirena loved her, but they didn't understand her. She couldn't allow herself to think about them. She was embarking on a new life, and her only concern could be for Malcolm and his happiness.

Wren placed her portmanteau by the door of Malcolm's apartment, then allowed herself a moment to catch her breath. Fortunately, she had been able to slip out of the house unnoticed and had managed to heft the trunk to the corner of the avenue, where she had hired a hack.

Downstairs, Malcolm's landlady had asked her impertinent questions and then snapped her mouth shut when Wren had stabbed her with an icy look. It was obvious the woman knew her betters when she met them. Grudgingly, she had pointed out Malcolm's door and watched as the young girl with the imperious attitude struggled up the stairs with the trunk. Arms folded across her buxom bosom, the landlady shrugged her shoulders. It was none of her business, she thought, as long as the rent was paid. And a long time coming that was, too! Perhaps the young miss would set things aright. If not, the girl's presence at least gave her a lever for having the dashing Malcolm Weatherly thrown out on his elegant ass.

As Wren sat atop her trunk just outside his door, Malcolm stood before his dressing table, holding a package. Gently he unwrapped the cloth. The black velvet slipped through his trembling fingers as he fumbled with the folds. His eyes shone with greed; his lips were slack as he spread out his treasure with tenderness. The light filtering through the worn draperies spun a halo of gold and glitter upon the King's collar. Even as he looked at it he couldn't believe it was here, in his possession. It had almost been too easy.

Because the goldsmith had assumed he was working under great secrecy and hadn't wanted to call attention to his shop until after the collar had been delivered, he had failed to hire a guard. At first Malcolm had been thwarted by the heavy iron bars on the jeweler's windows and door. But the day he had spent studying the small shop on Cheap Street had been worthwhile. Upon first inspection, it had appeared that the shop was self-contained and that the only way to the upper floors of the building was by the outside stairs. Then, shortly after noon, Malcolm had looked up and seen the jeweler pass by one of the windows on the second floor. Having kept himself in full sight of the outside stairs and not having observed the goldsmith use those stairs, he had rightly assumed that there was also an entrance to the second floor from within the shop. And the second floor's door and windows were unbarred. Late that night Malcolm had climbed to the second floor, the lock on the door giving easily under the pressure of his knife. It had been simple thereafter to locate the route to the floor below and help himself to the collar.

Malcolm was mesmerized by it. Made of heavy gold and large enough to go around a man's waist, the piece was intricately wrought and set with precious stones. Fiery diamonds were the largest of these, offset by sapphires and golden topaz. The sunlight caught each facet of the gems and highlighted their brilliance.

The sudden knock on the door made Malcolm start with such force that he found himself trembling. Guilt-ridden, he quickly wrapped the collar in the jeweler's velvet and hastily pushed the cloth into the bottom drawer of the dresser.

"Coming! Who's there?" he called, struggling to keep his voice under control.

"Malcolm! It's me, Wren!"

"Wren!"

The door swung open and Wren threw herself into his arms. "I had to come," she cried. "I couldn't stay away any longer. I love you, Malcolm."

"What are you doing here? I told you how it was. Please go home, Wren."

Not to be put aside again, Wren pushed her way into the room. "I won't go away. I came to be with you, for always. No, don't say anything; hear me out first. I know how noble you're being. I know you don't want me to do without the things I've always had. But you're wrong, Malcolm. I haven't always had them. I know what it's like to do without. I know what it's like not to have enough to eat or to pay for lodgings. I didn't always live with Sirena and Regan. I was almost ten years old when Sirena found me and took me to live with her. Before that, I'd been living on the streets or worse. I had to work for my living. Only one person in the world besides Sirena was ever kind to me, and that was Lottie, a foxy old crone. So you see, darling, I haven't always been a spoiled little pet. I knew what life was like for the people in the slums even before I could walk."

Malcolm regarded her with increasing astonishment. Not only had Wren misled him about being the daughter of the van der Rhyses, she'd also lied to him about who she was. An urchin, a street urchin born in the London slums, and now she had the audacity to suppose she might be good enough to wipe his shoes!

Before he could utter a word, Wren was in his arms again. "When will we be married, Malcolm? You can't send me back, you know. I've already told them I was coming to you. I . . . I even told them we were lovers," she lied, hoping he would believe there was no turning back for her, desperate to convince him she had given up everything just to be with him because he was so important to her. She couldn't let him send her back now that they were together again, now that her arms were around him and she was so close to belonging to him forever.

"Did you bring any money with you?" he asked curtly.

"Only my allowance that I've been saving. Thank the Lord I didn't pay my dressmaker's bill. Altogether I've over fifty pounds," she announced proudly. "A very nice start for a married couple. Here," she said, holding out her purse.

"This isn't going to go very far," Malcolm snapped. "The least you could have done was to bring some jewelry or something we could sell."

"Please don't look so upset," she pleaded. "Everything will work out, you'll see. Truly it will."

"Truly it will," he mimicked in a whining voice. "Well, truly it won't. You don't seem to understand, Wren. Go home."

"Don't, Malcolm. Please don't send me away. You said you couldn't afford me. Well, you won't have to. I'll work, I'll do anything, only don't send me home."

"Two days ago I said I couldn't afford you." He glanced covertly at the dresser, where the collar was hidden. "Now I don't want you. I don't need you anymore." He chuckled cruelly, thinking about the price the collar would bring him. "Go home, you silly schoolgirl!"

"No! I won't! I'm not a silly schoolgirl any longer. You need me, Malcolm. You do." She was in his arms, her mouth seeking his, her lips parted, her tongue searching for his. She pressed herself against him, felt his warmth against her, was aware of a rising urgency in him.

His arms came around her, tightening, pulling her toward him. The exhilaration he had experienced over the stolen collar was emphasized by the offerings of this beautiful girl. Yes, she was right. He did need her. For the moment.

"You see, darling," she whispered against his mouth, "you do need me. You want me."

"You're so right, Wren. It's time I learned what you are all about."

The harsh tone of his voice and the rough way he pulled her toward him, crushing her mouth beneath his, startled Wren. This wasn't the Malcolm she knew. That Malcolm had been sweetly passionate, tender, hesitant.

Suddenly fear gripped her as she stared at him. She had expected to see her love mirrored in his eyes; instead, she saw hot, burning coals. His lips tore heedlessly at hers while she stood frozen with terror. His hands worked at the buttons on her dress, and he grasped her breasts in a careless, hurtful way. His breathing was harsh and labored as he bent her backward, his mouth never leaving hers.

Wren knew what was happening and was powerless to stop it. All protests died in her throat, and she fought him with every ounce of strength she could summon. This couldn't be Malcolm. Not the Malcolm she knew and loved. This was someone else, a perverted creature with only lust, not love, on his mind.

The pain he was inflicting on her with his urgent thrusts was hot and searing, unlike any pain she had ever experienced in her life. She wanted to scream till her lungs burst, and yet no sound came forth. His fingers wrenched her flesh, and he sucked at her nipples until Wren prayed she would die. The agony and shame she felt were more than she could bear, but the dull void of love lost engulfed her and rendered her senseless with a force greater than any physical attack.

The torment and degradation continued. Wren's young body was stiff with shock as Malcolm drove into her again and again. Her insides felt hot, swollen, as if they were being torn to shreds by the ceaseless force of the man's deep thrust. Blood seeped between her legs as she tried vainly to beat at him with her small, clenched fists.

Her attempts were futile against his strength as he savored her smallness, savored the fact that she was a virgin no longer, exulted in his possession of Wren and the collar both in the same day. He had always wanted to do this to her, ever since the first night he had kissed her and known that one day she would give herself to him. Malcolm hadn't wanted Wren to give —he had wanted to take! When his passions had gone beyond his bearing them, she would coyly pull away from him and straighten her gown, pleading her stupid virginal morals and saying something about his being naughty. Naughty! When his loins had ached for release and his blood had refused to cool!

Half-conscious from the brutal attack, Wren felt Malcolm go limp, his deep thrusts abating as he remained inside her, his mouth on hers, his saliva merging with hers till she wanted to gag, to rid herself of him.

Malcolm got to his knees and gazed down at her half-naked body, then hurled the final insult at her. "Your friend Sara's body is far more beautiful than yours; her breasts are larger, rounder and softer. She came to me willingly and we were together as one, each of us giving and taking. You're like a lump of clay," he jeered.

Wren lay on the floor, making no move to cover her nakedness. What did it matter now if he saw her or compared her with Sara? Nothing mattered anymore. How could she have thought she loved this cruel, taunting man who was preening before the tarnished mirror, arranging his clothes as though nothing had happened? She wanted to cry, felt the need to shriek and howl, but she couldn't. All she could do was stare at the man who was tying his cravat with a nonchalance that frightened her more than if he had shouted and cursed at her. She saw his booted foot above her, but didn't believe, couldn't believe, he would kick her. She took the blow full in the left breast and rolled over in pain, retching as she did so. He stepped over to the dresser, fumbled in the bottom drawer and withdrew a black bundle.

"I'm going out now to see if I can turn this pittance you gave me into a sizable wad of money. I'm locking you in here; if you aren't here when I return, I'll hunt you down like an animal, do you understand? You wanted to come here and stay with me; now you've got your way. Don't think you can go running off to Regan to tell him how badly I used you. I'd be forced to kill you first. I want no screaming and yelling when I'm gone, or I'll have the landlady call Bedlam and tell them your mind snapped and you should be committed." His toe prodded her in the armpit as he tried to make her roll over. "Tell me you understand what I've just said to you." Wren nodded to show she understood, and Malcolm laughed. "You can't come close to a comparison with Sara," he called over his shoulder as he walked through the door and then locked it.

The sound was final, terminal, as Wren staggered to her knees. She sank down on the lumpy mattress and pulled the spread over her battered body. Had he meant what he had said? Would he do as he had threatened? She admitted she was afraid to find out.

"Please, God, send Regan and Sirena to me. I didn't mean what I said. Please help me," she prayed aloud.

She sat huddled under the spread for what seemed an eternity. Finally she crawled from the bed and searched for her clothes. What time was it? She should light a candle. Was he coming back, and if he did, what would he do? Please, God, help me, she begged over and over as she dressed.

At last she fell into a fitful sleep, only to awaken and cower in a corner of the bed when she heard a key in the lock. The door was thrust open, and Malcolm and four burly seamen entered the room.

"There she is, there's your prize," Malcolm chortled drunkenly. "Get up," he ordered, staggering over to the bed and dragging Wren by the arm to the middle of the floor. "I lost you in a game of cards to these fine gentlemen," he hiccuped. "Take off your clothes so they can see what they're getting."

"Please, Malcolm, you're drunk. You don't know what you're doing. Please don't do this to me," she pleaded tearfully.

"If you won't do it, then I'll do it for you," Malcolm leered, pulling at her gown and ripping it down the front till her body was exposed to the slavering seamen. "There!" Malcolm cried, lunging backward till he fell on the bed.

Wren tried to cover her body with her hands, but the men pulled and jabbed at her, each intent on doing what he wanted with her. She allowed it. She permitted it. She told herself she had no choice. She suffered and survived the onslaught. She knew it was the only way she would live to see another day.

Chapter Eight

Caleb didn't like the speculative looks Aubrey Farrington was bestowing on him. Once before Farrington had favored him with such looks, and he had ended up in a confrontation with Dick Blackheart. However, in all fairness to the gambler, there had also been an expression of deep regret in his eyes at the time. Caleb knew in his gut that if he looked more carefully into the old man's eyes, he would see that same regret now. His gut also told him it was time to cut his losses and let Farrington shift for himself.

If Sirena and Regan could cut their own losses and return to Java without Wren, then he could do the same thing for a few pounds. Farrington wasn't worth the aggravation Caleb was going through.

Cal's eyes traveled the length and beam of the ship and back to Farrington. There was something about the gambler that ate at him. Surely he wasn't getting maudlin about the old rake. If not, then why did this feeling of responsibility hang so heavily on his shoulders?

"If you'd just tell me the straight of it and stop beating around the bush, perhaps I could help you," Caleb said briskly. "I'm wise to your tricks, Aubrey.

You can't get away with what you did to me years ago. I know something's wrong and I want you to tell me what it is. And don't think for one minute I believed you when you swore you were virtually a pauper on the brink of bankruptcy. I made it my business to sniff around and ask questions. I also made it my business to check out your creditors, and do you know what I found out, Aubrey? They told me your credit is magnificent. At first I thought they were talking about someone else, not my old friend Lord Aubrey Farrington."

"Listen, Cal, I had a brief run of good luck and came into a small inheritance, and that helped me clear up a few debts—personal debts," the gambler whined.

"Children whine, fools whine, and you're neither," Caleb said coolly. "This is the last time I'm going to ask you what's going on. If I don't like your answer, you'll end up with a stomach full of bilge water."

"A small, personal business venture. Nothing which need concern you, Cal. Truly, there's no need for you to give it another moment's thought. As a matter of fact, I've been seriously considering the idea of retiring and taking a sea voyage. For my health," he added piously.

"If you're contemplating a sea voyage, that can only mean the law is either hot on your heels or breathing heavily down your skinny neck. It was a mistake on my part to reoutfit this ship, wasn't it? You allowed me to go ahead, make all the arrangements and have the handbills printed, and now you tell me you're considering a sea voyage. Good fortune to you, Aubrey. I'm sailing the *Sea Siren* on the morning tide, so I imagine this is the last time we'll be together. I do wish you well." Caleb nodded curtly and made ready to leave the ship. If ever the old fox is going to talk, now is the time, he thought to himself.

"Where are you heading? Back to Africa or Java?" Farrington asked as he followed Caleb to the gangplank.

"Wherever the sea takes me, I suppose. The *Siren*'s hold is empty, so I'll make good time wherever I go. My business affairs can manage themselves for at least a year, giving me a little time to see the world. Although I must admit I have a hankering to feel the trade winds and see my homeland again." Caleb watched Farrington's reaction to his noncommittal answer with a covert glance.

"Ah! To be young again! To go wherever fortune leads! You are truly blessed, Cal. Would that I were young again and free! The end of my story might be quite different indeed. So you say you might go on to the colonies? I hear America is the gateway to a young man's dreams," Farrington said wistfully, his sharp eyes never leaving Caleb's face.

"No, I didn't say I was going to America, you just did," Caleb answered flatly. "But I have had contact with the Dutch West India Company. Did you know they have fur traders working in their commission in the colonies?"

"No, I hadn't heard," Farrington lied. "Why, did they approach you? Surely they can't suppose you'd be interested in giving up the sea for a life in the woods skinning animals." Farrington gave a mock shudder.

"Not quite, Aubrey," Cal laughed. "At this time they have a small development of Dutch settlers somewhere in a place they call the Connecticut Valley. They're looking for someone to exchange goods and money for the skins. It hardly seems like an adventure to me."

"The colonies, you say?" Aubrey questioned. Then he suddenly held out his hand for Caleb to shake. His eyes turned cloudy and vague. He couldn't involve the boy again, not after what he had done to him the last time, the gambler ruminated. At least then he had had excuse enough. Dick Blackheart had bought up all his debts and held his very life on a thread. Turning Caleb over to the scurvy pirate had been a matter of survival. This time it would be unconscionable. There were ships' masters, men who were operating on the edge of the law, men who would willingly take a chance for a price, men who did not value their reputations and convictions the way Caleb did. After all, Farrington scolded himself, a man must have some pride, some small measure of self-respect. However, Caleb wasn't a boy any longer. He was a man, and capable of looking after himself. Self-respect and pride be damned! He'd ask him. All Cal could do was say no, walk away and call him an old reprobate. Well, he'd been called worse.

"A drink, Cal, before you leave?" Aubrey suggested softly. "A little small talk and another drink. I have something to tell you, something you may find very interesting, a little matter we can both profit from." Aubrey's watery old eyes implored Caleb to accept the offer, and he smiled when the younger man dropped his sea bag in anticipation of Aubrey's fine imported rum.

Caleb settled himself on a tack box and marveled at the beautiful day, a day rare in England as far as he was concerned. He took a long drink from the rum bottle and passed it back to Farrington to show that he was ready for any and all secret confessions on the gambler's part. A gull swept down, screeching and hawing, only to take wing and soar westward. "Amazing wing spread," Caleb remarked, somewhat startled by the intrusion.

"Yes, amazing," Farrington agreed. "However, I detest the things, as I have to clean their droppings from the deck several times a day. I'm not really a bad sort, Cal. In here," he said, placing his hand on his chest, "I am a loyal and conscientious person. I try to do my bit for my country, and if some moneys find their way into my pocket, so much the better. If I don't do it, then someone else will." He took a healthy swig of rum.

"Do what?" Caleb asked curtly.

"I'm getting to it; just give me time to get my thoughts in order. I want you to understand that when I was first approached to do . . . to do this . . . this . . . well, when I was first approached, I said no. I said I didn't want any part of it. Then when Baron Sinclair himself came to me and said what a noble gesture I would be making, I had second thoughts. After all, Cal, the Baron is a highly respected man, and we both know he wouldn't do anything that was . . . illegal. In all fairness to me, though, I did not commit myself on his first visit."

"How many visits did it take till the price was right?" Caleb demanded as the bottle of rum found its way to his lips again. By the looks of things, it was going to take the whole bottle and then some for Aubrey to get to the point.

"Three, four—who remembers?" Farrington said vaguely, reaching for a fresh bottle and uncorking it with a loud plop. He drank greedily, savoring the warmth and fire of the Jamaican rum. Another gull swooped down, emitted its loud, screeching complaint and then left its droppings next to Farrington's booted foot. He pretended not to see them as he inched away to lean more comfortably against a coil of neglected rigging.

"Well?" Caleb prodded impatiently.

Aubrey gulped, swallowed the rum in his mouth and sat up straight. "I've been smuggling, if you like that word, tariff-free supplies and transporting Puritans to the American colonies for a price."

"You what?" Caleb exploded. "You're an ass, Farrington!"

"Among other things." The gambler smiled. "As I said, if I didn't do it, someone else would. Actually, I started out transporting the Puritans and then worked into the smuggling little by little. Sinclair doesn't know about that end of it, and I'd just as soon he never found out. It hasn't been easy. My last captain was hung by the neck at dawn's first light on the last voyage. The passengers were thrown into the sea and my cargo sacked by vicious pirates. The captain had no experience, though he came highly recommended."

"What happened to your ship?"

"Only the good Lord knows. Now, my present problem is this. I have accepted money and given my word that I would have a ship ready to sail. I not only accepted the money, I spent it. My life isn't worth a farthing," he said pitifully. "There's this one zealot who I know is going to do something terrible to me. He's got the fires of Hell burning in his eyes. I need you, Cal, and I need the *Sea Siren* to take these people to the colonies. Whatever you can get for the cargo will be yours free and clear as your fee for the sailing. What do you say, my boy? Will you do this one small favor for an old friend?"

"You don't want much, do you, old friend?" Caleb replied quietly, sobering immediately from the impact of Farrington's words. He wasn't surprised at the man's request; he had known it would be something for which he, Caleb, could swing by the neck.

Seeing Caleb's hesitation, Farrington pressed on. "It's your cup o' tea, my boy. Adventure, profit and women. Why, you could clean up and have the adventure of your life! I have it on fact that the women in the colonies are beautiful beyond compare. And hungry, if you know what I mean." He winked. "Hungry for *real* men, not like those plaster saints who care more for their prayer meetings than they do for warmfleshed, fair-haired women. A few months of your time, profit from your Dutch company, women, adventure . . . who knows? Perhaps you'll even want to become a partner with Sinclair and me!"

How well the old buzzard knew him. In one breath he had said the two things that appealed to Caleb: adventure and women, and not necessarily in that order.

Farrington, refusing to lose any ground, continued. "You can hold your own against any odds. I've seen you at your best and at your worst. I'd feel very relieved if you'd take on this . . . this mission." He was beyond sobriety and he knew it, but he couldn't relinquish the bottle to Caleb till he heard his answer. "Think of it in terms of helping human beings."

"For a price," Caleb laughed. "You wouldn't surprise me if you sold your soul to the devil. You're an ass, Aubrey."

"Old Horny wouldn't want it, and you're right, I'm an ass, but then most men are in my position. You've agreed, so that makes you an ass, too." He hiccuped drunkenly.

Caleb grinned. He hadn't said yes and he hadn't said no. The old fool had known he would do it; he wouldn't have become so sotted otherwise. "You're right, Aubrey," Cal said, getting to his feet. "I'm going back to the Baron's to say my good-byes to Sirena and Regan, and I'll be back late this evening. At that time you damn well better be sober and have everything in readiness. I'll sail as soon as the *Siren* is outfitted and supplies are aboard."

Farrington waved a limp hand to show he understood and winced as another gull left its droppings, this time on the tip of his shiny boot. He peered at the mess through bleary eyes and shrugged. Loud snores grated on Caleb's ears as he departed the frigate, a wide grin on his face.

He hated going back to the Sinclairs' house. He had heard about the fiasco between Sirena and Malcolm and Wren. When Wren was discovered missing, he had been the first person Regan had come to, hoping that Wren had run to him. Regan and Sirena were in a foul, depressed mood over Wren's departure. If the day ever came when Caleb decided to take a wife, he'd make damn certain she was kept under lock and key with a cloth stuffed in her mouth. How could one little slip of a girl cause so much commotion and heartache?

Well, he couldn't worry about Wren now, especially after what she had done to him. Damn women! For now it might behoove him to stop by Sinclair's offices and announce that he was now a third partner in Tyler's illegal enterprise. He wondered vaguely how stiff the penalty was in this country for privateering. Whatever it was, he wouldn't dwell on it. He had committed himself to Farrington, and he would keep his word. In a few days he would feel the roll of the decks beneath his feet again. What matter if he was going to the new land, America? By picking up his orders from the Dutch West India offices, he could even add to his profit.

An uncomfortable feeling settled between his shoulder blades. By now he should have some definite direction in his life, some goal to work toward, like his father had when he first worked for the Dutch East India Company. It was true he was in his father's employ and that he ran the offices in Africa, but that wasn't his business. A man needed something he could claim as his alone. Something he sweated for sixteen hours a day, so that one day he would have a legacy to leave behind. And here he was, getting ready to take to the sea to transport human cargo to another land. He felt footloose, adrift, aimless. When he returned, he would take a long, hard look at his life and decide where he was going and what he would do.

Caleb considered himself a man, equal to his father, yet Aubrey Farrington constantly referred to him as a boy. Was there something about his makeup that the old man could see and he couldn't? Was there something invisible that marked him as a boy? "Bah!" He spat into the road. He was a man and he knew it. If he were to take a testimonial from every woman he had bedded in his life, each one would vouch for the fact that Caleb van der Rhys was a man.

The late-afternoon sun drifted in through the single window, lighting an array of dancing motes on the worn carpet. The bed loomed large and ominously on the far side of the room, its iron frame gleaming dully against the age-dimmed wall. Wren huddled in a corner, her back against the wall. Her dark, luxuriant hair tumbled down her shoulders and draped her pale face. She was very still, as still as death. Only her eyes were alive, watchful, fearful, burning with horrors known and horrors yet to come.

How could she have let this happen to her? How could she have been so blind? There was no excuse for her. To have thought even for a minute that Malcolm had cared for her, loved her, now seemed to her the height of sublime stupidity. How could she have been such an idiotic, romantic fool? Regan and Sirena had been right when they had said she wasn't ready for marriage, that she really didn't know Malcolm. Oh, God, she moaned to herself, to think I doubted Sirena! Now that she knew the kind of man Malcolm really was, she realized Sirena could never have instigated the little scene she had come upon in the garden. Sirena loved Regan; she would never have encouraged Malcolm to become her lover. And Sara! Why hadn't Wren listened to Sara? If she had only done that now, this very minute, she would be safe with the two people she loved most in the world.

A blue haze of cigar smoke wafted in her direction, causing her to wrinkle her nose and wipe at the tears forming in her eyes. Malcolm and his cronies sat at a small table in the center of the room, playing cards. None of them had glanced in her direction for the last half hour. She toyed with the idea of crawling past them and slipping out the door, but she knew her attempt would be futile, and she was also afraid of Malcolm's booted foot. She had never believed that a man could be so vicious. No, that wasn't true. She had known the evil natures of men. As a child, she had endured the festering alleys and the beatings of men like him, and she had survived. At the age of eight she had fought for food to stay alive and run from the terror that the darkness and the streets had imposed. Only old Lottie had been her friend before Sirena had rescued her. What was it the old woman had said? "Ye need eyes in the back of yer head and yer wits as sharp as a razor's edge." And Wren's wits were sharp, had been sharp, but with the good life Sirena and Regan had provided, she had forgotten, thinking she would never have to use street tactics again. If one wanted to survive, one did what one had to, whatever the cost.

Wren was so deep in her thoughts she almost missed hearing the conversation at the table. "I saw three ships sail at noon," one card player said as he swilled his ale and then wiped the back of his hand across his mouth. "The *Cavalier,* the *Vancouver,* and the *Michaelmas!* What I wouldn't have given to be aboard one of those ships as a passenger!" He laughed raucously.

"In two days' time the wharves will be empty for a while," another offered. "The last to leave will be the *Sea Siren.* She sets sail tomorrow, or so the scuttlebutt goes. There's something fishy there, my friends. That ship is sailing with an empty hold, and that can mean only one thing."

"What's that?" Malcolm asked, his eyes on his unlucky cards.

"She's one of those ships that sets sail empty and then picks up human trade, in a manner of speaking," a third seaman volunteered drunkenly.

"After this round of cards, I'm flat," Malcolm groaned pitifully.

"Mayhap we should sign on the *Sea Siren*. I heard the captain was asking round for good seamen this past day," the burly man closest to Wren said. "I would have added my X, but when he said the port o' call was none of my affair, I changed me mind. It's suspicious, all right. Sailing time is midnight. Under dark of night . . ."

"Dark of night what?" Malcolm demanded, throwing in his cards.

"Where's your mind, Weatherly? When ye be doing something ye ain't supposed to be doing, ye do it under cover of darkness. Seeing as how you're the proper gentleman and all, I can see why you wouldn't know something like that!"

Malcolm let his eyes travel to the corner of the room where Wren was huddled, afraid to move. His drunken mind whirled with triumphant thoughts of the royal collar, and his renewed ego demanded he celebrate his success with a woman. He had to get his hands on Wren, but he knew the seamen would cut him down if he made a move toward her. She was theirs, won by them, and they meant to keep her.

"Look here, Beasley, I have a pound note left. Why don't the lot of you go down to the wharves and do some nosing around and see what you come up with? Bring back some rum, and we'll have a party with the little lady in the corner." Malcolm knew the promise of drink and a party would make them more amenable to his wishes. "I'll have her as docile as a newborn kitten by the time you get back. Get a move on, lads, and let's see which way the wind blows. It's just possible the *Sea Siren* will sail with contraband."

"So what if she does? What use is that to us?" the man on his right demanded. "What can we do with contraband? Where've ye been, man? Smugglin' ain't what it used to be. Now the only thing as what gets smuggled is supplies and fancy yard goods to the colonies that ain't been taxed by yer Royal Highness. They ain't worth the trouble to fence. The only one what makes any profit is the man what's got the ship to sail the stuff over to America."

Malcolm's mind raced. "Yes, but you and I and everyone else knows about the stir that's sweeping the streets. The King's jeweled collar has been stolen. I just wonder if this *Sea Siren*'s departure has anything to do with that. I've heard of the captain—I've even met him. Caleb van der Rhys is his name. He's quite an enterprising gentleman who's been employed by the Dutch East India Company. It wouldn't surprise me in the least if this is a Dutch plot."

The men looked at each other and then at Malcolm. "He could be right," one of them acknowledged. "That's all the talk, the stealing of the King's collar from the goldsmith's. What better place to fence it than in America? I've heard some very rich men live there now and that the colonies are almost civilized."

"From what I've been told about the value of them gems, a man could buy the whole of the colonies and live better than the King himself."

Another seaman spoke up. "Don't go using our prize," he warned Malcolm, jabbing a finger in Wren's direction, "or we'll run you through. You hear me, Weatherly? We'll ask the little lady ourselves when we return. And if there's no talk about gems aboard the *Sea Siren*, you'd best plan on holding lilies in your hands." His small, beady eyes underlined the menace in his voice.

"You'll see I'm right," Malcolm said with more bravura than he felt. Damn the girl. As soon as they left, he would go out and see about booking passage somewhere. These men were more than he had bargained for. He would have to get an advance on the collar from Farrington. What good was the promise of a fortune to him when he didn't have enough pocket money for food? And what did he care if these toughs ransacked van der Rhys' ship in their search for gems? His collar was safe with Aubrey Farrington.

"Not so fast, Weatherly. Beasley here will stay behind just in case you get any funny ideas. If he makes a false move, Beasley, slit his throat," the sailor instructed his cohort.

Well, that takes care of my little plan, Malcolm fumed inwardly. Now I'll have to wait and see what happens on their return. He threw himself on the bed, a morose expression marring his handsome features as he forgot about Wren and his intentions. He knew he had to get away from these ruffians before they killed him. But how? They weren't about to let him out of their sight, because of all the money he owed them. They would keep watch over him, like a cat ready to pounce on a bird, until he took them to his banker. But what would he do in the morning when the banker advised them that his account was bare? He couldn't put them off any longer by saying the man was out of town for a few days. They meant to take him to the bank themselves.

While Malcolm contemplated his dim future, Wren was busily plotting her own. Beasley was sitting with his back to her, seemingly oblivious to her presence as he swilled what was left of the ale. All the tricks and wiles she had used in the dark alleys of London came back to her, and she was once again living in the streets and beneath the bridges, emerging only at night to scavenge for food. When you lived like an animal, you learned to behave like one. And you fought like one. She had to make her mind go back to the alleys and byways and remember what she would do if she were cornered as she was now.

Long moments became minutes, minutes lengthened into an hour, and the room darkened with the setting of the sun. Malcolm was asleep on the bed, snoring peacefully, as though he hadn't a worry in the world. Suddenly, as though being pricked by a thousand pins, Wren raised her head and saw Beasley staring at her. There was no mistaking the look in his eyes or the intention she read therein. He would have her again, would force his burly, stinking body on hers. She had no weapon. All she had were her hands and feet, but she would use them to protect herself, or die trying.

Slowly she rose to her full height, her amber eyes molten and glowing as she watched Beasley's appraisal of her. She moved wordlessly to the rough table, lifted the almost empty pitcher of ale and poured the liquid into a tankard. Taking a sip, she banged the cup down in front of Beasley, noting the marked appreciation in his narrow eyes.

"That's better, wench. I always did like my women friendly," he jeered.

Wren managed a weak smile and sat in the chair opposite him. Lottie's words came back to her as though she were still eight years old and it were yesterday. "Always make do with what ye have, child. If it's only yer own hands, make do. Catch a man unawares and he's little more than yer own size." Still smiling, Wren leaned back in the chair and lifted the hem of her skirt. Extending her leg upward, she slowly began to remove her stocking, allowing Beasley's eyes to linger on the soft flesh of her inner thigh. Then she rose and worked the buttons of her dress, moving around the table to stand near the seaman, close enough to hear his ragged breathing. All the while her mind raced; she could do it, she knew she could. Before she had been frightened, racked with despair because of Malcolm's evil. Not any longer. If her plan failed and she died, then so be it. She would cling to the last breath, but at least she would die knowing she had tried to save herself. She glanced toward Malcolm, still asleep on the bed, his mouth slacked open

133

in an unattractive manner. How could she ever have thought she loved him? If he awoke suddenly, she would have to do to him what she had done to Caleb, what she should have done to Malcolm the instant she entered his room.

Keeping a watchful eye on Beasley, who was draining the last of his ale, she tested her stocking for flexibility. One loop and a knee in his back, careful to stay away from his groping fingers, and it would all be over. The amber eyes were alight as she slipped behind him, and they roared to a blazing fire as she brought up her knee and curved the stocking tightly around his throat. Beasley began to fight, his hands warped into claws stretching backward for a moment before they tore at the silk at his neck. Closing her eyes, terror twisting her mouth into a soundless scream, Wren gave the stocking a vicious yank and choked off the last of Beasley's air.

Malcolm opened his bleary eyes and took in the scene before him. It was the thud of Beasley's body hitting the floor that had brought him to the full awareness of the danger he was in.

Crouching low like a wild animal readying itself for attack, Wren advanced a step, then another as Malcolm, mesmerized by her feral look, tried to back away. Once again the amber eyes breathed flame as she stalked him, aiming for the fire tongs resting near the burning grate. Another step and she would be able to reach them. The moment her hand grasped the metal device, Malcolm's foot shot out; she raised her weapon and slammed it down across the side of his face. Blood spurted profusely from the deep gash. She lifted the tongs and again lashed out, this time rendering him a stinging blow to his head.

Reeling backward, Malcolm could do no more than bring his hands to his wounds, his mouth mewing his agony at what she had done to him. Wren advanced again, this time jabbing the tongs to his midsection. Again and again she attacked him, till he fell to the floor, begging her to stop.

"You took me like an animal, treated me like an animal, and now I'm doing the same to you. Which of us, Malcolm, will survive? *I* will, because I'll be gone when your cutthroat friends return. They'll blame you for what happened to Beasley. Your life will be worth nothing. Nothing, Malcolm." She stood back, her quick, ragged breathing slowly returning to normal, and laughed. The sound was unlike anything Malcolm had ever heard. It frightened him more than the wounds he suffered and more than what he knew would happen to him when the seamen returned.

Through a red mist he saw her remove the stocking from Beasley's thick neck and roll it up her leg. Daintily, she buckled the buttons on her slippers and smoothed down her dress. "I'll be leaving you now, Malcolm. If you ever come near me again, I'll do to you what I just did to your friend." And then she laughed once more. It was her laugh not her threatening words, that made him crawl blindly in search of escape.

Outside, in the cool evening breeze, Wren and the darkness blended as one. She slithered down one narrow alley after another, her old life coming back to her as she made her way. People lived all their lives in dark alleys, leaving their sanctuaries only at night to fight for the very food that would enable them to last one more day. She had done it before and she could do it again. One more day, and then she would sneak aboard Caleb's ship. She couldn't allow herself to think beyond that point. For now, she had to get through the rest of the night and find a place to stay until the *Sea Siren* was ready to sail.

She was no different now, she told herself as she carefully stepped over the cobblestones. She had been beaten, used and abused, but she was still Wren. She had her mind, her heart and her wits, and she had come through the battle intact. It never occurred to her to consider the fact that she had just killed one man and maimed another. To survive, you simply did what you had to do.

Chapter Nine

The velvety darkness was like a shroud cloaking the girl scurrying down a series of crooked alleys. Only once did Wren lift her eyes to get her bearings as she stealthily made her way from Briarthorn Lane into a maze of even narrower alleys and cul-de-sacs. It had to be here, that small doorway with the chipped wood and rotten hinges. Lottie would help her. Lottie would take her in her arms and crush the breath from her slim body, all the while mouthing words of comfort. She would smell the same—sour and dirty. Wren smiled to herself. Lottie would slap her soundly and cuff her behind the ears for her absence all these years. If the old woman was mean enough tonight, Wren might even receive a swift kick on her shinbones to show that Lottie wasn't losing her touch. Lottie was queen of the maze, and every derelict came to her for help at one time or another. If you were on Lottie's good side, you never went hungry and you always had a blanket, even if it was full of bugs. Lottie's philosophy was simple: if the straights saw bugs crawling over you, they left you alone. A few open sores never hurt anyone, and soap and water was a killer.

The maze. Wren turned this way and that, trying to get her bearings. Ten years was a long time. She had to remember. She put her fingers to her temple and forced her mind to quietness. She had just light-fingered a gent and relieved him of his purse, and he was chasing her. Which way had she gone? Memories flooded her weary brain, and she sprinted to the right and then to the left, the gent more than a memory. She ran and ran till the splintered door with its rusty hinges loomed before her. Thank God for the big yellow ball in the sky!

Drawing in a deep breath, she rapped sharply three times at eye level and then gave the door a resounding kick, as she had done years ago. She repeated the process three more times before a raspy voice demanded to know who was beating down the door at this ungodly hour.

"Lottie, it's Wren! I have to see you—please let me in!"

"Ye can't trick me, girl. Me Wren is living with the gentry, lo these many years. Now, give me the straight of it or ye'll be in the arms of the law. Me own law!" the voice said harshly.

"Lottie, it's true. I'm Wren. I ran away and I got myself in trouble and need your help. Listen to me! Remember the time we rolled two drunks we thought were sleeping, and one of them slashed at you with his knife? I came up from behind and kneed him like you taught me. You still carry the scar from the elbow to the wrist on the outside of your left arm. Please, Lottie, let me in. I have nowhere else to go."

Wren waited, her heart pounding, for the old woman to slide first one heavy bolt and then another.

Suddenly she was wrapped in plump arms, the sweet sour smell of the woman's sweat engulfing her. She was safe. Lottie would take care of her.

"Come in here to me parlor," Lottie cackled gleefully. "I knew it was ye all along. I was jest punishing ye for not being in touch with me all these years. But ye came back to old Lottie. Tell me what ye look like. Have ye grown into a beautiful young lady like I said ye would?"

Tears burned Wren's eyes. She couldn't be blind, not old Lottie! "I'm a young lady, but I don't know if you could truthfully say I'm beautiful. What happened, Lottie? How did you lose your eyesight? Who's taking care of the maze if you can't . . ."

"Don't ye fret, girl. I'm still queen of the maze," the old woman said quickly, hearing the anguish in Wren's voice. "But to answer your question, a gent from the other side of town took a torch to me and burned off me hair and blinded me. I've been like this for four years now. Ye ain't asking what happened to the gent."

Wren laughed. "I don't have to ask. He's dead and his body was chopped in two and dumped into the Thames."

"Right ye be, little one. Old Lottie can see more without sight than most people if they had four eyes. Me senses are keen, and the men—they look after me much the same way I looked after you. I can hear a footfall at the beginning of the maze. I heard you, and I heard you stop to get your bearings; and if I know you, my girl, you stood there trying to decide which way to go. I heard every step you took. Any time I wanted I could have had old Bart on ye quick as a whistle. But I didn't. I wanted to see who had the wits to try and come into the maze."

"You have to help me, Lottie. I've gotten myself into some trouble and I don't know what to do. I don't have a shilling to my name and I'm ripe for Newgate. I killed a man tonight!"

If Lottie was surprised at the girl's words, she gave no hint. "Sit here and let me get you some food and ale. Me larder was just stocked today by the generosity of a farmer on his way to market. Bart relieved him of his wares, and we can eat till tomorrow and still have plenty left over. When your belly is full, you can cope with anything." She handed Wren a thick wedge of cheese and a chunk of soft, moist bread. "And for a sweet, we have a basket of honey buns."

"Bless old Bart," Wren sighed, relieved to be among friends.

"I've got some cold mashed turnip if ye want it," Lottie volunteered as she ladled the vegetable into a thick yellow bowl.

"Want it! I'd kill for it," Wren said softly. "I haven't eaten in days. Lottie, if I live to be a hundred, I know that I'll never taste food this good."

"We'll be giving your praise to the farmer the next time we meet up with him," Lottie cackled. "Eat now, till your stomach won't hold another morsel, and then we'll talk."

When she had finished eating and emptied her cup of ale, Wren felt her eyes grow heavy but forced herself to remain awake. She had to talk to Lottie and beg for her help. Lottie would know what to do. In a halting voice that grew stronger with the telling, she repeated what had happened to her, leaving nothing out.

Old Lottie listened to Wren, her sightless eyes focused on a point of past memory. "One thing I'm not understandin'. Why in Heaven's name did ye come here? Not that I don't want ye, understand. My house is always open to my little Wren. Only what about the van der Rhyses? Ye be sayin' how much they love ye and all, so whyn't ye go back to them and tell them what's happened to ye?"

"Oh, Lottie," Wren cried, "I can't. I can't! I couldn't face them now, not after what happened to me and what I've done. And after the way I doubted Sirena? The things I said to her? I wouldn't blame them if they never wanted to lay eyes on me again. Oh, Lottie, I just can't go back!" she sobbed, covering her face with her hands.

"If this Sirena loved ye like a mother, I don't see why not, child. Ah! Yer so young, ye don't know how forgivin' a mother's heart can be."

"Don't make me go back, Lottie. Please. I . . . I've got to get away from London for a while. I can sail with Caleb. When the time's right, he'll take me back to Sirena and Regan. But right now I couldn't face them. I've betrayed their love, their trust!"

"Hush, now, child," Lottie soothed. "We'll do it any way ye like. But ye can't stay here, not that I don't want ye, but now that ye've led the fine life, ye can see this is no place for ye. I'd give ten years off me life if ye'd stay, but ye can't and that's the straight of it. We'll have to think of something. This Malcolm sounds like a proper weasel to me, and what ye did to him was too good for the likes of him. I doubt if the law will be after ye for the killing, and those others ye said went to the wharf will run for cover like the river rats they are. Ye'll sleep now, and I'll have some of the men go to the wharf and see about this *Sea Siren* ye been telling me about. How could yer own brother desert ye like this?" she grumbled.

"He didn't desert me, Lottie. He doesn't know. And he isn't my brother, you know that."

"Thank God for that," Lottie muttered under her breath. She might be old and blind, but she had heard the girl's voice change when she mentioned Caleb's name. "Lie here on this cot, and when ye wake, Old

Lottie will have everything come right for ye. Here," she said, handing Wren a dingy coverlet.

"Is it full of bugs?" Wren asked sleepily.

"Scores of them, and a proper nest or two at the hem. Ye don't bother them . . ."

"And they won't bother you," Wren laughed, rolling over and pulling the filthy rag to her chin.

Lottie waited till Wren's breathing was deep and regular before she clapped her hands sharply. Within minutes three men walked into the room and stood there patiently. From the depths of her shapeless dress Lottie withdrew a pouch of gems and fingered its contents deftly. She spoke softly, urgently, and the men showed no emotion at her orders. They shook their heads to indicate they understood, one of them held out his hand for the ruby she had selected, and they departed as quietly as they had come.

A single tear trickled down one wrinkled cheek as Lottie laid a rough, caloused hand on Wren's sleeping head. She knew the girl was beautiful, as beautiful as she herself had been in her younger days. Out of a hidden pocket she withdrew a comb of sorts and tried to straighten her straggly, ill-kempt hair. Eventually she gave it up as too much of an ordeal, and a colony of head lice scurried down her back. Now, why had she gone and disturbed them? She settled herself in an old, battered cane rocker and waited for the lice to make their way back to her wild mane of hair before she, too, fell asleep.

The wharf was alive with voices and movement and torchlight as Caleb's crew readied the *Siren* for tomorrow's sailing. Men hauled provisions while Aubrey Farrington tapped his elegant cane on the deck, his watery eyes missing nothing. "Thank you, Lord, I knew you'd see it my way," he muttered as a bare-chested seaman hoisted a wooden crate to his shoulder.

Caleb sat nonchalantly on a tack box, his eyes as alert as Farrington's. If there is a King of Fools, I'm it, he told himself. Any time the old gambler looked as he did now, Caleb knew he was missing something. He'd make damn sure he searched the *Siren* from top to bottom before he sailed. The old fox had something up his sleeve, and it wasn't cards or his arm.

"How many, Aubrey?" he asked, blowing a fragrant cloud of blue-gray smoke in the gambler's direction.

"One hundred or so, give or take a few. You have plenty of room and then some. Don't start fretting, Cal. Everything has been taken care of."

"That's the part that frightens me," Caleb snapped. "When you take care of things, I always wind up on the short end of the stick. It will be dawn soon; we should both get some sleep."

"Sleep!" Aubrey shouted. "And let these men rob us blind! Never! I'll stay right here till dawn. If you feel the need for some sleep, you go right ahead. I'll watch things for you."

"And who is going to watch you? My mistake was not putting a leash around your neck the first time I met you. I'll just stay right here, and if you're half as smart as you think you are, you'll stay within my line of vision."

The gambler nodded agreeably. "Whatever you say, Cal."

"You know, Aubrey, before this ship sails I'm going over her from stem to stern to see what it is you're trying to have me smuggle to the colonies for you." Caleb watched him with narrowed eyes. Farrington wasn't a gambler for nothing. His face remained impassive, even a little sly.

"I'll ignore that insult because we're such good friends. For shame, Cal. How could you think I'd try to pull the wool over your eyes?"

"You said it, Aubrey. *Try*. You can't. I don't want

142

to find myself on the high seas carrying something a bastard bunch of pirates want. I have no intention of getting my throat slit or having my passengers harmed because of some fanciful whim of yours. From stem to stern, remember that."

The desperation on Farrington's face was almost lawless. In the bright moonlight Caleb could see the frenzy in the old rake's eyes. His voice softened unexpectedly, throwing the gambler off guard. "If you'd just tell me what it is you're trying to get me to take, we might come to some kind of terms. Realize, Aubrey, that I'm smarter than you and that you can't get away with anything. If you try your usual tricks, then all these . . . these passengers, as you call them, will be waiting dockside when I set sail—alone."

Farrington took one last look at Caleb's smoldering dark eyes and wavered, straightened his slumped shoulders. "For the last time, I don't know what you're talking about. I'm not hiding anything on your ship, nor do I intend to. I may be old, Cal, but I'm not a fool."

For a minute Caleb almost believed him—until he squinted in the moonlight and saw the same look of desperation in his eyes. He sighed. He would search the ship, as he had said, and woe be to the old man if he found something other than rotting wood and rats.

When the last store of provisions was safely put away in the galley, Caleb strolled on deck, dawn but moments away. He loved the beginning of a new day, but his gut churned at what this day might bring. He had to have been a fool to agree to Aubrey's plans. Well, it was too late now; he had given his word, and he would have to sail for America as promised. He glanced about restlessly, and realized he wanted a woman. He wanted one now. With everything going on around him, he wondered how he could even think about women at a time like this.

He pushed the thought from his mind and settled

himself against a roll of sail. Somewhere, someplace, someday, he would find a woman full of wonder and excitement, a woman who would love him the way he would love her. They would make love the first time to his satisfaction and the second time to the satisfaction of both; each time they would be tantalizing and incomprehensively cruel with each other, yet gentle, so very gentle, as if their lovemaking were an assault and a confession at the same time, as if it had to illustrate a confusion in themselves that was imperative for both to understand. If he sailed the world over, he wondered if he would ever find such a woman and if he would recognize her for what he wanted her to be, needed her to be, in order to make him complete. I'll know, he told himself, a touch of arrogance on his face. I'll know.

Malcolm Weatherly stood in the lavender shadows of early dawn, his torn and ragged cheek throbbing painfully. He couldn't see at all out of his left eye. He was afraid. More afraid than he'd ever been in his entire life. More afraid than when he had heisted the jeweled collar right from under the King's nose. What would become of him now that his handsome face had been ruined by that bitch Wren? If he ever got his hands on her, he'd be certain to do the same thing to her, so that she would have to hide out for the rest of her life. He'd make certain no man ever looked at her again.

He glanced around to get his bearing. For a moment he was confused. Somehow he thought he had come farther, was closer to the wharf and Farrington's derelict gambling ship. The deep, black fear rose in him again as he realized the sky was getting brighter by the minute. He forced himself to think and to take stock of his situation. He looked no worse than some of the water rats who frequented the seamy wharves and the taverns scattered along the rancid alleyways.

In his condition he doubted if any of his acquaintances would recognize him, and the rats would take him as one of their own. The worst that could happen to him was that he would get rolled and beaten as just another drunk. He raised his good eye to the east and quickly closed it. Christ, he must have pulled the muscles in the injured side of his face, and now it was bleeding again, the blood seeping into his eye. Rage at his circumstances swept through him, and in that moment he swore to himself that if Farrington gave him one false look or word, he'd kill him on the spot and take back his booty. If he got caught, then that would be that. He was ruined in society now, so nothing really mattered anymore.

He moved crablike, his injured shoulder slumping, along the grime-infested walls flanking the alley. When he came to the end of the cul-de-sac, he blinked at all the activity down on the docks. There was young van der Rhys, shouting at Farrington in a harsh voice. Malcolm was too far away to make out the words, but even from this distance the gambler looked afraid. That's good, good for me, Malcolm told himself. Farrington was leaving, his elegant walking stick making quick, light taps on the rough boards. Malcolm would give him just enough time to clear the wharf and then would follow him and take matters into his own hands. The gambler was a spry old gent, crafty and cunning, but he would meet his match in Malcolm Weatherly.

The moment the old man made his way onto the deserted open street, Malcolm shouted hoarsely and waited. Aubrey Farrington turned, his blank look quickly dissolving into one of fear when he saw the dandy's injured face. "Lord luv a duck. Weatherly, what happened to you?"

"Never mind what happened to me. I want to talk to you in your rooms and get myself taken care of. Help me."

"And why should I be helping the likes of you? We had a business deal and it's over. I owe you nothing except your share of the gems, and you agreed to wait till they were sold. I owe you nothing," he repeated firmly, making a move to walk away.

"You bastard," Malcolm gritted through clenched teeth. "Either you help me or I swear I'll find my own way to your rooms and set fire to them and roast you like a chicken."

Aubrey Farrington abhorred violence and threats, especially those made against his person. "Very well," he said coolly, "but let me tell you that I am no doctor and the sight of blood makes me ill. I can't tend to your wounds; I know nothing about them and I have no intention of learning. A physician is what you need. From the looks of things, you might lose that eye if you aren't careful."

"It's my eye, and if I'm not worried, then you need not be, either. You'll take care of me, you old sinner, or you'll never set foot outside your rooms again. I mean it, Farrington."

The gambler knew this was true. Weatherly was worse than Cal. His faded eyes went skyward and he begged silently, Why me? All I did was cut a few corners. I take a little from here to pay there, and if it weren't for me, those poor souls, the Puritans, would be sitting here waiting for the ax to fall. Remember that when You judge me. He lowered his eyes, careful to note that Weatherly's feet were just behind him. Even if he managed to shake loose of him, where would he go? Best to get on with it and rid himself of the vermin.

Inside his comfortable quarters, Aubrey fetched a basin of water and set to work. His touch was not gentle as he poked and prodded Malcolm's slashed cheek. His tone was cold and clinical as he spoke. "There's a smart cut on your eyeball and your face needs to be sewn. I can't do it."

146

"What happens if it isn't sewn up?"

Farrington treated him to a disgusted look. "I told you, I'm no doctor. The wound will heal the way it is if it's kept clean, but your face will be distorted. Forget the eye—it's gone. If the cheek wound is taken care of and sutured, you might end up with a red welt running from your eyebrow to your chin. In time it may fade, and then again, it may not. For God's sake, man, I told you I know nothing about these things." As he carried the basin to a table in the corner of the room he couldn't resist a parting shot. "You just might secure employment in Newgate or Bedlam and scare the prisoners and patients into obedience."

Malcolm ignored the callous words. The next time he peered into a mirror would be time enough to determine the state of his looks. For now, with his wound clean and bandaged, he had other matters to attend to. "Is it true that van der Rhys' ship is sailing today? No lies, Farrington."

"Yes," Aubrey said, returning to the center of the room, "his ship sails tonight with a full hold of passengers. Why?"

"Because you're going to get me on that ship. It's not safe for me here any longer. What's her destination?"

Farrington drew in his breath sharply. "The colonies, and then on to Martinique to sell our little . . . prize." He cast a quizzical glance in Weatherly's direction, uncertain whether he should have told him the collar would be leaving England with the *Sea Siren*. "What's the matter, man? You're white enough to have seen a ghost."

"I . . . I didn't know van der Rhys would have any part of this." He thought of the toughs he had sent down to the wharf to nose around the ship for any hint of jewels. If he were to lose the collar now, he would be left with nothing.

"The captain of the *Sea Siren* knows nothing about

the King's collar. He thinks he's on a mercy mission to help some Puritans escape the country. And you can rest at ease; the collar has not yet boarded the ship. Why your sudden concern?" Farrington asked uneasily.

"It's just some talk I heard. You're certain no one else knows about the jewels?"

"As certain as I am of my own name," Farrington assured him. "However, if you think for one minute that you're going to 'guard' the prize, you're mistaken. You're a thief." the old man exclaimed.

"And just what the hell does that make you?" Malcolm spat.

"A fence. And an honorable profession it is. I just make sure everyone gets what he wants, and then I take my commission. Thievery," he continued in a pious tone, "is the work of the devil. My hands are clean. I deal only in honorable professions."

Malcolm tried to sneer but gave it up and let his facial muscles relax. "And I suppose gambling is an honorable profession?"

"What's a man to do? If people want to throw their money away, can I stop them? I'm an honorable man dealing in honorable professions." Farrington's tone was virtuous, his eyes sly as he observed the effect of his words on the wounded, suffering man.

"Bah! You talk like an old fool, and I'm losing my patience. I want to be on that ship when she sails. Arrange it, Farrington. I don't care how you do it. Just do it. You'd be wise if you smuggled me aboard without van der Rhys' knowledge. I know I can trust you, Farrington, to do whatever is necessary." Malcolm's voice was cold, his face deadly with its disfigurement.

"You're insane, Weatherly. Van der Rhys has the sailing list, and there's no way an extra person can be smuggled aboard in broad daylight."

"You'll think of something. Arrange for some food

for me, get me some decent clothes and put it all on my tab."

Aubrey's mind raced. What in the hell was he supposed to do? Cal was breathing down his neck; this vulture was threatening to kill him. Even if he managed, somehow, to smuggle Weatherly aboard the *Sea Siren,* he knew he would never see his share of the profits from the King's jeweled collar. His contact in Martinique would pay over the vast sum to Weatherly, and that would be the end of Farrington. If there was one thing he hated, it was missing out on the final result of anything, especially if he had been in at the beginning. The only thing he hated worse was an empty pocket or purse. He had no choice but to make the crossing with Cal to protect his investment. He would confide in Cal to be certain he didn't find himself dead. A three-way split was better than no split at all. As long as he retained possession of the collar, he could call the shots. Yes, he would confide in Cal and then figure out a way to smuggle Weatherly aboard. Cal's cabin, a few greased palms—well-greased—and the matter should be settled to his and Weatherly's satisfaction.

I must be getting old, he mouthed silently as he made his way down the narrow stairwell to see the landlady, who, for a few flowery words and a quick peck on the cheek, would supply him with food for the vermin resting upstairs in his favorite chair. The things he had to do to stay alive in this cruel, heartless world! He sighed heavily as he knocked on the landlady's door and flinched when she opened it and said, "Coo! And if it isn't himself this beautiful day."

The things he had to do!

Chapter Ten

Lydia Stoneham woke up and lay perfectly still. She always woke up with fear in her throat. She went to bed with fear churning throughout her body, she ate in fear and she existed in fear, as she had done every day of her life since she had married Bascom Stoneham at her parents' insistence. She was afraid of everything—if she ate too much or if she didn't, if she spoke too much or too little, if she soiled her dress or kept it spotless—which meant, in Bascom's eyes, that she did nothing, even though her hands were red and cracked from the harsh lye soap he made her use. Cleanliness, he enjoyed repeating, was next to godliness. But most of all, she was afraid of her husband, Bascom. Of what he was and what he made her do. Obscene, filthy things that he insisted she perform in the name of the Lord so that she would be purged. How, she wondered anew, could those disgusting acts ever purge her? They were degradations matched only by the ugliness contained in his gaunt face and needle-thin body. She admitted to herself that she hated him with a passion she had never known in love.

As always when she thought of her deep aversion

to him, like now in the early hours of the morning, she trembled and shook, and tears welled in her hyacinth-blue eyes. They were tears of self-pity and remorse, for herself and for others like her who were forced to live out this farce of a life.

She squeezed her eyes shut to stop the tears, when Bascom's skinny leg reached out to touch her foot. He would feel her trembling and, like the insane person he was, assume it was a trembling based on sexual desire. If she lived to be a hundred and protested every hour of the day that she trembled from fear and not from any sexual desire, he would never believe her. He was convinced that she lusted after him even in her sleeping hours. And, wonderful husband that he was, first he would allow her to give in to her bodily urges, at his insistence, and then he would force her to pray to God for forgiveness. If there was a God, why didn't He intervene? Why did He permit her to be subjected to Bascom's madness?

She had to stop her trembling, had to force herself to get up and dress. Once she was fully clothed, Bascom couldn't see or feel her quaking body. But it was too late. His clawlike hands were working their way up under the thin nightdress. She wanted to scream as one bony hand cupped her full breast and the other stroked her flat stomach. She fought back a retch and lay still, hoping that he would tire and fall asleep again. That had never happened yet, but she always hoped and sometimes even prayed.

Bascom's head moved slowly toward the back of Lydia's neck, and then his tongue flicked out to lick at the warm spot at the nape. His head burrowed into her skin, her bright red hair shielding him from the sunlight filtering into the room. His tongue worked slowly while his hands were feverish in their pursuit of her soft, yielding flesh. Roughly, never releasing his hold on her breast, he rolled her over onto her stomach. Her eyes were closed. That is good, he told himself. She is begging for forgiveness, as I have taught her, while allowing me, her beloved husband, to have my way with her and to bestow on her unparalleled delight. Every muscle in her body was quivering, and behind her closed lids he knew her eyes were burning, fervently for him, and for the sexual pleasure he could give her.

He played with her, fondling each breast till its rosy crest became taut and erect. His hands moved slowly downward and began to explore the soft, warm place between her thighs until her tightly closed mouth opened and she moaned . . . in desire . . . for him. Always for him. His mouth found its way to the hollow in her throat and again his tongue flicked this way and that, traveling to the cleft between her breasts and then to the taut tips, which he licked and sucked on greedily, her moans ringing in his ears. He removed her nightdress and his own nightshirt and edged closer to her, the sharp, protruding bones of his emaciated body digging mercilessly into her. He was behind her, his organ between her thighs, his hand crushing the softness of her breasts. "It's time, Lydia. Say it now."

"Forgive me, Lord, for lusting after my husband's body. Deny me that which my body seeks for fulfillment. Forgive me, Lord, for my weak flesh," Lydia intoned loudly to be sure Bascom heard and did not make her repeat the words.

"I hear you, child, and I shall deny that which you ask. I am your lord and your savior!" Bascom shouted, his voice dramatic in the quiet of the room, as he thrust his throbbing manhood into her.

It is true . . . my flesh is weak, Lydia sobbed silently. If only he would . . . just once . . . How can he do this to me day in and day out? She felt him move away and knew what was coming. He got out of bed and stood by the edge, pulling her upright toward him. His skull-shaped head, its stringy hanks of hair falling over his eyes, bent to her breasts and he nipped at their pink erect circles. His hands caressed her haunches and then slid slowly upward till they rested on her shoulders, forcing her to her knees till her mouth was level with his manly pride. He lowered his eyes and watched her open her mouth. How obscene she looked. How could a woman degrade herself this way? He would make her do penance for this. He would make her kneel and pray till her knees were raw and bleeding and she was hoarse from her entreaties. Disgusting harlot! His eyes became glazed and a convulsive urgency seized him, causing him to shudder and cry out repeatedly. He was in agony because of what she had forced him to do in the name of God.

Lydia sat back on her haunches, her eyes downcast and full of shame. She took the blow squarely on the side of her face and didn't flinch. She had to pay for what she had done, what she had made Bascom do in order to save her soul from the devil.

Bascom reached for his Bible on the night table and opened it. "We must pray now for your wantonness. We will both ask God to spare us of more of these doings. He knows you for the harlot you are, and He will come to me in a vision and tell me what to do with you. Pray, Lydia," he commanded.

"Dear Lord, I am the harlot Your disciple says I am. I am full of lust, which must be driven from my body to purify it so I may serve You in any way You choose. Forgive me my weakness and make my husband strong of mind and body so he can bear my defects. Spare me, God, from Your wrath, but take pity on me and show me mercy." Her voice was flat and dull, and she repeated the words over and over until Bascom was fully clothed.

"You may get dressed now. Tonight, aboard ship, we'll pray again for your soul. Tell me that you want me to pray for your soul, Lydia."

"Yes, Bascom, I want you to pray for my soul," Lydia said tonelessly.

"My parents and my sister, Sara, are waiting for us downstairs. When we go into the dining hall, be sure to keep your eyes lowered, or everyone will know what you've just done. They'll all see you for the obscene harlot you are, and then they'll be forced to pity me. Pity me!" he screeched, his eyes burning madly. "If that happens, God will punish both of us. It is only you, Lydia, who need to be punished. It is you who must constantly fight these bodily urges and conquer them. Perhaps one day, if you pray long enough and hard enough, you will be saved from yourself and will relieve me of this cross I bear."

"Yes, Bascom, I will do as you say," she agreed, pulling her petticoat over her head and tying the laces across her bosom. I know there must be another God besides the one you pray to, she said silently, and to that God she dropped to her knees and prayed, tearfully, not for forgiveness, but for help in ridding herself of the insane zealot who was her husband.

Lottie opened the door leading to the maze, tilted her head to one side and listened. Three pairs of footsteps. The men were returning. Quietly she closed the door and sat down in the cane rocker. A scrawny yellow cat leapt into her lap and purred loudly. Lottie's dirty fingers, their nails cracked and split, stroked the cat gently, her unseeing eyes on the sleeping girl. What was going to happen to her? In her heart Lottie had known that one day Wren would escape the maze and marry a fine gentleman who would love her devotedly for all his days.

Three quick knocks on the stout door, the low-placed kick, and Lottie was off the chair, the yellow cat spitting his outrage at being dumped so unceremoniously on the hard floor.

"No wasted words, just the quick of it," Lottie commanded the men.

"The *Sea Siren* sails at midnight. The ship carries no cargo, only passengers to the American colonies. Puritans. We managed, at great expense, to purchase this outfit." Bart handed Lottie a parcel. "The girl should be able to slip aboard and go unnoticed. If they have an accurate head count, then we'll have to divert a woman passenger. Lucas here has agreed to that little task. Either way, the girl will be aboard when the ship sails. Seth pawned the ruby and got nearly two hundred pounds by holding a knife to the pawnbroker's throat. Did we do well, Lottie?"

"Very well, Bart. I couldn't have done better myself," Lottie said, laying a hand on his arm to show she was proud of his accomplishments. How well these thieves looked after her since she lost her eyesight. Why, even old Seth gave her a bath twice a year and never once paid attention to her flabby body. He soaped her like a baby and dried her off as if she were his own mother. These little things made life bearable.

"I left breakfast for ye in the other room," Lottie said happily. "Eat hearty, old friends. I'll wake the child now and ready her for her journey."

Lottie stroked the sleeping girl's tangled hair and ran her gnarled hand over one smooth cheek. She showed no emotion when she felt her wet cheeks. The child was crying in her sleep. "Come, Wren, it's time to rise and make ready for a new day. Come." She shook her gently, and when Wren sat up, she gave her the parcel. Quickly she explained what Wren was to do and where she was going, and patted her fondly on the head. Wren retired to a curtained-off section of the room to change her clothes. When she had finished dressing herself in the black Puritan garb, her hair pinned beneath the starched white cap, she came back and sat down next to Lottie at the table. She

155

ate her breakfast quickly, ravenously, licking her fingers to indicate her appreciation of the food.

"Listen to me, child," Lottie said, holding out a pouch. "Here is a hundred pounds. This other little sack is full of gems. Guard them both well, for it's all ye'll have when ye get to America. God only knows what ye'll be finding there, and this will be all ye'll have between starvation and survival. I'd give ye more if I had it, but I have the men to look after."

Wren's eyes widened. "It's too much, Lottie. I can't take it all. Half will do nicely. I'm strong and I can find work when I get there. You may need this for yourself and the others."

"Nonsense, child. We can always get more. This is to be yer nest egg against the future. Ye don't know what that strange land is like, and it might not be a fit place for a woman lookin' for work. Ye keep it and use it wisely."

"I wish I weren't going, Lottie, but I know I can't stay here. To do so would be to place all of you in danger. I'll never be able to repay you for your kindness."

"I need no payment. Seeing ye safely aboard ship will be payment enough. However, if ye have a mind to, ye can be doing me one small favor—if the opportunity presents itself, that is."

"Anything. Just tell me what it is," Wren urged.

"Seth said a man named Aubrey Farrington will be aboard the Dutchman's ship. He's known as the foxiest cardsharp in these here parts. A day or so before ye get to yer port, seek him out and engage him in a game of cards. Use every trick I ever taught ye. Fleece the old gent for every cent ye can. And after ye win, tell him the win was for Lottie. He'll know what yer talking about. Will ye do that for me?"

Wren nodded, a wide grin splitting her gaminlike face. "Every trick, Lottie?"

"Every trick," Lottie repeated firmly. "Seth overheard him talkin' with young van der Rhys, and that's how I know he'll be aboard. It's an old, private score ye'll be settling for me. It was the one and only time in me life I got fleeced, and it still don't sit well. I want ye to even up the odds for me."

"I'll do it, and as soon as I get to America I'll post a letter to you with your winnings or send them on the next ship that sails for England."

"Child, I don't want no winnings. Keep them. I just want him to know I ain't forgot and that I don't need 'em. I want to see him bested. To do that, ye'll be using this deck of cards." Lottie dug into one of the pockets of her tattered gown. "Whatever ye do, don't lose them. Ye remember the markings, don't ye? Seth was the best forger in all of England, and his steady hand has no equal. Just look at the tail feathers of them peacocks and ye'll see the markings clear as a bell."

"I remember, Lottie. You have my word."

The three men entered the parlor with smiles on their faces for Wren. "Me and Lucas will be leaving for the wharf, and Seth will be back for Wren when it's time," Bart said quietly. Lottie nodded and the thieves went out, the yellow cat at their heels.

Aubrey Farrington stationed himself near a porthole in Caleb's cabin so that he could observe Malcolm Weatherly being brought aboard. Van der Rhys had eyes in the back of his head and the instincts of a cat. Keep him occupied and his mind clacking away, Aubrey told himself, and hopefully he won't get suspicious. When Cal learned of the gambler's little coup, he would be bug-eyed.

"All right, Cal, I can see that the gig is up and there's nothing to do but 'fess up to you," Aubrey rattled away. "It's simple, really. With you gone and the gambling fever at a low, I found myself hard pressed for a little cash, so I agreed to—to put a friend of mine in touch with a . . . lady I once knew, and then he—"

"Heisted the King's jewels," Caleb finished flatly. "I knew you were behind that caper the minute I heard the news. You might as well have drawn a road map, Farrington. It smacked of your devious hand. The only thing that surprises me is that you haven't been caught yet." Caleb's face was tight and grim, but his eyes were speculative. "How much, Aubrey, on the black market?"

"Nothing less than a king's ransom!" Aubrey crowed smugly. "I've arranged for the transfer of the collar in Martinique. I'm sailing with you, Cal, to protect my investment."

"Nice of you to tell me," Caleb remarked coolly. "Somehow I knew you would. Now, tell me where the jewels are, in case one of my men decides you're taking up space and need to be eliminated. I wouldn't want this little trip to be for nothing."

"You disappoint me, Cal. You know the rules a gambler lives by. I never reveal my hand."

"If that hand's about to be cut off, you will. For now, though, I'll let you keep your little secret; but remember, the day I decide I want an answer is the day you'll babble like a court fool."

"That seems to be a fair bargain," Farrington replied blandly as he twirled his elegant Cavalier hat between his fingers. "Very generous of you indeed, Cal." He turned to go, his uneasy stomach quieting to a purr. By now, Weatherly was safely ensconced in the bowels of the ship, securely sequestered in the locker box.

"One last thing, Aubrey. Even shares. Agreed?"

"Anything you say. You can trust me. Even shares it is."

"Then you'll have no objection to signing this little document in the proper place," Caleb went on, extending a piece of paper and a quill. "Cutthroat pirates aren't the only ones who have walked the plank, remember that. This is my ship and I'm the captain. Do we understand each other, Aubrey . . . old friend?"

"Perfectly." Farrington smiled, put his signature to paper and strode from the cabin. A pity he had never learned to swim as a youth. He hated cold black water. But it will never come to that, he assured himself as he made his way to what would be his new home for the balance of the journey. He needed a drink, maybe two or three, to settle his stomach. Two-way splits were for fools. Three-way splits were for the feebleminded. Winner-take-all was the way it would be. All he had to do was figure out how to eliminate Weatherly and give Cal the slip, and he would be the winner.

The minute Farrington had left, a broad smile creased Caleb's face. Whom did he think he was fooling? He could have had the jewels in a minute if he had wanted them. Aubrey had lived by his wits too long. Where besides on his person would he keep them? And that rakish hat with its plume! What better place to hide something than the most obvious one of all?

Wren sat quietly while Lottie dozed in the cane rocker. Her mind whirled. She felt nothing, no emotion whatsoever. She should be feeling something, anything, to prove she was still alive and the same person she had been. She was sailing under an assumed name, in clothes stolen from God knows where, on a ship captained by her stepbrother, who was not to know she was aboard. She had a deck of marked cards that would enable her to cheat, and a hundred pounds and a cache of gems stashed next to her bosom. She had misjudged Malcolm, been raped and almost killed by his hand and his friends, and Sirena and Regan, those dearest to her heart, were lost to her forever.

She was going to a new land overrun with savage Indians. How had all this happened? she questioned herself. Because I was a fool, she answered as tears trickled down her cheeks. She felt a small measure of comfort in knowing that if anything terrible did occur on the sailing, she could always plead with Caleb to intervene. Surely he wouldn't desert her. She wiped at her eyes with the back of her hand and looked around the squalid room.

She had lived like this as a child; actually, she had lived under worse conditions until Lottie had found her and taken her in. The days when she had slept in alleys with garbage keeping her warm were behind her. She didn't have to think about them any longer. They were lost to her forever, and now she was going to a new land and a new life. She would have to survive on her own. She had learned her lesson well. Never trust anyone. Trust was for fools. She had believed and trusted Sara and Malcolm, and look what had happened to her! Sirena and Regan had trusted her, and see what she had done to them! And that bastard, Caleb, trying to seduce her in the garden. She hoped she had crippled him for life so that he could never take advantage of another young woman. Mentally she placed him in the same category with Malcolm and then wiped him from her mind. She would survive or die trying, and if the latter happened, she would endure it by her own hand—no one else's.

The stool Wren was sitting on teetered suddenly as she tried to make herself more comfortable till Seth returned. She wished she could see outside. She knew the moon was full, but layers of grease and dirt covered the windows with a smudgy grayness, eliminating all signs of moonlight. She blinked as she saw a parade of roaches cross the table and envelop a chunk of bread lying on a cracked plate. Within seconds the bread looked as if it were alive as it shriveled to nothing but crumbs. They have to eat, too, she told herself; they have to live just as I do. The spindly legs of the stool creaked again as she looked at Lottie. How could her old friend live like this? "Because she's never known anything else," Wren muttered aloud. Bart and the others, they never knew anything else either. You did what you had to do to keep body and soul together; if something better came along, then you were lucky enough to taste the cream on top of the crock. "Damnation!" she spit through clenched teeth. She had lived with the garbage, slept under it and tasted the cream. She had no taste for garbage and swill and from now on she would have only cream.

The door opened silently this time, and the yellow cat was first through the opening. He leapt onto Lottie's lap and snuggled down in her filthy skirts. Seth nodded slightly. Wren rose first, and then Lottie. Neither woman said a word. Wren turned and followed the man through the doorway without a backward glance. She knew Lottie was crying silent tears as she cradled the cat in the crook of her arm. There were no tears left for Wren van der Rhys to cry.

"I'll be givin' ye me good-luck charm," Seth said, holding out a portion of a sow's ear as they hurried down the alley. Wren accepted the offering of the silken talisman with a smile.

"I'll take good care of it and pray that it brings me as much good fortune as it has brought you." It was all he had to give, and both knew it brought no luck, for if it had, Seth wouldn't be living like Lottie and taking care of her.

"Step lively, little one, and as soon as ye see a cluster of those black and white birds, mingle with them and make your way up the gangplank like ye belong with them. Don't look about, and keep your eyes down like the women do." He squeezed her arm lightly and whispered, "Good luck, lass."

Wren nodded and moved ahead quickly. She

spotted a family of Puritans gathering near the frigate and slipped in among them, her head and eyes downcast. She knew every nook and cranny of the *Sea Siren* from the times Caleb had sailed to Java, and she could outwit anyone who might get in her way on board. Sirena had pointed out various hiding places to her and how she could dart from one to the other if a hunt were on for a stowaway.

She saw Caleb's boots first and realized she had to pass him. Her head lowered, she scuttled by him and knew from his stance that he hadn't given her more than a casual glance—if he had done even that. Cattle, animals, that was all they were to him. Human beings didn't sleep in the confines of a ship's hold. Human beings lived in houses, ate proper food and slept in proper beds. How many of these people would survive the trip? The older ones, with their pale skin and brittle bones, would never last it out. The dampness of the hold and the lack of fresh air would make them develop coughs, and they would be buried at sea before the voyage ended. Regan had told her this and she believed him. She wondered if Caleb had explained these facts to the people before he had agreed to captain the ship. Not likely. Why should he care, as long as he got what he wanted? Men were all alike. If they couldn't get what they wanted with their charm, they took it by force. Whatever she had left she wasn't giving up, either by charm or by force. If there was any charming to be done, she would do it; and if it came to exerting force, she could do that, too.

A pole jabbed her cruelly in the side. "Move on, now, you're holding up the line," a harsh voice demanded, prodding her again. An angry retort rose to her lips, but she stifled it. Not now. She looked up to see who had jabbed her. Satisfied that she would remember the man's face, she quickened her pace and climbed down the ladder into the dark hold.

The *Sea Siren* secure, Caleb gave the order to weigh anchor. He cast a critical eye at the moon, measuring the stiff wind that bracketed the vessel. It was good sailing weather, better than he could have hoped for. His gut churned as the ship slid from her berth into the open water of the Thames. Six weeks with that ragtag passel of religious fanatics! In his eyes they all looked like somber penguins, intent only on converting souls and preaching fire and brimstone. Especially Bascom Stoneham, with his blazing eyes and self-righteous rantings and ravings. "Spare me from his daily visitations from the Lord," he muttered under his breath. Did Puritans ever do anything else but pray? he wondered. A vision of Sara in her black garb flashed before him as he gave the wheel a hard turn. She wasn't so docile, and her brother's teachings looked as though they had fallen on deaf ears as far as she was concerned. Without her clothes, he imagined she would be a fine figure of a woman. It was going to be a long sailing, and what better way to while away a few hours every now and then? He would have Farrington suffer with Bascom's prayers and preachings. That would keep Bascom occupied and at the same time do the old reprobate some good. Aubrey could benefit from exposure to religion. It was time somebody made an effort to save that curmudgeon's soul.

With the ship sailing almost of her own free will because of the strong sea breeze, Caleb let his thoughts wander, as he always did the moment the *Siren* and he felt as one. He hoped that when Sirena and Regan found Wren, they would have a safe journey back to Java and the sons they loved so deeply. And Wren, where was she? His lips tightened and an imaginary pain attacked his midsection. Wherever she was, he knew she was in trouble. Trouble followed her, settled around her, and if he was any judge, it was her middle name. The grim set of his jaw lessened when he re-

163

membered how warm and soft she had felt in his arms, how ardently she had returned his kiss with the promise of more to come. Sweet, virginal Wren. "Spitfire" was more like it. His lips tightened again when he recalled how he had rolled on the ground in pain, his groin on fire. Suddenly he laughed. Sara's face had just swum before him, and she was asking him if he had spells. He'd show her the kind of spells he had before this trip was over! But where had Wren gone? Was she with that fop Weatherly? Surely she wouldn't be foolish enough to marry him. But just for spite she might. She had learned too much from Sirena. Wren was strong-willed, and had an ungovernable temper and a tongue that should have been forked. Yes, Sirena had taught her well. In his gut he knew they would cross paths again, and when they did, she wouldn't be a schoolgirl any longer.

Aubrey Farrington, resplendent in his sea attire, as he called it, marched on wavering legs to the wheelhouse, his face pale and his hands trembling. Caleb took one look at him and pointed to the railing. He listened as Farrington retched while holding his stomach as if it were going to drop to the deck.

"Whatever you do, don't eat today, Aubrey," Caleb advised with a chuckle. "Serves you right for coming along. God's punishing you for not trusting me. You might have this miserable sickness for the entire length of the journey. Seek out Bascom Stoneham and ask him to pray for your relief."

"Bastard," Farrington hissed as he once again leaned over the rail. "I've lost today's breakfast, lunch and dinner. There's nothing left in my stomach."

"You're being punished, Aubrey," Caleb continued to taunt the gambler. "If you should waste away entirely or find you can't maneuver around, what shall I do with your body? You'd better tell me now where your prize is."

"I'm not going to die, so don't concern yourself, you insufferable bastard. You're enjoying my agony, aren't you?" Farrington said weakly as a fresh wave of nausea swept over him.

"Couldn't happen to a nicer person. Go below and lie down. Sooner or later dizziness will overtake you, and you might fall and get hurt. I've no mind for setting bones this trip, and yours are so old I doubt if they could be mended. Splinters. There's no hope for you, Aubrey."

The gambler was too weak to retort and gladly took the arm of a seaman named Peter, who helped him to his cabin. He barely reached the rough bunk before renewed attacks of nausea overcame him.

The Puritans settled themselves in the hold, three yellow smoking lamps lighting the darkness. Wren glanced around, trying to see if Sara was aboard. The blond girl was sitting next to her mother, an unhappy look on her face. Mrs. Stoneham looked as if she were praying. Wren carefully inched her way to a dim corner and sat down, drawing her knees up to her chin. She lowered her head and fell asleep almost immediately.

In what seemed like only moments later she was jarred awake by a prod to her leg. "Wake, sister, we're about to pray." Wren blinked. She thought she had just seen the devil. She swallowed hard and got to her knees and bowed her head with the others. An hour later she fought the urge to laugh at the preaching man whose eyes were blazing with a vision of the Lord. She lifted her head defiantly and stared at him. She had had enough, and her knees hurt.

Bascom Stoneham stared back at her and said, "Lower your eyes, sister, while I pray for your soul. Never look upon me as I preach, for I am the Lord's emissary. You are but a poor sinner and have no right to gaze upon me as I spell out God's Word. Sinner!" he shouted. "You're all sinners, and I've been sent to save your souls! And I will save them! Pray with me now and ask for forgiveness. Sister, I won't tell you again to lower your eyes. If you don't, you'll be punished at day's end."

Wren giggled. How could the likes of him punish her? Such a skinny, scrawny, ugly man! How could the Lord pick such a man to do His work? Evidently his mother was wondering the same thing, for she raised her eyes and met Wren's. If she recognized the girl, she gave no sign but lowered her eyes again, a look of outrage and disgust on her face.

"Now," Bascom continued, "repeat after me: We are all sinners and must ask for forgiveness and also for punishment so that our souls can be purged and we can walk among decent people and do God's work."

Wren was beside herself. This time she raised her head and spoke loudly. "What if we haven't sinned, but have been sinned against?"

"Who is that who dares to speak while I say the Lord's words?"

No voice answered the preacher's question. Wren lowered her head and folded her hands into a pyramid, a smile parting her lips. Hypocrite, she said silently. Punish me, will he? Damnation, her knees hurt. If this was what this trip was going to be like, she had best get herself out of there, and quickly. She would ask the next seaman she saw to send Caleb to her. She'd rather deal with Caleb than with this devil standing before her.

"Every sinner in this room, stand up and tell the Lord what you've done, and I'll forgive you and pray for your soul!" Bascom shouted, his eyes blazing and spittle forming in droplets on his mouth. Wren looked up. Everyone was standing but her. She knew in her heart she wasn't a sinner, and she'd be damned if she'd stand up. And if that insane man took it into his 'ead to punish her, she'd give him what for in a

166

hurry, just like she had given Caleb, although, from the looks of things, he wasn't endowed with Caleb's manly attributes. She giggled at the thought and felt a viselike grip on her arm.

"You dare to laugh when I'm preaching the Lord's words and asking for purging? You dare to make a mockery of what I'm doing for these poor souls who have sinned against the Lord? Just this noon the Lord favored me with another visitation. He told me to be wary of those who refused to repent and to cast my eye upon them. You are a sinner, sister," Bascom declared loudly. "By the set of your jaw and the defiant look in your eyes I can see that you were the one the Lord was talking about. You must repent now, before it's too late. Together"—he waved his arms around the hold—"we will save you."

"I haven't done anything, and I don't need to be saved. I'm here by mistake. Captain van der Rhys is my brother. I'm Wren van der Rhys. I was expelled from school along with your sister, Sara."

Every head in the room turned and then immediately snapped back; all eyes were downcast. Wren ripped off the white cap and her hair tumbled free. She swirled the dark tresses about her shoulders and shook his arm away. "I've decided I don't like it here, and I'm leaving. Now," she said adamantly.

"Every sinner says he's done nothing and has no need to be saved. Yes, I recognize your name, and that's why I'm going to devote myself entirely to saving your soul. The others are well on their way to being purged through my mighty efforts and my daily visitations. And we'll hear no more of your going topside. You'll go on deck only when I say so. For now, you will do penance and ask the Lord to forgive you for talking to me in such a manner. But first," he said, dragging her to the front of the flock, "you will tell your brothers and sisters what your sin is. Then we will all pray for you."

"Damnation!" Wren spit. "Well, if you must know, I play cards." As an afterthought, she added, "On Sunday."

"Heathen woman!" Bascom admonished, aghast at her words. "If you promise to mend your ways now, this moment, in front of my flock, I will not have you punished at day's end."

"But why should I do that? I always win. I don't want to give up my evil ways. I enjoy a good game of cards and a glass of wine. That doesn't make me a sinner and I don't wish to repent. Call my brother and let me out of here," she demanded.

"All in good time. All in good time." Bascom rubbed his hands together. "For now, you will kneel and pray. I shall go on deck and speak to your brother myself. I shall tell him of your wicked ways and that I'm going to purge your very soul and welcome you into the Lord's hands."

The moment the hatch had closed on Bascom, Sara was at Wren's side, her mother with her. "I see you and I hear you, but I don't believe it," Sara said coolly. "How could you hold me up for ridicule before everyone and say I was expelled from school? What are you doing here and why are you dressed that way? I thought by now you'd be married to Malcolm and that both of you would be living the life of leisure and luxury." She felt ill as she waited for Wren's reply. She had to know what had happened to Malcolm.

"Malcolm is . . . was . . . actually, Malcolm is . . . dead," Wren began lowering her eyes in chaste Puritan fashion "He developed some sort of . . . of pox and just . . . he just died. In my arms," she added hastily. "I decided it was time for a little adventure, and the . . . opportunity to sail on Caleb's ship came up and I jumped at it. As for these clothes, I've always had a secret desire to dress like this. Is there anything else you want to know, Sara Stoneham?"

Not for the world or for every ounce of silver in all of England would she tell what had really happened. She wouldn't bare her soul to anyone. Sirena had always told her to carry her hurt in her gut and maintain a serene face. That way you could look at the world and let it look at you, and only that deep core within knew how wounded and hurt you really were. And she was wounded and she was hurt, but she couldn't dwell on it; otherwise it would eat her alive.

"That's a baldfaced lie if I ever heard one," Sara snapped. "Malcolm was all right several days ago. How could he have developed a pox and died?" Please, God, don't let it be true, she cried inwardly.

"And you called *me* a scatterbrain! I loved Malcolm, you know that, with all my heart. Do you think I would be sitting in this rotten hold dressed the way I am and listening to that—that—ass of a brother of yours if my dear Malcolm were alive? Well, do you?" Wren shrilled.

"Malcolm couldn't die like that. I know him—he would have fought the disease, had the best physicians Why are you doing this to me? I thought we were friends!"

"He did fight it . . . like the man he was, and I am your friend; that's why I'm telling you what happened." Wren forced a tear to her eye and let it trickle down her cheek. "I've lost him forever."

Sara wasn't about to give up. "I heard no word of an epidemic before we boarded. Poxes are passed from one person to another. Bascom would have said something. Your brother wouldn't have let us sail if there was a chance any of us might catch the disease. After all, Malcolm was in contact with all of us at the Sinclairs'."

"I know. You shouldn't sit so close to me, Sara. I held Malcolm in my arms before he . . . before he . . ." Another tear found its way to her eye and dribbled unchecked down her cheek.

Sara rocked back on her heels, her face ashen. "It can't be . . . it just can't be. Someone so alive as Malcolm can't be . . . dead."

Wren felt a brief stab of remorse, but it was short-lived when she remembered what Sara had said about her affair with Malcolm. While she hadn't believed it at the time, she knew now that it was the truth. "You'll live, Sara. I'm living with my grief, and if you ask that dotty brother of yours to pray for you, he will. He loves to pray for all us sinners. And you're a sinner, Sara," Wren said virtuously.

Oh, God, it can't be true, it simply can't be, Sara repeated to herself. Wren wouldn't lie to me. She must be telling the truth. Why else would she be on this Godforsaken ship bound for America? Now, what was *she* going to do? And what if her suspicions were right and she was pregnant? That was all Bascom needed to know. He would have her cast out of the community, a marked, evil woman.

Wren watched Sara and her mother return to their former places and lie down on the plank floor. Her eyes closed, almost as if she were praying. She leaned against the wall and waited for Caleb to come down the ladder to take her topside.

While Wren waited, Bascom sought out Caleb in the wheelhouse and promptly told him of his sister's plight.

Caleb was stunned. "Let me be sure I have the straight of it, Stoneham. Are you telling me my sister is in the hold, dressed like a Puritan and claiming she plays cards and cheats at them—on Sunday? And that she's tired of her devious little trick, so she says, and wants to come topside? You think you can save her from her evil ways with prayer, and you don't want me to intervene? Now, is that the straight of it?"

"Every last word, Captain van der Rhys. I know I can save her. It will take time, but I'm confident

170

that when the Lord visits me tomorrow, He'll have answers for me. Answers for your sister, too."

Caleb threw back his head and laughed. Bascom was shocked at the captain's mirth. This was certainly no laughing matter. Sara had told him van der Rhys was prone to fits, so what could he expect?

"Very well, Stoneham, I will not intervene. If my sister has embraced your religion, then she should be free to make her own decisions. You're probably right, and all she needs is prayer, an abundance of it. As for that wicked card playing, you have to break her of that. Why, her whole life could be ruined!"

"She said she wins all the time," Bascom declared piously.

"I'm sure she does, and she probably cheats, too. You have to keep a sharp eye on women these days. You're right, prayer is the answer. Good luck to you, Stoneham, and if there's anything I can do, just call on me. Give my sister my warm regards and tell her I hope she mends her wicked ways before the journey's end."

Caleb watched Bascom wind his skinny body down the ladder to the hold, and then he doubled over in laughter. "Well, Preacher," he addressed Stoneham's back, "I don't know which of you has met your match, but this should prove to be interesting, if nothing else." He laughed again, his white teeth gleaming.

In the hold, Wren sensed Bascom's presence before she opened her eyes. "Why are you standing there?" she demanded. "Take me topside to my brother."

"Your brother has asked me to deliver a message to you. He said to give you his warm regards, and since you have embraced our faith, he knows you will mend your wicked ways with prayer. Your brother is a sensible man, even if he takes fits."

"Fits! What are you saying? Take me topside or I'll go myself!" Wren shouted, getting to her feet, only to be pushed back onto the hard planks.

"Don't you understand? You aren't going topside at all. You're to remain here with us so we can pray for you and purge your soul. Your brother does not want you up above. Now, do you understand?"

"I understand, all right. It's you who doesn't understand. Isn't it time for the Lord to pay you another visit? You better get ready while I leave. You can pray and purge someone else."

"You're worse off than I thought. Make up your mind that you aren't leaving here. If necessary, I'll have you tied up by some of the men."

For the first time since boarding the ship, Wren felt a stab of fear. This crazy man meant every word he said. Perhaps when he slept, she could sneak up the ladder. After all, her passage had been paid for; she wasn't a prisoner. That's what I'll do, she decided. I'll give in to him now, and as soon as he falls asleep, I'll leave.

Almost as if he could read her mind, Bascom told her, "If you have any thoughts of sneaking away while I sleep, you can cast them from your mind. Members of my flock will guard you. This is for your own good, and your brother agrees, so you might as well come to terms with our decision. Now, let me get my Bible and we'll read aloud—together."

Angry beyond words, Wren lashed out with her arm, which was immediately pinned to her side, Bascom's face within inches of hers. She smelled his stale breath and saw his limp, stringy hair hanging down his cheeks as if through a magnifying glass. His eyes took on a glassy look, like that of the card players to whom Malcolm had lost her. She felt his hand move up her arm to her shoulder and then down to the swell of her breasts. He moaned slightly as his breath caught in his throat. "Are you a fallen woman, too?" he asked hoarsely, saliva moistening the corners of his mouth.

"Not till now," Wren said through clenched teeth as

she forced his hand from her bosom. "I think your calling is prayer, and you can leave the lovemaking to those who know how to go about it."

The blow Wren received was hard and fast, coming straight across her face. Her head reeled as she tried to bring her eyes into focus, and she was amazed to see that not one of the preacher's flock was looking at them. They were like trained animals, she thought wildly as she again fought off his searching hands. No one would ever touch her body again unless she permitted it, and this perverted man of God was not going to lay a finger on her. She cupped her hands together into one large fist, and aiming directly at his chin, sent him sprawling backward. Like a cat, she crouched quickly over him. "If you ever touch me again with so much as a finger, I'll kill you." She lowered her voice to a bare whisper. "I've killed before, and I'll have no qualms about doing it again. Now, do *we* understand, Preacher? If my brother doesn't want me topside, that's all right, but that doesn't give you the right to think you can take liberties with my person. You can pray till the moon is full, but don't expect me to do the same. And as for your flock members, remember this. Once you kill one person, it's easy with the others. Now, if you'll excuse me." She grimaced, then made her way back to her own secluded corner. When she sat down, she was trembling from head to foot. God in Heaven, what had she gotten herself into? Damn you, Caleb, she muttered to herself, all the while keeping her eyes on Bascom Stoneham. Her stomach churned and her breathing was rapid, her pulse quick. Old Lottie had told her about men like Bascom when she was a child, and she had never forgotten. They were sick in their heads, Lottie had said. Visits from the Lord, indeed! Wren sniffed.

Bascom's eyes were dangerously cold when he stumbled to his feet. As cold and malignant as a snake's. It was just as well Wren couldn't see them from this distance. If she had, she would not have slept a wink that night.

One day ran into the next, with Wren becoming more hostile toward the ranting preacher. He forbade her to go topside with the others for the usual afternoon airing; instead, he made her kneel for hours on end, although she refused to pray aloud. If it were the last thing she did before she died, she would make Caleb pay for the humiliation Bascom was making her suffer. It wasn't as if she didn't believe in God—she did—and she prayed daily in her own way. Unfortunately, she thought morosely, He wasn't seeing fit to answer her prayers. She would have to take matters into her own hands, as she had done in Malcolm's room when she had killed the card player and wounded Malcolm.

The body stench in the close confines of the hold was making her nauseous, and she had seen Sara vomit more than once. Bad weather had prevented Bascom from taking his flock topside for its daily allotment of fresh air. Wren was sick of it all. She was sick of Bascom, sick of Sara with her vacant eyes, sick of Mrs. Stoneham and her simpering expression. Only Lydia, Bascom's wife, appeared to be normal —or what passed for normal, Wren thought. Lydia had given up her airing three days ago and knelt with Wren in the position of prayer. Later she had tried to explain her husband to Wren, who had scoffed at her. Tears had gathered in Lydia's hyacinth eyes and she had gone on to say Bascom was different and that one had to get used to his strange ways.

"Never!" Wren had exploded. "He's insane. Why do you put up with him?"

Lydia had cried, great heart-rending sobs, and said she had nowhere to go and no one to turn to. Bascom provided a roof over her head and food for her stomach.

"But there's more to life than a roof and food," Wren had protested. "You're young and healthy and strong. There are other men who would take care of you and love you. Take Peter, for instance. I've seen the way he looks at you when he brings us food."

When Lydia had returned to the other side of their quarters to see to Sara, who was retching wildly, Wren had sighed and blessed herself. "The devil made me do it, God. She deserves better than that fanatic. Help her. If You can't see Your way to helping me, then help Lydia."

Now, satisfied with repeating these same prayers, Wren settled back into a sitting position, withdrew her deck of cards and looked at the colorful squares. Damnation. Here she had the tools to win a fortune, and she was locked up like a common criminal. If she could just figure out a way to get her hands on Bascom's hoard of money, she would be set for life. The heavy pouch of gold he kept tied around his waist was the only thing that prevented him from going over the side of the quarterdeck rail in a strong wind. He was so thin and brittle that he would have taken to the wind like a dry leaf. Besides getting even with Caleb, Wren promised herself that somehow she would leave the ship with Bascom's cache. Lydia had said that as soon as he reached America he was going to have a stonemason carve his likeness for his new church. America didn't need a likeness of Bascom, not if she had the real thing. If Wren could persuade Lydia to bolt, she would share Bascom's wealth with her. The idea seemed more than fair to Wren, and she smirked to herself as she slid the deck of cards into her pocket.

Chapter Eleven

The *Sea Siren* rode high on the waves as she dipped and rocked amid the white-capped peaks. Although it was high noon, the sky was black and threatening, the wind buffeting wildly. Caleb cast an anxious eye at the crow's-nest and the man in it trying valiantly to gain a secure hold on the rigging. All hands kept their eyes peeled on Caleb, knowing instinctively by a nod, a shrug, a movement of his leg, what he wanted them to do, since his voice couldn't carry over the wind.

All thoughts fled from Caleb's mind as the storm gained in intensity. He felt strangely exhilarated by the force of the elements and knew he had a battle on his hands. The tang of the salt air was like a balm as he gripped the wheel, the wind howling through the rigging and the close-reefed sails. Gigantic swells, whipped into curly white combers by the gale, rolled in continuously from the north. Spindrift flew in flakes, stinging his face as he fought to master the wheel. Hands gripping the slick, stout mechanism, which was nearly as tall as he, Caleb stood erect, man and ship brazening nature. Lightning flashed, illuminating the dark, spectral clouds scudding across the sky. Rain had not yet begun to pelt the decks, but it was out there, waiting. Making ready for the onslaught, Caleb lashed himself to the wheel as Sirena had taught him to do.

Minutes seemed hours and hours an eternity. The storm now raged in full fury. Blinded by the savage downpour, Caleb kept the ship true to her heading. His body was battered by the elements; his hair beat against his face and twisted about his neck like insistent, strangling fingers. When his physical strength began to ebb, an iron determination to survive became his mainstay. Nothing would stop him from conquering this storm. He had ridden out worse in the *Siren* and always lived to sail another day.

Below decks, Bascom braced himself in the confines of the hold, the wind and rain pounding in his ears. His flock was kneeling in prayer of its own accord. Most of the Puritans had never been on a ship before or been exposed to this monster that was howling and shrieking above. They held on to each other, secure in another's touch. Bascom himself was elated, and his eyes gleamed in the flickering light. This was God's way of punishing all sinners. And the biggest sinner in his flock was Wren van der Rhys. He would take her topside in the storm, and if she survived, then she would know that she was one of God's chosen few and that He forgave her her sins. Bascom knew she was a harlot, a jezebel, a tainted woman. She had probably lain with a hundred men. He knew it as sure as he knew his name was Bascom Stoneham, messenger of the Lord.

He would drag her forcibly by the scruff of the neck, if necessary, to the quarterdeck and make her kneel there, her eyes and head raised to Heaven, and if she still refused to pray to the Lord, he would do it for her.

A vision was coming to him and he closed his eyes. He saw Wren kneeling on the slippery deck, her arms reaching out . . . to him . . . to help her. Her clothes were ripped and tattered, her breasts bared, one long leg and thigh silken from the slick rain. He was helping her . . . His breathing became ragged and his eyes narrowed to slits as the ache in his loins grew more pronounced. When he felt the exquisite release of pain, he would know the Lord had purged her soul.

Wren flailed out with both fists when Bascom bent down to drag her to her feet. "Take your hands off me. Help me, somebody!" she shrieked to be heard over the crashing waves that beat against the ship. "I'll kill you, you lecherous bastard!" she screamed as she lashed out with her foot to give Bascom's stick-thin leg a vicious kick. No one made a move to help her. All of them would merely stand by and allow this crazy person to take her topside in the storm. She screamed her protests and continued her struggles, to no avail.

She was almost comical in her entreaty as she prayed to the real God to help her. "Please, God, don't forsake me now; deliver me from this madman who is bent on killing me." Bascom was shouting for his God to purge her soul, that he was doing everything in his power to follow the instructions of his visitation.

Caleb was stunned when he saw the two figures hurl themselves onto the deck. Now, what in the name of holy hell was going on? He tried vainly to see if any of his men were about, but all were secure in their posts and following his previous orders. He couldn't leave the wheel. All he could do was watch the macabre scene below. His ears rang with Wren's cries for help, and for the first time in his life he felt powerless. His heart hammered in his chest, not from the storm, but from fear for Wren.

Bascom lost his hold on the screaming girl when a wave leapt the side and crashed down upon them.

Wren struck out and grabbed at a water barrel standing next to a heavy tack box. She managed, amid the vicious downpour, to wedge herself between them and at the same time loop the thick ropes around her wrists. She hung on for dear life, the waves and the rain beating against her like a drum.

Bascom was shouting words and prayers to his God, words and prayers which sounded obscene to Wren's dulled mind.

Lightning raced across the sky like a fleet-footed runner, and Caleb saw a swell coming and groaned. She would drown or be washed over the side by the force of the water. He drew in his breath as the rain lashed against him, beating him, clutching at him, trying to claim him, trying to claim Wren. Caleb wasn't a religious man, calling on God only when he felt the need, and those times had been few and far between, but he prayed now. Please save her. Surely He would hear that it wasn't a prayer for himself.

Wren had seen the wave at the same time Caleb had, and she drew in a mighty breath. She had to hold on. She wedged herself tighter between the barrel and the tack box till the rough wood cut into her ribs. It was all she could do. The rest was in His hands. Her eyes were tightly closed, and so she missed Bascom's departure from the quarterdeck to the stern rail as the elements washed him from her sight.

Caleb watched helplessly from his position at the wheel. He saw Bascom being swept along and saw Wren's indrawn breath. If she could just hold on long enough and not lose her grip, she might make it. The tightness in his shoulders was the searing pain of a branding iron.

The ship heaved with the force of the swells; the masts groaned with the weight of the saturated rigging. Rhythmically, the *Siren* rose and fell as she rode the turbulent waves. Caleb guided the vessel from the trough to the crest of each gigantic wave. For moments the *Siren* would balance dizzily on the crest, then plunge steeply into the next trough as though dropping off the edge of the world.

For hours the storm persisted, each hour an eternity that took his toll on Wren and Caleb. He couldn't see her, didn't know if she was alive or dead. She could have been washed overboard. As for that preaching emissary of the Lord, he had to be dead. Nobody that evil—and Caleb had decided he was evil—deserved to live. But Caleb had never lost a man at sea. How would he explain to Sirena and Regan that he had let Wren go overboard? They would never understand, nor would they ever forgive him. Especially Regan, who loved Wren as if she were his own flesh and blood. Regan would pierce him accusingly with those agate eyes of his. Regan would never forgive him.

He experienced a loss that he had never known before. Wren. How well he remembered the feel of her, the warmth of her slim body. Even then he had realized he wanted to know her better, the way a man knows a woman. The way Regan knew Sirena.

He felt helpless. He was more tired than he'd ever been in his life. There was no sign of the storm's abating. How much longer could he take this torture? As long as necessary, an inner voice answered. His shoulders slumped and his head rested on his chest. He couldn't be beaten, wouldn't be. Imperceptibly his shoulders straightened, and with every ounce of willpower he possessed, he raised his dark head. His body leaning against the wheel, he could feel the burn marks on his rib cage from the lines holding him, and he knew that when he removed his hands from the wheel, his skin would be torn and bloody. He could bear the physical pain, but he would carry the hurt in his soul for the rest of his life. The thought of Wren's body being hurled about beneath the relentless tides was more than he could bear. A single, lone tear formed in his eye and clung to the lash. Only once before could he ever remember a tear coming to his eye, and that had been when Sirena had told him Regan was his father. The tear had clung precariously to his thick lash and somehow, miraculously, found its way back into his eye. No one had even seen that tear; no one had known his gut-searing joy on hearing those words. His great head slumped and he felt the tear drop from his lash. He had shed his first tear. And he had shed it for a woman. No one would ever know that except him. In that moment he understood he would have given his life if Wren could have been saved. He couldn't love her, could he? He barely knew her, but in some strange way he had always been drawn to her. Ever since the first time he had seen her.

Caleb had gone to visit Sirena and had been in the library of her London town house when Frau Holtz had entered with an enchanting little girl at her side, dressed all in pink. The first time he had ever heard her name, Sirena had said it. "Come here, Wren. There's someone I want you to meet. He comes from the Spice Islands and his name is Caleb. He is Mynheer van der Rhys' son."

Wren had been staring at him, oblivious of the new frock she wanted to model for Sirena. She had moved toward him slowly and asked softly, in her little girl's voice, "Do you know the Sea Siren?" Her brown-gold eyes had been lit from within like tapering candle flames.

Caleb had laughed, his strong, white teeth catching the light. "I know the story very well. She was a beautiful lady." He had taken a step closer and dropped to his knee. "I think she was almost as beautiful as you are," he had said, taking her hand and bringing it to his lips. His smiling eyes had sobered as he had gazed at her.

When she had spoken, it had been quietly, and her

181

words had startled both Frau Holtz and Sirena. "I hope the man the Sea Siren loved looked like you."

Caleb had temporarily torn his gaze away from Wren and glanced at Sirena. After a brief period he had whispered, "I hope he looked like me. I would be proud to have someone like the Sea Siren love me."

Wren had smiled, a knowing smile, adult beyond her years. "When I grow up, I'm going to be like the Sea Siren. Then I can . . ." She had hesitated. "Will you wait for me to grow up?"

Wait for me . . . wait for me . . . The words echoed in his head, words said by a little girl, in a little girl's voice; yet, as they gathered in intensity, they became the words of a young woman with a woman's voice, and they resounded over and over in his head. *Wait for me . . . wait for me . . .* And the words became the song of the sirens who beckoned to sailors at sea.

The storm persisted in its outrageous assault on the *Sea Siren* for another twelve hours. Caleb had long since slumped against the wheel, believing he was half dead. Yet his numb arms continued to steer the ship to a safe course through the swells and stinging spray.

An hour before dawn the storm wore itself out and the waters calmed to a mere boil. Peter, the first mate, and Harkin, the second mate, untied Caleb from the shoulder-high wheel and carried him to his cabin. Farrington was called in. He looked at Caleb with awe and pity and immediately set to work. No matter what he had ever said or done, the old man loved Caleb like a son. He performed healing ministrations to the best of his ability and sat back to wait.

When Harkin next appeared in the captain's quarters, he was carrying Wren's limp body. Farrington raised his gray brows in astonishment. The second mate gently placed Wren on the bunk opposite Caleb and spoke in a somber tone. "I don't know if she's even alive. I found her half in and half out of the tack box. Her shoulder's been wrenched by the rigging and has to be snapped back in. I've seen it done, but I could never be the one to make her suffer that pain. And while she's lying here more dead than alive, that preacher's out on deck, hale and hearty, praying for our souls. He's saying we're all going to Hell and it's up to him to save us from the devil's clutches. I want permission from someone, now that the captain is laid up, to throw him overboard."

Farrington waved Harkin away, his gaze intent on Wren. He peered down at her white face and noticed that the bodice of her gown was torn, revealing deep red welts peppering her sides. Her ribs were bruised at best, if not broken. Harkin was right. She was more dead than alive, her breathing ragged and raspy. Yet if her shoulder was to be snapped to, no better time to do it than when she didn't know what was happening to her.

"Harkin, come over here and help me with her. And if you're not man enough to make a good job of it, send me someone who is. I'll hold her neck and shoulder, you do what must be done with her arm. And make a good job of it, man, or it's the captain you'll be answering to." Aubrey's voice was gruff and revealed little of the pity he was feeling for Wren. His knowledge of medicine was limited, and he relied on common-sense remedies. Warm blankets, hot tea, bindings for the wounds and tender, loving care.

Farrington was unwavering in his care of the young couple as he tended and mended their battered bodies as best he could. Both spoke in delirium from time to time. Wren would cry out pitifully, "Caleb, help me!" And the man in the next bunk seemed to answer her. "Wren! I'll wait for you . . . Wren!" his cries tortured and heart-rending.

Though exhausted from bathing their fevers and changing the dressings on their wounds, Farrington refused the help of the crew and spurned the suggestion that one of the women from below assist him in his care of Caleb and Wren. He would allow no one to touch them save himself, and he spent the long hours stretched out on the floor between their bunks.

By the end of the third day Caleb was lucid but in severe pain. Aubrey grew fearful. "Cal, it is I, Aubrey. You must lie still. You've been ill for days with a raging fever. I'm almost sure your ribs are broken, but I couldn't chance taping you up for fear I would do something wrong and pierce a lung. I'll do it now, but you must remain still. Cal, do you understand me? Just nod your head." Caleb nodded weakly. Sensing his need to talk, Aubrey warned him not to make the effort till he was bandaged and resting comfortably. Again Caleb nodded.

He was as weak as a newborn infant and barely had the strength to lift his head. Aubrey had to balance his shoulder and neck as he wrapped strips of cloth around his rib cage. The effort left Caleb exhausted, and he fell into his first natural sleep. The old dandy sighed. Caleb would be hale and hearty in good time. It was the girl who worried him. By now she should have come around. There were periods when she was so still, so pale, locked in the embrace of a deep, unnatural sleep, and other times when she would cry out for Caleb to help her.

When Caleb awoke the following day, the first thing he heard was Wren's voice calling to him. For a moment he was back in the thick of the storm, lashed to the wheel, hearing her cries for help. His tortured eyes sought out Farrington's. The old gambler pointed a finger at the other bunk, and Caleb's eyes widened in shock. The enormity of what he was seeing hit him full force. She was alive—and calling for him! He struggled weakly to get up, and the pain that shot through him brought him back down on the hard bedding. "Tell me, Aubrey, how bad is she?" he rasped faintly.

Farrington shrugged. "I'm no physician, Cal. I

think she may be dying. She's been calling your name, but that's all she says. Her fever's been raging, just like yours was, but you met your crisis and conquered it. Her ribs are bruised and her shoulder was dislocated, though not too severely. Harkin and I saw to setting it, but I can't say we didn't do her any harm. She's been developing chills these past few hours, and I've covered her with as many blankets as I could lay my hands on. Harkin keeps me supplied with heated bricks from the galley, but nothing seems to help. There isn't much more I can do. I'm sorry, Caleb."

"It's my fault. I never should have let that preacher get his hands on her. There must be *something* you can do," he pleaded.

"All we can do is wait," Farrington said miserably.

"To wait is to see her die," Caleb moaned. Then he remembered when Sirena's son Mikel had been ill and had violent chills. She had taken his small form into the bed with her and held him close. Her body warmth had been all the small boy had needed, and the chills had soon ended. His mind refused to remember that little Mikel had died two days later. Wren wouldn't die! She couldn't die!

"Bring her here, Aubrey, and place her beside me. Don't look at me like that, you old fox. My body warmth is all we have. Strip her down. I can't get her warm if she's wrapped in those sweat-dampened rags. Be gentle and be careful, Aubrey."

Ignoring his pain, Caleb slid over close to the wall to make room for Wren. The effort of his movement left him breathless and lightheaded.

Aubrey gently laid the girl beside Caleb and discreetly looked the other way while Caleb enfolded her in his arms. He cradled her next to him and murmured soft words which were indistinguishable to Farrington. The gambler decided it was time to go topside; he wouldn't watch what wasn't meant for his eyes. Only men hopelessly in love looked as Caleb had when he had taken the shivering girl in his arms.

"Caleb, help me," It was the barest whisper, and he almost failed to hear it. He held her closer, careful of her injuries.

"I'm here, Wren, I'm here."

Throughout the long, endless day Wren cried out for Caleb and he would answer, his mouth pressed against her ear. His strong, sinewy arms enfolded her, and from time to time he kissed her cheek in tenderness.

During the night, as her chills began to abate and her sleep became lighter, her words became clearer as she cried for Caleb. He listened to them, his heart breaking for her as, bit by bit, the episode concerning Malcolm came to light. At first he hadn't understood when she had whimpered with fear. But as the night wore on and he continued to whisper words of comfort, she told him about Malcolm's losing her in a card game to the rough and surly seamen. Her eyes squeezed shut as though she were reliving the horror of the rape; she breathed the words over and over. Only the sound of Caleb's voice seemed to assuage her as he gentled away her tremors. Toward dawn, Wren seemed disposed to answering simple questions, and Caleb knew without a doubt that the horror she had described was much more than a nightmare. It was the horror of truth.

Hatred boiled in his heart when he thought of Malcolm and what perfidy he had enacted upon Wren's innocence. The desire to kill, crush, destroy, throbbed through his veins. He tried to tell himself he was experiencing the reaction of any brother who has learned that his sister was used and raped. But as Wren settled into a more natural sleep and nestled her body closer to his, drawing strength from the warmth he offered, he realized his pain went much deeper than that of a brother. With very little persuasion, he could love

Wren. He could erase the tortures she had undergone in her first physical contact with a man. The inner strength of Wren's ability to live with that violence filled him with awe and respect. He himself had witnessed the devastation that rape could have on a woman. He had been with Sirena through the worst of her trials, and he was familiar with the courage and resiliency that were necessary to go on with life.

Remembering what had been enacted upon Sirena and imagining what had been done to Wren, Caleb wrapped his arms more protectively about the girl who slept so trustingly in his arms, a haze of moisture in his eyes making a nimbus of the single lantern light flickering in the darkness.

By midafternoon of the following day Wren's fever had broken. Caleb climbed gingerly from the bunk, careful not to disturb her. She was sleeping her first natural sleep since the storm. He held his bruised sides carefully and motioned Farrington, who had peered in to check on them, to go topside.

After dressing, Caleb stood looking down at Wren, a great lump in his throat threatening to choke off his air as he remembered the things she had told him the night before. Again a surge of protectiveness swept over him, existing simultaneously with the hatred he felt for Malcolm Weatherly. His hand reached out to brush away a stray lock of hair that had fallen over her cheek, but he quickly withdrew it. He wouldn't allow himself to feel anything other than brotherly toward her. Wren needed time to heal, not to find herself thrown into the midst of another love affair. After what she had suffered, how could she ever learn to trust another man? It had taken Sirena what had seemed a lifetime to overcome the memories of what she had suffered before she could admit her love for Regan and go into his arms with trust and confidence.

Caleb told himself he had no time for waiting

games. Wren was his sister, or close to it, he amended. He would find his satisfaction with a woman who would understand his need was just for that. For satisfaction. If Wren wanted someone to talk with, he would be there for her. He couldn't allow his feelings for her, which were dangerously beyond those of a friend or a brother, to get the better of him.

Once out on deck, Caleb walked on wobbly legs to the wheelhouse to see how his first mate was faring. Satisfied that the ship was still keeping a true course, he made his way with Farrington to the quarterdeck. In a voice the gambler had never heard before, Caleb thanked him for his aid and for ministering to Wren.

"There's no need for thanks, Cal. I saw my duty and I did it. You would have done the same for me," Aubrey said offhandedly.

"What you say is true, Aubrey. But this is the second time you've stepped in and come to my rescue. The first time was in the Owl's Eye Inn, when I was about to be rolled by the doxie's accomplices. I'm in your debt."

"Just get me to Martinique, where I can unload this store of riches that has fallen into my hands. That's all I want from you, Cal. You've been like a son to me. Oh, I know you lose patience with me, and sometimes I'm insufferable, but if there's one thing you must believe, it's that you are truly like a son." There was an almost humble note in the old man's voice, and Caleb was surprised. Just when he thought he had the old fox figured out, Farrington did something that cancelled all his previous wrongs.

Well, he didn't have time to worry about Farrington now. Now he had to concern himself with Wren and how he was going to get her back to Sirena and Regan. And then, he thought to himself murderously, I'll get that bastard Stoneham and wring his goddamn skinny neck till he looks like a dead chicken! There was little he could do about Weatherly until he returned to Eng-

188

land, but he swore he would seek him out if it took a lifetime. And when he found him, Weatherly would curse the day he had ever set eyes on Wren.

Back in his quarters, he leaned over the sleeping girl till he had assured himself her breathing was deep and normal. She had a little coloring in her cheeks and he knew she would mend, perhaps not as quickly as he had, but she was alive and would continue to stay that way if he had anything to do with the matter.

Slowly he descended the ladder into the hold of the ship and found himself in the midst of a prayer meeting. Rage coursed through him at the fanatical look on Bascom Stoneham's face. Without stopping to think, he reached for the prayer book Bascom was reading from and flung it across the wooden floor. Gasps and sharp exclamations of horror rang in his ears.

"I've met fools in my day, but none your equal," Caleb growled. "Do you realize you could have killed Wren by taking her topside during a storm? It's a miracle either of you is alive! From now on, you and the others will stay here in the hold. It matters little to me if you like it or not. I've given orders to my men to report to me immediately the first time one of you sets foot on deck. Do we understand each other, Stoneham?"

"Heathen unbeliever!" Bascom cried piously. "Your sister needed to be purged for her wrongdoings, and what better time than during one of the Lord's miracles of nature? You yourself just said it was a miracle we both survived, and that's exactly what it was—a miracle! If you no longer wish us to go on deck, then we will stay below with the rats. But I want to implore you to take pity on my sister and allow her a little fresh air daily. She's been ailing since the start of the voyage, and nothing we do seems to help. Sara," he called, "come here."

Sara rose to her feet and walked slowly toward her brother and Caleb. She tried to smile, but her stomach felt so queasy she gave it up and grimaced as though in pain. Caleb frowned. If he did what the preacher asked, he would be running a damn nursery. Sara did look ill, though. He couldn't leave her down here with her brother and not feel guilty.

"Very well, she goes topside with me." There was no need to tell Bascom that he would quarter her in his cabin with Wren. The less that God-fearing gentleman knew, the better off everyone would be.

Sara followed Caleb docilely up the ladder and trailed him to his cabin. She showed no emotion at the sight of Wren asleep in the bunk, and Caleb thought it strange that she, as Wren's friend, did not inquire after her health. It seemed as if Sara had blindly accepted whatever story Bascom had told his congregation regarding Wren and the storm and his part in her near death.

Caleb watched Sara slide into the empty bunk and pull the cover up to her chin. The dark hollows around her eyes and the decidedly green cast to her complexion evoked in him a thread of pity for her mal de mer. The girl looked almost gaunt, and he found himself hoping it was only seasickness that was troubling her. The last thing he needed aboard ship was an outbreak of typhoid or the plague. He was about to reconsider the judiciousness of placing Sara in the same cabin with Wren when he saw her eyes close in a kind of painful sleep. Unable to bring himself to disturb her again, Caleb settled himself on a tack box and thrust his legs out before him, careful not to place undue pressure on his bound midsection. A little warm air, a mug of rum and a dash of sunshine were all he needed, and before long he would be in fine fettle.

Chapter Twelve

Aubrey Farrington was fast losing his patience with Malcolm Weatherly. "You'll live," he said callously. "You have no choice; you knew that when I made the arrangements to bring you aboard. You agreed; it's as simple as that."

"Listen to me, you weasel. I've had about all of this that I can stand. I need some hot food and fresh air. This locker box is like a hellish pit, and if you don't figure some way to get me out at night and filch me some decent food, I'll kill you," Malcolm threatened. "It's as simple as that."

A chill washed over Farrington. Weatherly was brutally ugly. Gone were his dashing good looks and his debonair manner. Now he was scarred, his eye blinded and a vicious, crusting scab running the length of his face. His once elegant manners were now those of a hunted animal. "I'll see what I can do, but I'll make no promises. Caleb is resting on deck. If the opportunity presents itself, I'll smuggle you some hot food. As for the fresh air, it depends on who is about and standing watch. I told you all this in the beginning and warned you there would be days when you would go hungry. You agreed. If you want to jeopardize all of our efforts, do it. Cal will have you shackled down here, and then where will you be? In case you aren't familiar with the nautical mind, let me tell you that this locker box is a brig when the occasion demands it."

Weatherly's lip curled and he stifled the urge to lash out at the old man. He couldn't allow him to have the last word. "Then see to getting me some clean clothes. These rags aren't fit for the likes of me. They smell," he said curtly.

Aubrey Farrington did not reply as he walked out the door. Some people were ignorant beyond insult, he muttered to himself as he threw the heavy iron bolt on the outside door. He smiled at the terminal sound. If he had his way, that sod would rot in there and no one would be the wiser. Only he would know. Himself and his maker, and as his years were drawing to a close, he knew he had better stay on the straight and narrow if he wished a seat in Heaven. He wasn't exactly a religious man, calling on his God only in times of stress—acute stress. He was, however, superstitious, as were most gamblers. He smiled and wrinkled his nose. Weatherly was right. Rotten fish smelled better than he did.

Back on deck, Farrington approached Caleb and was told about Sara.

"I'll be taking over your cabin; that means you move in with the crew," Caleb said firmly, disregarding Farrington's look of displeasure at being ousted from his small, comfortable cabin. "And if you see that bastard Stoneham step one foot off that ladder, call me immediately. I've already alerted the crew. And, Aubrey, I want you to see to the women's wellbeing. Take their food to them and keep an eye on Wren. It will be a couple of days before she can walk the decks. I'm placing their care in your hands. I don't know what ails the Stoneham girl, but I'm sure you'll find a remedy."

Farrington heard the ring of iron in Cal's voice and knew better than to protest. He had seen the tired look in his dark eyes and realized his friend was in pain. But now Aubrey had to be both a jailer and a wet nurse!

Later that evening, while Sara was out on deck, Caleb let himself into his former cabin to look in on Wren. She was lying on the bunk, her slight form barely making a mound beneath the coverlets, her face pale and wan against the pillows. Yet she gathered her strength and smiled up at him, the gratitude in her eyes magically kindling them to flames.

"I'm glad to see you looking alive. How does your shoulder feel?" he asked her, tenderness in his voice.

"Much better, thank you," she whispered, her eyes never leaving his face.

"Have you everything you want? Are you thirsty?"

Wren nodded in affirmation. He lifted her gently to a half-raised position and placed a glass near her lips. She sipped slowly, barely having the strength to swallow. "You shouldn't be alone; I'll have someone come and stay with you." Just as gently he lowered her to the pillow and moved toward the door.

"Caleb, wait," she said hoarsely, her voice weak and thready.

Almost as though he knew what she was going to say, he hesitated in returning to her side. He crossed the cabin slowly, trying to assume some of his old swagger in spite of his injuries. But he realized it would be better to have it said than to keep running from it. If anything, it would be more painful for her than for him.

"Caleb, I . . . I have the feeling that I've . . . did I say anything to you about . . . about . . ." It seemed impossible for her to voice the words. It was unnecessary. From the pain in his eyes she knew she hadn't been dreaming. She had told him everything about

Malcolm, or at least enough for him to put the pieces together to comprehend what had happened to her.

"Caleb, I couldn't bear it if you turned away from me. Do I disgust you?" she asked weakly, the effort of speaking nearly taking her breath away.

Instantly he was down on one knee, his face close to hers. "Never," he assured her, his voice threatening to break. "I think you are the bravest, most courageous girl . . ." It was impossible to continue.

"I know what happened to the Sea Siren. Frau Holtz told me. And I knew that if she could go on with her life, so could I. But I couldn't bear to have you look at me with pity, Caleb. That is all I ask of you."

"Never, Wren, only with admiration. And I promise you something else. When I get back to England, I'll search out that bastard and make him pay for what he's done to you. I swear it. He'll never draw another breath once I find him, no matter what it takes." The vindictiveness in his voice frightened her, and she calmed him with a light touch to his cheek.

"Hush. There's no need for that. Every time Malcolm looks into a mirror he'll remember what his lust cost him." Slowly, and with great effort, she insisted on telling him what she had done to escape the seamen and Malcolm. She admitted killing the ruffian and waited breathlessly for a look of horror to fill Caleb's eyes. When she saw only respect and admiration mirrored there, she relaxed and felt cleansed by her confession.

"Sleep now, little one," he told her, placing a gentle hand on her forehead, afraid that the strain of their conversation would mean the return of her fever.

Obediently she closed her eyes. Just before he stepped out of the cabin, she called to him. "Will you come and see me again?"

In that long moment before he answered her, sleep

claimed her, and her face became peaceful and serene.

Two days short of a fortnight found both Sara and Wren up and about. Caleb, completely mended, had resumed his duties as captain of the *Sea Siren*.

It was an hour past noon when Wren looked deeply into Aubrey Farrington's eyes and said, "Thank you for saving my life. I'll never forget it. I don't know how I can ever repay you for what you've done and for the care you've given me."

Aubrey blinked and frowned slightly at her words, and at that precise moment Wren won a permanent place in his heart. She looked different to him somehow. More womanly, more sure of herself. He hadn't known her before, but she had had the face of a girl when Harkin had carried her into Caleb's cabin. He couldn't explain it, and he was probably thinking through his hat, as Caleb called it. So he would mark it down to a foolish old man's wandering mind. Or did he have some preconceived opinions of her because Caleb had said she was flighty, irresponsible, spoiled, and had a tongue as sharp as any shrew on the wharf?

"You owe me no thanks. I did what anyone else would have done. You owe your true thanks to Caleb. He is the one who saved your life and knew what to do when your fever reached a peak. I was out of my depth, but he wasn't. You should be talking to him and not me."

Sara sat quietly and listened to the exchange between Wren and the gambler. She was puzzled. She and Wren had spoken very little since the day Caleb had brought her up here. Wren slept for long periods, and when she did awaken, she seemed to prefer her own company and to remain quiet. Sara didn't really feel like talking either, and, at best, the long silences were companionable. She wondered if she should confide in Wren, tell her what she feared. Sometimes it helped to talk to someone, even stupid, frivolous Wren. Once she had tried and been stunned at the look in Wren's eyes. But Wren wasn't a silly schoolgirl any longer. She seemed different now, more assured . . . more womanly. Besides, what could Wren do except listen and then make a cutting remark, as had been her custom when she didn't like something? But Sara didn't think she could bring herself to tell Wren that the child she carried was Malcolm Weatherly's child. She couldn't. Then what was she to do? If Bascom ever found out, God in his Heaven couldn't save her.

She shuddered, and Farrington was immediately concerned, thinking she was having another attack of mal de mer. She smiled and said she was fine. He looked relieved. Taking care of two ailing women appeared to have bested the old man. Perhaps he would help her when they got to America. He was experienced, wise to the ways of the world. And old men liked young women. If she approached him carefully, she might be able to wrap him around her little finger and have him dancing to her tune. There was Caleb to consider also. After all, hadn't he taken pity on her and brought her to his very own quarters so that she could recuperate from her malaise? Caleb and the gambler seemed to be fast friends, and if she remembered correctly, at one time Wren had said they were partners. If she behaved smartly, perhaps she could pit one against the other and come out the winner. Tomorrow she would put her ideas into action and get the feel of things. Tomorrow was a new day. She needed this long night to map out a plan that would guarantee her safety from Bascom when they reached America. A plan whereby she and the child growing in her womb would have sufficient funds to enable them never to want for anything. All she needed to achieve her goal was a sound plan.

One day ran into the next, the mid-May weather becoming softer and more inviting. Sara and Wren barely spoke to each other, with Wren alternating between periods of depression and anger when she realized Caleb had made no move in her direction since she had explained what had happened to her. He had come to see her on several occasions, that was true, but only when Sara or Farrington had been in the cabin. Since she had recovered, her attempts to seek him out had not been successful. Each time she ventured near the wheelhouse, one of the crew would hurry her back to the deck, telling her the captain had no time for women's chitchat.

If it was the last thing she did before she left the ship, she would give him a piece of her mind for letting her rot in that dreadful hold with Bascom Stoneham. And if Caleb thought that helping her pass her feverish crisis served as his atonement, he was sadly mistaken. He couldn't face her. That was just like a man. He does his dirty work and then runs and hides, afraid to stand up and get his comeuppance. Well, she wouldn't let him get away with *that!*

Gulping back a well of tears, Wren hated to admit that Caleb's avoidance of her had begun just after she had told him she had killed the seaman and maimed Malcolm. How the sight of her must repel him! She had driven him away with her confession just as surely as if she'd hefted a club in his direction.

She sat in her hard wooden chair on the deck and idly played with the deck of cards Lottie had given her. Since the order had been given that none of Bascom's flock could come above, the decks were painfully absent of people walking about, conversing in hopeful voices about the new lives they were going to lead in America. Even Bascom's fire-and-brimstone preachings were missed. "Like a stone removed from my shoe," Wren muttered, refocusing her attention on the thin cards which slipped through her fingers.

She hated the idea of tricking Aubrey Farrington into a game of chance now that she had gotten to know him so well. He treated her kindly, like a grandfather, and she liked his sly smile and disarming wit. How could she bring herself to cheat him after all he had done for her? Damnation! But there was still the promise she had made to Lottie to settle an old score with Lord Farrington. She decided she would make it up to him later.

Sara appeared on deck, her sea legs making her movements graceful and unhurried. Every hand working with the rigging or sheets stopped what he was doing to watch her as she tossed her long, silvery-blond hair over her shoulders and pretended not to see the flirting looks cast her way.

Vain bitch! Wren thought uncharitably. I know she's going by the wheelhouse, I know she's going to wave to Caleb and I know he's going to wave back. The crew never stopped Sara from visiting the wheelhouse, just Wren. "Damn you, Caleb," she said viciously just as Aubrey Farrington sat down next to her, his eyes on her playing cards.

"What have we here?" he asked, a surprised look on his face.

"Aubrey!" Wren cried in surprise. "Sit down and talk to me for a while. I feel like such an outcast on this damn ship. Sara looks at me as if she's blaming me for her brother's insane behavior, and Caleb hasn't come near me since I managed to get up and walk. You're the only one who will talk to me. Sara mutters from time to time, but it's not the same as talking." Then she laughed. "I see you're looking at these cards. I like to shuffle them; it keeps my fingers limber. For when I play the spinet," she added hastily. "And I like to look at the birds on the back and imagine where they come from." At Farrington's skeptical glance, she continued. "When I was in school we studied nature and the woodland creatures,

198

and I quite fell in love with plumed birds. So colorful and bright, they take your breath away. Don't you agree?"

"To be sure, to be sure," Aubrey said. His skepticism had changed to amusement. "Do you know how to play? Cards, I mean."

"Yes, but not very well. Ladies don't play cards. I just like the pictures of the birds. But if you want to pass some time, perhaps you could teach me what you know, and then later on we could play a real game for . . . for money. I have five pounds I could wager."

An hour later Aubrey rose and stared down at Wren. "My dear, you have a natural talent for this game. For someone who just likes to look at the backs of the cards, you did remarkably well. If we had been playing for money, you would have skinned my purse."

"Beginner's luck, Aubrey. If we had been playing for money, I doubt I could have been so lucky. Are you sure you taught me all you know? Somehow I thought card playing was more difficult."

"It's only difficult when you cheat at the game. And I would never do that," he said virtuously, raising his eyes to the heavens.

"Nor I," Wren echoed just as virtuously. "Being a cardsharp is the same as being a thief."

"You're so right, my dear. What do you say to a short stroll on deck before dinner?"

They chatted companionably as they made their rounds. When Wren saw Sara enter the wheelhouse, she faltered in her step and her eyes smoldered and sparked angrily. Then she turned abruptly, anxious to get back to her quarters, and left Farrington standing there perplexedly.

Aubrey saw Caleb nod to Sara and motion her to sit down. "It's the wrong choice, Cal," he said quietly, and wandered off.

Sara seated herself and folded her hands primly into the folds of her thick black skirts. How pale her hands looked, she thought, with their delicate tracing of blue veins. She was thin, much too thin, unable to eat for fear the rocking of the ship would make her vomit. Her liquid-blue eyes appeared to Caleb to be gentle, yet sad. What was she doing here? he wondered.

She knew she had to say something or he would begin to think her as addlepated as Bascom. "Captain van der Rhys, I've come to thank you for allowing me to stay on deck. I feel much better now that I've gotten my sea legs, and if you wish, I can return to my . . . my brother and the others."

Caleb watched her closely. Captain van der Rhys, she called him. In Tyler Sinclair's house she had called him Caleb quite freely and had openly flirted with him. Women! His voice was soft, barely above a whisper, as he replied, "I was planning on seeking you out later to see how you were faring. I feel reassured to hear you are on the mend and have your sea legs. For a while I thought I was captaining a hospital ship."

Sara moistened her lips with the tip of her tongue and gazed up at him. She was annoyed at the way he was staring at her. His eyes traveled from her mouth to her throat and down to her breasts. His face wore an amused look and his eyes were openly mocking as he made no effort to conceal his approval. It had been a long time since he had had a woman. He made a mental wager with himself that he could have her in bed within the hour.

"It's time for me to turn the wheel over to my first mate. Would you like me to show you around the *Sea Siren?*"

Sara's eyes lowered. "I'd like that very much, Captain van der Rhys."

Caleb's expression continued to be amused as he

handed over the wheel to Peter, who grinned at him knowingly.

As they strolled along the deck, Sara spoke quietly. "Does this invitation to walk with you mean you no longer find me unattractive?" It was a bold, blatant question, and Caleb answered in kind.

"I found you very attractive back in England, and I find you very attractive now. But I like to be the one who does the pursuing. I've found over the years that when a woman sets out to snare a man, she usually has some use for him. Do you, Sara Stoneham, find me useful in some way?"

Sara laughed, the first genuine laugh she had uttered in months. "And if I did, do you think I would admit it? Why don't we agree that if we were to find a convenient room with a bed, I would find you useful?"

Caleb laughed also. "I guess that means you no longer fear my fits."

Sara raised her eyes and smiled happily. "I've learned to live with many things not to my liking over the past months, I think I can learn to live with your fits." Out of the corner of her eye she noticed the openly speculative looks the seamen were giving her and Caleb. It was good that they noticed. Later she would need them to bear witness that she had lain with the captain.

Caleb's shoulders tensed as he approached Peter's cabin. His gut told him he would be sorry for this little adventure, and he almost made an excuse to turn back. But it was too late. They were already through the door, and Sara kicked it shut with her foot and leaned against it, her eyes wide with invitation. Caleb took her in his arms and she flung her arms around his neck, her lips slightly parted. He kissed her savagely, his tongue exploring the sweetness of her mouth. Then he drew away and carefully chose the words he wanted to say. "This means nothing other than what it is." His sun-bronzed hand tilted her chin upward, bringing her face to his.

"But of course. A moment of passion, of bodily release, nothing more. I understand, Caleb," she said, moving toward him and locking him in a tight embrace. The pulsating throbbing in her breasts made her cry out as she returned his ardor with total wantonness.

Their clothing in a tangled heap on the floor, Caleb lay down next to Sara and pulled her close. His movements were slow, almost lazy, as he played with her body. His mouth was brutal in its intensity as he brushed and teased her silken skin till the rosy crests became taut and erect.

Sara's tongue became a live serpent as it traced the outline of Caleb's mouth, darting inside, treasuring its warm moistness.

He kissed her eyes and neck and the hollow of her throat, where her pulse beat so wildly she thought she would faint. His hands were demanding as they swept across her thighs and found the warmth between her legs, sending her into a breathless frenzy of desire with each caress of his fingertips. When she thought she could no longer bear the feverish pitch to which he had brought her, he drove into her, again and again. Crashing waves of fire coursed through her as she cried out his name over and over.

Later, lying side by side, she stroked his cheek with gentle fingers. Perhaps now she could live again, love again and find some kind of happiness, regardless of Malcolm. Her body had responded to his passions, and that was all she needed to know for the moment. She watched Caleb's eyes close, his face content in the aftermath of their lovemaking. How well he had enjoyed her, crying out her name as she had forced his from her lips.

When sleep had overtaken him and his breathing had become deep and regular, Sara crept from the bunk and dressed quietly. She paused for a moment to stare down at him and admitted regretfully to herself that she had no feeling for Caleb other than that of physical satisfaction. He was an artful lover, demanding, overpowering, exciting, yet Malcolm would always be the man she wanted, the man she hungered for and craved. However far away from her Malcolm was in death, she would always remember the urgency of his hands, his mouth, his entire body. Her need for him went beyond the physical boundaries of sex, hers was the need of love.

Perhaps, Sara thought, in time she could learn to love Caleb van der Rhys. The next time she joined him in bed she would practice all the things Malcolm had taught her. Today was too soon. As it was, the Dutchman had been surprised to discover she was not a virgin. What would he say when he found out she was pregnant and claiming him as the father of her unborn child? It didn't matter what he thought. It mattered only what he did. Caleb van der Rhys was an honorable man. And honorable men always did what clever women said they should do.

Caleb woke, immediately aware of where he was and what had occurred between him and Sara Stoneham. He stretched his long-muscled limbs and felt them come to life. There was no denying he was much better, recovering nicely from the injuries he had sustained during the storm. A man had to be in fine fettle to satisfy a woman the way he had just satisfied Sara. He could still hear the sound of his name on her lips as one wave of passion had followed another. He smiled, self-assured that his injuries had in no way affected his performance in bed.

He supposed he should be feeling somewhat guilty about Sara. He knew he entertained no thoughts of a deeper attachment to her, except perhaps another encounter beneath the sheets. He had no desire to play the part of a love-sick puppy. It had been a pleasurable interlude, and somehow he had the impression that little Miss Stoneham was more versed in the arts of love than she had let on. And he hadn't been disappointed to discover that she wasn't a virgin. Virgins, he told himself, are bothersome creatures. He was tired of breaking them in for some other man to enjoy. He'd take a woman of experience any day.

As happened so often lately, whenever his thoughts were on women, somehow they traveled to Wren. He would have to seek her out and explain to her that his plans included taking her back to Sirena and Regan, even if that meant bringing her all the way to Java. And the sooner the better. Why did he keep postponing the inevitable? Before long he would have to face her, something he had been avoiding to keep from remembering how she had felt beside him in the bunk, his arms wrapped protectively about her. How she had called his name and how he had answered. How he had buried his face in her wealth of dark hair and groaned at his inadequacy to make her well. She couldn't mean anything to him, he wouldn't allow it. She was a sister of sorts. A street urchin whom Sirena had defended and generously adopted. His only obligation to her was that of a brother bent on avenging his sister, regardless of her insistence that she had avenged herself. Then why did you give orders to the crew to bar her from the wheelhouse? a niggling voice questioned.

How well he remembered the first day he had seen Wren. The image of her as a child was almost impossible to keep from his thoughts. As well as the sound of Sirena's hushed murmur to Frau Holtz that Wren was his destiny. Why did those words persist in revolving around his head? He must not have heard correctly. How could a woman be a man's destiny? Bah! he snorted as he swung his legs over the side of the bunk.

One leg in his trousers, he stopped and almost fell to the floor. Sirena had been Regan's destiny. He had known it before either of them. "God, help me," he muttered as he shoved his other leg into his trousers and hastily donned his shirt. He needed fresh air and the deck beneath his feet. He needed to look at the ocean and see the breakers. The sea was his destiny, not some two-legged creature with eyes like tapered candle flames.

While Sara had whiled away her idle hours with Caleb in the first mate's bunk, her brother had been telling his flock that the sinners above deck were the devil's handiwork and he would save them all. His prayer book clutched in his bony hands, he called for each member to stand in front of him so that he could personally convince them, just by the touch of his hand, that he was the Lord's chosen messenger and, as such, would drive the devil from this ship. If necessary, he exhorted, he would captain the ship himself.

Lydia Stoneham was the first to stand before him and hold out her hand. "Please, Bascom, speak with Captain van der Rhys and ask if the women might not go on deck just for a few moments. The heat down here is unbearable and the stench is terrible. Tell him you're sorry and beg his forgiveness, if necessary." Her voice rose till it was a shrill shriek. "Damn you, ask him!"

Bascom raised his hand and hit her on the side of the head with the prayer book, stunning her briefly. "Profanity! You dare to use profanity in the presence of a messenger of the Lord! My own wife! Down on your knees, woman, and if the Lord doesn't strike you dead, you can consider yourself fortunate. My own wife! And in front of my flock!"

Lydia was beyond caring, beyond feeling. He was insane, and if he was a messenger of the Lord, then

205

she was his disciple. "I've had enough of you and your mealy-mouthed mutterings. I can't bear another minute of it, not another minute. I'm going up that ladder and I'm never coming down again. Did you hear me, Bascom? If I have to leap overboard, I will. I'll do anything to get away from you. You're insane!" she shot over her shoulder as she gathered up her skirts and raced up the wooden ladder.

When she emerged through the hatch and stepped onto the deck above, the seaman standing guard could only regard her with surprise, unsure of what he should do. He couldn't push a woman back down the ladder. Captain van der Rhys hadn't said what he should do if a woman came up the ladder and tried to escape. Before he could decide what course of action to take, Lydia was running down the deck, sobbing heartbrokenly. She would throw herself over the rail and it would be over. Better to die than to live out her life with Bascom.

Blinded by tears, she paid no heed to where she was running and didn't see a pair of strong arms reach out for her. She shrieked as though in pain, thinking it was Bascom who had trapped her.

But these strong arms weren't Bascom's. And the square face with the strong chin weren't Bascom's either. This face had dark eyes full of concern and belonged to the first mate, Peter. "Easy, now . . . easy, now," he said softly. "What seems to be the matter? How did you get up here and where are you going?"

"Over the rail," Lydia gulped as she dabbed at the tears glistening in her eyes. "I hate him—I've always hated him," she blurted defiantly. "He's insane, and I'd rather die than go back down there. If you make me go back, I'll find a way to get up here again. Please," she implored, "don't make me go back down there."

"I won't make you go back, but I think we'd better

have a little talk with the captain." So she hated her husband and thought him insane, did she? It was the first sensible thing Peter had heard in weeks. She should know about the preacher, being married to him, he thought happily. She certainly was a pretty woman, and he did admire a pretty face.

When Peter ushered Lydia into the wheelhouse, Caleb groaned aloud. He was being overrun by females. "All right, the straight of it. What did *she* do?"

Peter suppressed a grin, his eyes twinkling merrily at Caleb's discomfort. "She said she was going over the side. She said she hated her husband and she refused to go back to the hold. She said if we made her go back, she'd find a way to get out again, and she also said she'd rather die than go back. The matter is in your hands, Captain," he concluded smartly, turning on his heel and leaving the wheelhouse.

"Mrs. Stoneham, it isn't easy operating a ship," Caleb began warily. "It takes one's full attention to navigate and stay true to the course. I have no time to settle marital disputes. Whatever your problem, it will have to be settled by you and your husband. There's no room topside for another female. I'm ordering you to go below to your husband."

"I suppose you're going to tell me you're a messenger of the Lord, too. Is that it? Well, I'm not interested in hearing any more messages. I've had enough to last me a lifetime. I meant what I said. I would rather be dead than go back down there to him. He's no messenger of the Lord. He's the devil himself. He's evil. He makes me do terrible things, makes the others do terrible things, too. He tried to make Wren obey him and she wouldn't. You can't send me back. I won't go," Lydia declared firmly, settling herself on a round stool near Caleb and the wheel.

Damn fool woman. Now what was he to do? "I'm the captain and you must obey me," he said, frowning at her docile look. She wasn't going to budge, he could feel it in his bones.

"It was your very own sister who gave me the courage to rebel at last. What kind of man are you to make me go back there so he can force me to do all those terrible things?"

"My dear woman, there are worse things in life than praying for forgiveness."

"I didn't do anything for God to forgive!" Lydia shrieked. "Weren't you listening to me?" Merciful God, was this strange person who was carrying on in such a state really Lydia Stoneham? Where had she gotten the courage to say something as bizarre as that she would jump over the rail? She couldn't swim and would go straight to the bottom! Belatedly, she covered her mouth and groaned inwardly. Who would blame the captain if he thought she was as dotty as her husband?

Caleb didn't want to ask her, but he did, almost knowing what her response would be. "What things, Mrs. Stoneham?"

Her face a bright crimson, Lydia spoke hesitantly, gathering courage as she went along, leaving out nothing, not even her own scorching humiliation, finally ending with, "I meant it, Captain. I'll leap over the side if you try to make me go back there."

Aubrey, you bastard, where are you when I need you? Caleb swore silently. He felt out of his depth with this woman seated before him. He couldn't send her back. What man in his right mind would subject a woman to such degradation? The only name that came to his lips was Bascom Stoneham.

Caleb whistled between his teeth, a shrill, sharp note that brought Peter on the run. "Take Mrs. Stoneham to my quarters and arrange sleeping accommodations for her with the other two women. They can take turns with the bunks. I don't care how you do it, just do it."

"Aye, Captain." Peter grinned as he gallantly escorted Lydia from the wheelhouse.

Whoever had said that men needed women was a fool, Caleb thought with a grimace. Or else that person hadn't known the women on his ship.

Chapter Thirteen

Bascom Stoneham felt the eyes of his flock on him. For the first time since he had become a preacher, he knew the emotion of fear. If he couldn't control his wife, how could he minister to and aid his followers? He had to do something, say something, and it had to be now, before the mass in front of him revolted. Even his parents were looking at him strangely. He cleared his throat loudly and opened his prayer book.. Deliberately, he lowered his eyes and read the printed words in a somber tone. The thick book closed with barely a sound. His eyes were hooded and his mouth grim when he began to address his congregation.

"I see now that all my prayers, all of your prayers, were not enough to drive the devil from my wife, Lydia. Sometimes the Lord works in strange ways. It has come to me that Lydia's fate is to be an example to all of us. Just this day I've perceived a vision.

Lydia is lost to us and can never return. But," he said, opening his eyes wide till the pupils were bare pinpoints, "we will continue to pray for her soul. Even though she is lost to us, we must never forget her. Now we are in a tunnel of darkness, but there is light at the end, and we will all walk toward that light while Lydia remains forever in the darkness with the devil at her heels."

If the devil was indeed at Lydia Stoneham's heels, she paid him no heed as she blurted her tale to a sympathetic Wren. "I'm so frightened. When we get to America, what will I do? How will I survive? What's to become of me?" she cried pitifully.

Emotion welled in Wren's throat. What *would* become of this gentle creature in a new land? What would become of Wren van der Rhys in the new land? It was her fault that Lydia had defied her husband and was now sitting next to her with no future before her.

She squared her slim shoulders and spoke confidently. "I'll take care of you, Lydia. I have some money, and we'll manage somehow. We're young and strong and we can surely find something to do in America. Something that will pay us enough money to live on. You must not worry, Lydia, promise me."

Lydia smiled and threw her arms around Wren. "I feel so good. So free for the first time in my life. I could sleep on the floor with the sleep of pure joy. And when I wake, I'll thank the Lord, *my* Lord, for giving me the courage to do what I did, and I'll thank Him for sending you to me to show me the way."

Damnation! Now what had Wren gone and done? She had saddled herself with another responsibility when, according to Caleb, she couldn't even take care of herself. Money. She had to get money for Lydia. If need be, she would badger Caleb to take her back to Java. How he would love to see her come crawling to him for help. She quailed at the thought. She'd make her own way and the devil take the hindmost!

It always came down to money. Aubrey Farrington had money, she was convinced of that. Bascom Stoneham had money. Bascom Stoneham had a lot of money. All the Puritans had entrusted their life savings to him. He had a fortune and she had a deck of cards. A deck of marked cards. And Caleb had money, probably more than Farrington. All she had to do was figure out a way to relieve each one of his hoard, and then she could set Lydia up in America and not have to worry about her. All she needed was a foolproof plan, and she herself would be comfortable indefinitely. It never occurred to her that she would not come out the winner. After all, she was the one with the marked deck, and even a professional gambler like Aubrey hadn't been able to spot the markings. By the time they reached America, Lydia would have so much money she would need someone to help her carry it off the ship.

Sara entered the cabin, her eyes widening when she spotted Lydia talking to Wren. She looked at both women and said nothing. The flush that rode high on Sara's cheeks didn't escape Wren's notice, and her jaw tightened. She knew where Sara had been recently and what she had done. Her heart pounded in her chest at the thought. Sara looked like the cat that had sat in the cream crock.

Lydia walked over to her sister-in-law and put her arms around the girl's shoulders. "I want to be the one to tell you that I've renounced your brother. It's better you hear it from me. I hope it doesn't upset you, Sara," Lydia said softly.

Sara grimaced. "Why should it upset me? Bascom is insane; we both know it. I'm just surprised that you had the courage to leave him. I could never understand how you tolerated him from the day you married him. Speaking personally, I think he's the devil reborn. I applaud you, Lydia."

211

Lydia tightened her hold on Sara and laughed. "It seems the three of us have the same opinion of Bascom. I'm glad to see that you're feeling better, Sara. I was truly worried about you when we were both in the hold. The sea air has worked its magic on you, and for that I'm glad."

"Sea air, my foot!" Wren snapped. "You can stop all this needless pretense, Sara Stoneham. I know what you've been doing and with whom, and you should be ashamed of yourself. Dallying with Caleb will get you nowhere, and it only cheapens you. He's a womanizer of the worst sort!" Her upper lip curled in distaste.

"Is that a note of jealousy I hear ringing in your tone?" Sara asked coolly. "Caleb isn't your real brother and you're simply jealous. Just the way you were with Malcolm because it was *me* he loved, not you. I told you, tried to warn you, but you wouldn't listen. It was only the van der Rhys' money Malcolm found alluring, Wren, not you!"

Wren's eyes glittered dangerously, sparks of fury lightening their depths. "Think what you will. I know Caleb, and if you have any serious plans, you might as well forget them. Caleb isn't the marrying kind. He plays with women the way children play with toys. Don't say I didn't warn you."

The slim blond girl faced Wren defiantly, the naked truth of her hatred for Wren written on her features. "I'm glad Malcolm is dead! Glad, do you hear!" she shrilled. "Now you will never have him! I told you he belonged to me! He was mine, and now he'll always be mine! Just the way Caleb is mine! I only wish you had caught the pox, too. I only wish you *were* with Malcolm—in his grave!"

Wren nearly staggered beneath the hatred in Sara's voice. Lydia, too, was aghast at what she had just heard. Sara, with a smirk on her face, lay down on the bunk and turned her back on the two women.

Wren felt the need to breathe clean air, to be away

from the stifling contempt which Sara exuded. She stumbled toward the door and Lydia followed, her hand ready to steady her new friend. Out on deck, leaning against the rail, Wren braced herself against the wind, the color slowly returning to her features. Lydia watched her anxiously, her own vivid red hair coming loose from its pins and whipping against her face. "I don't know what's come over that girl," she said tonelessly.

"What comes over a woman when she's been spurned by a man she loves?" Wren said, her words more a statement than a question. "Lydia, it's not true that Malcolm is dead. When last I saw him, he was very much alive, although somewhat the worse for wear. I told Sara he was dead only out of cruelty. I should go back in there and admit I had lied."

Lydia placed her hand on Wren's arm. "No, don't. It will do her little good. Better she thinks he's dead, for all the good he can do her. She has greater problems on her mind right now. Sara is with child."

"Do you know what you're saying?" Wren asked in a shocked voice, the terrible implications dawning on her instantly.

"It's true. A woman can always tell. It also explains the sickness she had below. I'm familiar enough with women when they're bearing a child. My own mother brought nine besides me into the world. I feel sorry for Sara when Bascom discovers it. He'll kill Captain van der Rhys for taking advantage of his sister."

"What makes you think Caleb is the father?" Wren demanded indignantly. "Caleb cannot be the father of her child, if she is in truth carrying a child."

"Then who?" Lydia asked quietly, watching Wren's face.

"Who?" Wren repeated. "I don't know who. I just can't believe it's Caleb." Damnation, it couldn't be Caleb, it just couldn't be! Wren's thoughts raced. There hadn't been enough time, the journey was

213

barely two weeks gone. An unbidden memory of Sara and herself in their room at Tyler's house, and Sara's boasting that she could have Caleb madly in love with her before dinner was over that evening, came to Wren's mind.

Will you wait for me to grow up? How often those words came back to haunt her. She had said them to Caleb the minute she had laid eyes on him in England, so long ago. *Will you wait for me to grow up?* Caleb had laughed and stared deeply into her eyes and said, "I may just do that." Damn liar, just like all men. Why could a woman speak with another woman and pour out her heart and be completely understood, whereas a man had to lie and twist the truth? Did that make him feel more manly, more worldly? Her lip curled as she muttered, "I may just do that." Damn liar. Caleb van der Rhys was a liar, and he had probably learned his trade from Regan.

Too bad dear old Caleb doesn't know what dear, sweet Sara has planned for him, Wren fumed inwardly. Instant fatherhood. Well, he can just stew in his own masculine juices for all I care!

Later, lying in her bunk, Wren admitted to herself that she was jealous of Sara. At the very least Caleb could have given her the opportunity to reject him. And reject him she would. Damnation, it was her inalienable right! He was making a fool out of her and she was allowing it. She would cut him down to size if it was the last thing she did.

"If you'll excuse me, ladies, I think I'll take a turn on the deck and see who's afoot," Sara said, looking from Wren to Lydia, defying either of them to make a comment. Neither said a word as she walked through the door.

"Twice in one day is a bit much," Lydia said pontifically. "She's like a harlot on the prowl."

Wren shrugged as jealousy once again coursed

through her. Damn you, Caleb van der Rhys, she thought murderously.

On deck, Sara carefully looked around and waited for Aubrey Farrington to make his appearance. For three days now she had seen him stuff leftover bread and cheese in his coat pockets. What did he do with it? If she could find out what Farrington was up to, she could go to Caleb and deepen his trust in her. She would say she wanted to help him and that whatever the old gambler was up to, Caleb should know about it.

Dressed in her Puritan garb, a black scarf around her bright hair, she stood waiting for the moon to take cloud cover. The spindly-legged gambler was late this evening. Perhaps he wasn't coming, she thought nervously. A footstep, another, and Aubrey Farrington came into view just as the moon ducked behind a dark cloud. She removed her stout shoes and pursued him stealthily.

Once Farrington stopped and looked over his shoulder to see if he was being observed. Sara crouched behind a thick roll of canvas and held her breath. Had he seen her? No. He was continuing his silent trek, and she was but a few steps behind him. She followed his cautious progress down the ladder of the fore hatch, her stockinged feet hesitantly finding the ladder rungs, and she dreaded stepping into the shallow pool of bilge water that sloshed rhythmically with the rise and fall of the ship. Plunging her feet into the murky, ankle-high depths and refusing to give her imagination free reign as to what unspeakable creatures might attack her from beneath the dark surface, she listened attentively for the sound of Farrington's treading water. Heeding her instincts, she caught up with him and winced from the light as he struck a flint to a tallow candle.

She stopped in midstride as she saw his arm reach out and slide back a bolt. After he had closed the

215

wooden door, she tapped her stockinged foot impatiently on the planks. Who was inside that room, and what was Farrington doing in there?

Crouching low, she crept over to the door and pressed her ear against it, trying to hear what was being said. A chair scraped on the floor, and the words spoken within were muffled, as though the people talking didn't want anyone to overhear them. She would have to wait; when Farrington left, she would open the door to see for herself, but first she would have to arm herself with some sort of weapon. God only knew whom the gambler was harboring inside. A cutthroat, a pirate, a murderer. She crept cautiously back to the dim recesses and fumbled around for something that would serve as a weapon. Her fingers fastened on a stout piece of board, and she clutched at it like at a lifeline. Now all she had to do was wait for Farrington to leave. Her stomach churned at the thought of what she might find behind the door, but she had to do it. She had to do it so that Caleb would be indebted to her and trust her. Lovemaking was one thing, but this was something else entirely. Men didn't like to be made fools of, especially by other men. Malcolm had taught her that at the very beginning of their relationship. Yes, Caleb would thank her.

What seemed like an eternity later, the door of the locker box opened and Aubrey Farrington exited, but not before he had looked to the right and then to the left, a wry expression on his face. Satisfied that no one was about, he slid the heavy iron bolt into place and quickly walked away, his pockets noticeably lighter.

Sara drew in her breath and tiptoed over to the thick wooden door. Surprise would be on her side. Whoever or whatever was on the other side of the door would think the gambler had forgotten something and was returning. Slowly she slid back the bolt, the stout board clutched between her knees. The moment the bolt slid back, she grasped the club and flung open the door. Lantern light cast an oily, yellow glow over the small area. A rough bunk stood against one wall, bare of mattress or bedding. On it lay a man who was slowly getting to his feet, muttering, "Well, what did you forget to tell me, Farrington?"

Sara gasped, all senses frozen, her breath locked in her lungs. It couldn't be! Her mind was playing tricks on her! "Malcolm! Is that you?" she cried in a shocked voice. "Malcolm, how can you be here? Wren said you were dead!" At last believing her senses, she rushed toward him. "Malcolm, Malcolm!" Her arms locked around his neck, and she buried her face in his chest. "Oh, Malcolm, I thought you were dead. My love, we've found each other, and I'll never let you go. Never!" she cried vehemently as she clung to him.

Malcolm was stunned. "Sara! How did you get here? Darling child!" he exclaimed, his mind working furiously to determine what advantage she could serve him. Suddenly he remembered his disfigurement. "Don't look at me, Sara," he pleaded. "I've suffered a misfortune that's seriously altered my appearance. That's why I left England, thinking I would never see you again. I'd rather suffer the fate of an outcast than bear the pain of having you see me as I am now." His words and tone were carefully calculated to elicit her pity. "It was always you I loved, darling Sara. Never Wren. Wren did this to me—to us," he added meaningfully. "I told her it was you I loved and would cherish for the rest of my days. She turned wild and took a hot poker to my face, saying if she couldn't have me, no other woman would. She tried to kill me, and there are days I wish she had. Anything rather than have you see me this way. I broke your heart and knew in my own you would never have me after the way I had made you suffer. Now I'm disfigured, a horror, and it's too late, my darling Sara. Please forgive me."

217

"Malcolm, darling, I love you, and a little scar couldn't change my devotion to you. If it did, what would that say for my love? Let me look at you, please, darling."

Slowly Malcolm turned the left side of his face toward the light, his anxious eyes willing her to tell him that his disfigurement wasn't as hopeless as he imagined. Sara's face whitened as a gorge rose in her throat. God! What had she just promised to this monster? Fighting to regain control of herself and to hold in check the trembling that had seized her, she wrapped her arms about him, pity for his condition and fresh hatred for Wren consuming her. Wren had done this to him—purposely, vindictively, with malice. Wren had reduced Malcolm to hiding in the depths of a ship, afraid to show his face in public, nearly maddened by the loss of the one thing which had been his mainstay besides herself—his good looks.

Her mind rambled and raced, jumping from the past and then into the future. A future with a man who resembled a gargoyle. The scab on his face was crusted; his forehead was puckered from the burn; his blinded eye stared sightlessly from behind a contorted eyelid that would never close again. Never again would Sara dream of being the envy of other women when they saw her sported on Malcolm's arm. She would be the object of their pity. Women would run away from Malcolm in terror instead of pursuing him. Oh, God! she thought wildly. Why had she followed Aubrey Farrington down into the reaches of Hell?

Malcolm's hands tightened about her, seeking, pressing, attempting to arouse.

"You smell, Malcolm. Poor darling," she added hastily, "doesn't that old man provide you with soap and water?" There was no way Malcolm was going to seduce her in this stench-filled room, smelling like a rutting pig. She had to get out of here before he overpowered her. Merciful God, she didn't know which eye to look into.

"Did you hear what I said to you, Sara? Your friend, Wren, did this to me. What are you going to do about it? I know from Farrington that she's aboard this ship. If I could get out of here, I'd finish her off myself."

"What would you have me do with her, Malcolm? Why did she do this to you? I don't for one minute believe that story you just told me. Wren's not violent, excepting her tongue. She is aboard ship, that's true. As a matter of fact, my sister-in-law, Wren and I share Captain van der Rhys' cabin." Her voice took on a sudden lilt when she mentioned Caleb, which didn't escape Malcolm's attention.

He sensed her withdrawal and was engulfed with rage. "Say it, Sara. My face offends you. Suddenly you find you no longer love me. You're comparing me with your Captain van der Rhys, and I come out a poor second. Say it!"

Sara suddenly felt very powerful, more powerful than she had ever felt in her life. "Actually, Malcolm, you sicken me. You're right, I no longer love you. I doubt if I ever did love you. And yes, Caleb does come out first. Any day now I expect a proposal of marriage. It's over between us, Malcolm. It was over the day you decided you wanted Wren van der Rhys and her dowry. I wasn't good enough for you, and now I've decided that you aren't good enough for me. Good fortune to you, Malcolm. When we get to America, perhaps they'll employ you to frighten off those savage Indians." She enjoyed her cruelty toward him. "And don't worry, I won't give away your secret. I'll tell no one that you're hiding down here with the rats. By the way, why *are* you hiding? Passage for this voyage was very cheap. It wouldn't have anything to do with the captain's seeking retribution for something you've done to his sister, would it?" Seeing her suspi-

219

cions confirmed in Malcolm's expression, she laughed, the sound mirthless and harsh in the stillness of the locker box.

Malcolm wanted to slap her, to hit her till her teeth rattled, but he knew she would fight back, and he had already had a taste of what a woman would do to protect herself. He no longer had any control over Sara, and the realization frightened and emasculated him. All he needed was another jab to his good eye, and he might as well lie down and die. Women were the root of all evil. He had heard that Sara's brother was always spouting off about the evil that festered in a woman's breast. How right Bascom was.

"Ta-ta, darling," Sara cooed as she slammed the door behind her and quickly shot the bolt home.

The darkness of the ship and the soft lap of the water against the sides was like a balm to Sara's uneasiness. She felt as though a mountain had been lifted from her shoulders. She was free of Malcolm, free of Bascom and free to go to Caleb. Caleb was her answer, her salvation.

Sara's feet took her up the fore ladder, through the hatch and onto the deck. There was no one about, only the seaman on watch in the wheelhouse. Vaguely she wondered where Caleb was and if he knew of the fugitive hiding belowdecks near the bow of his ship.

As she walked quietly toward the cabin she shared with Wren and Lydia, a queer feeling within her body made her hesitate. She waited, as women had from time immemorial, for the featherlike quickening to occur again. The child. Her and Malcolm's child. Sudden fear struck her. God! What if seeing Malcolm the way he was now had marked the child? Heaven forbid it be born with a hideous disfigurement brought about by its mother seeing its father! Suddenly Sara began to giggle, a light chortle at first, which built to ringing peals of laughter that brought tears to her eyes. Even now Malcolm could not allow himself to be honest with her. He had tried to use her again, to win her over with pity, to lie to her and think her stupid enough to believe him, pity him and even love him. But she had been smarter this time, craftier.

How ugly Malcolm was now. Gone were the abundant good looks which had always attracted women to him. Now his glance was sly, feral. His words seemed slick and well rehearsed. Never again would he be a strikingly handsome man who could win a woman's heart just by the grace of his looks alone. What could he have done to Wren to make her take a poker to his face? That was the only thing Malcolm had said that Sara could believe. The only thing that would move Wren to violence was an attack on her person. Sara laughed again, the sound ringing out over the water, the note of hysteria rising to a shrillness. So Wren was no longer a virgin. That was the only thing she would protect with her life; Sara knew it in her heart. Malcolm must have tried to seduce her before the wedding and Wren had refused. Malcolm, not used to refusal, had become violent, and Wren had reacted in the only way she could. Dirty scum, Sara thought, he deserved whatever he got.

It never occurred to Sara that just hours before she had lain in her bunk dreaming of Malcolm. Now she had to concentrate on Caleb, definitely the better man of the two. Her child needed a father and she needed a husband to save her from the outraged scorn of the community of Puritans. She sniffed delicately and continued with her stroll as if it were something she did in the middle of every night. Her hand caressed her burgeoning belly and her thoughts whirled in crazy circles. No one would stand in the way of what she meant to have for herself. Slowly, her footsteps led her in a circular course around the deck.

A seaman was coming on duty to take the watch, and in the darkness he bumped into her. He lifted his lantern to identify the woman and was perplexed when he saw the expression in Sara's eyes.

"Can I help you to your cabin?" he asked politely. "You shouldn't be out here this time of night. It's too easy to fall overboard—" He broke off his words, the flesh on his back rising as though a goose had just walked on his grave. In the dim light of the lantern Sara's eyes were wild and staring, her lips drawn back over her teeth in a soundless, mirthless laugh. When she at last seemed to notice him and the light, he had the feeling that a sly, demonic creature was peering out from behind her eyes. The seaman backed away, unable to take his gaze from her face, remembering the time he had taken a ha'penny tour of Bedlam and seen the stark raving madness on the faces of the inmates. His hackles still rising in warning, he backed away still further and broke into a run. As he ran he could hear the woman's laughter, demonic in its intensity, leaving the ranks of saneness and breaking into a possessed howl.

Back in her quarters, Sara stood looking down at the sleeping women, her thoughts vaguely disoriented. Ever since she had seen Malcolm, she felt somehow different. Her brain seemed fuzzy and her thoughts weren't clear. She stared down at Wren, moving closer to her bunk. There was something about Wren, something she should do, but what was it? Was it a secret? She had to think, to clear her head so that she would know what to do. She would talk to Bascom in the morning; he would know what to do about the problem. Perhaps if she slept, she would be able to remember what it was she was supposed to do in the morning. If she couldn't remember then, she would go to Bascom anyway.

Wren was not asleep. She watched Sara out of the corner of her eye, her heart thudding in her chest. Something was wrong with Sara. The girl's eyes were peculiar, and the way she was hovering over the bunk made Wren nervous. How pale Sara looked with the moonlight streaming through the porthole and casting a silvery aura around her, as if she were a ghostly specter. But it was Sara's eyes that frightened Wren.

Once Sara had settled herself in her own bunk, Wren realized there was no point in trying to sleep. The air in the cabin was very close, and she was fearful that her tossing and turning would disturb Lydia's sleep. A walk on the deck might help her sort out her thoughts. There would be no one about except the man on watch, and she doubted if he would pay her much notice. She had to think. The time had come to face a few truths.

The night air was brisk, yet it held the promise of the coming summer. She leaned against the rail and pondered the happenings in her life since Sirena and Regan had returned to England to take her back to Java. Why had she been so stubborn? Why hadn't she trusted their love and listened to them and done what they wanted? Now look at me, she wailed silently. What's to become of me? She also had Lydia to worry about, and the way Sara was behaving, it wouldn't be long before she would be saddled with her, too. She watched the dancing waves, eerie in the moonlight, as she pondered her problems. If she went over the side, she wouldn't have anything to worry about, she thought morbidly, but then that was the coward's way out. She had gotten herself into this situation, and she would have to extricate herself as best she could.

She was so deep in thought that she didn't hear the footsteps till a dark shadow caused her to turn her head. Caleb! She said nothing but returned her gaze to the water. Her heart pounded in her chest at his nearness.

How fragile she looked in the moonlight, Caleb thought. He said nothing but folded his arms and stared out across the water.

Wren wanted to shout at him and tell him what she

thought of him, but the words wouldn't come. Was she finally growing up? If so, it was a painful business indeed. She didn't have to be so physically aware of his presence if she didn't want to be. Then why was she? How close he was. Wasn't he ever going to say anything? Was he waiting for her to say something? She gulped and wet her lips, her knees trembling madly. What did he want? He wanted Sara. Her back stiffened at the thought and her jaw tightened. Well, he could have her, with her wild eyes, and he could have Bascom, too. The lot of them could sail off to the end of the world, for all she cared!

His voice, when he spoke, was soft, yet husky. "It's not wise for you to walk the deck at this hour of the night."

Her own voice matched his for softness. "I couldn't sleep, and the room was too warm. I wanted to feel the spindrift on my face." Was that soft, purring voice hers?

"How long have you been standing here?"

"Not long. If my being here upsets you, then I'll go back to my quarters. Caleb, I—"

Caleb touched her lips gently with his finger. "It doesn't upset me. I just don't want anything to happen to you." How soft her skin felt beneath his fingertip.

Wren moved slightly, his touch searing her mouth. She had to say something. "I guess I haven't done so well with things. I seem to have botched everything up. I'm sorry, Caleb." She looked up into his face, her features composed in the moonlight, belying the torrent of emotions that churned through her breast.

Caleb drew in his breath sharply. This beautiful creature standing before him couldn't be the same fire-breathing Wren who had so deftly defended herself when he had kissed her in Tyler Sinclair's garden. Nor the same girl who would have him believe she had killed a seaman and disfigured a man in self-defense.

He had to say the right words so as not to frighten

her and cause her to run off. "It's all right," he said gruffly. "Isn't that what a brother is for?" The moment the words were out he knew he had said the wrong thing. He wasn't her brother, didn't want to be her brother. That was the last thing he wanted. The vision of her as a child, staring up at him, flashed before his eyes. *Will you wait for me to grow up?*

Wren backed off a step and lowered her eyes. Her voice was so soft he had to strain to hear it. "Somehow, Caleb, I never thought of you as my brother. I'm certain you don't remember, but a long time ago, the first time I ever saw you, I fell in love with you, the way a little girl does with her schoolmaster. I remember . . . remember asking you if you would wait for me to grow up."

"And I said, 'I may just do that.' "

Wren's eyes widened and she smiled. Suddenly a brisk wind came up and penetrated her cloak and thin nightdress.

"You're cold," Caleb said, wrapping her cloak closer about her chin. "I don't want you getting chilled, not after what we all went through to make you well." He took her by the hand and led her across the deck. "Come into my cabin. I have a bottle of brandy, and it will warm you."

Obediently she followed his lead into the small cabin he had taken since giving the women his. It was lit by a dim, glowing candle, and when his hand reached out to lengthen the wick, she stopped him. "No, don't. It's so pleasant as it is."

He filled two snifters with brandy and handed her one. "Drink up. It'll ward off the chill. Then back you go to your bed."

"Don't treat me as though I were still a child," she pretended to pout. "I'm grown up, Caleb, or haven't you noticed?"

Caleb threw back his head and laughed. "I've noticed."

At his words a delicious tingle worked its way through Wren's veins, mingling with the warmth from the brandy. She felt drawn to him, yearned to have his arms encircle her as they had when he had helped her through her illness.

Caleb reached out and drew her to him. Her body seemed to have a will of its own as she moved into his embrace. Tenderly he covered her mouth with his and felt her lips tremble. His breath was warm upon her cheek, and his lips coaxed hers into a lingering kiss.

Wren felt his arms tighten around her, pulling her close against his lean, muscular body. She was aware of the warmth he offered and the tenderness of his arms. She knew without a doubt that he could have crushed her in a bone-breaking embrace, but his arms were gentle, holding, persuading, not brutal and forceful, as Malcolm's had been. The stubble on his chin scratched her cheek, making the soft contact between their mouths more gentle by comparison. This is Caleb, she told herself—Caleb, who would never hurt or degrade me. Yet the memory of what she had suffered at Malcolm's possessive, hurting hands and the indignities she had undergone at the hands of the seamen pervaded her consciousness.

Caleb held her, soothing away her tremblings with his lips, encouraging hers to part. He felt the slimness of her body through the light material of her nightdress, and the dual provocation of her high, full breasts against his chest. He slid his hands along her hips and pressed her firmly against his loins, taking pleasure from the warmth of her body against his rising desire. Her lips were soft and tasted of the brandy she had drunk. Her arms tightened around his back and her fingers lightly traced a path along his muscles. She felt so small, so pliable. He grew dizzy with his urgent need for her, a dizziness that climbed from his loins to his head. His desire for her became overwhelming, and his fingers found the opening to her nightdress. He wanted to rip the cloth from her body, to touch her flesh, to drink in her beauty, to be naked with her and make love to her.

Wren pulled her lips from his. In the frightened astonishment in her eyes he could read the lusty savageness on his own face. He felt himself beyond the point of judgment. No other woman had ever excited him this way, tantalizing him with her lips, teasing him with the pressure of her body against his. He knew only that he wanted, needed, intended to have the woman who had driven him to such passionate heights.

Indifferent to her terror, he picked her up and carried her over to the bunk. Dropping her down onto the mattress, he threw himself beside her, seeking her mouth with his own, his hands tearing at her flimsy nightdress in his eagerness for her silky skin and the place protected by her tightly clenched thighs.

Wren attempted to fight him off, making unintelligible sounds of protest, but he overpowered her by twining one leg around hers and pressing himself over her, reveling in the feel of her breasts against his chest. From deep inside him he growled, "I want you. I mean to have you."

Wren struggled, images of Malcolm and the seamen heightening her terror. She raised herself up in a sudden movement and crawled down the length of the bed. He caught her by the ankle and pulled her backward, attempting to cover her with his weight. She drove her fingernails into his wrist, savagely slashing at him, her other hand reaching for his face to tear at it. Their eyes met, each staring at the other—the friend and the foe, the trapper and the trapped, the predator and the prey.

Two tears welled in Wren's eyes and coursed down her cheeks, and from her throat came a desperately pleading voice. "Not you, Caleb. Please, I beg you," she whispered. "Never you!"

Caleb looked into her eyes for a long moment. Suddenly he reached for her and brought her into his

227

arms, kissing her tenderly and brushing the tears from her face. She buried her head in his chest, her body trembling with unshed tears and remembered terror. "I don't think I could ever have forgiven you," she sobbed, the hot tears scalding his flesh.

From out the mullioned windows of the sterncastle, the moon could be seen dipping into the ocean. Soon it would be light.

Like two abandoned children, they huddled together on the bunk, one forgiving, the other begging forgiveness. The hours passed and Wren's tears were dry; yet still she hid against his neck, and from time to time, at long intervals, she sobbed.

Caleb's desire had completely subsided, even to the point that he was indifferent to Wren's hand which had slipped between his legs. The weight of what he had nearly done to her lay heavily on him. He realized that he had almost brutalized her, and he was deeply saddened. Knowing that she had been raped and abused and denigrated, he considered his brutality and unquenchable lust unpardonable. And yet, she had pardoned him. She was holding him tightly and taking comfort from him. He cradled her, feeling the warmth return to her body, knowing that, above all else, he loved her. He wanted her, but he wanted her to desire him, to seek him as her lover. Bewildering thoughts rampaged through his head. How could she desire him when the very thought of giving herself to a man filled her with terror?

When the sun's first golden light stained the sky at dawn, Caleb remembered Regan's words. Patience, he had said. Nuzzling against Wren's fragrant drape of dark hair, Caleb once again tightened his protective embrace. Closing his eyes as a smile came to his lips, he repeated the word to himself. *Patience.*

Chapter Fourteen

The *Sea Siren* kept true to her course, rollicking amid the low swells, her sails full of wind and promise. The sun was just lifting over the horizon and glinted gold off the starboard porthole. Sara lay in her bunk, watching the progression of light as it cascaded through the mist-sprayed glass. At the sound of the door opening, she quickly closed her eyes and pretended to be asleep.

Hours before, she had awakened and noticed that only one figure occupied the adjoining bunk. Wren had gone out, and now she was returning. A rustle of whispers reached Sara's ears, and she recognized the other person's voice before Wren had shut the cabin door. Wren had spent the night with Caleb.

With an animalistic keenness, Sara knew that their meeting had been less than innocent. She could feel the heat coming from Wren's body across the room; she could almost smell the aura of sexuality surrounding her. For one instant she knew a sense of futility. She would bear her child, a bastard, a fatherless, nameless creature who would never have the advantages of honor attached to its name. Her fingers rode over the barely perceptible swelling of her belly, imag-

229

ining she could perceive the life within. She herself would be an outcast, branded with the mark of an adulteress, an embarrassment to her family and the object of derision.

No! she screamed silently. Never! She would have her way yet. Regardless of what she had to do, Sara Stoneham would become Mrs. Caleb van der Rhys, and the devil take the hindmost.

A corrosive jealousy burned through her soul. Wren! Wren had always had the best of everything. The best clothes, the best family, the most love . . . even Malcolm! Well, she wouldn't have Caleb. No matter what Sara had to do to stop her, Wren would never have Caleb!

Later that morning Sara descended the ladder into the hold to see Bascom. She tolerated her mother's inquiries about her health and felt herself rebel against her father's black looks. His expression seemed to accuse her of having left the flock for the conveniences and luxuries topside. Facing down his paternal disapproval, Sara drew her brother aside.

"I knew you would see the error of your ways and come back to your family," Bascom told her as he followed her over to the ladder, where no one could hear their conversation. "Come, it is time for our morning prayers."

Sara stared at him with unseeing eyes. "I have to tell you something. And you must listen to me and forget your silly prejudices."

Bascom peered at his sister and frowned. She looked peculiar. Perhaps the Lord was going to take her to Him. If it had to be someone's time, Bascom was glad it was Sara's. She was a foolish girl and served no real purpose in the world. Besides, the Lord willing, that way Sara would not live to disgrace the family. Now that he headed a congregation, his good standing and good name were all-important.

"What is it, sister?" he asked, his haunted eyes

scrutinizing her face. "Have you done an evil thing and want to pray for forgiveness?"

"Of course I've sinned. Everyone sins!" she answered impatiently. Her eyes were bright and almost feverish, glaring at the hard lines of his face. "I want to tell you a secret. Promise me you'll keep my secret till the ship docks in America. Give me your promise as a messenger of the Lord; I'll accept nothing less, Bascom."

"You have my word, sister. What troubles you? Confess to me, and we'll pray together to make it right."

"We could both pray till the cows come home, Bascom, and it wouldn't make my problem come right. I'm with child, brother. The father of my unborn child is being kept prisoner in the locker box of this ship. Wren maimed him horribly and he's disfigured. I thought him dead till I followed Lord Farrington, who was bringing him food in the middle of the night." Her eyes turned cunning as she watched Bascom pale and then flush a rosy hue. "This is your chance to get back at Wren for humiliating you in front of your flock. Trick her into the locker box and leave her with the animal who rests inside. She wants to take Caleb from me now. Captain van der Rhys," she amended. "Don't you see, Bascom? If I can trick the captain into thinking the baby is his, he'll marry me, and you won't be saddled with me or lose face with your flock. You can't afford another mistake; after all, your very own wife left you and is spreading all manner of lies around the top deck. Wren wants Captain van der Rhys for herself. She ruined the first man I loved, and now she wants to ruin Caleb, too. Say something, Bascom," she insisted.

"Merciful God, forgive this poor sinner . . ."

"Forget your merciful God and say you'll help me."

"Very well, sister. Tell me what it is you want me to do."

Sara whirled on him suddenly. Her eyes were blazing in her pale face. "I don't want you to do anything, you miserable excuse for a man! I'll do what has to be done myself! I just came down here to tell you to pray that I succeed!"

For the first time in his life Bascom Stoneham was speechless. He completely forgot it was time for morning worship. Somehow the devil had taken possession of Sara's soul, and that was almost more than he could comprehend.

While Sara sunned herself on deck and Bascom preached the horrors of sin to his congregation, Wren joked with and teased Lydia as she proceeded to teach her the basics of cards. Lydia teased and joked in return, delighted that Wren had returned to her normal, cheerful self. She suspected that Captain van der Rhys had a great deal to do with Wren's uplifted attitude, but she kept her own counsel.

Wren was bent on teaching her new friend how to act the foil for her own cheating, and Lydia proved to be an apt pupil. "But what if we're caught?" she asked fearfully of her teacher.

Wren sniffed disdainfully. "We're sailing the high seas. Caleb is the only authority we have to contend with. The worst thing that could happen to us is that he would throw us in the brig. Somehow I don't think he'll do that. Now, this is what we'll do. After lunch we'll entice Farrington into a simple game of whist, and when we see that he thinks we're not keen card players, one of us will suggest playing for money—and then we'll take all of his! Do you think you can do it, Lydia?" Wren asked anxiously. "I'm doing this for you, you know. When we get to America, you're going to need a great deal of money to live on."

Lydia's blue eyes were wide and incredulous. Her life had certainly changed since she had met Wren. She had divested herself of one husband, found the

232

first mate to her liking and openly flirted with him, become a card shark in a matter of a few hours and was now ready to fleece, with her accomplice's help, one professional gambler. She giggled. She was having the time of her life. "Of course I can do it," she replied confidently.

"Just keep your wits about you. Aubrey Farrington has the eyes of a hawk and knows every card trick and then some. Remember, look dumb, and always be surprised when you win. Tomorrow we'll have to think of a way to get Bascom up here so we can relieve him of his hoard. Today will be a sort of practice session. Just keep flexing your fingers so you can handle the cards with no wasted motion. Don't be nervous," Wren warned. "If either of us appears jittery, Farrington will become suspicious. Gamblers are a suspicious lot."

Lydia's eyes boggled. Wren was the most fascinating woman she had ever met. What a pity the captain didn't think so. Lydia shrugged. Wren was right—all men were bastards. She would reserve her judgment of the first mate, Peter, until she knew him better.

As Wren had suggested, the card game began after lunch and was still in progress as the afternoon wore on. Caleb, from his position in the wheelhouse, watched it with narrowed eyes. Aubrey was taking a beating, and it looked as if his bank roll was being depleted. Squeals of merriment from the girls every time they won made Caleb wince. Wren had never once looked in his direction all afternoon, and soon it would be sundown. He could feel in his bones that trouble was brewing and that somehow she would be at the bottom of it. Any minute now he expected Bascom Stoneham to charge up the ladder and drag his card-playing wife below, praying loudly all the while.

His shoulders tensed as he watched Wren, her dark hair flying wildly in the stiff breeze. Her laugh, each

233

time she won, chilled him to the bone. It was a damn good thing Aubrey had no vested interest in the *Sea Siren,* or he would truly have cause for worry. He saw the gambler rise and excuse himself with a motion indicating he would return—with more money, Caleb assumed.

A short while later Farrington appeared, his brow furrowed in deep thought, his hands clenched tightly into fists. Casually, he placed a gemstone next to the girls and nodded. Even from this distance Caleb could see Wren's eyes widen, and he heard Lydia giggle. Wren tilted her head and picked up the stone. She turned it this way and that in the dimming light, finally putting it between her teeth and biting down hard. For Christ's sake, Caleb fumed, she acts as if she knows what she's doing! She nodded to Farrington to show she accepted the gem as his bid. The gambler bit into his lower lip and threw down his cards. Wren's trill of delight was blood-chilling.

In the course of the next few hours, with the aid of lantern light, Aubrey Farrington tossed nine more gems into the center of the small ring and managed to lose each one of them.

Caleb knew in his gut, in every bone of his body, that Wren and Lydia were literally cheating the pants off Aubrey, and he was powerless to stop it. Serves the old fox right for gambling, he told himself, and to be done in by two women would be more than Aubrey could bear.

The game wore on long into the night, with both women winning consistently. The moon rode high in the sky when Farrington tossed what he said was his last gem into the ring. He looked at his cards, spat over the rail with uncanny accuracy and staggered to his feet. He was less than gracious as he stared down at the laughing women and said, "You two . . . ladies have got to be the smartest or the dumbest card players I've ever had the pleasure to come across. I know that you cheated me, but I don't know how. I'd appreciate it if someday you'd tell me how you did it."

Wren gurgled deep in her throat and Lydia smiled beatifically. "For shame, Lord Farrington," Lydia admonished. "We played fair and square and trounced you soundly. Let's not hear any evil talk of cheating, or we'll be forced to call you out. How would that look—two ladies dueling with a gambler? For shame, thinking such a thing!"

Caleb winced again and groaned aloud. "Women!"

Back in their quarters, Wren threw her arms around Lydia and both of them laughed hysterically. "We have a fortune here," Wren said, opening the palm of her hand. "We have to keep them safe, but where?"

"Perhaps Captain van der Rhys would keep them safe for us until we dock," Lydia replied hesitantly.

"You can just forget that idea, Lydia. We have to come up with a hiding place ourselves. The crewmen know we won all these gems, and some of them didn't look as if they would be above cutting either of us down for this little treasure."

Just after lunch the next day, Caleb knocked on the door to the cabin he had given over to the women. Hearing a bid to enter, he opened the door and found Wren and Lydia intent on a game of cards. Apparently Wren was teaching Lydia the finer points of the game. Sara sat sullenly on her bunk, repairing a ribbon on some feminine undergarment. He saw her eyes light when he stepped into the cabin, but he carefully paid her no attention. If Sara were one to kiss and tell, she would have done so by now, and Wren seemingly had no knowledge of what had transpired between the blonde and himself. So much the better.

Caleb signaled Wren, who left her cards on the table and moved toward him, a question in her eyes. He was planning to draw her outside on the deck to say what he had come to say, but then he decided there was little use in trying to be secretive. Shipboard was the last place to keep a secret, since everyone lived so closely together. Even with the Puritans, whom he had allowed to come above once again, everyone's business was everyone else's.

"I'd be honored if you'd share my dinner with me this evening, Wren. Gustave has promised something special from the galley." His eyes were warm as they rested on her, and Wren felt her heart skip a beat.

"When and where?" She smiled, relieving him of the formality of his invitation.

"Eight bells, my cabin. I'll just have come off watch."

When Wren turned back to her game with Lydia, neither woman had seen the burning hatred that banked in Sara's eyes. After taking her place at the table, Wren turned only once to glance at the blue-eyed blonde. Sara's stare was pointed enough to bore holes through her back.

Caleb watched the door close behind Gustave and turned to scrutinize the table which had been set for Wren and himself. It had been a long watch, and he looked forward to a leisurely dinner with her. A bottle of wine and two glasses dominated the center of the cloth-draped table, and he decided he would struggle with the cork before Wren appeared.

A light, tapping sound at the door announced her arrival. He bade her enter and was pleasantly surprised when he saw her. Her long sable hair was coiled around her head, emphasizing the graceful length of her neck and the feminine slope of her shoulders. She wore several layers of petticoats and a prettily laced chemise.

"Once before you came to this cabin without benefit of a dress," Caleb said softly, his voice husky as

236

he took in the ivory tones of her complexion and the womanly softness swelling above the top of her chemise. "Good God, woman, where are your clothes?"

"The Puritan garb is so dull and unfeminine," she pouted. "Lydia and I thought this would do me as well as a gown, and at least I feel pretty in it."

"You're beautiful tonight." His voice was low and his eyes enveloped her in an aura of rekindled desire.

Attempting to lighten the mood, Wren curtsied and played the grand duchess. "Thank you, kind sir. Would you care to kiss my hand?"

Caleb's eyes didn't brighten at her little jest. He was conscious of the long sweep of her neck rising above her nearly bare shoulders and the deep cut of her chemise, which brought into prominence the soft curve of her breasts. Remembering the last time he had kissed her and his dangerous responses, he didn't dare play her little game.

Sensing his reticence, Wren seated herself at the table and began to serve the dinner of chicken and precious potatoes. She proceeded to put on airs like an affected duchess and sought to make him laugh. Her humor rang false in his ears and clashed with his silence. They picked at their food without interest; only the wine was totally consumed.

Wren watched Caleb through lowered lids, feeling his tension. "Caleb," she began hesitantly, not certain where her words would lead, only knowing they had to be said in order to erase that terrible look of guilt from his eyes. "I want to confess that I don't regret anything that happened between us. Not a single action on your part. Since then, you have been extremely delicate . . ." She paused. "If I didn't know firsthand what a passionate man you are, I could never appreciate your consideration of my fears." Her voice was softly tender, her eyes pleading with him to understand her. "I feel I know you so much better, and that you understand me and that my feelings are important to you."

Caleb looked into her eyes, saw the pleading and confusion there, and felt his heart beat rapidly within his chest. She was trying to tell him that she wanted him, desired him, yet she was also trying to conquer the fears that Malcolm had instilled in her. Once again the deep heat of hatred rose inside Caleb, until he knew that if Weatherly were standing there before him, he would cheerfully kill him for what he had done to Wren.

Seeing Caleb's mouth tighten into a thin line and his eyes harden into gleaming chips of jet, Wren immediately regretted having reminded him of Malcolm's cruelty. Jumping to her feet, she rounded the table and placed her hands on his shoulders, feeling the knots of tension beneath the muscles in his neck. "Don't, Caleb. What's done is done."

He gazed into her eyes and saw the same understanding he had once seen in Sirena's eyes, the same concern. She, too, had once said the same words to him. "What's done is done, and where we go from here is what matters." He had marveled at the Siren's resiliency, and now he was finding it again in Wren.

Still gazing into the amber depths of her eyes, aware of her slim body and the scent she wore, Caleb pulled her wordlessly onto his lap, holding her against him as if she were a small child who had been frightened by a nightmare. Wren lifted her face for his kiss, allowing her lips to part beneath his.

He was aware of the pressure of her thighs and the thinness of her petticoats and the rising urgency of his own desires. The softness of her mouth and the delicate scent of her skin awakened a similar throb in his temples. His arm made a support for her while his free hand pressed her legs against him; he consciously resisted the impulse to touch her neck and the silky swell of her breasts, which were tantalizingly accessible beneath her low-cut chemise.

Their kisses became more passionate, more searching, and Wren responded by parting her lips still further. Tenderly, he advanced his tongue and was immediately regretful when he felt her stiffen and draw back. But suddenly her lips opened to him again and she returned his kiss. While he caressed her offered lips, slowly and lightly, she seized the hand that had been resting on her knees and raised it with a gentle movement until it lay against her breast. Beneath the thin cambric, he could perceive the perfection of her form and the stiffening of the coral tip beneath his palm.

Hardly daring to breathe for fear of frightening her, he allowed his hand to maintain its delicate contact with her breast. His thoughts were becoming unfocused and blurred because of the heady sensation of her lips greedily seeking his and the heat forming between her breast and his hand. Had he understood her action? Had Wren been making a conscious appeal for more intimate caresses, or had the placing of his hand upon her breast been merely a tender reflex?

Wren arched her back, her body extended toward him in an unmistakable offering. She felt his hand tremble where it touched her, and when he drew down the lace of her chemise, she was aware of a sudden burst of heat throbbing through her, igniting her senses to a flame of desire.

The pure, womanly curve of her breasts was bared to Caleb's view, and he was astonished by the silky whiteness of her skin, a whiteness all the more alluring in contrast to her throat and arms, which had been tanned by the sun.

His lips grazed her exposed skin tenderly, longingly, and with a sigh of pleasure she stretched herself in his arms, relishing the intimacy between them, aware of his desire for her, responding to him in a succession of undulating tremors which she knew were repeated within him.

For long moments their lips touched, their mouths searched, each straining toward the other as their desires mounted. Delicately, Wren detached herself from his arms and rose from his lap. She led him silently to his bunk, where she lay down and drew him close beside her, nestling her face into the hollow of his neck and tasting the salt tang from the spindrift which had misted over him during his watch at the wheel.

"Kiss me," she whispered, her voice barely audible in the cabin.

Responsive to her demands, he put his arms around her and sought her mouth. Edging slightly away from him, she tugged at the straps of her chemise until her breasts were completely bare to him. Fearing to surrender to his own wants, he hesitated to understand her action. Thoughts of the violence she had suffered at Malcolm's hands and his own vow of patience muddled his thinking. With a shy yet determined gesture, she lowered his head toward her bosom, offering herself to him, arching her back to bring her body into contact with his mouth.

Usually a demanding, impatient lover, Caleb acted with supreme tenderness, and instead of covering her breast with his mouth, he merely caressed the coral tip with a light flick of his tongue.

Wren issued a cry of surprise and delight, murmuring over and over, "Again, again."

Her demand freed him, allowing him to express his passion in a multitude of caresses with his lips and tongue, each more varied and intoxicating than the other.

Beneath the pressure of his hips, her legs had unconsciously parted and her petticoats had gradually rucked up, disclosing first a silk-stockinged leg and

240

then a firm-fleshed white thigh. Caleb closed his eyes to blot out the unexpected temptation, telling himself that he had promised patience with her, fearing he would be overcome with passion and force himself upon her. Yet he was aware of the close contact of their bodies, and his imagination was set afire as he pictured the nudity of her thighs and the center of her womanliness which was so near.

Wren jerked her head back, thrilled by the myriad caresses he was bestowing on her, oblivious to the temptation her parted legs offered, innocent of the nearly uncontrollable passions pounding through his veins.

To quell the desire to throw himself between her thighs and ravish her, Caleb slid from the bed and rested against the low side, his mouth teasing Wren's in a variety of warm, voluptuous caresses while his hands never strayed from her breasts. He murmured words of love and stirred her senses with his appreciation of her beauty. Her fingers tore at his fine lawn shirt, her lips seeking the hollow of his throat where she could feel his pulses throb. In a husky, impatient voice, she pleaded with him to remove his shirt. In his haste to obey her, he tore at the lacings, pulling the fabric over his head and tossing it to the other side of the cabin. Wren glided to the edge of the bed, turning toward him, her arms ready to enfold him, her eyes eagerly searching his newly bared midsection.

A wild temptation seized him . . . to outstrip her thoughts, remove what remained of his clothing and bring his urgent desire before her. Although he was increasingly aroused by this imagined gesture, his tender consideration for her sensibilities made him hesitate risking her alienation from him.

Wren allowed him no time for further reflection. She enclosed him in her arms and pressed herself against him, reveling in the sensation of her naked breasts molded to his bared chest. Her need to be

241

close to him bordered upon a hunger, a yearning, an all-consuming desire to make herself a part of him. Her lips traced a pattern of a thousand interlaced designs; her fingers explored the finely honed muscles of his back and made a tentative survey of the hardness of his midsection.

His hands played in her hair, tangling the long sable strands through his fingers, grazing the soft skin of her cheek and stroking her lips as they came into fragile contact with his flesh. He gave himself up completely to her gentle ministrations and allowed himself to be transported beyond the threshold of mere physical satisfaction, finding he was able to contain his desires because of his most tender consideration for her needs and wants. He experienced heights of voluptuousness he had never known existed, and he marveled that he had discovered them at her shyly innocent, tentative touch.

He pulled back a little, away from her kisses, and in her hunger for him she drew him close again, making room beside her on the bed and fitting the curves of her body tightly against the long, lean length of him. Petticoats already rucked up above her knees, her motions pushed them still higher, displaying the harmonious roundness of her hips and the elegant stretch of her thighs, revealed in the dim lantern light.

Caleb was astonished to find his hand covering a portion of her bare thigh. His passion flared and his mouth sought hers with a deeper yearning, the sharp intake of his breath and the low sound of a moan coming from deep within his chest exciting her own heightened sensations, and she found herself exalting in his desire for her.

Prudently, he advanced his hand, wishing to prolong this unexpected contact without causing her to associate his intentions with the violence and degradation she had experienced at those other men's hands.

He knew in his heart and without a doubt that what was most important to him was not the conquest of her flesh but the conquest of her heart. He loved her without reservation, and the thought of doing anything which would destroy her trust in him was more devastating than an arrow shooting through his chest.

She was pleased by the touch of his hand on her thigh, and she too, sought to prolong that contact. Yet when her petticoats uncovered the whole length of her as far as the delicate line between leg and hip, she made an instinctive movement to drape herself beneath the lace skirts. But she didn't complete the gesture, and as though wanting to lose herself and erase her inhibitions in the rapture of his kiss, she moved her legs toward him.

Still Caleb hesitated, not wishing to alarm her, yet hungering for her, unable to draw her close enough, know her well enough.

His touch was light as he caressed her gently, stroking the inside of her thigh with a movement so soft, so gentle, that she relinquished herself to the delight she was experiencing.

Her acceptance of his caress provoked him toward further raptures. Their lips met, their tongues touched, her body molded itself against his, but when his fingers grazed the warm secret of her femininity, she instinctively closed her thighs, refusing him additional intimacy. Then, feeling him about to draw away, she seized his hand and stayed it in the place where her thighs met. He could feel the tension ripple through her body, the involuntary rigidness in her arms and neck, the sudden tightening of her mouth as it rested against his. Immediately regretful that he had initiated this resistance in her, he attempted to remove his hand, seeking to reassure her that he had no intention of submitting her to ravagement.

She demonstrated her reluctance to end this embrace by holding firm to his hand until her thighs relaxed their grip. With a deep, sensuous kiss, she offered him a victory over her constraints. A succession of tremors, long and passionate, coursed through her body beneath the warm contact of his hand, culminating in the blending of their lips as one.

The quiet night was broken only by the creaking of the ship and the low sound of his voice as he whispered lovers' words, telling her of her beauty, of the need he had for her, of his love. He spoke and she believed. His love was evident in the tenderness of his touch, in the adoration of his lips and in the emotion in his eyes when he looked into hers. She knew he would always keep her trust, knew the price his consideration of her was extracting. He worshipped her with his hands, protected her with his arms and loved her with his heart.

And, in return, Wren responded with her heart and soul. Loving him, being loved by him, knowing he understood her, appreciated her and intuitively perceived the woman behind the flesh, the soul beneath the intellect. The loving and the giving were enhanced by their mutual joy; their passions flamed by tender devotion, the treasure of their love cherished more fervently than a kingly prize. Wren had found Caleb and Caleb had found Wren; prophetically, each had found his destiny.

They were still; no words needed to be spoken; no kiss could demonstrate the emotions within them. Her voice was whisper-light, threaded with happiness; her words posed a question which was already answered in her heart. "Why did you stop, Caleb?"

He held her in his arms, his mouth pressed lightly against her brow. "Because, sweetheart, I will take you only when you ask me to."

"I couldn't have stopped you, and I would even have forgiven you. But I love you so much more, so much more completely, because you didn't insist . . ."

"Shhh. Hush, sweetheart. You needn't tell me. Don't you know, can't you feel, that our hearts speak to each other and make words unnecessary? Now hurry, fix yourself up. It's time I brought you back to your own bed. For now," he amended, his voice throbbing with a meaning that made her pulses dance.

Chapter Fifteen

She should have been one of the happiest women alive, Wren thought miserably as she leaned over the rail. *Should have been!* The last time she had been alone with Caleb, she had been certain she had found love. But in the two days since then, Caleb seemed to have little time for her, and watching Sara manipulate him fed Wren's jealousy as if it were a festering sore.

Caleb's face was grim as he made his way from the galley to the deck. His ship was infested with women! Every time he wanted to take a brief rest on deck, there was a woman occupying his favorite seat. The captain of a ship could expect certain calamities, but one of them wasn't a covey of squabbling women. Between Wren's arrogant hostility and Sara's persistent offerings to him, he was ready to pull out his hair. There was no reason for Wren's aloofness. What did she want from him? He had thought she loved him, but when he remembered their last night together, he had to face the fact that it was *he* who had professed his love, not Wren! Was she playing him for a fool? Damn! he cursed, realizing a dull aching in his loins. And he had been so considerate of her, of her fears, of her hesitancy to make love. How fitting! he laughed bitterly to himself, wincing from the uncomfortable ache. I denied myself and now she despises me for it!

He strode rapidly, hoping to avoid Sara and another one of her half-tearful pleadings to take her to his bed. He was fast running out of excuses. But he was too late. Sara was lying in wait, about to pounce on him. At least Wren was not around to witness this little maneuver of Sara's. He steeled himself in anticipation, hoping he presented a stern, forbidding manner.

"Caleb," Sara cooed, "how nice to see you on deck. You look tired. Was the watch strenuous this day?" Not waiting for a reply, she looked up at him and parted her lips in an inviting manner. Slowly, she let her tongue trace the outline of her mouth while she raised a hand to smooth a path on his cheek. "I have nothing to do, and I was wondering if we could have a talk." She paused briefly. "You see, it's about Bascom, and . . . well, it's just too difficult to stand here and try to explain. You have such a—what I mean is, you're so forceful and masculine—so unlike Bascom. I just need someone to talk to. Please," she pleaded, tears gathering in her eyes.

Damn it to Hell. He didn't want to talk to her in his cabin or to . . . he didn't want her in his cabin at all. Did she think him a fool? Evidently she did. He felt his face flush slightly and turned just in time to see Wren whirl on her heel and march out of sight. Son of a bitch! he almost howled. Once again Wren had misinterpreted what she had seen. Only this time there was no wounded expression, no hurt eyes. This

246

time there was a piercing look of hatred shooting from those glowing eyes. She had wanted to kill him on the spot.

Sara had also seen the expression on Wren's face, and she smiled. She could care less how Wren felt. Wren was merely a silly child who was inexperienced in the ways of men and the world, while she, Sara, knew just how to entice a man. Hadn't she just convinced Caleb to go to his quarters? Men like Caleb didn't talk when they had a woman behind closed doors. Men like Caleb did what was expected of them. Caleb would never admit to Wren or to anyone else that they had only "talked." With men like Caleb, the less said the better. It was enough that Sara made trips to his cabin. Let the others think what they wanted.

Damn brazen jezebel! Wren cursed all the way back to her cabin. Damn brazen womanizer, that's all Caleb van der Rhys is. If he couldn't get what he wanted from me, Sara will do just as well. Does he think I am stupid? The *very* next morning after *I* was with him, I saw *Sara* leaving his cabin. If he's going to take Sara to his bed, the least he can do is to do it in the dark. Oh, no, not Caleb! Broad daylight, for all the world to see! Dirty rotten womanizer—all he thinks of is one thing!

She threw herself on her bunk, a lone tear trickling down her cheek. One tear for Caleb. He wasn't worth more. Just one tear. She was so glad she hadn't given in to his lust! At least she could comfort herself that she hadn't allowed her flesh to weaken! Damn herself! She sniffed and blew her nose loudly as she got up from the bunk, banging her head sharply on the top board. She cursed again, long and loud, using every filthy expression she knew. Well, he could make a fool out of her only if she permitted it.

She sat for hours, perched like a bird ready for flight, figuring out how to destroy Caleb. She finally settled on the method of castration and racked her brain trying to remember how the Sea Siren had done in Chaezar Alvarez. It would come to her, and then she would do something. She swallowed as she recalled that Sirena had said there had been a river of blood. She hated blood. She would have to think of something else, some other way to make Caleb pay for all her sufferings. And I am suffering, she told herself. I can't eat, I can't sleep, she whined silently as she bit into a chunk of cheese and chewed rapidly. I'll hack off his leg at the knee, that's it, and then let's see if that jezebel wants a one-legged lover! And I'll chop off all of his fingers so he can't fondle Sara's pink-and-white flesh, she added as an afterthought.

She felt better. Once a decision had been made, the whole world looked brighter.

She was just stuffing another chunk of cheese in her mouth when Sara danced her way into the cabin, her dress buttoned sloppily and her long golden hair tangled and matted. Her lips looked bruised; her cheeks were flushed and her eyes sparkling. No woman had the right to look so . . . so alive and contented, Wren thought spitefully. She was the one who should be looking like the cat who had swallowed the canary. She would hack off all his toes—no, only five, because he would have only one leg, Wren added fiercely to herself. It seemed fair to her, ten fingers, five toes and one leg for making her suffer and putting her aside for Sara. Damn you, Caleb van der Rhys! She felt suddenly weak at the thought of what she was going to do to him.

"Wren, Caleb is so wonderful! Your brother is such a gentleman! I was so foolish not to have believed you all those times you told me how gallant he was. He knows how to make a woman feel like a woman." Sara eyed Wren suspiciously, wondering if she had noticed her clumsily fastened dress and disheveled hair. To her own disappointment, Caleb hadn't laid a finger on her. He had demanded she speak what was on her mind and leave him to tend to his duties. Certain that Wren would think she had spent the last hour in Caleb's cabin, she had made herself scarce by hiding on the afterdeck, behind several crates of chickens. When enough time had passed, she had returned to the cabin she shared with Lydia and Wren, hastily rebuttoning her gown, tearing the pins from her hair and biting hard on her lips to redden them and give them a passion-bruised glow.

"Shut up, Sara. I don't want to hear anything about Caleb and how marvelous he is. Just tell me one thing. How would you like him if he only had one leg, five toes and no fingers? Just tell me that."

"I think your jealousy has left you tetched in the head," Sara said loftily. "Is it my fault that your brother finds himself enamored of me? Well, is it?"

"You're a slut, Sara Stoneham! You throw yourself at him! Any man becomes an animal when a bitch in heat wags her tail!"

"The pot calling the kettle black!" Sara spit. "If you want to think I'm a slut, then go ahead and think it. Caleb, however, doesn't share your opinion, and that's all that matters."

"How could he know any differently? All he's ever known are sluts like you!" Wren shot back defensively. "But you're right. Caleb's opinion is all that counts, and if he loves you, then I wish you both well."

Sara yawned, stretching her arms above her head. "I think I'll take a little nap before the dinner hour." She fixed a sleepy eye on Wren and added, "Somehow your good wishes don't ring quite true. Is it my fault, dear little Wren, if Caleb prefers me?" Her voice dropped an octave and became sly. "It must be difficult to be rejected by a man, and doubly hard when you have been rejected by two men!"

Wren wanted to reach out and wring her neck or, at the very least, put her fist through Sara's sensuous mouth. Instead, she seethed inwardly till her stomach felt on fire. She had to get away from Sara, away from this cabin. Could she go on deck and chance running into Caleb? Never. She would go to the galley and talk to Gustave.

Out of the corner of her eye Wren saw Peter relieve Caleb from the watch. Damn! She had dallied on deck too long. Now she would have another confrontation with him, one she couldn't afford emotionally. Caleb worked his magic on her, and she was quicksilver in his hands. But not this time. Enough was enough.

A quick look over her shoulder proved that her long-legged gait was no match for Caleb's determined stride. He was just another womanizer, like Regan used to be. Like father, like son! Well, she wasn't going to be one of his "women." She felt his warm breath on her neck as he grasped her shoulder and spun her around. "Take your lecherous hands off me," she gritted. Shaking free of him, she proceeded to walk away.

Angered at her attitude, Caleb blasted out. "Just a goddamn minute, Wren. I want to know what's going on. Don't think you're going to pull one of your pouting acts on me like you do with Regan and assume it will work. If you have something to say, say it. Act like a woman!"

Grow up! Act like a woman! Didn't he know any other words? She whirled around, her eyes spewing fire, her small hands clenched into fists. Before she knew what she was doing or could even think about it, she had clasped both hands together and brought them up under Caleb's chin with every ounce of strength in her body. "I *am* grown up, or hadn't you noticed? I am a woman. As a matter of fact," she said viciously, "I think I'm too much woman for you to handle. You need someone like Sara to mew and weep on your shoulder. That," she spit, "is the only thing that makes you feel like a man!" An angry, hurt sob caught in her throat as she turned and raced down the deck.

Caleb rocked, stunned from her blow and at her words. Then he sprinted after her and this time pulled her to him from the waist. He held her in a viselike grip, his strong fingers digging into her shoulders. His eyes were mocking and full of devilment as he stared down into her flushed face. "You're jealous of Sara. My little bird is jealous of Sara." His marveling tone was more than Wren could bear.

She forced all emotion from her voice and spoke slowly and distinctly. "On the contrary, Mr. van der Rhys." She made his name sound like an obscenity, and Caleb gritted his teeth. "If the bed-hopping Sara is what you want, then she is what you shall have. Stay away from me before you end up giving me one of the social diseases that Sara is so fond of sharing with her . . . friends."

Caleb's face drained of all color at her words. Jesus Christ, that was all he needed, a good dose of the clap! Damn her eyes, was she lying? She certainly sounded as if she knew what she was talking about. Christ, was that subject something women spoke of? How many men they had— The thought was so horrendous that Caleb backed off a step and had to fight to get his breath. Damn her to Hell. He should have taken her by force when he had had the chance. He was less than a man, and, by God, if he did have the clap, she would have it by now, too. When a van der Rhys fouled up, he fouled up all the way. She had to be lying. Sara was a Puritan, and Puritans just didn't have things like that. Or did they? Sara certainly was knowledgeable, almost as professional as some of the whores he had known.

If he could have seen the wicked smirk on Wren's face, he would have killed her then and there. He stormed into his quarters. Before this voyage was over, he would have Wren in his bed with or without his social disease, and this time he wouldn't be a gentleman about her and her damn fears. This time he would act like the man he was. And then he'd wring her goddamn skinny neck and laugh while he was doing it. And he'd wring Sara's neck right along with hers. Women!

Sara wanted to strike out at Wren when she returned to her bunk. In the dim light Sara imagined she saw a warm smile on her face, a satisfied look a woman wears when she has just made love. The same warm, contented look she herself had worn so many times with Malcolm. She watched Wren with deep hatred as the girl snuggled between the covers and drifted off to sleep. She couldn't let Wren steal Caleb away from her. Caleb was hers. After all, he was the father of her child. How easy the words fitted once she had decided in her mind that Caleb was to become her unborn child's father. She had decreed it, and that was all that mattered. In time Caleb would come to accept it without reservation, if he thought of it at all. Caleb was an honorable man. Honorable men always did what they were supposed to do, and he was supposed to marry her. Men were also stupid. They believed what they wanted to believe. Men always liked to know that their seeds had sprouted. That made them feel manly and protective. And if there was one thing Sara needed now, it was protection. She couldn't allow Wren to steal Caleb from her. She had to do something and do it soon.

She lay for hours formulating one plan after another and then rejecting each of them for various reasons. Aubrey Farrington was close to Caleb, a confidant and good friend. Wren was in love with Caleb, any fool could see that. Farrington and Wren stood between "her" Caleb and "their" child. Therefore, they would have to be eliminated. A smile tugged at the corners of Sara's mouth, and her eyes took on a glazed, faraway look. She rolled over and slept, satisfied that she had at last decided on a plan of action.

On his way to the wheelhouse the following morning, Caleb's face was black with rage at his circumstances. All through the morning he watched the three women sun themselves on deck. Each time his eyes fell on Wren, his heart lurched. When he looked at Sara, his eyes became speculative and brooding. Lydia, on the other hand, brought a soft smile to his lips. When he saw Wren lean over the rail, an alien feeling washed over him. She tripped on the hem of her skirt and almost fell into the churning water. He gasped as his throat tightened. If she had gone over, it would be the end for him. How could that be? he questioned himself. The answer was simple. He, Caleb van der Rhys, loved Wren. Totally. As he had professed to her their last time together. Since the beginning of time, men had loved women. Why had he thought he could go through life and never truly experience that feeling? Because, since the beginning of time, women had been wily and devious and manipulative in regard to men, and he hadn't wanted to be trapped into those circumstances.

He wanted her. He needed her. God, how he needed her! Wanting her was selfish; needing her was as necessary as having to draw another breath. Would she listen to him? Not likely. Wren never listened. Then he would have to show her. Regan always said actions proved more than words. Some women liked the words, like Sara. Pretty words, lies really, pleased Sara. But then, Sara was a fool. Wren was not. He could tell her all the pretty lies and she would turn around and match him word for word, lie for lie, and where would he be then? Back where he had started.

He seemed to be having difficulty breathing as he gazed at her from time to time, and his loins took on a suspicious ache that only one thing could relieve, but he would die before he made another advance to Wren. A goddamn pity if he should die at sea within the next few days and go to his watery grave in a semicelibate state.

He forced his mind and eyes back to the endless expanse of water. When Peter relieved him after the noon meal, he would seek out Wren and try to convince her. Convince her of what? his mind shouted. He refused to answer his own question.

When Wren had tripped on the torn hem of her dark gown, Sara had thought to herself, Now, why couldn't she have gone over the side and saved me the trouble of— No, she wouldn't even think about that here in the bright sunshine. That thought was for her dim cabin during the velvety night. She glanced toward the sun and swiftly calculated how much longer Caleb would be on watch. A little more than an hour. By that time she would have contrived a way to meet him and throw herself into his arms for the benefit of Wren's watchful eyes. Her face was almost feral in the golden light, and Lydia nudged Wren, who refused to look in Sara's direction.

From time to time Wren allowed herself to be tortured as she gazed at Caleb's muscular body behind the wheel. How could he prefer Sara to her? She loved him, couldn't he tell? Why was he making a fool of her in front of the crew and everyone else? Because he was a hateful man, and that was what men did. Why did they think women were good for only one thing? And who taught them such things? Another man, of course. If Caleb wanted Sara, he could have her, with Wren's blessing. Never with my blessing, she sobbed inwardly. Oh, God, I love him so, she wanted to cry out for everyone to hear. I can't let him do this to me; I can't show him how he's hurt me. I can't bear it. Tears of anger and frustration gathered in her eyes, and she brushed them away impatiently. She would be damned if she would cry over Caleb van der

Rhys. Never! The man hadn't been born who was worth her tears. Her mind refused to listen to her heart, and she closed her eyes wearily, visions of herself lying in Caleb's arms and responding to his tender touches flashing suddenly before her. She leapt off her chair and strode down the deck as if the hounds of Hell were on her heels.

As she passed the wheelhouse she sent Caleb such a scathing, scorching look that he blanched. Now, what in the hell had gotten into her? he wondered. She was just like Sirena—all mouth and legs. His lean jaw hardened as he remembered how she had felt in his arms, how her long legs had pressed against his. Christ, he couldn't think of that now! Yes, he could. He wanted to bury his face in her wealth of dark hair and then twine it through his fingers as he drew her face to his in a long, passionate kiss that she returned with equal ardor. "Peter!" He'd be goddamned if he would wait another minute. He would go to her now, tell her now, and then drag her off to his quarters whether she liked it or not. She would like it! He would make her love it and him at the same time!

Peter loped into the wheelhouse, breathing heavily and wondering why the sound of his name had the ring of iron in it. Seeing the look on Caleb's face, he merely grasped the wheel and thought better of the question he had been about to ask.

Caleb took to the deck at a dead run, his bare feet barely touching the polished planks. He saw a wisp of black round the corner and increased his speed. He was upon her within seconds and had her pinned in his arms. His eyes were closed, his breathing heavy, as he forced her body close to his. She felt different. He had expected her to stiffen at his touch, and here she was, soft and pliant. *Aaah.* He opened his eyes and almost choked on his own saliva. At the moment his stunned eyes accepted that it was Sara in his arms, Wren came into view and saw them locked together.

Caleb would have sold his soul to the devil if he could have erased the wounded look from her face. But it was not to be. He knew in his gut that no matter what he said or how he said it, she would look right through him and not hear a word. Wren was lost to him forever. God in His Heaven would never be able to convince him otherwise.

Wren heard Sara say, "Darling Caleb, how wonderful of you to take time away from your watch to be with me," as she continued on her way. She would bleed later, in the privacy of her bunk, but not here for all to see.

Caleb stared down into Sara's eyes. "What are you doing here?" he demanded harshly, his eyes hard and cold.

"I'm standing here with you, in your arms. What a foolish question," she purred softly. While her tone was soft, her insides churned. She had seen the look on Wren's face as well as the horror in Caleb's eyes when he had realized just who was in his arms. Her mind raced as she squirmed, rubbing her body against his in an almost sensuous rhythm. She would make him forget Wren. He didn't need Wren; he needed her and their baby. He would be so happy when she told him that soon they would be parents. He would love her then. Caleb was an honorable man, and honorable men always loved their wives and families. Caleb wouldn't be any different. "Darling, shall we go to your quarters?" she asked breathlessly.

Caleb's terse "No," slashed through her like a whip. She recovered quickly and smiled at him, her eyes lowered demurely. "I understand. Daylight does pose its problems. I'll come to you tonight, after the moon is high. I'll spend the rest of the day thinking of you."

Before Caleb could reply, she had gone. For a moment he was puzzled. Her eyes had reminded him of something. Or was it someone? He couldn't think now; it would come to him later.

Two days passed with Caleb, according to Aubrey Farrington, acting like the devil himself. He was torn, anguished over the fact that he couldn't get near Wren. Each time he came within eyesight of her, she put as much distance as possible between them, and always her face mirrored that same wounded look and then deep hatred. The situation was eating him alive, and for the first time in his life he didn't know what to do. He was being boxed into a corner with his emotions running high for Wren, and at the same time he was fighting off Sara's bold advances, which were becoming increasingly more blatant. He knew he had always been desirable to women, but Sara was something he had not counted on, unlike any woman he had ever come across. She wanted him, desired him and intended to have him. He would have to tell her, and the sooner the better, that she could never mean anything to him.

Sara had been deliberately stalking Caleb for two days, and was horrified to discover that all her suspicions were correct. Caleb was lost to her. He wanted Wren, desired her and was fighting the way a man fights for a woman. Like a fool, Sara thought angrily. And stupid, silly Wren was playing right into her hands by running from him. Sara was wise to Wren. She knew Wren was running from Caleb in the hope that her unavailability would drive him mad with desire. Now, where had the silly little fool learned *that* trick? It doesn't really matter, Sara told herself calmly. Caleb is falling for it and making an ass of himself in front of his crew and the others. Wren will have Caleb in the palm of her hand in another day. Sara knew that just by looking into Caleb's eyes. Well, Caleb might love Wren, but he would be honorbound to her, Sara, when she told him of "their" baby. Caleb would then fall *out of* love with Wren and fall *in* love with her. She would make him love her. And to insure that happy occurrence, she would do away with the only two people in the world who meant anything to him. In his sorrow and grief he would turn to her and "their" child for comfort. Her eyes were sly as she watched the crew go about its duties. Sly and furtive and not quite seeing.

By noon of the following day Wren felt as though she were possessed by the devil. She wanted to wreak havoc, to kill Sara, to lash out at Caleb for his uncaring attitude toward her and for the humiliation she suffered at his hands. And, God help her, she loved him. Another day or so and they would touch land, and she would put as much distance between her and Caleb van der Rhys as possible. She would cut him out of her heart and make a new life, she and Lydia. She knew she was lying to herself. She could never forget Caleb, not ever. He was in her blood for now and for always. She amended the thought: she would *try* to forget him.

Lydia's heart ached for the sorrowing girl. She wanted to comfort her, but she knew that Wren preferred to be alone with her thoughts. She felt she should say something but didn't know the proper words. When she tried to speak to her, Wren's face closed like a book. She would suggest a stroll around the deck and then, when the moment was right, say something comforting. Wren refused the offer of a walk, pleading fatigue.

"Wren, my dear, has it occurred to you that you may well be doing Caleb an injustice? You haven't given him a chance to explain or to set matters straight. You aren't certain of all the facts. If things are as bad as you seem to think, then why has the captain been trying to talk to you?"

"Talk, my foot," Wren shrilled. "I know what I saw and heard. He's nothing but a damnable womanizer, and all he wants is another notch in his belt. He's mean and rotten through and through." Wren kicked out viciously at the bunk.

"No, he isn't, and you know it," Lydia defended the captain. "He's a fine man who loves you very much. I'm not wise like you, Wren, but I know what I read in his eyes. You are the one who is being mean and rotten. Forgive me for speaking to you like this, but someone must make you understand the man whom you're tormenting."

"Save your breath, Lydia. I saw him with Sara and heard the words she spoke to him. That meeting was prearranged, and every night she goes to him. She can have him. I wouldn't take him if he were offered to me on a silver platter. And you're wrong, Lydia. If Caleb loved me, as you said, he would keep the greatest distance between Sara and himself. Every time I turn around I see her draped over him in some fashion. I no longer care," Wren concluded loftily.

Disgusted, Lydia picked up some mending to while away the time. "Since you're an authority on the subject, I refuse to waste my breath, as you put it. However," she added, striving for the last and final word, "you're wrong about Captain van der Rhys. The day will come when you realize this, and then it will be too late."

"If that day should ever come, you'll be the first to hear of it, for I won't be around," Wren said wretchedly. If only what Lydia said were true, she would be the happiest woman in the world.

Why, why, *why* hadn't she proved the full extent of her love for him? Damn herself and her little girl's fears! Caleb had wanted to make love to her, the kind of love a man gives to a woman, and, Heaven knew, she had wanted him to. But after Malcolm and the seamen, she had been afraid. If only she'd been able to conquer her fears and behaved like the woman she longed to be. The kind of woman Caleb wanted and needed.

The afternoon hours crawled on tortoise legs toward evening and darkness. Sara was nervous and irritable, ignoring Lydia's feeble attempts at conversation. She ignored Wren completely. Wren was the root of all her problems. Ever since Wren had spent the entire night with Caleb, Sara had been rebuffed by him, and none too nicely either. This evening might be her last chance to make him want her again. Once she had told him of "their" child, things would be different. Things *had* to be different!

Unable to sit still after dinner, Wren went on deck for a breath of fresh air. As she glanced about her, she realized a storm was brewing from the west; from the looks of things, it was going to be a bad one. Already the crew was busy securing the ship for the onslaught of winds and rain that would pour down on her. She wondered what Caleb was doing and where he was at this exact minute. Had Lydia been right? Did Caleb really love her? Was he simply playing with Sara to make Wren jealous enough to crawl to him, as all his other women had done? If that was so, he was certainly going to have a long wait. She'd crawl for no man, especially Caleb van der Rhys.

What she could do was walk. She didn't have to crawl. Worms crawled. She had pride and Caleb had injured it, either knowingly or unknowingly. She could go to him and at least listen to what he had to say. Listening couldn't hurt anything. She could listen and walk away and ponder the matter, then make a decision later as to what he had had to say. Surely that couldn't hurt, and maybe she would be able to sleep peacefully and not have her dreams tormented by him. But before she did that, she would have to calm herself and collect her wits. She clung to the mizzen-mast as her heart began to pound at the thought of being near Caleb again.

While Wren considered her actions, Sara left the cabin and made her way directly to Caleb's quarters. She knew she had picked the right time. For some reason, when a storm was approaching or in progress, a person's emotions ran high. Caleb would be in fine fettle, and so would she. She could barely balance herself as she went along, holding her arms out against the bulkheads. She could almost feel his arms around her in his cabin as the storm raged outside. Caleb would protect her and keep her safe because he was an honorable man.

She reached his cabin, knocked on the door and waited. Realizing he couldn't have heard that feeble little sound with the wind howling the way it was, she opened the door cautiously and was almost blown inside.

Caleb looked up, startled, at the open door, which she didn't bother to close. He dropped the boot he was about to pull on and stood up, his face becoming mottled because of her uninvited intrusion. "What are you doing here?" he demanded harshly.

"That's a silly question for you to ask me, Caleb. You know very well what I'm doing here. Actually, I'm here for two reasons. One, to make love to you, and two, to make you the happiest man in the world. So far I'm the only one who knows the secret, but because it involves you, I'm going to share it with you. It's the secret that will make you the happiest man in the world. Sit down, Caleb, and let me help you with your boot," she singsonged, sending chills up Caleb's spine.

His mouth tightened. "Sara, a storm is approaching and I have to take the wheel. Look, I don't want to hurt you, but this . . . this lovemaking is not going to work. I don't love you; I never did. I love Wren, and I think you know that. I'm sorry, but I told you in the beginning that it was just a—"

"Fling," Sara again singsonged. "But," she said, wagging a playful finger under his nose, "that little fling has made me pregnant, and now what are we going to do?"

Caleb had bent down to pull on his boot, and when

he raised his eyes, stunned at her words, he saw Wren standing in the doorway. She, too, wore a stunned, unbelieving expression. Then she vanished. Sweet, merciful God. Of all the goddamned, ill-timed luck! Rage boiled in him as he pulled on his boot and got to his feet. He took Sara by the shoulders and shook her wildly. "Do you know what you just said? Do you know or care, for that matter, that Wren heard your lie? No, I see that you don't. I can count, Sara, and it's impossible for me to be your child's father—if there is a child. Your trick won't work, Sara. I'm not the father, and well you know it. I'm ordering you to go below and tell Wren that what she overheard was a lie! What you've done is despicable, and I can never forgive you for it. What we had was nothing more than a physical encounter. We both spoke of it that way, if you remember. No promises were made by either of us. I took you to be a worldly woman; you certainly acted like one. It was never my intention to deceive you in any way, and if you misunderstood me, then that becomes your problem. Not mine, never mine. You would be wise if you'd go below before the storm worsens. In the morning you can talk this matter over with your brother and seek your best course of action. I can't. I won't allow you to ruin my life with this false accusation."

Sara heard the words, understood them and nodded. "If Wren weren't here, you would love me—I know it. You would love me and our baby. You don't need me now that you have Wren and Aubrey Farrington. If you don't want to have anything to do with our baby, then I will do as you suggest. I will go to Bascom and have him help me. I don't want you to worry about our child. Somehow I will manage without your help. In later years, if you have the desire to see your child, I will not stand in your way."

Caleb stared at her, not quite believing what he was hearing. He knew damn well he wasn't the father of her child. What was wrong with her? And, for Christ's sake, why was he standing here wasting time worrying about what she was saying, when he should be concerned with the coming storm and Wren? Of all the damnable luck! He couldn't waste any more time; he had to get on watch. "See yourself out and be careful on deck," he called over his shoulder.

"Of course I'll be careful. I know that you're just upset now because it is difficult for a man to know he's going to become a father and that he'll have to put his wild ways behind him and settle down to a domestic life. Have no fear, Caleb. I'll walk with great care to protect our child."

It wasn't her words that sent a chill down Caleb's spine, it was the vulturelike look in her eyes and the singsong way she spoke.

After he had left, Sara sat for a long time on Caleb's bunk. Thoughts skittered through her brain like wildfire. She smiled as she picked up a shirt Caleb had discarded, and a brush. She held them against her cheek and then hid them beneath her petticoats. Her child would have these articles as remembrances of his father. They weren't much, but they were something. She looked around for an item for herself and picked up a pair of faded trousers. These few mementos would prove to her child that he did have a father.

She trotted happily out of the cabin, singing softly under her breath. The strong wind almost lifted her off her feet, but she held on to the masts with a firm grip. She had already made up her mind to ignore Wren, so there would be no problem. All she had to do now was wait.

Chapter Sixteen

A jagged streak of lightning danced across the sky, followed by a low, threatening roll of thunder. Sara drew her knees up and locked her arms around them, frightened of the ominous sounds coming from the heavens. Did she have the courage to carry out her plan? The idea of going anywhere near the locker box again terrified her, as did the idea of being near Malcolm again. I must do what must be done, she told herself, or else Wren will have Caleb and I will be an outcast with a child.

Almost as soon as the blackness overhead was silent, she moved on cat's feet toward Wren's bunk and shook her awake. "Shhh," she cautioned, a finger to her lips. "Come with me. There's something I have to show you. Be very quiet and follow me," she implored, "and don't awaken Lydia."

Startled by Sara's intrusion on her sleep, and even more apprehensive about the girl's strange behavior, Wren crept from the bunk and her place beside Lydia. Sara's glassy-eyed expression was the same one she had worn the night Wren had found her standing over the bunk she shared with Lydia. A flutter of fear tugged at Wren, but she disregarded it as Sara led her through the darkness, nimble as a cat.

Their trek took them below, into the belly of the ship, and they turned to the right, toward the bow. Sara had lit a candle stub and carried it in front of her, her hand protecting the feeble flame. Finally she came to a halt and put her finger to her lips to indicate silence. "I want you to see what's inside."

"Sara, are you all right? You don't look well to me." Now Wren's skin was crawling with fear, the hackles rising on the back of her neck, and she felt as though her hair were standing on end. This was crazy! Sara was crazy! What were they doing here in the belly of the ship, below the waterline with the rats? Wren wanted to turn tail and run, but she had come this far, and her curiosity was heightened by Sara's furtive attitude. She decided to humor Sara for the moment and then take her back to bed.

"Don't make a sound," Sara warned. "You're never going to believe what I'm going to show you! Be careful, now. When I open the door, we'll walk through and stand to the right. Stand perfectly still, and you'll see what I'm talking about."

Wren reached for Sara's hand, holding it tightly, feeling the pressure returned to her own fingers. As Sara slowly and silently slid the bolt and swung open the door, Wren's flesh crawled at the thought of what might lie behind it. Together they moved from the darkness into a room Wren recognized as the locker box, which was sometimes used as the brig. She moved to the right, as Sara had instructed, still holding the girl's hand. Before she had felt Sara wrest her hand free and heard her slip outside the door, she knew what was going to happen. The terminal sound of the bolt sliding across the iron flange greeted her ears.

She whirled, her fists beating against the stout door, screaming at Sara to set her free.

"It won't do you any good, my dear," said an oily, ugly voice.

At the familiar tone, the blood froze in Wren's veins and she slowly backed off, her arms held straight in front of her for protection. "Stay away from me."

"Oh, no, my little bird. I want you to see what you did to me." Malcolm turned and picked up the lantern and held it high over his head. Wren gasped and edged away a few more steps till her back was against the damp wall. "Do I frighten you? Ah, I see I do. Look at your handiwork and know that I'm going to return the favor. When I finish with you, there won't be a man who will look at you."

Wren tried to breathe through her mouth to avoid smelling the rotten stench that was everywhere.

"Come here, little bird, kiss me the way you used to and whisper all those pretty words. Damn you, come here! Scream, I see you want to. No one can hear you in the storm. Scream if you want to, I won't stop you."

Abruptly she was in his arms, his foul breath on her cheek, his hot, moist lips crushing hers. She stiffened and tried to free herself from his grasp. He was harsh and brutal in his handling of her as he tore at her clothing, exposing her breasts to his greedy mouth. Overcome with revulsion, she struggled vainly as his mouth moved again to hers. His lips were avid, searching, and she felt his tongue force her lips apart. The harder she struggled, the tighter his embrace became. He freed his mouth and let his lips travel down to her throat, and again they touched her silky skin. When his viselike hand grasped her breast, her eyes widened in fear and her breathing grew ragged. Loathing him, loathing herself because she was in this situation, she continued her struggles, which only made him more demanding. Cruelly, he twisted the soft flesh of her breasts until it stung. She whimpered with the pain and felt scalding tears course down her cheeks, knowing that no matter what she did, the inevitable was certain to happen.

Malcolm laughed lewdly as he taunted her with filthy phrases of what he was going to do to her and what he was going to make her do to him.

He threw her roughly to the dirty floor and was atop her in seconds. Holding her shoulders pinned to the floor, he kicked off his trousers and freed himself for his attack. He drove into her and smiled sadistically at her cries of pain and shame. Again and again he used her, each time more brutally than the last.

When he had finished with her, he pushed her against the wall and laughed. "When I'm through with you, that's all you'll be good for. To service men."

Wren lowered her head and vomited at her feet, adding to the stench in the room. God, help me, she prayed silently.

Back on deck, Sara found her way to Aubrey Farrington's quarters and tiptoed inside. Her eyes gleaming wickedly, she lifted the club she carried high above her and brought it down on Farrington's head.

Without a backward glance, she walked through the door and out to the deck. The night was velvet black, the only light a streak of lightning frolicking across the ebony sky. Quickly she tossed the bloody club overboard and stood back to wait for the driving rain that would thunder down on the decks. Her eyes were blank, her body limp. When she felt she had been sufficiently soaked from the heavy downpour, she ran screaming to the wheelhouse. Caleb looked at her in shock. He heard the words but couldn't believe his ears. Wren had jumped overboard and Sara couldn't save her. Christ!

"All hands!" he shouted to be heard over the storm. "Man overboard!" What in the goddamn hell was *that* going to do? All around him was inky blackness and torrents of rain. The swells were higher than the ship. She didn't have a chance. No one, no matter how excellent a swimmer, could survive those waters during a storm. "All hands!" he repeated hoarsely.

The first mate looked at him and shook his head. "Captain, there's no way. You know that better than anyone. Go below. I'll take the wheel."

Caleb left the wheelhouse in a daze, Sara on his heels. "What happened?" he asked, his gut on fire with the effort of his words.

"I don't know. She said she wanted to go out for a breath of air. I told her not to go, that there was a storm. I begged her, pleaded with her," Sara babbled as she brushed her wet hair from her forehead. "She's dead, isn't she? I should have tried harder, but she was so strong and I'm so weak. I tried, truly I did. Please tell me it isn't my fault. You know how strong-willed Wren always was. Once she got an idea into her head, no one could shake it loose. Something was bothering her. She had acted peculiar all evening. Say it wasn't my fault, Caleb, please say it wasn't my fault. I refuse to believe Wren would kill herself because she had seen me and heard what I said in your cabin."

Wren was gone. Dead. She had said she was grown up and had looked at him the way a woman looks at a man whom she loves, and now she was gone. Dead. Given over to the sea. He groaned and buried his head in his hands.

"Caleb, say it wasn't my fault," Sara cried wretchedly.

"Go below, Sara. We'll talk later. I want to be alone."

She couldn't be dead. Not Wren.

The storm raged far into the night. Caleb watched it and listened to it with unseeing eyes and unhearing ears. His thoughts were only on Wren. Torrents of rain beat against him. He felt nothing, numb to his surroundings. The crew, intent on keeping the ship secure, could offer him no aid. He needed his time alone to accept what had happened. It was his fault, and he would have to live with it for the rest of his life. Thoughts of Sirena and Regan crept into his mind from time to time, and he quickly rejected them. He would have to deal with them some other time and in another place. If he were lucky, the storm would claim him, too. He couldn't go back. By now God only knew where Wren's lifeless body would be. He wondered how long she had fought the turbulent waters before she had finally succumbed to the inevitable. Why?

A vicious bolt of thunder ripped down and rolled out to sea as the question entered his mind. Why? Why would Wren leap overboard in the middle of a storm? In her own way she was as feisty and fiery as Sirena had been. Their meeting on deck a few days before was hardly reason for her to go overboard tonight and end her life. She had eaten a hearty dinner, too; he himself had seen the empty plates. It was Sara and her damnable lie!

He rubbed his temples with unsteady hands and then felt the stubble on his chin and cheeks. He should go below and change his sodden clothing and shave. When the seas calmed, he would have to assemble the crew and officiate at a makeshift service of sorts for Wren. He couldn't do it. But as captain of the ship, he had to. Why? The question tormented him. Over and over he repeated the same question. Why?

His legs stiff and cramped, he stood and stretched his aching arms. Empty arms. Again he felt the stubble on his chin. Why? He would ask Aubrey if he had noticed anything. Perhaps Wren had said something to him. He had a keen, if not slick, mind, and sometimes he was damn intuitive. Aubrey might know something.

In his cabin, Caleb shed his water-soaked clothing and donned dry clothes. He shaved and gave himself a wicked gash across his cheek to which he applied a dab of alum and then flinched. Why?

His shoulders slumped as he made his way to Farrington's quarters. If Aubrey didn't have an answer for him, what would he do? Sara claimed she knew nothing. Lydia might know something. That was unlikely, or she would have made her way to him during the storm. She seemed a sensible, forthright woman and genuinely fond of Wren. Perhaps she didn't know anything. But that was also unlikely, since Wren shared the same cabin with her.

He didn't bother to knock but opened the door, calling Aubrey's name as he entered. As he made his way to the bunk, he drew back in horror when he saw why Farrington hadn't answered. The old gambler's mouth was agape in a soundless cry. His dead eyes stared out from beneath a lethal wound. Caleb swallowed hard as he bent his ear to the gambler's mouth. Nothing, not even a faint breath. His fingers sought the pulse in Farrington's throat. No faint beat. Aubrey Farrington was dead. Caleb's mind refused to recognize what his eyes were seeing. Tears stung him at the injustice of it all. What was happening on his ship? Who would do such a dastardly thing? Farrington had never hurt a soul, and when it came down to the wire, he could always be counted on to do the right thing. Who? Why? Tears filled Caleb's eyes for the old man who had no one but Caleb to mourn him.

A white-hot fire took possession of his mind and body as he stormed his way to the main deck, cursing and bellowing so that the hands needed no call to report to their captain. Caleb was like the devil incarnate as he told the drenched crew of Aubrey's death and Wren's going overboard. "It's too much of a coincidence, and before we dock in America, I promise you the guilty party will hang by the neck. Now search this goddamn ship from stem to stern and see if there's a stowaway we don't know about. I want that bastard brought before me so I can stare into his eyes and know why he did this. Peter," he shouted hoarsely, "bring that son of a bitch Stoneham here. Now!" The order was thunderous.

Minutes later Bascom Stoneham was standing before him, a prayer book clutched in his bony hands. He waited, a feral look on his face, for Caleb to make his intentions known. If he was shocked at the captain's words, he gave no sign. "We can all attest to the fact that none of us left the hold. Your own man, guarding the ladder, will bear this out. You must look elsewhere for your guilty party," he said arrogantly.

Caleb took a step forward and grasped Bascom's shirt in his fist. "You might have been in the hold, but somehow, some way, you're responsible; I feel it in my gut. Get him the hell out of my sight before I kill him!" Caleb shouted.

Sara stood next to a weeping Lydia, watching the confrontation with wide eyes. She felt her legs go weak with relief when Bascom was dragged off to the hold. Now she had only one problem to contend with, the search. She had to get below and somehow waylay any intruders in the locker-box area. She would offer her services in the search, saying she couldn't stand by and do nothing. She would cry and plead if she had to. She couldn't let one of the men find Malcolm and Wren. She had killed once and felt no remorse. She could do it again!

Her eyes took on a fanatical gleam as she watched Lydia weep and wail. "Blow your nose," she said curtly. "I can't stand your sniveling. Go back down to your quarters and cry there. You're doing no good here. I'm going to help in the search, and you're only getting in the way."

Lydia, used to obeying orders, turned and walked away, crying loudly and dabbing at her eyes with the hem of her skirt. She had lost the only friend she had ever had. Now what was she to do? And who had killed Aubrey Farrington and why? Why would Wren jump overboard? Why? Lydia might not be as smart or worldly as a man or more experienced than some women, but she knew one thing for a certainty. Wren van der Rhys would never kill herself. She knew this as well as she knew she needed to take another breath in order to live. Someone on this ship had killed Aubrey Farrington and caused Wren to go overboard. Who? Why?

The *Sea Siren*'s rain-swept decks, fore, aft and below, were alive with activity as the crew began the search the captain had ordered. Sara picked up a lantern and joined the men down the slippery deck, her long, heavy skirt caught in her fingers. She was intent on getting to the confines of the deepest regions of the ship before anyone else did. She held the lantern out in front of her, pretending to search in the darkest corners below decks. When she reached the locker-box area, she halted in her tracks and began to swing the lantern to and fro, humming to herself some senseless ditty that pleased her for the moment. Wouldn't silly old Wren be in her glory if she knew she was indirectly responsible for the activity aboard ship?

When her soft humming began to irritate her, Sara began to move about again, fighting the temptation to slide back the iron bolt and look inside. Let them rot, both of them. They deserved to die, eaten alive by the rats that scurried in the darkness.

Gustave, the galley cook, held his lantern high as he made his way to the locker box. Seeing Sara standing there carrying her own lantern aloft, he stopped short, his mouth agape.

"I've already looked in there, and there isn't anything inside but enormous rats," she said. "I've looked all over this area," she whined pitifully. "Aubrey Farrington was my friend, a dear friend, and I felt I had to do my bit by helping with the search." She moved closer so that Gustave could see the tears trickling down her cheeks. "I'm so tired from all this searching that I feel faint. Please help me."

Gustave, only too glad to take a rest, gallantly escorted her to a stack of wooden crates. Carefully, as though he were handling eggs, he eased her down and set his lantern on the floor at her feet.

"Oh, my, that does make me feel better," Sara sighed as she opened the buttons of her dress and fanned herself with a handkerchief. "It certainly is sweltering in here," she went on, opening another button and bending forward slightly. Her cleavage had the desired effect, and the cook forgot why he was in the depths of the ship, intent only on a better look at Sara's ample endowments.

"Dear lady, you must let me help you back to the deck," Gustave said huskily.

"In a moment. First I have to catch my breath. While I'm doing that, why don't you look over there?" she suggested, pointing to a dark corner. "I've looked everywhere else, but whatever you do, please don't open that door. I couldn't bear to see those big old rats run by me. Why, a dozen of them ran right by me when I opened it before. But I didn't let that bother me. I looked all over that room and saw nothing but more rats. I swear to you, it was more than I could bear, but I forced myself for the sake of my friend Aubrey Farrington," she declared breathlessly, leaning over again to peer at her dusty shoe. "Mercy me," she continued to babble, "a person just isn't safe anywhere anymore, and I had put so much trust in Captain van der Rhys." Sara watched the cook carefully to see how he was taking her blatherings; she was confident that she had indeed pulled the wool over his eyes. "Just keep looking," she trilled to the startled Gustave. "We do want to tell Captain van der Rhys that we searched every inch of this blasted ship, as he ordered."

"Yes, ma'am," Gustave said happily. After he had satisfied himself that nothing or no one was lurking in the dark corner, he made his way back among the heaving packing crates and settled himself at Sara's feet to wait. For what he didn't know. She certainly looked like a lady, a distraught lady. His eyes went to the opening of her gown and her heaving breasts. How he wished he could reach inside that gown and touch her silky skin. Ladies like Miss Stoneham always had silky skin.

Sara watched him through sulky eyes and finally got up. "I think I feel strong enough to go back, if you'll just let me hold on to your arm." Deftly she buttoned her dress and stared primly ahead.

"Yes, ma'am," Gustave agreed dutifully. What had ever made him think a real lady like Miss Stoneham would be interested in the likes of him? She was the next thing to a saint, as his old mother used to say. Imagine a lady the likes of her coming all the way down here to help find the murderer of her friend. A genuine lady, there was no mistake about that.

Caleb's mouth became a tight white line when his crew stood before him and reported there was no stowaway on board. The *Sea Siren* was secure. He had known in his gut that the men would find nothing on the ship, but he had had to try. Now he would have to look elsewhere for the murderer of Aubrey Farrington. The crew understood what he was thinking, and each of them, save Gustave, wore a sullen look. Each had automatically become suspect.

His eyes on the sea, now calmed after the storm had spent itself, Caleb dismissed the crew and let his mind race. Wren must have been thrown overboard because of the gems. Whoever had done it must have thought Aubrey had more precious stones in his possession, and therefore had killed him. This solution was the only one that made sense.

The killer had to be a member of his crew. All the hands had watched the card game, making their own side bets on who was going to win, the ladies or

274

the gambler. They had seen Wren and Lydia wrest a fortune in gems from Farrington, and Wren carry the stones away. Two lives for a pouch of colorful jewels. How Caleb wished that the murderer had been Bascom Stoneham; then he could wring that bastard's skinny neck.

As the night faded into the light of day, he drove himself and the crew unmercifully. He felt no need for a woman and turned Sara away when she offered to comfort him. As if there were any comfort for him anywhere. He only wanted to do his penance so he could live with himself. Comfort was the one thing he didn't need or want.

Chapter Seventeen

Sara stood against the rail and made her final plans. When the Puritans, the crew and Caleb left the ship, she would slip below and slide the bolt. It wouldn't matter then, for afterward she would be long gone. Caleb would be busy on land with the funeral service for Aubrey Farrington, and no one would miss her. If she unbolted the door silently, she would not have to make a penance. She had decided hours ago that she couldn't leave the pair locked in, no matter how she felt about them. After all, Malcolm was the true father of her child, and she simply couldn't kill him. If he chose to die by not opening the door, then that would be his decision. As long as she left it unlocked, God couldn't punish her.

The *Sea Siren* was like a ghost ship. The crew kept to itself, each man suspecting the other and fearful to be caught alone at any time of the day without someone close by. While Sara was amused, Lydia was quiet and withdrawn, silent tears streaming down her cheeks. The small pouch of gemstones she carried between her breasts—Wren's legacy to her—was becoming worrisome. She would give it to Captain van der Rhys for safekeeping and reclaim the gems when she needed them. She might as well do it now and get it over with. Sara was growing more peculiar by the hour, and that constant humming of hers was about to drive Lydia mad.

She approached the wheelhouse hesitantly, but when she entered, her stance was firm.

"Captain van der Rhys," she said quietly, "I would like to speak with you for a moment." She withdrew the pouch from her bodice and handed it to him. "Will you keep this for me till we make port?" Tears gathered in her eyes as she added, "It's Wren's legacy to me."

Caleb was stunned and his back stiffened. "Are these the gems you and Wren won from Aubrey Farrington?"

"Yes, Captain. Wren gave them to me. She said I would need them to make a new life when I got to America. She only played cards with Aubrey Farrington so I could have what she called a stake to make a new life. She did it for me, and I can't bear it." She began to sob.

"When did she give them to you?" Caleb asked harshly.

"Right after the card game, Captain. The following day she said she was going to try to figure out a way to get Lord Farrington and Bascom into another game. She said these gems wouldn't last me too long and that I would need gold and Bascom had gold."

"Mrs. Stoneham, are you sure of what you're saying?" Caleb demanded.

"Of course I'm sure, Captain. I'm not a fool, as some people seem to think." She dried her eyes and glared angrily at Caleb. "It was someone on this ship, and I can't forgive you for not finding out who it was. And if you think it was my husband, you're mistaken. He's a coward, not a murderer."

Caleb's eyes were anguished and torn with guilt. Lydia felt sorry the moment she uttered the words, but they were true, she knew that. It was his duty to find the murderer. After all, he *was* the captain.

Long after Lydia Stoneham had returned to her quarters, Caleb sat hefting the small pouch in the palm of his hands. He was right back where he had started. If Wren and Aubrey hadn't been killed for the gems, then why had they been killed at all? Had they known something? Had they seen something? As always, his thoughts went to Bascom. According to the preacher's flock and to the guard on duty, Bascom Stoneham was as pure as an angel's wing. Caleb would just have to put him from his mind and concentrate somewhere else. The question was where? There was little time left. If the weather held, they would reach America in a few hours.

The *Sea Siren* straight on her course and secure, Peter herded the crew into Gustave's galley and motioned for silence. "It's time we had a few words," he said, not bothering to raise his voice. "I'm tired of looking at all of you with suspicion, just as you're tired of looking at me in a like manner. This ship will dock in a few hours, and we're no closer to finding out who killed Farrington than when we first began searching. Now, I'm not against our captain, because we've all done our jobs and haven't come up with anything better than he has. I'm casting my vote now that I don't sail the *Sea Siren* on her return journey until the murderer is caught. Those in favor say aye; those not in favor, nay."

A chorus of "Ayes" rang in his ears.

"If there's one among you who has an idea, a clue, something to go on, spit it out and we'll talk it over, and perhaps we'll come up with an answer. I've sailed with the lot of you, and it's my opinion none of you is guilty. We've crewed together for a long number of years, and this is the first trouble to hit us. Speak up."

"Peter is right," Jacques, a Frenchman, said loudly. "I would have placed my life with the lot of you and never thought twice. I don't think it's any of us."

"The Puritans in the hold, that divine preacher they have—what about him?" a seaman named Claude asked.

"The hold has been under guard at all times by one of us. Religious people like the preacher and his flock don't lie," Peter volunteered.

"There's a first time for everything," Jacques snapped.

"If what you say is true, that places the blame right square on one of us. Someone bludgeoned the old man and tossed the girl over the side."

Diego Sanchez stood up, resplendent in his brilliant scarlet shirt, and spoke softly. "It is bad luck to sail a ship with women aboard." He looked around to see the effect his words would have on the others.

The crew looked at one another and then at Peter, who was frowning.

"Diego is right," Claude said sourly. "Women are unlucky. Wherever they go there is trouble, and that's all we've had on this bloody ship since we set sail."

Heads nodded and sharp mutterings were heard as one man jostled another to make his point. All seemed in agreement that somehow a woman was involved. They were also in silent agreement that it couldn't be Miss van der Rhys, who had met her own untimely end, so therefore, it must be the preacher's wife.

"I disagree," Peter declared firmly. "Lydia Stoneham is a timid little thing and wouldn't have the strength to do Farrington in. It took strength to kill him." Heads nodded while the men mentally evaluated the only other woman who enjoyed the freedom of the ship—Sara Stoneham. She was tall, well fleshed and had muscular, long arms. Again there were vague mutterings and ominous curses. Only Gustave looked puzzled, out of his depth. How could they say such things about so fine a lady? he wondered. Why, she had been so distraught she had barely been able to walk, and still she had helped in the search. He should say something, make the men shut their filthy mouths. What did they know of fine ladies and how gentle they were? He sighed. Why waste his breath? All they would do was mock him. What did an old cook know?

Below decks, Sara paced the cabin, humming her sad little tune, her eyes burning feverishly. From time to time she cast anxious glances at Lydia, who sat quietly on her bunk, idly flipping Wren's playing cards.

Lydia watched Sara out of the corner of her eye, feeling her flesh crawl as the girl's nervous pacings seemed to take on an increased urgency. The humming sounded a trifle shrill, and she didn't like the way Sara was knotting and unknotting her hands. If only she had the nerve to tell Captain van der Rhys of her suspicions. He would think her dotty and perhaps blame her somehow, or, worse yet, make her go back into the hold with Bascom. Yet the captain seemed a fair man, and he had listened to her before and done what was right. Perhaps he would listen now, but would he understand and believe her? She could only try.

Sara, tiring of her pacing and humming, lay down on her bunk and closed her eyes. Lydia was off her bunk and out the door before Sara had time to open them. She made straight for the wheelhouse and waited for Caleb to motion her forward. Christ, he groaned to himself, now what? He forced a look of interest on his face as Lydia began to speak.

"Captain van der Rhys, I've anguished over this second visit today and decided that once I talk with you and tell you what I suspect, I will breathe easier. I may well be wrong, but then again I may be right, and you really should know. I'm saying this badly because . . . I don't want you to discount what I'm going to say because of Bascom. I'm not like him and the others. It's just that . . . what I mean is . . ."

Caleb was puzzled. He liked Lydia; she was a sensible woman who had shown great courage in her stand against her husband. He knew she had meant it when she said she would go over the rail if forced to return to her husband. He wouldn't admit it openly, but he admired her. He gave her his full attention and waited for her to get her thoughts in order.

Lydia squared her shoulders and primly folded her hands in her lap. "It's my sister-in-law, Sara, Captain. I know that she's . . . that she . . . is . . . is your lady, and that's why it is so difficult for me to say what I have to say. She's been acting very strange of late. She hums to herself, a nonsense tune, and her eyes are . . . are like Bascom's when he gets carried away, almost as if he's in some other world. Sara prowls the decks in the middle of the night, and she . . . she paces the cabin like a caged animal. May God have mercy on me, but I think she killed Aubrey

Farrington." She waited breathlessly for Caleb's eyes to lose their look of shock. "I feel it here," she said, placing her hand over her heart. "I don't know why she killed Aubrey Farrington, but I do know that she hated Wren. I see that surprises you. Sara had no love for Wren, and Wren barely tolerated Sara. Women know things like that." A ring of authority entered her voice. "It's up to you to find out the why of it all. Oh, one other thing. Sara is pregnant. She never said so, but the signs are unmistakable. I don't expect you to be aware of such things, and I don't know if it's important, but I felt I should mention it. Sometimes a woman will become crazed when she finds herself in that . . . delicate condition and without a husband."

Caleb almost choked in his attempt to get his words out. He wet his lips before speaking, and his voice sounded far away to his ears. "Tell me, Mrs. Stoneham, when did you notice Sara's . . . condition?"

Lydia flushed. "In the hold, shortly after coming aboard. She was nauseous every morning, which, of course, could have had something to do with the rocking of the ship, but again, a woman knows these things. Also, she has gotten a . . . little thick around the middle." The flush ran down to her throat and she closed her eyes. "Please, Captain, forgive me for being so forward and so blunt. I know a lady doesn't speak like this in front of a man, but I felt you should know. I don't want to stay in that cabin with her anymore," she blurted. "She frightens me."

Caleb felt as if the weight of the world had been removed from his shoulders. "Dear lady, whatever you want on this ship is yours, you have but to ask. You have just saved my life in more ways than one. If it won't cause you any anguish, you can have Farrington's quarters. One more thing, Mrs. Stoneham. In your opinion, why do you think Sara did this thing, if indeed she did do it?"

Lydia grimaced. She tapped her head lightly with

her fingers and said, "She's fey, unstable. I don't like speaking ill of my husband, but he is her brother, and perhaps it's a trait they were both born with. It happens sometimes," she insisted defensively, fearful that he didn't believe her. "Do you think, Captain, that what I said has any merit?"

"More than you know, dear lady. I don't want you to be afraid. I'll have the crew keep an eye on you. There's no cause for you to be alarmed."

Relief flooded through Lydia. He believed her, she could see it in the grimness of his face and the set of his jaw. Thank God she had had the courage to come and tell him!

Caleb watched her leave the wheelhouse with a lightened heart. How fitting it was that a woman had caused so much havoc and that another woman had set it to rights. He grinned and stared out across the great expanse of water. Very fitting indeed.

A nod of his head and Peter came loping into the wheelhouse. They held a long, low-voiced conversation. Peter's eyes widened, and then his face also became grim. He nodded several times and left to follow his orders. Perhaps the lady called the *Sea Siren* wasn't cursed after all, he thought.

Sara wasn't surprised when the first mate came to get her. She rose from the bed and followed him docilely to the hatch, where she descended the ladder to the hold. She was conscious of her surroundings, but her eyes were glazed and staring. Nothing mattered anymore. Her family could take care of her; she was too tired to care what became of her.

Settling herself next to her mother, who ignored her completely, she narrowed her eyes and watched the first mate and Bascom carry on a quiet conversation. She would tell Bascom it was all Lydia's fault that she had been returned to his keeping. That should set his hackles to rising, and perhaps he would leave her alone. All she had to do was ignore him the way her very own mother was ignoring her. Nothing mattered anymore. Not Wren, not Malcolm, not Caleb, and least of all Bascom.

Something niggled at her brain. Wren. It always came back to Wren. Of course, Wren would starve if she didn't take her food. Malcolm would starve, too.

"I'll take care of her," Bascom said curtly to Peter. "You can tell your captain that he's wrong about my sister. If he thinks she's acting strange, it's because of the fever she had. There's nothing wrong with her mind. She is as sane as I am." At Peter's skeptical look, he hastened to continue. "My sister doesn't know the meaning of the word 'violence.' Be sure to relay that message to Captain van der Rhys. If he fears for his crew, assure him that she's safe below with her family. Now, if you'll excuse me, we have a prayer meeting scheduled, and unless you're ready to become one of us, I suggest you go topside and leave us to our Lord."

Peter needed no second urging. He was up the ladder and gulping deep breaths of salt air in a matter of moments. Then he bounded into the wheelhouse and gave Bascom's message to Caleb. Caleb listened, his face granite-hard. He nodded and dismissed Peter and let his eyes drift back to the sea. What he hoped to see, to find, he didn't know. Before him lay only an endless expanse of blue-green water.

While Caleb scanned the vastness before him and Sara slept, Wren sat huddled in one corner of the locker box. How long have I been here? she wondered. Ever since the lantern had gone out, she had no way of knowing. She couldn't decide which was worse—staring at Malcolm's mutilated face in the light or having the rats play around her feet in the darkness. Isn't anyone ever going to check this damnable hole in which I'm being held a prisoner? What did Sara tell the others about my whereabouts? By now Caleb should have turned this ship upside down looking for me, she thought miserably. And where the devil is Farrington? Malcolm said he usually brought him food late at night and then took him out for an airing. Where *is* the old man?

After his initial brutal attack on her, Malcolm had left her alone, saying she wasn't worth what little effort he had to expend. To assure himself that Wren wouldn't cry out and reveal his hiding place, he had torn his shirt and bound and gagged her.

The bindings cut her wrists, and the foul, linty rag he had stuffed in her objecting mouth was rancid with the smell of him and choked her. She felt a fresh flurry of tremors ripple through her body, tremors of rage and fear, and in her heart she knew she was approaching the edges of despair. She began to pray.

Chapter Eighteen

As the *Sea Siren* tacked gracefully toward port at the mouth of the Connecticut River, Gustave completed the list of supplies he would need for the return trip to England. The galley had been scoured to his satisfaction, and he poured himself a large mug of coffee and went up on deck to view the approaching verdant landscape. His friend Diego meandered over and reached for the mug, helping himself to a long drink. They sat together companionably, neither talking.

Diego reached for the mug again, and after taking a few more swallows, began to tell Gustave of the plans for disembarking and dissembling the Puritans, who were gathering the last of their belongings in the hold before coming up on deck for their first glimpse of their new home. The conversation turned to Sara Stoneham.

"She's below with that preacher brother of hers," Diego stated, his mouth curling at the aftertaste of the bitter brew. "Just as well. That's one lady who could make me feel as though a goose were walking over my grave. Did you ever notice her eyes, Gustave? She looks like she's here, but the rest of her is out there." He waved his arms to indicate the vast reaches of Long Island Sound.

"I thought her to be a lady," Gustave said hesitantly.

Diego touched his temple and shook his head. "I had a sister who got like that once when she couldn't take her husband's carousing with other women. She died," he said bluntly.

Gustave rolled the words around on his tongue and decided he needed more clarification. "She died because her husband tossed in the covers with other women?"

Diego looked at the cook with disgust. "Yes and no. Something snapped in her mind, and she was never the same again. My sister was a lady, too," he said defensively. "One day she was fine and the next— poof!" He snapped his fingers. "It was terrible. Her husband cried for eleven days. He cried each day with a different child. They had eleven children," he explained to Gustave.

For some strange reason Gustave felt sick to his stomach. Miss Stoneham seemed like such a lady. But Diego seemed to know what he was talking about. He looked at the Spaniard craftily and asked, "Did your

sister ever do strange things, go strange places and . . .
you know . . . do things ladies don't normally do?"

"Like what?"

"Like would she ever go about at night with a lantern to places that were dark and full of rats?"

"I thought you said this was coffee," Diego remarked, peering at the dregs at the bottom of the mug. "I told you my sister was a lady. *No* lady, dotty or not, does things like that. You're disgusting, Gustave, even to think my sister would do such a thing. I'll wager you've been cooking with rum again, haven't you?"

"I was just asking," Gustave replied heatedly. "I didn't mean your *sister* did those things; I just asked if *women* did those kinds of things, other women. I would never say anything bad about your sister. If you say she was a lady, then she was a lady."

"Damn right she was a lady. She was a good mother, too." Diego cast a withering look in Gustave's direction, handed him back his cup and proceeded to change his boots.

Gustave sat in silence for a long time. Women were known to make fools out of men. He looked around to see if Diego had noticed his changed status from cook to fool. Diego was concerned only with his feet, so that had to mean Gustave was safe; he was the only one who knew what a fool he was. He sucked in his plump cheeks and began to whistle tonelessly as he made his way back to the galley. The first chance he got, he would take another look down in the bowels of the ship. Yes, that was what he'd do. It wouldn't hurt to take another look at all.

In the black darkness, in the deepest, most forward compartment of the *Sea Siren*'s hull, Wren and Malcolm waited. All motion of the ship had ceased, and the stillness was ominous. The slow rocking without the slight drag and pull of the force of the waves warned them that the vessel was either becalmed or at anchor.

Tears streaked down Wren's cheeks. They had been only a day away from land when Sara had tricked her into this hellish place with Malcolm. The *Sea Siren* had made port. She would rot in the stench-filled dungeon. She would die. Here, alone with the one man who hated her most in the world. Bound and gagged like the trapped animal she was. There was nothing, no word, no prayer, no hope, that could save her.

Above decks, Sara prepared to leave the ship in the last jolly boat. Several of the crew and two Puritans with whom she was not familiar waited alongside her for the jolly to beat the shore-rushing waves and follow the current back to the *Siren*.

Sara's thoughts were intent on the locker box holding her prisoners. Somehow she had to find the courage to sneak below and unbolt the door before she disembarked. No one was paying any attention to her; every eye was intent upon the slowly approaching jolly. Fear pervaded her body and chills danced up her spine. If she was to unbolt the door, she would have to be quick about it in order to return to the deck and leave in the last jolly. She was terrified at the thought of being alone aboard ship with a recently freed, half-crazed Malcolm.

She backed up a step, then two, and scurried to the hatch on the forward deck. After crawling rapidly down the ladder, careful not to make a sound, she inched across the keel line through the hull and made her way to the locker box by touch alone. It was as though her fever-bright eyes could penetrate the dark and perceive distinguishing touch marks. She had traveled the length of the hull a thousand times in her mind. Her fingers groped for the familiar outline of the door, searching for the bolt like a blind man's fingers searching for a tossed coin. Holding her breath, not daring to breathe, she silently eased the bolt free.

Immediately relief flooded through her. She had done it. She had freed them. They could walk out of the cell any time they wanted. She wasn't murdering them; she wasn't killing the father of her child. She had set them free!

Soundlessly she retraced her steps, her back hunched in a similar manner to those of the rats who existed in the dank darkness.

Hours later, Wren tried to ease her cramped position and stretch her legs. Malcolm must have heard her movement, because she sensed he was moving toward her. She cringed from him, dreading his touch, then felt him work the knots in her bindings. He loosened the gag from around her face and she spit it out. She was parched and dry, her mouth foul-tasting. She forced her lips to work, her jaw aching and sore.

"Don't touch me, Malcolm," she managed to utter hoarsely. "Don't touch me!"

"As if I'd want you," he sneered. "I won't waste my strength on a dead woman."

The truth of his words reconfirmed her worst fears. She would die here alone with Malcolm. "The door," she croaked. "Damn you, Malcolm, try the door. Beat it down! Don't you understand we'll die in here?"

"We'll wait for Farrington. And don't try to scream. You'll have that rag stuffed back in your mouth before you can get out one syllable."

Wren shook her head, not realizing he couldn't see her in the blackness.

"Do you understand me?" he threatened harshly, his fingers digging into the soft flesh of her shoulder.

"Yes . . . I understand . . . What you don't seem to understand, Malcolm, is that we've put in at port. When I was thrown in here with you, we were only a day or two away from reaching land. We're trapped in here! Trapped!" Her voice rose. "Lord Farrington isn't coming back for you. He'll never find me!"

288

The intensity of her words struck Malcolm with an unbidden fear that she was right. Farrington would sooner see him dead than alive. Then the gems would be his.

Wren scrambled to her feet, rubbing her wrists where the bindings had cut into them. She was unfamiliar with the cell, and her searching, outstretched hands discovered it was even smaller than she'd imagined.

"Damn you, Malcolm, help me find the door. Get up and find it! Beat against it! There's always a watch aboard ship—he might hear us!"

"One more word out of you and I'll strangle you," Malcolm warned, alarmed by the strength she was suddenly exhibiting.

Wren's fingers found the hinges flanging the door, then groped for the crack between door and bulkhead. The edges of her fingers felt a cool draft blowing through the minuscule space. She began to hit the bulkhead, her hands clenched into fists, her throat aching to realize a scream. Her poundings met with resistance but still she beat with all her might. She moved to the left and heard her poundings sound hollow as she found the center of the door.

Malcolm seemed suddenly to realize what she was doing and began fumbling for her in the darkness to quiet her hysteria.

Soundlessly the door swung open, revealing a glimmer of gray light. Both Malcolm and Wren fell back, mouths agape.

"Sweet Christ, the door was open," Malcolm whispered in shock. "All this time the door was open."

Wren lowered her head into her hands. She could not take in the reality confronting her. She had spent eternal hours in Malcolm's presence, and all the while the door had been open. Sara had never locked it, and neither of them had thought to try it, accepting their prison sentence like a final judgment. "We're free?" she asked in amazement.

"Will you shut up!" Malcolm ordered. "We're free. All we have to do is walk out of here."

"Let me go, please let me go!" she pleaded, struggling to wrest herself from his grasp.

"Not so fast, little bird. I'm not done with you yet. I'll still get some use out of you. But never fear, we'll leave here together."

"Where? Where can we go? Please let me go!"

"Shut up," he commanded. He knocked her down to the floor, pinned her beneath his weight and covered her mouth with his hand. He felt around the floor with his free hand and found that for which he searched. Quickly he had her bound again, the gag choking off her air and rendering her silent.

Wren's eyes were wild with fury and she kicked out at him with her foot.

"Try that again and I'll leave you here, and this time I'll lock the door myself." Wren was immediately docile, fearing he would carry out his threat. "All I need are the jewels from Farrington and a little cash money, and I'll be set for life," Malcolm plotted, his voice low and calculating. "And you, my little bird, will bring a nice ransom. Sara told me your brother captains this ship."

Tears coursed down Wren's cheeks. She was lost and totally alone. Caleb wouldn't give a tinker's damn about her. He had Sara and their coming child to occupy his mind.

"It'll be interesting to find out what your brother thinks you're worth. I'm going topside to see what's about and if I can find some food and water. I'll come back for you."

He whirled around and disappeared out the door. Several minutes later he was slowly climbing the ladder to the forward hatch, which he lifted cautiously. He took great gulps of air, and the stiff breeze whipping about nearly made him dizzy.

The sun was low in the sky; there was no sign of

anyone on deck. Straining his neck, he peered over the hatch side, across the deck and through the rail. Land. Green, inviting land. It would be another hour till dark. He spied the two-man dinghy which swung from lines over the starboard bow. He would take Wren with him in the boat. Upriver. When the time was right and he had her secure, he would seek out van der Rhys and name his price.

Malcolm waited, almost fearfully, for darkness to descend. He had to take care of the man on watch— kill him, if necessary—before he could lower the dinghy and head upriver. Well, he had proved that he was good at waiting; as a matter of fact, he excelled at that. Another hour, perhaps a little less, and he could set out on what he considered the last leg of his journey that would lead him to God only knew what. If it was the last thing he did, he would get those jewels from Farrington and a handsome ransom for Wren. He would set himself up like a king on one of the islands and have people wait on him hand and foot. He would have a different woman for every night of the week. If his scarred face troubled those about him, he would simply kill them. In time they would learn that he was a power, a force to be reckoned with. Money could buy anything. It could buy people; it could buy whatever service he required. It could even buy physical love.

He tilted his head upward. The dark clouds rode the new moon like a novice rider on horseback, and he crept toward the wheelhouse. He smirked to himself. The stupid guard would probably be drunk, relying on the man in the crow's-nest to warn of any approaching intruders. On silent feet he attacked the guard from the rear, grasping him around the neck and jerking him off balance. Then he smashed the seaman's head against the stout wheel before he let the guard crumble to the deck. The man wouldn't be doing anything for a long while. By the time he woke up, if ever, Malcolm and Wren would be long gone, armed and gone.

Malcolm went to the galley for some food, which he threw into a sack, and then made his way to the dinghy, which he lowered into the water. He sat down to rest for a moment and get his bearings. Satisfied that everything had gone the way he had planned it, he relaxed and sighed deeply. A few hours of hard rowing and he would be far enough upriver. He would find a safe place to secure the dinghy and then take to the woods on foot. He'd keep Wren tied so she couldn't escape, and then he'd rest himself. By nightfall he could return to port with his ransom demand for Wren. Everything was working out just the way he had planned it.

There was no fear in Wren, just white-hot fury. She knew now that Malcolm wouldn't kill her, but he could make things so miserable for her, she might wish she were dead. There was nothing she could do, and that only added to her rage. When the door was flung open, she let her eyes do all her talking. If the hatred that burned from them could kill, Malcolm Weatherly would have fallen lifeless before her. He pulled her roughly to her feet and pushed her ahead of him. She didn't balk; there was no point in angering him further.

"Down the ladder, and one false move out of you, and your face will be ugly in comparison to mine," Malcolm said, untying her hands. "I'll be right behind you," he added ominously.

Wren rubbed at her wrists and did as she was told, the gag almost suffocating her.

Malcolm wasted no time putting the dinghy into motion, dipping the oars deep and pulling back, every muscle in his back bunching into knots.

Wren cursed him with her eyes every time the oar struck the water. God, how she hated him! She had to try to get away from him somehow. Bound and gagged like she was, she knew there was little chance he would take his one good eye off her, let alone free her. As soon as he had tossed her into the dinghy, he had bound not only her hands but her ankles as well. If he fell into a fit of rage and decided to toss her overboard, she would be dead within seconds. It would be to her advantage to lie perfectly quiet and not antagonize him in any way.

Every muscle in her body stilled as Caleb's face swam before her tired eyes. How clearly she could see him, and if she willed it, she could remember the feel of him next to her. How good had he felt, so hard and so warm. She had fitted so perfectly in the cradle of his arm, and he had told her that in gentle whispers. She had felt as though she had come home, home to Caleb, where she belonged. Always Caleb. How gentle and warm, so very warm, he was. She had been a fool and was still a fool. She could have fought Sara for him, could have asserted herself. Instead, she had taken the coward's way out and run. She always ran instead of facing up to her problems. She should have gone to Caleb and poured out her heart; he would have listened and understood. And now he was lost to her forever. He would marry Sara because she was pregnant, and part of Wren's life would be over. Wren could never love anyone the way she loved Caleb. Caleb was part of her. He was her destiny. Sirena had known that, just as she herself had known. Why hadn't Caleb been able to recognize it, too? He had said they were as one, but that already seemed a long time ago. From the beginning she had been like an open wound to him, and she had merely made matters worse for herself. She was stupid and silly, just as Sara had always claimed.

As Caleb stood near the open gravesite, his glance was drawn to his ship anchored offshore. A feeling washed over him that, if he looked hard enough, he would see Wren. Calling himself a fool, he redirected his attention to the ceremony taking place.

Aubrey, Lord Farrington, was being laid to his final rest. Caleb had insisted that burial be on land, knowing how much his old partner had disliked the sea.

The crewmen were present, and their heads bowed as they waited for Caleb to find the proper words. Clearing his throat, he managed to say simply, "He was my friend. His only sin was his love for life and adventure, and for that I ask forgiveness in his name."

His hand shook slightly as he threw a clod of dirt into the yawning grave. Tears misted in his eyes and he turned away, unable to watch as the crew heaped the black, rich earth onto the simple coffin.

"Captain, I have to go back to the galley before I take shore leave," Gustave said somberly, respectful of Caleb's grief. "Can I leave you a plate for supper? Peter said you would be spending the night aboard ship."

"I'll see to my own supper, Gustave. Don't put yourself out. Join the men and have a drink for Aubrey. He'd like that."

"Aye, Captain, as soon as me and Diego get back."

The sleek, three-masted frigate dipped and rose at anchor in the gentle swells of the Sound as Gustave made his cautious way across the deck. From time to time he cast an anxious glance over his shoulder, even though he knew no one would be watching him. They were alone on board, he and Diego and Claude, the watchman. Still, he had the feeling someone or something was peering at him through the dark. Yellow lanterns lit the perimeters of the deck and he stood a moment at the rail, relishing the breeze on his leathery cheeks and sparse gray hair.

Why do old men make fools of themselves over a pretty face? he questioned himself. The captain would have his hide nailed to the mizzenmast in short order if there was anything in the locker box besides the rats. He shuddered in the warm June breeze as he pointed his feet in the direction of the forward hatch. He couldn't put it off any longer; he had to go below and see what the locker box held.

His bare feet were soundless as he continued his trek below decks. He stopped once and drew in his breath, feeling unseen eyes boring into the back of his skull. He cocked his head to the side like an inquisitive sparrow but could see nothing in the ghostly shadows. Still the feeling persisted. He swallowed hard, the thin knob in his neck bobbing up and down as if to a lively tune. He was almost at the locker but still couldn't shake the impression of unseen eyes. "Who's there?" he demanded, and half jumped out of his skin when Diego's voice shot back at him.

"What in holy hell are you doing down here? Don't tell me that swill you've been cooking has finally gotten to your brain and rendered you senseless!"

Although Diego's tone was gruff, Gustave knew immediately that something was terribly wrong. He held up his lantern and looked into his friend's face.

"We've got to get off the ship and back to the captain," Diego said in a lower voice. "I was just above and found Claude. He was hit over the head. He'll be all right in a few days, but he never seen who done it. Another thing—the two-man dinghy is missing. I know we didn't use it to go ashore. It's supposed to be hanging over the starboard bow in case of an emergency." The hairs on the back of Gustave's neck stood on end. His gaze left the cook's face and centered on the locker-box door. "What in hell are you doing down here, anyway?" he added.

Gustave debated a moment, then motioned Diego to come closer. Quickly he explained why he was going to the locker box.

Diego's eyes widened and he shook his head. "You're right, my friend, the captain will nail your hide to the mizzenmast in short order. The captain is a great one for setting an example," he muttered in sympathy as he followed Gustave and his bobbing lantern. "How about a few short snorts before you throw open that door?" he suggested as he withdrew a rum bottle from his baggy shirt front.

Gustave accepted greedily and drank as if he had been parched for months. He handed back the bottle, which was now nearly empty.

"I said a few short snorts, not half the damn bottle. Do you know what I had to go through to steal this?" Diego grumped as he brought the bottle to his lips and finished it off. Then he picked up a stout board which could have smashed the skulls of ten men with one wicked swipe. "A man should be prepared for any and all emergencies."

Gustave nervously wiped his sweating palms on his tattered trousers. "Let's get it over with. I'll throw the bolt and you go in first, with the board straight in front of you. I'll be right behind you with the lantern held high."

"Why is it every time you get yourself into some kind of mess, I'm the one who has to get you out or go first so you don't get yourself beaten to a pulp?" Diego grumbled as he hefted the board in anticipation of Gustave's arm movement with the bolt.

The cook sucked in his breath and threw the bolt on the third try. "Because you're my friend and I pulled you from shark-infested waters when you were but a wee lad, that's why, and you owe me your life," he replied.

"That was over thirty years ago, and I've more than paid my debt," Diego snorted, charging into the foul-smelling room, Gustave at his heels.

"Son of a bitch! I was sure. I was so sure." Gustave held his lantern high, the light filling the shadowy depths of the empty locker box.

The simple funeral service over, Caleb's mood darkened. Farrington had been laid to his final resting place, and now that the others were settled, he had nothing more to do but return to the ship. He knew he would feel better if he could instigate a real fist-pounding, no-holds-barred fight with someone and get himself beaten to a pulp. He was alive and Farrington was dead. His eyes grew wild as he looked at the soft mound of earth and then at Peter, who was shuffling his feet. "It seems that we should be doing something else, saying something else. This is so . . . so final."

"Death is always final," Peter mumbled. He, too, was grieving for the lively gambler. Many a long talk had passed between them, and he had genuinely liked the man, as had the rest of the crew. Death always left the living in agony. He had never seen Caleb in such straits before, and in his heart he knew the captain was grieving more for Wren than for the gambler. There should have been another body to bury. Caleb was grieving twofold.

Peter stepped aside. He didn't want to intrude on Caleb's grief, and yet he didn't know what action to take. He couldn't just leave him standing there with nothing to do and nowhere to go except back to the lonely ship. He would give up his liberty and return with his captain and Lydia, who, because of her desertion of Bascom, was no longer welcome in the Puritan community. They would have something to eat and a little rum, and after a good night's sleep Caleb would feel better. At least Peter hoped so.

"Come, Captain," Lydia said gently. "It's time to go back to the ship. It's been a long day, and it has taken its toll on all of us." Carefully, so as not to startle him, she took his arm, and Peter took the other. They made their way back to the dock and climbed into the jolly. All was quiet on their path across the water; no sound permeated the ebony, star-filled night.

Once back on board the *Siren*, Caleb was surprised to find Gustave and Diego waiting for him. Gustave's leathery face was tormented and the old man picked nervously at his hands.

"What's troubling you, Gustave?" Caleb asked. "Didn't burn down the galley, did you?"

Haltingly, and glancing at Diego for support, Gustave told the captain about the incident with Sara and the locker box, the subsequent attack on Claude and the missing dinghy.

Within minutes they were at Claude's side, and Lydia began ministering to him as he lay on his bunk. Water, clean cloths and a medicine box were before her as she set to work. Caleb and Peter hovered, offering advice and help. "I think," she said firmly, "that it would be better if you left me to my chores and went topside." Her tone was gentle but firm. "Better still, go to the galley and see if Gustave left any broth in the larder, and if he didn't, make some." It was an order. Caleb looked at Peter and Peter looked at Caleb. Both men shrugged and headed for the galley.

Peter struggled to collect his wits. What kind of order had that been? An order from a woman, no less! The captain and his first mate didn't make broth in the galley. The cook made the broth. Where in the hell was Gustave? Then Peter remembered the captain had dismissed both Gustave and Diego to pursue their liberty. And quick they had been to leave the captain's sight after confessing about the locker box! So he would make the broth and maybe a sweet, too, while he was at it. He hoped Caleb didn't have two left hands when it came to measuring, like Gustave had.

In less than an hour Gustave's spit-and-polish galley was a disaster, and Caleb and Peter were no closer to a simmering broth than when they had first started.

"Begging your pardon, Captain, but this tastes like water with a fishy taste. I think you're supposed to put in bones or dried meat and then let it cook."

"I did that," Caleb said belligerently, a fine bead of perspiration dotting his brow and upper lip.

"All I can say, Captain, and I say it with all due respect, is that if the patient drinks this 'broth,' it will kill him. I never tasted such vile stuff in my life. It's worse than Gustave's swill!"

"What do you suggest?" Caleb demanded.

"I'm no cook and neither are you. I think we should have a drink and ponder the matter. Maybe it will taste better if it cooks longer," Peter said, uncorking a bottle of rum. "Gustave cooks everything from sun-up to sundown. I've decided it just has to cook longer." His face darkened to that of a thundercloud. "And another thing, Captain. If you botch up this broth, Miss Lydia is going to blame me, and then where will I be?" He took a deep gurgle from the bottle and continued. "I've had my eye on that fair lady for a long while now, and whatever you do in this galley is going to come home to roost on my shoulders. Add some rum," he suggested, handing the bottle to Caleb.

"So that's the way the wind is blowing." Caleb grinned and added a dollop of rum to the pot.

"Pour, Captain, pour, don't trickle it," Peter said, tilting the bottle with a heavy hand. "Yes, that's the way the wind is blowing. She's a fair-looking woman, and she would fit real nice right here." He indicated the crook of his arm. "Any woman don't fit here, well, then she's not my kind of woman." He shook his head decisively.

"I know just what you mean." Caleb remembered how Wren had fitted into his arms and how wonderful she had felt next to him. He drank deeply, relieved now that half his burdens had been lifted from his broad shoulders. He handed the bottle back to Peter, but not before he had added another "dollop" to the simmering pot of broth. While Peter finished off the rum, Caleb was busily uncorking not one but two additional bottles.

"One for you and one for me," Peter hiccuped.

"Well, don't think I'm putting mine in the pot," Caleb protested indignantly.

"You're the captain. I'm only the first mate. Rank always fills the pot." Peter smirked.

"Who told you a thing like that?" Caleb demanded.

"Gustave, that's who," Peter lied as he brought the bottle to his lips, missing his mouth. He cursed loudly as he wiped at his bare chest.

"That sounds right to me," Caleb agreed drunkenly, now lacing the pot liberally. "You're right, I am the captain of this ship."

"And a damn good captain you are. You're the first captain I ever sailed with who knows how to make broth. Even the damn cook doesn't know how to cook," Peter laughed happily.

"I know, and it's a damn shame, too. I pay good wages and the crew expects to eat hearty and all we get is slop. My provisions are the best money can buy. Gustave ruins everything. This will be the first decent meal we've had in days."

Both of them peered into the pot.

"I thought this broth was for the guards. Why are your eyes watering, Captain?" Peter asked, staggering back from the strong fumes rising from the pot.

"Damned if I know. Must be from the onion I put in there," Caleb said, wiping at his eyes.

"That was no onion, it was a potato. Gustave ran out of onions days ago." Peter uncorked another bottle of rum and passed it to Caleb. "That's for the pot. You're the captain, and you shouldn't have to put yours in the pot. I'm the first mate, and it wouldn't look right if I did, so let's just use this bottle for the pot and forget about sharing."

"That sounds right to me," Caleb said, dumping the contents of the third bottle into the pot. "We seem to have quite a bit here, Peter, enough for an army. We'll eat hearty tonight."

"You're a good man, Captain, even if you did get off to a bad start with all those . . . those . . . holy people on board."

"I know. I can't stand them," Caleb whispered confidentially. "They've been nothing but trouble, and now you tell me you have designs on the preacher's wife. The question is, does the preacher's wife have designs on you?" he chortled, waving his rum bottle in the air and narrowly missing Peter's head.

Peter nodded sagely. "She looks at me and then looks at the floor."

"That means she likes you, and yes, she does have designs. I'm an authority." At Peter's look of disbelief, he laughed loudly. "Even Regan says I'm an authority. Married ladies can be trouble, especially when they have husbands."

Peter nodded again. "I'm expecting the worst," he said slowly and distinctly. "The very worst."

"That makes sense. That way you won't be disappointed if the preacher doesn't give you trouble. Bottle's empty," Caleb announced, flinging it across the room.

Peter laughed as the glass shattered in all directions. "You broke it, and Gustave goes barefoot in the galley. Now you have to clean it up."

"I'm the captain. All I do is steer this damn ship and cook broth. You have to wield the mop."

"Sounds fair to me." Peter peered into the pot again and reeled back, his hands to his face. He stumbled, righted himself and stared into Caleb's dark eyes. "I think, Captain, that you put just a little too much rum in the broth."

"How can you tell? Too much is never enough. If you're worried because the fumes unclog your nose and burn your throat, that doesn't mean anything. It's cooking away. See how thick it's getting?" He backed away from the cookstove and fell heavily against the doorframe.

Two hours later, her patient resting comfortably, Lydia set out for the galley to see how Peter and the captain were faring.

The fumes from the cooking pot drove her back into the passageway. Cautiously, she poked her head around the corner of the door, all the while dabbing at her eyes. Caleb was sprawled on the floor, snoring loudly, a rum bottle clutched in one hand, the other shielding his eyes. The first mate was trying, unsuccessfully, to wield a mop over what looked like broken glass. He wore a look of disgust as he scattered the fragments and drank from his bottle at the same time.

"And what do you think you're doing? Who made this mess? Who's going to clean it up?" Lydia demanded.

At her words, Peter dropped the bottle and the mop and clapped his hands over his ears. "Isn't it bad enough I can't keep my eyes open? Do you want to make me deaf, too, with your caterwauling? Don't look at me for this mess!" He smirked as he pointed a shaking finger at the prone captain. "He did what you ordered, and he's the one who made this mess. All I did was watch. I think it's going to be the best damn broth you ever ate." He nudged Caleb gently with his toe. "Pity he won't be awake to try it." He took one step and then another toward the rum-laden pot and crumpled to the floor. Loud, lusty snores permeated the galley as Lydia threw her hands helplessly in the air.

What did she have to lose? All the while wiping at her eyes, she ladled out a generous portion of broth for her patient. It would either kill him or cure him. If the captain cooked it himself, it had to be worth something. It looked like pure, undiluted, hot rum to her inexperienced eye.

Even through his rum-induced sleep Caleb was aware of a deep-seated restlessness, and he tossed and turned in his bunk—the same bunk he had shared with Wren when she had been beset by fever-ish chills and he had wrapped her in his arms and shared the warmth from his body. In his grief-tormented dreams he heard her cry out, "Caleb! Help me!"

Wren tossed fitfully in her sleep, her mind scream-ing Caleb's name over and over. Hours later, Mal-colm shook her roughly and pulled her to her feet. He loosened her bonds, and Wren stumbled as the blood rushed through her veins. Her feet on dry land gave her no comfort. She looked around but could see only inky blackness and dark, spectral-looking trees. She was standing in mud and slime up to her ankles. There was no means of escaping the man who was securing the dinghy to an enormous tree on the shore-line. Where would she run to in this infernal darkness? With the way her luck had been of late, she would run straight into some wild animal's lair and be chewed alive for her intrusion. She gulped and decided to take her chances with Malcolm.

Malcolm pushed her ahead of him and pretended to look around. If she couldn't see in the dark, what could he see with one eye? she wondered nastily. She was about to voice her opinion and then thought better of it. "I'm hungry and you damn well better feed me," she snapped. "If you think Captain van der Rhys is going to pay out good money for me, I better be hale and hearty or the price will go down."

"Shut up," Malcolm grated. "Get over there by that tree. I'm going to tie you to it, around the waist. You can maneuver your hands and feet. And if you don't shut that mouth of yours, I'll gag you again."

"You want me to shut up? I'll shut up, but not before I tell you that you are without a doubt a ring-tailed son of a bitch!" She felt better for expressing her opinion of him, coining Sirena's favorite phrase for an insufferable bastard.

Malcolm ignored her words and dragged her toward the tree. "I won't tell you again to shut that mouth of yours. This is your final warning. Once I gag you, that means no food. It's immaterial to me if you die. I can get the ransom from your brother even if you're dead. Dutchmen like bodies to bury."

Satisfied with the tight knot on the rope that bound Wren to the tree, he handed her some cheese and bread. "No more until tomorrow evening, so you better make it last," he said coldly as he gave the rope a vicious twist. It cut into her ribs, but she didn't flinch.

Wren bit off a piece of the rancid-smelling cheese and devoured it. She would eat the bread and cheese now; for all she knew, he might decide to kill her within the hour. That remark about the Dutch liking bodies to bury bothered her. If she was going to die, she would rather die on a semifull stomach.

She cast a critical eye toward the sky. Soon it would be dawn. What was going to happen then? Would he leave her here tied to the tree? Of course he would; he had no other choice. Then he would go back downriver, seek out Caleb and demand the ransom. That meant she would be tied here for another day. Already she could feel the pull of the rope around her waist. If she kept perspiring, the rope would tighten more cruelly. She wished she had more clothes on to protect her from the burning sensation she was beginning to feel. It was impossible to remain perfectly still. Fidgeting was a habit she had been born with.

Malcolm toiled to start a small fire within the

cluster of trees, more for light than for warmth. The balmy June weather was holding, and the studding of stars in the black velvet sky abated the threat of rain.

The moment the flint sparked, he sat back on his haunches and glanced about him. This was as good a place as any, he thought. Far enough away from the water to be safe from discovery by a passing boat. The woods were dense here, a shield from observing eyes.

Soon he would approach van der Rhys and find Farrington. For now, he had to sleep, to regain his strength. A few more days wouldn't alter his course and would only serve to increase van der Rhys' anxiety for Wren. Malcolm knew he would need all his strength to face a man as formidable as Caleb van der Rhys.

Chapter Nineteen

Leaving Peter and Lydia to tend the wounded crewman, Caleb had come ashore to make a cursory tour of the fortress settlement of Saybrook town, which rested at the mouth of the Connecticut River, in the heart of Pequot Indian territory. Owing to his colossal hangover from the night before, it had nearly been dusk when he left the *Sea Siren,* and the great gold ball in the sky was dipping rapidly into the thick tree line on the west as Caleb made his way down the hard, dusty road inside the protective walls of the fort to the office of the Dutch West India Company, as it was known in the New World.

Caleb had been in Saybrook two years before when he had arranged for tobacco, the "Imperial Weed," to be transferred from the Virginia colony to the office at Saybrook for shipment and distribution through the Company. The progress made by the settlers since he had last been here was at once visible. A wide expanse of forest surrounding the fortress, had been cleared, a precaution that aided visibility in case of an Indian attack. Several hundred people now lived in Saybrook town, many of them merchants and skilled craftsmen. Farms flanked the territory, the boundaries of their property lines hugging one another for security, and all roads led to the fort.

Caleb quietly opened the rough wooden door of the Dutch West India office and immediately upon entering knew something was wrong—very wrong. He could see it and he could smell it. The office was dingy and bare of everything save a primitive desk and a stool. A map, tattered and ragged at the edges, was hanging by one nail on the far wall. A lantern, empty of oil, was carelessly flung into a corner. A man Caleb had never seen before lolled drunkenly on the stool, his feet propped on the desk. Loud snores resounded through the room. Caleb raised one booted foot and knocked the man's moccasined feet to the floor. His anger was immeasurable. Was everything concerning this voyage destined to go amiss? A familiar heaviness swelled in his chest as fleeting thoughts of Wren and Aubrey Farrington crossed his mind.

"What . . . who?" the man muttered, trying to orient himself and failing miserably.

"What the hell do you call this?" Caleb shouted.

"You're a disgrace to the Company. Where's Galt?" he demanded.

"And who the hell are you to be asking me any questions at all?" the man retorted angrily as he wiped at the spittle drooling from his mouth with the back of a filthy hand.

"I'm Captain Caleb van der Rhys, and I'm here for the yearly report and to take the furs and tobacco back to England on my return voyage. Where have you been storing them? But first I want you to tell me where Galt is and explain this sorry mess!"

The man swallowed hard. He had known that sooner or later this day of reckoning would come. He only wished he had been better prepared. The man standing in front of him didn't look as though he would listen to an explanation, much less an excuse. But why should he give a damn? His wages were already a month late in arriving. By rights he owed this bastard nothing.

"I'm waiting," Caleb said through clenched teeth, fighting the urge to strike out at this slovenly figure.

"My name's Conrad. Galt is dead, attacked by a small band of renegade Indians months ago. The furs were stolen, the storehouse emptied, and this is all that's left. If you think I'm going into those Indian camps to make your bastard burghers rich and me dead, you have another think coming. The raid was long overdue and everyone knew it was coming. Those thieving Indians stole everything they could get their hands on. They emptied the storehouses, plundered—they even took two of the women!"

"Why?" Caleb shot out, remembering the good relations between red men and whites which had existed two years before.

"How the living hell should I know? Who knows why an Indian does anything? They're savages and don't think like humans," Conrad grumbled, his eyes avoiding Caleb's.

"I asked you why and I expect an answer!" Caleb grabbed Conrad by his shirt front and pulled him to his feet, staring down into the older man's eyes with contempt.

A new respect for Caleb dawned in Conrad. This was the first white man, besides the stray Jesuit priests who sometimes wandered through Saybrook on their way to the upper reaches of the Hudson Valley, who had ever admitted the Indians had a reason for committing their ruthless acts. Conrad could understand the prejudice against the Indians. The settlers were taking land which belonged to the tribes, pushing the Indian out, a subject which was defended with a heated self-righteousness but was nevertheless a cause for guilt. And, too, it wasn't easy to live under constant threat of attack. That was reason enough for the settlers to hate the red man. But Conrad himself had no such stake in the New World. Once his contract was completed with the Dutch West India Company, he would go home to Holland, hopefully richer than when he had left.

Now, with Caleb's inquiry as to why the Indians were prompted to pit themselves against the colonists, Conrad decided he deserved an answer. "On second thought, Captain van der Rhys, I'm going to tell you why the unrest exists between white and red. But you won't like the answer, and there's nothing that can be done about it. The Dutch West India Company is responsible." Conrad curled his lip in distaste and ran a hand through his sparse hair. "We, the pragmatic Dutch, with our 'Christian' approach to the aborigines. Bah! Lip service! The burghers of the Dutch West India Company are more interested in making money!"

As Caleb listened to Conrad's now mostly sober words, a colorful and true picture of the circumstances emerged.

At first arrival in the New World, the Dutch

company had established friendly relations with the Indians and managed to make its home base in the wonderful, deep harbor of Manhattan Island. Within a relatively short time the thriving colony of New Netherland and its capital, New Amsterdam, had become one of the most powerful footholds in the New World. This productive tranquility, however, was short-lived. Two years before, just after Caleb's last voyage to America, the incompetent Wouter Van Twiller had been replaced as governor of New Netherland and as regional head of the Company by a man named Willem Kiefft. Kiefft was a bigger thief and an even worse administrator than Van Twiller had been. The new governor's way of dealing with the Indians was to extort from them levies of corn, wampum and especially furs for the "protection" afforded by New Amsterdam.

"So you see why the Indians stole back the furs and emptied the granaries," Conrad concluded. "They stole to give the booty to the fat governor, Kiefft. I'm no Indian lover, but they have to live, too! It's extortion, pure and simple. Pay up or be decimated. That's the message our humble governor puts out."

Caleb shook his head, trying to absorb what Conrad was telling him, knowing that no matter how much rum the man had consumed, he was speaking the truth.

"The Indian traps his furs honestly, sells them to the Dutch West India Company and then has to turn over one hundred percent profits to Kiefft in New Amsterdam. Their women and children are hungry. I don't blame them for stealing, and that's why you see me here—drunk. I can't stand seeing another Indian come in here begging for food for his children. If I had any to give, by God, I'd give it! And to hell with your fancy burghers in Holland just waiting for their profits. Hand over my wages and the place is yours," Conrad said, hitching up his trousers. "And you're welcome to it!"

"On whose authority does Kiefft extort these levies?"

Conrad laughed. "How would I be knowing?" he sneered. "The likes of the governor don't see fit to confide in the likes of me. So if you'll just hand over my wages, I'll be departing your premises."

Caleb counted out the man's wages, his face a mottled mask of rage. The first order of the day would be to get a replacement for Conrad and then pay the governor a visit, an unexpected visit. Tomorrow, after sunup, he would find a horse and set out for a look at the governor's ledgers. It would be interesting to see how Willem Kiefft had prospered.

Caleb sat down on the wooden chair, propped his feet on the flimsy desk and then dropped them to the floor. He had seen a strongbox beneath the desk, full of papers. The Company's records, no doubt, for the trading post. He would take them back to the ship and go over them later. Now he had to think about what he had to do and how he was going to do it. He was one man, alone in a strange new world. The fact that he had been here when the trading post had first been established didn't alter the reality of the present situation.

During that trip he had spent his time wisely and to good advantage. He had established friendly relations with the chief of the Pequot tribe and smoked a pipe with him and his council members on the agreements between them. His relations had been so friendly, in fact, that on his departure the chief had offered him a gift of one of the young tribal maidens. Caleb had been hard pressed to decline the generous offer tactfully, and with tears streaming down Wildflower's face, he had sailed away with a brisk wave of his hand and a sly wink for the aging chief.

Now he had been told that the Pequots had rebelled and taken women hostages and stolen their own furs, furs meant for rich, elegant ladies in Europe. Something besides the levies must have stirred up the old chief. He had proclaimed that he was a peaceful man who only wanted to live out his days in his village and watch the young bucks grow to manhood. The men of his tribe were not warriors and were as peaceful as their chief.

When unrest settled in, everyone involved was threatened. Christ, what if the Indians decided to stage a war? Caleb mused. These settlers didn't know the first thing about fighting. They would be no match for the revenge-seeking Pequots. He shuddered when he remembered having heard that New Amsterdam matrons had used the severed heads of Indian men, women and children for a grisly game of kickball on the dusty streets. And the chief had remarked sadly, "Your governor laughed heartily. We did not go to war but turned our backs. Fence a dog or drive him into a corner, and sooner or later he will strike back." Those had been the only ominous words mentioned on the day Caleb had sailed back to Holland. Had that day come and gone? Were the Indians preparing for another attack, and would it be an all-out war against the ill-equipped settlers?

He groaned aloud at the thought of Bascom Stoneham wielding a weapon to ward off an Indian attack. Prayer wouldn't help Bascom if the Indians decided they wanted his scalp. Caleb seriously doubted that anything would help Bascom. But Bascom wasn't his worry any longer. The preacher would live here with his people and help build the church of his dreams. This was no time for Caleb to saddle himself with worrying about the good people settling this lush new land. The Dutch West India Company was of the utmost importance. The burghers had told Regan they expected and would accept nothing less than that New Netherland would attain the most powerful

311

position in the New World. Regan had agreed to their plan and sent Caleb to arrange matters. And Caleb had done what he had been told to do, and now everything was in a shambles.

First he would see the governor, and then he would go up the river to the Mystic fort of the Pequots and get the straight of it. Thoughts of renegade Indians with their deadly bows and arrows made him flinch. His hand went to his thick head of ebony hair and his mouth tightened. He was going in peace and would fly the white flag if necessary, along with the emblem of the Dutch West India Company. It was unfortunate he couldn't carry Kiefft's head on a pike to show his good faith. Kiefft had been installed as governor by the Dutch West India Company, but now, since Caleb's authority superseded Kiefft's, the governor's days were numbered as regional head of the Company in the New World.

Darkness enveloped Saybrook when Caleb closed the door behind him, the strongbox containing the piles of business papers riding on his shoulder. Great bonfires raged toward the sky, and women bustled about smaller cookfires, preparing the evening meal for their men.

From his position on the road Caleb could see Bascom leading his people toward the center compound, where the largest fire burned, for a prayer meeting before dinner. He frowned when he saw Sara walking behind her mother. A stab of guilt and remorse pierced him but was short-lived when he remembered that Sara's lies had most likely prompted Wren to go overboard.

Grief ripped through him. *Wren.* His loneliness was tangible and his sorrow weighed him down. How was he to live without her?

His feet directed him to the river and the jolly that would take him back to the ship, but his thoughts were centered on the last time he had been alone with Wren, when they had vowed their love to each other. How could she have believed Sara was carrying his child, regardless of what she had overheard? A flush of shame coursed through his veins. If he hadn't prided himself on being such a womanizer, and if he'd kept his hands to himself instead of on Sara, there would have been no recriminations. Guiltily, he recalled that even he had considered the possibility that he could have fathered Sara's child.

Choking back the taste of bitter gall, he broke through the clearing to the river. Wren was lost to him. He knew it in his head, but he would never accept it in his heart.

Chapter Twenty

Shortly after dawn, when only the earliest rising inhabitants of Saybrook were stirring, Caleb rowed ashore in the jolly and made his way around the back of the rustic Company building to the stables. One glance at the poorly fed, ill-kempt horses filled him with contempt for Conrad's inefficient handling of Company property.

After watering and feeding the three mounts, he finally chose one he thought would withstand the trip to New Amsterdam without mishap. After saddling his horse he led it from the stable and called to a small boy who was playing in the street. He reached in his pocket tossed the youth several coins and told him to curry the other two horses and lead them around the stable yard for exercise.

The boy, whose name was Sammy, was delighted with the coins and bobbed his head agreeably as he looked up at the tall man with the shiny boots. "I'll have to tell my mum, sir, and hand over the coins. Will that be all right?"

Caleb smiled. "It will be fine. Do a good job and you can do it every day. How old are you, son?"

"I'm seven, sir, but I'm big for my age and strong, too!" he said enthusiastically. "Could I be your ostler? My da' taught me everything about horses. And my family would be real pleased if I had the job. My da' has just about used up all our savings, and the store won't be giving out credit to the farmers. Governor's orders." The small face darkened with the injustice of the order and then brightened as he saw Caleb give his request deep thought.

"Governor's orders, is it? You're hired as long as you can do the job and your family gives permission. When I get back, we'll settle on a wage agreeable to your dad." So there was another matter to settle with the new governor. What right had he to claim that no credit be given to farmers?

Caleb sat tall in the saddle, urging his mount forward with a gentle hand and a firm pressure of his knees. He handled the animal with the same confident persuasion with which he mastered the *Sea Siren*. The steed surrendered to its rider, followed the well-traveled road out of Saybrook and turned west along the shoreline of the Sound.

Caleb squinted up at the sky and estimated he would find himself at the ferry landing well before dark. There he would take a ferryboat across the river to

Manhattan Island. As he rode his mind wandered away from the governor and dwelled more and more upon Wren. No matter how he tried to discipline his thoughts, they kept returning to her. At times he could see her so clearly in his mind's eye that he believed he could reach out and touch her.

Traveling along the tree-lined roads, he felt the salt breeze from the Sound freshen his cheeks. And always he thought of her, felt her amber-lit eyes following him, imagined he could hear the sound of her voice, low and husky as she called his name. Wren would always be with him wherever he journeyed. And always his heart would cry out for her and his arms would be empty without her, and for the rest of his life, and possibly beyond, he would know he had met his destiny and lost it.

Two hours before dusk found Caleb disembarking from the ferry which had taken him across the water to Manhattan Island. He thought of Peter Minuit, the first director general of New Netherland. Now that good man was building colonies in New Sweden, along the Delaware River to the southwest.

Regardless of his quarrel with Governor Kiefft's policies concerning the outposts and the Indians, Caleb could find no fault with his attentions to the burgeoning colony of New Amsterdam. The streets were in the process of being paved with the cobblestones many ships used for ballast, and the people looked well fed and prosperous. Construction had been accomplished at an alarming rate, and Caleb had to ask for directions to the Governor's Manse.

Skirting around the center of New Amsterdam to avoid the clutter of carriages and people, Caleb took a side road, prodding his nearly exhausted mount with his heels and encouraging it with his voice. Coming around a bend, Caleb saw a group of men riding toward him, accompanied by a two-wheeled cart into which was built a cage. He immediately recognized the yellow cockade of Dutch militiamen and was curious to see whom or what they had caged in the cart. As he passed them, he glanced into the cart and saw two Indians who were rail-thin from lack of food and had suffered a severe beating, no doubt from the hands of the militiamen.

"What've they done?" Caleb asked the leader of the party in an offhand manner, careful to keep any note of pity from his voice. He was aware of his own vulnerability, being alone on a back road with eleven or more men who were apparently proud of having captured the unfortunate Indians.

"Thieves is what they are!" came the fast reply, accompanied by a bitter, self-satisfied smile.

"We had reports of poaching and stealing from several farmers, and we caught the devils in the act!" another offered.

"What were they stealing?" Caleb asked.

"What else? Grain and food, and they were poaching the sheep and cattle. There was a band of 'em, and all got away except these two. We'll make a fine example of them, we will. When their friends see their heads on pikes, they'll begin to think twice about coming over here to do their dirty work."

Caleb again looked into the cage and was saddened by the apathetic expressions on the captives' faces. These red men were a far cry from the dignified, proud and noble Indians he was familiar with, and little wonder why. They were half starved and more than half dead from their beating.

"What's their tribe?" he asked, unable to distinguish any markings on them.

"Wappinger! And a fine bounty they'll bring."

"Wappinger! I've heard they were a friendly tribe."

"Maybe. But there's about a hundred of 'em stowed out on Staten Island, running away from marauding Mohawks. The governor don't care much about that, but canoeing over here and poaching is something else again. Indeed, these are the first we've captured, and we'll receive a nice purse for them, I can tell you that."

Rage against this sort of injustice filled Caleb, and he kneed his horse sharply and continued down the road, eager now to come face to face with Kiefft.

The long, tree-lined stone drive leading to the expansive Governor's Manse was well tended and landscaped. Politics must be paying well, Caleb told himself as his weary mount plodded up the drive at a slow pace. Huge tubs of flowers and evergreens dotted the wide veranda, and lanterns were strategically placed near the potted plants. Caleb knew it would be a magnificent sight at night. Whom did the governor welcome that he needed all these expensive trappings? The house and everything inside and out belonged to the Dutch West India Company. Things had certainly improved from the profits, just as he knew they had the moment he had opened the ledger he had found in Saybrook and poured over the spidery column of almost nonexistent figures.

Caleb tethered his horse and stomped to the front door. He smirked. Solid mahogany. Must have cost a king's ransom in this part of the world. He gave the silver knocker a vicious tug and stood back, waiting to be admitted.

He wasn't surprised when a liveried footman opened the door, making Caleb think for a moment he was back in England, where pomp and ceremony were a daily occurrence. "Captain Caleb van der Rhys to see Governor Kiefft," he said curtly.

"The governor retired early. His office in town would be happy to make an appointment for you, Captain. His lordship never sees anyone until after lunch." The footman's tone was haughty, and with the firm, no-nonsense hand of a practiced major-domo, he began to push Caleb out the door.

"Is that so?" Caleb snarled as he gathered the startled man's starched shirt front in one hand and lifted him off his feet, setting him down at the side of the door. "Now point out the governor's rooms and then go about your business. I come here representing the Dutch West India Company, and it will go hard on you if you don't do as you're told."

"I understand," the footman said, wiping his perspiring brow. "However, sir, the governor has . . . there is . . . the governor is a man of . . ."

"Lusty tastes and he has a whore in his bed," Caleb finished shortly. "Stand by so you can usher the lady out."

Caleb didn't bother to knock at the governor's bedroom door but thrust open the carved structure. The sight that met his eyes was so ludicrous he guffawed loudly. Twin gelatinous globes of alabaster flesh pumped furiously at something hidden from Caleb's eyes. The dual mountains quivered and then collapsed, accompanied by deep, guttural moans.

"I hope that is the end of it," Caleb laughed as he strode across the room and threw a cover over the fish-belly white flesh. He looked down at Willem Kiefft and hated him on sight. Bald, completely hairless, he reminded Caleb of an egg. The governor was without eyebrows or lashes, and his beady eyes glittered at the intrusion. His full, pouting mouth drew back, revealing tiny white teeth.

"Out!" The one word was a command aimed at the woman, who was already gathering her clothes together.

"Bellamy!" the governor shouted in outrage.

"If you're calling for your footman, save your breath. He has been informed who his employer is. Now, get your fat ass out of that bed before I do it for you. Put on some clothes and we'll talk. By the way, I am Captain van der Rhys, representing the Dutch West India Company."

Fear momentarily glassed the governor's eyes and then was replaced with arrogance. "Now, see here,

I'm the governor! Duly appointed! And that was my woman, and what right do you have to come barging in here?" His sensibilities returning, Kiefft assumed his usual bravado.

"By this right." Caleb tossed a scroll of parchment onto the bed. "You are correct about one thing, though. She was a woman. Somehow I would have thought a man of your position would be more discriminating than to employ the services of a common whore. And you are governor only as long as I wish. And I don't wish! So get the hell out of that bed. Now!" A dark crimson color stained Caleb's face, his mouth drew into a bitter, cruel line, and there was no denying the authority he exuded.

Kiefft reached for the parchment Caleb had tossed him and scanned the message. "I have not received a dismissal order from Holland. Until I do, I am the acting governor, and neither you nor any stiff, crackling paper is going to say otherwise."

"How much would you be willing to wager?" Caleb asked, reaching down and throwing back the coverlet. He moved slightly and pressed his knee into the man's groin. "That whore will never have to worry about being pounded to death again. Now, I want to know what's going on, and I want to know now."

The governor gasped for breath, his face tinged blue from the pain Caleb was inflicting.

"You're using up precious time and you're also turning blue. A fat man like you shouldn't take such chances with his health. Why is the warehouse empty? Where are the furs that were to be ready for me to take to England? If you try to lie, I'll kill you here and now."

"Take your knee . . . take it off and I'll tell you whatever you want to know," the governor croaked. Caleb eased the pressure somewhat but didn't remove his knee. The fat man gulped air and drew in a deep breath. "The goddamn warehouse is empty because the goddamn Indians stole the furs. Now, will you get the hell off me before you kill me?"

"Why did they steal the furs? The Pequots were a peaceful tribe when I was last here. Their chief is a man of honor and peace." ̄

"The old chief is dead. Sassacus is the chief now. He's no old man. He's a savage bastard, is what he is. He'd sooner cut out your tongue than look at you. He stole the furs."

"You aren't telling me why he stole them. I met Sassacus and I smoked the pipe with him and broke bread. If Sassacus has turned savage, then you made him that way. Tell me about the levy you fixed on his tribe."

The governor rolled his head. "A small matter to bring them into line. All they had to do was spend a few more hours trapping and they could come up with the furs. They want everything handed to them on a silver platter. That's what happens when you teach them our language and try to make them civilized. They're like mad dogs and they turn on you every chance they get. They're savages. They're not fit to polish my boots."

"What you mean is, they're too good to polish your boots. Were they good enough to lay that long, circular driveway and tend your lawns and flowers? What else are they good enough for? How do they work that off, you fat bastard?" Caleb gritted through clenched teeth.

"Someone had to do it!" Kiefft protested sharply, his heavy jowls quivering with tension. "For the pride of the Company! It's expected. While the Indians worked, they were fed. If extraordinary measures were needed to bring about their cooperation, then so be it!"

Caleb's lip curled into an ugly line, his distaste and contempt for Kiefft evident. "And a promise of food and a whip could insure their cooperation! Is that it?" he boomed. "Get up and get dressed. We've a long night ahead of us to discuss these 'savages,' as you call them. When I return to Holland, I want to be able to tell the burghers what an excellent choice they made in selecting you governor of New Netherland."

Kiefft bounded out of bed and ran to the adjacent dressing room in search of his clothes. He was frightened of van der Rhys, frightened of his authority and his contempt. A report from him to the right person in Holland would mean the end of his own governorship here in New Netherland. Kiefft knew he would have to watch his markers; if reform was necessary in this Dutch West India Company territory, it would behoove his own political career to see that he was the one who brought it about, instead of an upstart fresh from Holland in pursuit of grandeur and glory here in America.

Caleb sat down and looked around the room. It was decorated like a French brothel, a successful one at that. Rich burgundy draperies adorned the long windows, and heavy tapestries hung on the walls. A thick, tapestried carpet made him frown. The bedcovers were satin and luxurious, and he knew they whispered all night long to the naked bodies that cavorted between them. Gold goblets and a decanter of wine stood on a carved table next to the bed. Kiefft certainly didn't deny himself.

Caleb reached for the decanter and drank from it, swallowing deeply. He stretched out on a plum brocade chaise and stared at his booted feet. Mentally, he calculated his forthcoming discussion with Kiefft, knowing he could never turn the man's prejudice around but hoping he could somehow control his greed and subsequent mistreatment of the red man with threats of impeachment. Kiefft and men like him had stirred the cookpot situation between the colonists and the Indians into a boiling cauldron of discontent and fear.

Tomorrow he would see the other side of that fear.

He would ride north, past Saybrook, to the Pequot village on the shores of Mystic.

Governor Kiefft had given in to Caleb's demands too easily. The man should have fought to his last breath to retain what he had cheated to obtain. Instead, he had listened and nodded his head in agreement, promising to revise his methods of filling the Company's storehouses and administering justice to whites and red men alike. Something was afoot, Caleb knew it, and whatever it was, it boded ill for the Indian.

With a sinking feeling, Caleb admitted to himself that nothing he could say or do would turn the tide and prevent a confrontation between the Pequots and the settlers. At best, he could avert that disaster by going to see Sassacus and telling him of the governor's promised reform. He doubted that the Indian chief would listen to him, but he had to try. The Pequots were a small tribe, beset by problems from more aggressive and larger tribes—most specifically the Narragansetts. War with the settlers now would mean the complete annihilation of their people.

His conference with Kiefft had taken most of the night, and he had gotten only three hours of sleep in the governor's guest room before setting out to see Sassacus.

The nag which had carried him from Saybrook to New Amsterdam could never have made the return trip, and Kiefft had accommodated him with a russet stallion, complete with saddlebags brimming with food and drink. For this Caleb had been grateful, as it meant he would not have to stop in Saybrook overnight but could camp in the woods and arrive at the Pequot village well before noon the next day.

After spending a restful night in the woods, he rose early and continued his trek along the dense shoreline, his eyes watchful as the horse pounded the sandy terrain. From time to time he heard a bird call and knew that Sassacus's braves were warning their chief of a lone rider approaching.

The moment Caleb came within sight of the Indian fort, he reined in the horse and waited. He sat tall and straight, his dark hair falling low on his forehead. An Indian approached, his face inscrutable in the bright sunshine. Neither man said a word. Caleb allowed the stallion to trot behind the Indian at a slow pace, holding himself erect and proud.

The squaws and the children paid him no heed as they went about their tasks. One old man looked up from his pipe and went back to his dozing. A canvas flap was thrown back across the doorway of a small lodge, and Caleb dismounted and entered the dim room. A man sat cross-legged before a smoldering pile of ashes. He was dark-skinned and had bright, intelligent-looking eyes. His long black hair was coiled into a single thick braid hanging down his back, and his folded arms revealed rippling muscles.

"Welcome," Sassacus said, rising with one fluid motion. "How are you, Captain van der Rhys?" He spoke an almost perfect English.

Caleb held out his hand and the Indian grasped it firmly. Caleb caught his breath but made no move to withdraw his hand. The Indian smiled and nodded. "You've gained strength since we did this last."

Caleb laughed. "I'm two years older. Each year we gain strength." The Indian looked skeptical but accepted the statement. Both men sat down, Caleb deferring first to the Pequot chief.

"My people have watched the waters for many days now. I knew of your arrival in Saybrook." Sassacus eyed Caleb warily, to see if the honest, forthright man he had met two years ago was still present.

"I heard of the passing of your father, Sassacus. He was a great chief. Now you sit in his place, another great chief, and you look the part." Caleb grinned.

"If only it were so simple. Looking the part of a

great leader is not the deed done." The Indian smiled, showing square white teeth. "Many things have happened to our people. Many per—" He hesitated.

"Persecutions," Caleb volunteered.

"Many times the words do not come to my lips. White men talk many words. White men talk too much."

Caleb threw back his head and laughed. "Why talk when a grunt will do just as well?"

Sassacus looked sheepish. "My people think I am a god now that I know so many white man's words. I am pleased to see you, Caleb van der Rhys. My greetings to your honorable father."

"I'm here, Sassacus, to speak of the Dutch West India Company's business. I have just come from the home of the governor and bring his greetings. Also, I bring you word of his reform."

"Bah! It is too late for reform. The deed is done—empty promises. First we will eat. Perhaps lies and deceptions will sit better on a full belly."

When they had partaken of the simple food, Caleb leaned back on his haunches and studied Sassacus carefully. The chief's eyes shone brightly in the dimness of the hut, and the oil from his swarthy skin made him look as though he were perspiring freely. He too, was waiting, waiting for Caleb to say something, to make some sign that he knew there was more to discuss than the little that had transpired in the past hour. Each played a waiting game, each wanting the other to speak first to show there was no distrust in his heart.

Caleb took the initiative. "This could go on all day, Sassacus. I'm as good at waiting as you are. I learned much from you and your father on my last visit. No games, Sassacus. I can't help you if you won't confide in me."

The Indian nodded, his lean, hard body relaxed and he crossed his legs in front of him. As always when he spoke, Caleb was stunned by his clear tone and his almost perfect command of the English language. Without the braid and the buckskins, he might have passed for a scholar. "A crooked trader named Captain John Smith came to the settlement and aligned himself with your governor. He arrived about six months ago and set up trading posts along the Connecticut River. Your own people feared him almost as much as the Indians. I understand from some of your settlers that he drew a knife on the governor of Plymouth and spoke lewdly and contemptuously to the officials in the Massachusetts Bay. Everywhere he had been, he was charged with drunkenness and adultery. It's not a pretty story, Caleb, and one I do not relish telling you. As I said, your own people wished him dead. One night his ship was riding anchor at the mouth of the river, and a band of Indians, not my tribe, but Pequots nevertheless, swarmed aboard and massacred all hands, including Captain Smith. He had cheated us and raped our women. His cutthroats had raped small children and then left them to die. In truth, if it had been your people, would you have done less?" Caleb said nothing, motioning Sassacus to continue. "You've come at a volatile time, my friend. The Massachusetts Bay authorities have demanded that we surrender the murderers to English justice. We cannot do that," Sassacus stated firmly.

"My people are already at war with the Narragansetts and have made our peace with your Dutch brothers," he went on. "I will attend a council meeting of my people. We plan to agree to a treaty if it meets with our approval. They"—he made the word sound obscene—"want us to hand over the murderers along with a heavy indemnity. I will tell them that our people retaliated only because of the rape of our women and children and for the murder of our chief. They kidnaped him, Caleb, and after we paid the ransom, they sent us back his dead body. If this is your English justice, we want no part of it. I know that we must concede somewhere along the way, but we must have terms." Sassacus's voice was soft, almost humble, when he spoke again. "There are those who say the Dutch were responsible for the death of my father. In my heart," he said, placing a dark hand on his chest, "I know this is not true. Still, I cannot think for my people. I can only disagree and protest."

Caleb's own voice was soft when he spoke. "How soon will your people unite, and how soon will the war begin?"

Sassacus's smile was sad. "Ah, my friend, then you, too, see that war is inevitable. War solves nothing. Man must learn to talk and work out the problems. I was and am willing, but it is the white man who wants to pillage and plunder. The white man knows only war and greed." He leaned forward, his eyes imploring. "We were a peaceful people until the whites came here. We would have shared, but they took from us without asking. Would you allow what belongs to you to be taken by force without striking back? You can back a stray dog into a tree, but sooner or later he will find a way to free himself, and then he will become a wild renegade. I have hope for the meeting, but that's all it is—hope."

"What can I do? You haven't told me, Sassacus. I must know."

The Indian shrugged. He would say no more, and Caleb understood.

"Do you know what happened to all the furs?"

Again Sassacus shrugged. "Whose blood runs in your veins, Caleb van der Rhys?" the Indian asked harshly.

"You ask a foolish question for a wise chief. I agree with all that you've told me. Perhaps we can figure out a way to avert a war."

Sassacus laughed. "Now tell me who is being foolish. It is inevitable."

Caleb's face was troubled as he got to his feet. He

looked down at Sassacus, and his voice was stern when he spoke. "I see by your face and hear in your voice that you are hungry for war."

"Wise words spoken by a wise man," Sassacus said sarcastically. He rose in one fluid motion. "It is *your* people who will not listen! They will turn a deaf ear to you. For that I am sorry. There is something else you should know, Caleb van der Rhys. If it comes to war, and should we face each other in battle, I will fight to kill for what is mine. I want to be certain you understand what I am saying. If we meet in battle, one of us will die."

Caleb stared at the Indian for a long moment. "Understood, Sassacus."

The Pequot chief watched Caleb ride from the fort, his heart heavy in his chest. A pity all white men weren't like Caleb. He appreciated the relationship they had, one man to another, not white man and red man, but simply two men. Soon that would change, and it would be white man against red man, Caleb against Sassacus. Who would win? Sassacus's shoulders slumped. The white man always won. He squared his shoulders. Perhaps this time it would be different. Perhaps he could make it different.

He left the hut and walked to the clearing in the center of the fort. For a long time he stood there staring straight ahead of him. His bearing was proud as his eyes sought out one figure and then another. His jaw was grim, his high cheekbones lending a quality of arrogance to his face. Perhaps this time it would be different.

Chapter Twenty-one

While Malcolm Weatherly made his way downriver to confront Caleb and extort ransom for Wren, she was struggling to free herself from the ropes which bound her to a massive tree trunk. She cried in agony as the bands around her waist became tighter instead of loosening with her efforts. If she had to be grateful for one thing, it was the fact that Malcolm had secured her in a grassy nook close to the water's edge, shaded by goliath-like trees. If the sun were beating down on her, she wouldn't last the day. Already she was thirsty, and Malcolm hadn't left her any water. Her mouth was dry and her lips were cracked and sore, and the glimpses she caught of the fresh river water were maddening because it was unreachable.

She drifted between wakefulness and sleep, exhausted from her struggles. Suddenly, a crawling on the back of her leg awakened her. Images of horrible multi-eyed insects shot through her mind. Frantically she tried to reach the spot but could not bend forward. Revulsion constricted her chest and her spine stiffened as she became aware of a parade of red ants crawling up the front of her leg. She succeeded in brushing them off by rubbing her legs together, but they returned for the attack. A soundless scream leapt from her throat as the long, endless column of shiny red insects, their antennae quivering, inched farther up her leg, their grinding mandibles growing clearer and more horrible every moment.

While the inch-long red ants tormented Wren, Malcolm traveled downriver, his eye constantly searching out the terrain to the left and to the right. He sang loudly and lustily as his oars dipped and spurred the dinghy onward. He should be in sight of the settlement soon. An hour, perhaps less, for his business, and then back to the woods. He was pleased with himself that things were going according to plan.

He rowed contentedly. Soon he would be face to face with Aubrey Farrington and collecting his half of the jewels. He had decided long ago that he wouldn't wait for the gambler to sell them off in Martinique. He wanted them, and he wanted them now. He could sell them wherever and whenever he wanted. And with the ransom money from Caleb, he would have ready cash, which was the main thing for the time being. His world was slowly coming to rights.

There they were—the sails of the *Sea Siren*. Malcolm maneuvered the dinghy to the left and got as close to the shoreline as he could. He swiftly calculated the distance and decided it would be a small matter to cover it on foot. He worked slowly and efficiently to beach the dinghy and then broke off branches from the low-hanging trees to camouflage the small craft.

He reached the shore rapidly, his heart pounding in his chest. Only once did he falter even slightly, and that was when he saw a new grave with a stout wooden cross on it. He stepped over it lightly, paying it no heed, and continued his short journey.

Malcolm walked through the stockaded walls surrounding Saybrook, and after making certain no one had seen him, quickly skirted behind the buildings as he searched for the offices of the Dutch West India Company, where he knew he would find Caleb. He was well aware of his disfigurement and realized he could never go unnoticed for long among the people of the settlement. Hunkering down against the stable wall behind the Company's office, he waited, squinting his one good eye up at the sky. It was only an hour or so past noon. He was prepared to wait all day if necessary. He had already waited over two days in the woods, and one more day would be worth the end results.

His patience was well rewarded. Within the hour he spied Caleb handing his horse's reins to a small boy and heard him give the lad orders to curry and feed the animal.

Quickly, like a wraith, he stepped out into the open and called, "Van der Rhys!"

Caleb turned at the sound of his name and for a full moment didn't recognize Malcolm. The change in his appearance was so startling . . . so pitiful. "Weatherly!"

"Why do you look so surprised? After all, it was your ship that brought me here. Of course, Farrington helped, but if you want the truth, I was hiding in what you call your locker box. I'd appreciate it if you could tell me where I can find the old man."

Caleb was stunned. He shook his head to clear it. "You were on the *Siren* all the time, and none of us were aware of it?" He shook his head again as he recalled Aubrey's late-night comings and goings. He should have known better, or at least suspected. "Your friend, and mine, rests over there," Caleb said, pointing in the direction of the new grave.

"No lies, van der Rhys. Where's that old sinner? We have business to take care of."

"Ask anyone." Caleb waved his hand around the settlement. "Somebody on board ship clubbed him to death the night before we touched land. We buried him when we docked three nights ago."

It was Malcolm's turn to be stunned. "What about the jewels—where are they? That old fox wouldn't go to his death without leaving some clue to their whereabouts."

"So that was what he was trying to hide! You've just given me the answer to his death. I could find no reason why someone would kill a harmless old man. You'll have to look elsewhere for your jewels, Weatherly. Whoever killed Aubrey Farrington has them," Caleb lied smoothly.

Malcolm was beside himself with rage. "I don't believe a word you're saying. I think you have the jewels —in fact, I know you do. Well, I'll just show you how much good they're going to do you. Listen to me, van der Rhys, and listen carefully, for I have no intention of repeating myself. I want those jewels, all of them, plus fifty thousand pounds sterling for your sister, Wren."

Caleb's face went blank and his limbs froze. "Wren is dead," he choked. Then he remembered the misery Weatherly had caused her. "As dead as you're going to be!" He lunged at Malcolm, who deftly sidestepped the attack.

Malcolm laughed, a tinny cackle that nearly froze the blood in Caleb's veins. "She's not dead, but she might be soon. I have her safe and sound . . . for the time being. She was in the locker box with me. You look ill. Take some time, until noon tomorrow, to adjust yourself to the idea that your sister is alive and well . . . as I said, for the time being. You deliver the jewels and money to me tomorrow, and you can have her!"

"If you're lying to me, Weatherly, I'll carve you up in little pieces and feed you to the sharks!" Caleb's teeth were clenched as he advanced a step and then another. Malcolm held his ground, although his heart pumped rapidly.

"Keep your hands to yourself, van der Rhys. I said she's alive and well. I'll turn her over to you tomorrow on the noon hour, providing you meet my demands. Any tricks and she gets it." He made a rough motion of running his hand under his throat to show his intent.

Caleb understood the action all too well and also that the former dandy would do just as he threatened. For now, it would have to be his way, but tomorrow was another day and he would be off guard. Caleb remained still, knowing in his gut that if he made a move or said a word, he would kill the man standing before him. For now, he would have to wait. That Wren was alive was all he needed to know. There must be something to all that praying, after all.

Caleb squatted down on the dusty road, in full view of every one of the settlers. His legs were rubbery and his arms trembled. That damn mist was clouding his vision again. When he was in control of himself, he looked up. Malcolm Weatherly was gone, almost as if he had never appeared, had never said the words that made Caleb a whole man again. Tomorrow was another day.

Malcolm ran through the woods fronting the riverbank, hardly daring to breathe. So one small thing was not in his favor. Now, who could have killed the old man? The Dutchman was probably right—someone who wanted the jewels. Malcolm could almost see the jeweled collar in Caleb's hand tomorrow at noon. He had it—he wasn't fooling Malcolm. Somebody might have killed Farrington thinking he had it, only to realize after the bludgeoning that the jewels were in the Dutchman's safekeeping, probably hidden in the ship's safe. A child could have figured that out with one look at the sea captain's face. Tomorrow the jewels would be in his, Malcolm's, pocket.

Cautiously he made his way to the dinghy, stopping every few seconds to see if he was being followed. Satisfied that he wasn't, he removed the branches and carried them deeper into the woods, to be used again the following day.

As he rowed the boat swiftly upriver, he glanced at the sky. He was right on schedule. He would be back before sundown. He felt surprisingly good, good enough for a little play with Wren. Maybe this time she would welcome him. And if she didn't . . . If she knew what was good for her, she would, and he would make that clear before he untied her.

Wren was in agony; the clawing red ants were all over her, beneath her garments and in her hair, and one of them seemed to be caught in her thick eyelash. She let out a shrill scream and then fainted.

Two small girls playing in the woods stopped in their tracks as the high-pitched wail reached their ears. Hearing no further cries, they tiptoed on moccasined feet to where they thought the sound had come from. They held hands and giggled slightly at this small adventure. A wounded bird perhaps, and they would nurse it back to health. A small animal caught in a snare, and they would free it so it could return to its natural lair. The smaller of the two, who resembled a precocious squirrel with her bright, merry gaze, nudged the taller one and pushed her forward. At the sight that met their eyes they backed off quickly and held a whispered conversation with much pointing and stamping of feet. The smaller girl tilted her head to one side and advanced closer, taking in Wren's dark gown. She looked at her friend, and they both nodded. The taller girl ran down to the river and came back with her hands full of mud. Together they ripped off Wren's clothing and smeared her with mud from head to toe. They clucked their tongues in sympathy when they noticed the ants in her hair. Another brief conference and another trip to the river. Within minutes Wren resembled a grotesque river monster.

The two girls sat back on their haunches and surveyed their handiwork. They had a problem. Should they go back to the fort for help, or should they try to take the "creature" with them? Could they make a litter and carry her? How? Again they put their heads together and whispered. Within minutes they had removed every lace on their persons, from those on their moccasins to the ties that bound their hair. Fir branches were broken by the smaller child's standing on the taller one's shoulders and swinging from a branch till it collapsed. Then, they tied the branches together and dragged Wren's unprotesting body to the makeshift litter.

The mudpack seemed to be working; Wren had come to and was feeling better. She wanted to say something to the children but knew they wouldn't understand. She tried to thank them with her eyes and a gentle touch of her hand. She wanted to tell them to hurry, to get her out of here before Malcolm returned. Her gaze became pleading as she motioned to the rope they had removed.

It was the smaller child who understood first. Gesturing wildly and pointing to the rope, she danced around in agitation. Her companion nodded solemnly to show she, too, understood, and bent to help her friend with the litter. They made their way deep into the woods, certain it was the wisest route to follow. Every so often they stopped to smooth the pine needles and cover their tracks. Their eyes met from time to time and expressed their awareness that this was serious business, and it wasn't just the boys in the fort who knew how to do things. Chief Sassacus would be proud of them, proud because they had helped a white sister. If they were lucky, he might even give them a sweet to suck on. Already the little one's tongue was tasting the rock candy she adored.

By the time they reached their village, they were completely out of breath, their titian skin wet with perspiration. They dragged the litter the last few feet to a shady tree and stood back expectantly, each rubbing at the blisters on her hands from contact with the rough bark.

The women of the fort meandered over to the litter and stared down at Wren and then at the girls. Each began to babble, and much hand waving ensued. The girls looked at each other when one of the women said Sassacus was downriver. There would be no sweet. Disappointed at this news, they ran off to pick berries, their mouths watering.

The children had probably saved Wren's life, the women agreed. But who was she and where did she come from? Because there were no answers to their questions, they lifted Wren gently and took her into one of the lodges, where they worked industriously to wash off the dry mud and to apply fresh, wet compresses all over her body. Their eyes met when they saw the raw rope burns around her waist, but they said nothing. A white woman who had been tied up somewhere meant trouble. They placed Wren on a clean blanket and then sat down around her.

Wren relaxed within the protective circle of women. She knew they were Indians and that they meant her no harm. The children had managed to bring her here and now she was safe, away from Malcolm and his deranged ideas and threats. These women, with serene understanding in their eyes, would never harm her, she was convinced of that. Her eyes closed wearily and Caleb's face intruded into her dreams.

The women took turns sitting in the tight circle. They watched the girl with compassionate eyes as she slept fitfully, calling on someone named Caleb to help her. They rolled the strange name around on their tongues so that they would have it right when they told it to Chief Sassacus on his return.

Malcolm felt elated as he stepped from the dinghy. By this time tomorrow he would have the ransom and the jewels and would be well on his way to a new life here in the colonies. He would set himself up in grand style and have servants wait on him hand and foot. He would be a generous employer and would lavish his servants with good food and fine lodgings. Money, he thought, could buy anything.

It was too quiet. There should be leaves rustling, small animals running through the underbrush. Even the birds were silent. Something was wrong. His jubilant mood of moments ago disappeared. What could have gone wrong? He had left Wren securely tied. He had the dinghy and he had seen Caleb, and he knew for certain that he hadn't been followed.

Malcolm's good eye nearly popped from its socket when he saw Wren's gown lying on the ground, covered with a lacy pattern of holes made by the red bugs. His mind refused to accept the visual evidence before him. What is holy hell happened to Wren's dress? he asked himself. Did she free herself? She couldn't have, he answered silently. Someone must have helped her escape. Who? He looked around and felt the first rumblings of fear in his gut. This was Indian territory, after all.

He reached down and picked up the tattered dress, trying to imagine what had happened. It was too much for him to comprehend, and he slumped against the tree. All his fine dreams of mere moments ago were shattered. There would be no fine house and no servants. Not only would the ransom be lost to him, but the jewels would be lost as well. He had nothing. He had never had anything except a pocketful of dreams, and now that was gone, just like his handsome face. His eyes burned with tears and the injustice of it all. What was he going to do now? Without Wren, van der Rhys would kill him. Unless . . . he wiped at his eye with the back of his hand . . . unless he could come up with a plan to outwit van der Rhys and get the gems and the money first. How? He couldn't think. All he knew was that he didn't want to die. He couldn't die; his whole life was ahead of him. But, he sobbed silently, I can't have any kind of life without money and someone to take care of me. I don't even have a weapon to defend myself against Caleb. I have to think—to come up with some sort of plan. He prayed that wherever Wren was, it was far away from Caleb. And, he thought maliciously, whoever has her, I hope it's the Indians and that she's strung up somewhere for all the grief she's caused me. Whatever is happening to her, she deserves it.

Malcolm made himself a small campsite and settled down to sleep. Normally, under the present circumstances, he would have slept with one eye open. Now, thanks to that bitch Wren, he couldn't even do that. However, because he was so tired and needed to sleep, he would simply have to take his chances.

Dawn crept up on him and woke him with tenacious fingers. He stirred, trying to orient himself to his surroundings. He itched; God, how he itched. In the early light he could barely make out the red bugs that were crawling all over him. He screamed shrilly and ran down to the river and dunked himself, hoping to wash the crawling insects from his person. At least now he knew what had happened to Wren's gown. He had dreamed of that tattered garment all night long, wondering, imagining, what had made those holes. Now, if he could just figure out how she had gotten loose, he would feel less anxious.

He shivered in the cool air as he made his way back to the campsite. He had no blanket to warm

337

himself, and his flint was wet. He sat with his arms wrapped around his knees and cursed everything in sight. That didn't alter anything, but it made him feel better—until he started to think about how Caleb would react when he found Wren was gone. Malcolm had to find a way to wriggle out of taking Caleb to where Wren was supposed to be. He would just demand the ransom brazenly and give him directions; if the bastard didn't like it, that would be that. No ransom, no information. After all, one didn't divulge everything. Caleb was probably thinking the same thing—no Wren, no ransom. It would be a stalemate, and it would depend on how hungry Caleb was to see that bitch Wren. Malcolm would have to act convincingly; otherwise he would have to give up that scheme and start all over.

He settled himself as comfortably as he could and was soon asleep again, his dreams now invaded by a tall, dark-haired Dutchman who chased him from one end of the Saybrook settlement to the other, finally catching him and locking him in the locker box aboard the Sea Siren. He woke, drenched in his own sweat. There would be no more rest for him now. He rekindled the fire and sat shivering as he nibbled sparingly on the food he had brought with him from the ship.

Sometime during the morning hours his eye became glazed and his mouth curled down, making him look more grotesque than before. When he walked down to the water to wash himself, he stared at his reflection for a long time; for some reason the face that gazed back at him pleased him and at the same time frightened him.

His movements were slow, sure and precise as he readied the dinghy for his trip to Saybrook and Caleb. He stuffed the sack of provisions beneath the bench-like seat, placed the oar in its lock and then stood back to survey his campsite. The fire was nothing more than charred embers, with a few smoldering coals that hissed at him when he kicked out with his foot to scatter the ashes. He decided to leave Wren's gown as evidence that she had been here. Caleb would want proof, and the gown was as good as anything.

Malcolm sat down before the dying fire and stared morosely at the hole in the sole of his boot. Not only was there a hole in his boot, but there was also a hole in his stocking through which pink-gray skin glared up at him. A man shouldn't have holes in his boots, he thought. Caleb van der Rhys' boots flashed before him—soft black kid that cleaved to his legs and looked as though they had been made expressly for him. And what did *he* have? Boots and stockings with holes in them. All that would change as soon as possible. The first thing he would do with his money would be to find a bootmaker and order a dozen pairs just like Caleb's. And the second thing he would do would be to order seven pairs of stockings, one pair for each day of the week. If he had boots without holes and fresh stockings, no one would look at his face and see his disfigurement. He knew this was a flimsy rationalization, and he grimaced in despair. Why was he fooling himself? In his gut he realized that his life was over and van der Rhys had won. Even that bitch Wren had won by getting away from him. He was alone. All he had was a little food, the rags on his back and the dinghy. A man deserved to have more. A lone tear trickled down his cheek and he wiped at it angrily. His entire predicament was all Wren's fault. Women, he decided, were not even a necessary evil. Yet they made fools of men and caused wars, and a few besotted men had even lost empires because of them. A fierce, scorching hatred erupted in him and he spit vehemently. One way or another, they always won, always managed to come out on top and stand laughing at some man. Or was it just he? Women didn't laugh at Caleb van der Rhys; it was the other way around. The thought caused Malcolm such anguish that he rolled over on the ground and pounded his fists into the still-warm embers of the fire.

He had wasted enough precious time with his woolgathering. He had to begin his journey.

Chapter Twenty-two

When Caleb rowed away from the *Sea Siren* to meet Malcolm, his thoughts were only on Wren. God, he had thought he would never see her again or feel her in his arms. And now, within hours, he would have his dearest wish come true. There would be no more sleepless nights, no more recriminations. He would do, say, whatever she wanted as long as she loved him. He would lay down his life for her, if that was what she wanted. The thought stunned him and he grinned to himself. If that would make her happy, he would do it unflinchingly. God, how he had envied Regan with his love for Sirena! And now he had the same thing, the same wonderful thing that had made Regan a whole man. He would hold her in his arms and whisper all the right words in her ear. He would say them over and over until she begged him to stop. God, how he loved her! And how he hated Malcolm Weatherly! It had taken every ounce of his self-restraint not to have killed Malcolm on the spot when he told him about Wren. But Caleb hadn't, because if he had given in to his vicious impulses, he would never find Wren. If he had killed Malcolm, he would not be feeling what he was feeling now, this deep love for another person, the desire to give his life to Wren's happiness. After he had found her and held her in his arms, he would kill Weatherly and toss him to the sharks for fodder. He had never killed a man out of pure hate, but there was always a first time for everything.

Idly, his booted feet scuffing the dusty patch of ground he was now standing on, he watched Bascom Stoneham lead his flock to the outer perimeters of the settlement. His eyes narrowed slightly as he saw Bascom cup the elbow of a young girl in a possessive manner. His eyes narrowed again as he spotted a young man weaving his way through the ranks of the Puritans with a look of determination and purpose on his face, and not to attend a prayer meeting. Even from this distance Caleb knew the young man was interested only in the stiff-backed girl being escorted by the preacher. He recognized impending trouble when he saw it. But the Puritans were no longer his concern. His only concern now was for Wren. He turned his back on the parade of Puritans and watched both the shoreline and the woods for Malcolm to make his presence known. He was a patient man, and he would wait forever if in the end he could hold Wren in his arms. That terrible mist is covering my eyes again, he groaned inwardly. One of these days— He didn't finish the thought, because when his vision cleared, Malcolm was standing about ten feet away from him.

Caleb hadn't really expected Wren to be with him, but he had secretly hoped that maybe Malcolm would decide to turn her over at the point of exchange. He should have known better. The weasel wasn't going to give an inch, and from the looks of the stout club in his hand, Weatherly wasn't taking any chances on Caleb's emotions. Caleb wanted to kill him, to strangle him with his bare hands and hear him beg for the mercy that he would deny. At last he forced the words from between clenched teeth. "Where's Wren?"

Malcolm laughed, a shrill sound that sent the hackles on Caleb's neck to twanging. "First the ransom and the jewels. Now!" Malcolm demanded arrogantly as he waved the club in the air. "And no tricks, van der Rhys, or you'll never see her alive. Toss it here for me to see."

There was nothing for Caleb to do but toss to Malcolm the oilskin pouch he had hidden inside his shirt before leaving the ship. Malcolm laughed again as he stuffed the pouch inside his own shirt, satisfied that Caleb had kept his end of the bargain.

"All right, you bastard, you got what you wanted. Now, where's Wren? I'm warning you—if she's been harmed, I'll kill you." Caleb said this so softly, Malcolm had to strain to hear him.

"She's upriver. Ride the shoreline, and when you come to the bend with the cove and the sandbar, head to your right. That's where I made camp. Wren is tied to a tree, just waiting for you."

Caleb's heart turned over at the words. "Oh, no, we go together, and if you're lying, I'll kill you on the spot."

"I'd like to oblige you, van der Rhys, but I have other fish to fry. And this club I'm holding makes for the odds on my side. If you want your sister, you'll have to get her yourself, without any help from me. And if I were you, I'd get a move on, for the camp is infested with red ants that can eat a person alive." He added nonchalantly, "I wouldn't waste any time if I were you."

Dark sparks of fury shot from Caleb's eyes and Malcolm backed off, the club held out in front of him.

"It'll take more than that measly weapon to get

me," Caleb gritted as he reached out to grab it from Malcolm's shaking hand. They fought like animals, with Caleb having the advantage over the wiry Malcolm. Weatherly gouged and scratched, fighting like a woman, while Caleb struck out with his fist, letting it find its mark in Malcolm's good eye. He was momentarily taken off guard when Malcolm screamed shrilly in his ear. That moment was all Weatherly needed to race off into the woods and disappear from Caleb's sight.

Caleb leapt on his horse and dug his heels into the animal's flanks, enraged because he had to rely on Malcolm's word that Wren was alive and safe. But he had to believe that!

As Caleb's horse pounded the sandy riverbank, Malcolm raced wildly through the woods, going in circles in his blind panic. His vision was poor, and pain creased his head in spasms as he continued his erratic flight. Soon, he gasped to himself, I should be out of the woods and near the dinghy.

Exhausted, he fell to the ground and cried, the sounds like those of a whimpering child. He had to find a safe place where he could hide from Caleb. Caleb would kill him as soon as he found Wren gone. Pitiful mewing noises came from Malcolm's mouth as he wiped at his eye that was rapidly closing, almost obscuring what little vision he had left. Where was there a safe place in this Godforsaken land? He couldn't live in the woods like a wild animal. If he did that, he would never have his fine house and his servants. Wherever he went, Caleb would find him. He knew it, accepted it. Now he had to go on, to look for a place that would be free from Caleb's searching eyes. If Caleb did manage to find Wren and she was dead, the Dutchman would devote the rest of his life to hunting down Malcolm and then would kill him in slow, easy stages.

Malcolm curled himself into the fetal position and

rocked back and forth, his soft moans of anguish shattering the quiet of the forest. He didn't want to die; God, he didn't want to die. Safety, that was all he needed, and he needed it only until Caleb set sail. He sat upright, his spine straight, as a thought occurred to him. Once before he had been safely hidden from Caleb's eyes. True, Farrington had helped him then, but he could make his way back to the *Sea Siren* and hide in the locker box right under Caleb's unsuspecting nose. Van der Rhys would never think to look there. Malcolm would row out to the ship under cover of darkness and creep aboard. He sighed. This was the answer to all his problems, he was certain. Survival was all that mattered. His survival.

Caleb crouched low on the stallion's broad back, making it easier for the animal to race across the soggy terrain. He rode for what seemed like hours, every muscle, every nerve in his body strained to the breaking point. From time to time he shouted Wren's name to let her know he was coming. Each time his cry was more muffled and carried away on the brisk wind. Perspiration dripped down his back and drenched the horse.

His eye peeled for the sandbar, Caleb almost missed it with the wind stinging his face. He slid from the galloping steed and rolled over several times. Then he was on his feet, shouting Wren's name as he raced into the woods. In his heart he knew she wouldn't be there; it was his mind that refused to accept the thought. His broad shoulders heaved and then slumped as he bent down to pick up a black rag. He blinked at the lacy, cobwebby holes and at the dried blood that was caked to them. He ground his teeth together in a helpless fit of rage as he poked a finger through one of the holes. This couldn't be happening to him. No, it was impossible. To have come this far and then have the joy snatched away from him. It was like drowning and coming up for air one last time, only to get pulled back down by the undertow.

The thought that he refused entry into his mind surfaced, and he looked at it squarely. What if this were a devious trick and Wren weren't alive after all? What if she had really gone over the rail, as Sara had said she had? What if she had been dead all along, and this was just some rotten, macabre joke of Malcolm's seedy little mind? "Oh, God," Caleb moaned. She couldn't be dead. His mind and heart could not accept that now. She was here, somewhere. There was blood on the gown, Wren's blood. He had to believe it was her blood and that somewhere, some place, she was free of Malcolm and alive. He had to find her. He had to clear his mind of all the cobwebs so he could think logically.

Caleb sat down, his long legs crossed in front of him. He forced his lean body to relax and let his mind take over. He would go with his original idea that Wren had been here tied to a tree as Malcolm had said. She had either escaped or been freed by someone. That person hadn't been Malcolm; therefore, it had to be someone who inhabited this section of the country. Only the Indians lived here. Caleb had ridden over two hours, at a hard and fast pace, to arrive at the sandbar. Another hour and a half and he would be at the mouth of the Mystic River and Sassacus's fort. Other Indian tribes inhabited this area, not just the Pequots. Any tribe could have found her and taken her for reasons of its own. Gory tales of Indians' vengeance made him shudder when he thought about them, and he forced them from his mind, refusing to believe Wren was anything but alive and well. A negative attitude would get him nowhere.

She could be anywhere, and if he didn't have a plan of action, he would go in circles for days or even months. The forest was all-encompassing, dark and forbidden to those who didn't belong. The thought frightened him. He would appeal to Sassacus, who knew the forest intimately. Sassacus would help him. Caleb would promise whatever was necessary to secure the chief's help and would work the rest of his life to repay his debt to him. He had no other choice, and he knew in his gut that the red man would help him.

The rough-hewn stockade gates of the Mystic fort opened and Caleb rode into the compound. He reined in his horse, visible to all, and waited. He knew that no message would be sent to the chief, informing him of his arrival. Sassacus had probably been aware an hour ago that Caleb was heading in this direction. When he was ready, and when he thought Caleb had waited long enough, the chief would come out and welcome him.

Caleb waited patiently, his eyes circling the huts and coming to rest on a small group of chattering women. An eerie feeling crawled up his spine, and his forehead became dotted with perspiration. He was used to seeing the Indians behave in a solemn-faced manner, their great dark eyes staring unwaveringly before them. Something must have happened for the women to be chattering the way they were. And they weren't paying any attention to him, which was equally strange. He shrugged, but the eerie feeling remained.

Sassacus pushed aside the canvas flap covering the doorway of his lodge and came out to greet his guest. His eye followed Caleb's to the babbling women, and he shrugged as if to say, "Women!"

"A small matter, probably something to do with one of the children. It's of no importance—a little harsh to the ear, but of no concern. I am pleased to see you again so soon, Captain."

"And I am pleased to see you, Sassacus," Caleb said, clasping the Indian's wrist in both his hands. "We must talk and then I must go back downriver.

But first I need your help." Once inside the chief's quarters, he explained about Wren and how he had found her gone from the woods.

Sassacus nodded. "We will help you. But only when it becomes light at dawn. One Indian tracking another Indian in the dark is a foolish waste of time. Each of us learned from our fathers how to hide tracks. The daylight hours will give us a small advantage. My men will set out at first light. I see this woman means much to you—here." He placed his hand over his heart.

"She is my heart," Caleb said simply, and smiled.

Sassacus returned the smile. "I understand. Now, tell me, what is the other thing that brings you here?"

"What have your chiefs decided? When will you start the war? You notice I said *when*, not if. I will go once more to the authorities and plead with them. More than that I cannot do. I sail back to England and Holland shortly."

Sassacus motioned for Caleb to follow him outside. He pointed toward the rising moon. "You understand, Caleb?"

Caleb felt a great sadness envelop him as he stared at the orange ball in the sky. "I understand. Before another full moon the war will have begun."

Sassacus nodded and his shoulders slumped. "By that time, my friend, you will be halfway to your homeland. We will not see each other again in this life. In the next one, perhaps we will stand side by side and hunt and fish like the brothers we are. I must do what is right for my people, just as you must do what is right for yours. We both understand this. You are my friend and I am yours. Nothing—war, man, Indian or white—can change that."

There were no words to say, and if there were, Caleb could not have uttered them for the knot that was choking him. Instead, he placed his arm around the Indian's shoulder and went back with him into the lodge.

Sassacus smiled. "We will eat and drink, and you will tell me of this woman who has captured your heart and I will lie to you and tell you all the women in the village want me as their man." At the concerned look on Caleb's face, Sassacus added, "You must not pity me. At some distant time, if you want, grieve for me and my people. If just one white man grieves for one red man, then we have made progress. It will be up to the others who follow me to continue where we have left off. Is that not so, Caleb van der Rhys?"

"That is so, Sassacus."

Wren woke, disoriented in the dimness of the hut. She didn't move, but her eyes took in the squaws and their watchful attitude. A feeling of incredible loss swept over her. What had she lost? Certainly not Malcolm. Tears sprang to her eyes as she remembered the name falling from her lips when she had surrendered to sleep. Caleb. Had something happened to Caleb? Why did she feel this way? She had to get up, move, do something.

Two of the Indian women, sensing her intention, gently pushed her back onto the blanket with a motion for her to lie still. Wren obeyed. She slept again, her arms folded across her chest. How empty they felt. Arms were meant to hold someone. "Caleb," she cried aloud heartbrokenly.

The women looked at one another and again repeated the strange name—Ca-leb. Soon Chief Sassacus would make his rounds of the fort, and then they would tell him of the strange name and how they came to have the white woman in their hut.

Sassacus walked around the compound as it began to come alive for the start of a new day. How he loved these quiet, gentle people who were entrusted to his care. He prayed that he would always have the wisdom to do the right thing where they were concerned. And if he couldn't do the right thing, he prayed that his people would forgive him.

As he neared the squaws' lodge, he waited expectantly for the women to bid him entrance. There was something they wanted him to see. A treat of some sort. His eyes widened when he saw a white woman lying on a blanket and gazing up at him with bright amber eyes. He had to clap his hands to quiet the women as they all babbled at once, pointing to Wren and then to the children and always ending with the word "Ca-leb."

Wren moistened dry lips and looked up at the tall chief. "I think they are trying to tell you that I have been calling that name in my sleep. I am Wren van der Rhys. I sailed with Captain van der Rhys from England and was kidnaped by someone who hoped for a ransom." A note of hysteria crept into her voice as she gazed at the Indian. "Where am I? What is this place?"

Sassacus dropped to his knees, stunned. "You are a van der Rhys woman?" he asked incredulously. "Caleb and I are old friends. I am Sassacus, the chief of my people. He was here last night and we talked for many hours. I did not know of your presence here." He shrugged. "My people do not always see fit to tell me all things immediately. I cannot chastise them, for I see that they have taken excellent care of you."

Wren smiled. "Yes, your people must have taken very good care of me, for I feel much better. I am glad you are Caleb's friend. Tell me, do you know where he is?"

Sassacus smiled. "I see much love in your eyes for him. I will have my men take you to him soon. You will be returned to your people. We wish you no harm, you must believe that."

"I do believe that, and I wish to thank you and especially the children who brought me here. Is there something I can do, some way I can repay you for your help?"

"Seeing you back with your people will be payment enough. Caleb is my friend, and you will be my friend. Now, you must allow the women to remove these compresses and clean you up. They will bring food and you will eat. When you have rested and are able to travel, you will be on your way to your people." He smiled again, a dazzling smile of happiness because he would be able to do something for his friend Caleb.

Chapter Twenty-three

Caleb rode into Saybrook and handed over the reins of the stallion to the young boy, Sammy. He was tired and discouraged. There was a deep ache within him, an emptiness that only Wren could fill. To have come so close to finding her and to lose her again! Damn that Weatherly! The first order of the day would be to find him and wring the truth out of him.

He looked around the bustling settlement and was impressed by the amount of activity at this early hour. Sounds of furious hammering pounded in his ears. Bascom's congregation was hard at work building its new homes with the aid of the present settlers. Before long, there would be a hundred new houses. Progress had already been accomplished on the construction of the new church. The skeleton was up and men were busy nailing planks to the timbers.

Caleb slouched against a stout oak tree and watched the proceedings as the men worked in companionable silence. Companionable, that is, until Bascom arrived on the scene, prayer book in hand. He shouted to be heard over the noise of the hammers and waited for the men to acknowledge him. The workers held their tools loosely in their hands, and at the exchange of words that passed between Bascom and them, Caleb almost guffawed aloud.

"It's time for a prayer meeting. Lay down your hammers and join me in asking the Lord for forgiveness for our sins and to help us see the light of His ways. My flock waits over there," Bascom said, pointing a bony hand.

"We can't rightly be attending your meeting," a red-faced, burly man protested. "We have a goal set for us each day, and until it's met, we have to keep on with the building. We could do with a few more hands. How about yourself, Preacher?" he sneered.

"Prayer and forgiveness are more important than work, even if that work is building a house of the Lord," Bascom declared virtuously.

"You won't be thinking like that if those redskins come riding in here, Preacher," the man shouted. "We work from sunup till the moon is directly overhead. We do our praying on Sundays." He motioned the workers to resume their tasks and lifted his own hammer to bang in a nail.

"One can never set aside just one day for the Lord. Every day is for the Lord. That's something I'll have to teach you, and teach you now. There must be no dissension among us now that I've arrived." Bascom drew himself up to his full height. "I am the Lord's messenger."

One of the settlers grinned at another and muttered, "Then deliver your message some place else." He banged a nail with undue emphasis to make his point.

Rather than lose face by continuing an already lost argument, Bascom turned angrily away from the area.

"The Lord wasn't using all His wits when He sent this preacher to us," the burly man said to a worker near him. They laughed heartily, the sound reaching Bascom's ears as he strode off. He knew they were laughing at him and mocking him. His thin lips tightened. He'd call down the wrath of God on the lot of them for ridiculing him! Things hadn't gone right ever since Lydia had walked out on him. Each day he could see a look of speculation on the faces of his flock. If a man couldn't control his own wife, how could he minister to and aid his own people? And dotty Sara certainly wasn't helping his image. Today he planned to ostracize her in front of his congregation. Unmarried women who found themselves with child had to be punished for their sins. He would see that she was punished severely.

The sun was already low in the west when Wren and her small entourage of Pequot braves followed the trail south through the dense Connecticut woods to the Old Saybrook settlement. The late June weather held a warm promise for the summer about to emerge upon the land. Songbirds were singing their last song before roosting at dusk, and a gentle breeze wafted up from the Sound. Wren's heart sang with happiness at the thought of being reunited with her people, and she was grateful for the superb care the Pequot women had given her. She still bore nasty welts from the rope Malcolm had used to bind her, but the minuscule ruddy insect bites had all but disappeared because of the cooling mudpacks the Indians had administered.

Because of the hostilities between the colonists and the Indians, the braves indicated to Wren that it was time to leave her, here by a small stream that fed into the river. They would go on alone to find either Captain van der Rhys or his first mate, Peter, and alert them to her whereabouts. One brave, noting the concern on her face, motioned to the sky and pointed at the sun, dipping his arm slightly. She understood that this undertaking would be accomplished before dark.

Alone in the lengthening shadows, Wren rested alongside the stream, delighting in the reflection of the sun's reds and golds upon the water. The trek along the trail had been difficult, and she had sensed the Indians' eagerness to complete their task and immediately return to their camp. The woods offered no safety these days to a small band of red men who might encounter a hunting party of white men. Before Wren had left Sassacus's fort, one of the squaws had offered her a beautifully stitched buckskin dress, complete with intricate beadwork and fringes along the hemline. Her long dark hair had been bound with rawhide thongs atop her head to bare her neck to any cool breeze. But the day had been hot and the trail dusty, and Wren looked longingly at the cool water rushing past her.

Impulsively, she stood up and stripped off her dress and moccasins, stepped forward and tested the water with her toe. Wishing for a bar of perfumed soap, she waded into the stream and found that at its deepest level it was waist-high. As she submerged herself, she was uncertain if she trembled from the cool water or from the prospect of seeing Caleb again. Always Caleb. He had been uppermost in her mind throughout the trek back to Saybrook. She had no idea what his reaction to her might be. The last she had known about him before being trapped in the locker box with Malcolm was that Sara had claimed he was the father of her child. Knowing what an honorable man Caleb was, Wren was certain he had married Sara by now.

A sob caught in Wren's throat, but she was determined not to cry. She was a little girl no longer. She was a woman. Perhaps if she had behaved like a woman, had shown Caleb how much she loved him, instead of letting her fears override her passions . . . She willed her mind to come to a halt, to accept things the way they were, not the way she wished they could be. Yet she couldn't discipline her memories. Caleb's face swam before her time and time again . . . his night-dark eyes sweeping over her, warming her skin with an unseen flame, letting her know she was beautiful and desirable . . . his mouth taking possession of her, his strong, white teeth nibbling at her lower lip in tender, teasing touches . . . his arms, hard and powerful, capable of crushing her and yet so tender, so gentle and persuasive. She remembered the feel of his thick thatch of hair beneath her fingers, the way his lean, steel-hard thighs had pressed against her legs, making her weak-kneed and helpless. She heard the sound of his voice, confident and commanding when giving orders to his crew, soft and murmuring when he whispered love words into her ears. The crinkles of humor at the corners of his eyes, the almost invisible little scar near his upper lip . . . everything . . . everything . . . was Caleb.

Wren lifted her eyes and saw him standing there. At first she thought he was a figment of her imagination, so great was her desire to see him. He stood tall, feet planted apart, arms folded akimbo across his chest. He was still, as still as the giant oak behind him; only his eyes were alive . . . alive with the joy of seeing her. Slowly he stretched out an arm, extending it toward her, reaching out for her. All doubts left her; all answers were there to be seen in his eyes.

As though in a dream, she floated toward him. Oblivious of her nakedness, untouched by the breeze that chilled her wet skin and ruffled her hair, she emerged from the stream, arms extended, her heart in her eyes.

She was in his arms, holding him, being held, knowing her world had come right again, finding her answers in his eyes, on his lips.

Caleb was speechless with a happiness so deep and wondrous, it filled his soul and throbbed through his veins. She was real, she was here, in his arms, and he would never let her go.

Two long tresses trailed down from her tumbled hair, framing her lovely face. Her skin shone golden in the last rays of the sun, making her body appear as though it had been carved from copper. He held her close to him, pressing his hands possessively against her hips.

Lightheaded, delirious with joy, her legs trembling beneath her, she clung to him for support and felt herself being lowered to the shady bank, knowing he was beside her, wrapping her in his arms, cherishing the feel of her and the love he offered.

She offered her lips and possessed his in return. She offered her body and enslaved his passions. A hundred times his lips touched hers, seeking, finding, caressing. A thousand times his hands stroked her; still he could not satisfy his desire for her. She intoxicated him with her beauty: the elegant length of her legs, the clear curve of her thighs, the sleekness of her haunches, the provocative appeal of her breasts. It was toward these visual signs of her beauty that he directed the ardor of his caresses and kisses.

Wren thrilled beneath his touch and turned herself voluptuously in his arms, encouraging him to voyage again with his lips along her supple thighs, allowing him access to the threshold of her sensuality, maddening him with her responses, inspiring his caresses.

With closed eyes and his name upon her lips, he led her into the kingdom of love.

The night air was warm and soft. When Wren awakened, her first thought was of Caleb. For an instant she thought she had only dreamed he had come to her, loved her. She realized she was alone, her naked body covered by his shirt. Thinking they had been separated again, she gave a frightened start and sat up. The first stars of evening twinkled in the darkening sky.

A splash from the stream attracted her attention; a plume of white shot up as Caleb threw the water over his body. Wren was mesmerized by the sight of him. The water swirled about his hips, revealing to her view the hardness of his chest, his well-muscled arms, the strong column of his neck, the proud set of his head. Droplets glistened off his skin like jewels, his panther-dark hair tumbling over his brow.

She rose, casting aside his shirt, and waded into the stream, oblivious of the chill, knowing only that she had to be near him, to feel his arms encircle her once again.

Around them there was no movement save for the flow of the stream and the scud of distant clouds. A night bird issued a song that strummed through their veins and pounded at their pulses, reawakening their desires. She stood before him, an arm's reach away, and faced him proudly, shoulders back, head erect. "You understand. I have no regrets." Her voice was soft, a whisper in the night. "Not a single action do I regret. I surrendered myself to your embraces, responded to your caresses. I know no regret." Her eyes burned with unspoken questions.

"I sensed in you a hesitation, a withdrawal. No matter how slight, it was there." His voice was deep and husky with emotion. His mind whirled with arguments and approved of the consideration he had given to her fears; his imagination summoned up visions of Wren's total surrender to him, to his love for her.

She lowered her eyes. "You know me well. You know me through and through. There's not an inch of my body whose response to your touch you do not know. But what do I know of you?" Her words were less than a whisper.

He reached for her hand, drawing her closer, guiding her hand to him and laying it upon his chest. She placed her head on his shoulder with a movement already familiar and one that he loved. Her hand, lightly touching his chest, trembled slightly on coming in contact with his skin. Then, in a slow and delicate progression, her fingers slid along his body, awakening in him a tidal wave of desire that rippled down to his aching loins.

He caught her up in his arms and carried her to the mossy bank, laying her gently upon their discarded clothing and coming to rest beside her. The moon was in his eyes, the stars in hers. With tender advances she learned the mysteries of his body and became the mistress of his soul.

Wren, his enchantress, summoned his passions and invoked his love. Each sensual caress that she learned from him, she turned about and practiced upon him, captivating him, enslaving him. A cry broke from his lips, a sound of passion and joy, and the cry became her name. *Wren.*

At daybreak Caleb waited impatiently for Sammy to saddle his horse. His thoughts were on the coming day, and when he spoke to Wren, Lydia and Peter, his tone was curt, almost abrasive. "Stay within the confines of the settlement. There's no telling when I'll come back. See about setting in ship's stores. If and when the situation between the Pequots and the colonists comes to a head, I want us to be well out to sea." His dark glance rested on Wren's upturned face, his meaning clear. He wanted no harm to come to her. Now that he had found her again, he wanted to keep her near him, always.

As Lydia and Wren walked off arm in arm, Caleb motioned Peter aside. "Weatherly is still lurking about. I know it as well as I know my name. He can't live in the woods forever without coming into Saybrook at some point. That can only mean trouble for all of us, especially for Wren. Keep a sharp eye out. I'm placing both women in your hands. Don't fail me, Peter."

"Aye, Captain. And we'll see about setting in ship's stores as well as rounding up the crew. If you see any of the louts hanging about New Amsterdam while you're there, be sure to tell them to high-tail it back to the ship before their scalps are on a redskin's belt."

Caleb took a last look in the direction that Wren and Lydia had taken. He ached to see her face again and hold her in his arms. Determinedly, he mounted, turned his steed in the direction of New Amsterdam and headed out of the settlement. What he hoped to accomplish by confronting Kiefft one last time was based more on elusive dream than on tangible reality. Sassacus had meant every word he had said, and war was inevitable. Were the colonists prepared? Would they be a match for the Indians with their knowledge of the woods and their deadly bows and arrows and stealthy attacks in the middle of the night? He shuddered to think of what an Indian rampage could do to the young town of Saybrook. For that reason alone, he wanted to take Wren and his crew as far away as possible. He had lost Farrington and had come so close to losing Wren that he couldn't chance it again.

While Caleb continued his journey, Wren and Lydia spoke with the women in the settlement and listened intently as one of them gave directions to a thriving berry field. Lydia's eyes sparkled as she made plans to bake pies for that evening's dinner and make preserves for the ship's galley.

"If we pick the berries, will you give us flour?" Wren asked the smiling woman. An agreement was made, and Wren herded Lydia in front of her.

As they walked down a dusty road, Lydia talked all the while about pie baking and said the secret lay in lemon and butter. She fretted that here there would be no lemon for her pies, and was busily improvising a replacement when Wren placed a hand on her arm and forced her to stop in the middle of the road. "Look," she whispered.

Lydia drew in her breath at the sight of her husband leading Sara into the center of a circle of people. Tears stung Wren's eyes on seeing Sara's unkempt look, her hair in wild disarray, her gown torn and tattered. Sara raised an arm to cover her face, either in shame or from fear.

"What's he going to do?" Wren hissed, fear for Sara alive in her face.

"Oh, no," Lydia moaned. "He's going to disown her as a sister, and then he'll make his parents come forward and do the same thing. He'll announce to all the people what she's done and how God is punishing her. Oh, Wren, we can't let him do that to Sara. She deserves better. I know," she said quickly, seeing the tight look on Wren's face, "what Sara did to you, but that's over and done with, and because of that you have Caleb. Always remember that because of Sara you have Caleb. And she no longer has the full mind she once had. You have only to look in her eyes and see the madness that rests there. My pity is for the child she carries."

"What will happen to her?" Wren asked as she glanced around to see if even one person would intervene in Sara's behalf. No one stepped forward.

"What would you do if a messenger of the Lord stood before you and said he had the answer to Sara's salvation? It's simple, really: Bascom will banish her. He'll take her by the hand and lead her from the circle, and from that moment on, she will belong to no one. She will have to forage for food like a wild animal, and she'll learn to live like one. According to Bascom, that is God's punishment. Sara will go completely mad and eventually die. He did this once before to a poor old soul who had told him she had no more coins to give the Lord. Bascom said she was giving her money to the devil and visiting a local tavern. She eventually threw herself into the river. Bascom prayed for her soul."

"My God!" Wren exploded. She looked at Lydia and grinned. "Do we wait for him to start his rantings and ravings, or do we snatch her out of that damnable circle here and now?"

"I'll agree to anything if it gets us out of Bascom's sight. Now!" Lydia declared firmly, her head high.

"Will he try to stop us? Perhaps we should arm ourselves with some sort of weapon. Here," Wren said, picking up two stout sticks. "If he makes one false move, club him."

"Of course he'll try to stop us. This is a big moment for Bascom. It isn't every day that a messenger of the Lord gets to ostracize his very own sister!" Lydia snatched one of the sticks from Wren, and before Wren could gather her wits, Lydia had marched ahead, waving the makeshift weapon in front of her. Wren had to run to catch up to her. Together they elbowed their way through the tight circle of praying men and women.

Bascom read their intent the moment he spotted the sticks clutched in their hands. "You're not welcome here," he said harshly, advancing to the center of the circle to stand next to Sara whose manner was docile, as though she were a child waiting to be punished for some trifling, mischievous act.

"As if I care what you think, Bascom Stoneham!"

Wren scoffed disdainfully, raising the stick over her head. "We're taking Sara with us. We'll take care of her!"

"Oh, no, you won't! Sinners, both of you! Do you think I would trust my sister to two sinners?" he screamed in outrage as Lydia raised her stick, too.

"The only sinner around here is you for what you're planning to do to your own flesh and blood. If you were truly a messenger of the Lord, you would forgive her, not turn her out to live like an animal in the forest. You're the sinner, Bascom!" Wren shouted to be heard over the mutterings of his flock. "Sara goes with us!"

"Sara stays!"

Wren and Lydia lashed out at the same moment, one cracking Bascom on the head, the other jabbing him in his midsection. He fell on the ground, dazed. Wren reached out to grasp Sara, as did Lydia, before the confused Puritans could take action.

"My God," Lydia wailed, "she won't move!"

"Then drag her, but get her out of here!" Wren groaned as she bent to pick up her stick to ward off any possible attack from Bascom's followers.

Bascom's followers, however, merely stood there, stunned, their mouths agape. Wren grabbed Sara by the arm, and she and Lydia managed to drag the girl from the circle of speechless onlookers.

"Damnation, Sara, if you don't pick up your feet, I'm going to leave you here!" Wren stopped a moment and tilted Sara's head upward. There was no sign of awareness in her eyes. "You were right, Lydia. She doesn't even know what's happening. Hurry, before that ranting, raving bastard decides to come after us. I can barely understand how you ever married that man and lived with him and still were able to keep all the brains God gave you," she scolded as they dragged a limp Sara down the dusty road and out of sight.

"We have to rest, Wren. Sara's a dead weight. He won't come after us. I'm sure. And if I'm not mistaken, this is something else that will give Bascom's flock pause about the merits of its spiritual leader."

Panting and struggling, they managed to prop Sara against a gnarled old oak tree. The moment they released their hold on her, she slid to the ground. Wren grimaced but made no move to lift her. "I'm trying to be charitable, Lydia, I really am, but I don't have the strength to get her back on her feet. What in the name of God are we going to do with her? Don't even suggest taking her back to Caleb's ship. He would kill both of us and ask questions later. He's had all he's going to take from Bascom and his relatives."

"Sit down, we have to think," Lydia mumbled. After several minutes of silence, she said, "Maybe the Indians will take her."

"If that's the best idea you can come up with, you better stop thinking," Wren grumbled.

"What *are* we going to do with her? If we can't take her back to the ship, then there's nothing we can do. This isn't England, Wren. There is no housing here unless you build it yourself. Somehow, I can't see either of us taking on *that* task. And Sara needs care and constant looking after. For now, we can both do that or take turns, but what will happen when it's time to sail?"

"Maybe your idea of the Indians wasn't so bad after all. A hut is a lot easier to build than a house. All we really need is some sort of shelter that will protect her from the elements. Surely there must be some kind soul who would take pity on her and let her live within the confines of this settlement," Wren said hopefully.

"Don't count on it. These people are a strange lot. They don't understand that Sara is mind-sick. They fear things like this and say it's devil's work. Whatever we do, we have to do it ourselves. I know in my heart it won't be long before Bascom disgraces himself." Lydia paused. "I know his appetites for young girls. Saybrook is too small to contain that kind of secret. As soon as he's out on his ear, I *know* Sara's parents will come to her rescue. If only we could find someone to care for her until then. Do you recall seeing that old Indian woman tending a fire when we started out earlier?"

Wren nodded. "She looked as if she was mixing something in a pot. Come to think of it, what's an Indian doing here if all these people are afraid of them? A deal!" she cried excitedly. "Maybe we could lure her away to care for Sara. We could give her all those gems that we won from Farrington. Indians love trinkets."

"But Caleb was going to return them anonymously to the King," Lydia fretted.

"The King doesn't need them. His neck is fat enough already," Wren sniffed. "Besides, I won those gems fair and square in a game of cards. Caleb has no right to make decisions about my property."

"But you gave them to me and I gave them to Caleb for safekeeping," Lydia said dejectedly.

"Then we'll just have to steal them back. Where did he put them?"

"In a strongbox in his cabin," Lydia answered.

"You stay here with Sara, and I'll go back to the ship and get the stones. If I find Peter along the way, I'll send him to you. Don't let Sara out of your sight. See if you can't get her down to the river and give her a good dunking; she smells."

"Does this mean we aren't going berry picking and won't have any pies for dessert?"

"Perhaps the children will pick them for us if we give them a stone or two. All children like pretties. Or I could give them one of the playing cards with the pictures on them." She jumped to her feet and scrambled off.

"Oh, God," Lydia groaned as she watched Wren disappear around the bend. She shrugged. Somehow or other, she knew they wouldn't have to pick the berries or bake the pies. Somewhere in the settlement there was a person who was just waiting for Wren to make him a target for her conniving ways. Lydia could taste the pie already, even though there wouldn't be any lemon juice to add the finishing touches.

On her walk through the small settlement Wren stopped from time to time, carrying on low-voiced conversations and waving her arms for emphasis. Lydia would have her pies.

Back on board the ship, she hurried to Caleb's quarters and searched out his strongbox. With a steady hand she dexterously worked a hairpin into the lock, and soon the pouch of gems was in her hand. Better hers and the old Indian woman's than the King of England's. He had enough jewels and would never miss these.

An hour later she was dragging an unwilling Indian woman by the arm to where Sara sat propped up. It looked as though Sara hadn't moved since Wren had left. Lydia verified this wearily.

"Now comes the hard part," Wren said. "We have to communicate to this woman that we need a shelter and want her to take care of Sara. How are we going to explain that Sara is . . . is . . . isn't right in the head?"

"She already knows," Lydia grimaced as the Indian squatted down and peered at Sara with bright shoe-button eyes. The woman tapped her head and then shook it vigorously. Lydia grimaced again. "I think that means she's not interested."

"I think you're right, Lydia. But we have to convince her that the most important thing in the world to her is taking care of Sara. Maybe if we tell her about the baby, she'll feel differently."

"She'll feel differently, all right," Lydia said sourly. "Try. You don't have anything to lose."

"Damnation, Lydia, I don't know how to converse with an Indian!"

"I trust you. You'll think of something; you usually do."

"Madame," Wren said imperiously, "we need your help." She gestured with her hands to indicate they wanted a hut. She pointed to the woman and then to Sara to show she wanted her to care for the not-too-bright girl.

The old woman shook her head and uttered one word. "Loco."

"A temporary state of affairs," Wren continued. Then she made a cradle with her arms and rocked back and forth, pointing to Sara.

The Indian woman still shook her head and held up two fingers. "Loco," she said.

"There's nothing to do but show her the gems and see what she does," Wren grumbled. She withdrew two emeralds and a shimmering ruby and held them out in the palm of her hand The old woman's eyes lit up and she cocked her head from side to side. First she looked at the stones and then at Sara, as if she were weighing the worth of both.

Lydia and Wren held their breath, waiting to see what she would decide. The gems won out and she reached for them. This time it was Wren who shook her head negatively and again made motions for a place of shelter. After much gesticulating the old woman scurried off and returned sometime later with several long branches and some sheets of bark. Deftly, she set about erecting them into a makeshift shelter. When she finished, she held out her hand for the gems. Again Wren shook her head and pointed to Sara. With no wasted motion the old woman had Sara up off the ground and in her arms. She dragged her under the shelter and both girls clenched their teeth and winced at the thump they heard. This time when she held out her hands Wren placed the gems in her dark palm.

Dramatically, Wren dusted her hands and laughed. "We did almost a day's work. Convincing that woman to take care of Sara was more work than cheating Farrington for the jewels. If anyone deserves berry pie for dessert, it's us."

"There seems to be some commotion going on," Lydia said as they neared the center of the settlement. "All the people have stopped what they were doing. Look—even Bascom is paying attention to the man who's speaking. It must be serious if Bascom would interrupt his prayer meeting!"

"Then let's see what it's all about," Wren said, pulling Lydia by the arm.

"Do you always have to be in the thick of things? Peter is there; he can tell us what's happening. Why don't we just wait here and let him come to us?"

"That won't do. I like to hear things firsthand. Walk faster, Lydia, before we miss something." Wren quickened her step.

"Whoever the man is who's doing the talking, he certainly is dressed for society and not this wilderness. Wren, he must be someone important." Her own curiosity aroused, Lydia matched her steps to Wren's long-legged stride.

The two women made their way to where Peter was standing and waited for the man to continue speaking. They were too late; he was turning and walking away, his face hateful and mean. Peter looked at the women, and his face, too, wore a strange expression.

"What's going on?" Wren demanded. "Who was that man, Peter? Why is he dressed in those elaborate clothes?"

366

Peter shrugged. "He said he was Willem Kiefft, the governor. He means trouble for Caleb and for us, too. He's calling us Indian sympathizers and traitors to our own kind. Do you see the looks we're getting? Walk with me, quickly now, and don't waste time. We're going back to the ship."

The women needed no second urging. They, too, heard the mutterings and saw the unrest that seemed to be gripping the people. "Why wasn't Caleb here?" Wren fretted as she forced her legs to keep up with Peter's loping walk.

"Does this mean we're not going to get the berry pies? I knew I should have picked the damn things myself and made them," Lydia grumbled.

"For shame, Lydia. Blasphemy coming out of your sweet mouth," Wren chided.

"I don't feel particularly sweet right now," Lydia said, glancing over her shoulder as they sped to the shoreline.

"Peter, tell us what happened. What was he saying? Why are those people looking at us that way?"

"Politics! Kiefft isn't happy about Caleb dictating to him and holding him under the knife of the Dutch West India Company. He said the captain was ready to toss him out on his ear. I know the captain, and it wasn't his ear he was about to be tossed out on." Peter hurried the two women along to the riverbank and the waiting jolly boat. "Kiefft wants the settlers to unite, to break away from the influence of 'interlopers,' as he referred to the captain. There was all kind of talk about being sacrificed to the Indians for the profits of the Company. Add to that the promises he has no intention of keeping, and it spells trouble for the captain and ourselves. Did you notice that when he walked away, he took three men with him, the most influential men in the settlement? They reminded me of puppets waiting to have their strings pulled."

"Will we be safe on board?" Lydia asked, a quiver in her voice.

"We're going to do our best," Peter said softly, his hand reaching for hers, causing Wren to wish with all her heart that Caleb were here to reassure her. "I doubt if they'll do anything tonight, but we have to prepare ourselves. There's no way of knowing if the captain will make it back from New Amsterdam tonight or even tomorrow. We're on our own, and each of us will have to depend on the other."

"But why?"Lydia protested. "We did nothing! The captain didn't do anything wrong!"

"Little matter when a man like Kiefft decides which way he's going to jump. I don't think his grievance is against us. Mostly it's against the captain and the ship. The last thing he wants is to have the *Siren* pull into port without the cargo he guaranteed to the Dutch West India Company. I've seen seeds of unrest planted in the past, and I've also seen the results. They aren't too pretty."

"I'll be damned before I let them touch Caleb's ship!" Wren snapped.

"That goes for me, too!" Lydia avowed, hands on her hips, red hair tossing, blue eyes full of fire. "That's not just a ship to me, it's a symbol of my independence!"

Peter's stomach churned. Two women and him. What kind of showing could they make against a band of angry settlers who were looking for a good fight and some sort of retribution, just or not? Not much, he told himself. And why had the captain given the crew shore liberty? The men were scattered all over Hell and creation, probably drunk as lords and no good to anyone even if he could track them down.

"We have a good number of daylight hours left," Wren said. "If you feel that something might happen tonight after dark, then we should think about taking some precautions the moment we're back on board.

I don't know exactly *what* we can do, but one of us is bound to get an idea. I'll die before I let them harm the *Sea Siren!*" A chill washed over her when she remembered that the *Sea Siren* was really Sirena's maiden ship, the *Rana*. If she let anything happen to this ship, the van der Rhyses would never forgive her.

Bright afternoon sunshine faded into soft twilight as the trio battened down the *Sea Siren.* Secure in the knowledge that they had done all they could, for the time being, they dragged tack boxes to advantageous lookouts and proceeded to keep watch.

Chapter Twenty-four

The same twilight that wrapped the *Sea Siren* in its arms slowly descended on the Pequot fort. Sassacus liked this time of day when the children were tired and played quietly as their mothers cleaned up after the evening meal. Soon it would be time for the chiefs to take their places at the council meeting. For hours the young men worked, laying the twigs and gathering the dried-out logs that would make the bonfire stretch to the heavens.

Sassacus looked around the compound at the newly erected lodges that housed the representatives of the other Indian chiefs. They would remain inside, eating the sweetmeats the women had prepared as they waited to be called to the meeting. Each would come out adorned in his richest attire and then sit cross-legged, face impassive, eyes blank.

He should be in his own lodge, dressing, but he hated the thought of being cooped up. He wanted the soft night around him with the brilliant stars overhead and the rich smell of the earth wafting up to his nostrils. His eyes traveled to the stockade fence and he cringed. He hated the sight of it. Man, red or white, did not belong behind a barricade. Children and women should be able to walk about freely without fear. This was a white man's fence, this ugly log structure that glared back at him in the lavender light. The white man built stockade fences to ward off the Indian, and the Indian built stockade fences to ward off the white man. It made no sense. His eyes were sad and troubled as he reached out a hand to touch the rough bark. He and his people were prisoners of the white man, even though there were no guards outside the heavy gates. He knew in his heart that he and his people had seen the last of their peaceful days. He had to do what was best for them. If that meant going to war, then he would go to war with the other chiefs. They would unite and hope against impossible odds that they could regain that elusive thing called peace.

As Sassacus pondered and weighed his problem, Bascom Stoneham strolled from the makeshift quarters that had been allotted to his flock, his eyes on a dark form directly ahead. He neither saw nor appreciated the quiet star-filled night or the soft evening sounds that meant people were living and breathing and loving in this tiny village. His thoughts were full of lust and what he was going to do when he came upon the young girl walking along the river.

His voice was sharp, hostile, when he grasped the

frightened girl's thin shoulder. He turned her to face him his grip painful and strong. Her name was Anna and she was frightened, as any child of thirteen would be. She swallowed hard, tears gathering in her eyes at the pain the preacher was inflicting on her. She wanted to cry out, but the eyes boring into her forbade it. She swallowed again and tried to speak.

"You must not speak in my presence. I feel a visitation coming on," Bascom said, forcing the girl to her knees. "Clasp your hands and pray with me. Pray to the Lord and beg Him to forgive you for straying from your parents. I saw the way you've been looking at the Emery boy and the way he's been looking at you. Pray to the Lord that He drives your lustful wants from your body. Pray," he commanded.

Fear coursed through Anna as she again tried to speak. Saliva gathered in her mouth and dribbled down her chin. "Truly, Preacher Stoneham, I was not lusting after William Emery. Our eyes met once and I lowered mine immediately. It was an accident."

"A sorry story, indeed, and one I cannot believe," Bascom intoned piously. "I know what I say. You have the body of a woman, and all women lust after men. You throw your wanton bodies before men and flaunt your wares like a hawker. Disgusting!" he all but spit. "Now, pray, and don't stop till I tell you, or I'll have a long talk with your parents about your wicked ways."

Anna dropped her eyes and bowed her head, muttering and half moaning prayers she didn't know she knew, saying words that had no meaning to her. Saying anything to keep the preacher from telling her parents of what he called her wicked ways.

While Anna prayed, Bascom positioned her more carefully in front of him and forced her head upright. "Close your eyes when you pray to the Lord!" he cried in an excited voice. His hands worked feverishly with the belt buckle of his trousers as the girl's prayers invaded his ears. Quickly, before she knew what was happening, Bascom forced his manhood to her mouth, his bony hands gripping her head. His body moved in a frenzy as the girl choked and sobbed.

"Wanton slut," Bascom shouted hoarsely as he thrust her from him and snapped his buckle together. "I'm going to take pity on you and not tell your parents of your sinful ways. I'll stay here all night and pray for your soul. The devil's blood runs in your veins," he muttered as he opened his prayer book and then dropped to his knees.

Anna rubbed her hands across her mouth and ran, her eyes blinded with tears. She wasn't a wanton slut, she wasn't! She ran till she collapsed, exhausted and numb. She had to tell someone. Who? Billy Emery? She cradled her head in the crook of her arm and sobbed, great racking sobs that tore at her very being. "I'm not what he said I am. I'm not!" she cried over and over. Eventually she slept, and it was Billy Emery who found her hours later and carried her back to her worried parents.

At seventeen, he felt very manly as he approached Anna's parents and smiled to reassure them the girl was safe, only sleeping. No one noticed the dried tears on her cheeks except Billy, and he promised himself he would find out why Anna had been sobbing. Morning would be time enough. He was also the only one who noticed that the preacher wasn't anywhere to be seen. And that, he told himself, is unlike Bascom Stoneham, who likes to be in the thick of things with his prayer book. The young man's eyes narrowed to slits as Anna's father took her from his arms and carried her off to her bed.

Caleb had never been so angry in his entire life. Sassacus was right—the white man was stupid, even ignorant. The men sitting before him with their glasses of wine, their jovial attitudes and their elegant clothes made him want to kill. They heard him out and then laughed. Ridiculous! Sassacus? There was no fight in Sassacus. Sassacus liked the white man. Unite? The Pequots were so scattered they couldn't unite as one and make war. They knew the white man was superior and would take what he wanted. Who really cared if those savages had been here first? You had to be strong and eager to conquer new worlds. The white man was strong; he had already proved this. Even if the Pequots did band together, they would be no match for the English and the Dutch. There might be a skirmish or two, but those bastard savages would be put in their place.

Caleb watched the men raise their wineglasses and drink to the demise of the Indians.

A portly gentleman, attired in a crimson waistcoat with a ruffled shirt, slapped Caleb resoundingly on the back. He was already drunk, and his facial muscles hung slackly as he tried to bring Caleb's angry face into focus. "You, van der Rhys, think you have control of the Dutch West India Company. You don't," he blustered. "We do what we think is best. You come sailing into port and think you have all the answers. You don't—as Governor Kiefft will soon show you!"

Caleb seethed and fumed but realized he couldn't argue with a group of drunken men. And from the looks of things, that was a state more common to them than sobriety. He was on his own. The letter giving him full authority from the Dutch West India Company meant nothing to these sodden fools.

Sassacus took his place before the council fire, his spokesman calling the names of the visiting chiefs. Although they were not in the Pequot fort in person, their representatives answered to their chiefs' names. When all were assembled, they sat side by side, forming a straight line. Sassacus, on the far side of the fire, faced them. Through the flames he could see the visages of his enemies.

There sat the spokesman for Miantonomo, chief of the Narragansetts, who had no love for the Pequots. When Sassacus had approached Miantonomo nearly a year before with terms for an alliance, he had been cruelly rejected.

Beside the Narragansett, rested the representative for the Mohegans, speaking in the name of Chief Uncas. There was no friendship to be found in this face, either. Little more than two months earlier, sixty Mohegans, who were related to the Pequot tribe, had set out from Hartford town with ninety militiamen. When their loyalty had been doubted, Chief Uncas himself had soon reassured the English by attacking a nearby hunting party of Pequots and returning to the militia with four heads and one prisoner. This prisoner, nephew to Sassacus, had shown great courage; he had lost his life by suffering an atrocious torture: one leg had been tied to a post, the other to a frisky horse.

Even the spokesman for Ninigret, chief of the Eastern Niantic warriors, was no friend to the Pequot. Sassacus had learned that afternoon that Ninigret was joining with nearly six hundred Narragansetts and, with the English, was preparing to attack the Mystic fort.

It was into these hostile eyes that he peered, stating his pleas. "All red men are brothers. We are all of the Algonquian family and language. We are brother to the Narragansett, the Niantic, the Mohegan and the Mohican of the Hudson Valley. We who are the children of the earth must live for the earth. Now it is the Pequot time to face his enemy. But soon, very soon, each of you will suffer the fate of the Pequot. Our bones will rot and make the earth richer, more fertile.

374

We will become fodder for the white man's crops as he fishes our streams and hunts in our woods."

Sassacus spoke slowly and precisely, to be certain they understood and would deliver his message to their chiefs. "We are the people. We will die. All of us. Women. Children. There will be no heritage. The leaves will fall and cover our graves, and within the lifetime of the eagle, there will be none to say that a red brother lived on the land."

It was difficult for Sassacus to keep his shoulders straight, his head high and proud, as he left the ceremonial fire and walked to his lodge, where he would await their answer. Would they stand beside their brothers, the Pequots? Even as Sassacus crossed his legs and lowered himself to the floor, he knew his people would face their destiny alone.

The shadows of twilight had deepened before Malcolm withdrew from his hiding place in the woods and pressed forward, tripping and falling over vines and rocks. The swelling over his eye had eased since his battle with Caleb, and he had enough vision to see where he was going.

He trekked for hours until he saw lantern lights winking in the settlement of Saybrook. He was familiar with the territory. During the past two nights, he had skulked into the compound to forage for food and had succeeded in garnering eggs, early radishes and peas from kitchen gardens, and, wonder of wonders, a stray chicken. Belly full, confidence high, he stood still, orienting himself in the darkness and determining the best way to get to the riverbank without being seen.

He crept through the trees as silently as he could, stopping every so often to see if he was being observed. His thoughts rumbled with curses, damning Wren and Caleb van der Rhys. He knew that Caleb's influence in the region was far from minimal because of his position with the Dutch West India Company. Owing to the fiasco Malcolm had brought about with his attempt to ransom Wren, van der Rhys had no doubt placed a bounty on his head. There was no welcome for Malcolm Weatherly anywhere in this new world. His only chance for safety lay among the masses in England. There, among the riffraff of the slums, his disfigurement would be accepted, almost unnoticed.

Excitement coursed through him. He was so close to precious safety—the ship! He was almost to the shore and even from this distance he could see the *Sea Siren*'s sails and masts stabbing the dark sky. She was close, close enough for him to swim out to her. She had been his haven once before, taking him away from England, and she would be his haven again. He looked around, held his breath and was just about to weave his way to the sandy, gritty strip of land that would lead him to the Sound when he heard a voice, soft at first, then raised in anger. Malcolm drew back fearfully and waited. The voice was familiar, one he had heard before. He strained to distinguish the words, but with the rustling of the branches overhead and the soft lap of the water, he could only make out sounds. He crept back through the trees, careful to be quiet.

It was the preacher! And two other people. No, one other person. The third person seemed to be hiding, peering around a tree. A woman was with the preacher. Malcolm leered. This was something he understood. The preacher was out dallying with another man's wife, and the husband was waiting to catch him in a compromising position. Malcom shook his head. Whatever happened to Bascom, he deserved it. Malcolm certainly wasn't going to intervene. He had enough problems of his own without adding more to the list. He would just wait and see what happened.

He watched in shock as Bascom forced the girl to her knees and then prevented her from getting away. She was clumsy, not like that sure-footed she-cat, Wren. Bascom had her in his clutches before she could get one foot solidly planted in the sand. She was crying, sobbing at what the preacher was making her do. So it wasn't a mutual feeling of lust. This Malcolm understood also. His eye went to the figure standing behind the tree, and he wanted to urge him on, to shout at him to take the preacher by the neck and throttle him for what he was making the girl do. From the looks of things, the preacher wouldn't have to wait for God to punish him. The man behind the tree would do it for Him.

Malcolm saw the glint of a knife in the moonlight and the direction in which it was traveling. He winced. There were other ways to die, better ways, less painful ways.

The man, whoever he was, had things well in hand. He was leading the girl away, his arm protecting her from the grisly sight at their feet. Malcolm saw the knife fall to the ground and fought the desire to rush to it and pick it up. Instead, he crawled silently on his hands and knees to the water and struck out for the ship.

Ahead of him, Malcolm could see the dark hull of the *Sea Siren* against the starlit sky. He swam, kicking with his feet, straining one arm in front of the other, willing himself to reach his goal.

Minute after agonizing minute passed; from time to time, exhausted, he rolled over on his back and floated. Still the ship seemed no nearer. His arms ached and trembled. His legs were cold and becoming stiff. Each breath he took seemed to fill his lungs and expand his chest and was squeezed out of him as though he were trapped in a vise. His clothing and the pouch of jewels, still stuffed inside his shirt, weighed him down; a cramp jolted through his calf muscles.

The *Siren* continued to elude him. Glancing back, he saw that he hadn't even swum half the distance. In the darkness the shoreline was nearly impossible to discern. The inky, black waves became his enemy. Overpowering him, filling his mouth and nose, shutting out his air. Valiantly, he struggled onward, one goal in mind—the darkness of the locker box, where no one would find him. Safety. Security. Almost a homecoming. His exhausted muscles refused to work in coordination. It was increasingly fatiguing to keep his head above water, to gasp the next breath.

Tears mixed with the swells of the Sound. Tears of self-pity and rage against the injustice of his fate. He had come so close to having it all, everything, and now he had nothing. And it was all because of Wren. She had actually killed him back in the flat in London when she had robbed him of his one marketable asset —his good looks. Even Sara hadn't wanted him after she had seen his ruined face. Wren had destroyed him as calculatingly as if she had put a knife to his heart and pierced it.

The black waters closed over his head. Once. Twice. He felt himself going under for the third time, and instead of uttering a prayer of contrition, he heard himself cry out wretchedly, "Wren!"

Chapter Twenty-five

Caleb rode his mount hard and fast, stopping once for a few quick hours of much needed rest. When he awoke, darkness had settled around him. He had wasted too much time rounding up the stragglers of his crew. Traveling alone was much quicker, and he had instructed the men to wait for him to make port in New Amsterdam, where they would take on additional stores for the return trip to England.

The horse's hooves tore up chunks of turf as he raced toward Saybrook. Ahead of him, Caleb could see lanterns and torches lining the riverbank. On perceiving so much activity near the water, he rightly assumed it had something to do with the *Sea Siren*. Dismounting, he cautiously approached the thronging colonists from the trees and soon realized they were discussing the fate of his ship.

It was several moments before he began to understand that Kiefft had paid a visit to Saybrook and convinced the settlers that Caleb and his crew were Indian partisans, supplying the Pequots with weapons and spying on their behalf. It was a ridiculous statement, yet Caleb knew there was nothing he could say to refute it. Tempers were high and hostilities were fed by fear. The Pequots offered a very real threat, and he *had* been with Sassacus on several occasions.

Peering through the trees toward the ship, he felt his stomach tighten. She was a good mile out into the Sound. Without a chance of retrieving his jolly, it would be a long swim.

Suddenly a cry went up. "The preacher! The preacher, Stoneham!" the voice shrilled. "He's dead! Murdered!"

Caleb's ears pricked as he listened. One man, whose modish clothing revealed he was not one of the settlers but was probably one of Kiefft's men, linked Caleb's name with Bascom's murder. Outraged, the throng drew closer to the water, looking toward the *Siren* and waving clenched fists.

Knowing it would be only a matter of time until they ventured out in their boats to attack the ship, Caleb also knew it was time to take his chances.

He ran as though his life depended on it, and it did. Gasping, his long arms giving him momentum, he skidded to a stop at the river's edge. One quick look over his shoulder at the advancing colonists, and he leapt into the murky waters of the Sound. When he surfaced some distance from the shoreline, he kicked off his boots, the shouts of "Murderer!" and "Indian lover!" ringing in his ears.

His feet free of the weighty boots, he struck out just as his own jolly was launched from the shore, full of shouting, cursing men, intent only on his capture. Another quick look over his shoulder told him four members of his crew who had returned to Saybrook were behind him. Their intent was the same as his.

As Caleb's arms slashed through the water, he realized how the past days had taken their toll of him. Farrington's death, Sara's duplicity, Wren's supposed death and then her miraculous reappearance, along with his hatred for Malcolm Weatherly, had left him drained of emotion. Too many sleepless nights worrying what might or might not have been with Wren were now in the past, and he had to force his body to keep moving in the churning black water. He had to reach the ship and Wren. He was tired. The crewmen were almost abreast of him, and they had hit the water after he had. He had to make it; he couldn't fail now, not after all that had happened. Deep, even strokes would bring him to the *Siren.*

Lifting his head as his arms knifed through the water, he saw the four crew members, two each abreast of him. They were good men, his men, and they knew that his strokes were less than even and measured and that his breathing was ragged, much more so than theirs. If he faltered, they were there. Determination and anger raced through him. He couldn't let the crew bring in its captain. He'd die first. Even if he slowed, as long as his strokes were measured, he would make it.

Wren stood on the quarterdeck of the *Sea Siren,* her face softly lit by the gimbaled lantern. Her anxious gaze was fixed on the commotion ashore, when suddenly she realized what she was seeing. "Peter! Look! It's Caleb!" Excitement rang in her voice and mingled with her anxiety.

"Aye! And it seems as though four of our men have finally found their way back to the ship!" His eyes were pressed tightly against the ship's glass as he looked toward shore. "And look what's behind them and gaining distance!"

Wren peered out, her hand shielding her eyes from the lantern's light. In the distance, behind Caleb and the crewmen, was the *Siren*'s jolly boat, manned by Kiefft's men, their muskets raised and ready to fire.

Peter ran to the foredeck, hoisting the winch which would lower the second jolly. "I'll row out and pick them up. You and Lydia go below and lock the cabin doors."

"I'm going with you," Wren stated, lifting her skirts in preparation of climbing down the Jacob's ladder.

"No, you're not! Stay below—that's an order!"

"I'll be damned if I'll go below and hide like a criminal. My running and hiding days are over, Peter. I'm going with you!"

"And leave Lydia alone? You must stay here. Now, do as you're told. Now!" Peter thundered.

Wren gulped and seized Lydia by the arm. "We'll do as you say. Hurry, Peter."

With the boat lowered into the dark water, Peter cast a last, longing look at his Lydia and slid down into the jolly. Every muscle in his back bunched into knots as he dipped the oars and then swung back, only to dip and swing again. There they were, he could see them struggling in the churning tides. He prayed he would reach them in time. The governor's men were fast closing the distance. Soon they would be within shooting range.

On deck, Lydia was trembling with the force of her fear. "Wren, I'm frightened," she whispered. "Why is this happening? Why would Governor Kiefft do this?"

"You heard what Peter said before. What better way to insure that Caleb never makes his report to the burghers in Holland? This way, we will all be victims of mass hysteria, not of coldblooded murder."

"Wren, we have to do something. If they come aboard . . . I've heard what men can do to women . . ."

"They're not pirates, Lydia, they won't rape us. That's not what they have in mind. Right now they just wouldn't want any witnesses to say what really did happen." Wren's voice conveyed a confidence she did not feel. "Be brave, Lydia. When Caleb comes aboard, he'll know what to do." She hugged Lydia close.

Several shots rang out through the darkness. Kiefft's men were firing on the swimmers and Peter.

"Dear God! They're firing on our men!" Lydia squealed.

Wren's heart constricted in panic, her amber eyes flashing with rage. "Lydia! Come with me. We have a gun, too! The ship's cannon."

"The cannon! You must be crazy! We can't fire that!"

"Why not? Caleb said it's always loaded. All we need to do is add powder. Do you know where it's kept?"

Lydia glanced at the cumbersome, lethal cannon whose muzzle pointed through a bay abaft the starboard beam. She froze with terror.

Wren seized her shoulders and shook her. "Do you know where the powder is kept? It's in the stern, in the magazine!" Lydia shook her head in the affirmative, like a puppet whose string had been pulled. "Get it!" Wren ordered, pushing Lydia toward the stern. "If you can't carry it, roll it down!"

Wren ran down the starboard side, stopping at each gun sight, peering over the gunwale to assess the best aim. At sea, the crew would bring a ship about for the best firing vantage. Trapped on a sandbar the way they were, there was no chance of doing that. The best she could do was choose the cannon facing the target; then hope and pray that when she fired it, it would at least alarm Caleb's pursuers and give him time to get aboard safely. Cannon 2 on the starboard beam seemed to fit her specifications.

Lydia came forward, hunched over, carrying the twenty-pound powder cask on her back, supporting it with a rope drawn forward over her shoulders like Wren had seen peasants do in Java. The cask thudded to the deck and spilled open, saving Wren the trouble of breaking into it. "How much powder do we use?" Lydia gasped.

"I don't know. But I've seen it done before, when Regan was testing the guns on his ships in the Batavia harbor. Help me, Lydia. There's little time left!"

The women worked quickly, uncertain of what they were doing. At the last moment Wren remembered to use the long plunger to tamp down the powder. Exerting all their strength, they rolled the gun into place. Wren grabbed the lantern and lifted the chimney, holding the naked flame to the fuse. Squeezing her eyes shut, she fired the cannon. It reeled backward on its mounts from the force of the explosion.

An oily, inky cloud exuded from the gun, and when the smoke cleared, Wren hardly dared to look, fearing that somehow she had miscalculated and that Caleb and Peter had also taken the brunt of the shot.

"Look! Look!" Lydia squealed. "I see the jolly and our men! Throw down the ladder so they can board!"

Caleb had one foot on the ladder, a dumbfounded expression on his face. "Did they fire on us or on Kiefft's men?" he muttered. "That was too close for comfort."

Wren was loading the cannon again when she felt a hand on her shoulder and swung around, a silent scream in her throat. "Caleb! I didn't know what to do. We thought Peter wouldn't get to you in time, and those men were firing at you!" She collapsed into his arms.

"Hush, now! You did everything just right. You saved our lives and gave us the time we needed." He hugged her to him and then released her, shouting orders to the crew.

"Peter, there's little chance we can keep them from boarding the ship," Caleb said. "The cannons were meant for long-range firing. Once they're on board, we've lost firing range. We'd better prepare to fight." He drew Peter aside. "Listen to me carefully. If they manage to board and the fight is all to their favor, set

384

fire to the *Siren* and go over the side. We'll take our chances in the water."

"Aye, Captain. And I'm sorry about the sandbar. I panicked with the responsibility of the women. If only the tide had been right, we could have turned the ship around and headed for sea. It's my fault, Captain, and if anything happens to you and the others, I'm to blame."

"There's no blame being placed on your shoulders, Peter. You did the best you could, and that's all I ask of any man. Tomorrow the tide will be right and we'll sail away from here. I hope," he muttered under his breath.

At the first sound of the grappling hooks, Wren's eyes took on a feverish glaze and her body began to tremble. Kiefft's men wanted Caleb, and the only way they would get him would be to kill her first.

She flinched at the sound of a pistol being cocked, and then another and another. The four crew members were stationed broadside, while Peter stood a little to the left of Caleb to give him backup support should his volley miss. Where was Lydia? "Lydia, where are you?" she hissed.

"Shhh, over here. See, I have a rapier, too."

"Good. Use it, don't just hold it," Wren whispered back.

"It's the same principle as jabbing a hairpin, isn't that so?"

"Oh, Christ," Caleb moaned to Peter, who rolled his eyes at Lydia's words.

"Yes," Wren told her, "but be sure that you use force."

There was no time to give Lydia an exercise on the finer points of fencing. Wren was only glad that as a little girl she had pretended to be the infamous Sea Siren and that Regan had seen to her lessons himself.

Over the port rail climbed Kiefft's men, aided by

colonists from Old Saybrook. The decks became alive with sharp cries and mayhem. Lydia jabbed out with her weapon, delaying an attacker until Peter could see to him himself.

Wren waited in the darkness, undecided where she was needed most. How could eight people survive this attack? she wondered fearfully. She refused to speculate whether or not she could actually use a rapier to kill a man. Her fencing lessons had been child's play, meant more for form than for actual defense. Her mouth became a thin line of concentration as she emerged onto the deck, the sword clutched in her hand.

She stepped over two fallen bodies and advanced warily on an unsuspecting man bent upon cutting Peter down from behind. The point of her blade plunged deep into the back of his neck, and he dropped before her. She pulled her weapon free of his resisting flesh and grimaced, but the expression on Peter's face was all she needed to keep going.

Again and again she lashed out, mentally counting the odds against them as three to one. She jabbed and feinted, cracking one man over the head with the rapier's handle, only to stun him. Lydia saved her in the nick of time by running her own rapier through the man's arm. Peter finished him off.

Wren was seized with a panic which choked off all reason. Averting her eyes from the gore, she backed against the foremast, weapon held loosely in her hand. One of Kiefft's men advanced on her, his eyes raking her and taking in the sword she held. She was an easy target, stunned by panic, immobile with fear. Even as he approached her, she was defenseless against him. He wielded a cutlass, held at a menacing angle, ready to slash out at her if she made a move.

Her mouth was dry, her gaze fixed; she was helpless. None of the polite and genteel lessons she had learned from Regan had prepared her for this. Just as the man's hand reached out for her, she turned to run. He grabbed for her viciously, pulling at the fabric of her skirts, tearing the stitches at the waistline. The material trapped her legs and caused her to sprawl onto the deck.

A soundless plea rose to her lips as he ripped the fabric away from her legs and feasted his eyes on the elegant length of her legs stripped bare to his view. Frozen by terror and what she read in his face, Wren was paralyzed. Amid the frenzied happenings around her, she knew there would be no help from anyone: only herself. Slowly, unseen by her attacker, she groped the deck near her side, searching for the hilt of her rapier. Just as her fingers found their target, he lunged for her, naked lust casting dark shadows over his eyes. The tip of her weapon found his breast, and with a deliberate, unhurried action, she plunged it deep into his flesh. Rolling onto her side, she avoided his dead weight falling on top of her. "That was for you and all the Malcolms of this world!" she screamed, beyond the edge of panic now and into the grip of deadly willfulness. "No one will ever do that to me again!"

She had killed before and she had done it again; *would* kill still again, if necessary, but never would she allow herself to be at the mercy of a man's lust.

Silently she crept from her seclusion near the foremast and took stock of the situation. Her eyes widened as she watched Caleb square off against a burly attacker who wielded a wicked cutlass. Another of Kiefft's men was creeping up behind him, his intent only too clear.

With a wild whoop Wren was on the man's back, smacking him over the head with the hilt of her weapon. Startled, Caleb turned and took a blow on his shoulder. He grinned as Wren slid from the dead man's back, her eyes gleaming in the dim light. It couldn't be possible! Her dark hair was flying about her shoulders and her skirt was gone, revealing her long, curvaceous legs. With her tattered clothes and wild hair, she looked just like the Sea Siren.

"I couldn't let him kill you. Not after I've only just found you again." She smiled. "Are we winning or losing?"

Caleb threw back his head and laughed. "You might look like the Sea Siren, but she'd never ask a question like that. Look around—we've repelled them for the time being. But they'll be back." His expression changed, his voice became deeper, his eyes lingered on her face. "Sweetheart," he said, gathering her into his arms, "I, for one, am proud to fight beside you."

"Then you believe they'll come back?" she asked, her eyes darkening with an unspoken fear.

"Aye, sweetheart, we can almost bet on it. Are you frightened?"

Wren clutched at him, her lips close against his chest. "Yes," she whispered, her voice barely audible. "I'm frightened that something will happen to one of us." She lifted her head and looked directly at him, her eyes filled with meaning. "I want you, Caleb. I love you and I want you to make love to me. If something should happen . . . I don't want to die without knowing you completely, totally."

Caleb's eyes grew darker with pent-up desire. Wren, his beautiful Wren, had at last become a woman. A woman who loved and wanted to be loved. Wordlessly, he lifted her into his arms and carried her across the deck, taking her to the captain's cabin. And as he did, he whispered against her ear, telling her of the first time Regan had made love to his Siren, there in the same cabin, behind the shroud of an isolating fog.

Wren touched her fingers delicately to his lips. "Shh. Ours is the first love, the only love. Never have two people loved the way we do. Ever since I was a little girl I've wanted to be like the Sea Siren. For the longest time I hadn't even dreamed that Sirena was that woman and that Regan was her handsome captain. But I'm grown up now, Caleb. And the only woman I want to be is your woman."

With his foot he swung the cabin door shut, his mouth closed over hers, his heart filling with an overpowering love for her. He worked the laces of her bodice, stripping her of the confining cloth. Her clothing came away piece by piece, and always his mouth kissed and tasted the freshly exposed skin. She was naked in his arms, turning her body beneath his caresses, offering herself, tempting him again and again with her sighs of pleasure and low moans of passion.

Finally, having little patience for the restrictions his own clothing imposed, he broke away from her, tearing and ripping at the material, eager to be naked in the arms of the woman he loved.

Wren's senses soared and whirled, making her dizzy with yearning and a deep hunger for him. Gone were the fears she had known. She was a woman, Caleb's woman, and she wanted him, needed him, demanded he possess her. She answered his caresses with a sizzling response that bordered on an animal lust. Wantonly, she explored his body with her lips, brazened the most sensuous caresses and invited him to partake of her passions with an exquisite joy.

Caleb delighted in his bewitching partner, withholding the moment of completion to savor her charms further. He rejoiced to find his desires met by hers. In the darkness he perceived her through his fingers, through his lips, and was intoxicated with their love for each other.

Straining toward him, throbbing with unfulfilled desire, her body rose and fell in rhythmic obedience to an instinctive yearning. And then a cry came from her: "Take me! Have me! Make me your own!" She pulled him to her, gathering him into her, making his flesh a part of her own.

Hours later, sitting on the quiet deck, Wren snuggled deep into Caleb's arms. "Did you really think I looked like the Sea Siren?"

"For a moment I really did. But there's only one Sea Siren and only one Wren. Do you understand?"

"Yes," she breathed contentedly. "You love me because I'm who I am."

Caleb frowned and then laughed. "That's exactly what I'm saying, but somehow when you say it, it sounds different."

"That's because men use too many words when action is needed." Her silken arms embraced him, her lips covered his.

"Caleb, tell me about the boys back in Java. I can't wait to see them again. I was in England three years, and Wynde was just a baby when I left."

Caleb's voice took on a faraway tone as he recalled the last time he had seen his half brothers. "I imagine they've grown at least a head taller since I've seen them. At times they're so much alike I can hardly separate them in my mind. Let's see if I have it right. Thor is the oldest. Strong and domineering and quite aware of the responsibility of his younger brothers. Then comes Storm, serious and inquisitive, always asking 'Why?' Rein is third in line." Caleb laughed, remembering. "Rein is always complaining that he gets left out of everything, but he's the most headstrong of them all. Sometimes I think he gets himself into trouble just to gain attention. And Wynde is the baby. He's still hanging on to Sirena's skirts, but that will soon change. You see, I know a secret."

At the mention of a secret, Wren's head popped up from his shoulder. "Tell me. I love secrets."

"Sirena is expecting another child. By now she and Regan should be in Java awaiting the birth. I pray it

390

will be a girl. Regan will need a daughter now that I'm taking you away from him."

"I wonder what Sirena will name the baby if it is a girl. All the boys managed to be born during some of the worst storms in Java's history."

"Knowing Sirena and Regan, could you expect anything else?" Caleb asked, laughing. "Regardless of the weather when this child is born, Regan said if he had a daughter he would call her Fury."

"Fury," Wren whispered, trying the name on her lips.

Caleb smiled again. "Regan will have his daughter, and she'll be born during a storm, and she'll carry the name Fury van der Rhys. Sirena will see to it."

All through the rest of the night the crew of the *Sea Siren* was on watch, scanning the water and the shoreline.

"What do you think, Captain?" Peter asked in a whisper, careful not to wake Wren, who was sleeping contentedly in the crook of Caleb's arm.

"I don't think they'll be back anymore tonight, but tomorrow will tell another story. The only thing that saved us is the fact that they're not fighters but farmers, men of the earth. There was no heart in most of them for what they were doing. As their friends fell at their feet, some of them went over the side. God alone knows how many will return in the morning. How one man can and did make such a mess of things, I'll never understand." Caleb shook his head. "I find it hard to believe that Kiefft would kill innocent people just to prevent me from going back to Holland to make my report. We're playing a waiting game for now. If it weren't for the sandbar . . ."

". . . we'd be out to sea by now," Peter said softly. "Captain, I . . ."

"I told you I place no blame on you for our circumstances, nor do the women or the crew. Full tide will get us out of here."

"Only if full tide arrives before Kiefft and his men."

"We can't think of that now," Caleb said as he shifted slightly to ease Wren into a more comfortable position. Then he dozed off.

When the first pearly gray streak of light heralded the coming dawn, Caleb blinked and was instantly awake. Joining Peter at the rail, he watched as dawn fought the darkness for supremacy. His eyes, like Peter's, were on the shoreline. Even from this distance they could make out hurrying figures and frenzied activity.

"Two more hours till full tide," Peter said morosely.

Caleb's gut rumbled and his face became a mask of hatred for what his eyes were seeing. They would all be killed. He would never make it back to England and Holland and would never live to enjoy his new life with Wren. There were at least fifty men assembling on the shore. As each minute raced on, more arrived carrying guns.

"Captain, look! Upriver! Do you see what I see?" Peter cried excitedly.

"By God, I do, and I don't believe it!" Caleb exclaimed, tossing his seaman's cap in the air. "It's Sassacus!"

"How many canoes do you count, Captain?"

"At least two dozen."

"They're coming to help. Never have I been so glad to see an Indian in my life!" Peter shouted hoarsely.

"Peter, they're not coming to fight. Sassacus will not intervene between the white men, just as I wouldn't intervene between the red men. He's bringing those canoes to pull us off the sandbar. Lord, if I live to be a thousand, I'll never forget this sight. Order the crew on deck to help secure the lines. Make fast work of it. Sassacus timed it just right. As soon as we're free of the sandbar, the tide will carry us out. The settlers will have no stomach for a fight on water with all those Indians. They would be hopelessly outnumbered and it would be a slaughter."

Caleb drew in his breath as he watched the Indians strain with their paddles to cross the Sound. Their bodies gleaming with sweat, they surrounded the *Siren* and worked to free her from the spit that held her down. A mighty lurch, and the lady crashed into the water.

There were no happy shouts from the Indians at the success of their efforts. Their expressions were staid, placid. They didn't understand why they had done what they had, only that their chief and the captain, who was a white man, were friends.

No words were spoken, and Caleb raised his hand to his head in a jaunty salute to Sassacus, who returned it in kind. This time Caleb put a name to the damnable mist that clouded his vision. He was shedding tears for a friend he would never see again. How could he ever repay his debt to the courageous Indian?

A single tear formed in the corner of Sassacus's eye and he wiped at it unashamedly; at the same time Caleb ran the back of his hand over both his eyes.

"Another time, another place, Caleb van der Rhys, and we will again be brothers," Sassacus said softly.

Only Wren was close enough to Caleb to hear him say, "Look for me in that other world one day, Sassacus, and we will hunt and fish together, good friend."

CAPTIVE SECRETS

For Chelly Kitzmiller, Dorsey Adams, and Jill Landis

Author's Note

There are many species of hawks to be studied. For this novel I chose the goshawk because I fell in love with the winged creature's capabilities. I was astounded to find that a hawk, if hand-raised, could become a loyal pet capable of deep affection, anger, and jealousy. They're also generous, offering tidbits of their food to those they like. They love to tease and provoke for a gentle caress. They adore sparkly stones and bright colors. Often they "borrow" items and return them days later. Their prowess in the air is nothing short of incredible. They can fly a mile high in the air and rocket downward almost as fast as a speeding bullet and can literally stop in midair, work the wind, and continue downward or onward. They're loyal to their owner, mate, and young, and will kill any attacker with their talons, their only weapon, if they feel threatened. They're also known for their long-distance flying, sometimes six to eight hours at a time and often through the entire night.

I ask your indulgence and to believe, as I do, that there really could have been a Gaspar and Pilar in 1665.

F.M.

Prologue

Java, 1665

The old salt smacked his lips over toothless gums, relishing the moment the stranger standing before him would hand over the jug of rum.

The stranger was tall, muscular, with the torso of a tree trunk, arms full of hard muscle that rippled beneath the fine lawn shirt he wore open to his belt buckle. He was bronzed by the sun, a seaman by the look of him. The old man narrowed his eyes, trying to see around the cataracts that filmed them. Handsome, he thought. Hair as black as a raven's wing and eyes the color of . . . He searched for a word from his past to describe the stranger's eyes. Coal-black, like pitch. He'd never seen such black eyes before, and these held something else he'd never seen: contempt. Oh, he'd seen his share of emotions over his eighty-six years, but always love, hate, anger, or vengeance. He blinked his bleary eyes for a better look, but the film blotted out the fine details of the man's features.

"I would hear your tale, old man, and for the pleasure of your company the jug is yours." The stranger spoke quietly, his voice deep and . . . educated, the old man decided.

"And what name do you go by?" he asked, eyeing the jug greedily.

1

"Is it important?" the man asked blandly.

"A man needs a name when he drinks with another man. Every mother gives her babe a name. Mine is Jacobus."

The stranger debated a second before replying. The old lush would finish off his jug and not remember a thing. Lies always come back to slap one in the face.

"Luis Domingo," he said at last, and smiled—a flash of white teeth in the hazy lamplight that reminded Jacobus of a shark at feeding time.

Luis Domingo . . . The old man rolled the strange-sounding name over his toothless gums and thick tongue. He'd never heard it before, but then, his memory wasn't what it used to be. "You smell of the sea. I like that. Sit down and I'll begin my tale if you'll pass that jug along." When the stranger slid the bottle across the table, Jacobus snatched it and brought it to his lips. After a hearty pull, he wiped his mouth with the palm of his hand and sat back with a contented sigh.

"She had the face of an angel, the Sea Siren did. She was so beautiful, even her enemies fell about her feet. Her heart was pure, and she always spared the unfortunate souls who sought to attack her. Mind you, she fought fair. Oftentimes she would switch from a cutlass to a rapier without a misstep. Razor-sharp they were. Shiny like a hawk's eye and just as deadly. I seen her myself, hundreds of times, as she danced across that black ship like the sea sprite she was." He paused to take several long swallows of the fiery liquid in the jug, then picked up on his words immediately.

"There wasn't a man at sea that didn't hunger for the Sea Siren. Her eyes saw everything at a glance. Like emeralds they were. Her hair was black as yours, and it rode her head like a raven's wings. Her skin was like cream in a crock. She carried a wicked scar on her arm that men would have died from, but not the Sea Siren. There wasn't a man that could best her in a duel. Not a single man.''

Jacobus's voice became dreamlike as his memories took him back in time. ''The black ship she sailed was like a ghost. One minute it was there and the next minute it would disappear. Into nothing. She had this laugh that carried across the water. Made many a man's blood run cold,'' he said in awe.

''They could never catch her, and hundreds tried. She ruined the man who was the head of the Dutch East India Company. Sank his ships because his men raped and killed her sister. She swore revenge on the bastards and killed every single one of them—fair and square.

''The Dutch East India Company put a price on her head, and handsome it was, but to naught.''

''You make her sound like a saint in a costume,'' Domingo said coldly. ''She was a pirate and she pillaged and plundered ships, so how can you say she—''

''If you know all about her, then why are you asking me to tell you what I know?'' Jacobus said, bristling at the stranger's words. ''I seen her hundreds of times. Once she smiled at me, and it was like the Madonna herself gazing on me. She never hurt those who didn't deserve to be hurt. She never kept a thing from the ships she boarded but let her crew have it. Rights of salvage.''

The old man swigged again from the bottle, and then continued, his words slurring slightly. ''I think she came down from heaven. That's my own opinion, because she . . . she would just disappear in a cloud of fog. You could hear her laugh ringing across the water when she was victorious. My hair stood on end. Such strength she had, it wasn't human, I can tell you that. I seen her the day she dueled with Blackheart. He was twice her size and twice her weight, and she cut him down. 'Course he was maimed from his first encounter with her, so he wasn't starting even with her. That blade danced in the sun, I can tell you that. Blood rivered the decks of that frigate.'' Jacobus lowered his voice to a hushed whisper. ''That black ship was . . . magic. She sailed high on the water with a speed I've never seen. Never!'' The old man sat back once more and gulped from the bottle.

Domingo leaned forward on his chair, his dark eyes piercing the old man like twin daggers. ''Do you expect me to believe this garbage that a woman, even a beautiful woman sailing a black ship, is something mythical?''

The anger in his voice jolted Jacobus, who looked up groggily. ''Real or magic, I don't know. I told you what I seen,'' he said fearfully, suddenly aware that the stranger's eyes were angry and calculating. All sign of contempt was gone.

''Where is this infamous black ship now, and where is the Sea Siren?'' Domingo asked harshly.

The fine hairs on the back of Jacobus's neck prickled. He'd said too much. He had to hold his tongue now and not give away the fact that he'd been a member of the Sea Siren's crew. The rum jug beckoned, but he set it on the table. If this stranger had a mind to, he could rip out his tongue and . . . ''Only God knows,'' he blustered.

Domingo laughed, a chilling sound in the sudden hush that had descended over the tavern. ''Does this Sea Siren's god allow her to kill and maim and . . . disappear into thin air? A fine story from a drunken sot.''

Jacobus did his best to meet Domingo's dark gaze. ''It's not a story, it's true. There is a Sea Siren, and there is a black ship. I don't know where they are. No one has seen either for over twenty years.''

Domingo's eyes turned to slits as he leaned across the table. ''Is she dead, old man? Is the Sea Siren and that black ship at the bottom of the sea? Tell me the truth, or

I'll wring that stringy neck of yours. Or is this a fairy tale?''

Jacobus shook the man's hands off his shoulders. "It's no fairy tale. Go to the offices of the Dutch East India Company and see for yourself. A wanted poster has been hanging there for twenty-five years. And when the Sea Siren is needed, her ship will sail again. You mark my words.''

Domingo stomped from the room, the laughter of the tavern's patrons ringing in his ears. Were they laughing at him? Was it all a trick of the old sot's? Tomorrow at first light he'd go to the Dutch East India offices and see for himself. This was the closest he'd come to actual proof that the legendary Sea Siren really existed and wasn't a figment of his father's imagination. The Sea Siren and the deadly black ship she'd captained had ruined his father.

Domingo's head reared back as he bellowed into the night. "If you're alive, I'll kill you for what you did to my father! No quarter given!''

Chapter One

Cadiz, Spain, 1665

Furana van der Rhys fingered the costly material of her ball gown, a gown of her mother's choosing, with deep sadness. She would wear it this once, and then it would be packed away with all her other worldly possessions. The sadness in her indigo eyes deepened as she gazed around her bedroom. For many years she'd slept in this room, cried in this room, fought and played with her brothers in this same room . . . and always at the end of the day she prayed.

For days now she'd kept herself busy packing up her things in huge brass-bound trunks that would be carried to the attic when she left this house, this room, for the last time. There was very little left now to prove she'd inhabited it all these years, save her comb and brush and the jewelry she would wear for her birthday ball. When the clock struck midnight she'd be twenty-one years old. Parents and old friends would toast her and say good-bye. Only then would she smile.

At noon the next day she would leave for the convent, where she would lead a cloistered life until her death. It was the only thing she'd ever wanted. For years her parents had denied her entrance into the convent, saying she was too young and didn't know her mind. Finally they'd agreed that she could follow her vocation when she was twenty-one and of age. Just a few more hours. . . .

Fury, as her parents called her, walked away from the elaborate ball gown to stare out at the bright sunshine she loved. She'd been so happy here, growing up with teasing, boisterous brothers, climbing trees, sliding down trellises, and chasing after her siblings as they played game after game.

Doubts assailed her, and immediately she started to finger her rosary. She was doing the right thing, the right thing for her. Only once had she questioned her vocation—when her four brothers were lost at sea aboard the *Rana*. After their deaths, she was all that was left to her parents; only she could provide grandchildren to carry on the ancient lineage. But the thought of herself with a man—and a child of that union—brought a rush of color to her cheeks. A man, a strange man who would covet her . . . want to make love to her . . . Her lips moved faster, fingers furiously working the beads in her hand.

A fluffy cloud sailed overhead and dimmed the sun for a moment. Fury blinked to ward off tears. Of course she would miss the sun and the bright blue sky. She would miss a lot of things, at first. But she would adapt to the cloistered life, learn to sleep on a straw pallet, adjust to the perpetual gloom of the convent. The vow of silence would be hardest to accept, but that was years away, not until her novitiate was over. She would be ready then.

The rosary at an end, Fury pocketed the beads. If she hurried, she could say another in the chapel before lunch, this one for her parents. It was going to be so hard for them when their only remaining child stepped aboard the ship that would take her back to Java. Will I have the strength to leave, Fury wondered, to say good-bye to those I love with all my heart? She had to trust in God that her leavetaking would be bearable for all of them.

The chapel was small, intimate, built for her mother by her father, who was not of his wife's faith. It had been a labor of love, and any who entered to worship thought it a beautiful place, peaceful and holy. Fury herself had from her early years kept fresh flowers on the small altar—mostly jasmine, her mother's favorite. The rosary found its way to her hand, familiar prayers tumbling from her lips. *"I believe in God the Father : . . ."*

Sirena van der Rhys crept close to the chapel, her emerald eyes full of unshed tears. She knew Fury would be inside, but she could not bring herself to cross the threshold. Her daughter, the most precious jewel in her crown, would soon be lost to her forever.

Sirena swallowed past the lump in her throat. Fury was so beautiful. Long-limbed like herself, and with the same tawny skin, but with her father's indigo eyes and square jaw. She had Sirena's hair, but Fury's was thick and curly, cascading down to the small of her back. As a child she had changed her hairstyle seven times a day, delighting in using all manner of jeweled combs and sparkling hairpins. Once she entered the convent, they'd shave her head and make a pillow of her hair.

Sirena raised her eyes heavenward. "Why?" she whispered. "Why are you doing this to me? You've taken everything from me—my parents, my firstborn, Miguel. Wasn't that enough? Five sons I've given up to you, and now you're taking my only daughter. You're punishing me, aren't you? For all those years I sailed the seas to avenge my sister and uncle. I renounced you as my God, and now you're claiming what is yours. What kind of God are you, that you leave me with nothing? Miracles are for other people, not the likes of the Sea Siren, is that it?"

Sirena's knees buckled and she would have slipped to the floor but for her husband, who had come up silently behind her and now caught her in his arms. "I have no God anymore, Regan," Sirena whispered to him. "He has forsaken me. I will never say another prayer. Never!" she cried against his shoulder as he carried her away from the chapel entrance to their bedroom at the far end of the casa.

Regan felt his throat constrict as he gently lowered his wife to the bed. Memories of Fury, their beloved little girl, washed over him in wave after wave of anguish. He remembered her birth—during the eye of the worst storm ever to attack Java. It had been a difficult labor, but he had seen Sirena through it. The child had squalled furiously at the first smack to her bottom. Regan recalled his words from that long-ago time: "This one is a fury, Sirena!" he'd said proudly as the storm descended on Java. When they christened the tiny bundle a month later, it was he who said she was to be called Furana. "So you'll never forget the *Rana*," he'd murmured to his wife. Now he struggled in his mind for the right words to tell her that things would be all right. But he knew they wouldn't be. He knew this beautiful woman so well, knew her better than he knew himself. The moment Fury left their lives, Sirena would climb into the same shell she'd closed about herself when their other children died. She would be lost to him. And when that happened, his own will to live would shrivel and die.

Sirena met her husband's anxious gaze with shimmering, tear-filled eyes. She knew him so well, knew exactly what he was thinking, and she wanted so much to say the words he needed to hear. She loved this man with every breath in her body. He was so handsome, with his fair hair and bronze skin. Her Dutchman. They'd gone to hell and back and survived, but this . . . At last she shook her head and smiled at him.

"I'm all right now, darling," she said, brushing away her tears. "And I promise that I won't put you through any more misery. In the past my grief consumed me, but I won't let it happen again. When we sail for the Americas tomorrow at sundown, this life will be behind us. You have my word. Come, now we must get ready for dinner. Fury will be waiting for us.''

Regan was almost dizzy with relief at his wife's words. And when Sirena reached up and kissed him full on the lips—a long, lingering kiss—his pain melted away, and he forgot everything but the love he bore for this, the most beautiful woman in the world.

While the house buzzed and seethed with preparations for her birthday ball, Fury perched on the wide windowsill of the secluded breakfast nook at the back of the house. She loved this sunny spot and her feathered friends waiting outside the window. Fury's eyes scanned the birds, looking for Gaspar, the wide-winged goshawk she'd found as a wounded nestling and raised with care. Gaspar was always the last to arrive, and he did so with silent fanfare, his wings flapping with authority. The smaller birds, Gaspar's offspring, took wing and circled overhead until his perch was steady. Fury giggled as they flew down to take positions to the left and right of their impressive sire. She was reminded of a row of soldiers awaiting orders, she the general in command. She clapped her hands and watched in amusement as twenty pairs of eyes turned to watch her expectantly.

''Ladies first.'' She smiled as she held out a handful of meat scraps flavored with congealed bacon fat. One by one the birds ate their fill, pecking daintily from the palm of her hand. When they finished she said, ''Shoo,'' and as one they flew to separate perches in the trees.

Gaspar waited patiently for the words that would signal it was his turn. And as always, it was her scarred arm, thonged with leather, that he perched on—the right one, scored deeply in several places from a long-ago battle to save him from the talons of a huge marauding kite. "For you, my darling," Fury crooned. "Eat like a gentleman." And he did, allowing her at the same time to tweak his long beak with her soft touch.

"I'm going to miss you, Gaspar, and all the others, too, but I have to go," Fury murmured. "I'll never forget you." Gaspar cocked his dark head and stared at her with his shiny eyes. "I know you understand everything I say. From the day I saved you, we . . . it must be like that special feeling a mother has when her baby recovers from a sickness after she nurses it through the night. You'll always belong to me, Gaspar. And you'll be well taken care of when I've gone, that's a promise. Now it's time for you to get out of this hot sun. Go, and later I'll have a special treat for your little ones. Take this to Pilar for now," she said, holding out two small chunks of bacon fat. Gaspar took both pieces in his talons and flew high into the trees, where Pilar sat with her fresh crop of nestlings. Fury had christened the two tiny birds the moment they'd emerged from their protective shells: Sato and Lago. She had no way of knowing from the vantage point at her bedroom window if the birds were male or female. And she'd never see the little ones take wing for the first time. A single tear dropped to her hand. She would miss them terribly. Another tear fell on her hand as two pairs of dark eyes watched from the branches overhead. Wings flapped and leaves rustled as the young woman wiped away her tears with a lace-edged handkerchief.

"Fury," Sirena called from beyond the closed bedroom door, "is it safe to come in?"

Fury smiled and opened the door to her mother. "Yes, they're gone, Mother, dinner is over. I think Gaspar knows I'm leaving. Pilar, too. It makes me very sad."

It was on the tip of Sirena's tongue to beg her daughter

one more time to change her mind, but she resisted the impulse. Fury loved Gaspar and Pilar as much as she loved her family—in a way, they were *part* of her family—but she was willing to leave them behind. "The cook will take good care of them, darling."

"I know, Mother, it's just that Gaspar is like a child to me. I will worry about him and Pilar, I can't help it." She shook her head and sighed. "I'm not very hungry. Would you mind if I walked through the garden for a while?"

"Of course not, go along. But I'd like you to take a nap before the ball. Will you do that for me?"

"Of course, Mother, but only if you promise to take one, too."

Sirena nodded, not trusting her voice, and gave her daughter a kiss as she left the room.

"She has so many good-byes," Regan said hoarsely. "Every bird, every animal in the garden, will get a pat and a few words of loving remembrance. My God, Sirena, what did we do wrong to make our daughter want to leave us like this?"

Sirena toyed with the food on her plate and tried to speak past the lump in her throat. "Is it possible we loved her too much? . . . Oh, Regan, we can't talk about this again, it's killing me." Sirena's eyes flew to the wall above the sideboard in the dining room. Crossed rapiers, hers and Regan's, gleamed in the filtered sunlight. "He's punishing me, Regan, you, too. I know you don't believe in Fury's God, but this time you must believe me. We're being punished."

Regan's clenched fist pounded the table, causing china and silver to dance in front of their eyes. "I refuse to believe that! I won't believe some . . . spirit controls our lives, our daughter's life. I never understood all those holy words you say over wooden beads. It's demented. If there is a God, why did he allow your sister to be raped and killed? And our sons. What kind of God would allow our flesh and blood to be lost at sea? Why did he allow you to suffer so, and why is he taking Fury from us? How many times you called me a heathen, Sirena, because I don't believe. Twice now you have renounced this God of yours. Is it going to help matters? Is Fury going to stay with us? The answer is no.''

Sirena lifted her head, her green eyes sparkling dangerously. How many times they'd had this same conversation, and always it ended in anger, with each of them going for their rapiers and threatening the other with death. ''Damn you, Regan, not today! I refuse to fence with you.''

''And I have no time to fence with the winner,'' came a soft voice from the dining room threshold.

Regan and Sirena whirled about, surprised. Then Sirena laughed, the tense moment between her husband and herself broken . . . which had been Fury's intention. Always before when husband and wife worked out their hostilities with the rapier, it was the daughter who fenced with the winner. Every bit as artful as Sirena, she also had the stamina and hard-driving determination of Regan. She'd lost only one match, and that had been several years before. Now she was better than ever with a rapier. The cutlass was another story altogether. Her father had worked with her for hours at a time, strengthening her weakened right arm until even he had admitted they were evenly matched.

Fencing was an art, a sport, and Fury excelled at it just as she did at everything. She knew she brought tears to her mother's eyes when she plucked the strings of her guitar and again when her nimble fingers slid over the spinet that sat in the drawing room. Her voice was trained, thanks to her mother, and she often sang for guests.

They'd given her everything, these wonderful parents, big strapping brothers to love, a fine education, their love, this beautiful casa to live in . . . everything parents gave a child, and now she was casting it all aside.

Sirena gazed warmly into Regan's eyes. "She's right, darling, today is not the day to vent our hostilities." She rose to embrace her husband.

Watching them, Fury smiled. Now she knew *exactly* what her parents would be doing later instead of fighting.

"I think that I will check on the progress in the ballroom," she drawled. "Guests should be arriving in a few hours. I want to make sure there are enough fresh flowers." Sirena winked roguishly at her daughter as she and her husband glided from the room.

As Fury walked through the halls, she thought about her parents and their wonderful life. They loved passionately, quarreled just as passionately, and nothing would ever separate them. They lived and loved for each other. She thought it miraculous the way their love had survived all these years. "There are other kinds of love," she muttered to herself as she picked a wilted leaf from a flower arrangement. Love *had* to be more than just physical— passion-bruised lips, sweaty bodies, touching and caressing . . . When she was fifteen her mother had tried to explain about that side of it, but she'd felt too much shame to listen. *That* had been a mistake. She should have tried to understand instead of harboring such wicked imaginings. Right now, this very second, her parents were probably . . . touching, feeling, kissing . . . Swallowing hard, she ran down the corridor like a wild boy past her parents' bedroom. Face flaming, she made her way to the pond in the garden, where she dropped to her knees and splashed cool water on her burning cheeks.

The air around her churned as Gaspar and Pilar, their huge wings creating an umbrella over her, finally settled on her shoulders. Fury sighed. "You always know when something is troubling me, don't you, Gaspar? Pilar, you get back to those babies right now, do you hear me? I'm fine. Gaspar, make her go back, the babies might tumble from the nest."

Gaspar daintily moved on her shoulder until one large wing nudged Pilar. Pilar tucked her head down and pecked Fury's cheek before she took wing.

"You have to be stern with her, Gaspar, she's a mother now. You must make sure nothing happens to the little ones. It's your responsibility to care for them until they can fly themselves. Look at me. Tomorrow I leave this nest and head for Java. It's time for me to leave and be on my own, to find my destiny. It's been so wonderful, but all things must come to an end. Come here, Gaspar, I need to hold you, to feel the beat of your heart, to know I'm the one who has saved you so that you could find Pilar and . . . and . . . make . . . babies like Sato and Lago. It's natural that this should happen for you, for others, but not for me. I promised myself to God, so these worldly emotions are not for me. You can go now," Fury cooed. "Go ahead, I'm fine now. Pilar will peck your eyes out if you don't behave yourself."

"Haw!" the huge bird squawked. Fury laughed as Gaspar flew toward the trees. "Haw!" his mate answered. Everyone, even the birds, had someone.

Fury flirted with her image in the mirror, twirling this way and that way to assess the effects of the costly gown on her lithe figure. Miss Antonia was to be congratulated: with this particular dress, the seamstress had achieved perfection. Her mother had chosen the design, but she had picked the color, a deep azure blue that complemented her indigo eyes and honey coloring. She loved the deep cleavage and the way the dress fell away from her tiny waist in deep swirls. Miniature seed pearls and sparkling gemstones were randomly sewn over the gown and along the length of the hem and sleeves, winking and shimmering every time she moved. Her mother would be delighted.

She'd dressed her own hair, piling it high on top of her head with ebony ringlets curling and feathering about her ears and neck. A veritable waterfall of diamonds graced her ears and slender throat. She would be the belle of this particular ball—her parting gift to her mother and father. They expected her to enjoy herself, to dance with all the eligible gentlemen and to flirt shamelessly. And she would; it wasn't too much to ask, and she was more than willing to create one last memory for her parents.

She was ready with minutes to spare, enough time to add just a smidgin of color to her lips and cheeks. Next she eyed the sparkling diamond garter her mother had given her when she was seventeen. It was decadently wicked, but as long as she was going through all the motions, she might as well put it on.

She braced one long, tawny leg on the dressing table bench and secured the garter a few inches above her knee. It fit as perfectly as it had the day of her seventeenth birthday. Cheeks awash with color, she walked to the mirror, skirts in hand, and stared at the precious gems adorning her thigh and felt a rush of heat through her body. She turned from the mirror in time to see Gaspar land daintily on the window ledge, his talons securing his position. "Haw."

"My sentiments exactly," Fury said, quietly letting her skirts drop. "I don't like the way this makes me feel, Gaspar. It . . . it makes me feel . . . so . . . sinful.

"I can't wear this," she muttered. "I don't know what Mother was thinking of when she gave it to me." In a frenzy she released the catch of the garter and threw it on the bed, where it shimmered like a snakeskin. Her color still high, she ran to the basin of water on her nightstand to wash her hands.

"Lord, forgive my sinful thoughts. I'm trying to do . . . to act . . . I'll never think such thoughts again," she gasped.

"Gaspar, Gaspar," she said, an hour later tripping over to the huge bird. "You've never seen me looking like this, have you? At first I felt rather silly, as though I were dressing up in Mother's clothes, but now . . . I rather like the way I look. It's just for this one night," she said, stroking the bird's velvety feathers.

His perch secure, the bird dipped its head and pecked at the dangling diamonds in her ear. Fury smiled. "I saw your babies fly. You should have warned me somehow, Gaspar. They were wobbly, but Pilar was right behind them. It was wonderful. Tomorrow they will fly farther and the day after still farther. The basket was a good idea, one of my better ones," Fury cooed to the hawk. "They all told me Pilar wouldn't make her nest in it because I touched it, but I knew better because you carried it to the trees for her. I feel like crying, Gaspar, and I don't know why. I'm going to miss you and this house and everyone. Part of me doesn't want to leave, that little part of me I'm selfishly withholding from God. That small part that is me, Furana. I want to give entirely of myself, but—" One large wing fluttered and opened to spread over Fury's dark head. For a moment she allowed herself to lean against the bird's hard chest. "Don't forget about me, Gaspar," she choked. "I must go now. I'm going to be late."

The hawk's eyes never left the girl until the door closed behind her. "Haw, haw, haw!" he screeched. An answering sound echoed down from the basket perched high in the breadfruit tree. The bird's talons dug deep into the chair back as his huge wings lifted outward. He swooped about the room, heading straight for Fury's bed. His talons dug into the coverlet until his grasp on the diamond garter was secure. His surge through the open window was swift and sure as he soared upward to his mate. "Haw, haw!"

"My God, Regan, she's a vision of beauty," Sirena whispered as Fury entered the ballroom.

Speechless, Regan stared at his daughter. She looked exactly like her mother. He wanted to say something, to compliment this child of his, but as always at moments like this, his tongue stuck to the roof of his mouth.

Fury assumed her position in the receiving line, and the formality of her birthday ball began. She smiled charmingly, every inch her mother's daughter as she greeted the guests who'd come to wish her well. When the last guest sailed through the flowered archway, Regan raised his hand to the musicians, their signal to start the music. Instantly a handsome young man claimed Fury and whisked her onto the dance floor.

"She's more graceful when she fences, don't you think?" Regan observed to Sirena as he saw his daughter stumble over her partner's foot.

"She gets her clumsiness from you," Sirena muttered. "We Spanish are light of foot, graceful, and demure." Regan chuckled as his wife glided away to mingle with her guests.

"Sirena, my dear, however did you manage all this?" Doña Louisa asked as she waved her arms about the flower-decked ballroom.

Sirena smiled and squeezed her friend's arm. "With a great deal of patience, Louisa," she said. "The flowers were brought in this afternoon from the greenhouses. I wanted to make sure they didn't wilt. Darling, you must try some of the rum punch we've laid out; it's a family recipe— Oh, there's Don Carlos. I must speak to him, Louisa. We'll talk more later, I promise.'' With that, Sirena hurried off into the crowd.

She had to admit that the great ballroom did look like something out of a fairy tale, with the monstrous crystal chandeliers and matching sconces that winked and twinkled with the dancers' movements. The musicians were dressed in impeccable white with crimson cravats and cummerbunds that set off the scarlet blooms surrounding the dais where they strummed their guitars. They were playing a lovely ballad, and more couples swirled onto the dance floor in time to the music.

Sirena moved to the rear of the room to check the serving tables. Her practiced eye told her everything was in order. The Spanish lace that had been in her family for ages was pressed and draped to perfection on the long tables, and she knew the linen skirts under the fine lace held no wrinkles either. Satisfied that the dining room and buffet tables could not be improved upon, she turned and peered over the heads of a young couple ready to move onto the dance floor. Fury whirled by in the arms of a dashing young man who devoured her with the eyes of a puppy, warm and adoring.

Catching sight of her mother, Fury grimaced, either at her own clumsiness on the dance floor or at her partner's obvious devotion. Sirena winked at her daughter to show she understood perfectly and then lost sight of her as the crush of dancing couples swallowed them up. Suddenly, Sirena found herself blinking back tears, and she hurried away.

When Fury lost sight of her mother, she returned her attention to the engaging young man in her arms. Ramon was everything a girl could wish for—charming, well brought up, and classically handsome, with olive-toned skin and ink-black eyes. He was also sweating profusely, and at last Fury took pity on him. "It's beastly hot in here, Ramon, would you like a breath of air? I know I would."

"Yes, yes, I would," he replied eagerly, his heart beginning to pound as she linked her arm in his to lead him off the dance floor and through the wide double doors to the veranda. If only he could kiss her, hold her face in his hands and kiss her until . . . He stumbled, and Fury's tinkling laugh made him bolt for the open door.

"What is it, Ramon, do you feel faint?" Fury asked as she noticed the young man's trembling shoulders.

He hated Fury's sisterly tone. "No, it's just that I—I had this sudden urge to . . . kiss you in there," he said, waving toward the ballroom. "You look so beautiful, *carida*. Everyone always said your mother was the most beautiful woman in Cadiz," he blurted out, "but they're wrong, you are."

Fury stepped backward, aware suddenly that the air about them was no longer still. Trees rustled overhead, a familiar sound. Gaspar was close, probably perched on the veranda roof observing her. She craned her neck to peer past the lanterns that were strung along the sloping roof.

"What is it?" Ramon asked, looking about uneasily.

"Nothing, why do you ask?" she replied, her eyes searching past the lantern light for some sign of the hawk. "You said you wanted to kiss me; well, here I am." At twenty-one, Fury had yet to be kissed. Now she decided it was time. She moved closer to her young man, holding up her head, eyes closed, and puckering her lips in a classic pose of breathless anticipation.

Ramon swallowed, his Adam's apple bobbing in excitement as he licked at his dry lips nervously. He reached out and grasped Fury's shoulders with both hands.

How long did it take to kiss someone? Fury wondered

peevishly—and then a sudden rush of air in the warm evening startled her. She knew it was not Ramon.

Her eyes snapped open the next moment as she heard the sound of wings. Gaspar and Pilar swooped down from the veranda roof, and there was nothing playful about their descent. In the lantern light she could see the birds' glittering eyes as the tips of their huge wings bombarded Ramon, knocking him over the veranda railing. Fury knew instantly that the birds were merely warning the young man: their talons were curled; otherwise they would have ripped Ramon to shreds. But *he* knew nothing of the kind.

Forgetting herself, Fury hiked up her skirts and leapt over the railing. "No!" she shouted sternly. "Gaspar, no! Pilar, no! Now look what you've done!" She tried to stifle her laughter at Ramon's ungainly position in the oleander bush. "He's fainted. No doubt from fright."

Gaspar circled overhead, his eyes intent on the figure on the ground. "He wasn't going to hurt me," she called softly. "Kisses don't hurt. I . . . wanted to see what it felt like."

Pilar's wings flapped twice before she headed back to her perch in the trees. Gaspar circled the couple several times, his wings flapping angrily before he headed back to the veranda roof.

Fury knelt over the prostrate young man. "I'm so sorry, Ramon . . . Ramon, wake up. It's all right." Fury leaned down and kissed him lightly on the lips. She blinked and then kissed him again, just as lightly, savoring the feel of his lips beneath hers. She wondered then what it would feel like if he were awake and responding. She sat down amid the oleander leaves, her elbows propped on her knees.

"Fury, what in the world . . . ?"

Fury looked up into Sirena's emerald eyes . . . and

sighed. "It's a long story, Mother, and I don't think you'd believe it. It's not what you think."

Sirena dropped to her knees to peer at Ramon. "He looks like he was attacked. Darling, did he fight over you?"

"What's going on?" Regan demanded, hurrying down to join his wife.

Fury laughed then, a delightful tinkle that wafted through the garden as she tried to explain what happened. "He's not dead, is he, Father?" she asked anxiously.

Regan felt for a pulse, then shook his head. "I doubt it, but he looks as if he was damn near frightened to death."

"My God, Regan, what will we tell his parents?" Sirena asked anxiously.

"Nothing, Mother. Go back with Father, and I'll . . . I'll think of something to say when he wakes up. He's going to be embarrassed when he comes around, and doubly so if you're here."

Sirena nodded. "She's right. Come along, darling, and let's leave these two . . . lovebirds to their explaining."

Regan shivered when her laughter, so like Fury's, rippled about him. How was it possible they could be alike in so many ways and yet so opposite in others? Could two predatory hawks truly be emotionally tied to his daughter? If one of his men had told him such a story, he'd never have believed it.

"I'll be damned," he muttered as he suffered through a second dance with his nimble-footed wife.

"Damn you, Fury, if you didn't want to kiss me, all you had to do was say so instead of knocking me over the railing!" Ramon grumbled as he got to his feet.

"It wasn't me," Fury said, stifling a giggle at the look on his face.

"What do you mean, it wasn't you? There wasn't a soul out here but us." His voice carried the full weight of his indignation and bruised pride as he swiped at the crushed petals and leaves on his clothing.

"It was Gaspar. He's on the roof. I guess he thought you were going . . . to hurt me," Fury explained. "You're lucky, Ramon, he and Pilar could have torn you to pieces. He was playing." She smiled indulgently.

"Playing!" Ramon cried. He eyed the huge bird uneasily, afraid to move toward the veranda. Fury linked her arm through his and led him around the garden to the wide, white steps.

"They kill, and you keep them as pets. It's insane," Ramon sputtered. "Their wings alone could crush a person to death and those feet . . . My God, Fury, they'll turn wild when you leave!"

Fury sobered instantly. She'd thought the same thing more than once. "They have their little ones now to protect; they'll miss me for a while, but I don't think they'll . . . You're wrong, Ramon. If the servants continue to leave food for them, they'll stay here. They're the way they are because I saved Gaspar once from the talons of a kite. It's his way of repaying me."

"And you're scarred for life. Your mother told my mother you almost lost your arm," Ramon said heatedly.

"Well, I didn't, and that's behind us. You're not hurt, only your dignity is wounded. No one knows but us, and I won't mention it."

"Well, I certainly don't intend to stay *here* any longer, not with that . . . that *vulture* guarding your every move! Good night, Fury," Ramon muttered, and marched toward his parents' waiting carriage.

Fury sat down on one of the veranda's wicker chairs. She supposed she should be upset, but she wasn't. Ramon was such a . . . boy, even if he was her age. Kissing him would have been like kissing one of her brothers.

The shadow was ominous as it sailed gracefully into the lantern light to perch on the veranda railing. The bird's glittering eyes stared at the girl, and one wing lifted slightly in apology. Fury inclined her head and smiled.

"Apology accepted," she said softly.

The bird soared upward, the white tips of his wings eerie-looking in the yellow light.

Inside, the musicians were readying the guests for the quadrille. It was her party, and she'd been outside far too long. Fixing a smile on her face, she sailed through the door to join in the dance.

Regan stood on the sidelines and watched his wife and daughter on the dance floor. His eyes sparked dangerously as he noticed Sirena's partner—a slick, overdressed dandy twenty years younger than his wife—blatantly attempting to seduce her. His wife, he noticed, was flirting outrageously.

Suddenly he laughed. There was a time when he would have hauled the younger man out to the veranda and whipped him soundly for such behavior, but he'd mellowed over the years. She was his, she always was and always would be. He was the one who sat across the table from her, and it was his arms that enfolded her at evening's end—he who made wild, passionate love to her until break of day. While he may have mellowed, his passions had not. She still excited him beyond comprehension. All she had to do was look at him, smile or wink, and he wanted to snatch her by the hair and drag her off to his lair.

He could watch her now and feel sympathy for the man twirling her around the dance floor. No one but Regan van der Rhys would ever taste Sirena's charms.

Sirena whirled by again, her tinkling laughter swirling about him like a soft caress. He played the game and scowled, to his wife's delight. Then he looked around, and noticed that the eyes of all his guests were on Sirena. She was easily the most beautiful, the best-dressed woman in the room, or perhaps the second best. It was hard for him to make that particular decision when he compared her with Fury.

The dance ended with a loud fanfare. Sirena smiled at her partner and placed her hand on his arm as he escorted her to Regan, who was still scowling. Sirena lowered her lashes and then inclined her head slightly. Regan blinked at the searing passion he saw in her eyes. Involuntarily, his loins twitched. Sirena laughed, her gaze now bold and openly seductive. "Later," she cooed as she was whisked away in the arms of another guest.

"Jesus Christ," Regan muttered under his breath. Later was still hours away. She always did this to him, and he always reacted in the same way. Just as she was his, he was hers, and she was letting him know it. He inched forward, and as Sirena danced by, he mouthed, "I love you." She smiled radiantly and blew him a kiss. He was the envy of every man in the room, and he loved the feeling.

Watching them, Fury flushed at her mother's open display of love for her father. Then she laughed—to her partner's delight. Unlike her mother, she'd never flirted or pretended to like men much. It might be fun to try. She smiled and stared into her partner's warm gaze.

"You look especially handsome this evening, Diego," she purred, her hand on his arm tightening imperceptibly.

Diego stiffened and then relaxed. This wasn't the Fury he'd grown up with. And what about Ramon? he wondered. Wasn't he her favorite? He'd seen Fury go out to the veranda with him, yet she'd returned alone. "Did you kiss him?" he blurted out.

Fury laughed gaily. "But of course, and if you draw me closer to you, I'll kiss you too . . . on the cheek," she murmured, and slipped from his arms to those of another as the dance ended and another began.

Suddenly Fury realized she was having a wonderful time, something she'd thought impossible, as she flitted from one partner to another like a bird. Out of the corner of her eye she became aware of a tall, handsome stranger, a guest of the Parish family. In another second her partner would swoop her by the Parishes, and if she so desired, she could smile at him the way her mother did. Without a second thought she turned her head and stared directly into the eyes of Doña Louisa's guest. What would it be like to kiss *him*? she wondered. She laughed, a gay, throaty chuckle—much to the surprise of her partner, who wondered what it was he'd said to make her laugh.

Breathless from her dancing, Fury walked over to her parents. When she turned back to give the handsome stranger a demure smile, she saw that he was not even aware of her! No, he was too busy bowing low over her friend Daniella's hand and ogling her low-cut gown. Daniella was blushing and making cow eyes at him in return. Annoyed with herself, Fury turned to meet her mother's gaze.

"He didn't come through the receiving line, so he must have arrived late," Sirena said softly. "I'm surprised that Doña Louisa hasn't brought him over to be introduced. Handsome devil, almost as good-looking as your father."

"No one is as handsome as Father," Fury said loyally. She wondered if he would ask her to dance; good manners dictated it, but this man, Fury decided as yet another man led her out onto the floor, this man did not abide by rules of any kind. She flushed again, wondering where and how she'd come by such a thought.

"You look angry, Fury," her partner observed quietly.

"Angry? Me? How absurd!" No, she wasn't angry, Fury told herself. She was . . . *jealous*—jealous of Daniella, an emotion she'd never felt before. She hated it. "Ruiz, I really could use a breath of air if you wouldn't mind." Cheeks burning, she almost ran from the ballroom to the coolness of the veranda.

"It's such a beautiful evening, isn't it? I love the darkness with the stars and moon for light. Look how silvery everything looks. It's so . . . so romantic, don't you think?" She didn't wait for Ruiz's reply but rushed on. "I wonder how many lovers have kissed and embraced under the stars. Thousands, probably. Even the animals like darkness, it protects them, but there's no one to protect lovers except . . . Why aren't you saying anything, Ruiz?"

Ruiz smiled wryly. "Because you haven't given me a chance. Fury, we've known each other since you came to Spain at the age of eight. In all those years I've never seen you act this way. Is it because you're leaving tomorrow for . . . your holy life, or is it that you're beginning to realize you're making a mistake? I—I couldn't help but notice the way you looked at Don Parish's guest. We've been friends a long time, Fury, and if you want to talk about this, I'm willing to listen. You have my word that it will go no further."

"Even to Daniella's ears?" Fury teased. "Were you jealous when she danced with . . . him?"

"Yes, very. Daniella told me she wants a man who makes her blood sing. I don't think I'm that man," Ruiz said ruefully.

"How is that possible, to make your blood sing?"

Ruiz shrugged. "I have no idea, but Daniella said that's what every woman wants from a man. If I knew how to accomplish that, I'd probably be the most sought-after man in all of Spain.''

Fury contemplated him with thoughtful eyes. "I think Daniella was teasing you, Ruiz."

"No, she means it. I would marry her in a minute, but she won't have me."

"Because . . ."

"I don't make her blood sing." Ruiz threw up his hands in disgust.

They stood together for several moments in silence, staring out across the manicured gardens. At last Fury turned to Ruiz and placed a gentle hand on his arm. "Come, let's go in, Ruiz. I have to speak to my mother, and it's almost time for the food to be served. Father plans on making a toast or two. . . . And I wouldn't worry about Daniella. She'll soon see what a wonderful person you are. I believe that, I truly do."

He drew her arm through his and began to escort her back inside the ballroom. "You'll never know, will you? You'll be off praying for all of us, and we'll never see you again. You'll never know who will marry whom and who will have children." He stared down at her with wide, troubled eyes. "Oh, damn you, Fury, why are you going off to some damn-fool convent never to be seen again? It's not natural!"

Fury stopped in her tracks. It was true, everything Ruiz said. Soon all her friends would be just a memory.

"And another thing," he continued bitterly, "don't go praying for me. Pray for yourself. . . . Oh, never mind," he muttered. "Happy birthday!" And with that, he stomped off in Daniella's direction, leaving an astonished Fury to return unescorted to her parents.

"Mother, can I ask you something?" she said as Sirena took her arm and drew her in beside her. "It's . . . what I mean is . . . Ruiz said something to me out on the veranda just now that . . . Well, it seems impossible, but he did say it, and I was wondering . . . Does Father . . . does he make your blood sing?''

Sirena laughed. ''Twenty-four hours a day, my sweet. From the first moment I saw him. Come, let's ask your father the same question.'' She turned to her husband, who was several feet away chatting with an elderly gentleman. Catching his eye, she beckoned discreetly.

Regan excused himself and joined his wife, giving Fury an affectionate smile. ''Yes, my dear?''

''Regan, Fury has a question for you. Do I make your blood sing?''

Regan stared first at his wife and then at his daughter. He fought the laughter bubbling in his throat when he. saw from his daughter's face that she was quite serious. ''Yes, my darling daughter, she does. The moment I laid eyes on her, she captivated me. My blood has never been still. It's called love, Furana.'' Regan held her chin in his hand and stared into her eyes. ''I truly regret that you will never experience this particular emotion.''

''I, too, regret it,'' Fury said, so softly her parents had to strain to hear the words.

Suddenly, to break the moment, Regan clapped his hands and announced a toast. ''Well wishes for our daughter's birthday!'' Waiters appeared as if by magic with elaborate trays full of crystal goblets filled to the brim with sparkling champagne. A chorus of Happy Birthdays reverberated throughout the ballroom. Regan raised his hand, and once again the musicians took their places. He bowed low. ''Señorita, I believe this dance is mine,'' he said gallantly.

Tears streaming down her cheeks, Sirena watched her husband and daughter trample upon each other's feet as they whirled and twirled about the room to uproarious applause. When at last the music stopped, the dancers limped off the floor to another round of applause.

"I think our guests are getting impatient," Regan said, beaming down upon his lovely daughter, "so let me get your dinner partner and we'll get things under way. I hope you don't mind, sweetheart, but so many of your young men clamored for the honor of escorting you in that we thought it most politic to accept the invitation of Don Parish, who has volunteered his guest to do the honors. Stay right here and I'll be back in a moment."

Sirena heard her daughter's gasp and smiled. So, she mused, her daughter's blood *was* capable of singing.

Luis Domingo was as tall as Regan, broad-chested with narrow hips and well-muscled legs that strained slightly against his immaculate white linen trousers. His eyes were dark and as inky black as his hair, a lock of which tumbled over his forehead. *Handsome* was the only word Fury could think of as her father introduced him.

"Furana, may I present Luis Domingo, Don Parish's house guest. Señor Domingo, my daughter, Furana."

"Señorita, it is my pleasure," said Luis, bowing low over her hand.

Fury was unprepared for the timbre of his voice, deep and oddly compelling. Unaccountably, she blushed and withdrew her hand, averting her eyes demurely. "Bewitching," he murmured.

"What—I beg your pardon?" Fury stammered.

"He said you were bewitching," Regan said sourly.

White teeth flashed in amusement as Luis held out his arms. Fury's heart skipped a beat at the feel of her escort's hard, sinewy arm. This was no boy like all the others. She wondered what Gaspar would do to *this* man if he kissed her.

Domingo gazed about him at the lavish banquet tables

with their rainbow-hued waterfalls. His dark eyes took in the fine crystal and silver and lace. This ball had to cost a fortune, he reflected, probably more than he earned in a year. But that would all change . . . soon. He smiled at Fury. "Forgive me for staring like a field hand, but I've never seen anything to equal this," he said with a wave of his hand. He took a plate and began to fill it from among the countless delicacies spread out before them.

"It's my birthday." There was a note of apology in her voice. "My parents wanted this to be an elaborate affair since it will be the last . . . what I mean is . . ."

"You're leaving to enter the convent tomorrow." He nodded. "Doña Louisa explained it all to me. There's no need for apologies—unless you're uncertain of your vocation."

She flushed. "I guess I was apologizing, and no, I'm not uncertain. It's just that we Spanish tend to do things in a grand way." She was babbling, she knew, but she couldn't help herself.

Again Luis smiled at her. "But you're half Dutch," aren't you?"

Fury stared at her escort with unabashed admiration. His was a beautiful smile, endearing somehow, she thought. "Yes—I—I am half Dutch," she roused herself to reply. "But my upbringing has been Spanish. My mother is Spanish, my father Dutch. . . ."

White teeth flashed. "Yes, I know," he said. With a flourish, he offered her a plate piled high with pink shrimp, squab, and lobster on a bed of rice.

Fury stared at it with bewildered eyes. "I can't possibly eat—"

"I'll help you finish it," Luis assured her. "Doña Louisa insists that one never go to the table twice—in public. I would prefer to eat on the veranda, if it's agreeable."

Obediently, Fury followed alongside him, praying Gaspar would just this once leave her alone to enjoy the attentions of such a fascinating man.

As the couple ate, they talked of inconsequential things, the weather, the beautiful casa she lived in, the tropical flowers that scented the air, her parents.

"I think I've been doing most of the talking," Fury said at last, folding her napkin neatly beside her plate.

Luis laughed. "It's your birthday. I understand that once you enter your order you will take a vow of silence. This is something I cannot comprehend."

"You are not a religious man, then?"

"I believe in God, if that's what you mean, but I don't spend all my time in church praying. Goodness must come from here." He touched his chest.

Fury remained silent, her eyes drawn to his hands. They were the largest she'd ever seen; she wondered if they were rough and callused. Then she looked up and found him staring at her intently, so intently that she flushed. Obviously, he was waiting for a response. "I—I believe that most people believe in God, some more than others," she said hesitantly. "There are those who call on Him when they need something and forget about Him the rest of the time. I've known I was meant for the convent since I was ten or so, but I waited until now for my parents' sake. . . . But enough about me," she said, clapping her hands to dismiss the subject. "What do you do . . . Luis?"

As he gazed into the depths of her blue eyes, Luis suddenly found himself wanting to tell this lovely creature everything about him . . . every secret he'd ever held close to his heart. But did he dare? And, even more to the point, would she understand? "What do I do?" he said lightly. "I turn up in unlikely places and escort beautiful ladies to dinner. . . . No, actually, I spend most of my time looking for the marauder who ruined my father's small company—which certainly isn't proper dinner conversation at a birthday ball.''

Fury blinked at Luis's startling response. She was utterly mesmerized and wanted to hear more, but . . . ''I think Doña Louisa is trying to attract your attention,'' she said reluctantly. ''She's usually the first to leave a party. I—I would like to thank you for your kind gesture this evening. . . .''

Dark eyes scalded her. ''You were a damsel in distress, it was my duty.'' His voice was suddenly as mocking as his countenance.

Fury's eyes sparked. ''I didn't realize it was such a chore—or is it that I'm going into the convent and you feel you can't waste your time with someone who . . .''

''Yes?'' he prodded.

''Nothing, señor,'' she said stiffly. ''Thank you again. I enjoyed our talk . . . for a little while.''

Luis bowed low and then brought her hand to his lips. His dark eyes caught and held hers. ''Might I ask a favor?''

Blood rushed to Fury's cheeks, and her heart started to pound. He was going to ask if he could kiss her. Not trusting herself to speak, she nodded.

''Pray for me that I find the marauder who ruined and killed my father.'' An instant later he was gone, weaving his way through the clusters of people in the ballroom.

Fury turned and ran down the veranda steps into the darkest part of the garden. She knew her cheeks were flaming; even her ears felt hot. She clutched her chest as though the movement would still her heart.

The handsome Spaniard hadn't wanted to kiss her. No, *she* had wanted him to kiss her. Now she felt shame and wished for her rosary. She would pray through the dawn, begging God's forgiveness for her wicked thoughts, and then she would pray for Luis Domingo—not for the vengeance he sought, but for his immortal soul.

The moment the last coach clattered down the cobblestone drive, Fury embraced her parents. "It was a wonderful party! I think everyone had a wonderful time; I know I did. Thank you so much. I'll never forget it. Never!"

Sirena hugged her, then pulled back to smile into her daughter's eyes. "It's almost dawn, darling. Why don't you try to sleep for a little while. Your father and I are exhausted. Shall we have breakfast around nine o'clock?"

Fury nodded. "That sounds wonderful, Mother." She kissed both her parents and hurried off.

In the privacy of her own room, she removed the confining gown and petticoats and laid them over the back of a chair with a weary sigh. Her jewelry was placed in a velvet-lined jewel cask, to be turned over to her mother before she left. Then, clad in a soft silken wrapper, rosary in hand, she dropped to her knees at the side of the bed and bowed her head. Her lips moved soundlessly. When, hours later, she raised her head and opened her eyes, it was full light.

She looked around, disconcerted for a moment. A shaft of sunlight speared across the room, bathing the clock on her night table in its bright light. Fury peered at the numerals and realized she had less than thirty minutes to dress for breakfast.

Breakfast was a tense affair: Sirena on the verge of tears; Regan grim and tight-lipped, staring at his plate.

"It's a beautiful day," Fury said brightly.

"Good headwinds. The *Java Queen* will get off to a good start," Regan agreed soberly. "Your mother and I made the decision for the *Queen* to sail with an empty

hold. She'll ride high in the water, proof that she carries
no cargo. Any marauding pirates will think twice about
attacking a ship without cargo. It's for your safety, Fury.
Ronrico Diaz is the best seafaring captain, next to myself,
that I would trust with you and the *Queen*.

"I don't like it one damn bit that you made us both
promise not to take on passengers. I know what you said,
that you wanted to pray and be alone with your
thoughts," he said when he saw that his daughter was
about to protest. "You'll have the rest of your life to
pray. You should have company, people to talk to, to dine
with. I don't like it one damn bit, and neither does your
mother." Frustrated, Regan banged his fist on the table,
and Fury flinched.

"I don't give a damn about the revenues," he continued. "I do give a damn about your sailing alone with a
crew and no passengers to keep you company. It doesn't
matter if the crew is loyal and hand-picked or not. We're
giving in to your wishes because you begged us, and in-
dulgent parents that we are, we can deny you nothing. In
our hearts we know Captain Diaz will protect you with his
life."

Fury thanked both her parents with her eyes. She
smiled. "I have as much faith and trust in Captain Diaz
as you do, Father. I've known the crew of the *Queen* for
years. They won't let me fall in harm's way. I need this
time alone. Please, you must tell me that you understand.
Mother?"

Sirena smiled at her daughter, tears shimmering in her
eyes. "No, there's no one better than Diaz," she echoed.

"Sixteen weeks will see you in Java. We've arranged
for you to go to our house and rest before . . . Father
Miguel will be waiting to personally escort you to the
convent doors. It's all been arranged. You must promise

me, Fury, that you won't deviate. . . . What I mean to say is . . ."

Fury leaned across the table, her voice earnest yet quiet. "Mother, I'm twenty-one years old. I've sailed with both you and Father since I was five. I can take care of myself. Please don't worry about me. If I remember correctly, you yourself were quite notorious at my age. And as for you, Father," she added impishly, "what would the world think if they knew the governor of the Netherlands was married to the infamous Sea Siren?"

"They would think I'm a very lucky man." Regan grinned. "As far as the world knows, the Sea Siren retired long ago and was never heard of again. Sometimes I think she was a myth myself, the way she disappeared into the mist. Someday, Sirena, I want to hear how you pulled that little trick. And don't tell me it was black magic, either."

Mother and daughter smiled at each other. Clearly there were some things this husband-father didn't need to know. Theirs was a secret Fury would carry with her to her new world of silence. Sirena winked roguishly at her husband and laughed when he scowled.

"What time will you and Father leave for the harbor?" Fury asked, watching them with affection and delight.

"The *Java Star* sets sail at six o'clock. You'll be six hours at sea by the time we get under way," Sirena said quietly. If it weren't for the anguish she felt over Fury, she'd be looking forward to visiting Caleb, Regan's son by a previous marriage, along with his wife and Regan's grandchildren. But she had little heart for the journey now.

"Be sure to give Caleb a big kiss for me and tell Wren my prayers are with her and her brood," Fury said brightly. "It's going to be wonderful for you to see the children. How long will you stay?"

Regan sent Sirena a pointed glance. "As long as your mother wants. We have no itinerary. I've resigned my post as governor and am now fully retired. Perhaps we'll end up in Java at some point in the future. If we do, we'll leave word at the convent.''

Fury stirred spoon after spoon of honey into her coffee. They'd gone over all of this before, at least a dozen times, she thought sadly. Another hour and she would walk out the door for the last time. She dreaded the last good-bye, imagining her mother clinging to her, crying, while her father stood by, stone-faced, angry that she was deserting them. But she couldn't help it—at last the future was hers. She would be doing what she was meant to do: serve God for the rest of her life.

''Do you have the bishop's letter, Fury?'' Sirena asked suddenly. How many times she'd wanted to kick herself for giving her daughter that damned acceptance letter. Had she kept it, Fury would not be leaving them now.

''Yes, Mother, and also the letter from Father Sebastian. You mustn't worry.''

With a bittersweet ache in her heart, Fury gazed around the breakfast room, memorizing it with her eyes. She'd always thought it the homiest of all the rooms in the casa, and it was her favorite, even over her pretty bedroom. Potted blooms in clay pots graced every boundary of the red-tiled floor. Wispy ferns hung from straw baskets near the multipaned windows, all favorites of her mother. The table and chairs, whitewashed iron with persimmon-colored cushions, were also made by her mother. She particularly loved the ancient chestnut tree, outside the wide triple window, that held Gaspar's nest high at the top. He always knew when she was at the table and would come to perch on the sill . . . until today.

''Mother, has Gaspar been at the window?'' she asked suddenly.

''No, he hasn't. Perhaps the party kept him awake and

he's sleeping.'' Sirena smiled wanly. It was so easy to
indulge this child, she thought.

"I don't think Gaspar ever sleeps," Fury said fretfully.
"I think he understands that I'm leaving." She leaned
across the window seat and whistled to the huge hawk.
The leaves remained quiet.

"Maybe he's fishing." Regan grinned. "Don't worry,
sweetheart, he never goes far."

Fury smiled at her father's small joke. She knew he was
trying to keep the moment light for all their sakes, and
she appreciated it. Now that she was within minutes of
departing, she felt strangely at odds with herself. Knowing
she might never see these beloved parents of hers
again . . . Then she straightened her shoulders and willed
her eyes to remain dry. This was what she wanted, had
begged and pleaded to be allowed to do. She wouldn't
back down now. "I'll just run upstairs and get my things.
I heard the carriage arrive a few minutes ago. I'll be down
in a moment."

Fury fled the room, afraid the tears she felt burning her
eyes would overflow. Upstairs, she bolted into her room
and ran to the window, her handkerchief clasped to her
mouth with a trembling hand. Again and again she called
to the birds, but there was no response. Tears slipped down
her cheeks as she craned her neck to peer high into the
trees. All she could see was the umbrellalike leaves, and
none of them stirred in the soft, warm morning air. "Oh,
my fledglings," she whispered, "not even to say good-
bye?"

Slowly Fury gathered her traveling cloak and vanity case.
This awful feeling of suddenly being alone, deserted by the
winged creatures she loved . . . she hated it. She was halfway down the long, winding staircase when she stopped,
eyes wide with sudden understanding. What she was feeling
her parents were feeling, only more so. She was their flesh

and blood, created from love. Their hearts must truly be shattering. She'd been only a temporary guardian to Gaspar and Pilar. The knowledge nearly undid her. Fighting the sob in her throat, she continued down the stairs to join her parents.

"Let me lean on you," Sirena whispered to her husband, devouring Fury with her eyes.

"Only if you let me lean on you, too," Regan whispered back.

"Well, I'm ready," Fury said when she reached them. "I couldn't see Gaspar or Pilar. I guess they're out . . . with the little ones."

Sirena bit down on her lower lip and was rewarded with the salty taste of her own blood. She'd promised herself she wouldn't cry, and by all that was holy, she wouldn't. She didn't want her daughter to remember her as a sniveling, cowardly weakling.

Outside in the bright sunshine, their good-byes were brief, almost aloof. As the carriage rumbled away, Fury moaned and gave way at last to her tears, eyes fixed sightlessly on the road ahead of her. If she had been able to look back, she would have seen her mother crumple against her father's unsteady form. But she would not have noticed Gaspar and Pilar, whose glittering eyes charted her course down the road.

Once the carriage was out of sight, Pilar immediately took wing and headed for the basket in the chestnut tree. When Gaspar was satisfied that she was safe in the top of the tree, he spread his wings and soared high overhead.

Tears streaming down her cheeks, Sirena pointed to the large hawk circling overhead. "He's going to follow her, Regan. Mark my words."

Regan gathered his wife in his arms and stroked her dark head, his eyes on the huge bird. "How do you know this?" he asked in a shaky voice.

"Because he loves her. She saved his life and provided for him all these years. I also have this feeling that he will not . . . let her know he's near. I feel he's going to take our place and . . . protect her."

Regan laughed. "Protect her from whom, God?" The moment the words were out of his mouth, he wished he could take them back.

Sirena stared into her husband's eyes. "There's a special affinity between that hawk and our daughter, and if there's one thing I know, it's that he will protect her with his life. By the time the *Java Queen* reaches Java, those two fledglings in that nest up there will be fully grown. And I like those odds, Regan, I like them very much. I feel much better now, knowing that Fury sails with an escort of four. And as for God, He will have to take His chances the way the rest of us do."

Regan nuzzled his cheek against his wife's glossy black hair, knowing better than to debate the matter further. "Let's walk through the garden, Sirena, before it gets too hot. We are creatures of leisure today. A cooling bath, a short nap, and if you feel in the right frame of mind, a little lovemaking before we sail."

Sirena laughed, the sound tinkling about the garden. She was more than pleased that her husband of so many years still found her desirable at the oddest times.

Overhead, Pilar's wings flapped once at the sound of Sirena's laughter and then stilled. Her diamond-bright eyes never left the strolling couple.

Chapter Two

Saianha, South Africa

The justice was old, his footsteps heavy and unsure as he climbed from the carriage. He cursed his age, the dry, dusty road, and the fact that he was here at all. He'd wanted nothing more than to disregard Amalie Suub's petition, but honest man that he was, he knew he had to at least consider her request.

Sudam Muab looked up at the three-tiered house that had once been Chaezar Alvarez's castle—or kingdom, as Alvarez preferred to call it—before his untimely demise years ago. He'd never forget that day as long as he lived. The servants had carried in the self-appointed king's body, his manhood carved from his loins by a wicked-looking woman wielding a rapier and cutlass—or so said the wide-eyed servants.

The small town had buried the body at sea, but he couldn't remember why. Along with everything else these days, his memory was failing him. This would be his last major decision before turning the reins over to a younger man.

Rotted jungle vegetation all but obscured the fairy-tale house that was once a kingdom for the crafty Spaniard who had built it to his specifications. Muab supposed that if someone had enough money and the inclination, the jungle could be hacked away and the house restored. He'd been

41

the one who had insisted on having the property posted, believing that at some point in the future, Alvarez's heirs would arrive to claim it. But they hadn't. From time to time he'd come out to check on the place, never sure why.

He remembered the day Amalie Suub had walked into his cramped offices, one year ago. She'd said she was daughter and legal heir to Chaezar Alvarez and that she wanted to claim what was hers by the time she reached her twenty-first birthday, which was now a few days away. To support her allegation, she'd presented a marriage contract legalizing Alvarez's union with Amalie's mother. Muab suspected it was a forgery. In any case, he wasn't sure it mattered anymore. The house and holdings, which consisted of furnishings that were full of mildew and rot and two ships that should have been sunk years before, along with a small grove of nutmeg trees, were all that Alvarez had left behind.

Muab mopped his perspiring brow. No one would chastise him if he made a decision in favor of Amalie. If there was a way for her to restore the house to its original splendor, she would make a fitting queen.

The old justice laughed. Amalie Suub, daughter of a king and a slave woman. His rheumy gaze fell on a round shield dangling haphazardly from a tree. It was rusted and pitted from the elements, but the old man knew that if he were to throw a rock at it, it would clang, and the sound would reverberate for miles. He'd heard stories that the shield was always hung to herald a guest's arrival.

Well, he'd come here for a reason, and he'd best get to it so he could return to the relative comfort of his offices. All he needed was one thing, one piece of paper with Chaezar Alvarez's signature. Amalie had suggested he look here. There was no reason in the world to suspect he would find anything in the house after all these years; on the other hand, there just might be something . . . courtesy of Amalie Suub. For example, there would undoubtedly be something in the house to verify Amalie's copy of her mother's marriage contract. The girl was no fool; that much he'd decided after their first meeting.

The justice cleared the sweat from his eyes as he tramped through the choking vines and flowers that obscured what was once a decorative stone walkway. The huge teakwood door was closed tight, possibly locked, and he could not budge it.

"Warped," he mumbled as he picked his way through the rotting vegetation to the back of the house. This door yielded to his touch. He entered a huge, sunny kitchen with an open fireplace that took up one entire wall. Huge chopping blocks and tables were scattered about, testament that at one time there were many guests to cook for. But even here the jungle had crept in. Vines twisted up the walls near the windows. Bright red and purple flowers hung from shelves as though designed that way. Reedy shoots, various forms of underbrush, forced their way up through cracks in the tile floor, and he thought he saw a snake slither away.

Farther into the house, rotting vegetation made him gasp for breath. He tried to breathe through his mouth, walking from room to room until he came to Alvarez's study.

It was once an impressive compartment, the private sanctuary of a successful man. Now it was full of worms and rotting leaves and flowers. The books lining the shelves would probably crumble to the touch. Everywhere he looked there were thick black patches of mildew. His eyes strayed to the desk and the six long drawers that Amalie told him held Alvarez's papers. One paper with one signature was all he needed. Just one paper. . . .

The moment he found it, he backed out of the room. It had been far too easy, but he didn't care. The law was the law; if the signatures matched, then this property and anything else Alvarez owned would go to Amalie, his legal daughter.

Muab matched up the signatures in the murky light that struggled through the stained-glass windows Alvarez had brought all the way from Spain. Satisfied, the old justice deposited both pieces of parchment into the cloth bag he carried. All that remained was to affix his signature to several documents and write a letter to Alvarez's superiors in Spain, which they would probably ignore the way they'd ignored his other three letters asking them to forward the Spaniard's belongings. As he made his way to the carriage, Muab had already determined that the beautiful Malayan was now the owner of all that Alvarez possessed. In the Spaniard's life it had been a kingdom of untold riches. In death it was nothing but rotting timbers and stone. What Alvarez's daughter would do with it he had no idea, and he didn't care. All he cared about right now was returning to his cool offices by the harbor.

Amalie Suub stepped onto the same trampled vines and flowers Justice Muab had trampled. It was all hers now, she thought happily. Not that it was much, but it was better than the shack she'd lived in with her mother until her death.

She walked around the estate, her eyes calculating the cost of refurbishing the mansion her father had lived in with her mother, who had been little more than a slave to his whims. All she needed was money, lots of it. And short of selling her body, there was little chance of laying her hands on the kind of money she would need to restore this magnificent house and grounds. The ships, of course, would require even more to make them seaworthy.

Amalie sat down on the steps leading to the wide double teak doors, her long, tawny legs stretched in front of her. She hiked up her thin, worn dress well above her knees.

Men liked her legs, white men especially. Some had even fought over her charms, and she'd been elated, knowing she was desired in their eyes. One of her favorite pastimes was dreaming about the day she would own a pair of shoes with heels so she could walk in front of a man the way the grand ladies did who attended her father's fancy balls.

It was beastly hot now. She knew she could go inside where it was cool, but the house wasn't really hers yet. Oh, yes, she'd sneaked inside after her mother's death just to look around. She'd found her father's journal the first time, but it had meant nothing to her then because she couldn't read or write. Thanks to the missionary who'd taken her under his wing, she could now do both. In fact, she was so adept, she helped the missionary with the younger children.

Father Renaldo was the reason she was sitting here now, the reason she'd had the nerve to appeal to the justice for aid. And thanks to him, she owned something at last—and that's what she had to remember. No slave owned anything, even the clothes on his back. She alone was the exception.

From the moment she'd created the forged marriage contract she'd stolen from Father Renaldo, she'd never thought about the deed again, only its outcome. True, she was Chaezar Alvarez's daughter, but only an illegitimate one with no rights at all. Her expert forgery had changed everything; now she was respectable, not that it was going to do her any good. Unless . . . She laughed, an eerie sound that echoed in the jungle surrounding her. She looked up as the birds in the branches took wing at the sound. Cat's eyes, yellow in the golden sun, watched them circle higher overhead, then lowered to stare sightlessly at the foliage.

Over the past years, before Father Renaldo's tutelage, she'd been an expert thief. Twice she'd been hauled before the burgher, only to be let go when her eyes promised things old men only dreamed of. The day Father Renaldo rescued her, at the age of seventeen, he'd made her promise not to steal again. And, as a show of good faith, she'd turned over the six diamonds she'd found in her mother's possession at her death—jewels stolen from her father at his death. Perhaps it was time to reclaim those diamonds as her rightful inheritance.

Amalie smiled. The world, she reflected lazily, was made up mostly of the weak and downtrodden, people like Father Renaldo and her mother. And then there were the others, greedy people like herself who dared to take a chance.

Amalie's eyes sparkled dangerously. She needed money, more than even the town burghers had, and the only way she could get it was to steal from those who had it. But how?

She brushed impatiently at the long black hair falling over her eyes. One thing she'd learned: When you stole from someone you had to be quick and fast. Proof of that simple fact was in her father's journal, written in his own hand. A master thief himself, he'd met his match, according to several entries, in a scantily clad, long-legged woman who roamed the seas pillaging and plundering any ship that crossed her path. Amalie had devoured the words until she knew the entire journal by heart. And at the back she'd found a dozen drawings of the long-legged woman, all done in fine detail. While knowing little of art in any form, she'd realized the sketches had been done by a man obsessed. Every conceivable pose the artist could imagine had been rendered in fine India ink, right down to a wicked scar on the woman's arm.

It was this same woman, named the Sea Siren in the journals, who, according to her mother, had carved the manhood from her father's body. A witness to the event, her mother had regaled her with tales of how she and the other servants had silently applauded the deed. And the moment she'd known Alvarez was dead, her mother had raced to his room to steal those few small diamonds.

Amalie herself knew little of jewels, but there was no reason to suspect her father would have anything less than flawless stones. If Father Renaldo could be persuaded that they really belonged to her after all . . . and if she could convince him to sell them to the right person, she might have enough money to either refurbish the plantation or have one of the ships restored. She promised herself that she would decide later in the day when the evening meal at the mission was over and her time was her own.

Amalie Suub was beautiful, and more than one head turned as she picked her way through the small mission. She was as tall as most men, with a long, loose-legged stride, and her thin chemise did little to hide her shapely body. Perhaps her most startling features were her wide, white smile and her cat's eyes, a yellowish-brown that seemed to see everything at a glance. She knew the others envied her light skin and that if she lived in a different place, she could pass as a Spaniard. It was a fact that pleased her to no end—more so once she'd read her father's journal.

Father Renaldo watched Amalie as she ladled out dinner to the children. His spectacles were almost useless these days now that the white film had started to grow over his eyes. He could barely make out her features, but he could certainly smell her sharp, earthy scent. God, he told himself, had chosen to strengthen his sense of smell when He took his eyesight. Give and take.

He was worried about Amalie, afraid she would do something . . . terrible. The justice had been to see him three days in a row in his efforts to come to a decision. Renaldo had known for some time that his wayward charge had stolen a marriage contract from his satchel. But he'd said nothing. He understood how important it was for her to be more than just a slave's illegitimate daughter. When the justice had examined the marriage contract, he'd held his breath and waited . . . God forgive him. Then he'd heard the man's sigh of resignation, and at that moment he'd known that the plantation, as well as the name Alvarez, would be bequeathed to Amalie.

He could smell her now as she swished back and forth among the plank tables. For the first time he realized that he didn't like the smell, that he didn't really like Amalie. He felt sinful and bowed his head at his wicked acknowledgment. Amalie was a child of God, as were all children. *No, not this one,* whispered a voice deep inside him. *This one is a child of . . . the devil.* The old priest started to shake and tremble as his fingers fumbled for the rosary tied around his waist.

Amalie came up behind him, her bare feet soundless in the loamy earth. "Would you like me to read to you for a little while, Father?" she asked quietly.

The old priest felt his neck and face grow hot. "Not this evening, Amalie. I want to say my rosary."

"Father, I've been meaning to ask you . . . Can I have those stones I gave you?"

"Why?" he asked sharply.

"Well, they did belong to my father—and now, like everything else of his, they're mine. Or they should be. I was going to ask you to sell them for me, but I think the trip into town might be too much for you. I'm going to need the money to . . . for whatever I decide to do. Of course I will give some of it to you for the children. God would want me to be generous."

The priest flinched as though she'd struck a blow to his body. "Your mother stole the stones, Amalie. They won't bring you any peace. Still," he mumbled, more to himself than to Amalie, "I suppose the diamonds do belong to you. In the morning will be soon enough. Go along, child, read the Bible until it's time for sleep."

Amalie laughed, a deep, sensuous sound, and slipped away silently. Renaldo breathed deeply and almost choked on her animal scent. He heard her laugh again as she moved off, this time to her pallet. Involuntarily, he shivered and crossed himself.

Amalie Suub Alvarez was evil; he could feel it in every pore of his body. The old priest's hands worked feverishly on the beads in his hands. Over and over he said the familiar prayers. Always before they had comforted him, but not this evening—and perhaps never again.

Amalie awoke to a slow, sleepy dawn. As yet the birds were still cradled in their nests, their shrill early-morning cries minutes away. The others were asleep, the mission quiet and peaceful. Soon she wouldn't have to sleep under the stars with hundreds of others pressed close for warmth during the chilly nights. Soon she would be free of this damnable mission.

She closed her eyes and tried to picture the plantation alive with people and music. Her father had wanted to be a king, to live in grand splendor with the infamous Sea Siren as his queen. Instead, she'd killed him and sailed away, probably to her own death. If she, Amalie, were careful and planned every single detail, she could become a queen and resurrect the Sea Siren from her watery grave. It was an exciting thought. There would be obstacles, many of them, and primary among them was that she knew nothing about ships and had never been on one in her entire life.

Amalie sat up and hugged her knees. There were hundreds of books in her father's office, most of them about sailing. She'd looked through some of them, but they were full of rot and mildew, their pages either sticking together or crumbling in her fingers. At least her father's navigational charts were intact in their oilskin pouches, that much she knew.

A bright beam of sun shafted downward through the glossy leaves overhead, bathing Amalie in an eerie yellow glow. She moved out of the sun, muttering to herself as she left the room to prepare the morning meal.

First there would be the endless prayers, then breakfast, then cleaning up, then lessons. She hated it, but she'd gone on pretending because she needed this place and what it offered. After today, however, she wouldn't need this mission or Father Renaldo. Oh, she would stay on for a while longer—but only long enough to learn what was needed and to put her plan into operation.

Amalie's eyes flew to the priest's quarters as she padded down the hallway. It was possible the old man would die in the meantime. If he didn't . . . such things were simple to arrange. She smiled. At last her life was on a steady course.

After breakfast, Father Renaldo announced his intention to accompany Amalie into town. Instantly her suspicions were aroused; fear tightened like a vise in her chest as she scrutinized the old man. Why did he want to come with her? What was in his mind? Did he intend to thwart her plans somehow—perhaps even refuse to give her the diamonds?

Her yellow eyes narrowed. She didn't want him with her, but she had no choice. If he tried to get in her way, she would simply have to cut him down. They were adversaries now.

The moment breakfast was over, the old priest hobbled to the schoolroom, the children in tow. "Today," he said in a reed-thin voice, "there will be no lessons. Tomorrow is All Saints' Day, so you will fashion garlands of flowers for the chapel, and I want to see the biggest, the prettiest blooms in crocks at the foot of Our Lady. Saria will be in charge of the garlands, and Celeste will oversee the chapel arrangements. I'm going into town with Amalie and should return by sundown, but in case we are delayed, Rita is in charge of supper. Hurry now, for it will take many hours to do the flowers. And remember, they must be perfect.''

Amalie cursed under her breath, words she'd heard in town, words no lady would ever allow to pass her lips. Her best course of action, she decided, was to act as if nothing were amiss. She waited until they were alone and then approached the priest, forcing a note of cheerfulness into her voice. ''Do you have the stones, Father?''

''Yes, Amalie, I do. If you will prepare the horse and wagon, we can leave immediately.''

He listened as Amalie went off to hitch the old bay to the mission supply cart. He should have told her of his intentions. His conscience demanded she be told. Perhaps on the ride into town, he decided. All night he'd prayed for God to tell him what to do. He'd been a foolish old man, succumbing to the caress in a girl's voice—a foolish old man who'd thought he was doing the right thing by remaining silent in the face of deception. But she was Alvarez's daughter, although illegitimate, and nothing could change that.

The old priest sighed. Perhaps while he was in town he could go to confession. Father Juan would hear his sins and they'd talk afterward. It would ease his mind considerably. And tomorrow was All Saints' Day—God's way of giving him a chance to atone. He'd spend the entire day in prayer and fasting.

''Father, the wagon's ready,'' Amalie said, startling him from his sober thoughts. ''Please, allow me to help you.''

Father Renaldo suffered her touch as she helped him onto the hard, high seat. Before she snapped the reins she leaned over and said, "Father, I—I would like to see the diamonds before we start out."

Father Renaldo debated a moment, but only because he didn't want to touch the hard, bright stones. In his eyes they represented death. In the end he handed over the pouch, crossing himself imperceptibly. He wished he could see the girl's expression as she shook the glittering stones from their cloth bag into the palm of her hand.

"I hope they fetch a good price," Amalie muttered as she dropped them, one by one, back into the little pouch and tucked them away. "Thank you, Father."

The old man shook his head wearily. "I deserve no thanks for surrendering you to the forces of evil. Come, child, let us be on our way. I have no desire to travel during the hottest hours of the day."

An hour into their journey Amalie noticed that the priest was deep in prayer, his hands telling the rosary with an almost frantic intensity. He's afraid, she thought with sudden realization. He's afraid of me. We're bound together in this deception, and it's tearing him apart.

"Father, forgive me for asking, but why are you making this trip?" she asked, breaking the hour-long silence. "I appreciate your company, but the heat will shortly be unbearable, and we still have a long way to go."

The priest did not answer her; his lips moved silently in prayer. Amalie didn't repeat her question; she knew the answer. Father Renaldo intended to reveal the truth to Justice Muab. When she spoke again a little while later, her tone was light, conversational. "The sun today is particularly brutal, Father. And you're not well. Perhaps we should turn back," she said softly.

"No, no, I must get into town." He turned to her then, his rheumy eyes striving to pierce their prison of shadow. "Amalie, I cannot allow the justice to believe the lie I told him. I was blinded with what I felt was your need.

That house, child, will not make you happy. It's all based on lies, and I compounded those lies. Please . . . I want you to stay at the mission and help with the children. It's a good, honest life, and you are well suited to it. Forget that grand house and those rotting ships in the harbor. The diamonds are yours, although I feel in my heart they will only bring you misery and heartache. But as for the rest . . . Please tell me you understand,'' the old priest pleaded.

Amalie contemplated him coldly. "Of course I understand. Because I do not embrace your faith does not mean I am incapable of understanding. I simply disagree, which is my right. My father was a disgusting, treacherous, lustful man. He used my mother in ways that aren't fit for your ears to hear. I have a right to avenge her—and to see to it that I do not fall prey to the same fate. I refuse to die a slave, at the mercy of some man's whims of kindness or cruelty. This is my chance to live the life I want for myself—and neither you nor anyone else will stop me! Now, Father, I suggest you climb down from this wagon and return to the mission. Now. I'll go into town alone.'' Amalie reined in the horse and turned to the old priest with glittering eyes.

Father Renaldo heard the threat in her voice. Evil . . . He gripped his cane tighter in his gnarled old hand as he struggled down from the wagon. Walking back to the mission was better than forcing the issue now, here. He was no match for this one. Some way, somehow, he'd get word to the justice. His rosary in his hands, he began to trudge along the road, head bowed in prayer.

Amalie never looked back as she urged the old bay onward, to town.

Amalie arrived in town during the hottest part of the day without a drop of perspiration on her brow or a hair out of place. For the first time since starting out, she allowed her gaze to stray to the right and to the left as she observed the stately town houses of the rich traders and politicians. She particularly liked the grilled gates, manicured shrubbery, and long, circling drives. One day she, too, would have a town house here, she vowed.

One day she would ride into this town in a shiny black carriage, and every head in town would turn—the men's eyes full of desire, the women's full of envy. One day everyone would know and respect Amalie Suub Alvarez.

As the wagon clattered down the street, Amalie stared straight ahead; she was in the business district now, and she knew the shops were open, their proprietors lazing behind drawn shades. At the end of the street she tethered the old horse and ramshackle wagon and strode up the south walkway with her head held high. She was Amalie Alvarez—or she would be soon—and the sooner the people in town became aware of her, the better she would feel.

Her bare feet made slapping sounds on the wooden planks. Soon, she promised herself, she would have shoes to adorn her feet, as did all proper ladies. A splinter gouged her toe, but she kept on walking, her eyes searching for the gilt lettering that represented the jeweler's establishment. When she found it, she approached the entrance, heart pounding.

A cluster of bells tinkled as Amalie opened and closed the shop door. Sun ribboned through the windows, bathing her in a golden glow, shining through her thin chemise and outlining every limb and curve of her body. Grasping the small pouch, she walked up to the counter and shook the stones into the palm of her hand. She waited, her beautiful face impassive, for the arrogant-looking proprietor to get up from his chair and walk to the long counter that separated his offices from the entry area.

The jeweler's eyes widened at the sight of the girl in her

faded, worn dress. He almost ordered her out of his shop—
until he saw the stones in her hand. Greedily, he made a
move to pluck them from her palm, but the moment he
did she closed her hand into a fist.

"I want to sell these. I know they're worth a lot; how
much will you give me?" Amalie said, fixing him with
her cat's eyes.

"Where did you get these?" the jeweler demanded. "I
don't buy stolen goods."

"I didn't steal them; they're mine. Do you wish to buy
them or not?"

"I need to examine them first," the jeweler said, clearing his throat.

Amalie opened her hand and gave the jeweler one large
sparkling diamond at a time. She smirked as he licked his
lips, eyes aglitter. Obviously he hadn't seen many diamonds of this quality.

The man held the jeweler's glass close as he examined
each stone carefully. Amalie waited until he had replaced
the last diamond in the pouch. From underneath the
counter he withdrew a cash box. The small mound of guilders he counted out shocked her. She hadn't been prepared for this. Was it enough or not? She didn't know.
Taking a gamble, she shook her head.

"I want gold sovereigns, and this is not enough," she
said coldly, and waited, hardly daring to breathe. The man
replaced the guilders and withdrew another box. Again he
laid out a small mound, and again Amalie shook her head.
The man added two more sovereigns to the small pile of
gold. Again and again she shook her head, until she sensed
that the man was nearing his last offer. Should she take it
or not? Instinct warned her not to accept. "Add *all* of the
guilders, and I will sell the diamonds," she told him.

The jeweler snorted. "Ridiculous! They aren't worth

that much. I have to be able to sell these at a profit. This is my last offer.''

"What would you offer for me?'' Amalie asked quietly.

"Why, I . . . I'm a respectable man and run a respectable business. I—''

"Have a wife.'' Amalie's yellow eyes flashed. "But would she do the things to you I would do, Mynheer Jeweler?''

The jeweler licked his lips again. "What . . . what kind of things?'' he asked in a quivering voice.

She smiled. "Things to remember . . . things you'll take to your . . . grave.''

Slowly, seductively, Amalie leaned across the wooden counter, her cat's eyes dark brown now and moist with heat. The jeweler tore his hungry gaze from hers and looked down the front of her dress. He nearly choked at the sight. Amalie's smile promised untold delights as her tongue snaked out from between her teeth. She allowed it to caress first her top lip, then her lower lip. The jeweler moaned.

"All of the guilders, Mynheer. A larger pouch. Now . . . before—''

"Lock the door,'' the jeweler said hoarsely as he stuffed the gold into her pouch.

"No,'' Amalie said, walking around the counter. "You will find what I do to you much more exciting if you fear . . . the unknown.''

"Yes, yes, hurry. This is unbearable,'' he said, unfastening his trousers. He was suddenly shy, muttering under his breath, "I'm . . . I'm not very . . .'' His face reddened miserably.

"I can see what you mean, Mynheer. I know how to remedy your problem,'' Amalie said with a hint of sardonic laughter in her voice. "Trust me, Mynheer, you will never want to bed your sensible wife in her sensible

bloomers and corsets again.'' A deep growl of pleasure
ripped from her mouth as she lifted the chemise over her
head and stood before him naked in her splendor. The
jeweler's eyes rolled back in his head as Amalie pulled
him to the floor.

Several minutes later, sweat dripping from every pore
in his body, the jeweler squealed like a pig going to market. ''What . . . wha . . . *oh*!''

''Shhh, I am about to remedy . . . your problem, Mynheer.''

Amalie's touch was light, almost playful as she caressed, tickled, and prodded, her strong, muscular thighs
contracting against the jeweler's flabby limbs. Her face,
however, was impassive as she recalled other times when
she had been used and abused by some of the white plantation owners. Because she was tall and long-limbed, those
men had thought her impervious to pain and had not been
gentle. She'd promised herself that someday she would be
as cold and brutal with fat Dutchmen and foppish Spaniards.

Barely audible moans and squeals of delight from the
man beneath her brought her back to the job at hand. Her
fingers stiffened as they moved downward to the patch of
fair hair, and then lower still. With a lithe movement she
slid between the man's spread legs, her knees closing and
then widening against his manhood. When he yelped with
pleasure, she intensified the pressure.

Long, velvety hair fell over her face, a veil to hide from
the jeweler the contempt she bore him. She crooned soft
words, words pleasing and sensual to the prone man beneath her.

''You're hurting me!'' the jeweler gasped.

''But it feels good, doesn't it?'' Amalie cooed as she
pressed her knees against his throbbing testicles. When
she released the pressure, the man sighed, and Amalie

almost laughed. She waited a moment and then brought her knees together with such force, the jeweler's head jerked backward in pain. The palm of her hand shot forward and upward against his chin in a single, savage thrust. His eyes widened in disbelief, then glazed over as his life drained quickly out of him.

When Amalie had slid the chemise over her shoulders, she returned to the man lying on the floor. Working quickly, she pulled up his underdrawers and trousers, then dragged his body over to the chair he'd been sitting in. She continued to struggle with the man's enormous weight until she had him propped in the chair. Next, she scattered all his books and papers about the floor. Finally she came to his cash box. Without a qualm, she emptied it of all but a few gold coins, then jammed the lid so that it looked as though someone had tampered with it. She savored the feel of the pouch in her hand. Weight meant money, power, and leverage.

Without a backward glance at the jeweler, she let herself out the rear door of the shop into a deserted alley full of refuse and empty barrels. No eyes looked on her as she walked through the alley, her head high, her back ramrod stiff. She started to sing under her breath, a silly little tune the old priest had taught the children. She felt victorious. She had all but a few guilders of the jeweler's money, and she still had the diamonds.

Her next stop was the justice's office, where she stood waiting in respectful silence until he raised his head from the papers on his desk.

"I can see why you would be impatient after all these years," Muab said, nodding. "I affixed my seal to this proclamation earlier today, thinking you would soon come into town. As of now all of your . . . father's property and possessions, those that remain, are yours." He handed over a packet of papers and wasn't surprised to see the beautiful girl's hands tremble as she accepted it.

"Thank you, sir, for your time and trouble," she said quietly.

"Hrumph, yes, yes. You are now Amalie Alvarez. I've sent a letter off to the . . . to your father's superiors, informing them of this action. It is entirely possible they will respond, but unlikely. Give my regards to Father Renaldo," the justice said, dismissing her.

"I will tell him you send your regards."

The justice watched the tall girl walk through the door, wondering what she would do now. His stomach churned. It was wrong, he knew it was wrong, but . . . he no longer cared. He'd gone by the evidence, and in the end that's all that mattered. He wished the girl well.

The blazing sun boiled downward, but Amalie paid it no mind as she walked toward the harbor, shoulders drooping and head down in a subservient manner. For once she desired anonymity and knew full well that in her present posture the scurvy few at the harbor would virtually ignore her until she raised her head and challenged them with her yellow eyes.

The harbormaster was no stranger to Amalie. He'd always been civil when she appeared and asked to see the ships that belonged to Chaezar Alvarez. She also knew that he was a friend of the justice's and would now know that she was entitled to her father's property.

A monstrous banyan tree surrounded by thick greenery at the side of the road beckoned with promise of shade, and Amalie was drawn toward it. She needed time to think, to rest a moment, time to massage her aching, callused feet.

As she lowered herself onto a mossy patch beneath the old tree, she was suddenly assailed by doubt. Perhaps she should wait to visit the harbormaster, buy some clothes and shoes and come back another day. Those she would deal with now would regard her as a slab of meat, a slave's bastard child dressed in a worn, thin chemise that left nothing to the imagination. Would the gold in the pouch she held in her hand garner respect?

Her head snapped upward as another thought struck her. What would be the outcome in regard to the jeweler's death? Was there anyone who knew how much money he kept in his cash box—his wife, some family member, a shop owner? Had she left enough coins there to satisfy the authorities that burglary had not been the motive for his death? It had taken all her strength to snap the man's fat neck, something some men wouldn't be able to do. Certainly no one would suspect a woman. No, a simple crime of passion, a murder—probably at the hands of one bent on vengeance—would be the verdict rendered by the . . . justice, the same justice responsible for giving her her new life.

Satisfied that her interpretation of the incident would be shared by the authorities, Amalie rose to her feet in one effortless movement. She'd had all the rest she could afford, and as inviting as the tree looked, she had to move on. She straightened her shoulders and headed for the harbormaster's quarters.

Hans Wilhelm was a crusty old man with twinkling eyes and a hatred for soap and water. On his desk were two guns and a saber that he used or threatened to use on a daily basis. He was so fat he was grotesque, and his twinkling eyes were merely a trick of the light filtering through the wooden shutters. He was a hard man to deal with, and his only priority in life was to gouge as much money as he could from the owners of the trading vessels he dealt with.

Wilhelm leaned back in his chair, his belly jiggling with

his effort. His coarse shirt was stained with weeks of sweat, and he reeked of himself. Amalie breathed through her mouth as she entered his office and waited for him to speak. He knew why she was there; she could see it in his beady eyes. His voice, when he spoke, came from deep in his belly, gruff yet hollow-sounding.

"I've been waiting for you, Amalie, my dear."

"I want to know if you'll take the brigantine, the galleon, and the sloop and trade me a frigate." Amalie forced herself to sound casual, indifferent, as though she really didn't care one way or another what the harbormaster's answer would be.

Wilhelm's nostrils quivered. He smelled money. "Now, why would I want those rotten ships? And why would the likes of you be wanting a frigate?"

Staring at him, Amalie was reminded of a mound of dough with finger indentations. "I asked you a question, Mr. Wilhelm. If you can't give me an answer, I'll go to the Dutch East India Company. Or I can make inquiries elsewhere."

Wilhelm sighed wearily. "It would cost a fortune to have those ships careened, and they're rotted with teredo worm," he lied. "That will have to be taken care of before we can begin to discuss the possibilities you mentioned," the harbormaster said craftily. He wondered uneasily if this was some kind of trick to trap him. His fat stomach lurched when he remembered how he'd spent the money that came from Spain for repairs and harbor fees. Long ago he'd made up his mind to lie if any of the Spaniards' superiors ever came to claim the ships left in his care. He'd never been able to bring himself to the point where he would sell off or dispose of the ships out of fear that perhaps one day some fool would arrive with the proper credentials and claim the ships.

"I'm prepared to pay the bill . . . in full. But don't try

to cheat me, Mr. Wilhelm," Amalie said quietly. "I know how much upkeep costs per year. My father kept a ledger with all his debts."

"Yes, your . . . Mr. Alvarez was a crafty bastard." And so are you, he added silently.

They haggled for well over an hour until Amalie suddenly turned to leave. "We're getting nowhere, Mr. Wilhelm. Either you're interested or you aren't. I wish to settle this now. As to the frigate, I know there is one in the harbor that has been there for two years. Set your price . . . now!"

"All right, all right." Wilhelm waved a hand in the air as if tired of debate. "If you have a mind to, we can walk out to the wharf and see just how rotten those ships are."

"Both of us already know how rotten they are. They can, however, be salvaged, so why not finalize our business now? I'll return tomorrow, and you can have the papers ready for me to sign. I want the justice to oversee this transaction. I'm sure he'll want to send off another letter to my father's government, apprising them of the fact that I'm selling the ships to you. Is that satisfactory?"

After another twenty minutes of haggling, the final price was agreed upon. "I want the frigate careened and then taken to the cove at Saianha," Amalie said. "How long will that take?"

"A month, possibly less," the harbormaster said, rubbing his jowls thoughtfully.

"Good. Then it's a bargain?"

"Yes, a bargain." Wilhelm's eyes gleamed at the thought of how full his cash box would be.

Amalie nodded. "I'll return at eight o'clock in the morning. Will that be satisfactory?" Again Wilhelm bobbed his head.

Smiling, Amalie strode down the plank walkway to the harbor and stared at the row of ships in their berths. She knew immediately which ones were her father's, and she also knew where the frigate was. She shaded her eyes from the burning sun for a better look. To her, the frigate looked in worse condition than her father's ships. When she'd had enough of the brutal sun and the sailors' leering eyes, she retraced her steps and headed down a well-trod path to the town's only brothel.

Amalie hated the place and all that went on behind the curtains on the second floor, hated it because the women were used and paid a pittance for their bodies. Three girls from the mission were here simply because there was nowhere else for them to go.

At the back door of Christabel's establishment she called out and announced herself. Anyone who knew her would have been astounded at the look of compassion in her eyes as several young girls ran to her. How old and weary they looked, and none of them was as old as she. She stared into the eyes of the old hag who owned the brothel. "I've come to tell you that these *children* won't be returning to this . . . place," she said coldly, defying the hag to question her further.

Outside in the sultry late afternoon, Amalie explained to her charges that she was taking them back to her plantation, where they would live and work. "All I ask is your loyalty; if you can pledge that to me, then I will take care of you." The girls nodded, their eyes alive for the first time in months. "Then it's settled. I must stay in town this evening so I can be at the harbormaster's office at eight o'clock. We'll have to sleep in the wagon this evening, and we'll need food. One of you can go to the shop for it. I also need to know where I can hire some able-bodied men to crew my frigate once it reaches Saianha."

The girls giggled. The oldest, at fourteen, pointed to the path behind her. "All you have to do is waylay them on their way back from Christabel's parlor. Or we can do it for you, they know us.'' Three pairs of grateful eyes waited for Amalie's response. After a tense moment, she nodded.

''Waylay them, then—but that's all. Believe me when I tell you you'll never suffer at a man's hands again. It's getting late now, and I have no desire to be on this street once darkness falls. We'll come back after midnight.''

The children, as Amalie thought of them, huddled close together in the wagon, a huge banyan tree shielding them from the late-afternoon sun. For a while they whispered and giggled; then, eventually, they slept, sweet smiles on their faces.

Amalie sat on the ground with her back against the ageless tree, her long, honey-colored legs stretched out in front of her and her future secure in the pouch around her neck. Her head buzzed with the day's activities and the knowledge that by tomorrow she would have a frigate and a crew to man it. She would also have her father's mansion. The girls would clean it and keep house, but would there be enough money left to initiate the necessary repairs to make the place livable? There would have to be; she'd see to it.

A much more serious problem was what to do about the old priest and the dangerous knowledge he possessed. He alone could ruin her scheme. If walking back to the mission in the heat hadn't killed him, then she would be forced to deal with Father Renaldo more directly. It would be at least a year before another missionary would arrive, possibly longer.

She could move the rickety mission to her plantation. The children could live in the old slave quarters, and their first major task would be to clear away the jungle from the main house. She knew that the fussy, flighty town women would cluck their tongues at first, but in the end they would approve as long as the quarters held beds and were clean.

Amalie Suub Alvarez . . . protector of small children. Who would ever fault her?

Amalie's yellow eyes calmed, and as she relaxed she gave the appearance of a sleepy cat. Her plan, as she thought of it, had many parts. The children were the first part; she needed them to work for her. The frigate was the second part of the plan, and securing a good crew was the third part. The last part of her plan, the grand finale, hinged on the first three parts.

Excitement coursed through Amalie. It would be dangerous, deadly even, but if she didn't make any mistakes, she was sure she could assume the identity of the woman her father called the Sea Siren. An able crew would help her plunder the seas. Riches beyond her dreams would be hers. Her father's kingdom would be restored. She would be a queen and the children her loyal subjects. It was a perfect plan. The only flaw—if it could be called a flaw—was that her kingdom wouldn't have a king. Perhaps a prince or two, but never a king.

Amalie chuckled deep in her throat and dug her toes into the soft dark earth. Father Renaldo had always said one must anticipate problems and work them out before they became major concerns. There would be problems. She had no wicked scar on her arm, for one thing. The pictures in back of her father's journal denoted a terrible scar that ran the length of the sea witch's arm. Yes, the scar was going to be a problem, but it could be dealt with if she was willing to endure pain and disfigurement.

But how would she explain her sudden wealth? The thought had been in the back of her mind for days now. Anticipate, anticipate . . .

Amalie bolted upward, her cat's eyes lighting with sudden inspiration. The justice had said he was sending a second letter to her father's superiors in Spain informing them of his decision. Months from now she could say her father's holdings in Cadiz and Seville had been transferred over to her. The yellow eyes gleamed. The only person who could dispute her was the justice, but he would have given over his post by then. And he was a very tired, very old man, looking forward to his retirement.

Her plan, Amalie decided, would have no flaws, none at all.

A long time later, when the slice of moon rode high in the heavens, Amalie stirred. It was cool now, with a light caressing breeze. Overhead, stars sprinkled the sky in the velvety night. The birds had been silent for hours, and not a sound crept to her ears. It was time.

She walked on callused feet to the wagon, betraying her uncertainty as she roused the girls and asked, "How do we do this? Should we walk through town or . . . ?"

One of the girls giggled and said, "No self-respecting lady walks about after dark unless she's escorted by a man. Christabel's place is past the harbor. I know another way to get there, but it is longer."

"Show me the way," Amalie ordered, relieved. She wanted no encounters with any of the townspeople.

In the following hours, Amalie made many promises. Some she would keep; others were mere words. There was no honor in what she was planning, and the only reason she knew she would keep some of the pledges was to stay alive herself.

Shortly before dawn she issued her last order to a swarthy seaman with a stubble of beard and a nose that had been broken in too many places to count. "One month from today you will sail my ship to the cove at Saianha. Once the ship is berthed there, you will live aboard until I am ready to set sail. You will have a home with me for as long as you need one, providing you do not betray me or cross me in any way. You will be well paid, and you will be richer than you ever dreamed. I demand only one thing of you, and that is loyalty. Do you agree to my terms?''

The seaman looked Amalie over from the top of her head to the tips of her toes. His eyes strayed to the little girls, all of whom he'd had over the past months. Mellow now with rum in his gut and his loins sated, he nodded agreeably, but his eyes were those of a shark in open water.

''Aye, one month from today I will be in Saianha,'' he replied.

Amalie watched as he stumbled down the road to town. She nodded to the girls. ''It seems I have the scurviest, deadliest crew imaginable. For the right price one can get *anything*.''

''Cutthroats,'' one of the girls whispered.

''Devils,'' said the second little girl.

''Vermin,'' said the third.

''Yes, all those things, but they will make us rich. They are men—stupid creatures who understand greed because money can buy them women and rum. But they don't think beyond that. I, on the other hand, am a woman, and there are no limits to what a woman can do, especially one who understands her adversaries.''

Amalie's plan was under way.

That morning, Amalie's business with the harbormaster was completed in less than an hour, and she was on her way back to the mission by nine o'clock, a satisfied smile on her face. The smile lasted for several hours—until she and the girls discovered Father Renaldo's body alongside the road. Amalie leapt from the wagon and cried real tears . . . of relief.

Chapter Three

The trees overhead were silent in the soft, warm breeze, an indication that Pilar was calm . . . for the moment. Jet eyes watched, their field of vision almost limitless as her young sailed up and then down, testing their newfound freedom.

Pilar's killing talons were tucked beneath her long, fluffy belly feathers and had been in that position for some time. Slowly, calmly, she ruffled her feathers, taking on the appearance of a dry pine cone, and then shook them free a second later. Shiny emerald leaves moved in the dry breeze as the huge bird was transformed suddenly into something swift and deadly. The houseboy standing under the tree dropped the pail of raw meat and ran as fast as his bare feet would carry him. Safely inside, he peered through the breakfast room windows, his eyes searching fearfully for Gaspar.

The hawks were his responsibility, the housekeeper had told him, and he had given his word to the van der Rhys that he would care for the winged devils until they were ready to move on. He hated and feared them and their deadly sounds.

The evil-looking male, Gaspar, had been gone for almost two days, something that had happened twice before since Miss Fury's departure. The female was not her usual calm self. "Devil birds," he spat out, and blessed himself before returning to his other duties.

Outside, the branches of the chestnut tree dipped and

swayed as Sato and Lago frantically sought purchase with their talons. Satisfied that her offspring were secure, Pilar soared to the ground, her talons digging into the wooden pail. She waited, wings tucked close against her chest, for her young to descend. The moment they left their perch she sailed upward. She watched as the young ate their fill and then returned to their perch beneath Pilar to wait for Gaspar.

The huge hawk returned as the sun was setting. Pilar fanned her wing and lowered it delicately over his tired body. He slept, his shiny eyes at rest, with Pilar next to him.

Six weeks to the day of Fury's departure, Sato and Lago were able to fend for themselves. Their glittering eyes watched as Gaspar and Pilar emptied the basket in the chestnut tree.

Gaspar ruffled his feathers before he soared straight up, Pilar in his wake. They circled overhead several times before they started their journey.

"Kukukukuku." Good-byegood-byegood-byegood-bye. For one startling second Pilar faltered, her huge wings dipping in the soft breeze. Then Gaspar tapped her wings with his own, his signal not to look back.

Their journey was just beginning.

Ronrico Diaz, the captain of the *Java Queen*, was a religious man, and he found himself looking forward to the late afternoons when Fury would walk about the deck and talk with him about her beliefs and her decision to enter the convent. He himself had two daughters who were nuns and one son who was a priest, and he constantly spoke of his family. Every night he prayed for this girl because he wasn't sure she was ready for God. So many rosaries, so many prayers tumbling from her lips, so many questions in her eyes.

"Miss Fury, do you think you will recognize Java once

we dock? It's been many years since you were there,'' he said gruffly.

"I think so. I was ten when we left, and my parents talked about Java constantly so that I would remember. I'm looking forward to seeing my old home again. You seem pensive this afternoon, Captain Diaz. Is something troubling you?''

"Yes and no. We're due for some bad weather shortly, I can feel it in my bones, and we sail with an empty hold. Cargo makes it easier to ride out a storm.''

"I have every faith in you and the crew. And to add to that faith, I will say some extra prayers. I thought . . . what I mean to say is, I was concerned that you might be worried about pirates. We're approaching dangerous waters, are we not?''

He patted her arm. "The *Java Queen* is a fortress, your father saw to that. There's no need for you to worry about pirates. They won't waste time attacking a ship that carries no cargo. In ten weeks you'll be safe and sound in your old home. I made that promise to your parents.''

"God sees to our safety, Captain Diaz. I myself have no fear. Long ago I placed my hand in His, and He will protect me, and you, and this crew. But I must admit I'm so bored, I would almost relish some excitement,'' she blurted out.

"What kind of excitement?'' the captain asked uneasily, wishing Regan van der Rhys had allowed him to take on at least a few passengers. But the governor had been adamant about the empty hold and not taking on passengers.

"Anything!'' Fury cried. "Captain, do you think the men would allow me to join in some of their games, the ones they play with cards and dice?''

"Your father would have me drawn and quartered!'' the captain exploded.

"My father isn't here. And I don't see what harm it can

do. Not every day, of course, just once in a while,'' she coaxed.

''They're a motley crew, and they swear and cheat,'' the captain told her. ''And they play for money. It's no place for a woman promised to God.''

''Would they swear and cheat with a woman promised to God? I think not. And I have money to play with. I see no problem, Captain.''

''They drink and tell bawdy stories,'' the captain said desperately.

''Captain Diaz, I was not raised in cotton bunting. I grew up with four brothers who were all hellions. I've heard all the bawdy stories. I'm an adult, Captain, and just because I'm entering a convent doesn't mean I don't know what goes on in the world.'' To drive her point home, she added, ''Don't forget how my father took us all to sea every year. He told me I needed a well-rounded education. I even know how to swear, what do you think of that?''

''I think it's a sin,'' Captain Diaz groaned.

''We're all sinners in one way or another. Captain, I wish to play,'' she said firmly. ''And tomorrow I would like to take the wheel for a little while if you have no objection.''

The captain had plenty of objections, but he wasn't about to voice them now. ''I'll speak to the men. If they say nay, there isn't much I can do about it. If they agree, then you . . . may participate. Now, isn't it time for your evening prayers?'' he asked sourly.

''So it is. I'll pray that you tell me during the evening meal that it's agreeable. Adios, Captain.'' Fury laughed all the way to her cabin.

Alone in her cabin, Fury realized she was more than just bored: she was lonely. She'd been at sea for a little over six weeks and still had ten more weeks to go before she set foot on dry land. Her rosary, always a source of comfort, found its way to her hand. She fingered the beads, but she didn't pray. The holy ritual did not comfort her; she felt angry and didn't know why. She made a tight fist of the prayer beads before she placed them under her pillow to gaze around her with somber eyes.

Her quarters were rough yet comfortable, with a few of her more treasured possessions scattered about. The cubicle was small, but she knew her room at the convent would be smaller still. She would have a candle, a pallet to sleep on, her prayer beads, and possibly a prayer stool.

In a way, Fury thought morosely, this long sea journey was to prepare her for her lonely life. The first day she'd rejoiced to be truly alone with God and her prayers. After several hours of repeating them, she'd tired of prayers, and her thoughts had strayed to her parents and her beloved brothers, to Gaspar and Pilar . . . and to Luis Domingo. She'd daydreamed of excitement and adventure and indulged in one satisfying reverie after another. The first time it happened she had wanted to pray, needed to pray, but the familiar, comforting words wouldn't come. And today she'd spent four hours on her knees willing the prayers to pass her lips, but to no avail.

"This *is* what I want," Fury whispered fiercely. "It's what I prayed for all my life, and now that it's almost in my grasp, it's slipping away from me—and it's my own fault. My thoughts are no longer pure. I've become selfish in my boredom." The realization that she'd cajoled the captain into helping her relieve her boredom sent scorching color to her cheeks.

"What kind of person does that make me?" she asked herself, mortified. Her conscience answered: *Human, normal . . . mortal.* "Yes, but my life has been promised to God," she protested. "I want everything. I don't want rules and taboos. I want . . . I want. It's that simple."

Fury stretched out on her bunk, hands reaching beneath the pillow for her prayer beads. They were her lifeline to God, a now tenuous bond that was slowly being severed by . . . herself. She wept tears of anger and humiliation that the life she'd planned so carefully was eluding her through self-indulgence and cant. At last, exhausted by her inner struggle, she slept.

Up on deck, the captain—an honorable man, for the most part—was attempting to persuade his crew to Fury's request. "It is a small favor I'm asking of you. Think of the girl and not yourselves for a change. What harm will it do to give up your grog for an hour or two? What harm is there in letting her win once or twice? And, it wouldn't hurt you to spruce up a little for the lady," he added meaningfully. "Now, I'm not asking you, I'm *ordering* you to do me this *one* favor!"

Tobias, the first mate, grinned crookedly at Diaz. "No need to shout, Cap'n. The men will act accordingly. When she loses all her money, the jig's up. She can't play without it—those are the rules. It'll be fair and square, Cap'n, you have my word."

The captain gave his first mate a gruff smile. To his surprise, he found he was looking forward to the confrontation between his salty crew of sea dogs and the little lady of God. It would do the scurvy lot good to act like gentlemen for a little while. And he seemed to recall Regan van der Rhys telling him that his daughter was a fair hand with the dice and the cards. "A female gambling shark" he'd called her.

The laughter rumbling in the captain's belly as he strode away made the back of Tobias's neck prickle. He stared after the old sea goat with suspicious eyes.

When Fury woke an hour later she was drenched with perspiration. She brushed at the fluffy tendrils of hair that clung to her cheeks and knew a quick wash and powder were in order before she dined with the captain in his quarters.

Normally, after a nap, she would rise and then drop to her knees and pray. Now she squeezed her eyes shut and willed a prayer to her lips.

Hail Holy Queen . . . Merciful Father, I implore you . . . What was *wrong* with her? Where was her God? Why wasn't He there to comfort her?

"You're testing me!" she cried, anguished. "And I'm failing miserably. I can't remember my prayers, my knees are sore, and my thoughts are far from pure. I'm contemplating a diversion to drive away my boredom. Why are You letting me do this? I don't understand!"

In desperation she dropped to her knees and reached for the wooden cross on her pillow. "Oh, my God, I am heartily sorry . . ."

For what? a niggling voice inquired.

"For failing my God," Fury murmured, weeping.

You cannot fail God unless He allows it, the tiny voice responded. *Perhaps He isn't ready for you yet.*

Fury shook her head. "I must be stronger. I know that. And I try to be . . . but it's the dreams, the terrible, sinful dreams. I cannot make them go away. I have no control over them!"

Your secret desires, the voice tormented her. *Women of God hold no secret desires. In your heart you aren't ready to embrace God.*

"*No!* No, that's not true! I love God more than life itself." But no matter how hard she tried, Fury could not deny the words. She *was* having sinful dreams, and she *was* dwelling on them, trying to decipher them, willing them in her mind to mean nothing.

Defeated by the knowledge of her own unworthiness, she rose from the bed to splash cold water over her face and rub her fiery cheeks with a towel. When she'd changed her dress and run a brush through her hair, she again sat down on the bed, reaching automatically for her crucifix. As her fingers caressed the figure on the cross, her eyes filled with tears. This wasn't supposed to happen. She was supposed to be happy, and she was more miserable than she'd ever been in her life.

The dreams were part of it—dreams of Luis Domingo and the hawks. Dreams could be explained away, even squelched if one had enough willpower. But the picture flashes she experienced when she was calm, her mind at peace—those truly bothered her.

Premonitions? Daydreams? Her head felt like a beehive, all jumbled sound and mindless fury. She had to think, and she had to think *now* about what she'd seen before she drifted into sleep . . . Gaspar and Pilar flying in a tight formation to reach her, their eyes seeking out the *Java Queen.* She shivered in the warm cabin. They were searching for her now, pursuing the ship. Soon she would know if these pictures were real or the devil's work.

The devil's work . . . She rubbed her knuckles against her eyes. That's why she couldn't remember her prayers: she'd allowed the devil inside her mind, and now she was no longer holy.

"Begone, Satan!" she shouted. "I renounce you in the name of Jesus Christ!" She waited, holding her breath, for the imagined holocaust.

The supper bell rang. Shoulders slumping, Fury slammed the door behind her as she fled, heart pounding, up the ladder to the captain's quarters. One picture pursued her as she ran—that of Luis Domingo wrapping his strong arms about her naked body. Shuddering, squeezing her eyes tight against the image, she careened into the captain's quarters, flustered and breathless, an apology on her lips for her unladylike behavior.

It wasn't until the galley cook served up a dessert of thick-crusted, greasy apple pie that the captain spoke about Fury's request. "They agreed," he said gruffly.

"When?" Fury asked, suddenly nervous.

"They're waiting topside for you now. Mind you they play for blood; it's more than sport with them."

"Thank you, Captain, I know it wasn't easy for you to . . . coerce the crew."

Diaz leaned back on his chair, a cigar clamped firmly between his teeth, watching as his slim young charge left the table to do battle with his band of sea serpents. He wasn't sure whom he pitied more—the girl or the men.

A purse of coins in her hand, Fury tripped over to the sterncastle and motioned to the men that she was ready to play. She fought the laughter bubbling in her throat at the sight of them. Their hair was combed but still wet, their beards trimmed, and they wore clean shirts. To a man, they looked embarrassed and uncomfortable.

Fury gathered up her skirts before she settled on her haunches the way the men did. She folded her hands primly in front of her. "Gentlemen, if you will explain the fine points of this game to me, I think we can be under way," she said, eyes twinkling.

Two hours later Fury looked down at the pile of coins next to her. Clearly she was the evening's winner. "However did this happen?" she asked innocently.

"I thought you said you never did this before," grumbled Basil, the second mate.

"Makes no difference, mate," Tobias said gruffly. "She won it fair and square and wiped us out."

"And to show you that I am fair and a good sport, I'm going to give you all a chance to win it back." Fury smiled sweetly. "Now, I'm going to divide this money into even stacks, and I'll cut the cards with each of you, winner takes the pile. Is that agreeable with you?" Slowly, reluctantly, the men nodded and gathered around her. "Good. All right, then"—she held out the pack of cards—"who wants to go first?"

Suddenly a brisk wind whipped across the deck, and a clap of thunder rumbled ominously in the distance.

"Let's make short work of this, mates," Tobias said, rising and brushing off his leggings. "We're going to have a downpour any second now."

Four minutes later Fury walked away with her three original coins in her hand. "Weather permitting, I'd be more than pleased to join you tomorrow," she called over her shoulder. "Thank you all for being so kind to me."

The crew stared at one another, their mouths hanging open. "She's better than any of us," growled Esteban, the cook.

"I never saw a lady spit on the dice before. In fact, I never saw a lady *roll* dice before," Basil said in awe.

"She didn't cheat, either. I watched her like a hawk," Javier, the bosun, said sourly.

Tobias grinned. "At least she gave us a chance to win our money back. I for one like the lady, and I think we all enjoyed the evening whether we admit it or not. C'mon, now, lads. It's time to secure the ship for the squall."

The storm, when it finally hit, lasted a full five hours. Not until the sea was calm again, lapping against the sides of the ship with rhythmic familiarity, did Fury relax enough to fall into an uneasy sleep punctuated by vague images of two black shapes riding a tall man's shoulders.

The following morning, when Fury knelt by her bunk, the prayers she couldn't remember came easily to her lips. She prayed aloud until her voice grew hoarse and her knees protested. She had so much to make up for, so many prayers to be said. Unbidden, a prayer for Luis Domingo tumbled from her lips. Heat spiraled up from the core of her being and settled on her cheeks. She said a rosary and then another for her wicked thoughts, and still they stayed with her.

She was angry now, with herself and with her God, who kept testing her over and over. Well, she'd had enough!

Fury washed and dressed and realized that she'd had nothing to eat, but she wasn't hungry. She'd walk along the deck and soak up the warm sun. Perhaps she'd read or write a little in the journal she'd kept since childhood. When her mother had given it to her many years before she'd whispered, "For your secret thoughts, darling." She'd been afraid to write down her secret thoughts, though, for fear her inquisitive brothers would somehow find the journal and mock her.

The crew nodded to her amiably as she strolled along the deck. Fury sighed as she settled herself on a caned lounge with her book. Today was going to be like all the other days—slow-moving and boring.

The following days crept by on tortoise legs and then swept into weeks, and Fury's routine was always the same: she ate, she slept, and she prayed—or tried to pray—and at night she gambled with the crew. At best it was a monotonous and predictable business, and she realized she hated it. Her devotions were more sporadic now, less intense, and she constantly questioned her God. Daily she prayed for a sign that she was doing the right thing. At first she felt dismayed when her prayers went unanswered, and then she grew angry and demanding, even to the point of threatening to abandon her vocation altogether.

At some point—she wasn't sure exactly when—the notion struck her that she was being tested not by God, but by herself. The realization left her so unnerved that she forced herself one morning to sit down with her journal and make two lists—one of everything she loved and was giving up and a second of everything she would gain once she entered the convent. Even after several hours' concentration, her second list was pitifully short; still she clung stubbornly to the conviction that, despite her threats, she was meant for a life devoted to God. "I'm going into the convent," she declared fiercely, "and that's all there is to it!"

Suddenly the sun was blotted out overhead. Fury raised her eyes, and for a moment her heart stopped when she realized what she was seeing. She ran to the rail and shouted, "Here! *Here!*" Her arms flailed in the air as she cried out, bringing Tobias running to her side. "It's Gaspar and Pilar! I can't believe it! They've found me!"

The weary hawks worked the wind, racing down, then up, literally hanging in the warm breeze. Fury's heart pounded in her chest as the majestic birds made one final circle and then sailed gracefully to the deck.

Tears streamed down Fury's cheeks as she reached out to stroke "her beauties," as she called them. Pilar lifted one huge wing in greeting. Gaspar, his glittering eyes triumphant, leaned toward his mistress and laid his head against her cheek.

"I knew you would come, I felt it in my heart," she whispered. "Oh, I'm so glad you're here—I've missed you terribly!"

She turned to Tobias, smiling at him through her tears. "They're exhausted, and probably haven't eaten for ever so long. They need food and a basket—wide, but not deep. Please fetch them for me," she said.

Warily the captain came up behind her. "I see it, but I don't believe it. Your father told me about these birds—killers, aren't they?"

Fury laughed. "Nonsense. Wild hawks, perhaps, but not killers, these two. I raised both of them from the time they were mere fledglings. They're completely loyal to me. As long as I'm not threatened in any way, they'll remain quite calm. Can you imagine, flying all this way! You look surprised, Captain Diaz." Fury laughed. "I can tell you exactly how they got here. They can fly six to eight hours straight. They roosted in ships, and when possible they probably flew along the coast, stopping in ports like . . . like people!'' She gurgled with laughter. ''Who cares how they did it? They did it, and they're here safe and sound. Not to mention exhausted.'' She crooned softly to the weary birds, stroking their sleek backs. She swallowed against the lump in her throat when she noticed how many feathers both hawks had lost. She thought her heart would burst with love for the birds.

Diaz watched as Fury stroked the hawks' silky backs, her delight and pleasure in them evident on her face. It was the happiest he'd seen her since she boarded the *Queen*. But he didn't care what reassurances she made; these were hawks, and hawks were killers. He wanted no part of them.

''I cannot conceive how you flew all this way and actually found me,'' Fury whispered to the exhausted birds. ''I know I'll never understand, but I thank you for coming.'' Tears blurred her vision as Gaspar and Pilar leaned forward to touch her cheeks with their beaks. She yowled her pleasure then, sobs racking her body. The hawks looked at each other. They'd never heard these sounds before. They rustled their wings, stretching them to cover the girl's head and shoulders.

Tobias, on his way back with the basket in hand, stopped dead in his tracks at this display of devotion from two birds of prey. He inched forward cautiously, then set down the basket and slid it with his foot toward the rail. In his other hand he held a bucket of salt pork. With the hawks' glittering eyes on him every second, he lowered it to the deck, and then without a word withdrew as quickly as he could, heading for the crew's quarters and the keg of rum the men had stowed away there.

Fury dried her eyes and reached for the basket. When

she spoke, her voice was soft, a comforting caress. "We have only two more weeks before we reach land. Until then you can rest, both of you." She pointed to the mizzenmast and held out the basket to Pilar, who clasped it with her talons.

Pilar turned into the breeze and with barely a ruffle of her wings, the stately bird sailed upward on the gentle breeze. Gaspar and Fury watched until the basket was secure in the rigging. The moment Pilar's head disappeared, Gaspar swooped downward and with one talon lifted the bucket of meat. His wings fanned as he, too, caught the breeze, and he swooped upward. Fury clapped her hands in delight. "Rest, you've earned it," she called up to them in a lilting voice.

Fury's faith, which had slowly been deserting her since her journey began, was now restored. She clasped her hands reverently and murmured, "You sent them, I know You did. Forgive me, God, for doubting. Forgive my doubts."

She gave no thought to the fact that when she entered the convent, the hawks would have to leave her . . . once and for all.

The *Java Queen* was three days away from the Port of Java when a storm lashed across the ocean. It was the worst of his career, Captain Diaz declared worriedly as he ordered Fury below decks until the faltering storm had subsided. "If it ever does," he added mournfully.

"I have to get Gaspar and Pilar," Fury cried, running forward to the rail. "They'll die up there with no protection!"

Diaz grabbed her arm. "I'm *ordering* you below, Miss Fury. *Now!*" He spun around and bellowed for his second mate. "Basil, take this girl below decks and lock her door!"

The moment Basil reached out for Fury's arms, two

black shapes swooped across the quarterdeck, screeching their disapproval. Fury wrenched free of Basil's hold and fell to her knees in the driving rain. "Go below!" she screamed to the birds. "I'll try to follow you."

Gaspar flew ahead of her, Pilar at her back, her powerful wings urging the frightened girl on toward safety. At the top of the ladder Fury turned to look behind her, but all she could see was the blackness of Pilar's outfanned wings. Gaspar was above her, she could sense his presence. Choking and sputtering, she slid down the ladder and landed flat on her back. Gaspar fluttered down the hold to her side, and Pilar, talons curled beneath her, joined him.

Amid the muted howl of wind and water, Fury struggled to a half-sitting position, her eyes on Gaspar. Twice she tried to get on her feet, but Pilar's wing tips held her down. "Hawhawhaw," she screeched.

Suddenly the deafening sounds of the storm above decks lessened and Gaspar was alongside Pilar. Fury watched as Pilar dropped her wings to wipe the rain from Gaspar's drenched feathers.

On her hands and knees Fury crawled to her cabin, the hawks urging her forward.

Safe in her cabin, she sat on the edge of her bunk, the hawks perched on the mahogany footboard, their gleaming eyes finally at rest.

Above decks the sea boiled and the heavens split as Captain Diaz steered the galleon under her close-reefed sails. He kept her bow pointed as near into the wind as possible, but never dead into the eye of the storm. Gigantic waves, whipped by the gale into curly white combers, rolled continuously from the west. Spindrift lashed out with unrelenting fury, stinging his face as he fought the wheel.

The maelstrom demanded his full concentration. Powerful seafaring hands, rough and callused, gripped the stout wheel. Lightning flashed, illuminating the dark, spectral shapes of clouds scudding across the sky. This rain could kill him, he knew, drive him overboard, beat the strength from his body. He'd once heard Regan van der Rhys liken the rain to a vampire draining a man's vitality bit by bit until he could no longer stand erect. Already the savage torrent was whipping up his nostrils and down his throat, choking off his air supply, pounding him to nothingness. The bastard wind was going to drive the *Queen* to destruction if he didn't regain his strength and do something.

Diaz realized something in that moment of fear. It wasn't the storm that frightened him out of his wits, but the thought of what Regan van der Rhys would do to him if anything happened to his daughter.

Fearing the worst, Diaz grappled with a length of sailcloth to lash himself to the wheel, but it was ripped from his numb hands by a violent breaker.

Minutes seemed hours and hours seemed eternities as the storm raged. Diaz was blinded by the brutal downpour but kept to his heading by sheer instinct. Suddenly a crashing breaker and a yowling cannon of wind exploded behind him. He had no time to think or pray as he was carried away, crashing and sliding in the unholy cataclysm. No man heard his screams as he was swept over the side.

Fury knew the moment they lost course. The huge galleon listed, righted, then rolled almost on her side. She was thrown from the bunk, her body crashing against the wall. Dazed, she struggled to her knees.

"The captain's lost control of the wheel," she moaned to the glowering hawks. "This storm will carry us off our course, back out to sea!"

The galleon's hold on the monstrous roiling ocean was weak—she was in dire need of ballast. Fury rolled from one end of her cabin to the other as the *Queen* fought to remain upright under the first mate's hands.

She was beneath the hawks now at the foot of the bunk, her fear-filled eyes on their gigantic talons. Deadly talons. They could grasp hundreds of pounds and lift it straight into the air and still fly as though unencumbered. There was no other word to describe the hawks except to say they were powerful.

She cried out in despair, knowing full well there was nothing she could do to fight the battering storm and keep the galleon on her course. She'd manned the wheel on her father's ships hundreds of times, but always in calm waters. She was strong, but no match for this.

Her stomach heaved sickeningly. She'd never before given thought to her own mortality. If she died now at the hands of the storm and sea, she would never enter the convent, never, ever see . . . neverneverneverneverer.

She wished she knew more about eternity, that nebulous place after death. Her final accounting in the eyes of God. Was she clean and pure enough to enter the gates of heaven?

With one mighty shove she was on her feet. "Oh, God, I don't want to die, not yet. Please!" she shrieked.

The hawks' feathers rustled, the sound vying with the storm, their jet eyes on the girl.

She was upright now, holding to the bunk with a vise-like grip. "I must ask the impossible of you," she told the two hawks, whose eyes were fixed on her with uncanny comprehension. "Of you . . . and of myself."

When she made her way, weaving and stumbling, out of the cabin and down the passageway, they followed. Twice she was thrown against the wall with the violent pitching of the boat. At the ladder, she paused. She knew the hawks couldn't help her open the hatch to the deck; there was nothing for their talons to grasp. She swore then, words she didn't know she knew, words she'd heard her brothers hiss at one another when they were angry, words her father had muttered under his breath. With a strength born of desperation, she threw herself against the hatch door again and again, but each time the battering wind slammed it shut, her shoulder taking the brunt of the blow. She waited, counting seconds before she gave one last heave. A flurry of angry sound roared past her ears as Gaspar soared through the tumultuous wind, his talons securing a hold on the stout wood support. A second later Pilar was at his side.

Fury stumbled up and out, then fell to her hands and knees, fighting the wind and blinding water. She saw no one, but could hear the crew cursing and shouting as they struggled with the sail and rigging.

Her nails were broken to the quick, her hands and knees full of splinters as she crawled a few steps and then was driven backward by the ravaging wind. She had no idea how long it took her, but at last she reached the wheelhouse and pulled herself upright with the wheel for support.

Everywhere was black as India ink; the lanterns had all gone out. Fury's hands moved on the wheel and touched something cold and hard. Gaspar's talons. She moved her hand to the right: Pilar's talons. *How did they know this was what she wanted them to do?* An eerie feeling swept through her as she realized that her life depended on these hawks that were so tuned to her feelings. She would have cried for joy but she was too frightened. In the very core of her soul she knew no force on earth could make them relinquish their hold on the wheel.

Fury felt silly and ridiculous when she shouted, "Steady on, mates, a true course to Java or dry land, whichever comes first!" The crew couldn't hear her, and if they did, she didn't care.

For hours the *Java Queen* heaved with the force of the surf, the masts groaning with the weight of the saturated rigging. The battered ship rose and fell in the angry, swelling sea. Fury steered her course straight and true—frightened, yes, but exhilarated and buoyed by the unshakable conviction that Gaspar and Pilar would see the *Java Queen* home safely.

The relentless wind and surging sea left with the last of the black night, and dawn appeared, gray and misty. Fury's shoulders slumped as a weary sigh escaped her. Gradually her ears picked up the jabbering sounds of the men as they emerged one by one from their posts onto the now gently rolling deck. They'd all survived, she thought in relief. The disbelief she read on their faces at the picture of herself and the hawks at the wheel made her smile wanly.

"Where's the captain?" Tobias asked uneasily, his eyes still on the hawks.

"I don't know." She shook her head. "I took the wheel from Eduardo."

"He ordered us to take cover when the storm was at its worst. There was nothing we could do but go over the side. We did our best, miss, so did the captain." He blessed himself to make his point. "Spread out, mates," he ordered the others, "and see what you can find."

Tobias turned back to Fury. "These birds steered this ship through the storm?"

Fury smiled. "I helped a little, but, yes, they did exactly that. And the three of us will be more than happy to turn the wheel over to you, Tobias. I have no idea where we are or how far off course."

Pilar's wings rustled slightly, and in the blink of an eye she and Gaspar were sailing upward toward the mizzenmast.

"Devil birds," Tobias muttered as he took the wheel.

"Would devil birds save your life and mine? We'd all be dead now without them. Remember that," she called over her shoulder as she stumbled out on deck.

Seven days later the *Java Queen* sailed proudly into the Port of Java. No one noticed the huge black birds at the top of the mizzenmast, their glittering eyes raking the harbor of their new home.

There was a tension about the crew that troubled Fury as she prepared to go ashore. Obviously they were uncertain of their future, which was understandable. They were without direction for the first time in many weeks. Without Captain Diaz they might find themselves stranded with no hope of returning or even of signing on to another voyage.

Fury stared at the pouch in her hands—it contained all the money she'd won from the crew over the long voyage. Coming to a decision, she sought out Tobias and handed him the velvet purse. "I'll have no use for this where I'm going," she told the first mate. "Please . . . divide it among the men. In the absence of my father and Captain Diaz, I urge you to stay aboard until matters can be arranged regarding your welfare. I myself will see to it tomorrow." She turned to those of the crew who had gathered near. "Adios, my friends." They nodded, their eyes full of relief as they prepared to carry her trunks to shore.

Fury's eyes roamed the dock until they rested on the familiar face of Father Sebastian. He was older than she remembered, his round hat sitting on his head like a fat pancake. She watched as he waddled to the gangboards leading to the wharf, his round, pigeon's body shaking with each step he took. "Welcome to Java, Miss Fury," he called. "You're as beautiful as your mother, and I would have known you anywhere."

Fury hurried down to meet him. "Thank you, Father Sebastian. I was hoping someone would be here to greet me. I'm most eager to reach my parents' home, but first I must go to the Dutch East India offices. Our captain was . . . lost at sea during a murderous storm. His family must be notified and provisions made for them and the crew."

Father Sebastian blessed himself as he escorted Fury to

his flat wagon. "Yes, of course. It's what your father would want. I never met a fairer man than Mynheer van der Rhys. In his last letter to me he said he was sailing to the Americas to see his son, Caleb. Did your mother accompany him?"

Fury nodded. "When their visit is over they will come here, or at least that was their plan. Circumstances . . . I've found lately that one cannot count on anything fully."

The priest favored her with a gentle smile. "It's about to rain, so I suggest we hurry. You remember the rains, don't you, my dear?"

"Yes, Father. There is very little about Java that I don't remember." She gazed about her fondly. "I loved it here, and that's why I chose to enter the convent here. . . . Is Juli still at the house?"

"Yes, and she's looking forward to serving you as she did your mother."

Fury smiled. "She'll have exactly one week to fuss over me. I hope you told her it would just be temporary."

"I told her," Father Sebastian said quietly. The priest's eyes were fretful as he snapped the reins and urged the horse forward.

"The Dutch East India offices are just up the street here. And afterward I'll drive you to the house." He gazed up at the darkening sky. "I think," he said, reining his horse to a halt, "that we did beat the rain by a scant second or two. Step down, child, and run into the offices. My hat will protect me. I know how fussy you ladies are about your hair." Fury raced for her father's old offices just as fat raindrops began to splatter.

The man behind the desk stood up in greeting, his hands outstretched. "It's uncanny," he said, a look of awe on his face. "I don't know who you resemble more, your mother or your father. The best of both, I suppose."

"Captain Dykstra, it's nice to see you again. I have a

letter for you from my father. Will tomorrow be soon enough to deliver it?''

"Tomorrow will be fine." He searched her troubled eyes for a moment, then escorted her to the chair beside his desk. "Please sit down for a moment. The rains will let up shortly. And I can see by your expression that all is not well. Tell me what's wrong."

Dykstra rubbed his chin thoughtfully as Fury spoke. At least the girl was safe, but that wouldn't stop Regan from flying into a rage when he heard this particular piece of news.

"Ronrico Diaz was an able-bodied seaman, one of the best. Your father and I both sailed with him on many occasions. His family will be well taken care of, I assure you. I myself will arrange a service with Father Sebastian. The crew's wages will be paid, of course. In the meantime they can stay aboard until a decision is made regarding the *Java Queen*'s next voyage. If they have a mind to, they can sign on with another ship."

"And a bonus, Captain Dykstra. They've earned it," Fury told him.

Dykstra laughed. "Ah, your mother's daughter through and through! That's exactly what she would have said. Your father, on the other hand, would have offered extra rations of rum and ale."

"Both, then," Fury said firmly.

"Done!" Dykstra boomed.

She clapped her hands in delight. "My father said you were one of the fairest, most honest men he'd ever met . . . after himself."

"I always say that myself," Dykstra agreed, nodding pleasantly. "Tell me, who brought the *Queen* into the harbor?"

"I did . . . in a manner of speaking. But I had a little help."

"Well done, my dear. Your parents will be proud of you." He turned to peer out the window behind him. "Ah, the rain is letting up. You'll want to be on your way to a nice long bath and a hair wash, no doubt. Well, the house is ready for you. We'll talk later, and you can tell me tall tales of that rascal father of yours."

Fury grinned. "Only if you tell me of some of your escapades."

"I'll walk you to the wagon; I want a word with the good Father," Dykstra said, offering her his arm.

Midway to the door, Fury's eyes fell on the cork board attached to the wall. "Is that what I think it is?"

"The infamous sea witch? Yes, it's been hanging there for twenty-some years now. I think every man on Java was in love with her. She's become a legend. She nearly destroyed the Dutch East India Company, something your father did not take lightly. He didn't have a peaceful day until the witch retired from her plundering ways. I met her once," he murmured, his eyes fixed on some long-ago memory. "She was the most beautiful, most magnificent woman I've ever seen."

"Were you in love with her, too?" Fury asked quietly.

"Yes, unfortunately."

"Do you think she'll ever roam the sea again?" Fury asked.

He glanced at her. "It's strange you should ask me that. A few weeks ago a bark sailed in for repairs, and there was talk of a black ship off the coast of Africa. The men aboard swore it was captained by a woman. Every so often such tales are whispered about. That's why the legend of the Sea Siren will never die. I live in dread of the day she might return to the sea. Of course, if she just did away with the bloody pirates and left my fleet alone, I wouldn't mind."

Fury smiled. "A fairy tale, Captain Dykstra."

"No, my dear, the Sea Siren was no fairy tale. She was a live, flesh-and-blood woman with vengeance in her heart. And the black ship was indeed seen—the fear I saw in those men's eyes convinced me of that. As to the Sea Siren, I don't know," he said nervously. "Only time will tell."

Impossible, Fury thought as she settled herself in the wagon while the priest and Dykstra conversed in low tones. Her mother was the Sea Siren, and she was in the Americas. A rumor started by a drunken sailor—that's all it was. But the first moment she had to herself, she would visit the bend in the river where the *Rana* was hidden. The black paint had been stripped away long ago; she was just another frigate now and probably rotting away to nothing.

The knot of anxiety that formed in her stomach at Dykstra's words remained with her until the wagon neared the front entrance of the van der Rhys mansion. At first sight of the two story, white-pillared veranda and the massive, intricately carved mahogany double doors, Fury forgot everything but her delight in being back home. As always, the grounds around the estate were meticulously kept. Even now several gardeners went about their chores of pruning and weeding the brightly colored flower beds. The scent of spices and flowers permeated the air, and exotic wild birds called raucously to one another. The house, the grounds, everything reflected her parents' pride. Many years and much labor had gone into the completion of this manor house. The front steps had been chiseled out of the precious "pink marble" from the foothills of the China mountains. In Europe, her mother told her, craftsmen carved jewelry and statues from the deep red stone. Here on Java, a wily agent for the Dutch East India Company— her father—had used it for his front steps.

"Is it as you remembered, child?" Father Sebastian asked softly.

"Oh, yes, Father. Look, the servants are coming out to greet me. Let's see if I can remember them. Ling Fu, of course, Juli, Marion—and there's Valie!" Fury leapt from the wagon and ran up the cobblestone path, her eyes shining as she embraced those she'd known since childhood.

Impertinently Juli held her nose as Fury approached her. "Miss Fury, you are in need of a nice hot bath and clean clothes. Come inside with me."

Fury smiled fondly at the motherly housekeeper. "In a minute, Juli. I must talk to Father Sebastian before he leaves." She beckoned to the old priest and drew him to one side.

"Father, you said you had a letter for me from the Mother Prioress. May I have it?"

"Tomorrow is time enough for such things, my daughter. Go along now to your bath and a nice bed with clean sheets. We'll talk over breakfast."

"Very well, tomorrow it is," Fury called gaily as she ran up the steps to her old bedroom.

Tomorrow . . . tomorrows always come, the priest thought sadly, watching her. The child was so happy, and tomorrow he would destroy that happiness. Sighing, he settled himself in the wagon and was about to drive away when suddenly his horse shied and snorted, nostrils flaring. Two monstrous birds sailed directly overhead, momentarily casting great shadows across the sun. The priest had never seen such huge, black-winged creatures. He watched them for a moment as they hung suspended in the light breeze. It was an omen, some kind of omen. He blessed himself and began to pray.

From her position in the high bed, propped up by frilly pillows, Fury stared through the open windows into the soft dark night. The heavens and the stars looked different here, on land. *Everything* felt and looked different here.

This was her home, and she was happy to be back at last, but it didn't feel right somehow.

Her girlhood room was offering no comfort this night, exhausted as she was. A thousand thoughts, doubts, questions, assailed her—questing demons that tormented her and destroyed her peace of mind. At last, realizing that sleep was out of the question, Fury swung her legs over the side of the bed, threw on her wrapper, and padded to the door. Maybe if she slept in her mother's bed . . .

Inside her parents' room, she gazed around her in admiration. Everything was exactly the way she remembered it. The beautiful, high-ceilinged compartment; the full-length windows that opened onto a terrace abloom with potted flowers of every shape and color; the furniture, dark and heavy, with colorful draperies and pillows in perfect complement. How often she'd run to this room crying over something or other! It had been a sanctuary in so many ways.

It was out these very windows, Fury recalled, caressing the polished teak frame, that her mother had escaped—sliding down the trellis into the bushes below to slip off to sea in her identity as the infamous Sea Siren. And when she'd returned it was Juli who'd helped her undress, Juli who had secretly washed the Sea Siren's costume and polished the slippery black boots. Juli, her father said, was the only person in the house, aside from Frau Holz, in Sirena's confidence.

This room was full of ghosts, memories of another time, yet Fury didn't feel as though she was trespassing. How wonderful and exciting it must have been for her mother to wield such power, to have big, strong, able-bodied men bow to her as their superior.

Fury stood in front of the full-length mirror at the far corner of the room and struck a pose, one her mother had taught her that had given her a slight edge during her fencing lessons. "En garde!" she called, hiking up her skirts to show an alluring length of leg. Laughing, she brandished a make-believe rapier in the direction of the open windows. Suddenly, Luis Domingo appeared in her make-believe drama.

"You're mine!" he declared, approaching her, his eyes mocking and murderous at the same time. "To the victor go the spoils, Siren!"

"Never! I'm promised to God!" Fury cried as she backed up one step at a time, her hands grasping a cut-glass perfume decanter from her mother's dressing table. "One more step, you detestable swine, and I'll cut you to the quick!"

The Luis Domingo of her fantasy roared with mocking laughter. "Forgive me, señorita, I see now that you are not the Siren I seek. My apologies for thinking you were that lustful, vengeful, beautiful woman. Go to your convent—that is where you belong!"

"You lie! You know you can't best the Sea Siren! You aren't man enough! Only one man can tame the Siren—and it isn't you, you insufferable toad!"

Domingo laughed, a deep, sensuous sound that set Fury's nerves to tingling. "I'm man enough. The problem is you, señorita. You aren't woman enough, and you'll never know if I'm lying or telling the truth because you belong to God . . . and God doesn't permit such things." His eyes raked her body with a boldness that both shocked and titillated her.

"A pity, señorita."

In a fit of pique Fury threw the decanter, which shattered against the wall behind her phantom tormenter. "Now you'll carry my scent forever. You'll never forget me! Never! Roam the seas in search of me until you die, and *you'll* never know if I'm real or not!" Domingo's laughter rang in her ears, so real that she almost swooned.

"Miss Fury, are you all right?" Juli called from the doorway.

Fury spun about, her cheeks crimson. "I'm fine, Juli. I—I was talking to myself. I always do that when I'm—"

"Upset." Juli smiled. "Your mother used to do the same thing, but her words were . . . more colorful. You've grown to look just like her except for your blue eyes. Will you be staying in this room, Miss Fury?"

"Why do you call me Miss Fury and my mother *juff-rouw*?" Fury asked lightly, hoping to draw the housekeeper's attention from the embarrassing pantomime she'd just witnessed.

"Your mother disliked the Dutch language; she said it was harsh and guttural-sounding. When you were little she instructed me to call you Miss Fury or señorita. The word *señorita* does not come easy to my lips, but if you would prefer it . . ."

Fury smiled. "Miss Fury will do nicely. I won't be here long enough for your tongue to get tangled up in words." She sank down onto her mother's bed with a sigh. "I feel so strange, Juli. Not like myself at all. At first I thought it was the anticipation of my return. But here, in this room, it's even worse." She lowered her voice, and Juli had to strain to hear the words. "One second I feel like a stranger, and the next moment I feel like I'm . . . my mother."

"That's only natural, Miss Fury. You are among your mother's things. When I come here to clean this room, I, too, feel her . . . spirit. Sometimes my memory takes me back, and my eyes fill with tears. When they spoke of the Sea Siren in town and the havoc she wreaked, I think every woman secretly cheered her. I know I did. Our lives have been dull and boring these past years."

"It must have been exciting," Fury said, eyes sparkling at the thought of such adventure.

Juli nodded. "Doubly exciting because your father lived

under this roof. Do you have any idea how we plotted and schemed and then worried and watched until she returned safely? I would give anything to have those days back again.''

Burning with curiosity, Fury beckoned Juli to her side. ''I've heard so many stories about my father. He says he knew all along, but my mother denies this. Do you think he did?''

''In the beginning, never,'' Juli declared firmly, sitting beside her young charge. ''Later he may have suspected, but he wasn't sure. You see, we all heard him storm about the house and curse the Siren every time she sank one of his ships. All he did was dream of ways to vanquish her. She made a fool of every man in Java; she brought the Dutch East India Company to its knees, and when she found what she was seeking, she . . . retired.''

Fury sighed. ''She's truly a legend. It's so hard for me to think of my mother as a bloodthirsty pirate. She's so gentle and caring. When I was ill she used to sing to me or sit by my bed for hours and tell me stories. And I know she loves my father more than life itself. I've never understood . . . what I mean is, there has been so much tragedy in her life. She suffered unbearable agonies aboard the *Rana* on her trips to Java from Spain. Her sister . . . her uncle, and then Miguel, her first child, and then my four brothers lost at sea . . . and still she's managed to survive and be happy with my father.'' Fury's voice trembled, and her eyes filled with tears. ''I don't believe I have that inner core of strength.''

''After death there is nothing,'' Juli said, smoothing back a lock of Fury's hair with tender fingers. ''Life is sunshine, warm breezes, and the hope that a new day will make things better. Isn't hope better than the blackness of nothing? I myself cannot imagine life without the sounds of the birds in the morning, the stars at night, and the beauty of the flowers that are all about us. One must make the best of one's life. Your mother had choices, and she chose to live each day to the fullest. You are most fortunate to have her.''

Fury smiled. "You really love her, don't you?"

"As much as you, and I was only her servant. She taught me to read and write. Once a year I receive a letter from her and a box of wonderful presents. When she appointed me housekeeper to this grand estate, I wept." Juli patted her hand and stood up. "Come with me, Miss Fury, there's something I want to show you."

"What?" Fury asked, curious.

"Shhh," Juli said with a finger to her lips. "The walls have ears."

In the housekeeper's room off the monstrous kitchen, Fury watched as Juli opened a huge brass-bound trunk at the foot of her bed. Inside was an overwhelming array of fine laces and silks and small wooden boxes, obviously all gifts from Sirena.

"Your mother has been most generous over the years," Juli said softly, rummaging through the trunk. "She said I should consider these things as part of my dowry. What she didn't tell me was where I was to find the man to give them to. . . . Ah, here it is!"

Eyes wide, Fury watched as the older woman untied the string from a roll of goatskin. "I wrapped all of it in this oiled skin to protect it," she explained, working carefully to separate the skin from the treasure it concealed. When she had succeeded, she held out her arms to Fury, who accepted the bundle reverently.

How shiny the black boots were, she marveled. She could see her reflection in them. The shirt was blindingly white, tattered in places but neatly mended, as was the abbreviated skirt, which had been stitched together in the middle the way a man's drawers were. The red-and-black bandanna was folded neatly.

"They still smell of the sea," Juli whispered. "They smell of . . . *her*."

Fury nodded, unable to speak, her eyes on the cutlass. "How many men did . . . do you suppose . . . ?"

"Only those who deserved her hand, Miss Fury, no others."

"My mother once made a costume and tried it on, but it didn't make me feel like this. These things are . . . so real."

"I didn't know what to do with them," Juli told her. "When she gave them to me she said they belonged here because it all started here and there was no place for them where she was going. She said the Sea Siren was dead. Perhaps I should have destroyed them, but I could not bring myself to do it, and I was glad I hadn't when I heard of your brothers. I thought for certain your mother would return and search the seas for them. I waited and waited, and she didn't come, so I put them away, but I never forgot they were here."

Fury itched to try on the neatly folded clothes, but it was to the cutlass that her eyes kept returning. At last she reached for it and picked it up. "Dear God, this is heavy!" she gasped.

"Be careful, Miss Fury, it's razor-sharp," Juli cautioned. "I stone it down from time to time."

"A rapier is very different from this," Fury said as she did her best to brandish the wicked-looking blade. "My father had one of these, but he's very strong. This is a man's weapon. Where did she get the strength to use this?"

Juli smiled. "Your mother told me once that everyone has a hidden source of strength that rises to the fore when needed. She wasn't dealing with swooning women, she was fighting to survive the only way she knew how. She drew on that strength. That's why she's alive today. You have that same strength, Miss Fury, inherited from both your mother and father.''

Fury groaned as she rent the air with the cutlass. "I feel like my shoulder is being pulled from its socket," she said wryly.

Juli began to laugh, but the sound died in her throat as two black shapes flew into the room with a wild rush of feathers. Crossing her arms over her ample breasts, she backed against the wall.

"Merciful God, what . . . !"

Fury giggled. "They won't hurt you, Juli. Believe it or not, they followed me all the way from Spain. This is Gaspar and this is Pilar. I raised them from fledglings, and now they're my friends." She rolled up the sleeves of her wrapper to show Juli the scar on her arm. "When Gaspar was still a nestling, he was attacked by a full-grown kite. I saved him, but was badly scored in the process. It's turned out rather like my mother's scar, don't you think?"

Juli nodded, her eyes full of fear. "It's an omen. A bad omen," she said.

Fury laughed. "No, no, it's simply a bad wound that healed. There's nothing about it that can be construed as an omen."

The hawks were on the floor now, their talons gripping the carpet as they minced their way to the goatskin packet. Pilar's wing tips rustled as she flicked out at the shiny black boots, her eyes glittering at her reflection. Gaspar, more intent on the cutlass, moved closer. He circled Pilar and the packet twice before he was satisfied that nothing was amiss. Then, with a wild flutter of his wings, he swooped up and out of the French doors, Pilar following in the wake of the breeze he created.

Juli's hand flew to her throat. "What . . . ?"

"They're curious," Fury said lightly, trying not to show her own unease. "Perhaps they picked up my mother's scent."

"They—they look like devils straight out of hell!" Juli cried, crossing herself. "You aren't going to leave them here when you go to . . . Not here!"

Fury sighed and crossed to the window, peering out. "I tamed them, Juli. I truthfully don't know what they'll do when I leave. They've never had to forage for food, and they'll die if they aren't fed."

"Please, Miss Fury, don't ask me to feed them," Juli pleaded. "Ask anything else of me, but not that!"

"Once they get to know you, they won't hurt you," Fury said reassuringly. "All you have to do is put their meat in a pail and leave it for them. Let's do it together while I'm here. Later, if you're still afraid, have one of the djongos do it." She turned away from the window. "Come, let's put these things back."

From their perch on the low stone walls outside Juli's room, Gaspar and Pilar watched as Fury helped the housekeeper replace the costume and cutlass within the protective goatskin. Gaspar's eyes glittered as the lid of the trunk was raised and then slammed shut. Pilar's eyes were on the brass handles at each end of the heavy trunk.

Fury slept fitfully in her mother's high, wide bed, her dreams invaded by demons with talons, disguised as mortals. When she struggled awake, darkness was still caressing the dawn, loath to unleash the soft lavender that would herald a new day.

Minutes later she entered the kitchen, washed and dressed in a gay cherry-red day gown, and found Juli at the table sipping coffee. "I gather you, too, didn't sleep well," Fury said bluntly.

When she'd seated herself, Juli rose and stood next to

the chopping block, her cup of coffee in her hands. It would never do for her to forget her place. Her tongue, however, was something else.

"Why are you up so early?" Fury asked. "You needn't worry about making breakfast for me. All I really want is coffee."

"I'm baking for Father Sebastian," Juli explained. "He has a ferocious appetite in the morning, and then I make up a basket for him to take back to his parish. Your mother always had us do that."

Fury smiled. "It would seem that little has changed here; why is that, do you suppose?"

"People change, not places," Juli said, shrugging. "If this house changed, you would be unhappy. You have wonderful memories of it. Your parents knew you would return from time to time, and really, what is there to change? The herbs on the windowsill grow and are cut and grow again. The floor and walls will last hundreds of years. My chopping block has a few more cuts and nicks, but otherwise it, too, will last a lifetime."

"I guess what I remember most is the smell of nutmeg and cinnamon and the little frosted cakes," Fury murmured. "Once I asked my mother if a person could get drunk on the smell of spices and flowers, and she said yes. Do you know, Juli," she said suddenly, "that a man can make a woman's blood sing?"

Juli's round, dark eyes widened. "Now, where did you hear such a thing?" she gasped.

"From my mother. She said my father has always made her blood sing, and that's how you know you're in love." Fury propped her chin in both hands and gazed dreamily at the housekeeper. "I wonder how that feels."

"I don't think either one of us has to worry about that," Juli said grumpily as she punched down a mound of dough on the floured board. "You're going to the convent next week, and I'm here in this house with no men about."

Fury laughed. "Speaking of men, I think I'd like to take a walk in the gardens before Father Sebastian arrives," she said. She kicked off her slippers and hiked up her skirts. "Would it be too much trouble to serve him outside?"

"Of course not, and you will be served, too," Juli said bossily. "Once you leave here you will be fasting and eating rotted fish and God knows what else. You will eat breakfast with Father Sebastian."

Fury grinned. "Now I understand why you and my mother got along so well; she can be just as bossy. Well, I humored her, and I will humor you, too. Pink ham and golden eggs on a fluffy cloud." She laughed as she raced out to the garden.

Out of Juli's sight and hearing, however, the laughter died in her throat. There must be something wrong with her, she thought. She'd never felt this way before—uneasy, on the verge of tears all the time, achy and . . . lonely. The bad dreams were with her all the time now; no wonder she had shadows under her eyes. And her appetite was completely gone. In fact, she didn't care if she never ate again. What was wrong with her?

"Dear God," she cried suddenly, "I didn't say my morning prayers!" In the whole of her life she'd never forgotten the important ritual. "Now, *that's* an omen," she said sourly.

But she didn't rush to clasp her hands in prayer. Didn't raise her eyes heavenward to beg forgiveness. Instead, she walked around the gardens to the long drive in front of the house to wait for Father Sebastian.

An hour later, when the priest clattered up the driveway in his wagon, Fury was the picture of misery and dejection. The elderly cleric noted the shadows under her eyes and sighed. He'd intended simply to hand over the letter he'd brought and leave, without having to witness its effect on this beautiful girl. But seeing her here, looking so wistful, so alone, he changed his mind.

"Good morning, Father," Fury called, running over to meet him. "It's a lovely day, isn't it? Juli is going to serve us breakfast in the garden."

"Good morning, my child. Yes, I think I would enjoy a light repast on this beautiful morning. . . . Furana, I've brought the letter as promised. But I'm afraid the news it contains may not be to your liking."

"Thank you, Father," she said, frowning as she accepted the heavy vellum envelope the priest was holding out to her.

Father Sebastian watched as Fury read the letter from beginning to end several times and tried to digest its contents. He'd been expecting outrage, tears, a fit of temper, and was almost disappointed when she looked up at him, dry-eyed, and said, "I don't understand."

The priest fanned himself with his pancake hat. "The bishop himself ordered the nuns to Surabaja, where a deadly fever has broken out," he explained gently. "They've been gone for over three months and aren't expected to return until next year. There is also a possibility they may not return to Cirebon at all. Much depends on the sisters' stamina and endurance. Several weeks ago the bishop told me three of the sisters had fallen prey to the fever. For now, Furana, I'm afraid you must remain here."

"Is the convent closed?" Fury demanded.

The priest frowned, puzzled. Was he hearing relief in the girl's voice? "No, it isn't·closed. There are three old nuns who were not well enough to make the journey. The bishop gave them a special dispensation. But the gates are locked and chained, and no one is to be admitted. I take in a wagonload of food once a month; I ring the bell to let them know it's there, and then I leave. Those were my orders from the bishop. If you wish, you may make the next journey with me, but you cannot speak to the nuns. Nor will they let you see them.''

Fury's eyes filled with tears and her voice trembled. ''What am I to do, Father? What if they never return? What will become of me?''

The elderly priest regarded her compassionately. ''Child, God works in mysterious ways, and we must not doubt His wisdom. Perhaps you were not meant to enter the order.''

Fury gazed off into the distance, her eyes narrowed against the glare of the early-morning sun. At last she sighed and turned back to Father Sebastian.

''I think, Father, that you may be right. God has chosen this way to tell me that for now, at least, I am not meant to join the Holy Order. I must accept it. I have no other choice.''

Father Sebastian nodded. ''Those are my thoughts exactly, Furana. We both must accept God's decision.''

''I suppose that means I am now mistress of this house— and my first duty in that position is to escort you to breakfast. Your arm, Father,'' Fury said, and gave him a tremulous smile.

Chapter Four

The tall, lean, bare-chested man standing so easily on the bow of the *Silver Lady* bore little resemblance to the distinguished gentleman who had attended Fury van der Rhys's birthday celebration in Cadiz. His dark eyes took on a brooding quality as he stared out at the sparkling blue of the ocean. He'd felt out of his element at that party in his crisp linen suit and neat cravat; generally he preferred the casual dress he affected on shipboard: a loose flowing shirt and dark trousers tucked into soft leather boots that were kept polished every day.

Absentmindedly, he massaged his month-old beard with one sun-bronzed hand. It itched like hell, but he scarcely noticed; his thoughts were far away, back at the grand casa in Cadiz. "Too ornate," he muttered. The young women attending the birthday celebration had been silly creatures . . . with the exception of Fury van der Rhys. The food had been too rich, the musicians and decorations too costly—all memories of a life he himself had been obliged to give up many years before, thanks to the witch they called the Sea Siren.

Luis Domingo lifted his spyglass to search the sea for any sign of other ships. He'd worked too hard over the past fifteen years trying to rebuild his father's shipping company to let this first commission fall into the hands of bloodthirsty pirates. Someday when he was as rich as Regan van der Rhys he would count the cost of all the sleepless nights and missed meals and paid-off debts. Someday . . .

Luis allowed his thoughts to carry him away as the *Silver Lady* sliced through the water, her Spanish colors billowing in the light breeze. This was a lazy time of day for him, the winds calming, the air still, the smell of the sea teasing his nostrils. He was relaxed now, so relaxed that he found himself drifting back in time, back to the single moment that had changed his life forever. At the age of eight he'd had no idea what death meant, but he remembered how it felt when one of his father's friends had told him that his father would never be returning to their fine house.

Domingo snorted. Fine house indeed! His mother had been forced to sell that house as well as the furnishings and hire out as a domestic to some of the richer families in Cadiz. She'd been only fifty years of age when she died, but she'd looked twice that, bent and crippled from hard work and not enough nourishing foods. Domingo's eyes narrowed against the pain of that memory.

All that was changed now, thanks to his diligence and hard work. He'd worked like a slave, day after day, just to pay off his father's debts. Fifteen long years of blood, sweat, and even tears that none had witnessed save his sweet, gentle mother. A pity she wasn't alive to see the results.

Once he'd paid off the debts, it had taken him two more years to earn the money to outfit the two remaining ships that belonged to his father. He'd had small consignments, but none like this one, and none that yielded enough profit for anything but the barest necessities. This particular commission was a lifelong dream of his father's and one the man would have accomplished if it hadn't been for the sea witch.

For the thousandth time, Luis ran the route over in his mind—he'd memorized the navigational charts. Cadiz to the Canary Islands and on to Cape Verde, and from there to Gabon, where he would weigh anchor, seek any needed repairs, and lay in fresh supplies. Three days at the most in port and then on to Cape Town, where he would lay in his most precious cargo, ivory. Then northeast to Madagascar and from there to the Sunda Strait and his last port of call, Java.

He closed his eyes as he envisioned his full hold, bales of shimmering silks, ivory, and spices. Coffers full of pearls, barrels of tobacco and molasses that would fetch a king's ransom—providing he wasn't accosted by pirates. There was no doubt in his mind that he would be a rich man when he returned to Spain, rich enough to set up a household and think about marrying . . . someone as beautiful as Furana van der Rhys.

A light breeze tickled the sails of the *Silver Lady* as she skimmed among the small breakers. "Tighten sail," he called as his eyes searched the vast ocean.

"Aye, Cap'n," came the reply.

Soon he would sail into Cape Town with the mysterious cargo that he kept in his quarters. He had no idea what he carried in the enormous brass-bound trunk that had been delivered to the harbor just as he was about to sail. The royal communiqué the imposing man offered identified him simply as an emissary of the Spanish Crown and ordered the captain of the *Silver Lady* to keep the trunk sealed and secure in his quarters at all times. Upon arrival in Capetown, it was to be delivered to one Amalie Suub Alvarez, who would then sign a letter of acceptance that was to be delivered to the Crown on the return journey. Finally, and most impressive, he'd been paid in advance for this service, something unheard of in the shipping business.

Luis found himself staring up into the rigging, his eyes searching for flaws or weaknesses. In an instant he was scaling the intricate maze of ropes with ease, while his crew watched him warily. None of them relished the tongue-lashing they would receive if the rigging proved unsatisfactory.

Out of the entire crew only Julian Castillo, the first mate, had sailed with Domingo's father. He'd been a boy not yet out of his teens when he'd signed on with the elder Domingo and frightened out of his wits the day the Siren had cut down his captain's ship. Pressed for details by the authorities, Julian could only say that the Siren was as deadly as she was beautiful. Over the years his boyhood memory turned fanciful, and he began to embroider his stories with more detail: ''The Sea Siren is stronger than any man, with a laugh that tinkles off the waters like an eerie sound from hell before she disappears into a black mist!'' In truth he remembered very little, what with fear of going over the side and the possibility of becoming shark fodder; but he did remember the terror he felt when he first saw the black ship approach the *Spanish Princess*.

Julian frowned, heavy brows drawing together across his forehead. His head pounded fiercely, as it always did when he tried to remember a detail, something that was said as he cowered in fear. Always it was the same when he fought the mists of memory: his head would pound so unbearably, he couldn't think. He wanted to remember, for Luis Domingo's sake. Perhaps someday . . .

Luis slid down the rigging, his movements agile as he landed gracefully on his feet. He nodded to his crew, who relaxed perceptibly. Whatever he'd imagined he saw was fine, and no new orders were given. Once again he picked up the glass, but this time, as he returned it to its case, a vague feeling of apprehension settled over him.

''Cap'n, I'd like a word with you,'' Julian called.

Luis shook off his uneasiness and grinned at the first mate. ''My ears are yours, Julian.''

''If you've a mind to, Cap'n, I think you could pick up some sandalwood at our next port of call. I know several merchants who have storehouses full of the wood and are just waiting for the right moment to strike a business deal. There's still some room in the hold. I don't pretend to be up on the latest female trends, but I did hear that the ladies of Seville have been begging for treasure boxes made from the fragrant wood. I'd say they'd fetch a pretty penny if the right craftsman was commissioned. Tack a fancy price on one of those little boxes and every lady'll want one.''

"That means an extra day in port,'' Luis said thoughtfully, stroking his bearded chin. "What the hell, a man can't have too many sidelines now, can he?'' He clapped Julian on the back. "If the price is right, we'll take on as much as we can carry. Advise the crew we'll be making port at this time tomorrow.''

"Aye, Cap'n.''

As Julian strode down the deck, Luis stood alone, measuring the sea. In the last hour the wind had increased steadily, and before long the waves would be churning furiously. Another hour and they'd be in for a stiff storm. He'd be fighting a southerly wind, where his course now lay, and he might have to veer off to the west if the gale increased.

Hours later, with the storm behind them and a mug of freshly brewed coffee in his hand, Luis congratulated his crew. "Well done, men. In a few hours we'll make port, and the drinks are on me. It's up to you to find your own women, though,'' he added, chuckling.

To a man, the crew saluted their captain. They would eat, drink, and bed as many wenches as possible in the time allotted, and while Domingo had said the drinks were on him, they knew he wouldn't join them. It was an arrangement agreeable to all.

The *Silver Lady*'s arrival in the Sandalwood Islands was as smooth as silk, each member of the crew doing his job to perfection—their reward, ten hours on land to do whatever they wanted. Once Luis had agreed on a price for the sandalwood, Julian stayed long enough to supervise the loading and then departed to enjoy a few hours of freedom with the pouch of coins Luis handed over.

"We sail with the tide, Julian," Luis said, his eye on the fragrant wood being loaded into the hold. Julian was right; it would fetch a tidy price, more if he could find a suitable craftsman with whom to share the profits.

A little before dawn the next day, much to Luis's delight, a staggering Julian led the brigade of drunken boisterous sailors to the *Silver Lady*. They saluted their captain, vapid smirks on their faces. "Hell of a night, Cap'n," Julian said, his words slurred. He threw an arm over Luis's shoulder in a sweeping gesture that almost knocked them both off balance.

Luis grinned and helped his first mate stand upright. "So it would seem. All right, look sharp now, men, this berth isn't what the *Silver Lady* is used to."

The crew fell into step, all signs of drunkenness gone as if by magic. Luis watched in amazement as sail after sail was loosened or tightened, the grips on the rigging as expert as always. He nodded and took his place in the wheelhouse. Later, when the ship was in calm waters, he knew the men would groan and moan and hold their heads and retch over the railing, the cook standing by with pails of strong black coffee laced with mint for their sour stomachs. But for now they would work like dogs to do his bidding—because they respected him. He never asked them to do anything he wouldn't do himself. He was a fair man, as fair as his father before him. Over all, he was proud and pleased—proud of them, and pleased with himself.

As his hands manipulated the wheel, he noticed with some concern that the *Lady* seemed cumbersome. Her hold was too full. If pirates did attack him, he wouldn't stand a chance, he reflected. They could fight, but one well-placed shot broadside and the *Lady* would be done for. He frowned.

Perhaps his desire to make an extra profit from the sandalwood had gotten in the way of good common sense.

It was almost dusk, the most hateful time of day for sea captains bent on reaching port unharmed. It was almost impossible to see clearly what lay ahead—which made it the most advantageous time for pirates to attack. Luis turned the *Lady* in the sultry breeze as he ordered his men to climb into the shrouds and watch the seas.

As the days wore on, Luis's apprehension increased. He was sailing in dangerous waters, waters familiar to pirates and unfamiliar to him. What chance would he have in the event of an attack? If he could just make Cape Town and unload most of his cargo, he would feel safe. Two more days, he told himself over and over. Just two more days.

The *Silver Lady* was no more than twelve hours from Cape Town when Luis spotted the ship off his starboard bow. "Sail ho!" came the cry from above. "She's black and she carries no colors!"

Luis pressed his eye to the round circle of glass, but in the failing light he couldn't distinguish colors. "All hands, prepare for attack!" he shouted.

"All hands ready," Julian shouted back.

"She's traveling at five knots, Cap'n," called the mizzen watch. "She sees us but isn't changing course! She's going to pass us by!"

Luis stood on the bow, the glass to his eye. It was a frigate, black as ink with sails to match. The hairs on the back of his neck prickled as he waited and watched. He didn't realize he'd been holding his breath until the frigate sailed ahead, paying his ship no mind.

The crew was on deck, clustered around him, jabbering. They'd all heard the tales of the magical black ship and her long-legged female captain.

"Men in the rigging—"

"A man at the wheel—"

"No sight of a woman—"

"She carries no flag or name. Is it the . . . ?"

"I don't know," Luis growled. "Carlos, fetch Julian. Tell him to report to me here on deck!"

Moments later the first mate faced the captain in the eerie, yellow lantern light. "It gave me a bad turn there, Cap'n. I never thought I'd see that ship again."

"*Is* it the same ship, Julian?" Luis demanded. "How can you be sure?"

"In twenty years, Cap'n, this is the first time I've seen a black ship. I can't swear it's the *same* ship, but it put the fear of God in me, I can tell you that!"

"Did anyone see a female aboard?" Luis called out. To a man, the crew shook their heads.

"What does it mean, Cap'n?" asked Julian.

"I don't know," Luis replied. "But I'm damn sure going to find out the minute we reach Cape Town." He thrust the glass at Julian. "Keep your eye dead ahead. I'll be in my quarters."

The door closed securely behind him, Luis drew a deep breath. So, it wasn't a fairy tale after all. His eyes narrowed as he stared sightlessly at the navigational charts spread out before him. How many black ships with black sails could there be? As far as he knew, there had been no reports of any in the previous twenty years. He tried to swallow past the dryness in his throat.

There really was a black ship.

The black frigate sailed on under close-reefed sails toward Saianha, her new home. In the moonlight, skimming over the breakers, she gleamed a deadly silver—as deadly as the owner who waited impatiently for her delivery.

Chapter Five

Cape Town

Amalie's attitude was one of proper subservience as she waited for the ladies of Cape Town to give their approval. Although she appeared calm, her insides were churning. Just the evening before, she'd practiced her poses for hours, taking long, deep breaths, casting her eyes downward, placing a gentle hand on one of the younger children's shoulders to show protectiveness, allowing a small, winsome smile to touch her lips. She was tired now with the strain she'd been under for the past several days. In a few minutes the women, with their pursed lips and disdaining glances, would either approve of her as guardian to the children or shake their heads, indicating other arrangements would have to be made.

Amalie raised her eyes, meeting those of the woman closest to her, the spokesperson of the small, tight group. Her expression gave away none of the hatred she felt for these women with their flowered dresses and ugly hats and sensible shoes, their smug, self-righteous faces. She drew an imperceptible breath when the biddy nearest her spoke.

"Everything seems to be fine, the sleeping area is adequate, your food storage area free of vermin, and the hymn and lesson books properly marked. I see no reason why you cannot continue as you have been. I think all of us agree that you're doing a fine job with the children.''

Amalie watched as each woman nodded agreement. This time she allowed her timid smile to flourish, not out of gratitude, but rather at the long hairs jiggling at the corners of the woman's mouth. ''Whiskers,'' she blurted out aloud, unable to stop the word from escaping her lips.

''I beg your pardon?'' the woman said stiffly.

Amalie smiled, showing perfect pearl-white teeth. ''Forgive me. My Dutch is not so . . . bad . . . good?'' The little girls at her side giggled knowingly. Amalie's command of the ''master tongue,'' they knew, was perfect.

Heads held high, the dowagers hiked up their skirts and marched back to their waiting carriage. Amalie waved cheerfully as they drove off without a backward glance, and the moment they were out of sight she broke into gales of laughter. To the children's delight, she mimicked the town women, down to tweaking a set of imaginary whiskers. When she had had enough of her little frolic, she clapped her hands.

''Enough! Back to work, and there shall be a treat when I ring the bell.'' The children scattered, each to an assigned job.

It was over and done with, the visit she'd dreaded for weeks. Now she could breathe easier and get on with the business at hand. She looked around, pleased with what she saw. The stone cutters were making wonderful progress on the house. Another two months and her father's house would be restored. In just one month Lucy, the oldest of the girls, had transformed the surrounding jungle into a profusion of brilliant, fragrant flower beds. When the house was finished she would have flowers in every room, on the veranda, too. A pity, though, that it took so many hours to weed and cut back the jungle.

Amalie's tawny cat's eyes looked to the sun; it was time for her daily walk to the cove, to search the waters for some sign of her ship. It should arrive today, tomorrow at the latest, if they were on schedule.

She hurried back inside, into the kitchen, where she searched for and found the footgear she'd bought in town two weeks before. One pair of ladies' opera pumps, in sumptuous black silk, and a set of high walking boots in soft black leather . . . She loved them, but she hated the way they felt on her feet. The children had giggled and teased her when she paraded in front of them, turning her ankle with each step. Each day she forced herself to wear them for a little while, first the silky black shoes with the narrow heels and then the buccaneer boots, which encased her legs up to the thighs in leather, rubbing and chafing against her tender flesh. Already she had several blisters on her feet, but it was worth it. Soon she would be able to wear the dainty black shoes with ease—just as the town ladies did.

Amalie slipped on the leather boots and reached for her father's spyglass, which she kept on the kitchen shelf. Each time she used the glass she knew she was one day closer to seeing her ship arrive. The knowledge sustained her though all the long hours of waiting and watching. It had become a ritual—walking down to the cove and watching for her ship—and, like most rituals, it was now an end unto itself.

The footpath was neat and well tended, flowers on each side, to guide her through the jungle. Each day, as they worked, the children managed to cut away a little more, clearing away the vines and plants that seemed to grow overnight. In another week the entire path to the rise where she stood sentinel each afternoon would be free of growth.

Today there was one less worry riding her slim shoulders, one added cause for jubilation. The thin-lipped, narrow-minded Cape Town ladies were back to minding their own business and would stay out of her affairs—for the time being. When next they came to call—*if* they did— she would be able to meet them at her guarded gates dressed in her finest and tell them what they could do with their good intentions. She laughed, a devilish sound that sent the birds squawking and fluttering to the tops of the emerald-leafed trees.

By the time Amalie set foot on the rise that afforded her a clear view of the cove, she was drenched in perspiration and had to drop to her haunches to rest. All about her the jungle steamed in the midday sun, sending out spiraling, heady, intoxicating scents.

Amalie loved this little sanctuary, as she referred to it. No one, not even the children, could find her here once she'd left the portion of the path that had been cleared. She'd discovered this copse with its wild ferns and brilliant jungle flowers long before she'd embarked upon her present course, but even then it was a place to daydream and make plans. This was where she had come to read her father's journals; here she'd always felt like a queen. Once she'd come at twilight when the first stars dotted the velvet blanket of night. Childishly she'd called on the heavens to avenge her for her mother's sake . . . to grant her the power to destroy those who would stand in the way of her rightful inheritance. For hours she'd cried out her anguish—begged and pleaded, bargained and wheedled—and in the end she'd returned to the mission convinced that it wasn't enough simply to wish for what you wanted. You had to scheme and plot and then act on your plans the way she was doing. And, she mused, you had to be prepared to eliminate anything and anyone who stood in the way. The determination to succeed was what had brought her to where she was.

On her feet now, oblivious to the steaming jungle and

her own sweat-drenched body, Amalie brought the spyglass to her eye in search of her ship. Blue sky merged with sun-spangled ocean as she scanned the horizon. Nothing.

Angrily, she shook the spyglass and looked again. Damnation, where were they? Was it possible she'd made a mistake in trusting Wilhelm to get her ship to her in time? Of course, weather conditions hadn't been the best of late, and repairs had probably taken longer than anticipated. She'd wait a few more days before she sent out an inquiry. What else could she do?

Amalie tossed the spyglass to the ground and followed it there. Glum-faced, she watched as a brilliant feathered parrot flew down from its perch in the jungle shrubbery to peck at the glass with his beak. Then, with a sigh, she turned away to contemplate the horizon. Her wonderful new future seemed to be growing more elusive with each passing day. Was it doomed to failure? The thought had never before entered her mind, but what if—

Suddenly she bolted upright, squinting into the distance. Startled, the parrot squawked loudly, ruffled its emerald plumage, and flew off to a nearby branch. Amalie snatched up the spyglass and focused it carefully. Yes, there it was—a small dark dot on the distant horizon. It had to be her ship; it just *had* to be! She waited, hardly daring to breathe. The moment her eyes could see the ship without the aid of the spyglass, she let out a whoop of pure joy.

The black ship was finally here.

Her black ship.

Amalie rushed to the edge of the rise, forgetting about the parrot now sitting serenely in a low-lying cluster of colorful frondlike branches. He squawked once and then again as Amalie's wildly swinging arms knocked him from his perch. Instantly he retaliated by diving at Amalie's left arm. His beak ripped into her, digging tenaciously at the soft flesh on her inner arm, and he was dragged with her as she tumbled over the side of the rise and rolled to the bottom. Screaming in pain and outrage, Amalie tried to shake him loose, but he only clung harder, his beak buried in her flesh. The moment she rolled to a stop, the parrot gave a vicious tug, tearing her arm all the way to the inside of her elbow before freeing himself and flying high to safety in the trees.

Her eyes filling with horror, Amalie stared at her injured arm and at the blood spurting in every direction. Hurriedly she tore at her skirt to bandage the wound, leaving dirt and bits of leaves clinging to the edges of the jagged opening.

It was a good ten minutes before she had calmed down enough to think rationally. She knew she could bleed to death if she didn't close the wound and wrap it tightly. But first it would have to be cleaned. With water. . . .

On that thought she leapt into the cove and thrust her arm into the cool, clear water, shivering in the sunshine as all around her turned pink with her blood. Then she waded out, trying to keep the wound closed while she searched the underbrush for a plant with healing properties. In a frenzy she slapped three pale green leaves onto the bleeding wound, unsure if they would help or not, then bound her arm, using her teeth to pull the cloth into a tight knot.

Eyes full of alarm, she watched as blood continued to soak through the makeshift bandage. The next moment— just as the black ship weighed anchor—she was back in the cove, floundering in the water with her arm submerged. Again the sea around her turned pink. Amalie moaned. She could feel herself growing weak from fear and loss of blood; if she fainted, she might slip under the water and drown. The realization made her scream, the sound carrying over the water like an eerie wail. She thought she saw one of the men from her ship dive overboard just before she surrendered to darkness.

When Amalie regained consciousness, she was on the ground and surrounded by several of the scurvy-looking men she'd hired to crew her ship. All wore looks of confusion. She fought off a wave of dizziness as one of the men helped her to her feet. Her arm, she noticed, was neatly bandaged with a filthy rag. "Has the wound stopped bleeding?" she asked hoarsely.

"Aye, but it needs tending," the man holding her said gruffly.

She tried to see his face in the fading light. He was the youngest of the crew and the least verbal, if she remembered correctly. Later, when she wasn't so weak, she'd think about the fact that he and the others around her had probably saved her life.

"I have to return to the house," she said, "but I don't think I can walk."

"Aye, we thought of that. I'm to carry you," the young man said in broken Dutch. Portuguese, Amalie decided as she allowed herself to be cradled in the man's arms. She turned her head in the direction of the crew.

"Stay with the ship until I tell you otherwise," she ordered them, then sank back with a moan and allowed herself to be carried away.

There was disgust on the faces of the men as they marched to the jolly boat waiting at the shallow end of the cove. Delays for whatever reason meant money lost—and all because of a woman's weak stomach and faint heart.

"She damn well better be prepared to make us rich," grumbled the oldest of the crew, a man named Miguel.

"Women are good for one thing and one thing only,"

sneered another. He massaged his groin openly to make his point.

The others smirked as they remembered the way Amalie's thin, wet shift clung to the curves of her body. Miguel fished his one and only coin from the knot in his blouse. "Her nipples are this big!" He pursed his mustached lips into a round O. "When the time is right, lads, we'll all have a piece of her, and that's a promise!"

"What's your name?" Amalie asked the young man who was carrying her so effortlessly.

"Cato, miss. Are you feeling stronger?" He liked the way she felt, all warm and wet with her long hair swirling about his bare arms. He'd never had a woman the way the others had, although he'd boasted about it along with the rest of them. "I see lights up ahead. Would you rather walk now?" he asked tentatively.

Amalie smiled. "I think I can walk if you'll allow me to hold on to your arm. It was kind of you to carry me home. Are you the one who bandaged my arm?"

"Aye, miss. You lost a lot of blood. The dressing should be changed right away. The saltwater helped to clean the wound, but then you put those dirty leaves on. . . ."

"I didn't know what else to do. I was so afraid I would bleed to death that I did the first thing I could think of. I'll have one of the girls clean and dress the wound. I'm sorry you had to ruin your shirt," Amalie said softly as she looked at the man's bare arm.

Cato shuffled his feet as he stared into the clearing. The large house looked grand to him in the yellowish light, grander than anything he'd ever seen.

As Amalie neared the house, the four girls from Christabel's ran up to her, smiling shyly at Cato. "It's all right, Clara," Amalie said quietly. "This is Cato. He's a friend. Lucy, fetch some food for him before he leaves." She turned to Cato. "I'll send word to the ship when I'm ready to sail. Thank you for helping me."

Cato shrugged and shuffled his feet, refusing to meet Amalie's gaze. As he was led away, he glanced back at her, his gut churning as he remembered the way the crew had leered at her limp body when he'd pulled her from the cove.

"Handsome and dashing, even if he's a common seaman," Clara crowed as she removed the bandage on Amalie's arm. A moment later she exclaimed in horror at the sight of the open wound. "Mother of God!"

She ran off to the kitchen for medical supplies and was startled to find Amalie laughing wildly when she returned. "What is it? What's the matter?" she asked, alarmed.

"Fetch me my father's journal, Clara, I want to show you something," Amalie said. When Clara returned a moment later with the tattered book, Amalie leafed through it until she found the page she wanted. "See this!" she cried delightedly.

Clara gazed down at the drawing of a woman in scanty attire, her left arm poised in midair as she brandished a cutlass. Down the inside of her arm ran a jagged-looking scar, which the artist had magnified with red ink. Her eyes widened as they returned to the site of Amalie's injury.

"If I'd planned it, I couldn't have done it better," Amalie told her, grinning. "Some things, I've come to learn, are better left to chance."

"Is there much pain?" Clara demanded as she sprinkled on the healing powder brought along from the mission.

Amalie shook her head. "It's a pain I can live with. Go to bed, Clara. If I need you, I'll call. Tomorrow we have much to do now that the ship is here."

"I'll stay until you're asleep," Clara insisted. "You

thrash about in your sleep, and you might injure your arm.''

The moment Amalie had drifted into a sound sleep, Clara left the room with the journal in her hand. In the kitchen, she turned up the wick in the lamp and stared down at the drawing. This wasn't God's hand, of that she was sure. It was the work of the devil. God's wrath was going to come down on all of them, she was sure of it. She blessed herself.

She owed her life to Amalie, as did the others. Without her intervention the four of them would still be working in Christabel's brothel. She'd prayed to God on a nightly basis to be freed from Christabel's bondage, and nothing had happened until the day Amalie appeared. Was she one of God's emissaries, or had she been sent by the devil?

The others, younger than Clara, saw Amalie only as a savior and didn't think beyond the fact that they were finally free of Christabel and had a roof over their heads and all the food they could eat. Should she talk to them? She wondered, frowning. But what could she say? Was it wrong of Amalie to want what was rightfully hers? No, she decided, but it was a sin to plunder ships at sea. Of course *she* was a sinner too. They were all sinners. But they'd been forced into sin. This plan of Amalie's was deliberate.

Clara squeezed her eyes shut and prayed. *Please, God, forgive us for what we're going to do. And as soon as Amalie has enough to restore this fine house, make her stop so we can all live simply and honestly.*

Her hands trembling, Clara walked down a long hallway to Amalie's room. Satisfied that her benefactress was sleeping peacefully, she left the journal and returned to her own pallet, where she said a rosary before falling into a restless slumber.

* * *

It was a full week before Amalie was able to move about with ease. Tired and weak from a three-day fever, she allowed the girls to coddle, admitting only to herself that she rather liked the attention. Clara insisted that she spend part of every day sitting in the shade of a banyan tree, her wounded arm free of its bandage, to receive a dose of the sun's beating rays. "It will help heal and dry that monstrous scab," she said knowledgeably.

After several hours, when her arm started to itch badly, Clara would move her to the veranda and pour whiskey over the wound, wincing when Amalie screamed in agony. But it had to be done. And as the days passed, Amalie found that the process grew less painful, a sure sign that the wound was almost healed.

One afternoon, after she'd awakened from a brief nap in the sun, Amalie became aware of a commotion at the far end of the veranda. The children were squealing with delight. They had a visitor.

She stared at the stranger through narrowed eyes. He was taller, more muscular, than any man she'd ever seen. More handsome in his fine lawn shirt and ink-black trousers. What was he doing here? she wondered. What did he want? Her heart took an extra beat when the man turned to stare in her direction. He was devilishly handsome.

When he continued to wave his arms and point in her direction, Amalie swallowed fearfully. Surely Clara and the others wouldn't allow him near her. She didn't want to see anyone. Nervously she waited as Clara approached her, certain the jeweler's death was about to be laid at her feet.

"What is it, Clara?" she called out. "Who is he, and what does he want?"

"His name is Luis Domingo, and he's from Spain," Clara replied, eyes sparkling. "He said the Spanish Crown paid him to bring a trunk here to you. And you have to sign this paper because he has to return it to Spain. He's a sea captain on his way to Java. He wants to talk to you, Amalie.''

"No," Amalie said, shaking her head. "I don't want to talk to him. And I can't use my hand yet—you'll have to sign the paper for me. Here, stand in front of me so he can't see what you're doing. Did he say what's in the trunk?''

Her tongue caught between her teeth, Clara signed Amalie's name in a shaky hand. "No, it has a seal on it. He's handsome, isn't he? Are you sure you don't want to talk to him?''

"I'm sure. You told him I was ill, didn't you?" Clara nodded. "Good, now return this paper to him, thank him, and offer him a cool drink. And while he's drinking it, find out what he's carrying on his ship. Be vague, as though you're making polite conversation." She watched with narrowed eyes as Clara hurried away.

Luis Domingo gazed admiringly at the manicured gardens as he waited for the cool drink the young lady was bringing him. Relieved at last to be rid of the huge trunk, he glanced down at the spidery signature on the heavy vellum. Amalie Suub Alvarez must be very old—old and waiting to die. He allowed his eyes to sweep the grounds and the shrouded figure reclining on the cane chair under the spreading banyan tree. He thought he smelled death.

The drink was cool and tart, and Luis gulped it down in two long swallows. He wiped at his brow, aware that his neck and armpits were soaked with sweat.

"I'll walk with you to your wagon, Señor Domingo," Clara offered.

Luis looked over his shoulder. "Is she going to die?"

Flustered, Clara stammered, "Wh-who?"

"The old lady. Is she going to die?"

"Ah, no, no, she . . . No, I don't think so. Tell me, Señor Domingo, what do you carry in your ship? Jewels, spices, silks? My mistress likes me to . . . to tell her little stories. I'll make one up about you and tell it to her this evening before she goes to sleep."

Luis laughed, a sound that carried on the breeze across the garden to Amalie, whose eyes popped open. She liked the deep, masculine sound.

"Well," she demanded peevishly after Luis had left, "what did he say?"

Clara clapped her hands in excitement. "Everything, all manner of riches! He's so handsome, isn't he, Amalie? He's sailing to Java and then back to Spain to sell everything he's picked up in his travels. Isn't that romantic? And bringing you that trunk all the way from Spain—and then delivering it *personally*! What do you think is in it?"

Amalie's brow furrowed. "It's probably papers and ledgers of my father's. I don't even want to look at it. Have the boys carry it down to the cellar. Now, tell me, when is Señor . . . Domingo leaving for Java?"

"Two days. He said he would sail with the tide." Clara hesitated. "Amalie, you aren't . . . you wouldn't . . . But you aren't well enough yet!"

Amalie smiled. "In another two days I'll be fine. Now, Clara, I want you to go to the cove and ask Cato to come here. But first have the boys take the trunk to the cellar. I want it out of my sight." A trunk full of the trash of her father's life. Why would the authorities think she would want such a thing? To be rid of it, of course. Chaezar Alvarez had been a blight on the Spanish Crown. Well, she didn't want his wretched refuse, either. She had more important things to worry about.

Two days . . . just two more days . . .

* * *

Amalie set foot on her ship shortly before she gave the order to set sail. She had come aboard with little gear beyond the scanty costume she'd recreated and the high buccaneer boots, which she'd secured in her cabin. She would have plenty of time to don them once Domingo's ship was sighted, and she had no desire to let her crew see her naked legs before she absolutely had to. Now, looking around at the surly faces of her crew, she knew she was about to make her first concession.

"No seaman worth his salt sails on a ship that carries no name. It's bad luck," Miguel snarled. "We don't care about colors, but we do care about a name." The others lined up behind Miguel and chorused their agreement, even Cato.

Amalie was on uncertain ground. She knew nothing about naming a ship, but it was obviously a matter that had to be settled immediately or she would have a mutiny on her hands. That she did understand. She struggled to come up with a meaningful name, one that would strike fear in her crew and those of the ships they accosted.

"From this moment on," she called out, "the ship will be called the *Sea Siren*! If there's one among you who objects to this decision, he may leave now." When no one moved, she nodded. "So be it."

This was the moment the crew had waited for—the moment she herself had waited for. Could she do it?

"To your posts," she cried, her hands tight on the wheel, heart beating wildly. Book learning was quite different from real-life experience, she was discovering. She forced herself to relax, the warm salt air a balm to her body. Gradually she began to feel confident and exhilarated.

The frigate skimmed out of the deep-water cove, over the white-capped breakers, and into open water. Amalie caught the smirk on Cato's face as he faced several of the crew. Obviously a wager had been placed on her capabilities, and she'd come through a winner—as had Cato. She liked the idea that he had not bet against her, and her eyes thanked him before she turned the wheel over to Rego, her first mate.

Now it was time to walk about *her* ship. She'd lied, cheated, stolen, and killed to arrive at this moment. She smiled as she strolled the deck, aware that the crew's eyes were on every step she took.

The newly named *Sea Siren* was a sleek, three-masted frigate that was skillfully demonstrating her prowess in what Amalie thought of as her maiden voyage. She sported fresh decks scrupulously scoured and a sterncastle whose varnish was just beginning to dry. And it was all hers. No one was ever going to take it away from her.

Amalie turned and swayed on the rolling deck. She took a deep breath and then another; she couldn't afford to get seasick, not when things were going so well. Any sign of weakness on her part would be seized by the crew as justification to take matters into their own hands.

Cato appeared out of nowhere, startling her. "It takes awhile to get your sea legs. It'll help if you eat something. If you like, I can bring a bit of food to your cabin. Miguel says we should sight the Spaniard by nightfall."

Amalie looked into Cato's anxious blue eyes. "So soon?" The young man nodded. "Very well, fetch me some fruit and a little bread. I'll be in my quarters."

Amalie had never before set foot aboard a ship. It was all a new experience for her, but one she liked . . . very much. Her cabin was small with a bunk, a chair, and several shelves. It was clean and smelled of soap and the sea. The bundle on her bed drew her eye. Soon it would be time to don the costume.

She tested the hard bunk, then sat back with an uneasy sigh. Everything she'd planned was about to happen. What if the men aboard Domingo's ship put up a fight and she lost her crew? What if the Spaniard captured her and turned her over to the authorities? Her resolve hardened as she recalled the anticipation on the faces of her men. None of them had any intention of backing down or putting up a weak fight. If need be, it would be a bloody battle with no quarter given, of that much she was certain.

Amalie drew in her breath as she buttoned the stark white blouse. She was nervous, unsure of herself, and she didn't like it at all. Even the sight of the rapier didn't comfort her, and the cutlass only made her wince. With her injured arm there was no way she could hold it, much less wield it. She could, however, attach the cutlass to the belt at her waist and carry the rapier. Two weapons might even enhance her resemblance to the notorious Sea Siren and force Domingo's crew to think twice about fighting back.

She pulled on the boots, grimacing as the leather abraded her blistered feet, then hobbled out the door and up the ladder. Once secure on deck, she struck the classic "Sea Siren" pose—legs astride, rapier in hand—and silently dared her crew to comment.

Watching her, Cato drew in his breath with a sharp hiss. She was magnificent. Her long hair streaming behind her in the gentle breeze, the black kid boots cuffed at the knees, the soft white shirt tied in a knot at her waist, those long, slender legs . . . Jesus, he wanted her, as did every man aboard ship, and he would fight to the death for her. He had heard tales of the infamous Sea Siren, and he'd bet a year's wages that there wasn't a man at sea who could tell the difference.

Amalie did her best to hold the spyglass steady as she scanned the horizon. She forgot about everything—her uneasiness with the crew, even the stinging pain of her blisters and chafed thighs—the moment she sighted the minuscule speck in the distance. "Sail, ho!" she cried.

"Where away?" Miguel shouted.

"Straight ahead," came a reply from high in the rigging.

Amalie swallowed past the lump in her throat. "Loosen sail, full speed. I want every minute to count. Remember what I told you—our attack is to be quick and deadly if necessary." She leapt down from the bow and raced to the stern, where she climbed onto a pile of rigging atop a water barrel. With her legs spread to steady her, she was a Valkyrie, the frigate her Valhalla. She threw back her head and laughed, the sound ripping across the water like the wind.

The *Sea Siren* drew ever closer to her prey, and Amalie knew the moment Luis Domingo had focused on her with his glass. She read the fear and loathing in his face and laughed again, this time in triumph.

"Make no false moves, Captain," she called out as the two ships came within hailing distance, "or my men will make short work of you and yours!"

In reply Luis Domingo brought up his cutlass and lashed out at Amalie's men as they leapt aboard the *Silver Lady*. It took all of thirty minutes for Amalie's cutthroats to subdue Domingo's nine-man crew. Outnumbered and pinned to the mast by Cato, Domingo could only curse his revenge as he watched his cargo being carried off. His eyes spewed hatred at the beautiful creature on the stern of the ghostly black ship.

An eternity later Amalie gave him a low, sweeping bow, her rapier slicing through the twilight. Luis tried to blink the sweat from his eyes, staring in disbelief as the long-legged creature blew him a gentle kiss with her fingertips.

"I'll kill you for this!" he shouted. "I'll hunt you down and rip you limb from limb!"

"You aren't man enough," Amalie called out, chuckling. "This little assault was nothing compared with what I could have done if you had angered me. As it is, I'm feeling charitable, so I'm allowing you to keep your sandalwood, your ship . . . and your life. You have much to thank me for, Captain."

"I'll die before I thank you, you thieving bitch!" Luis spat out.

"That can be arranged, too." Once again she offered him a mocking bow. "Perhaps next time. Until we meet again, Señor Domingo, thank *you* for your generous contribution to my well-being."

It was fully dark by the time the black ship had melted into the night.

For hours Luis swore he could hear the Sea Siren's evil laughter as he cursed and stormed about his ship. "All of this," he snarled, "and not a shot was fired! Pinned to my own goddamn mast! She'll pay. I swear before God that she will pay!"

"We were outnumbered, Cap'n," Julian said nervously. "It was like this when she attacked the *Spanish Princess*. We had no time to react, and we were loaded down with cargo. Only that time the Siren sank the ship. Today she was generous." He peered out into the night and shuddered. "You don't suppose she'll come back and ram us, do you, Cap'n?"

Luis snorted. "She won't be back. She's sailing off to dispose of my cargo, God only knows where. Pirating is a handsome business, all profit." He turned to glare at his first mate. "You're sure that woman was the same one who struck down the *Princess*?"

"I swear on my mother, Cap'n. Did you see those long legs and that midnight-dark hair? Her laugh is the same, too. My blood ran cold when I heard it."

"It's easy to laugh when you're victorious, Julian. But she won't always be victorious; I'll see to that," Luis said, his voice so deadly quiet, so ominous, that Julian crossed himself involuntarily.

"Aye, Cap'n." It was on the tip of his tongue to tell Luis that his father, the elder Domingo, had said the same thing before he died.

"Swab these decks and get me a Bible so we can give the dead a Christian sea burial. . . . Three good, honest, hardworking seamen cut down—I swear I'll make her pay for this!"

"Ay, Cap'n," Julian said, sighing as he watched his captain stride away. How did a person exact revenge on a ghost? For twenty years had passed since her attack on the *Spanish Princess*, and the Siren was still as young and beautiful as ever. No, she was an evil ghost, and mere mortals would never stop her. The only thing to do was pray.

All night long Luis Domingo prowled the decks of the *Silver Lady*. It was all true, every word the old man had said.

The Sea Siren lived.

Chapter Six

Java

Dawn, Fury thought, was always a happy time for her parents because it signified a new day, a day to be cherished and lived to its fullest. She, too, had come to think like her parents, rising early to watch the sun ascend the heavens. Today, however, she would have preferred the impenetrable mask of night—a Stygian ally to hide her shame and bewilderment. Shame, because somewhere deep inside her she was relieved that the bishop had denied her entrance to the convent. Bewilderment, because now she had nothing to do until her parents arrived. *If* they arrived. Her parents, she knew, were not creatures of schedules. They could very well decide to stay in the Americas for years.

The early-morning dew soaked Fury's delicate slippers as she strolled through the garden, but she barely noticed. She gazed about in the soft grayness, knowing that in just minutes the garden would be ripe with color and scent. All around her would awaken to greet the new day, as had she, but to what end? Without a purpose in life, and the means to fulfill that purpose, one day was much like another—empty and joyless. She was sick to death of needlework and books. Prayer, too, had become a chore that rarely soothed the agitation of her mind. It wasn't that God wasn't responding to her devotions; it was that she had no patience to wait for that response. Everything was in God's time. Time . . . How she hated the word. Time could be an eternity. It was entirely possible that she could wither away and die of . . . loneliness, she thought morosely.

Fury wiped at her eyes, certain the tears shimmering on her lashes would spill over. She knew she was indulging in self-pity, and determined at once to make every effort to change her empty days and evenings. Today, for example, she would go into town to visit with Father Sebastian and offer her services to the parish. It was the least she could do.

By now it was full light, the slight breeze warm and flower-scented. Fury drank deeply of the early morning; in a short while, the air would be heavy and hot. But she was getting used to that. In the month since her arrival, she'd found herself adapting to her old home with ease. Boredom was her only problem. There were simply too many hours in the day.

Her arms full of fragrant blooms, she made her way back to the house to change and by midmorning was ready to leave for town. The sun beat down upon her as she climbed into the flat wagon and nodded to the djongo who would take her to Father Sebastian's rectory. She was dressed simply in a yellow-sprigged muslin dress with long sleeves, her ebony hair pulled back and swirled on top of her head. She knew she should be taking a hat or at least a parasol to ward off the fiery rays, but she loved the way they tinted her fair skin to a rich honeyed hue.

By the time they'd reached the village, Fury was limp with the heat and soaked with perspiration. But at least here the air was slightly cooler, and a gentle breeze blew in off the village quay. She drew in a deep breath, savoring the tang of salt air.

The village was small and laid out along the tiny waterfront. Many of the gabled rooftops were tiled, giving them a sense of permanence. This village, crowded as it was between jungle and water, seemed to have a timelessness about it, unobtrusive in its surroundings. As the wagon rounded a bend in the dusty road, the hamlet disappeared. The small parish church was nestled at the end of the long, narrow street, and to its right sat Father Sebastian's house. In another minute she would be there.

They were just passing the Dutch East India offices when Fury gasped in horror. The djongo turned his head, startled.

"What is wrong, missy?" he queried.

Luis Domingo . . . here, in Java? It wasn't possible! Yet there he was, going into the Dutch East India offices. "Faster, Ling, make the horse go faster," Fury ordered. He can't see me like this, she thought wildly. Dear God, what must I look like?

"Horse hot, missy, no go faster."

"Yes, yes, I know. I'm sorry. . . ."

There was no place to run, no place to hide. He was turning now at the sound of the wagon wheels, and she was close enough to see his frown of puzzlement. Obviously he was trying to remember where he'd seen her before. Then, mercifully, they were past him. "Turn around, Ling, and see if that man is staring at us," Fury said breathlessly.

"Much look, strange look, on man's face," Ling reported. "Man still looking," he added a moment later when he turned for a second look. "Padre's house, missy. You wait, I help you down. Horse need water and shade tree. I wait over there," he said, pointing to a small lot on the opposite side of the road.

Fury almost swooned as the old priest led her into his cool study. Concerned, he immediately ordered a cool drink and then had his housekeeper lead her upstairs to "freshen up." The child needed to talk to him, that much was obvious; but why now, he wondered, wringing his hands in agitation, why at this particular time of day? Luis Domingo would be arriving within minutes. And Domingo, unlike the delicate young lady upstairs, was in a murderous frame of mind and hell-bent on revenge. And he knew why. Father Sebastian peered out the window nervously. The moment he'd heard about Domingo's experience with the infamous Sea Siren, he'd personally canvassed the town until he'd found Jacobus—who was now, this minute, secure in the rectory sleeping off his last jug of wine. God alone knew what would happen if Domingo accosted the old sea barnacle now, in his current state. Better to keep them apart, at least for the time being.

"Merciful Father," the old priest murmured, fingering the beads of his rosary, "grant me the wisdom to help Señor Domingo, and show me the way to protect Jacobus . . . and," he added, eyes twinkling, "if You have the time, allow me a little insight into Miss Furana."

The priest started when the garden bell tinkled and Fury reentered the room at the same time. In a matter of minutes Luis Domingo would walk through his door.

"There's no time for explanations, Furana," he said hurriedly. "Go upstairs immediately and stay there until I call you. Señor Domingo will walk into this room in a few seconds, and I—I doubt he will take kindly to your presence at this time. He's rather . . . overwrought."

Fury's eyes were full of questions, but she knew better than to argue with the gentle priest. Without a word she headed for the rectory staircase and took the steps two at a time, the way she had when she was little and her brothers had chased her about the house. She reached the top just as Luis Domingo announced himself.

What was he doing at Father Sebastian's? Fury wondered. Flattening herself against the stairwell wall, she listened as the Spaniard repeated the story of his ruin at the hands of the nefarious Sea Siren. . . .

An hour later, after Luis had finally calmed down enough to listen to reason, Father Sebastian blessed him and showed him out. Instantly Fury descended the stairs, her face full of shock, eyes disbelieving.

"It's not true, you *know* it isn't, Father," she cried. "The Sea Siren . . . Father, it's impossible! Why would he tell such a lie? You should have said something, told him that my mother is in the Americas. Why didn't you?"

"Child, listen to me. It's understandable that you're upset, but think for a moment. How would it look if I suddenly appeared to know so much about the Sea Siren? I admit I was fearful of giving away some of my knowledge. It is imperative that I protect those who have seen fit to take me into their confidence. All Señor Domingo knows is that he lost his cargo to a woman dressed as the infamous Sea Siren who captained a black ship that was identical to the *Rana*." The priest rubbed his eyes wearily. "When I first heard the story in the village, I immediately brought Jacobus here. It was Jacobus who told Luis Domingo his version of the Sea Siren months ago, in exchange for a jug of rum. I think we should put our heads together and—"

"And what, Father?"

"I don't know, child, I don't know," Father Sebastian said, gnarled fingers clutching at his rosary as if to a lifeline.

Fury shook her head. "I don't understand why he came to you. You're a priest, what would you know of pirates and cargoes?"

Unconsciously, the priest began to knead the hard beads. "Comfort, words of wisdom. Why did you come here, Furana? You yourself seek comfort and a solution to your . . . problems. Why should Señor Domingo be any different?''

Of course he was right, thought Fury. She was reacting emotionally, something her mother had always cautioned her about. ''I assume the whole town knows now,'' she muttered. She threw up her hands and started to pace the tiny study.

''I'm sorry now that your parents confided in me,'' Father Sebastian said softly. ''But when your father became ill, Sirena thought it was because of her . . . activities on the high seas. Even though Regan isn't of our faith, I prayed with your mother for days on end.'' He sighed. ''Lord, I wanted to tell that young man he was mistaken, but I am bound by the promise I made to your mother.''

Fury nodded. ''Yes, of course. But we must do something, Father. We can't allow these tales to flourish, and yet we can't openly defend the Sea Siren. That would cause suspicion. I—I need time to think.''

''What do you want me to do, Furana?'' the priest asked quietly.

Fury paused, frowning. ''If you could go to the Dutch East India offices and see what Mynheer Dykstra knows, that would be most helpful, Father. . . . And then I'd like you to bring Señor Domingo to the casa tomorrow evening for dinner. Together we might be able to clear up this whole sorry dilemma.'' She cocked her head to one side, considering. ''Tell him only that's he's been invited to the van der Rhys casa for dinner. He'll assume that my parents issued the invitation, and I would prefer it that way. I rather think this meeting between us should come as something of a surprise. It's entirely possible that the man is lying. Other sea captains have plundered their own ships for personal profit. He could be doing the same thing.''

''I'll pray for a solution to this problem,'' the priest said, suddenly feeling out of his depth.

Fury spun about, eyes glinting dangerously. "You do that, Father. Perhaps praying will work for you. It certainly hasn't for me, of late. As far as I can determine, God has forsaken me. And now He's seen fit to burden me with this very *earthly* problem—quite fitting, don't you think, Father?"

"That's blasphemy, child," Father Sebastian said, aghast. "You're distraught. You must not denounce God because of this unfortunate incident—or for *any* reason. Hell is—"

"Right here, Father. I'm walking in hell now and have been for the past month. You might pray about *that*, if you've a mind to!" Her face flooded with indignation, Fury fled the parish house. It wasn't until she was safely back in her room at the casa that she regretted the way she'd spoken to the priest.

It had to be a lie, a trick of some sort. The question was: Why would Luis Domingo pick Java of all places to fabricate such a tale . . . unless he was up to something? Nothing else made sense. The man had to be acting on the tales Jacobus had told him, salvaging his cargo for his own personal gain—*in the name of the Sea Siren*. Damn his eyes!

By God, she'd find a way to stop him. All she had to do was sit down with a clear head and figure out a way to end the tales of her mother once and for all. First, though, she'd begin a journal, while things were still fresh in her mind. Tomorrow, after dinner with Domingo, she'd have a detailed report for her mother to read so she'd know her daughter had acted in good faith on behalf of the Sea Siren.

It was late afternoon when Fury retired to the garden to gather more flowers for the house. She felt better having committed her thoughts and anxieties to paper. She'd also planned a simple but tasteful dinner for the following evening. Her dinner gown would be simple, too, since all her good clothing had been left behind in Spain. Perhaps she could find something appropriate among the things her mother had left behind.

When her basket was full, Fury retraced her steps to the house down a long, winding stone walkway. A circling breeze forced her eyes upward, and she watched as Pilar and Gaspar sailed down to perch on the banister of the garden terrace. Setting the basket on a glass-topped table, Fury walked over to the hawks, stroking their silky heads and crooning soft, warm words of affection. Both birds ruffled their feathers. Gaspar inched his way across the banister until he was even with the basket of flowers. One talon reached out for a soft purple bloom. Daintily, so as not to crush the delicate flower, he inched his way on one talon back to Fury and Pilar.

Fury held her breath. Who was the flower for—herself or Pilar? Please let it be for Pilar, she prayed. It was a game she'd played with the birds back in Spain. Before, the flower had always been for her. Now she nodded slightly to Gaspar. He offered the bloom to Pilar, who seemed to take an eternity before deciding to accept it. A minute later it was Pilar who inched her way toward Fury to offer the mangled bloom.

Fury laughed in delight and clapped her hands. ''Wonderful! Now you understand about giving and receiving.'' She placed the flower in her hair over her ear and bent low so the birds could observe what she'd done. ''Well done, Gaspar. Thank you, Pilar.''

The hawks preened, their feathers whispering to each other before they soared upward. Fury danced her way into the huge kitchen to hand over the flower basket to the cook.

Later, on her way upstairs to her room, she decided she

would wear a flower in her hair when she dined with Luis Domingo and Father Sebastian.

Fury was exhausted when she woke the following morning. She'd dreamed all night, terrible dreams. First her mother and father had spent hours screaming at her, berating her for not redeeming Sirena's good name. Then Luis Domingo had taken over, accosting her with a wicked-looking cutlass and threatening to kill her mother. In her nightmare she'd run from the Spaniard until she was breathless, searching desperately for the cave where he'd stashed his cargo. And then, just as she'd been about to uncover his lair, she'd awakened.

Thieves always tried to blame someone else, Fury decided as she threw open the windows and savored the flower-scented air. Overhead in the thick umbrella of green leaves, she heard a soft rustling. Her beauties . . .

She called to the hawks and was rewarded by the sight of a sleepy Pilar parting the branches overhead with her wing tips, her glossy head peeking through the emerald leaves. Fury waved listlessly, and within moments both birds were perched on the balcony railing, eyes glittering and intent. They remained motionless as she stroked their heads, murmuring soft early-morning words of greeting.

"I wonder," Fury mused, "if there is a way for you to . . . spy on Luis Domingo." She must be out of her mind, she thought. The hawks were intelligent but certainly not capable of spying. Still . . . "It would be nice if you could follow him and report back. You know, scratch me a message or bring me something to prove he really was attacked by a pirate." She giggled, her usual good humor returning. Gaspar's wing wavered and then wrapped itself around her shoulder. A moment later Pilar, the less affectionate of the two birds, followed suit. "I know, I know," Fury gurgled, delighted, "you are going to take care of everything. Well, I'm going to take care of you right now and give you your breakfast, and then we're going to take a look at the *Rana*.''

Fury wondered what could possibly be accomplished by running down to the cove where her mother's old ship was berthed. The *Rana* must be rotted through and through by now, probably unsafe to board. Still, it would be wonderful to see her again and know once and for all that no pirate had restored her and taken her out to sea to pillage and plunder. At the very least, seeing the ship would reassure her.

Buoyed by the prospect of taking action—any kind of action—Fury dressed, breakfasted, and fed the hawks, then strode out to the stables.

She had always loved the pungent smell of this place. As a child she had played and romped and hidden in the straw, daring her parents to find her, squealing in her high, child's voice when her father pretended not to know which particular pile of straw she was hiding in. So many pleasant, wonderful memories.

''I'll take Starlight,'' she told a young stable boy. ''Fetch her out and I'll saddle her myself.'' Starlight was a spirited roan mare with a perfect white blaze and three white stockings. Fury loved her and tried to ride out with her for at least a little while every day.

The stable boy, no more than twelve years of age, stood back as she threw on the saddle and secured the cinch. His eyes almost popped from his head when the two hawks swooped down, their talons spread to secure a perch on the back of the leather saddle. Fury laughed, her long hair billowing backward between the two birds as she spurred Starlight to a fast canter. The boy stared after her, blessing himself as the huge birds flapped their wings and screeched.

After a minute or two Fury tightened the reins, forcing

Starlight to a trot. The humidity was at its heaviest, and it would be at least an hour before they came to water. She kept her eyes to the ground as the roan picked her way daintily through the vine-covered trails. This particular track held years and years of growth, so much so that at last she was forced to slip from the roan's back and tether her.

She wasn't absolutely sure of her way, but she seemed to recognize certain outcroppings and fern glades. The thatched hut where her mother had hidden things she wished to keep secret. It was just a lean-to now. Fury had been to the cove only three times—once with her mother, once with her father, and once with all four of her brothers. That time, the five of them had sneaked off without telling anyone, and as they'd stood on the rise looking down at their mother's ship, they'd played a game, each of them getting the chance to be captain. At the end of the day they'd all been in agreement—none of them would ever fill their mother's shoes when it came to pirating games on the sea. They'd all been punished upon their return, and Fury had cried, heartbroken—not because she'd been sent to bed without dinner, but because she would never be the Sea Siren.

The hawks were overhead now, working what little breeze there was to stay as close to her as possible, both of them screeching their displeasure at these strange new surroundings. Fury felt like screaming herself as she beat at the vines and vegetation choking off the path. She was sweating profusely, and her long hair was hanging in lank strings about her face. She ripped at the neck and sleeves of her dress to bare her arms and shoulders to the stagnant air. It occurred to her that she was making a mistake: all this time and trouble merely to look at a decaying, rotting ship. But she plowed on determinedly, wiping her face with the tattered sleeves of her dress. Above, the birds circled lazily in the blazing sun.

A minute later she felt a cooling breeze wash over her and knew she was almost to the rise above the cove. She stopped, her heart hammering in her chest. Please, she prayed, let the ship be there.

The hawks were ahead of her now; even at this distance she could see they were ready to swoop down and meet her at the rise. She ran then, not even feeling the branches that scratched her bare arms and legs. Another few feet and she would be in the clearing.

Like a child, Fury covered her eyes, delaying the moment of discovery. Finally, unable to stand the suspense a moment longer, she took her hands away—and stared in disbelief at the frigate. Even from this distance she could see that the ship was in perfect condition, her decks and railings gleaming. And black as tar.

Fury swayed dizzily. It was impossible; the *Rana* was supposed to be safely anchored and rotting away to nothingness. God in heaven, how was this possible?

Should she scramble down the bank and swim out to the ship? One look at the sun told her she had to head back to the casa or she would be late for dinner. Tomorrow she would return—properly dressed. She needed time to think, time to consider. . . .

All the way back to the house Fury's mind raced. Someone had kept the ship in repair; more than that, she was completely outfitted and ready to take to the sea. But who? Was it the same person who had plundered Luis Domingo's ship? Was it perhaps Luis Domingo himself? Soon she would have her answers.

Fury galloped into the courtyard at full speed, reining Starlight so abruptly that the mare reared back, her front hooves pawing the air, the hawks screeching as they dived downward and then up. As the stable boy ran to help her, she slid from the horse and dashed to the kitchen doorway.

Inside the house, she tore up the stairs like a whirlwind, calling over her shoulder, "Juli! Draw me a bath and get my clothes ready," and shedding her torn gown at the top of the stairs. She left her petticoats and both shoes in a pile outside her door.

Juli came hurrying over, eyes dancing with amusement. "Everything is in readiness and has been for some time," she said tartly. "I am well aware that the van der Rhys women tend to do things at the last moment. Rest easy, Miss Fury, your mother always said it was fashionable to keep a man waiting."

"Not this lady," Fury muttered as she slipped into the tub of steaming water. "Ooooh, this is hot!"

"How else will we get all the . . . What *are* you covered with?" Juli demanded. "And what are we to do with your hair? It will never dry!"

"It's dust, Juli—dust and sweat and Lord only knows what else. Oh, *how* will I ever be ready in time?" Fury wailed. "What—"

"I'll think of something, Miss Fury. Now hold still while I . . ." Juli frowned in concentration as she dunked, rubbed, and scrubbed Fury within an inch of her life. When she stepped from the tub she was again rubbed and patted until her skin glowed. Powder permeated the air, as did a fragrant scent that made Fury's head reel. At last Juli smiled. "Intoxicating! You'll have to dress yourself while I see about . . . Ah, I have just the thing for your hair. Your mother left it behind. Many times she, too, would return late from one of her excursions, and her hair, like yours, took forever to dry. Your father never suspected. I'm so glad I saved it."

Thirty minutes later Fury was fully dressed in a rich tangerine silk dress with long, loosely cuffed sleeves and

gores of silk swirling about her ankles. She felt elegant
and quite grown-up, especially since the dress had belonged to her mother and fitted her perfectly. No jewelry
was needed to adorn the timeless elegance of the gown,
but she definitely wanted a flower in her hair—only it was
soaking wet.

"I found it, I found it!" Juli cried exultantly from the
doorway. "It's just as dazzling as it was the day your
mother wore it for the first time. It's called a skullcap,"
she said, fingering the delicate circle of fabric. "I remember when she had it made. It took hours to sew these tiny
pearls and brilliants over the silk. See the way it curves
here at the edges. You can either cover your ears or . . .
Try it on, Miss Fury."

A moment later Juli clapped her hands in delight. "You
look like a royal queen! Remember to hold your head up
because the crown of the cap is the heaviest. As your hair
starts to dry it could slide off."

Fury frowned. "It is heavy. Perhaps a coronet of
braids . . ."

"There's no time," Juli said, shaking her head. "Father
Sebastian and a very handsome gentleman are waiting for
you on the veranda. And now that you aren't going into
the convent," she added meaningfully, "it wouldn't hurt
you to . . . flirt a little. You are your mother's daughter,
after all."

Fury flushed. "How did my mother tolerate your bra-
zenness?" she demanded.

"Your mother taught me to speak my mind. If she were
here, she'd tell you the same thing."

"Is he really that dashing?" Fury asked, giving herself
one last look in the full-length mirror. "I met him only
once at my birthday ball months ago. He didn't . . . what
I mean is . . ."

Juli giggled. "He didn't make your blood sing, eh? Well, he will tonight, young lady. He will tonight."

Luis Domingo's manners were impeccable, his eyes glowing with admiration as he bowed low over Fury's extended hand. "You cannot be the same young lady I escorted to dinner a few months ago," he murmured.

"Oh. And why is that, Señor Domingo?" Fury asked coolly.

"You were merely pretty then. Tonight you are ravishing." He pressed her hand once, lingeringly, then let it go. "Then you were but a sweet child; now you are a formidable young woman."

Flustered, Fury remained silent as she led the way into the house, where Juli served wine in elegant crystal goblets. The moment they were seated, Fury fixed her gaze on Luis and spoke directly. "Father Sebastian tells me that your ship was attacked by . . . some woman."

Father Sebastian's jaw dropped, his eyes flying first to Fury and then to Luis Domingo. With a sinking heart, he saw Domingo's jaw tense.

"Not *some* woman," Luis replied, "The infamous Sea Siren herself. She plundered my ship and made off with all my cargo, with the exception of some sandalwood."

"Come now, señor," Fury said casually, sipping her wine, "even I remember the stories about the Sea Siren, and I was only a child. If there is such a person, she must be quite old by now. You described a beautiful young woman to Father Sebastian. How do you explain that? I, too, have seen the picture that hangs in the Dutch East India offices, and Mynheer Dykstra, a good friend of the family's, told us that picture is over twenty years old."

Luis shrugged. "I cannot explain it. I can only tell you what happened. My men were present. She was there and she was real and the frigate she sailed was black as Hades," he said coldly.

Fury decided to try another tack. "Señor Domingo, there must be hundreds of black ships that sail the seas. You did say this attack occurred at dusk, the deadliest time of day for sea captains. Perhaps it was the lighting that made the frigate look black."

Luis's eyes darkened. "Would that same lighting also make white sails turn black? And how do you explain the woman herself? She talked to me—I didn't imagine *that*. I tell you, she was real and she was beautiful, much the same as she was described to me."

The priest sipped his wine and regarded Luis thoughtfully. "How close were you to this female pirate, señor," he asked, "and how old would you say she was?"

"Stern to stern," Luis replied, "and young. Beautiful, deadly . . ."

"And an impostor!" Fury said, waving her hand in the air. "Surely a man of your vast experience has reasoned that out by now. Fairy tales, señor, are for children, and this particular tale has been told over and over until it's become real. The Sea Siren is either dead or, more likely, retired from the sea."

Luis was on his feet, his mouth a tense, grim line. "Am I to understand you're calling me a liar, señorita?" he said quietly.

Fury remained seated and offered Luis a serene smile. "No, señor, I am merely saying I *think* you're mistaken. An able impostor is the only logical explanation."

"How is it you know so much about this scourge of the seas?" Luis demanded.

Fury flushed. "Señor, the Sea Siren was no scourge! It is true she wreaked havoc on my father and almost ruined the Dutch East India Company. If anyone is an authority on her, it is my father. She never plundered for cargo; she had a mission, and when that mission was fulfilled, she retired. It's that simple. Your female pirate is an impostor, and I simply cannot believe otherwise!''

''I'll be goddamned to hell!'' Luis exploded. He turned to Father Sebastian. ''Is that what you think, too, *Padre*?''

The elderly priest hesitated; clearly this discussion was not to his liking. ''Twenty years, señor, is a very long time for a woman not to age,'' he said reluctantly. ''On the other hand, you and your men were *there*—and you seem so sure . . . Tonight I will pray for a reasonable explanation.''

''In the meantime,'' Fury said sweetly, ''let us put such talk aside. I believe our dinner is ready. Señor . . . ?'' She beckoned, motioning to his chair.

Luis struggled with himself, but in the end common courtesy and gallantry prevailed, and he took his seat without further comment.

Midway through the meal, Fury realized that Father Sebastian was the only one at the table actually paying attention to the food. She and Luis were merely going through the motions for the sake of propriety. Conversation consisted of the weather, the beautiful gardens, and the mysterious trunk he'd delivered to Saianha. At the mention of Chaezar Alvarez's wife, Fury's eyes widened. Even Father Sebastian stopped eating.

''Señor Alvarez had a wife?'' he asked incredulously.

Luis nodded. ''Does that surprise you?''

Father Sebastian shrugged and resumed eating.

''Señor Alvarez was a competitor of my father's years ago. It was said that he was enamored of the Sea Siren, as was every man in Batavia, even my father.'' Fury stared into Luis's dark eyes. ''My father never once mentioned his having a wife.''

''Perhaps it is my mistake.'' Luis proceeded to relate the terms of the Spanish commission and the delivery he'd made to Saianha. "I merely assumed it was his wife. The name on the manifest was Amalie Suub Alvarez. The woman appeared to be quite advanced in age and in ill health when I delivered the trunk. I did not actually meet her, however. I don't suppose it matters one way or the other."

"No, I don't suppose it does," Fury said thoughtfully.

Luis regarded Fury just as thoughtfully in the ensuing silence. She was every bit as beautiful as her exquisite mother, he reflected. And as sharp-tongued. Nothing would get by this one. Earlier, he'd been quite open in expressing his thoughts and losing his temper—which he wished now he'd controlled—and she'd shown a depth of spirit in matching him that he'd had to admire.

"Tell me, Miss van der Rhys," he said abruptly, "if I'm not being too presumptuous, why did you have a change of heart in regard to the convent?"

Fury crossed her fingers under the table. "I decided I couldn't give up the outside world. I thought I had a noble religious vocation, but I was proved wrong once I returned here to Batavia. Isn't that so, Father Sebastian?" she asked quietly.

"Hrumph, yes, quite so," the priest replied, forking a large piece of fowl onto his plate.

Luis's eyes narrowed. Something was going on between the priest and the girl—a secret of some sort. "What will you do now?" he asked nonchalantly.

"I plan to help Father Sebastian in the parish until my parents return from the Americas," Fury told him.

"So you can stay close to God, I assume," Luis muttered.

"Yes." Fury glanced at the open doors leading to the wide veranda. Luis's eyes followed her gaze, and he heard a slight rustling noise from among the trees outside.

"It's very warm this evening, don't you think?" Fury asked sweetly.

Luis nodded. He wondered suddenly if he was falling in love with this beautiful young woman. He'd been attracted to her the first time he'd met her, although then she'd seemed no more than a delightful child—and one promised to God, at that. Now, however . . .

Fury looked up at that moment and caught him staring at her. The flush on her cheeks made him smile inwardly; he was responsible, he knew, for the color creeping up her long, slender throat. What would it feel like to caress that delicate column of ivory? he wondered. To follow it with his lips, down . . . down . . .

Breathless, Fury tore her eyes away and placed her napkin across her plate, the signal that dinner was at an end. She wondered if she dared to take the Spaniard for a stroll through the garden with the hawks on the veranda, then decided it would be most unwise under the circumstances. Instead, she led the way into her father's library, where Juli served coffee and offered cigars. Both men declined the tobacco but accepted brandy with their coffee.

"I hope you won't think ill of me, child, if we make an early departure," Father Sebastian said, placing his coffee cup on the silver tray. He stood and took her hand in his.

"Of course not, Father," Fury said warmly, "but you're welcome to stay the night if you like." She turned to Luis. "Señor Domingo, must you return to town also? But you'll want to see about your cargo, of course. What will you do? Can you possibly recapture what was taken from you?"

"I plan to put a price on the Siren's head," Luis declared bluntly. "I have all the time in the world now to search her out and bring her to justice. Believe me when I tell you there will be no mercy shown her."

Fury smiled. "I believe you, Señor Domingo, but first

you have to find her. I wish you would believe me when I tell you it is an impostor who ravaged your ship. In any case, I wish you success in your endeavor. If I hear any news from Mynheer Dykstra, I will be sure that you are informed.''

At the wide front doors, Luis brought Fury's hands to his lips, his eyes boring into hers. ''I thought you were beautiful when I first met you, but here in this lush tropical paradise, I realize you are exquisite. You remind me of someone I've seen somewhere,'' he said thoughtfully.

Fury blushed furiously. Her hands were trembling so badly, he had to be aware of it. ''My mother, perhaps. People say we look very much alike.'' Her voice was as shaky as her hands. No man had ever had this effect on her before.

He nodded and released her hands, stepping back to don his cape. ''Perhaps. *Buenas noches, señorita.*''

Fury nodded and smiled. ''Perhaps you will return when your emotions are . . . calmer,'' she said, one eyebrow lifted suggestively.

He bowed low before her. ''I'd like that very much.''

The moment the darkness swallowed the two men, Fury ran to the kitchen, her cheeks on fire. ''Juli!'' she called.

Juli came hurrying in, her eyes dancing with mirth. ''Is your blood singing, miss?'' she asked playfully.

''Of course not,'' Fury blustered. ''But he *is* handsome, isn't he? He said *I* was exquisite. And he kept staring at this . . . this cap on my head. For all I know, he thinks I'm bald.'' Both women doubled over in peals of laughter. Fury handed the sparkling headpiece to Juli.

''I watched from the kitchen,'' Juli told her. ''He hardly ate, and his eyes never left you. Definitely enamored. You could probably twist him around your finger—if you wanted to, that is,'' she added brazenly.

Fury laughed. "I have to admit I was flattered. Tell me, did you listen to what he had to say about the Sea Siren?"

"Every word," Juli said, nodding. "I'd say the señor is quite intelligent and able to make sense of the puzzle you've set for him. You must be very careful. . . . Now," she said, clapping her hands, "I want to hear about your trip to the cove. How did you find the *Rana*?"

Fury was somewhat puzzled by the teasing manner in which Juli asked the question, but she was too excited to pursue it. "Oh, Juli, you won't believe this, but the ship is moored out there! She's *seaworthy*. I expected her to be a hulk and rotting from top to bottom. It's been so many years! Who could have . . . Someone found her and . . . Why are you smiling, Juli?" she demanded, unable to stand it a moment longer. "What do you know?"

"As you know, Miss Fury, I have many brothers—seven, to be exact," Juli began, eyes twinkling. "When your mother started sending me all those gifts and purses of money, I wanted to do something for her in return. So, I talked the matter over with Father Sebastian, and he suggested we condition the ship and careen her. My brothers did it. And they did a wonderful job! She's as seaworthy as she was in your mother's day. But this I swear, Miss Fury—whoever it was who attacked Señor Domingo's ship did not to do so with the *Rana*. No one but your mother would dare to take her down the River of Death."

"Then who attacked Señor Domingo?" Fury asked.

Juli shook her head. "I have no idea. But if you should decide to take matters into your own hands—to hunt down the impostor who is posing as your mother . . . well, you now have the means to do it."

Fury swallowed past the lump in her throat. "Juli, I've never sailed a ship on my own. I've taken the wheel, but my father and mother were with me. When I was younger

I sailed with my brothers. A ship the size of the *Rana* needs a goodly crew. I can't . . . I couldn't . . ."

"Who else?" Juli said forcefully. "You are your mother's daughter. When Sirena was tested, she found she had the strength, the will, the determination, to overcome everything in her path to reach her objective. You are no different. We could wait to see if this impostor plunders other ships. I can have my brothers frequent the harbor and saloons. They're bound to pick up some information, if there's any to be gathered. If the piracy of Señor Domingo's ship is an isolated incident, the whole matter would best be forgotten. But if not . . ." She felt no need to complete the sentence.

Fury's heart fluttered in her chest. Juli was right: she could study her mother's navigational charts, brush up on her seafaring skills—and wait to see if this impostor struck again. If she did, the *Rana* would be ready to exact revenge . . . with an able captain at the wheel.

"Would you like me to make you some hot chocolate before you retire?" Juli asked, watching her. "If you plan on riding out to the cove tomorrow, you'll want a good night's rest."

"I am tired," Fury agreed. "Chocolate would be wonderful, Juli." Warm chocolate to soothe her, she reflected, with her mother's navigation charts and thoughts of Luis Domingo to keep her company. . . .

Fury sighed. She'd be lucky if she got any sleep at all.

While Fury sipped at her chocolate and pored over the *Rana*'s charts, Luis Domingo was sipping wine with Father Sebastian in his study, wine that Juli had added to the basket of food she'd sent along with the priest.

Father Sebastian was tired, and he was worried. Life, he decided on the way back to town, had been far too quiet. This man was going to turn everything upside down.

He just knew Fury was going to do something foolish, something that might later come back to haunt Sirena van der Rhys, and ultimately he would he held responsible. Dear God, how will I ever explain this to Regan? he wondered, shuddering at the thought.

"Are you all right, Father?" Luis asked with concern.

Father Sebastian swallowed the last of his wine and immediately poured a second glass. If nothing else, the Madeira would help him sleep. "A little tired, my son, but the trip out to the van der Rhyses' estate always makes me feel good. Tell me, what did you think of Furana?"

Luis paused to consider the question. "She's beautiful. Spirited, I'd say. I didn't see that in her the first time I met her. Then she was . . . perhaps 'peaceful' would be the right word. Now she seems to be fretting over something. I'd like to see her again when my affairs are straightened out. But I've no intention of . . . distracting myself until I've tracked down the Sea Siren and brought her to justice."

Father Sebastian blanched. "How do you intend to find her? I don't see what you can possibly do now. The woman is gone, along with your cargo. If—and I say if—she's as proficient as the Sea Siren, you will never find her."

"Then I'll set a trap for her."

"What sort of trap, Señor Domingo?" the priest asked, frowning.

"I think it wiser not to voice my plans, even to you, Father," Luis said apologetically. "I would like to ask you a question, however."

"Yes, my son?"

"In all the tales you've heard of the Sea Siren, do they always refer to a scar on the inside of her arm, a scar so wicked it defies description?"

The priest nodded. "I believe so. From here to here," he said, rubbing the inside of his arm from wrist to elbow.

''Then she shouldn't be too hard to find,'' the Spaniard said, his eyes narrowing.

Father Sebastian felt a prickle of alarm race up his spine. Fury's arm was scarred as badly as her mother's. ''The Sea Siren is dead!'' he said harshly.

''And I tell you she's alive,'' Luis insisted. ''I saw her with my own eyes!''

''No, my son. You saw a woman *pretending* to be the Sea Siren.'' He was on his feet now, weaving his way to the staircase. ''I'm very tired, Señor Domingo, so if you would take pity on an aging man and see your way out, I would appreciate it.''

The Spaniard regarded the priest with eyes as cold as death. So, he thought, the holy man did know something! ''Wait, *Padre*,'' he called out. ''Please, just a moment more.''

Father Sebastian paused and then turned to face Luis, his hands feverishly working the beads around his waist. ''Yes, Señor Domingo?''

''Father, what I said to you moments ago, my confession as to my plans, I'd like you to consider it just that— a confession. A sacred trust. Never to leave this room.''

The priest nodded, his eyes infinitely weary. ''You need not worry. I have never broken any of my vows in all my years. Your . . . plans are safe with me. Now, if you'll excuse me . . .''

Luis's eyes smoldered as he watched the gnarled figure make its way to the staircase. ''We'll talk again. *Buenas noches,* Father.''

Luis Domingo closed the door quietly behind him. The night was warm and dark. He stood on the stone step, savoring the flower-scented air before he reached into his pocket for a cigar. When the tip glowed brightly, he began his long walk back to the *Silver Lady*.

Turning at one point to take a last look behind him, he

saw two yellowish lights wink on the second floor of the parish house. The good Father and . . . who else? The drunken old man from the tavern, no doubt. Earlier in the day the tavern owner had told him the sea salt had trudged off with the priest.

Luis drew deeply on the cigar. Now, what possible connection could a priest and an old sailor have in common? He stopped in his tracks and blew a cloud of blue-black smoke in the still air. An old man, a nervous old priest, and a young girl who'd just changed her mind about entering the convent . . . A conspiracy?

As he strolled down the hard-packed road, Luis allowed his thoughts to drift. Nothing else made sense. It had to be a conspiracy. Clearly he would have to interrogate the officers of the Dutch East India Company and anyone else who could remember back to the Sea Siren's reign of terror.

By the time he boarded his ship, his thoughts had turned inward. Grimacing, he tossed the remains of the cigar overboard and headed to his cabin. What kind of man was he that he would suspect a priest, a memory-fogged old man, and a sweet, innocent young woman? He cursed himself for his shabby, uncharitable thoughts, and wondered what would happen in heaven if the good Father, Fury van der Rhys, and he bombarded God with prayers that were in direct conflict with one another. Whom would that unfathomable Spirit help? The holy man, of course, and the young religious woman.

''Son of a bitch!'' he said as he climbed into his bunk. Then he threw back his head and laughed bitterly. ''Son of a *bitch*!''

Chapter Seven

Luis Domingo struggled with the rage that threatened to engulf him. Exactly thirty days earlier the *Silver Lady* had been attacked and plundered, and he was no closer to finding the pirates now than he was on that fateful day. No other sightings had been chronicled. He knew the captains and crews of the ships he'd questioned, as well as the government officials and town merchants he'd interrogated were wondering by now if he'd lost his wits. He was the nightly topic of dinner conversation, but he was too angry to care. For weeks he'd done nothing but seek information, and at last he was forced to acknowledge that there was none to be had, a realization that only increased his anger. No man liked to be made a fool of.

He was standing at the harbor now with the rest of the tradesmen, watching a brigantine limp into port. He wondered what account her captain would give when he set foot on land. His ship carried a monstrous-size hole in her stern; apparently the attacker had gotten off a good shot broadside. The Spaniard hated himself for hoping the marauding pirate had been the sea slut, as he now referred to her in his mind. But if it was the same woman who'd attacked the *Silver Lady*, Batavia would finally have to take him seriously. And if the brig's cargo had been meant for the Dutch East India Company, they would go after the pirate themselves.

Luis let out his breath in an exploding sigh when, the instant he set foot on land, the captain started to babble almost incoherently about the famous Sea Siren. All heads turned in Luis's direction.

Luis moved closer to the Dutch East India's manager. "What was she carrying, Dykstra?"

He shrugged bitterly. "A goddamn fortune in cloves, nutmegs, and silks. . . . Look, now is as good a time as any for me to apologize for doubting you. Twenty years is a long time . . . you can't blame people for being skeptical about the sudden reappearance of a legend."

"What are you going to do?" Luis asked.

"What I would do myself if I weren't too old—hunt her down and bring her back in irons." He turned to Luis and smiled. "Which is just what I'm going to hire you to do."

Luis laughed mirthlessly. "I cannot conceive of any commission I'd rather undertake. You may consider me hired."

There was no answering laughter from the Dutch East India's manager. "Excellent. Señor Domingo, if you'll follow me back to the office, I'll be glad to discuss terms with you. I have full powers here, and I'm a fair man, as fair as Regan van der Rhys, who held this job before me. The last time the Siren was in these waters, the company was almost ruined because we waited too long to act on the information we had. I won't allow that to happen this time."

Luis bit down on his lower lip. "I, too, consider myself a fair man. I think we'll be able to come to an agreement."

"This time I want the woman captured," Dykstra emphasized. "You're going to have to forget about being noble because of her sex. There's no such thing as courtesy on the high seas. I don't care what condition she's in, as long as you bring her in. Do we understand each other?"

Luis nodded. "How much time do I have?" he asked.

"As much time as it takes," Dykstra said, mopping at his flushed face. "Within reason, of course." If there was one thing he wanted to avoid, it was to retire from the Dutch East India Company under a cloud. He wasn't sure Luis Domingo was the right man to send after the Siren, but he was the only man available. He was almost certain Regan van der Rhys would approve his choice.

Luis mopped at his own brow as he and Dykstra left the docks. "I'll need to talk with you at length. I want to know everything you know about the Sea Siren and the parts you and Regan van der Rhys played during her reign of terror. He brought you into his confidence, did he not?"

"Of course," Dykstra wheezed, struggling to keep up with the Spaniard's brisk pace. "We were . . . are the best of friends. Regan van der Rhys is the man who . . . I wouldn't have this position if it weren't for the mynheer. Come, have supper tonight at my house. I have an excellent cook, and later if you . . . feel . . . have the desire, we can . . . ah, visit another very old friend of both Mynheer van der Rhys's and mine."

Luis smiled. "Are you referring to Clarice's . . . establishment?"

Dykstra laughed. "So you know Clarice. Of course everyone knows *of* Clarice, but there are few people who *know* her, if you take my meaning."

"Perfectly." Luis inclined his head in acknowledgment. "I'd be honored to join you for supper. I'll look forward to a pleasant evening, then."

Alone in his offices, Dykstra stared moodily at the patch on the wall where the picture of the Sea Siren had hung for so many years. He would miss looking at it every day now that Domingo had just left with it, claiming it as his own. The portrait had somehow become quite dear to him; he'd almost come to regard his possession of it as a sacred trust of sorts, bequeathed to him by Regan van der Rhys as his successor, so to speak. But there was no way in hell he was going to believe the Sea Siren of his early days was back in business. It simply wasn't possible. Regan had personally given him his word that the infamous wench had retired from the sea.

Dykstra leaned back in his chair and hooked his booted feet over the edge of his desk. He should be in a flap of rage over the sacking of the company's ship, but he wasn't. This was what had been missing in his life—the excitement he and Regan used to experience when the Siren was at sea. He liked the feeling of anticipation, of single-minded purpose. Domingo was going to be another Regan, he could sense it. He threw back his head and laughed when he thought about how Clarice would probably give him pretend virgins for the rest of his life as thanks for introducing Luis to her "girls." Clarice was always properly grateful, he reflected fondly. Goddamn, life was suddenly interesting again.

All the way home, Dykstra fantasized about the evening ahead—he and Luis Domingo . . . and Clarice's women. By the time he walked through the front door of his tastefully furnished house, he'd bedded all of Clarice's nubile virgins, leaving his leftovers for the rest of the town's patrons. In his mind he was a happy man. What a story he'd have for Regan when next they met!

At the thought of his old friend, Dykstra turned unexpectedly moody. He remembered how badly Regan had wanted to capture the Sea Siren—so badly, he hadn't been able to think about anything else. Dykstra had never understood Regan's decision to let her go. When pressed, Regan had merely said that one could not hold a spirit captive. There had been something in the man's eyes that had puzzled him at the time, something he'd mulled over for many years. It wasn't like Regan to let anything get away from him if he wanted it, and he'd wanted the Siren so badly, he would have killed anyone who stood in his way.

The bottle of rum on Dykstra's desk beckoned. He was on his third glass when he slapped at his unruly gray hair. "Oh, God, no," he muttered as he sorted feverishly through the papers in his desk. Somewhere he had a miniature of Regan and Sirena. Hell, he didn't need the rendering to remember what Sirena looked like; all he had to do was look at their daughter. He threw his hands in the air and yowled his outrage.

They were close, he and Regan, the way men are who boast about their conquests. Regan would never have let the Siren out of his clutches, which could mean only one thing: *Regan had had the Siren in his clutches all along.* Goddamn, why hadn't he ever figured it out before?

Sirena van der Rhys was the Sea Siren! She retired from the sea when Regan married her. What a stupid clod he was! How Regan and Sirena must have laughed at him—no wonder Regan had never endorsed him for the governorship.

But if Regan's wife was the infamous Sea Siren, what did it mean? he asked himself, trying to think everything through clearly. For one thing, he allowed, the story about Fury going into the convent could all be a ruse. Regan and Sirena were too protective of Fury; they would never have allowed their only daughter to come all the way to Batavia to enter a convent alone.

"Son of a bitch!" Dykstra bellowed suddenly. *Fury* was the mysterious legend come to life—a true reincarnation of the infamous Sea Siren. How could he have been so blind?

Dykstra fingered the rum bottle clumsily, then set it aside. He'd had more than enough to drink. Domingo would be arriving soon for dinner, and he'd need his wits about him when entertaining the Spaniard. His eyes narrowed as he contemplated the evening ahead. Should he apprise Domingo of what he suspected or keep his thoughts to himself until they could be proved? Everything came down to proof, and there *was* some sort of proof, something he couldn't remember, something Regan had told him . . . what was it? Damn the rum, he wasn't thinking clearly! Coffee. He still had time for plenty of thick, black coffee.

Dykstra struggled to his feet. The proof . . . what was the proof? he persisted, his pulses pounding with the effort. Perhaps if he stopped thinking about it, it would come to him. He made his way to the kitchen and ordered coffee from his startled housekeeper. "Fetch it to my bedroom. I'll take it while I change for dinner," he growled over his shoulder.

Goddamn it, what was the proof?

Relaxing in his bath, Dykstra forced his mind to blankness so he could restructure his thoughts. It wasn't the Siren's legs or her breasts, although Regan had gone on and on about how beautiful they were. So what in the goddamn hell was the proof?

Dykstra's hand slapped at the soapy water. The scar! *That's* what it was. Of course, how stupid of him to forget. Regan had said he'd observed the vicious, wicked scar when he fought with the Siren. It ran the entire length of her arm, and that's why she always wore long sleeves. Indeed, he could not remember a single instance when he'd seen Sirena's bare arms. All her gowns bore long sleeves. Dykstra's bushy brows furrowed. Fury's arms, too, had been covered the day she'd appeared in the Dutch East India offices. Was it part of their plan? he wondered.

"*What* plan?" he asked himself, disgusted. He could sit in his bath all night and still be wondering come dawn. Maybe Regan had nothing to do with any of this. Maybe it was all Sirena. The possibilities seemed endless.

Goddamn it, he realized sourly, now he had a pounding headache. If he didn't get rid of it, he'd have a miserable time at Clarice's.

* * *

Luis sensed a change in the Dutchman when he arrived. He was pensive and morose, then almost surly whenever he spoke. Never one to let things simmer if he could bring matters to a boil, he spoke harshly. "Are you having second thoughts about hiring me, Dykstra?"

Dykstra looked up, startled. "Not at all. I simply have a damnable headache. I've been realizing that my—my superiors will no doubt pressure me for a swift resolution to this . . . this wretched business, and with my retirement imminent, and the governorship opening up . . ." He smiled sheepishly. "Well, you may just imagine how this is going to look on my record. It has nothing to do with you, Domingo. My offer still stands."

Luis nodded. "As does my acceptance."

"Excellent. In that case," Dykstra continued, "there's something else I wanted to tell you—a piece of information I'd forgotten until today. The Sea Siren has this scar . . . Regan told me he'd actually seen it once. Apparently it runs the entire length of her right arm. That will be all the proof you'll need in verifying . . . when you capture the witch."

It was almost midnight when the two men left Dykstra's home and headed for Clarice's establishment.

"You flatter me, Mynheer Dykstra, by bringing this dashing young man to my house," whispered Clarice, a ravishing, voluptuous woman of indeterminate age. She turned to Luis with a wide smile. "Obviously, señor, you are a man of culture who knows his own mind. I like that. How may I be of service?"

Luis threw back his head and laughed, a deep, resonant sound. "I'd like a very long-legged young lady whose breasts are no more than a handful," he drawled. "Eyes as blue as sapphires and hair as black as sin. A pretty smile. A woman versed in *all* the ways of pleasuring a man. And when she grows tired, have five or six others form a line outside my door. Any questions, madam?''

Clarice shook her head. "I believe we can accommodate you, señor. I knew a man like you once with appetites much the same as yours. He never left this house unsatisfied."

"We'll see," Luis called over his shoulder as he made his way to the second floor.

"My God, where did you find this one?" Clarice hissed to Dykstra the instant the Spaniard was out of hearing. "He cannot be serious in his request—I need all my girls; tonight is one of the busiest nights of the week. I'm going to charge him by the hour," she hissed again. "Who will pay for this night of debauchery, Mynheer?"

Dykstra shrugged. "Señor Domingo is my guest, so I will pay. It is of no importance. Now, to *my* wants . . ."

"I know, I know, three virgins," Clarice purred. "Do you think they grow on trees, Mynheer? But for you, anything."

"How old are they?" Dykstra asked, one eyebrow lifted skeptically.

"Old enough," Clarice replied with a casual wave of her hand. "They just arrived yesterday. I've been saving them for you."

It wasn't until he was removing his trousers that Luis realized he'd described Fury in telling Clarice what he wanted in a woman. The one she'd sent him was called Naula, and it didn't take him long to learn that she was hellfire and damnation when she wasn't being angelical and ethereal.

Within minutes Luis found himself moaning as he throbbed and pulsated, nearly out of his mind with desire. Naula transported him to such dizzying heights, he soon gave himself up totally to her expert ministrations. Up, up, up she led him, until finally he exploded into slick wetness. He was aware of Naula's smiling face as he relaxed into the soft bedcovers.

"Devil," he managed to gasp.

"Yes," Naula whispered. "Will you tell Clarice I pleasured you?" she teased, her fingers trailing intricate patterns down his chest.

"Jesus Christ, hell, yes . . ." He moved to lie on his side, his dark head nuzzled between Naula's creamy, round breasts.

"What shall I tell the other . . . young ladies waiting outside your door?" Naula asked coyly.

"Tell them to . . . to disappear."

Naula's laughter tinkled about the room. "That's what Clarice said you would say. Mynheer Dykstra said *he's* the only man here who can . . . service *all* of Clarice's young ladies." She laughed impishly as she worked her tongue inside Luis's ear.

Luis's long legs were suddenly over the side of the bed. "They said *that*? Then maybe we should play a little trick on Clarice and the mynheer."

Naula leaned over and trailed her fingers down his back. "The kind of trick Mynheer van der Rhys used to play with Mynheer Dykstra?"

"Which was?" Luis asked, curious.

"They always boasted of their prowess, but the truth was quite the opposite . . . you understand, señor? The girls kept their little secrets because they were generous men. And since Mynheer Dykstra is paying for your night's entertainment, I see no reason why you can't turn his own trick back on him. If you like," Naula said, nibbling at his shoulder, "I can help you."

Luis's heart skipped a beat. He *knew* this young woman could very well kill him with her bedroom skill. He wondered how it was that Dykstra was still alive.

He was on his back again with Naula leaning over him,

one round, pink-tipped breast sliding back and forth across his lips. Desire swelled in him a second time.

"What shall I tell the others?" Naula whispered, pressing the length of her silky body against his own.

"To come in, of course," Luis groaned. "I'll think of something."

Naula pouted as she walked naked to the door and motioned for the others to enter. The girls, one more beautiful than the other, giggled when Luis drew the sheet up to his neck.

One of them, more brazen than the rest and sinfully beautiful, walked over to the bed and pulled back the sheet. Luis's erection died immediately. A second clucked her tongue in disapproval, while a third wagged a playful finger under his nose. A fourth crept to the edge of the bed, her breasts spilling from their gossamer covering. "If you like, señor, we can make this a night you'll never forget," she murmured.

Luis swallowed and tried to speak, but his tongue had grown thick and somehow incapable of forming words. He settled for a nod. Goddamn, Dykstra certainly knew how to make a man happy.

Naked bodies whirled about him as the covers were thrown from the bed. Every inch of his body was oiled and massaged. He felt himself being poked and prodded in some places while others were reduced to lacy, shivering trails of ecstasy. Just when he thought he couldn't stand it another second, he felt five pink-tipped tongues lapping the sweet-smelling coconut oil from his entire body. At some point his ankles and wrists were pinned to the soft mattress as one deft pink tongue trailed the length of his entire body. His growl of pleasure was so intense, the women smiled knowingly as he struggled to free himself. The moment Naula's sheath imprisoned him, the others freed his wrists and ankles and tiptoed from the room.

Luis was aware of the droplets of perspiration on Naula's face as she rocked over him, bringing them both to a dizzying crescendo of fulfillment.

From somewhere far away he heard a faint whisper. "You'll sleep like a newborn babe, señor." A whispery kiss feathered his parted lips. "Very few men have given me as much pleasure as you have."

The moment the door closed behind her, Luis was wide awake, wondering if making love to Furana van der Rhys would be half as satisfying as this. His last conscious thought before drifting off was to wonder what it would be like to make love to the Sea Siren.

Luis woke at midmorning to a light tapping at his door. He mumbled something, then immediately rolled over and went back to a half sleep. A moment later he became aware of muted noise and activity in his room and jerked to wakefulness, thinking Clarice operated a day shift of sorts.

They were lined up, all five of them, dressed in proper day attire and looking every bit the same as the town ladies. Only their eyes were merry and devilish when they pointed to the tub full of steaming water.

Of course, he needed a bath! He reeked of himself and Naula, not to mention the coconut oil. He was aware for the first time of the bits and pieces of feathers from the pillows sticking to his oiled skin. Willingly he allowed himself to be led, by five giggling females, to the inevitable.

An hour later he was so clean, he literally squeaked. Every inch of his skin had been prodded, poked, rubbed, and scrubbed. He squinted at his glowing skin. In his entire life he'd never been this clean.

Breakfast, they said, would be served in the dining room. Luis dressed quickly. Clarice, he decided, managed a full-scale operation that ran smoothly. He'd been in many a brothel, but none like this.

It was past the noon hour when Domingo and Dykstra

tripped down the whitewashed steps of Clarice's establishment. "How was your evening?" Dykstra asked him.

"Superb," Luis said, shielding his eyes from the glare of the sun. "And yours?"

"Equally superb. Clarice certainly knows how to treat a man. We must come back again."

"By all means." Luis grinned.

"Meanwhile, back to business," Dykstra said coolly. "Before leaving the office yesterday I gave orders to have one of the company's frigates readied for the evening tide. If you are ready to begin, that is. If not, tomorrow will be soon enough. I think we covered everything last evening. If there's anything else . . ."

Luis rubbed his chin thoughtfully. "No. From here on in I'll manage. I'll be aboard the *Silver Lady* until it's time to sail, should you need to get in touch with me. Otherwise, I'll plan to sail with the tide. The sooner I get matters under way, the sooner this will be resolved."

"Remember, Domingo, I want her—one way or the other!" Dykstra said as they parted at the Dutch East India offices.

Luis nodded and strode off. One way or the other . . . If necessary, could he kill a woman, even one who'd robbed him of his dream? He prided himself on being a gentleman. A poor gentleman, thanks to the sea witch.

As he leapt on board the *Lady*, he decided he could kill a woman if his life was in danger. But the woman hadn't yet been born who would ever get that advantage over him again. No woman was as strong and powerful as a man. This he believed implicitly.

While Luis Domingo was transferring his belongings to the Dutch East India's ship, Fury van der Rhys was slipping and sliding down the rise that bordered the *Rana*'s berth. She looked back to the top and waved to Juli, who was busy untying a bundle from her stiffly starched apron.

"Hold out your arms!" she shouted. Without thinking, Fury stretched out her arms and caught the packet.

"What is it?" she called up. Juli brought her hand to her forehead in the age-old maritime salute. Fury laughed excitedly as she slipped into the water. Minutes later she was climbing the rope ladder that would lead her onto the *Rana*'s decks.

Dripping water, the bundle tied around her neck, Fury hauled herself up on deck and looked about her, her face full of awe. This was *her* ship now. Strange feelings rushed through her as she touched first one thing, then another. Her mother's ship . . . Her mother had fought and killed aboard this ship to avenge her sister's death. She'd made love down below with Fury's father. How many times, Fury wondered, had she cheated death on these same decks? Suddenly the urge to swim back to shore was so strong, she had to grip the rail to keep from bolting. She dropped her hands to her sides when she saw Gaspar and Pilar work their way down in the warm breeze. "You're a welcome sight," she called. She stroked the birds' sleek heads, laughing as Pilar pecked at the bundle around her neck. "I don't know, maybe it's a mid-afternoon snack. I suppose we could eat it now."

How curious they were, these beauties of hers, she thought as she undid the twine around the bundle. The hawks rustled beside her quietly, their black eyes glittering with alarm at her gasp of surprise as she withdrew her mother's costume from the bundle. She could imagine Juli smiling at the thought of her reaction. She brought the fine lawn shirt to her cheek and swore she could smell her mother's scent. The birds inched down the brass railing, their eyes never leaving her face. "Stay here," she ordered, "I'll be right back."

In her mother's old quarters, Fury shed her wet clothing. Above deck she could hear the birds and knew they wondered what she was doing. She herself was wondering the same thing. Whatever it was, she knew it was something she *had* to do. What she was feeling, right now, this very minute, was quite different from what she'd experienced when she'd first dressed in the costume—the day she'd arrived at the estate. That had been amusing; this was real. So real, in fact, that she raced up to the wheelhouse and gripped the wheel the way her mother had hundreds of times, the way she herself had when she'd brought her father's ship into port with the aid of Gaspar and Pilar.

Where were they? Frantically she looked around and saw Gaspar take wing and soar straight up out of sight. Pilar remained on the railing. She frowned; the two hawks never separated from each other unless they had to—or in case of danger. She raced to the bow of the ship, her eyes searching for Gaspar.

In the distance she saw Juli, who was waving frantically, as though trying to tell her something. Fury shielded her eyes and saw the housekeeper sweeping her arms about in wicked, slicing motions. Of course, the rapier. She remembered seeing both the rapier and cutlass below. Juli must have had one of her brothers bring the weapons on board earlier. She ran to the cabin and brought the weapon back on deck. Razor-sharp and wicked as sin, it was; she flexed it, her stance secure as she danced back and forth across the deck. "En garde!" she cried as the blade nicked and sliced at the warm air.

She was the Sea Siren.

On the rise Juli smiled her approval. "Now, little one, you'll know what it's like to feel alive." She watched the pantomime below with bated breath, her eyes taking measure of the young woman who feinted, dipped, and slashed at an imaginary opponent. "You are your mother's daughter," she whispered at last.

Down below, Fury was filled with a sudden fierce pride. She was instantly all things—courageous, beautiful, daring, accomplished—all the things her mother was before her. She *was* the Sea Siren.

"Quarter!" she shouted triumphantly. "Quarter and your life is spared, señor!" Of course she would spare the Spaniard's life, the way her mother had spared Regan's. How could she do less? she thought, elated. She laid aside the rapier and ran below again to return with the heavy cutlass that was her father's.

Fury's thoughts were swept away when she noticed Gaspar circling overhead, working the wind to descend. She shielded her eyes from the sun and saw something gleaming and sparkling in his talons. In the blink of an eye Pilar was off the rail to catch the shimmering bangle. A second later she was holding it out to Fury.

"My garter! Gaspar, wherever did you get this!" she cried as she fingered the glittering diamonds. "The last time I saw this was the night of my birthday celebration. Gaspar, you took it! How wonderful! You brought it all this way." Tearfully, Fury nuzzled the bird's sleek head. "You could have given this to me any time since I've been here, but you waited till now. Why?"

Both birds cocked their heads and regarded her with keen eyes.

Fury sighed. "I won't pretend to understand, but it's obvious that you mean me to wear this." Quick as a flash she secured the glittering circlet around her thigh. "Ooohhh, I feel so deliciously wicked," she purred. "And now I understand. Before I was . . . pretending. This garter makes me real." She clapped her hands to show her approval and watched as the birds soared high overhead. They would play now, delighted with their little trick.

Vivid blue eyes stared down at the winking diamond garter. Long, tawny legs flashed in the sun as Fury brandished the heavy cutlass, nicking and slicing the air about her.

A long time later, exhausted at last, she returned to her cabin to shed her costume. When she walked back on deck she was Fury van der Rhys.

"I watched you. You *were* the Siren," Juli said excitedly. "I want to hear what it was like walking about the ship. And what did those damnable birds give you?"

"Juli, it was the most wonderful experience!" Fury exclaimed. "I felt as if I were bewitched for a time, and then when Gaspar brought the garter, I was me again. Oh, I can't explain it! I was slicing at Señor Domingo and making him beg me—I was going to spare his life the way my mother spared my father's. I never felt like that before. It was make-believe, a pretend game. And now it's over," she concluded sadly.

"Hardly," Juli muttered. "I think it's just beginning. If we're lucky, your clothes will dry before we reach the house. Tomorrow is another day, Miss Fury."

Fury nodded. "Yes, another day."

She was on her way up the stairs to retire when Juli came running up to say that Father Sebastian had just arrived and was waiting to speak with her on the veranda. Fury hurried out to him.

"Father, what is it?" she cried anxiously. "What's happened?"

"I'm not sure, but I thought you would want to know. The talk in town is that Mynheer Dykstra hired Señor Domingo to find the Sea Siren. The señor sailed with the tide on one of the Dutch East India's ships. Yesterday, a brigantine belonging to the Dutch East India Company limped into port. Her captain said she was attacked by the Sea

Siren. She was shot broadside and all the Dutch East India's cargo plundered. It's just like before. The town is . . . they're saying all manner of things. The merchants are putting a price on her head and the Dutch East India Company is adding its own. Every able-bodied ship is going to sea to hunt her down—dead or alive, they say.''

''Did anyone actually see the . . . the impostor?''

''The entire crew of the plundered ship, and that makes Señor Domingo's story true. We never should have doubted him,'' the old priest said sourly.

Fury considered his words, brows furrowed in a pensive frown. ''Father, don't you find it just a little bit strange that Señor Domingo is the one hired by the Dutch East India Company to find the Sea Siren?''

''Not in the least. He's young and strong, and he actually had words with the woman. He was the logical choice. Mynheer Dykstra is too old to be hunting down the likes of this woman. It makes sense.''

''Not to me, it doesn't,'' Fury snapped. ''Perhaps they're in this together. *That's* logical.''

''Furana!'' cried the priest, shocked. ''Mynheer Dykstra is your father's old friend. He would never do anything so base. You should apologize for such a wicked thought. Although—'' he hesitated.

''What?'' Fury demanded.

''Both men were seen coming out of—''

''Where?'' Fury prodded when he seemed disinclined to continue.

''Clarice's . . . establishment. At midmorning. Today.''

''Oh . . .'' The information was a blow to Fury's pride. She knew her face was scarlet as she led the way into the library, where she rang Juli for refreshments.

''You'll stay the night, Father. I insist.''

''Yes, thank you, child. I don't think I'm up to the trip back this evening.''

Over coffee, Fury and Father Sebastian discussed other, inconsequential matters, but Fury's mind was whirling with thoughts of Luis Domingo in Clarice's establishment. True, her own father had gone to Clarice many, many times— or so her mother had said. But the idea of Luis Domingo in the arms of an experienced whore made her body hot all over.

"Have you ever seen the women who work for Clarice?" she asked at last, unable to stand it a moment longer.

"My, yes—and it would be hard to tell they weren't town ladies," the priest said piously. "Quite elegant they are when they shop. Only the finest. Very young and pretty."

"How pretty?" Fury asked, wanting to bite off her tongue for voicing the question.

Father Sebastian leaned back in his chair, his eyes far away. "Very beautiful, I believe. The prettiest one is Naula. Clarice considers her a prize among all the girls." He turned away then, embarrassed at the turn their conversation had taken. "Why are we talking about this, child?"

Fury tossed her head defensively. "You brought up the subject, Father. I have no interest in brothels or the people who frequent them. Señor Domingo's personal affairs are of no interest to me whatever," she added, eyes flashing.

"I thought we were discussing Mynheer Dykstra and the Spaniard," the priest said fretfully. "Am I . . . did I forget something?"

"No, of course not. You're just tired. I'll ring for Juli and have her show you to your room. Good night, Father."

"Sleep well, child."

A few minutes before midnight Fury rapped softly on Juli's bedroom door. "These brothers of yours," she asked when Juli beckoned her inside, "all seven of them, where are they?"

"In town. Why, Miss Fury? Has something happened to Father Sebastian?"

"No, no, nothing like that. If your brothers can crew my ship, I can sail on the morning tide. We need to send someone into town and arrange with them to meet me at the ship."

"Who? Are you sure you want the servants to know . . . Oh, I see, you want me to go into town. You are like your mother," Juli grumbled as she began to dress. The housekeeper's eyes widened when she took a good look at Fury and realized she was dressed and planning to make her way through the jungle in the darkness. "Miss Fury! You can't possibly—"

"The moon is bright, and I'll take Gaspar and Pilar with me. The stable boys think me daft as it is. A moonlight ride won't surprise them at all, and I'll try to be quiet. You'll have to send someone to care for the horse, though.

"Promise your brothers they'll be well paid," she whispered as Juli slipped out the door.

Later, on her way to the stable, Fury wondered where she was going to get the money to pay Juli's brothers. Perhaps Mynheer Dykstra would advance her some money without asking too many questions.

Fury saddled the mare and led her into the courtyard. Then she clapped her hands lightly and was rewarded with a *swoosh* of dark air. Somewhere in the darkness the hawks were waiting for her.

Fury didn't like the darkness. She never had. On the ride to the cove she tried to pray but soon gave it up in favor of an easier task—imagining the face of the whore Naula described by Father Sebastian. Beautiful, he'd said. Well, there was no one more beautiful than her mother. If the faceless Naula were half as pretty, she was indeed worth looking at. Had the famous Clarice assigned Naula to Luis Domingo? Probably, Fury decided. He was the type of man who would command only the best, the most experienced women. Lord, she hated her thoughts. Luis Domingo meant nothing to her, and if she sailed the *Rana* out to sea in search of him, she'd be endangering her life.

Fury's throat constricted as she thought of all the others who would be looking for the Sea Siren—Luis Domingo would not be alone. What chance would she have against a gaggle of cutthroats eager to claim the price on her head? And it was *her* head. Nowhere in this world was there a woman who could even come close to impersonating her mother . . . except for herself.

Fury followed the jungle slope down, finally reaching the tiny beach that cupped the cliff-framed cove, and approached the ship. It took only minutes to pasture the horse and swim out to the *Rana*.

Soaking wet, she made her way to the wheelhouse and the maps and charts she would need to steer down the river and out to sea. She prayed that twenty long years had shifted the rocks that gave the River of Death its name. If not, she would need every ounce of skill to somehow skirt the killing rocks at the ocean's edge.

Fury's touch was reverent as she unrolled first one map and then another until she found what she wanted. If she was unlucky enough to be seen, she would sail around the west tip of Java. "Anyone in pursuit will think the sea swallowed me whole," she muttered. This map of the eastern isles was going to be a blessing.

Her slender fingers trailed across the old maps her mother had sailed by. There was no reason to believe she couldn't manage the trip. Still, she didn't feel at all as confident as she had the previous day when she'd come aboard. Of course, then she'd had the costume and the weapons. They made the difference. Dressed as she was now, she was a lady, a visitor on board ship. It was a feeling she didn't like at all.

Below in her cabin she stripped off her wet clothing and slipped into the costume she'd worn the day before. As if by magic, the same feeling returned. Before she allowed herself to think about her transformation, she was on deck, cutlass in one hand, rapier in the other.

Confident now, she strutted up and down the teakwood deck, getting the feel of the black boots, the diamond garter winking in the lantern light. Suddenly she stopped, eyes wide with the realization that she was different here aboard the *Rana*. Her hand measured the weight of the rapier, and she knew in that second she could wound, maim, or kill if she had to. Furana van der Rhys might flush, blush, and simper in the presence of Luis Domingo, but not this seafaring hellcat.

She was striding again, the heels of her boots thumping on the deck as she tried to make sense of what she was thinking and feeling. Long ago, when her mother rode the seas, she lived under a dual identity, an identity that served her well. She was able to transform not only her outward appearance, but her personality as well. On land she was as capable as at sea, and she didn't need the scanty costume or the *Rana* to be the Sea Siren. Fury, however, needed both to assume her mother's old identity. "And that doesn't say much for me," Fury muttered, one hand still clutching the hilt of the rapier.

The peaceful cove was a haven . . . for now. Fury leaned on the railing and stared across the moonlit water. She could still change her mind if she wanted to. She could forget about the impostor riding the seas and Luis Domingo as well. She could even go back to Spain. So many choices. . . .

Suddenly the hawks grew restless from their position on

the mizzenmast, and Fury picked up the sound on the water at the same moment. A boat was headed their way.

The boat was small and crowded, the occupants' whispers carrying across the water. Immediately Fury dropped the rope ladder over the side of the ship. All but Juli climbed aboard.

"I'll secure this vessel at the deepest end of the cove," Juli called up. "Good luck."

Fury's heart pounded as she greeted Juli's brothers. All were young, agile, and in the darkness she was unable to read their expressions. She called out to Juli, her voice betraying the anxiousness she was feeling. "Juli, how much did you tell them . . . what are their feelings . . . what did their wives . . . Juli, you can't leave me like this and not . . ."

Juli closed the distance between the *Rana*'s bow and the jolly boat she was in. "They are not afraid, if that's what you want to know, Miss Fury. They are big, hulking men, as you can see, and even if they were afraid, they'd never voice their fears in front of a woman. We have their wives to thank for allowing them to sail with you. *They* understand what it is you are doing. I gave away no secrets, if that is what you are fretting over, although one would have to be very stupid not to know what is going on. The less voiced the better. I will tell you this: they fear those damnable birds."

"Gaspar and Pilar!" Fury said in a shocked voice. "But they won't harm your brothers. Speaking of harm, Juli, each day that goes by, there are more and more people who know . . . for years this was the best-kept secret in the world, and now all seven of your brothers know, Father Sebastian knows, and it wouldn't surprise me at all if Luis Domingo knows, not to mention the imposter who roams the seas."

Juli's voice turned thick with displeasure. "My brothers, to a man, will swear allegiance to you. There is no one else who can be trusted. If you are having second thoughts, now is the time to voice them," she growled.

"No, no, I guess I'm just nervous. It will be light very soon and time to sail."

"Godspeed," Juli called over her shoulder. "I'll pray for your safe return."

Fury turned to face her crew. They were clean and freshly shaved, and had curious, honest eyes. Immediately, Fury regretted her words to Juli. They were there to help her. All were young but none as young as herself. All were married with children, Juli had told her several days earlier. The wages she would pay them would not make them rich but would make their lives more comfortable. None of them seem surprised at her scanty costume, and none were leering at her. She felt safe and realized one source of her anxiety was gone. Now it was time for business.

If her crew of seven felt uneasy, it wasn't noticeable to Fury as the *Rana* skimmed out of the cove beneath her sure, if unpracticed, hands—down the winding river, over the white-capped breakers, and . . . into open water. She hadn't expected such a rough sea, and it took all her strength to hold the frigate steady. Above her she could see Gaspar and Pilar, sentinels on the mizzenmast, their jet eyes on the rolling breakers. Over and over she told herself that she was the *Rana's* master.

Two hours later a wild wind started to blow in from the west, signaling an impending storm. Excitement coursed through Fury as she gripped the wheel. She felt Gaspar and Pilar swoop down to perch on the high-backed chair that was bolted to the floor, their talons digging into the heavy mahogany. Their presence gave Fury renewed strength. If she could bring the *Java Queen* safely into port, she could certainly ride the *Rana* through any rough weather.

The course she plotted was one of pure instinct, one she felt a man such as Luis Domingo would follow. If she was wrong, she'd have to live with her mistake. She hoped that Father Sebastian's information was accurate. She had to assume that the Spaniard would set sail in one of the Dutch East India's brigantines, which would give her a definite advantage. If she was mistaken—if he was sailing a frigate much like her own—he would be making top speed. She had to outmaneuver as well as outguess him.

Where would he head? If there was a storm, the brigantine wouldn't heave to under a reefed main topsail. Instinct told her the Spaniard would take the northern shore to reach Sumbawa while she was following a course along the southern shore of Java. Most likely he'd head for the shore off the island where the last Dutch East India ship was attacked. Weather and speed permitting, she could rendezvous there with the angry sea captain. Bali, she decided, the most beautiful island off Java's eastern tip, was his destination. Now it was hers as well.

The storm was savage in its intensity, but of short duration. Fury rode it out under her own prowess, the crew cheering her on. When she turned the wheel over to Mandu, Juli's oldest brother, there was open admiration in his eyes. "Well done, Capitana." Fury beamed her pleasure at his words. Her mother's old crew had called her capitana, too. "I'd be obliged, Capitana, if you'd take . . . your feathered friends with you," Mandu added uneasily.

Fury laughed and snapped her fingers. The birds spread their wings with a loud swish before they sailed upward among the rigging. Mandu turned his head to look over his shoulder.

"Think of them as being on *our* side, *our* protectors,

not just my own,'' Fury suggested, smiling. ''As long as you do nothing to alarm them in regard to me, they are quite docile.''

Mandu gave a brief nod. ''Aye, Capitana.''

Out on deck, Fury called for all hands. ''*We* did well, men,'' she told them. ''Another day, and if my predictions are right, we should meet up with our quarry. Bali would be my first thought, but he may make Sumbawa, depending on his headwinds. For now we've earned a brief rest.'' She turned away, dismissing her small crew. ''I'll be in my cabin.''

Down below she grinned gleefully. Shorthanded as they were—a frigate generally required a crew of at least twelve—they'd done better than she had a right to expect. Good men, a good captain, and a good ship were all that was needed. Now she could relax for a moment.

On deck, the crew whispered among themselves. For a woman, this young lady had handled the frigate as well as any man. For once their sharp-tongued sister had been correct in her assertions. All they had to do now was secure the ship and allow the warm trade winds to spur them onward.

Ten hours later a cry of ''Sail ho!'' came from the rigging. The spyglass was in Fury's hands in a moment.

''Does she sport a Dutch flag?'' she shouted.

''Aye, Capitana, and she's tightened sail. She's spotted us. Her captain is on the stern.''

''All hands on deck! Mandu, steer this ship directly broadside.'' To the others she shouted, ''I want no shots fired until I give the order. We aren't here to fight. Do you understand?''

Never in her life had she experienced such excitement. Her heat thundered in her chest and her pulses thrummed. Something niggled at her, some little-known thing she should have done and now couldn't remember. . . . Lord, of course, the lip and cheek color!

In the blink of an eye she raced to her cabin and dabbed from the little pot Juli had added to her satchel at the last moment. It was Juli who remembered her mother scrubbing the vermilion paint from her cheeks on her return.

Back on deck, Fury raced to the bow of the ship. Feet firmly planted and slightly apart, her hair billowing behind her, she waited, a smile on her face.

"Remember now, veer off at the last moment," she called to her crew. "I want the captain to think we're going to attack, until the very last second. She's loosening sail. The men are in the shrouds. I can see them unfurling the sail! We have only a few moments of daylight left. We're almost broadside!"

As the last vestige of daylight relinquished its hold on the dark gray of early night, Fury felt her hand caressing the hilt of the cutlass at her side.

Luis Domingo, captain of the *China Jewel*, stood on the stern, his face full of shock at the figure of the woman outlined in the murky yellow light. Cutlass in hand, she made a low, mocking bow in his direction.

"We mean you no harm, señor, unless it is your intention to fire upon us," she called to him.

He should give the order to fire; he couldn't understand why he wasn't. He knew his men were ready and waiting for this female witch to make some move that would warrant an attack. He also knew the *Jewel* could not outrace the sleek black frigate. So he waited, his dark eyes narrowed to slits. "We carry no cargo; this is a scouting voyage only," he called.

"I'm not interested in your cargo, señor. I've been tracking you since you left port. Take a good look at me, señor!" Fury ordered. "I am not the pirate who plundered the *Silver Lady*! You were mistaken, and I demand an apology."

"You'll get no apology from me, you sea slut," Luis snarled. "You robbed my cargo. I saw you, I talked to you. No woman makes a fool of me!"

"You'll regret those words, you miserable Spaniard!" Fury cried. She didn't stop to think. She was a whirlwind of motion as long legs flexed and then leapt. In a split second she was aboard the *China Jewel*, the tip of the cutlass pointed six inches below the Spaniard's belt.

Stunned, Luis stepped backward, followed by the scantily clad woman wielding her cutlass. "I could kill you this very second," Fury said, her voice ominously quiet. "All it would take is one downward stroke. But I told you I meant you no harm. You should have believed me."

She inched closer, the cutlass secure in her hand. "Listen to me carefully, señor. I never killed for the sake of killing. I never plundered for my own benefit. My reign on the sea was a cause, and when that cause was laid to rest, I retired. Until today I have not been aboard that frigate out there for twenty years, nor have I attacked any ships."

"Then how do you explain the Dutch East India's brigantine?" Luis snapped.

"She was beset by an impostor, as were you. I don't know who, or why this . . . this person chooses to masquerade as the Sea Siren, but I shall find out."

Fury took a step backward and lowered the cutlass a fraction. "And now," she said mockingly, "I believe I came aboard for a reason . . . an apology. Proceed, Captain." When Luis remained silent, she whipped up the cutlass to slice the buttons from his shirt, then returned it to point directly at his groin. "I'm losing patience, señor."

Grim-faced, Luis shook his head. "No apology, Sea

Siren, not from my lips. I know what I saw, I know what I experienced. What you say may or may not be true; I am, however, willing to concede your point—if you will but *show me your arm*."

Fury drew away, startled and at a sudden loss for words. At that moment there was a loud, *swoosh*ing noise from above. Both Fury and Luis looked up in time to see Gaspar and Pilar swoop down, then soar upward again, their wings rustling as they circled the Spaniard in a menacing orbit.

"What the goddamn living hell is *that*?" Luis shouted as he doubled over.

Fury laughed. "*That*, señor, is called retribution. Those birds can kill you as quickly as I can. Right now they're quite angry, as you can see. If I *ever* hear you or your crew refer to me as a sea slut again, I'll unleash them on you so fast, your head will spin."

Luis observed the circling hawks for a moment or two, then returned his gaze to Fury, eyes glinting with rage. "Another time, another place, Siren, and we'll face off again."

"On your knees, señor!" To the birds, Fury called, "Watch him till I'm back aboard."

Luis stared, mesmerized, as incredibly long legs leapt high above him. He sucked in his breath when she landed gracefully aboard the black frigate. The sound of her laughter raised the hackles on the back of his neck.

"Admit it, señor, I outmaneuvered you!" she called, offering a salute with the tip of the cutlass.

"Never!" he cried passionately. "I could have drilled you broadside. But I was in a charitable mood."

Again Fury's laughter tinkled across the water. Her crew as well as Domingo's knew she was the victor, no matter what he said.

The hawks swooped down with deadly intent, only to

sail upward in their own wake as Fury called, "Enough!" He watched in amazement as both birds flew into the black ship's rigging.

Until this moment he'd been unaware of the fog rolling in. Even now it shrouded his decks, creeping upward. All he could see of the woman aboard the black frigate was the diamond garter twinkling in the misty light. Then . . . nothing. *She always disappears into the mist,* the old sea salt had said.

A long time later, a tankard of ale in his hand, he asked his first mate, Julian, for his opinion. "Was it the same woman?"

Julian frowned. "I don't recall seeing that diamond garter on the woman who attacked the *Queen,* and I know there were no birds. . . ."

"What about the first time, when she attacked the *Spanish Princess.* Did you see a garter or those damnable birds then?"

"It was so long ago, Captain, and my memory isn't what it used to be. The birds I would remember, but the garter, I'd have to say no. Women . . . acquire baubles and wear them at a whim. It's possible she confiscated it from somewhere. She is more beautiful than I remember. The red lips and cheeks I remember, and those long legs . . . aye, Captain, a beautiful woman."

"How old do you think she is?" Luis asked.

"You would be a better judge of that than I, Captain. Young, I'd say."

Luis's brows knitted in thought. "No more than twenty, I'd say. The real Siren would be in her fortieth year or thereabouts." He threw up his hands in disgust. "Women!"

"You saw the scar?" Julian asked.

"No, but it's my gut feeling it's there. She must be real, she has to be real."

"Flesh and blood?" Julian demanded fearfully.

"As real as you and I. I could feel her breath on my face. I want her," Luis growled.

"As does every man jack aboard this ship," Julian said. "She's a devil angel if ever there was one. She strikes the fear of God in me, I can tell you that."

Luis sat alone for the rest of the night, secure in the knowledge that his ship was in Julian's capable hands. He searched his mind for ways he could have reacted differently, things he could have said and done. She hadn't exactly made a fool of him, but she'd definitely had the advantage. Only a fool would have attacked the odds once she boarded the *Jewel*.

Beautiful honey-colored legs, eyes that were more blue than the sky. So very beautiful, more beautiful than any woman he'd ever met. Strong, capable, sense of humor. Her remembered laughter sent chills up his arms. His last thought before retiring to his cabin was that this was one woman not to be taken lightly. As he drifted off to sleep, he wondered once again what it would be like to make love to the exquisite sea creature.

In her bunk Fury lay still, trying to stem the trembling that threatened to overtake her. It was over; she had successfully carried off her plan. She truly believed she was the victor, although no battle had been waged and no blows struck for either side.

Not until dawn was she able to give definition to what she was feeling: her blood was singing, and all because of Luis Domingo.

Chapter Eight

Saianha

Amalie leaned against the cave opening, her pose one of nonchalance. It was backbreaking work carrying the cargoes of the many ships they'd plundered to this safe, secure cave, not that she was doing any of the work. As each crate or barrel was stored inside, she logged it in one of her father's old ledgers. Later, when she felt it was safe, she would dispose of the goods to the highest bidder, preferably in Spain. She wondered idly when and how much; she had no idea what the contents of the cave would yield in the way of money. She also had to allow for the crew's share. No matter, it was close to a fortune.

It was a beautiful evening, warm and star-blessed. She was glad to be on land. While she liked the sea and the rolling ship, she knew she could not create a life for herself on the water. This was where she belonged; the ship and the sea were merely the means to insure that the rest of her life would be charted to her satisfaction.

The note she'd made in the margin of the ledger irritated her. In order to transport the contents of the cave to a ready market, she would need a brigantine, perhaps a galleon, possibly two. There was no way she could purchase the ships, since she had no ready money and nothing to trade for them. She would have to commandeer them at some point and drive the crew overboard. But where would she secure the ships until it was time to sail for Spain?

Another problem, and one she thought about constantly, plagued her as no other. How long would her crew be content with things the way they were? Already they were grumbling about money and the risk to their lives every time they accosted a ship. For six months now she'd been able to calm them, promising them anything she could think of to ward off a mutiny. The only alternative was to kill off those who became too verbal in their complaints or demands.

Amalie logged a cask of coffee beans and another of nutmeg, the men cursing as they rolled and dragged the heavy barrels into the recesses of the cave. Tomorrow they would sail on the morning tide in hopes of overtaking a galleon with an escort of two, all heavily loaded with ivory, a prize that was unequaled among their current plunder. A prize the Dutch East India Company could ill afford to lose. Amalie smiled in the darkness. Their loss—her gain. If she could just find a safe hiding place for the galleon and brigantines, she could keep the cargoes on board and not have to go through this time-consuming ritual of loading, unloading, and logging in.

She smiled again, grimly this time, when she thought of the price on her head. She knew in her gut there wasn't one among her crew—save, perhaps, Cato—who hadn't speculated on turning her in. That amount of money, plus all the cargoes, would make them rich for life. The whole fine mess was taking its toll on her, and she knew it. She slept little, and when she did, it was lightly. The least little sound woke her. Most of the time she was irritable and angry with the crew's sly looks and open greed. She knew she was going to have to do something soon to set an example, one they wouldn't forget.

Minutes later Amalie snapped the ledger closed and signaled her men that it was time to leave. She was last in line to slip and slide down the steep incline that led to the small harbor where her ship was anchored. Cato was directly in front of her. The tension between her shoulder blades told her that something was up. Miguel and some of the others must be plotting to waylay her, she reflected, or, worse yet, kill her so that all the cave's contents and her ship would be theirs.

"Cato, look at me," Amalie said. "This damned crew is planning something, aren't they?"

Cato kept his eyes fastened to the scrubby terrain and treacherous vines. "I'm not sure," he answered, his voice low.

Panic swept through Amalie. She needed these men, needed them desperately. She swallowed past the lump in her throat and tried to speak normally. "I'll cut out their gizzards, yours, too, if you align yourself with them."

Still, Cato did not respond. Desperate now, Amalie tried a different tack. "Cato, do you recall the conversation we had on deck one night while the others were sleeping and you were on watch? I meant every word I said. When my father's house is finally restored, I will live like a queen— and a queen needs a king. You and I could be very happy . . . as long as you don't cross me and do something foolish that we'll both regret."

Cato turned at last to speak to her—and in doing so lost his footing. Amalie reached out, her grip on his arm like a vise, and pulled him upright. "There now," she said softly, releasing his arm, "you're steady on your feet. Remember, I want to know your decision before we sail."

Cato nodded, his young gaze full of admiration. Amalie's strength and stamina never ceased to amaze him. But he'd be a fool to side with the woman against Miguel and his cutthroats. She would be sadly outnumbered, of that he was sure. He would tell the others, his friends, that they would be princes, and because he would be king he would grant them whatever they desired. She hadn't said anything about crowns, though, he worried. A queen and king always wore crowns and elegant robes. His spirits soared almost immediately when he remembered seeing the trunk with its heavy lock and emblem of the Spanish Crown. Crowns and costly robes would be kept in such a place. His spirits plummeted. His young, curious voice carried back to Amalie. "Where will you get a throne?"

Amalie chuckled deep in her throat. "I already have . . . two of them. They belonged to my father. Solid gold," she lied. "In need of polishing. It will be your first . . . kingly duty."

It never occurred to Cato that kings didn't do manual labor. He smiled in the darkness. Already, he could feel the costly robes about his shoulders. He would have to give some thought to the crown and how it would stay fastened to his head. Gold was heavy, and if the crown were studded with priceless gems, it would weigh even more. Wearing a crown was probably something one had to get used to, he thought smugly. He racked his imagination to come up with something he could tell the others princes wore. Possibly neck cuffs studded with rubies, emeralds, and diamonds. He almost choked on his own saliva when he thought of the others as his loyal subjects. He knew at that moment he would do whatever Amalie wanted him to do, even kill.

In her cabin Amalie changed from her coarse dress to the abbreviated costume responsible for Miguel's slobbering mouth. Cato was so young and probably no match for Miguel and his cohorts. She had doubts about her own abilities but refused to dwell on them. The impending confrontation was inevitable, had been from the start. Miguel's greed exceeded only her own. It would happen in open water, of that much she was sure, which didn't give her much time to prepare for the onslaught. An hour, perhaps two at the most, before the crew made a move. Her heart pumped madly in her chest with the realization the crew would openly attack her and try to kill her. How she defended herself and how victorious she was would set the precedent for her reign at sea. The previous altercations were what she considered necessary exercises to prepare her for the really important attacks like the one she was anticipating today.

Amalie flexed her injured arm. Daily she'd exercised with the heavy cutlass until she thought she would drop with fatigue. She was confident that she could outfight any man bent on attacking her.

The attack, when it came, was stealthy and deadly.

Amalie swiveled, cutlass in her hand, at the precise moment Miguel raised his arm to strike her down. The seaman's body had reflected off the shimmering water when the glass was to her eye, which gave her the split second she needed to square off against the hateful cutthroat. All about her were shouts of outrage and curses of rebellion as she brought up her arm to fend off Miguel's wicked blade. Up and down, to the left and to the right, she feinted, her agile body dancing away to thrust and jab.

"Kill me, will you?" she cried. "Not likely, you pig!"

The surprise and a quick moment of fear showed in Miguel's eyes as Amalie's lightning-fast movement sent him reeling backward. She pressed her advantage, parrying with an expertise he'd not known she possessed. His eyes widened when her blade sliced down, then upward, ripping not only his trousers, but his filthy shirt as well. The sight of his own blood brought obscenities spewing from his mouth. His own cutlass sliced through thin air as Amalie danced backward and then to the left, her cutlass whacking his arm at the elbow. She laughed when his ugly face contorted in pain.

"Whore!" Miguel roared, his blade lashing out at Amalie's scarred arm.

"Son of a whore!" Amalie countered as her blade sliced upward, ripping Miguel's ear from the side of his head. "You swore your allegiance to me and turned mutineer, and for that you and the scum that follow you deserve to die!"

Miguel's eyes were murderous with rage as he swung his cutlass, missing Amalie's own ear by a hair. Amalie thrust blindly, off balance as the seaman tried to pin her against the railing. Curses and dark mutterings rocked in her ears as she thrust the cutlass straight out, piercing Miguel in the middle of his stomach. She heaved mightily, ripping the blade upward toward his chest. Blood gushed from the gaping wound.

Amalie whirled then, her eyes glittering as she faced the circle of men that had formed around her and the unfortunate Miguel. She crouched, her hand beckoning the next volunteer who wanted to do battle. "Now, do it now, or from this day on you'll never know a moment's peace," she cried, "for I no longer trust you. I'll kill you when you sleep, when you're high in the rigging, when you're sotted with ale, or when you're playing a game of cards. I'll come up behind you and slice your head from your neck."

When no one moved, she straightened to her full height. "I see that wisdom has struck all of you suddenly. From this moment on you will never again question my authority. You belong to me now, body and soul. You will do what I say when I say it. And the first man who looks at me crossways will find himself shark fodder like Miguel," she warned them. "Now get rid of this vermin and scour these decks till they sparkle!"

The silence roared in Amalie's ears as she strode to her quarters. The moment the cabin door was closed and locked, she rushed to her bunk and buried her face in the pillow to muffle her cries of triumph.

She'd won. *She'd won!* She was now in total control of her ship and the men aboard. There wasn't one who'd have the guts to start a fight with her. Over and over again she played back the scene with Miguel. The exhilaration was overpowering, running like fire through her veins, until she realized what it was she was experiencing: the need to prove herself even more. And the only way she could do that was with a man.

Cato. Cato, with the young, strong body and dark, burning eyes. She would devour him, satiate herself, and make him a willing slave to her bidding. It would be a simple matter to drug the young man with her charms until he was addicted to her body as well as to her mystique. All she had to do now was wait until he brought her a mug of coffee and his hourly report on conditions topside.

Within minutes of the hourly bell, Cato arrived at her cabin carrying a steaming cup of coffee, and meat and bread on a tray. Amalie—or his queen, as he now thought of her—was sitting on the edge of her bunk, smiling at him. He returned her smile and gingerly set the tray on the small table next to the bunk. There was something very different about the way she was looking at him, almost as if she wanted him . . . to touch her. A core of heat curled in his stomach and then fanned outward to suffuse his cheeks with color.

"I want to thank you for—" Amalie jerked her head to indicate the upper deck. Cato nodded and turned to leave. "Wait, don't go," she called. "Come, sit here by me and tell me what the crew is saying. Have I anything to worry about?"

He wanted to tell her she would never have to worry

about anything; he wanted to tell her he would protect her from the likes of Miguel and any others who might have the same intentions. He wanted to tell her how beautiful she was; how he admired her strength and the way she'd attacked the man who was now feeding the sharks . . . But he didn't. His tongue was too thick in his mouth for words, and his body was raging with desire. Dare he tell her what he was thinking?

Hands trembling, he sat down next to his captain. "I . . . the men, they have all sworn allegiance to you, and this time they mean what they say," he began. "Miguel was . . . has always been . . . They're glad he's dead. You have nothing to worry about. I promise to keep my eyes and ears open."

"Thank you," Amalie said, and touched his arm in a gentle caress. Cato flinched as though he'd been struck.

"Would you like to touch me the way I'm touching you?" she asked softly.

Cato nodded, his callused hands reaching out almost of their own accord.

Amalie laughed deep in her throat, the sound primitive and sensual, demanding. "No, not my arm. Here . . ." She pointed to the cleavage between her breasts.

Cato closed his eyes as he buried his face in the twin mounds of creamy flesh, only half aware of Amalie's fingers fumbling with the buttons on her shirt. When at last her breasts were totally free of their confinement, she stretched and leaned back, relishing the artful working of his tongue, moaning her pleasure as she drew his head upward. Their lips met in a searing kiss that left both of them gasping. In a second their clothing fell to the floor as their bodies met and locked with each other. Amalie felt herself crying out as Cato's hands stroked her body, slowly at first and then urgently. She could feel a roaring in her head as the urgent caresses unleashed the wild, clamorous passion she'd so long held in abeyance.

Blood raced through Cato's veins as Amalie clawed at his back, her mouth burning beneath his. Frantically, low moans of pleasure and desire shaking her, she writhed beneath his hardness.

"Hurry, hurry," she murmured, tearing her mouth from his. With one hard thrust from Cato she arched her back, involuntarily crying out, her head rearing into the pillow.

Stunned with what she'd just experienced, Amalie clasped Cato's head to her breast as she crooned words of satisfaction. Minutes later she whispered, "Again, please, again." This time she moved to lie on top of him, her breasts crushing against his chest. Ever so slightly she brought her bruised lips to his, her tongue darting in and out of the warm recesses of his mouth.

Cato, his body slick with perspiration, his heart drumming, silently offered himself up to his queen.

Moaning with pleasure at her ability to arouse him with a mere touch, she crouched up onto her knees, straddling his firm body, her breathing hard and ragged, her motion rhythmical, drawing him deeper into her web.

Cato reached for her breasts with trembling hands. A low, fierce growl of ecstasy ripped from his mouth as Amalie once again brought him to the brink of exploding passion—only to stop all movement, leaving him burning for release.

"Beg me, plead with me," she whispered. "Tell me you want me, all of me, tell me there is no other like me."

Cato's eyes glazed as he repeated the desired words from the depths of his soul. "Don't leave me," he whispered as he drew her to him, their bodies entwined. "I need you," he gasped, surrendering to wave upon wave of passion. He could feel his heart hammering in his chest, every nerve in his body clamoring for satisfaction. "Please," he moaned.

"Yes . . . *Now* . . ." she whispered. They rolled as one, her powerful hands pulling his full weight down onto her.

He rode her like a wild stallion, hard and fast, plunging, withdrawing, until neither of them could stand the exquisite pain a moment longer. Amalie rocked her slick body against his, meeting each explosion of his passion with a tortured cry.

Cato had no idea how much time had passed until Amalie stirred next to him. He didn't care if he never went on deck again. This was what he wanted; this was what he would never forget. He reached out to stroke Amalie's face, and she smiled against his hand. "Did I please you?" he whispered huskily, his heart bursting with love. "Will I make a fitting king for you?"

Amalie smiled again, curling her naked body like a cat. "Of course," she whispered, and realized she meant the words. Cato was so innocent. She'd pleasured many men, more than she cared to remember, but not one had been interested in pleasing her. Only Cato. She tweaked his cheek playfully, wanting to bring a smile to his face.

"Will . . . will we do this again?" he asked in a hushed, pleading voice.

"As often as you like," Amalie replied. She gurgled with laughter when, minutes later, Cato swaggered from her cabin. In no way would she ever think of him as a boy again. In her heart she knew he'd never breathe a word of what had transpired between them. It would make little difference to her authority over the other men if he did, but it was nice to know he respected her enough not to boast about their lovemaking.

Stretching luxuriously, Amalie savored the feeling of satisfaction that welled within. She could still smell the musky scent of Cato, and it pleased her. With a little work, a little refinement, he just might be the perfect king for her domain. She detested the word *slave*, but Cato would make a willing one. She pressed her face deep into her pillow and imagined she was holding him in her arms, kissing him, making love to him. She remembered the way her body felt when he was deep inside her. Right now, this very moment, she wanted that feeling again and knew she would never have enough now that her passions had been aroused. Hours and hours . . . days, possibly weeks of doing nothing but making love and eating. Could one exist only on love? She wanted to find out, needed to find out, and she would.

Amalie slept then, her dreams filled with a tall, dark-eyed Spaniard who in no way resembled Cato. When she woke, it was fully dark, a bright orange moon shining through the mullioned window in her cabin. As she dressed she tried not to think about her dream and what it meant.

The moment her booted feet touched the deck, she heard the cry of "Sail ho!" from high in the rigging. Her heart leapt in her chest at the thought of another battle, especially now, when she didn't feel like fighting. Uneasily she took notice of the low, swirling fog. The smoky lamp pots added eerie shadows everywhere she looked. Perhaps it was an omen of some kind, a warning. . . .

Almost immediately she discounted the thought. A fog was a fog, and the smoky lantern pots were lights, nothing more. But she would have them extinguished in any case—lights could be seen even in fog.

"Where away?" she shouted, cursing when the spyglass offered nothing but swirling fog. She ran to the bow and brought the glass to her eye a second time, then craned her neck backward to peer into the rigging. "You're sure?"

"Dead ahead, Captain. She's traveling at five knots,

perhaps a little less, and she doesn't know we're on her stern,'' the seaman called softly, knowing full well that voices carried over the water. ''She's heavily armed.''

Darkness, Amalie decided, could either be one's enemy or one's friend. ''Douse all lanterns,'' she ordered. The only thing in her favor right now was the fog and darkness, since she was sailing in unfamiliar waters. One good shot could scuttle her frigate, and they'd all be joining Miguel.

At last she sighted them—the galleon and her two brigantines . . . loaded with ivory and perfect for her needs. She couldn't afford to make a mistake. Swiftly she motioned to Cato.

''We'll attack from the jolly boats,'' she told him. ''I want a dozen men in the water swimming alongside. The galleon won't expect such a feeble attempt—surprise will be in our favor. As soon as we have cloud cover, over we go. Have everyone gather round while I explain our plan. . . .''

Amalie's heart pounded as the jolly boats set out under cover of the thick gray fog, one to the left, one to the right, and the third directly in the wake of the galleon. The plan, she'd explained, required strict silence. Having her crew attack by stealth while she rendered the captain helpless would be their one main advantage. They were sadly outnumbered, and what she was planning was foolhardy. But she gave each man his orders and the promise of an extra dividend when splitting the prize. Bloodthirsty by nature, they could hardly wait to get their hands on the small convoy.

''Directly ahead,'' whispered one of the men from the water.

Amalie looked about but could see nothing save the eerie yellow glow of the galleon's smoke pots. Another few moments and it would be time to board. This attack, she thought excitedly, would double or perhaps triple the price on her head. Three ships at once! She almost laughed aloud as she slid over the side of the jolly boat.

Everything was going according to plan; even the thick, dark clouds cooperated, sailing across the sky to give her all the cover she needed. The moment her feet touched the galleon's deck, she crouched down, straining to make out the deck in the thick fog. One of the men jabbed his forefinger in the direction of the wheelhouse, and Amalie sprinted off in a half crouch, all senses alert to anything that might hinder her progress.

Seconds later one of the smoke pots hissed loudly in the water, her signal for them to attack as one—and all hell broke loose.

"All hands on deck!" the captain shouted into his horn. "To your stations! Attack! *Attack!*"

Amalie smiled in the darkness as she crept behind the captain. A minute later she had his hands pinned behind his back and her arm locked around his throat. "If you want to stay alive, Captain, order your crew to cease and desist. I want these ships. If you force us to kill your men, it will be your doing."

The captain tried to speak, but Amalie's arm was slowly cutting off his air supply. When he struggled, she merely increased the pressure. "Quietly, Captain, or I'll snap your neck. Now—order them into the jolly boats."

"Jolly boats?" the captain rasped.

"Of course. Do you think for one moment the Sea Siren would leave you in open water to die? I told you, I want these ships, not your lives. Make your decision *now*." Amalie released her hold on the captain and thrust him forward. She watched through narrowed eyes as he picked up the horn to obey her command.

It was all too easy, she thought suspiciously. Something was wrong. "I want to see your log," she told him, "and then I want a roll call—on deck. And if you do anything out of the ordinary, Captain, I'll run you through and pin you to the yardarm."

The captain was a fat man, his steps jerky and faltering with fear. Amalie jabbed his buttocks with the tip of her cutlass as she marched him to the quarter deck. Soon the crews from all three ships were howling their outrage at the near-naked long-legged apparition issuing orders in a voice stronger than any they'd ever heard from their own captain.

It was a bloodless battle for the most part, with only three men of the galleon's crew carrying slight wounds. To a man, her own crew emerged unscathed. In her excitement, Amalie searched for Cato and gave him a jaunty salute with the tip of her cutlass. "Well done!" she called. "Well done indeed."

"I never believed the story until now," the captain muttered.

Amalie turned to him with a smile. "What story is that, Captain?"

"That you were real. There were some who said you were a legend. Once before you all but ruined the Dutch East India Company. Are you here now to finish the job?"

Amalie merely shrugged. Let him think what he wanted. By the time he reached port—*if* he did—his story would be so outrageously magnified, she'd be hard-pressed to recognize it anyway.

The captain struggled to stand at his full height. He couldn't go over the side without one last attempt at bravado. He needed to show his crew he was not a coward. "They'll kill you, you know. There's a price on your head now that will increase when we reach port. The Dutch East India Company has hired a man, a crew, to ride these seas and capture you."

Amalie laughed. "You're all fools! There's no man out there," she said, motioning to the open water with her cutlass, "who can kill me. I'm a legend. Am I real, Captain, or am I a ghost? How is it that none of my men were hurt? How is it that I captured *you* so easily? If I were flesh and blood, could I do all these things? Think about *that* when you make your report to your company's officers."

The captain's eyes bulged with fear. A spirit, a ghost? He looked around at his crew, who were eager now to go over the side. By the time he turned back to Amalie, a low bank of fog had rolled across the deck, obscuring her form within its thick, swirling tentacles. The captain reached out to her with a trembling hand, but she stepped backward, to be enveloped completely by the heavy mist. It was as if she'd never existed.

Giving a low groan, the captain spun around and threw himself overboard. There followed splash after splash of water as his crew did the same. Amalie had to clamp her hand over her mouth to keep from laughing aloud.

"Secure these ships and make ready to sail!" she hissed to her crew.

"Aye, Captain."

Amalie watched the beginning of a new day from the bow of her ship, a steaming mug of coffee in her hands. There was a smile on her face as she admired her three latest acquisitions . . . a marvelous night's work. The ivory alone would make her richer than she ever dreamed. A few more ships to her credit, and she would soon have a flotilla. An *armed* flotilla.

Cato came up behind her. "Are we sailing home?" he asked quietly.

Amalie turned, her eyes softening in the early light. "No," she said. "Soon, though."

"What will you do next?" he asked. He was remembering the hours he'd spent lying next to her. He wanted to be there again, in her bunk, shutting out the world.

Amalie pretended to consider his question as she sipped her coffee. "I think we'll wait for the . . . person the Dutch East India Company hired to find me. He can't be far away. And I suspect he won't be as foolish as our fat captain. Silent and deadly, I'll wager. If he's who I think he is, then he feels he has a score to settle with us for sacking his cargo."

"The Spaniard?" Cato asked.

She nodded. "It makes sense, doesn't it? Who else would be angry and poor enough to take on the fruitless task of finding the Sea Siren? Remember, too, that we attacked his ship off the coast. For all we know, he could be sailing blind. He doesn't know we're in his waters, so to speak. He's either captaining his own ship or one belonging to the Dutch East India Company," she mused. "Until then, though, our immediate problem is where to hide these ships."

"The outer islands are riddled with hideaways and caves," Cato said, frowning. "If we found one, we can find others. Surely your father's maps will yield a suitable place. Perhaps a deep harbor, the one he used to store the unlimed nutmegs you told me about when we were in Saianha."

"I told you about that!" Amalie said in puzzled surprise.

"It was when I carried you to your house after you injured your arm. You spoke of many things then. I remember all of them," he said softly, proudly.

He was so boyish, Amalie thought, and yet manly at the same time. Her eyes warmed as she handed him her mug. "Have one of the men bring some food to my cabin. I want to go over those charts again."

Cato shuffled his feet on the deck. "Have someone bring

food to my cabin'' meant he wasn't to do the bringing. Steaming with jealousy, he stalked away, aware that Amalie's eyes were boring into his back. When she wanted *him*, she would let him know. If he wanted her, he would just have to wait until she was ready. Lovemaking on command. He spit over the side of the rail to show his displeasure. Maybe living as a king wasn't going to be so wonderful after all.

In her quarters, Amalie spread out the old maps and charts on her bunk, knowing full well it was going to take every bit of concentration to decipher her father's faded markings. Hours later her eyes burned with strain and her shoulders ached with tension. What good were the ships if she couldn't find a safe harbor for them? And the ivory— was it a good idea to leave it aboard the ships, or should she secure it in the caves with the rest of the booty they'd plundered? Her head reeled with all the possibilities. Becoming rich had been the easy part. The hard part, she now realized, was keeping the riches secure.

Returning to Saianha would be the simplest solution. In her own waters she might fare better, but then, what should she do with the plunder they'd already stored? She couldn't have two bases of operation, and yet . . .

Her head started to pound. If her crew became aware of her indecision, they might decide to take matters into their own hands. What captain would sail blindly with no destination in mind? She had to come up with something before she went on deck. She bent over the maps again.

Amalie could barely keep her eyes focused when, an eternity later, she sat back with a satisfied sigh. After hours of painstaking scrutiny, the oldest of the maps had yielded the perfect sanctuary: a deep cove at the end of the River of Death. There was something in her father's journal about the deadly river, something to do with the real Sea Siren.

Volcanoes and rocks . . . "the only explanation," he'd written in his cramped hand. But explanation of what? According to the chart in front of her, the mouth of the river had been closed off when twin volcanoes had erupted years before.

Amalie massaged her throbbing temples before she returned to the maps. Bits and pieces of her father's journal flashed before her, committed to memory. Of course! "The only explanation" meant the Sea Siren had sailed her ship up the River of Death, and that was how she'd outwitted all who'd been determined to capture her. Amalie felt giddy with the realization. How else could the female renegade disappear at will? If the mouth of the river was blocked at some point, surely over the years the elements had created another opening.

Her best calculations, allowing for a stint of heavy weather, placed her approximately seven days away from the river. She'd give the order to change course and head directly for it; with luck, the tides and currents over the years had rendered it passable. She could only pray that she wasn't making a mistake.

Amalie felt almost invincible as she strode up and out to the deck. How wonderful the balmy air felt, how clean and fresh! The throbbing in her temples eased with each long-legged stride. She had accomplished a feat the equal of any the Sea Siren had performed. And she'd become a woman in the true sense of the word. This strange, intoxicating elation had to be . . . happiness. It was unlike anything she'd ever felt before.

Hours later she was still on deck, her perch on a pile of rigging secure. Overhead, millions of tiny stars winked down at her while dark clouds, as soft as gossamer, sailed across the sky like graceful dancers. She'd lost all track of time and knew only that it was the dead of the night. She should have been sleepy, but she wasn't.

"I thought I'd find you here," Cato said softly. "You should be asleep." He reached out to caress her hair, and Amalie shivered beneath his touch.

"I don't want to sleep for fear I'll miss something," she said. "If I had my way, I'd never sleep. It's such a waste of time. We live only once, and every hour, every minute, should be savored. Sleep robs us of those precious hours and minutes."

Cato pondered her words. "In these hours, nothing of importance happens. Darkness is a time for . . . many things."

Amalie laughed throatily, the sound tinkling seductively across the rippling water. "One night we'll make love here on the deck under the stars. Would you like that?" He nodded. Amalie knew that even now he was consumed with passion for her. All she had to do was crook her finger and . . .

"There's a time and a place for everything, Cato," she said, smiling, touching his cheek. "Soon. . . ."

A bank of dark clouds scudded across the moon, blotting out the winking stars. "You see, if we were below decks, we would miss this blessed darkness," she murmured, gazing up at the heavens. "It's as though someone tossed a coverlet across the sky, bathing us in this dark velvet. Now we have only scent and feeling. The smoke pots are low. Once they're extinguished the blackness will be complete." She looked at him. "Does that frighten you?"

"No. Does it frighten you?" Cato asked curiously.

"Somewhat. If a ship were to come upon us, how would we see and retaliate? We would have to rely on our senses of smell and touch. A little difficult if one is to do battle, do you agree?"

Cato shrugged. "Unlikely."

"The moment we make a safe harbor, I want the galleon's weapons transferred to this frigate. It was foolish of me even to think of sailing this ship without cannon, but I did it, and it's not a mistake I want to repeat. Two expert gunners are all we need, providing they have excellent eyesight." Amalie could feel Cato's shudder.

"If I'm to die, I'd rather die at a man's hands," he said stoutly. "A man whose face I can see." His tone softened then. "If you wanted this frigate outfitted with cannon, it should have been done in port. It's going to be an awesome task, and there's going to be a war among the crew. Give some thought to unloading the ivory from the brigantine and sailing her. It will be a simple matter to paint the ship black if that's your intention."

"No," Amalie said harshly. "This is my ship. The *Sea Siren* belongs to me. It wouldn't be the same; I must sail *this* ship. At one time it carried its own cannon, but those bastards in town made off with them, thinking this ship would never be seaworthy again. It can be done, but until then I think we should sail only under cover of darkness. We have three ships to worry about now as well as our own, and we're short handed. We're ripe for the picking if another pirate ship accosts us. I have no intention of giving up what I have, Cato. I want you to apprise the crew of this. If there's any dissension, let me know."

The last of the oil in the smoke pot sputtered out, bathing the deck in total darkness. For a moment all was silent, and then suddenly Cato whirled about, his words hissing in the quiet moonlit night. It took a moment for Amalie to realize that he was talking to one of her men. A strange sail had been sighted three leagues westward, said the crewman, flying two colors, Dutch and Spanish.

The words whipped from Amalie's mouth. "Do we assume she's armed? How high does she ride? Cargo?"

"I recognize her," the seaman reported. "She's the backbone of the Dutch East India Company and is deployed to convoy cargo vessels and to fight off pirates. She's three-masted and carries square rigging. It's doubtful she's carrying cargo, she rides too high.''

Amalie peered about her in the darkness, seeing nothing. The night could work for her or against her, since the same darkness cloaked the unknown ship to the west. Her mind raced, and for the first time she felt unsure of her course. ''Has she spotted us?''

''Aye, but she probably thinks we're from her own company since her true colors still fly. The night is too dark for her to see us clearly.''

''Can we overtake her?''

''Aye, if we change course and leave the other ships behind,'' the seaman said. ''But then we have no cannon.''

Attack or not attack? Perspiration dotted Amalie's brow. ''Conditions are not . . . appropriate for an attack,'' she said, swallowing past the lump in her throat. ''We'll stay on course.''

''There are weapons aboard the brigantines,'' the seaman said boldly. ''We can be aboard in minutes.''

''To what end?'' Amalie snarled. ''A ship with an empty hold will do us no good. We have to find a safe harbor for the three ships we have now. A fourth, if we're lucky enough to snare her, will only compound our problem. She's no good to us. Pass the word, we stay true on our course.''

''What if she attacks us?'' Cato asked quietly.

''That's a different matter. If it happens, we'll deal—''

A volley of thunder ripped through the black night, drowning out Amalie's words and putting an abrupt end to her hopes of sailing on unseen. ''All hands on deck!'' she shouted as pungent black smoke whirled upward from the galleon. ''She's been hit broadside. All hands to the brigantine. Over the side. *Quickly!*'' A second volley of shots rocketed through the night and then a third, none of them finding their target.

The frigate was alongside the brigantine in minutes. Amalie leapt aboard, shouting orders to fire on the three-masted ship. "Shred her sails! Rupture her bow! Splinter her stern! I want that ship gutted and sunk! Move fast, men! The fool fires on his own ships!" She pointed to several scurrying seamen. "You, you, and you, shore up this ship—and be quick, or that beautiful ivory will sink to the bottom of the sea, where it will do us no good."

"You fire like women with babies on their hips!" Luis Domingo shouted above the cannon shots. "Do I have to come down there and show you how to do it? Open your eyes and fire on the target. Shot that goes to the bottom of the sea does us no good." Roaring with rage, his face white as sheeting, he glanced over his shoulder just in time to see a pair of beautiful long legs leap gracefully from the bow of the brigantine and land just inches from where he was standing. The Sea Siren!

"Enough!" she cried. "Give quarter or we sink this ship with all your men aboard! Think fast, señor, you have only seconds!"

"Never!"

"Never is a very long time. Never could very well be your eternity. I'll ask you again—give quarter."

"I said never!" Luis snarled. "I'll kill you before I yield. First you robbed my cargo with your cutthroats, then you had the gall to accost me a second time and tell me that it wasn't you at all but an impostor pillaging and plundering in your name." He took a step forward and spat in front of her, eyes murderous. "Liar! Sea slut!"

What was he talking about? For the briefest of seconds Amalie's blood ran cold and she wavered. "I—I had no intention of attacking your ship, señor. You fired first. As for your cargo, if you aren't man enough to defend what is yours, you deserve to be bested. Now fight like a man or go over the side! I gave you your chance and you ignored it.''

Amalie's cutlass lashed upward and then down quicker than the volley of shots ripping through the night. She feinted to the right, the tip of her blade slicing through the air. Suddenly a jolt of pain ripped up her arm into her shoulder as the Spaniard's cutlass met her own. She sidestepped neatly, drawing the blade down the length of his leg. Taken by surprise with the force of her strength, Luis staggered backward. Amalie seized the advantage and brought up the cutlass, using both hands to hack at the weapon in her opponent's hand. Recovering quickly, he jabbed at her midsection, but she stepped aside nimbly, her weapon arching upward. She feinted to the right and then the left, lashing out in every direction, hoping to make contact in the darkness. Again steel met steel, but this time she felt herself being driven backward, farther, farther, until she was forced against the ship's railing.

"Now it is *you* who will give quarter," Luis growled, drawing his cutlass against hers and pressing the weight of both to her heaving breasts.

"You speckled-shirted dog, I'll never give you quarter!'' Amalie gasped, and brought up her knee with all the force she could muster to trounce the Spaniard in the groin. He reeled backward, doubling over with pain. Amalie held the cutlass high overhead, about to bring it down on Luis's neck, when Cato appeared next to her.

"There's no need," he cried, staying her arm. "You've won. His crew and yours know you are the victor. They've all been disarmed; you'll have no further trouble with them. We can be on our way unmolested—why not let them keep their captain?"

Luis snorted at Cato's report. "Why don't you have

those goddamn black birds finish me off if you don't have the guts to do it yourself," he hissed.

Amalie paused, caught between Cato's declaration of victory and the Spaniard's puzzling words. *What black birds?* Suddenly she felt his hand on her arm, the fingers running up and down the heavy welt of the scar on her arm.

"Lying slut!" he roared. "If my life depended on what you call the truth, I wouldn't believe you. A fine tale it was! Send in your killing birds and be damned!"

Amalie lowered her cutlass, exasperated. "I don't know what you're talking about, señor. I don't want you and I don't want this ship. You fired on me. Ask yourself why I would attack a ship with an empty hold."

"I'd rather ask why you travel with a Dutch and Spanish escort," Luis countered. "Those ships belong to the Dutch East India Company. What are you doing with them?"

"I might ask you a question, señor," she said, ignoring his demand. "Why would you fire on your own ships? You ride these waters looking for me, and yet it's your own company's ships you shot at, not mine. Are you that poor a shot, or is it that you're afraid to fire on me directly since I scuttled the *Silver Lady*?" She laughed with the triumph of a conviction, then backed away from him until she'd reached the bow of the ship. "I have no more time to converse with you further, señor. Be sure it's a pretty tale you spin when you return to Batavia, and be sure to spell my name correctly on the wanted posters."

Luis watched as she leapt from his ship to the bow of her own. His eyes strained to pierce the darkness, trying to make out her diamond garter. He saw nothing save a flash of steel as she sheathed her cutlass. "Let's hope that diamond garter is still aboard these decks," he called loudly. "It might make all this worthwhile."

Amalie could hold her tongue no longer. "You've done

nothing but talk in riddles this past hour, señor. If you have a passion for killing birds and lust after diamond garters, look elsewhere. *Buenas noches, señor.* The next time we meet I'll kill you for no other reason than to please myself.''

''Twice! Twice she bested me. Or was it three times? Goddamn bitch!'' He'd see her dead before . . . Christ, what was the matter with him? He'd had her in his clutches and let her go. He'd believed her when she said she meant him no harm . . . the birds, where were the goddamn black birds? And where was her garter? ''All hands on deck!'' he shouted. ''Scour this ship! Find that diamond garter! Now!'' he thundered.

''You saw the garter, Julian! Where the hell is it?'' Luis roared his anger as he dabbed at the blood dribbling down his chest.

''Captain, I was too busy fending for myself. It's dark and I saw no garter on the sea witch's leg. I did see it when she came broadside at your last meeting. Perhaps she took it off herself. The sea witch is no different from other women. One day they put gemstones in their ears and around their necks, the next day they tie on velvet ribbons. The sea witch is a woman with flights of fancy. If you wish, I'll help the crew search for the garter. When you spoke of it to her, she didn't show any concern that I could see, which makes me think she simply wasn't wearing her bauble this night.''

''You can't trust women,'' Luis spat out. ''I went against my better instincts. I never should have believed her. She's right, I am a fool.''

''Why do you think she didn't—''

''Kill me? I don't know, unless she was enamored of my charms,'' Luis said bitterly.

''I saw it all, Cap'n. You could have taken her at any

time," Julian said loyally. "You held back because she was a woman, isn't that right?"

"She's incredibly strong," Luis hedged. "And skilled. I had no idea she'd be that good. Not even our first encounter . . ." He spun around to his first mate. "But she lied, Julian! I was halfway to believing her. . . ."

"We fired first, Cap'n," Julian muttered. "She did say she was staying true to her course."

"Then what in the goddamn hell was she doing with three ships belonging to the Dutch East India Company? Who the hell could see that dastardly black ship in this darkness? It could have been any ship. Tell me, Julian, did you see . . . sense anything different about this woman?"

The first mate shook his head. "Not a thing, Cap'n. Beautiful as sin. I suppose it's possible that she's going to escort the Dutch East India's ships back to port . . . safely." He shrugged.

"The day that happens they'll get whiskey in hell," Luis snarled. Frowning, he leaned over the rail to stare into the murky waters below. Was Julian right? Had he held back because the Siren was a woman—or had she bested him? To others he could lie, but not to himself. He searched his mind for ways he'd held back, given in to the strength of the woman, but only because . . . because . . . he wasn't sure in his own mind if she was the real Sea Siren or the impostor. Yes, he'd held back; he was certain. His breath exploded in a loud sigh of relief.

"Julian, I don't believe she was the Sea Siren," he said. "No birds, no garter . . . But whether I'm right or not, the next time *any* woman confronts me on the open seas, I'll forget what a gentleman I am. The next time I'll . . ."

The first rays of dawn saw Luis Domingo in his quarters with every map owned by the Dutch East India Company spread before him. He'd find the sea witch if it was the last thing he did. It was dusk when he flexed his shoulders and called for his first mate.

"I do believe I found the slut's lair," he drawled nonchalantly, pointing to a chart so old the edges were frayed and yellowed.

Julian peered down at the ancient chart, his face draining of all color. "The River of Death!" he said in a trembling voice.

Luis nodded. "Don't you see, it bears out everything that old sea salt told me months ago. Think back to the Siren's beginning reign of terror and destruction of the Dutch East India Company. Somehow she was privy to sailing dates and cargo manifests, which means she sequestered that damnable black ship somewhere in a deep harbor or hiding place that only she had the nerve to sail into. And what better place than the River of Death? Those simmering sister volcanoes would hold any sea captain at bay." He turned to his first mate, eyes glinting in the dim lantern light. "I'm convinced now that there are two Sirens. The question is: Which one is the impostor? Believe it or not, we've met both of them. Which is your choice?"

Julian paused, clearly taken aback. "I can't be sure, Cap'n, but the one tonight was damnably strong, and there was something about her voice, as though she knew something . . . knew her own power. They called her arrogant back then, so arrogant she believed she was—"

"Invincible. Exactly!" Luis jabbed a finger under Julian's nose. "She could be invincible and arrogant only because she knew she was safe and could disappear almost at will. The volcanoes created a vaporous black mist—the one the old sea salt referred to. Examine all this information, and the answer is right in front of you. If you recall, the Siren retired from the seas when the sister volcanoes erupted. See—on this map and this one, the entrance to the river was blocked, probably sealing her ship inside her sequestered cove. Now, this map''—he pointed to a recent rendering—''shows that the river is open. Quite natural with the various tides and currents. It's still narrow and would take much skill to skirt the rocky formations on either side. A frigate could make it, but it's doubtful a brigantine could sail past the opening. I plan to travel that river in one of the jolly boats.''

Luis tossed his marking chalk on the rough table and clapped Julian on the back. ''Better yet, the River of Death is so close to Batavia, I think we'll change course—sail for port and trade in this ship for another, one of those sloops with the rapierlike bowsprit. Dykstra was to take delivery of several on behalf of the Dutch East India Company; he probably has them by now. They say the bowsprit on those sloops is almost as long as the hull. The parade of canvas she sports makes her more nimble than a brigantine or frigate. And the square topsail, in favorable winds, gives an extra measure of speed, which is what I'm going to need. Eleven knots is nothing to sneer at. Dykstra said they were to be outfitted with twelve or fourteen cannon. Six would do us fine, less weight in favor of maneuverability.

''Yes,'' he went on, tapping his chin, ''that's exactly what we're going to do. Give the order to change course now. We'll lose two days at the most and, hopefully, pick them up once we have the sloop. What do you think, Julian?'' Luis asked as he rolled the charts and maps into goatskin pouches.

Julian nodded. ''I can think of no better explanation, Cap'n. But what if there is no black frigate once you're past the River of Death? How will we know if it's her haven?''

''We'll know,'' Luis replied. ''When people think they are safe, they become careless. There will be some sign,

I'm sure of it. If there isn't, we're no worse off. The most we lose is seven days either way. But I feel it here''—he pounded his chest—''those waters are her home.''

Julian left the captain's quarters to give the order to change course. Up on deck, he strode from bow to stern, savoring the warmth of the evening air. He could imagine no life other than this one. The sea was his mistress, the clear, star-filled night his wife, the elements his children, the captain his superior. . . . Still, now and then he wondered if he would ever see his mother country again. If the captain was smitten with the Sea Siren, it could be the death of all of them.

He wondered then, and not for the first time, why the Siren hadn't run the captain through. She had to be the real Siren because of her boast that she did not kill for the sake of killing. Nothing else made sense . . . unless she was the impostor and smitten with the captain herself. Damnation, he was developing a pounding headache. Women always gave him a headache; they were such demanding and unpredictable creatures. Diamond garters, black birds that killed, near-naked women who could fight better than most men . . . The world was changing too fast for him. Truly, he belonged at sea.

Chapter Nine

Batavia

Peter Dykstra nervously fingered the ends of his lace collar before knocking at the door of the casa. His heart thumped in his chest at what he was about to do: spy on and try to trick his good friend's daughter. Once and for all he was going to bring this puzzling matter to a conclusion. Whatever happened afterward would be in other hands, not his own, he decided miserably.

Over the dinner table, Dykstra was glad that poor eyesight was not among his various ailments. Fury looked ravishing in the candlelight; if he didn't know better, he would have thought he was sitting across from her mother. He warned himself to be careful with his questions. If what he suspected was true, he didn't want to alert the young lady. He remembered well her mother's hot temper, and there was no reason to believe the daughter wasn't similarly gifted.

"I'm so glad you could come to dinner, Mynheer," Fury said graciously, sipping from her wineglass. "I've become very lonely here. Gathering flowers to grace the rooms is not my idea of a productive life. How fortunate that you are a man and can do as you please. When I was a child I wanted to be a boy like my brothers and do all the things they did."

The perfect opening. "Good Lord, child, do you mean you'd like to go to sea or be a merchant?" Dykstra asked. "Did your parents ever tell you tales of the Sea Siren?"

Fury felt a hard nudge to her back as Juli removed the first course plates. "Of course, Mynheer Dykstra. My father openly admits to once being obsessed with the famous pirate. I thought it such a romantic story." She smiled dreamily. "I can't even begin to imagine what her life must have been like. So strong and powerful, men lusting after her, none strong enough to kill her. Conquistador, they called her. A better sailor than any man. What did you think of her, Mynheer?"

Dykstra hesitated. Obviously she knew what he was after. As wily and ingenious as her mother. "I always envied your father's meetings with her. There were many, you know. Of course, we have only his word for what happened during those meetings," he added.

"Your words seem to carry a double meaning, Mynheer," Fury said quietly.

"Oh, no, it's just that Regan and I were such fast friends, and both of us liked to boast . . . the way men will do with one another. I tend to think your father gilded his stories a little. I would have done the same in his circumstances." He shook his head. "It wasn't like Regan to let her go. I've never understood why he allowed it."

Fury's eyes narrowed. "He didn't *allow* her to flee, Mynheer. She escaped. He searched for years, every chance he could, until . . . my mother called a halt to his wanderings. And, eventually, she retired on her own—as I've been given to understand. My parents felt much admiration for so accomplished a woman. There aren't many women walking this earth or sailing the seas who can bring hundreds of men to their knees."

Dykstra felt himself bristling with suppressed rage. "She was no lady! Good women don't do the things she did. She deserved to be punished for her cruel deeds," he said coldly.

Fury flushed. "On the contrary, Mynheer, my father said the Siren was more of a lady than all of the women together in Batavia. With the exception of my mother," she added hastily.

Dykstra paused and took a steadying breath. "It sounds like you condone the Sea Siren's actions," he said, striving for a light tone.

"Mynheer Dykstra, the Sea Siren reigned over twenty years ago, before I was born. I admire what she did . . . and all for a cause that otherwise would have gone unpunished—" Fury broke off to stare directly into Dykstra's eyes. "Why are we talking about the Sea Siren now, at this particular time? Is it because of the bogus pirate who is sailing the seas? You'll never convince me she's the Sea Siren."

"How can you be so sure if, as you say, you weren't even born during her reign of terror?"

Fury could feel her skin prickling. Dykstra had something, some news, or else he was baiting a trap for her. "Mynheer Dykstra, this impostor is a direct contradiction to all the Sea Siren stood for. I wouldn't cross this one if I were you—she might come on land and run you through just for the pleasure of it. You see, that is the difference between the two; the real Sea Siren would never do such a thing. She's an honorable woman!" Smiling coldly, she placed her napkin on her plate and rose. "We can have coffee and brandy in my father's study, if you like."

Without a word Dykstra followed her into the study, his hand in his waistcoat pocket. She was suspicious—so suspicious, she was letting her tongue run away with her. It was time to close in for the kill.

In her father's library Fury did her best to relax and

play hostess as Juli placed the silver tray on a low table. "Sugar, Mynheer?"

"Please. . . . Fury, I have something I want you to look at."

"You sound very mysterious," Fury said lightly. She could feel Juli stiffen in the study doorway.

"When Señor Domingo first told me of the attack on his father's ship, the *Spanish Princess*, I was, of course, skeptical, as were the other men in town. But when he described the woman so carefully, I had to pay strict attention. For he *was* describing the Sea Siren—or at least the Sea Siren whose picture hung in the Dutch East India offices." Fury nodded to show she was following the manager's story.

"Well," Dykstra continued, "several days ago I was rummaging in my desk for something and came across this miniature painting of your parents, one your father gave me when he moved his family to Spain. I don't know what possessed me to alter this, but I did. Would you like to see it?"

Fury nodded, struggling to control her emotions. She knew full well Dykstra was watching her with sharp eyes.

"But this is outrageous, Mynheer!" she exploded a moment later. "My father will never forgive you for your . . . suspicions. You're making my mother out to be the Sea Siren! Where did you come by such an idea? No, no, it isn't possible."

"It's not only possible, it's probable," Dykstra declared. "And I'll take that probability one step further. I think you've taken her place."

Fury had the presence of mind to look astonished. "But why? After all these years, why would you think . . . for what purpose? Oh, it's too preposterous to even give credence . . . I'm appalled, Mynheer, that you would even *think* me—"

"Mynheer, where would Miss Fury get the Sea Siren's ship?" Juli interrupted, forgetting her place. "It's been said it was scuttled, rotting at the bottom of the sea. And Miss Fury has never left this house except to go into town. You can speak with any of the other servants if you don't believe me."

Dykstra ignored the housekeeper's outburst, his eyes on Fury and the color creeping into her cheeks.

"Mynheer Dykstra, it's a coincidence that I'm here in Batavia at this time," Fury continued, wary now. "I was to enter the convent, but matters were taken out of my hands when the sisters were sent away. There was nothing I could do. I'm waiting for my parents to return from the Americas later this year."

"When one practices to deceive, one must spin a web of lies and enlist cohorts to aid and abet the deception," Dykstra said gently.

Fury's eyes were furious as she stood to show the evening was at an end. "May I ask to whom you have told this ridiculous tale?"

Dykstra rose as well. "I'm afraid that's my business, Furana. From now on this house will be watched. Once and for all we will discover the Sea Siren's identity."

"How dare you!" Fury gasped. "Please leave this house—now! I will never forgive you, nor will my mother. My father's wrath I leave to you!"

The moment the door closed behind the Dutchman, Juli ran to Fury. "My God, how did he find out? What are we to do? If he has the house watched . . ."

"I suppose it's down the trellis for me under dark of night," Fury said shakily.

Juli giggled. "This is so exciting! Just like when your mother was roaming the seas. I never knew what each new day would bring. I knew it was going to be like before; I just *knew* it!"

"It's not as simple as Mynheer Dykstra makes it sound," Fury said thoughtfully. "I think there's more to all of this than he's let on. He and my father have been friends for over thirty years. Why is he turning on us like this? It doesn't make sense . . . unless he feels he's going to be passed over for the governorship, and is trying somehow to build up his reputation at my expense. He never would have dared to say such things, much less even think them, if my father were here. Do you think my defense of the Sea Siren was too strong?"

"Justly so." Juli shrugged. "He can't prove anything. Even if he suspects, he has no proof. For now you will simply do what your mother did when things became . . . difficult."

"What did she do?" Fury demanded.

"Took to her bed and said she was on a religious retreat. Locked her door and went down the trellis and out to the cove." Juli smiled, remembering. "The more dangerous it was, the better she seemed to like it. She positively bloomed when she was 'on a mission,' as she called it."

Fury placed a hand on Juli's arm, bringing her back to the present. "You said you had something to tell me?" she said gently.

Juli frowned. "I had something to . . . Oh, yes! And very important it is, too. My second brother's wife, Drucilla, cooks for a gem merchant's family in town. It seems this merchant has a brother in town who is also a gem merchant. Drucilla told me she overheard the merchant talking to Mynheer Dykstra about a shipment of *thirty* pounds of diamonds that is due to arrive here any day now."

Juli paused for breath. "Now, let me see if I remember this," she continued slowly. "It seems the diamonds belong to the Viceroy of Karwar, Dom Ignacio Carlos Xavier de Reness, third count of Surat. The merchant said the count obtained the diamonds in private trading and signed aboard as a paying passenger. It's the *Nightstar* and due to make port, as I said. She carries a very valuable cargo of Chinese silks, porcelain, textiles, and all manner of exotic products. Drucilla said the plan was to sew the diamonds into the count's clothing so that, in case of a pirate attack, only the cargo will be plundered. The count will be disguised as a seaman. It's his intention to return to Spain, where he hopes to restore his family's fortunes. But that's not all, Miss Fury!'' she cried as Fury opened her mouth to speak. ''Drucilla says Mynheer Dykstra has asked Señor Domingo to *pose* as the count and carry the diamonds himself. What do you think of that!''

Fury sank down onto one of the chairs, stunned. ''Thirty pounds of diamonds! If they're perfect gemstones, they'll be worth a king's ransom. That must mean the Dutch East India Company is accepting responsibility for safe transport. Obviously the count, whoever he is, is not capable of fending off deadly pirates if Señor Domingo is to assume his identity.''

''Has this information helped at all, Miss Fury?'' Juli asked anxiously.

Fury massaged her temples to ward off the headache she felt coming on. ''Matters like this have a way of becoming public knowledge. I don't think I would wager my diamond garter that the bogus Sea Siren is ignorant of this news.'' She rose and began to pace the study floor.

''All those diamonds,'' she muttered. ''Perhaps I should think along the lines of an escort for the *Nightstar*. I'll stay a respectable distance, and none need know I'm sailing a protective course. At the same time, I'll be returning home to Spain, for I seriously doubt my parents will come here to Java. . . . Yes, yes, I think I've arrived at the perfect solution.'' She turned to Juli. ''What to you think?''

Tears gathered in the housekeeper's eyes. ''You are your

mother's daughter through and through," she said softly. "I truly believe she would have made the same decision. I understand your desire to return home. And I am proud and happy to be a part of all this."

There was no doubt in Fury's mind that she could provide safe conduct for the faceless count and his diamond fortune, and Luis Domingo. No doubt at all.

At midmorning the following day a white-uniformed djongo arrived at the casa. He shuffled his bare feet, his eyes cast downward while he waited for Juli to take the invitation he held out to her.

Fury raised her eyebrows as she read, a smile tugging at the corners of her mouth. "Fetch me a pen," she ordered one of the maids.

"A soiree," Juli said, peering over Fury's shoulder. "The entire board of governors of the Dutch East India Company. What does it mean?"

"I think they are ready to choose my father's replacement, and since the logical choice is Mynheer Dykstra, they'll want my views—or rather, my father's views," Fury replied, scribbling a note of acceptance and thanks to her hostess, Matilda von Klausner. "Which might or might not explain his actions last evening. I'll have to think about that later. For now I'll have to think about a gown." She waved the djongo away and closed the door. "Juli, whatever shall I wear? I brought nothing suitable with me."

Hands on her ample hips, the housekeeper peered at Fury with speculative interest. "Are you handy with a needle, Miss Fury?"

Fury shook her head. "Are you?"

"I'm afraid not. And a week isn't very much time."

"Is there any material in my mother's trunks?"

"Oh, yes. There are two bolts of China silk that are

exquisite. Both are in perfect condition, but what good
will it do us?''

"What about your brothers' wives?'' Fury asked hopefully.

Juli snorted. "They mend. Where would they learn how
to sew for fine ladies? No, there is no one—not even in
town. Every seamstress will be overworked.''

"Then we must improvise,'' Fury said briskly. "Show
me the material. Perhaps something will come to us.''

"Something?''

"A solution,'' Fury said tightly.

"Hrumph.'' Juli snorted.

Minutes later Fury's bedroom was draped with the costly
bolts of material, one an emerald silk shot through with
silver, the second a lovely plum embroidered with gold
thread. "The emerald one, I think,'' Fury said, frowning.
"The plum is lovely, but I prefer the green. You were right,
Juli, it's magnificent! Now, if we just put our minds to it, I
think we can come up with a solution. . . .''

An hour later the two women were still staring at each
other and the fabric. Suddenly Fury gathered the handsome bolt of emerald silk and draped it around her entire
body. She swayed seductively for Juli's benefit. "What do
you think?''

"That's perfect, Miss Fury! A sari, the kind women of
India wear. We won't have to sew at all,'' Juli said in
relief, "providing we can cut a straight line with the scis-
sors.'' The brilliant silk was unwrapped and rewrapped
around Fury's slender form. "See, we'll drape this here
as a sleeve of sorts to cover your scarred arm. Your other
arm and shoulder will be bare. You can wear the diamond
garter on your bare arm, like this,'' she said, circling Fury's upper arm with her hand. "And diamonds in your
ears will add just the right touch. What do you think?''

Fury grinned. "I think I wouldn't be able to get along

without you. If we make a fringe at the edge, we won't even have to sew a hem. It's absolutely perfect.'' Fury pirouetted slowly, glancing behind her to catch the effect of the billowing fabric. ''I wonder if I will know anyone at the soiree beside Mynheer Dykstra and a few of the governors,'' she mused.

''I'm sure Señor Domingo will be there,'' Juli said slyly.

''That would be nice, I'm sure. He's never seen me in anything as breathtaking as this. The dress I wore to my birthday ball was fashionable, but of schoolgirl quality. And at our dinner I wore one of Mother's gowns. This will be something that will—''

''Make *his* blood sing,'' Juli giggled. ''We'll have to give you an elaborate hairdo and color your lips and cheeks as well.''

''For a public appearance?'' Fury gasped.

''Of course. Your mother loved to shock the local inhabitants. And she succeeded time and again. Your father would turn white with jealousy when men dropped at her feet. Yet he knew in his heart she was his. It was a game they played. Your father would huff and puff, and your mother would flirt so outrageously, it was sinful. It was all so wonderful back then.'' Juli sighed happily with her memories.

Fury sank down on the bed. ''I want to be like my mother, but I want to be myself, too,'' she said slowly. ''All the things I know about her and all the things you've been telling me confuse me sometimes. I don't want to impersonate her, Juli. On shipboard it's different, but not here. I have to be me, Fury.''

''But you are!'' Juli exclaimed. ''You picked the fabric you most admired. Your coiffure will be of your own choice. The garter is yours; your mother never wore one. It will be Fury van der Rhys who attends the soiree, not your mother.''

Fury hugged the older woman. "Thank you, Juli, you're a wonderful friend. I truly appreciate your help."

"It's my pleasure, Miss Fury."

Somehow Fury managed to while away the rest of the day walking in the garden and reading from an old book of poetry. She fed the hawks and had an early dinner, then retired to the privacy of her bedchamber.

As she undressed, she realized that she'd lied to Juli earlier when she'd said she was tired. She wasn't the least bit tired. In fact, she felt more alive—now, this minute— than she'd felt at any time since arriving in Batavia. She'd learned something, something she needed to think about seriously.

The silky sheet pulled up to her chin, Fury braced herself in her nest of pillows, the heady flower-scented evening air wafting through the open balcony doors to tease her nostrils. Now, at last, she thought she knew the answers to the questions that had plagued her all her life.

She loved her mother and as a child had tried to emulate her, taking pleasure in the compliments that compared her prettiness with her mother's. "So like your mother in every way." In every way . . . except one. In the beginning she'd savored the comparisons, especially when her father uttered them, but she always knew in her heart that there was only one Sirena. And at some point after the death of her brothers, she'd consciously tried to change her physical appearance—her hair, her nails, her mode of dress. But she couldn't change her features. With each passing day, she grew more and more to resemble her mother. Her expertise with the rapier, her sailing skill, all as good as her mother's. Her social graces she knew now had been sabotaged deliberately . . . by herself.

Her decision to enter the convent had been a last attempt to reclaim her own identity—to herself, not Sirena van der Rhys's daughter, not an exact replica of her mother, but

Furana van der Rhys, postulant, novitiate, and finally nun. Fully, totally committed to God.

All those prayers, all the rosaries, all the sore knees, weren't for God, they were for her—selfish prayers that would allow her to be separate from her glamorous, glorious mother. And the more her parents had argued with her, the more determined she'd been.

Fury sat up in bed as the hawks called gently to her from the balcony railing.

"Yes," she murmured as she crept from the bed. "You knew, didn't you. I don't know how, but you did; otherwise you wouldn't have followed me. You've been wonderful—true and loyal friends to me." She reached out to stroke them. "I don't know if I am meant for the convent. Perhaps it was an excuse for me to find a life for myself, a life of my own. I love my mother, but I don't want to be her. I want her to be proud of me for my own accomplishments. Clearing her name is something only I can do. And with your help I know I can succeed."

She laughed ruefully. "You see, I'm still uncertain how far my abilities will carry me. I've never had a price on my head, and I've never fought a life-or-death duel. I know I don't want to die, at least not yet. I want to love and be loved. I want my blood to sing when I wake in the morning, and I want it to be singing when I fall asleep at night next to the man I love, but my commitment to God . . . I don't suppose you understand a thing I've been saying, and that's all right as long as you're here. It's taken me ages to learn about myself, and tonight was my time to begin."

Gaspar's wing tip fluttered softly as it inched up to caress Fury's cheek. Not to be outdone, Pilar stretched and spread her wing around Fury's shoulder, her glittering eyes warning Gaspar that this was a woman's moment. Fury laughed with delight when Gaspar inched his way down the balcony. "Thank you," she crooned, then gently made *swoosh*ing motions with her hands for the birds to retire for the night.

Sleep proved to be elusive, however. So many words, so many thoughts . . . The explanation was too simple, Fury thought in dismay. How could she wipe away her commitment to God and the church in just a few hours, and with mere words?

Instantly contrite, she leaned over the side of the bed and fumbled for her rosary on the night table. "Holy Father, I haven't forsaken You," she prayed. "For so long I believed . . . still believe I am meant to serve You in whatever capacity I can. I will never again believe that You have forsaken me, this I swear. You are all about me. Show me what it is You want me to do. I can give up this life, I know I can. Forgive me, Merciful Father, for my sins. . . ."

The week passed slowly for Fury. She was aware of the men watching the casa and herself but refused to be intimidated by them. Each day she saddled Starlight and rode out to the rise to gaze down upon the *Rana*. She did nothing out of the ordinary, however, and Juli always reported to her when she returned that the men had not left their posts. She felt she was setting up a valuable pattern from which to draw on in the coming days.

On the morning of the soiree she sat gazing longingly at the bolt of China silk in her bedroom. She couldn't wait to be wrapped in its silky softness; she wanted to feel a man's arms—Luis Domingo's arms—about her, crooning sweet words under a bright moon and winking stars. She wanted so to attend this soiree, wanted to see Luis Domingo again. She wanted . . . craved . . . needed . . .

It was possible she was tormenting herself needlessly, for she didn't know if the handsome Spaniard would even be there. But that possibility was too painful to contemplate. He simply *had* to be.

Fury could feel tears of shame stinging her eyes at her lustful thoughts. But she couldn't stop them. Over and over she wondered what it would be like to make love with Luis Domingo.

"You aren't considered a real woman until you bed a man, and it doesn't matter if you're married or not," a school friend had whispered once. She had been the most knowledgeable about the man-woman union, as she called it, although neither Fury nor the other girls at the convent school had ever challenged her as to the source of her knowledge. "Men's tongues are like weapons on a woman's body," the young lady had declared authoritatively, adding that women had to be as aggressive as men in bed and make known their wants. "You must tell them what feels good, here and here," she said, pointing to various parts of her anatomy. "Can you imagine letting a man undress you and looking at *all* of your naked body!" Fury *could* imagine, and *that* had been the problem.

She was startled from her burning thoughts when Juli poked her head in the doorway. "Everything is ready, Miss Fury. My brother brought your garter from the ship early this morning. We should be leaving soon. You did say you wanted to stop by the parish house to see Father Sebastian. The sooner we start, the sooner you'll be conversing with the *padre*," she said cheerfully. "We can ask him if Señor Domingo will attend. Surely he'll know."

"It's of no importance," Fury said, as if it made no difference to her whatsoever. She could feel Juli's eyes on her but refused to meet her gaze.

"Of course it's important," the housekeeper chided. "You will be the most beautiful, sought-after young lady at this soiree. All of Batavia will be talking about the stunning, exquisite Señorita van der Rhys. I want that

Spaniard's eyes to pop from his head when he sees you. You wouldn't be a woman if you didn't want the same thing.''

Woman . . . Fury's heart thumped in her chest. ''You make it sound like a contest,'' she grumbled.

Juli nodded. ''In a manner of speaking it is. All the women try to outshine one another. And there is always a winner. Men flock around you in droves, they shoot daggers with their eyes at their friends when they're luckier than themselves, and you favor them with a dance. Even the married men have roving eyes. My advice is to flirt outrageously with one and all. With the ladies who will want to scratch your eyes out, be demure and polite, respectful of their ages and their corsets.'' This last bit of advice sent Fury into peals of laughter. Juli grinned. ''But if you plan on taking a breath of air, make sure it's with Señor Domingo and no one else, or tongues will wag for weeks. You want only the most handsome, the most eligible man, and he is the catch of the season.''

''There is one problem I think we've both overlooked,'' Fury said, standing. ''How am I to dance in this tight dress we've created? I can just see it unraveling while I'm on the dance floor. My petticoat will be such a shock.''

''Petticoat . . . petticoat . . . you don't wear a petticoat with . . . absolutely not. You'll look . . . fat and dumpy, like the ladies with corsets. No, no, no, the material must swirl and drape, there is no room for underpinnings.''

''None?'' Fury gulped. ''What if it comes loose by some . . . fluke . . . men are so clumsy . . . my God, I didn't think . . . no, I must wear . . . stop laughing, Juli. I could be exposed . . . good Lord, now what am I to do?'' Fury wailed.

''It's too late to do anything, so you might as well stop fretting about what *could* happen and concentrate on making it not happen. If you really don't want to dance, say you hurt your ankle. You'll think of something," Juli said loftily.

Fury's stomach turned sour when she thought of herself dancing unaware of the emerald silk unwinding until she was stark naked in Luis Domingo's arms, the guests hooting with delight. Dear God. She must have been crazy to accept this invitation and go along with Juli's idea for the dress—or was it her idea—damnation, she couldn't remember anything today. She turned to Juli and said sweetly, "I will personally throttle you with my bare hands if this dress so much as moves on my body." Juli blanched and shrugged.

"If it does, there will be hundreds of men wanting to make an honest woman of you." She almost hoped it would happen; nothing would stir up the party like a naked woman. Then she thought about Fury's promise. "I forgot to tell you that my brother said the prettiest girls from . . . you know, Clarice's place, are to be among the governors' escorts. Can you imagine! Of course the town *ladies* don't know they've been invited, because this time, it seems, the men are organizing the soiree." Juli laughed and clapped her hands with glee. "I can't wait to see the expressions on the faces of those dowagers!"

The town whores at the soiree! Fury felt light-headed. Father Sebastian had said Naula was the prettiest of Clarice's girls. Certainly she would be at the soiree on the arm of one of the governors. The idea of Clarice's girls at the party was so outrageous, Fury found herself laughing.

"I can't imagine what protocol is in a matter such as this," she sputtered, wiping her eyes. "Does one acknowledge them? No doubt the governors will expect a certain amount of . . . camaraderie among the women! My God, Juli, I never would have believed this. Perhaps there's no need for us to stop by the parish house now— undoubtedly Father Sebastian will be attending the soiree himself, if for no other reason than to keep the guests from tearing one another apart!''

While the two women laughed about Father Sebastian's role at the soiree, the good *padre* himself was finding nothing amusing in the situation, although he knew he could perform his duties as long as he kept his gaze lowered. However, it wasn't the evening's festivities that bothered him, but the letter he held in his hand.

The words on the stiff, crackly parchment were already committed to memory, but still he opened the letter and read it again, fingering the heavy gold seal that identified to the reader, as surely as the cramped, narrow script and ponderous signature, the source of the correspondence. The elderly priest was sorry that he'd petitioned the archbishop himself to grant Fury entrance to the convent. That permission had now been granted, thanks to his pleas—temporary entrance two weeks from Sunday.

Sighing, he slid the letter between the pages of his Bible and plodded wearily into the kitchen. Why couldn't he have left well enough alone? Now he would have to tell Furana . . . and he didn't want to.

"Say the rosary, say the rosary," came a squawk from the kitchen windowsill. "Pray for the living, pray for the dead. Sins are the devil's work, oh, yes, oh, yes, praypraypray!''

"Shut up," the priest grumbled, glaring up at the brightly plumed caged parrot. A moment later he hurried off as a knock sounded at his front door.

It was Furana and her housekeeper. Father Sebastian's eyes flew to his Bible. Not today; he couldn't tell her today. Tomorrow, perhaps, or the day after. "Lies are sinful, lies are sinful!" the parrot screeched as the priest opened the door.

"What a wonderful surprise," Father Sebastian said

hoarsely. "Thank you," he said, taking a basket of food from Juli. "I'll just take this inside." He made his way down the hallway to the kitchen, where he immediately threw a rag over the parrot's cage.

"Death to all sinners!" shrieked the bird before darkness descended.

"Tea, ladies?" the priest asked, returning to the parlor.

"No, Father, we stopped only to deliver this basket. We're on our way to Mevrouw von Klausner's house for the soiree this evening. I trust you will be there to give the opening blessing," Fury said, biting her lips to keep from laughing.

"Yes. I was rather surprised, but then, I am the only religious in town at this time. Tonight is . . . uh, rather unusual, but they—the governors, that is—have asked me specifically . . . and they have been most kind to many of my poor, unfortunate parishioners. . . ."

"Will Señor Domingo be in attendance?" Juli asked, rescuing the poor man from his obvious discomfort.

"Why, yes, I believe so. He was in port yesterday. I'm sure he will be there. Nau—uh, he needs some respite, as do most men."

Fury took pity on the priest. "Perhaps you shouldn't attend. I know it's going to be difficult for you. I could explain to Mevrouw von Klausner that you aren't feeling well."

Father Sebastian smiled warmly. "It's kind of you, Furana, but I'll be fine. You ladies had best run along now. I know how much time it takes for you to prepare yourselves for these occasions."

"Thank you, Father. Rest now, we can see ourselves out. And Father," Fury called over her shoulder, "I know your blessing will be appreciated by . . . everyone."

"Poor dear," she murmured as they made their way to the von Klausner house at the end of the street. "He's so torn between what is right and wrong. He will suffer torments over this." She giggled.

"We're going to be the first to arrive," Juli grumbled. "Your mother always said it was fashionable to be late, and people pay more attention when you're the last to arrive. Our timing is . . . inadequate."

Fury shrugged. "Even if we're the first to arrive, I can make sure I am the last to be announced. It makes no difference." *He's going to be here,* she thought, heart pounding. *I'll see him again.*

Excitement coursed through Fury as a clutch of djongos carried their small satchels and escorted them to their assigned rooms.

"Missy wish bath?" the djongo queried.

"Yes." Juli nodded briskly as she set about laying Fury's clothing on the bed. "Quickly, quickly." She frowned as the djongo minced his way out the door.

Fury's transformation was about to begin.

Every nerve in Luis Domingo's body quivered with exasperation at his circumstances. Here he was sitting aboard the *Silver Lady* smoking a cigar like one of Batavia's fat merchants instead of sailing the sea searching for the Sea Siren. He had Dykstra and the brood of governors from Amsterdam to thank for his idleness. Thanks to Dykstra, he would also be attending the soiree at the von Klausner house, an affair he wasn't looking forward to. He wasn't in the mood to salivate over coy woman and dominating mothers who thought him a good catch for their aging daughters. Of course he could have refused the invitation and sailed on the early tide, but he hadn't. The Dutch East India Company had hired him, and in their employ he would do as instructed.

Luis's stance, as he leaned against the mainmast, was one of unconscious grace. He blew a perfect smoke ring as he stared out at the deep blue of the ocean. He itched to take the wheel and sail until he came to the mouth of the River of Death. Nothing would stop him tomorrow; he would sail with the tide—under his own colors or those of the Dutch East India Company.

He hated to admit it, but he had the feeling that something was about to go awry, something he had no control over. He gazed out to sea, shielding his eyes against the sun's brilliant glare, searching for something—anything— that might give him a clue. He felt as though he were carrying a hundred-pound yoke on his shoulders, and he didn't like the feeling.

The sun dimmed momentarily, and Luis glanced upward. The sky had been blue without a trace of a cloud. He sucked in his breath as two dark shapes, wings spread, flew directly overhead, blocking the sun. *The goddamn black birds!* He swiveled to follow them with his eyes and was stunned a moment later to see them nest in the breadfruit tree at the von Klausner house. "Son of a bitch!" he muttered.

The hundred-pound yoke disappeared. The Sea Siren— the real one or the impostor—was nearby, either on land or hiding in a deepwater cove. He cursed himself for allowing Dykstra to talk him out of sailing to the River of Death. Instantly he was off the *Silver Lady* and boarding the ship he'd just brought into port yesterday. In moments he had his maps and charts out of their goatskin protection, his narrowed gaze tracing the route he would take tomorrow.

Nothing had changed since he'd looked at them last. Again his finger traced the route, up the river, farther, farther, until he came to the deepwater cove he was certain sequestered the deadly, sleek black ship captained by the Sea Siren. She was close; *this* was what he'd been feeling. Once again his finger traced the cove, this time until he came to the wide half-circle and solid wall of rock and jungle on each side. There was no reason to *sail* up the River of Death, he realized. He could ride at least part of the way and use his feet the rest of the time. He could leave now and find that goddamn black ship before nightfall. He had to. Time was his enemy, with the Spanish ship due in any day.

It was the diamonds, of course. She was after the diamonds, so there was no point in wasting his time searching her out; *she* would find *them*. And she was here: he could feel her. Close, by God, she was so close!

Fifteen minutes later Luis was riding hard. An hour later he realized he was hopelessly lost. All about him was steaming verdant jungle. To his eye, there was no sign of a trail or footpath. The horse, lathered and panting, was about ready to drop. Luis looked upward at the startling blue sky, expecting to see the black birds circling overhead. But the expanse remained serene and beautiful.

Ten minutes later he dismounted and tethered the weary animal. The blazing sun beat down on him as he struck out on foot, his hands ripping and beating back the choking jungle growth. Time soon lost all meaning, but he tramped on regardless. At one point he was aware the sun was well over his shoulder and that he should start back. Another thirty minutes, he pleaded with himself, just thirty more minutes.

Suddenly he found himself sniffing like a dog at a smell he would have recognized anywhere. Water . . . wonderful, glorious water. And something else: the faint sound of voices. He dropped to a near crouch and inched his way to the small sandy beach directly ahead of him. A cove, probably one of many, but would the Siren's ship be anchored in this quiet spot? He slithered to the edge of the beach under full cover of the thick, lush foliage.

Luis's heart thundered in his chest until he was certain

the men laughing aboard the black frigate would hear it. Black frigate. The Sea Siren's ship! His eyes searched out the battering ram on the bow. That he would never forget! By God, he'd found it, he'd succeeded where hundreds of others had failed.

He strained to hear what the voices were saying, then blinked in disbelief. They were having a discussion about children and furniture! Chatting and drinking coffee from a huge iron pot on deck. These were not common seamen. Christ, was it possible he'd made a mistake? He continued to listen, one eye on the setting sun.

A deep, pleasant laugh carried across the water as one of the men discussed his sister. The others seemed to know her, for only complimentary words were being used. Was the sister the Sea Siren? Luis wondered. A moment later he knew he'd found the right ship when another of the men mentioned "the *capitana*" and the sister in the same breath. "Even if she feeds those devil birds for the *capitana*, she's as fearful of them as we are." There was a chorus of agreement among the men. Luis found himself pounding the ground triumphantly. "I wonder if the birds will chaperone the party this evening," the man continued. "Can you picture that scene?"

Luis had heard enough. He crawled backward until he felt it was safe to stand erect. Then he spun around and tore down the path he'd created earlier. The inky night settled about him just as he sighted his horse. Breathing raggedly, he leaned against the animal's broad flanks.

By God, he'd found her . . . almost. He'd found her ship, and that was every bit as good as finding the she-devil herself. All he had to do, he thought as he climbed into the saddle, was alert the Dutch East India Company and block the entrance to the River of Death. Position men all along the perimeter of the cove to cut off any means of escape. Then he'd have her!

A sudden thought made him rein in the horse. Which one *was* she? Who was the real Siren—the one with the damn black birds or the other one? Both women had a scar; he felt somehow confident of that, although he hadn't seen them and had felt only one for sure. But on which arm? That was the secret . . . which arm? Left? Right?

Angrily Luis wiped his sweating forehead with his shirtsleeve as he spurred the horse onward. By night's end he'd have his answer. And he would remain quiet and not tell Mynheer Dykstra what he'd just discovered. For now.

The moment he reached the smithy he slid from the horse's back and handed the animal to a stable boy. He raced down the street to the town's one boardinghouse. Inside, he shouted for a hot bath as he flew up the staircase, ripping at his shirt along the way.

The startled bath boy rolled his eyes heavenward when Luis started to whistle. The señor was a happy man, he decided as pail after pail of water doused the Spaniard.

Luis was still whistling when, one hour later, he strolled down the plank streets dressed in a natty white linen suit, a fragrant cigar between his fingers. He was the only man to have found the Siren's lair, the only man. The knowledge was more powerful than any aphrodisiac.

Yes, Luis Domingo was a happy man.

Chapter Ten

Juli clapped her hands to shoo the von Klausner servants from the room with their empty water pails. She turned to Fury, who was sitting on a stool wrapped in a length of soft sheeting. "And now, Señorita van der Rhys, it is time to turn you into the most ravishing creature in all of Batavia. First, your hair. . . . Hmm, you smell divine, better than the entire garden at the casa."

Fury watched in the mirror as her hair was pulled and tugged, swirled and twirled, until she was barely able to recognize herself in the pier glass. Suddenly she was totally different from the proper young lady who had graced her previous life. She held her breath as Juli touched coloring to her cheeks and blended it on her high cheekbones.

"Now, do this," the housekeeper said, stretching her mouth into a wide grimace. She ran her index finger deftly over Fury's lips and blotted the excess. "See how white your teeth look against the color of your lips? Perfect! Just perfect," she pronounced. "And now the earrings. . . . "

A moment later Fury took a look at herself and gasped. "I don't look like me *or* my mother!"

"That's why it's perfect. Men will be groveling at your feet, all those crusty old Dutch governors with their . . . women. Señor Domingo will probably drag you off to his ship in front of everyone and make wild, passionate love to you all night long," Juli predicted, grinning.

Fury giggled. The prospect was not without appeal, although she didn't say so to Juli.

Musical chords from the spinet in the ballroom wafted upward to drift through the open French doors. "I do believe the party is beginning," Juli said. "Even up here I can hear the guests being announced. Oh, Miss Fury, you will create a stir when you walk in alone, more regal than any queen. Quickly now, we must drape this silk to perfection. I have it timed perfectly. Don't squirm, don't even move," she ordered. Fury's face burned as Juli deftly wrapped the luxurious silk all about her naked body. The housekeeper had insisted she wear no undergarments at all, and she'd been right: no matter how thin, they would have thrown off the look of the fashioned gown.

"Short steps only, Miss Fury." Juli walked slowly around Fury, inspecting every curve with a critical eye. "You can do it. Just remember that every woman in the room will be green with jealousy, and every man desperate for your favors. And now I have a surprise for you," she said, her eyes fairly dancing with excitement. "When I went downstairs for extra bath sheeting, I peeked at those little cards for the dinner guests, and guess who your partner is! Señor Domingo!"

Fury's heart began to pound. That meant she would have the handsome Spaniard all to herself for well over an hour. She laughed delightedly and pirouetted for Juli's benefit.

Juli tapped her chin with a stubby finger. "By next week I do believe we could sell this creation by the hundreds. We're the only ones who know it hasn't been sewn. We should give it serious thought. Now, remember, short steps or you'll fall flat on your face," she said tartly.

Fury twirled one last time in front of the pier glass, her

eyes drinking in the sight of her long, slender form. Suddenly the room was awash with sound and motion as the hawks swooped in to perch on the bedposts. Fury affected a low, sweeping bow, and Pilar fanned her wings in approval. Gaspar tilted his head to the side, then sailed across the room to land on the dressing table. He extended one claw, and Fury saw something sparkle in the clutch of his talon.

"The garter!" Juli cried. "You get it, Miss Fury. I'm not going near those birds."

Fury held out her hand, and Gaspar dropped the diamond garter into her palm. "They love anything that glitters," she said with fond indulgence as she fastened the garter on her upper arm. "Now what?" she asked Juli as the diamond circlet slipped to her wrist. "It's too big. . . . "

"Allow me." Juli unfastened the garter, one eye on the hawks as they watched her every movement. "See, we'll fasten it higher and move it to catch on this link. The little tail will be on the inside of your arm. No one will notice. . . . There! It's perfectly exquisite!"

Pilar's wings rustled and fanned out as she lifted herself up to hover above Juli and Fury. Gently, one wing tip lowered to tickle Fury's cheek. Gaspar flapped his wings until he, too, had a suitable draft to rise, and then both birds *swoosh*ed through the open doors leading to the balcony. Juli sighed with obvious relief as she ushered Fury to the bedroom door.

"Have a wonderful time, Miss Fury," she said, giving her a hug. "I'll try to peek from the landing."

Fury blessed herself as she walked out to the staircase that led to the wide central foyer. She told herself she was a make-believe fairy princess on her way to a ball where she would meet a handsome prince—and that was exactly what she was doing, she thought triumphantly.

Fury drew a deep breath when the von Klausners'

houseman announced, "Señorita Furana van der Rhys. . . ." She heard the collective gasp as she made her way down the receiving line—and she reveled in it. Head held high, she moved off to the right side of the room so designated for ladies, where she was immediately claimed by a gallant Spanish don who insisted on fetching her a glass of wine. While she waited for him to return, she allowed her eyes to search the room for a glimpse of Luis Domingo.

At the moment of Fury's announced entrance to the ball, Luis Domingo was being introduced to the board of governors from the Dutch East India Company and their charming escorts. He made a show of bowing elaborately over Naula's hand and received a brazen wink in return. Chuckling, he straightened—just in time to witness Fury's entrance.

"Regan's daughter," murmured one of the governors.

A second nodded appreciatively. "Exquisite creature. More beautiful than her mother. . . ."

"Magnificent gown, and I know nothing about women's clothes," pronounced a third governor.

The ladies, too, had much to say with their eyes and low-voiced mutterings.

"The gown must have cost a fortune. . . ."

"Absolutely nothing underneath . . ."

"Flawless gems . . . worth a king's ransom . . ."

"Scandalous use of face color . . ."

And then Naula's statement put it all in perspective for Luis:

"If that gorgeous silk were mine, I'd have made it Chinese style with an opening up to here." She pointed to the middle of her slender thigh. "Just high enough for a garter to show through the opening when I took a step."

Instantly Luis excused himself and made his way across

the room to Fury. His heart pumped furiously as he bowed low over her hand, his dark eyes glittering with admiration. Christ, she was beautiful. More beautiful than any woman he'd ever met. And possibly more dangerous as well. It was time to find out.

"Señor Domingo, how nice to see you again," Fury murmured. Her blood wasn't just singing, it was boiling in her veins.

"And I you," Luis said gallantly. "But don't you think it's time you called me Luis?"

The laughter around his eyes puzzled Fury, but she smiled and nodded. "Will you be in port long?" she asked. The handsome don, approaching with a long-stemmed goblet, glowered at Luis, then abruptly changed course and drank the wine himself.

Luis smiled. "I think I just intimidated the man who was fetching your wine. My apologies. Would you like me to—"

"No, thank you. He was merely being polite. It must be obvious to you, Señ—Luis, that the ladies here this evening are . . ."

"Jealous? But of course. They pale beside you, and isn't that something no woman wants to have happen?"

"I wouldn't know," Fury said airily.

Luis laughed. "Come now, I thought every woman"— he emphasized the word—"recognized envy as the highest form of flattery, particularly when exhibited by members of her own sex. Would you like to hear a bit of gossip concerning your gown?" he teased.

"Oh, dear, am I perhaps too . . . ?" She glanced down at herself in sudden apprehension.

"On the contrary. All of the . . . ah, governors' *escorts* were breathless with their comments. The one with black hair said if she had a length of silk, she would have fashioned it Chinese style, with a slit up to here, and worn a *garter*. The others seemed to agree with her taste.'' Luis watched Fury's eyes for any sign of agitation.

''How interesting,'' Fury said coolly. ''And what is your opinion?'' *My God, he knows, and he's baiting me. Damn you, Gaspar, if it weren't for you, I would have forgotten to wear this bauble.*

Luis pretended embarrassment. ''I like a length of thigh as much as the next man. I think I'd vote for the garter. They must be all the rage in feminine wear. The Sea Siren wears one. But then,'' he added lightly, ''women are creatures of whimsy, and fashions change so quickly these days. Don't you agree?''

''Absolutely.'' By now Fury wanted desperately to flee but knew she had to brazen this out and pretend to take Luis's words at face value. ''I think I would like that wine after all, Luis. If you don't mind . . .''

''It will be my pleasure,'' Luis said, and moved off to the far corner of the room.

By God, she *was* the one! He had her now *and* the place where she kept her ship. As he waited for a white-liveried waiter to pour wine into two long-stemmed crystal goblets, he began to laugh, remembering the look on Fury's face when he mentioned the garter. She thinks I suspect, but she isn't sure, he reflected. By God, it was the coup of the century!

Suddenly he sobered, recalling that whatever her game was, Fury van der Rhys—the Sea Siren of the diamond garter and black birds—hadn't harmed him when they'd met at sea. She'd merely said *she* had come out of retirement to seek the woman posing as herself, and he hadn't believed her. It was the other one, the impostor, who'd plundered his ships and then accosted him a second time. Christ, he was going mad with all this subterfuge!

''Thank you,'' Fury said demurely when he returned

with her wine. "I don't believe you responded when I asked how long you'll be in port."

"Another day at least. I have something I must do tomorrow, and if I finish, I'll sail with the tide."

Fury smiled. "You make it all sound so . . . mysterious."

"I suppose it is in a way. I think I've discovered, and this is just between us"—Luis lowered his voice—"the Sea Siren's lair."

Fury's fingers clutched the stem of the wineglass in a white-knuckled grip. "How . . . how interesting. Perhaps you might confide in me? Of course I won't breathe a word. I did live here for some of my younger years. I might know where this lair is."

"Would you believe it's possible to navigate the River of Death? I think that's how the Siren gets away. The volcanoes create a mist, and the steam from them mixes with the river to form a black mist they say she disappears into. Of course, my maps say the mouth of the river has been blocked for years. The volcanoes erupted during the Siren's reign of the seas. That's why she retired; she couldn't travel the river any longer."

"You almost make me believe you, Luis," Fury said sharply. "But everyone knows the river is still blocked. No one is brave enough to take a ship up that river. I think your theory is interesting, but not feasible."

"Tomorrow I plan to test it. The Dutch East India Company has a new sloop that will sail through with ease. I think the river's been open for years now. The currents and tides . . . you see, it's the only explanation."

"Tomorrow, you say?" Fury purred.

Luis nodded. "Tomorrow."

Fury sipped her wine. "Tell me, have you spoken of your theory to anyone else?"

"Good Lord, no. Do you think I want to give away the

biggest coup of my life? Then there's the reward, of course, and handsome it is. But I know I can trust you.''

Fury smiled grimly. "Have no fear, Luis, my lips are sealed.''

"Not forever, I hope,'' Luis said lightly. "Someday I should like to kiss those lips.''

Fury's throat closed, and her eyes smarted with tears. Frantically, she glanced toward the stairway for some sign of Juli.

"Oh, there's one other thing,'' Luis said, watching her intently. Again he lowered his voice. "Apparently the Siren sails with two huge black birds, deadly creatures. This afternoon I saw them fly overhead and nest not far from this very house. That can mean only that the Sea Siren is in one of the coves or inlets off the river. Don't you agree?''

Fury shrugged. "What would I know about such things? Deadly black birds, diamond garters, the River of Death . . . I only hope you aren't wasting your time. They say the Siren can outthink and outmaneuver any man.''

"I've heard that, too,'' Luis said mockingly. "I'll keep it all in mind. Now, would you care for a stroll in the garden? It's much too warm in here. You *can* walk in that dress, can't you?''

"Not very well, but yes, I would like to take a stroll. First, however, I'd like to go to my room for a handkerchief. If you'll wait for me, I'll join you on the veranda.''

It seemed to take Fury forever to make her way across the room and out to the candlelit foyer, where she spotted Juli talking in rapturous tones to the von Klausners' houseman.

"I have to talk to you. Now!'' she spat out, taking Juli by the arm.

"What is it?'' Juli asked, alarmed.

"Luis Domingo knows. He's been baiting me all evening. Somehow he's figured it all out. You have to go to the cove and tell your brothers to take the ship out and down the river. He knows it's no longer blocked, and he said he's going upriver tomorrow. We can't wait until then—it has to be done now! I hate to ask you to do this, but I can't leave, he's too suspicious as it is. I wouldn't put it past him to leave now just to satisfy his own curiosity. For all I know, he may already have been to the cove.''

"Where should I tell my brothers to take the ship? I see you haven't given that any thought. Well, give this some thought, Miss Fury, the man on the steps is starting to make my blood sing.''

"Tomorrow is another day,'' Fury said airily. "I expect you to bring back information. Your brothers have always lived here. Surely they know places. . . . I'll leave it to you, Juli. I have to get back before Luis suspects something. Oh, and Juli, take Gaspar and Pilar with you. Simply tell them to follow you and they will. Go along now,'' she said in her mother's firm voice.

"Dear Aldo, there's something my mistress wants me to do. I'm afraid we'll have to postpone our dinner in the kitchen. Perhaps we could breakfast together if you have a mind to. My mistress is soooo demanding,'' Juli simpered as she backed herself up the stairs. It wasn't till she was all the way to the top of the stairs that she realized she would either have to go down over the balcony or descend the stairs and go past Aldo, who would surely wonder where she was going at that time of night. And where was she to find the damn black birds?

He was so close, she could smell the faint scent of cigar smoke on his clothing, a scent reminiscent of her father. He had her elbow in the palm of his hand as she took dainty little steps in the tight gown. She could feel herself shivering in the warm air, shivers that had nothing to do with the balmy air.

The garden was exquisite, with colorful lanterns illuminating the intricate footpaths. A slight breeze carried the heady scent of jasmine to Fury's nostrils. She began to relax, savoring the feel of the air and the touch of the handsome man walking by her side.

They would miss the board of governors' announcement if they stayed in the garden, she thought, then realized she didn't care if she missed it or not. This was what she wanted. And she didn't want it to end.

Be bold and brash, Fury decided. She bent down to pick up her skirts only to realize there was no excess silk to hike above her ankles. She gave a light tug at the clinging wrapped silk—and immediately toppled over to land flat on her face in the grass. A furious flapping overhead in the darkness made her bury her head in the lush greenery to stifle her laughter. She knew the hawks would circle harmlessly and then return to their perches.

Luis was grinning from ear to ear as he reached down to help her up. "I guess I have to thank you for wearing that scandalous dress, for if it weren't for the dress, I wouldn't be about to . . ."

His lips were so close that Fury could feel his warm breath on her cheek. She closed her eyes in anticipation of the kiss she knew was coming. She wanted him to kiss her, expected it; after all, that's what this evening was all about. Another moment and his lips would be on hers. She would swoon, be all light-headed and warm all over. What was taking him so long? Perhaps he was staring at her, memorizing her face or simply drinking in her beauty. She opened one eye and then the other. He wasn't drinking in her beauty or memorizing her features at all. He was staring at something behind her. Something that was high in the air. The birds! She turned and almost lost her footing a second time. She should have fainted, she thought sourly.

"Isn't that your housekeeper hanging from the balustrade?" Luis drawled.

"My housekeeper!" Fury shrilled. "Absolutely not! Why would my housekeeper hang from . . . that woman doesn't look anything like . . . my . . . my housekeeper. How can you think such a thing? It's a trick of lighting, the lanterns . . ."

"Something seems to be attacking her . . . do you hear that noise?" Luis chuckled deep in his throat, a sound Fury took to be fear. "It must be those damn killer birds! You stay here while I get help!"

"That's not my room!" Fury lied brazenly.

"I don't think that matters right now. What matters is getting the poor woman down before she kills herself. Do you want her death on your conscience?"

"Well, no, but . . . look, she's got a foothold and is . . . she's over the side and back on the balcony. See, your anxiety was for naught. Poor woman was probably trying to get away from . . . from someone," Fury said weakly.

"Did you see those damnable birds?" Luis asked gruffly.

"No, I didn't see any birds, and I could barely see the woman," Fury said huffily. "I think we should go indoors. I feel a chill and I think I have a headache coming on."

"I wonder why that doesn't surprise me," Luis drawled.

"I beg your pardon, what did you say?" Fury asked fretfully as she started to mince her way on the garden path.

"What I said was we should get back to what we were doing before that ridiculous woman decided to escape from her lover."

Fury could feel herself stiffen as Luis gathered her into

his arms. She closed her eyes, knowing this time he *was* memorizing her features. His lips were so close, almost on hers. She could feel her heart begin to pound—or was it his? His lips were soft, gentle, and full of promise. She could feel his hand on her bare arm, the fingers trailing down, down . . . And then those same gentle fingers were on her back and working their way down her draped arm. Another second and they would find their way to the inside portion of her arm.

Suddenly, deep inside her a warning sounded. She didn't want to heed it, she wanted to remain in Luis's warm embrace, their bodies pressed tightly together. But some instinct prompted her to tear herself away. She took a few steps backward, a flustered look on her face, and then ran—ripping at the confining fabric of her gown, loosening it slightly. At the French doors she stopped to regain her composure, then smoothed back her hair and walked into the ballroom.

No one was paying attention to her; all eyes were on the dais, where the governors were about to make their announcement. She heard the words, and later they would sink in, but not now. Dykstra had been passed over for the governorship, and some faceless man she'd never heard of was being mentioned for the position.

He knows, he knows, he knows!

In her room, Fury unwrapped the shimmering emerald silk from her shoulder, tied it to the bedpost, and then twirled until she was standing naked in the darkness. She'd never felt this hot, this burning fire that was consuming her. Fear? Luis Domingo? In minutes she was dressed and on the balcony, peering into the darkness for a vine or trellis. There were none. Heart thudding in her chest, she climbed over the balustrade. Poor Juli. Poor Fury, she thought grimly as she closed her eyes.

* * *

Luis Domingo stood in the shadows, his dark eyes narrowed in amusement. Did she dare to jump? She could kill herself. When he saw her kick off her slippers, he moved out of the shadows and ran, knowing he didn't want the young woman to hurt herself no matter who she was, no matter what she'd done.

Fury squeezed her eyes tight and leapt, her arms flailing the air. At the same moment Luis stretched out his arms and caught her, his body jerking backward with the force of her weight.

"My God . . . what . . ."

"I have to assume this is a new cure for a headache," Luis drawled from beneath her.

"My God . . . what . . ."

"You already said that. . . . I think an explanation is in order, but if you prefer to . . . ah, ignore this situation, I can and will keep my lips sealed."

He knows and he's laughing at me. Sparks spewed from Fury's eyes. Damn, what would her mother have done in a situation like this?

She realized then that her body was literally covering his. She was so close to him, her lips almost on his. "Actually," she murmured in a shaky voice, "I was . . . was looking for you. Obviously you were closer than I realized." She cradled his dark head in her hands and brought her lips to his in a searing kiss that sent shock waves through her entire body. Luis's arms tightened around her, straining to bring her even closer.

She didn't care then if his fingers caressed her arm; she didn't care about anything but his lips on hers. Her body was demanding, ordering her to explore, to search . . . to seek and find.

"No," Luis said hoarsely as he thrust her from him. Fury blinked and looked at him, confused. "You don't know what you're . . . No. I can't. . . ."

Fury blinked again, then shame rushed through her. He'd been playing with her, he didn't want her at all! The kiss was . . . the same kind he'd given the whore Naula. Damn him to hell—he thought she was no more than a common wanton!

She was on her feet in an instant, her face fiery red. "Good night, Señor Domingo," she said coldly.

Luis could only stare after her, too stunned to move. The moment the darkness swallowed her, he cried her name, again and again.

Tears streaming down her cheeks, Fury ran through the dark, quiet streets until she came to the parish house. She didn't bother to knock but thrust open the door, calling the priest's name in a voice so tormented, the good father—who'd long since left the soiree for the comfort of his own bed—was downstairs in an instant, tripping on his nightshirt as he went along.

"What is it, child? What's happened? What time is it?"

"He knows, Father, he knows! I'm sure of it!"

"Who knows what?" the old priest demanded fretfully.

"Señor Domingo. He suspects who I am. My scar . . . the hawks, the diamond garter . . . I sent Juli to get the ship out of the cove before sunup. There is no other hiding place for her." Fury began to pace up and down the foyer, wringing her hands. "It's all over, Father. Everyone will know shortly. I suppose you know that Mynheer Dykstra was passed over for the governorship for someone I never heard of. He will never forgive my father and mother, or me, for that matter. Do you know why they wouldn't accept him, Father?"

Father Sebastian sighed. "Because he is getting on in years. They want a younger man, or at least that's what I think. I can't prove it. I saw the mynheer's face; he took the announcement badly, I thought. I tried to speak with him, but he stormed out of the house. He said if he

isn't good enough to be governor, then he is resigning as
the manager of the Dutch East India Company. The mynheer is a very bitter man and I can't say I blame him. I
devoted an hour of prayer for his soul.''

''Yes, yes, that's all well and good, Father, but about
my problem. If Luis Domingo tells Mynheer Dykstra,
the . . . they could send me to prison, Father. My mother,
too.'' The thought of her beautiful mother in prison turned
Fury's face white. She herself knew about prisons; she'd
been planning on entering one.

The elderly priest shook his head. ''They have to have
proof, Furana. A scar on your arm isn't going to convince
the authorities you're anything but who you are, a young
lady sent here to enter the convent.''

''A young lady who was *rejected*. Father, the authorities
will see it as a simple ruse. My mother's ship . . . I can't
let it be confiscated, she'll never forgive me. Once I secure
it, I'll return here and decide what I am to do.''

He should tell her now, the old priest thought. He should
walk over to his Bible and show her the letter from the
archbishop. But he knew he wouldn't do any such thing.
''What can I do, child?''

''If Luis Domingo is half as astute as I think he is, he
knows this is the only place I'd come to at this late hour.
Would you—would you tell him I came here to make a
confession because of my . . . my wanton desires?''

''Do you think he'll believe you came here in the middle of the night to confess your sins?'' Father Sebastian
asked gently.

''It's up to you to make him believe it, Father. The casa
is being watched by Mynheer Dykstra's men. I was going
to sail the *Rana* to provide Luis with an escort back to
Spain—at a safe distance, of course.'' She told him then
about the diamond consignment. ''I have to go back to the
von Klausner house now,'' she concluded, ''and believe

me when I tell you it's going to be much harder to get in than it was getting out. I have no idea how I'm going to explain my absence. The story will be all over Batavia. God only knows what Mynheer Dykstra will do.''

"You are your mother's daughter, Furana. Whatever happens, I'm sure you'll do the right thing,'' the priest said loyally.

Fury whirled. "I'm sick and tired of hearing I'm my mother's daughter! That sort of thinking is what got me into this predicament. Listen to me, Father. I will do whatever I have to to keep this secret. No one—not Mynheer Dykstra, not Luis Domingo—will reveal it. *No one. Now*, Father, you can pray for me!''

Fury had her hand on the doorlatch when Father Sebastian called to her. "Do you love Luis Domingo?''

Fury's bitter laughter sent chills down the old priest's back. Why, he wondered miserably, had he expected an answer?

Half in the shadows, Luis settled himself on an iron bench to await Fury's return. He could have followed her, but he'd wanted to remain in the garden and think about those few tantalizing moments in the grass. Whoever would have thought that the demure religious could be so passionate? Christ Almighty, he could have taken her right there! He still didn't know where he'd found the strength to stop himself.

A strange feeling settled over him. He tried to put a name to it, and when the elusive words finally surfaced, he almost choked on the thick gray smoke from his cigar. Protectiveness and love. For Fury van der Rhys. The thought was so mind-boggling, he rose and began to pace in irritation. It wasn't possible he could be falling in love with the young woman . . . it couldn't be! Yet his eyes kindled with desire as he recalled her entrance to the party. Every man in the room had wanted her, and he was no exception. He still wanted her, for all the good it was going to do him. He conjured a vision of himself, old and gray, unmarried and childless, living on his memories while Fury, in a nun's habit, prayed for his everlasting soul.

Luis stomped off through the garden in search of total darkness and solitude. As he turned to toss away his half-smoked cigar, he saw Fury out of the corner of his eye, contemplating the second-floor balcony. His heart began to pound. He wanted to go to her, tell her he would keep her secret and help her get back to her room, but he couldn't move. Forty minutes later he heaved a mighty sigh of relief when he saw her slide over the balustrade. He continued to watch, and twenty minutes after that the housekeeper appeared, pondering the same problem of reaching the second floor unseen. It was all Luis could do to keep from showing her the various footholds Fury had found. "First of all you have to hike up your skirts," he whispered, "there to the right, that's it, grab hold, now inch your way, little by little, ah, that's it, now to the left, slowly, there you have it . . . straight now . . ."

The attack, when it came, was so silent, so deadly, Luis barely had time to dive for cover. His heart pumped madly. From somewhere deep inside him words came, words he later could barely remember uttering. "I mean her no harm, for Christ's sake, I think I love her!" Did he say the words or did he—the sudden silence roared in his ears. He knew his hair was standing on end in the breeze the birds created. "Jesus Christ!" he fumed as he got to his feet. They were overhead, each working the gentle breeze, waiting, waiting for him to . . . what? for Christ's sake. Explain? "I'd never hurt her," he whispered. "I won't give away her secret. I won't," he said fiercely. "If you're going to do something, for God's sake, do it now!'' he commanded. He watched in horror as Pilar seemed to soar straight up in the air, her wings flapping in a frenzy in the light from the colorful lantern. She circled, her wings fanning the air, and then before he could blink his eyes she descended to within an inch of him, hanging suspended in the air, her wing tip feathering out to touch his cheek. So gently. ''Take care of her,'' he said softly.

''Hawhawhawhaw,'' came Gaspar's cry overhead.

''And on that note, I think I'll say good night to my hostess,'' Luis muttered in relief.

Luis wasn't at all surprised, a short while later, to find himself at the parish house. He looked longingly at the second-story windows. It was almost sacrilegious to wake the old priest at this hour, but he needed to talk to someone who wouldn't lie to him, someone who knew Fury van der Rhys, Peter Dykstra, and Fury's parents. His feet seemed to have a mind of their own as they walked up the path and onto the small porch of the parish house. He knew the door wasn't locked. The parish house as well as the church were never locked to those in need of prayer and a kind word.

Inside, Luis settled himself on the one comfortable chair, leaned back, and closed his eyes. Perhaps he'd missed his calling and should have entered the priesthood. It was so peaceful here. He imagined he could see tiny angels flitting overhead, plump little cherubs praying and singing. Because he believed in the *padre*'s God he knew there were such things. He found himself grinning when he patted his shoulder where he knew an imaginary angel hovered.

He could sit here all night; the *padre* wouldn't care. He had no desire to return to his boardinghouse or to the ship.

In fact, he'd even lost the need to talk with the good Father: best let him sleep.

Poor Father Sebastian, Luis thought, stretching comfortably. He was at the end of his life span; just yesterday he'd noticed the man's bowed back, his bent, gnarled hands. Was he in pain? Probably, Luis decided. Yet he'd never seen anything but compassion and goodness in the old man's face. No doubt at the end of the day he would sit in this chair and read his Bible, deriving comfort and the strength to endure one more day. Luis smiled, a sweet, gentle smile, and asked the Lord to allow the priest to live to be a hundred.

Would he be trespassing if he picked up the priest's Bible and read a verse or two? Perhaps he would find answers in this holy book. Or were the answers within himself? What exactly was it that he was seeking? Vengeance . . . yes, he was bent on vengeance for the death and ruination of his father. He'd almost forgotten about *that*. He'd been so intent on the future, he'd shelved the past.

Sudden anger ripped through Luis, driving all his peaceful thoughts into oblivion. He slammed the Bible onto the table. Honeyed words weren't going to change past injustices or make him forget about his father and what Fury's mother did to him. For in his mind now he was convinced that Sirena van der Rhys was the Sea Siren.

He should return to the ship and try to get some sleep. At least in sleep he wouldn't be tormented. He gazed around at the moonlight spilling into the room, and then, sighing, he righted the Bible on the little table, aware for the first time of the crackly paper underneath. Idly he opened the stiff paper and read the flowing script. He sat for a very long time, the words burning into his heart. When he at last folded the religious decree, he felt as though he'd been kicked in the stomach by a mule.

On stiff legs he made his way back to his ship, his thoughts as unyielding as his bones. There would be no sleep for him this night—and probably not for several nights to come.

Fury was lost to him . . . not that she'd ever truly been his, but this evening, for a few brief moments, she'd been ready to offer herself to him. And what had he done? He'd goddamn well turned away from her. If he lived to be a hundred, he'd never forget the look of shame and humiliation on her face—not at what she'd been prepared to do, but at his reaction to it. "You're a bastard," he muttered. "A low-down, scheming bastard!"

When the gray-laced dawn crept over the horizon, Luis was on the deck of the *Silver Lady* cradling a mug of three-day-old coffee in his hands that was so strong he could have eaten it in chunks.

The trade winds were cool and balmy as they rippled across the deck, but even they couldn't ease his tortured thoughts. Perhaps he should cut his losses and sail the *Silver Lady* back to Spain, begin all over. He had the rest of his life to make a fortune. He would probably never marry now, so he didn't have to worry about building a fine house and supporting a family. He could live at sea and call the *Silver Lady* his home.

As for the real Sea Siren, let her rest in peace. Her daughter would soon be peaceful enough in the convent, praying for all their wicked souls. The bogus impostor could have his cargoes, and may she never know a moment's peace from them. The hell with Dykstra and the Dutch East India Company. The hell with the diamond merchant he was to escort back to Spain. He would sail with the evening tide.

But before then, he decided, he'd take one last ride back to the cove, prove to himself once and for all that Fury really was impersonating her mother. If nothing else, he wanted to carry that proof back to Spain with him. It was important to him, and he wasn't sure why.

The sun was creeping into the sky when Luis began his trek through the jungle. Somehow he felt sure that he would find the cove serene, with no trace of the hateful black ship. Certainly he'd given Fury plenty of time to sail her out to open water. He wondered if she would ever realize what he'd done for her. On the other hand, she might realize full well that it was within his power to sign her death warrant. Even if he chose not to expose her and her ship, but sailed away without telling a soul, mightn't she convince herself otherwise? She would assume her ship was no longer safe here in the cove—and with no place to hide, she'd be open prey to any marauder on the seas.

Minutes later he reached his destination. Sure enough, there was no sign of the ship that had rocked so gently in the calm cove waters the night before. Any doubts about Fury's identity were now washed away, he thought grimly.

Over and over on his ride back to the harbor he asked himself if he could turn his back on Fury. It was his fault she'd rushed to move her ship, and it would be his fault if she didn't survive to enter the convent two weeks from today. Could he live with that?

The small town was alive with bustle and noise as Luis reined in his horse at the parish house. All the von Klausner guests were departing for their homes after a huge breakfast, as was the local custom. He wondered where Dykstra was. The entire board of governors would be leaving Clarice's about now, their morning baths and huge breakfasts a pleasant memory. Past memories were best forgotten, he thought sourly.

"Señor, will you join me for lunch?" the priest asked, opening the door in greeting.

"Yes, thank you," Luis replied. "But, Father, I must talk with you, it's very important."

"Can we talk over lunch, or would you prefer my study?"

"It doesn't matter. Father, you must speak with Fury. . . ." All his hopes and ambitions spilled out, along with the past evening's activities and his recent trip to the cove. "I was here last night, Father, I needed to talk with you. I was going to read a verse or two from your Bible, and the . . . the letter underneath fell to the floor. I don't know why I read it, there's no excuse I can offer for invading your privacy. I do apologize," Luis said gruffly.

"She doesn't know . . . about the letter, that is," the priest said fretfully. "She and her housekeeper left the von Klausners' just as the sun came up. I intend to ride out to their casa myself when the sun sets and tell her then. I'll give her a message if you wish."

"Tell her the cove and her secret is safe with me. She has nothing to fear from me. I'm sailing this evening."

"You have time to ride out and tell her yourself," the priest said.

"If you don't mind, Father, I'd rather not. In fact, I think I'll forgo lunch as well." Luis extended his hand. "Perhaps we'll meet again one day."

"If not in this life, then in the next one," the elderly priest said, walking with him to the front door. "I wish you a safe journey, Señor Domingo, and have no fear, I will deliver your message to Fury just as you instructed. Godspeed."

Father Sebastian watched the handsome Spaniard until he was out of sight. He didn't have much firsthand knowledge about love between men and women, but what knowledge he did have told him Luis Domingo was in love. Fury had been acting the same way, her face flushing any time the Spaniard's name was mentioned. The thought of her in a convent for the rest of her life was so upsetting, he walked into his kitchen and ripped the cloth from the parrot's cage. "Go on, say it!" he croaked petulantly.

"Say your prayers, say your prayers," the parrot babbled.

"Shut up!" he ordered, throwing the cloth back over the parrot's cage. "I don't need you to tell me to pray, it's all I do; it's what I do best." To his housekeeper he said, "I'm leaving now. I won't be here for dinner, I may not even return this evening. If you see me, I'm here; if not, I'm not here."

"Are you all right, Father?" the old woman asked, bewildered.

"No, I'm not all right, but don't concern yourself," he grumbled. "Just give me a jug of water to take with me and that umbrella you never use. I'm too old for this hot sun. And before you can say it, I don't care if the town thinks me daft or not."

Chapter Eleven

The River of Death

The sky overhead looked evil somehow, Amalie thought fearfully. Low gray clouds scudding together formed a thick blanket that dipped lower and lower until it was impossible to distinguish the fog from the cloud bank. But if she showed fear in any way, her crew would forget about Miguel and the allegiance they'd sworn to her. Open water at least gave a captain and his ship a fighting chance. Navigating this narrow river known for so many deaths would take every ounce of skill and determination. Amalie wanted nothing more than to squeeze her eyes shut and not open them until she had secured her ship in the first deepwater cove she came to. But she was hell-bent on a course from which there was no turning back.

Amalie was steering what she hoped was a straight blind run with one of her crew on the bow to warn her if she came too close to the dangerous rocks on either side of the narrow river.

Her hands gripped the wheel so fiercely, her knuckles showed white. She wanted to think about the real Sea Siren and the whispered diamond consignment her crew had picked up on that was due to arrive in Batavia. Until now it had all been so easy, a game of sorts; but no longer. The Spaniard's riddles finally made sense to her. The woman her father had written about in his journal was back on the high seas—and seeking revenge. Revenge against *her*, Amalie, for plundering the seas in her name.

Dare she set sail after the Dutch ship and the diamond consignment? Of course she dared; the diamonds were the reason she was steering this very ship up the River of Death. If she was successful, she, too, would retire from the sea. She'd return to Saianha a wealthy woman, able to live in luxury until she died.

The plan when they weighed anchor was for Cato to pilot the jolly boat into the harbor and sign on to the Dutch manifest. Seamen talked when they were full of grog. Rego would be in town waiting for Cato to inform him of the sailing time. But she'd have to be careful. The real Sea Siren, if she knew of the diamond consignment, would be on watch. She might even be noble enough to provide an escort for the Dutch ship. The thought was farfetched but not impossible.

Amalie's shoulders ached with the strain of constant vigilance. They were close now, almost there. . . . She watched, grim-faced, as Cato reached out and touched a jutting rock. They were all a hairbreadth away from disaster, and everyone aboard the ship knew it.

"Never again," she muttered to herself. "I never want to be this close to death again."

When at last Cato shouted, "We're clear, the cove is dead ahead!" Amalie did her best to straighten up, to look confident and assured. Fortunately only Cato knew how weak she was, how terrified.

"All that matters is you did it," he murmured. "Don't think back, think only of the present. We'll weigh anchor, and at first light I'll make my way back down the river and into town. I'll take the jolly boat as far as it's safe and travel the rest of the way on foot. Rego will return with the boat when I have the information you need."

Below decks in her cabin, Amalie gave in to her emotions. She huddled in her bunk, shivering uncontrollably. Tears of frustration, of fear and relief, coursed down her cheeks. She wasn't the Sea Siren. She was an impostor who couldn't even come close. That woman had been nerveless, her ability lawless. The Siren had relied only on herself, while she, Amalie, was dependent on her crew and others for information. Hers was a mission of pure greed; the Siren had sailed to avenge a wrong. There was no comparison no matter how much she wanted to believe she was every bit as capable and talented as the famous Sea Siren. "Even in death you robbed me, you bastard," she hissed to the four walls. "I wish you could hear me, Father," she spat out.

Amalie wanted to pray then, to the God she'd learned about in the mission. If she said the words she learned and remembered, it would be sacrilegious and only compound her spiritual being. That God would not forgive what she'd done.

When Cato looked in on Amalie, just before setting out in the jolly boat, she was sleeping, her tears drying on her cheeks. She looked so beautiful, he thought, her hand cupped under her cheek. Peaceful and saintly . . . He felt his loins stir, and he ached with his need. Softly he turned and closed the door behind him. He had his own mission now, one dictated by his love.

Juli clucked her tongue at her mistress. "You need sleep, Miss Fury. There's nothing you can do until one of my brothers brings word. Use that time to rest. Warm milk, warm chocolate," she coaxed.

Fury shook her head and continued her restless pacing. A sudden clatter in the courtyard sent her flying to the balcony doors. "It's Father Sebastian," Fury muttered as she turned from the window. "What do you suppose . . . ?"

"Nothing good, I'm sure," Juli said sourly as she moved out of Fury's way.

Fury threw open the heavy front door to stare anxiously at the priest. "What is it, Father, has something happened? Why have you come all this way so early in the morning? Juli, fetch a cool drink. And set the table for breakfast."

"No, child," the priest said, mopping his forehead. "No breakfast, but I would like a cool drink. Please, let us sit down. My bones grow older each day."

Fury waited in an agony of impatience as Father Sebastian drained his drink. At last he sighed heavily and leaned forward, his face so earnest she almost swooned with fear. Something had happened to her parents, she thought wildly. The elderly priest looked so sad, so forlorn.

"It's my parents, isn't it?" she blurted out. "Something has happened to them. That's why you're here."

"No, child!" cried Father Sebastian, obviously upset that his behavior had so misled her. "That's not why I'm here. . . . Last night, quite late, Luis Domingo came to the parish house. He entered, but he did not wake me, although he needed to talk. Instead, he . . . sought solace by picking up my Bible, and he . . . he read this." The priest drew out the parchment letter from the archbishop. "I meant to tell you about it earlier, child, but I couldn't. I so wanted you to enjoy the soiree and not concern yourself with this until it . . . This doesn't mean you have to . . . Forgive me, Furana," he concluded lamely.

Fury reached for the crackly paper, but the priest hesitated. "Before I give you this," he said, "I want you to know something. Señor Domingo asked me to give you a message. He said he'd been to the cove and seen your ship. He said your secret is safe with him. He's sailing with the evening tide. He read this letter while I slept and later apologized to me for having done so. You'll never see him again, Furana.'' The good father sighed heavily. ''I fear we've both misjudged the man. Mynheer Dykstra, however, will not be as generous as Señor Domingo. With him the matter is much more personal, I believe.''

''The letter, Father. Give it to me,'' Fury demanded. Her face betrayed no emotion as she read the contents. ''This says I have . . . two weeks . . . two weeks to do . . .''

''Whatever you want. Two weeks is fourteen days. A person could sail quite far in fourteen days. This time of year the trade winds are a sailor's dream. When one leaves the outside world for a religious vocation, one must leave his old world in peace, with no emotional ties. I . . . I told Señor Domingo he should come out here and tell you himself, but he declined. I wanted to say something to him that would ease his mind, but I couldn't say what he needed to hear. He knows who you are, Furana. And he's carried his vengeance against your mother for so long. He's turning his back on everything—his chance to seek out the impostor, his chance for a handsome commission to escort the diamond merchant back to Spain, everything.''

''We all make decisions we have to live with, Father,'' Fury said softly.

''He must love you very much to make such a decision.'' Father Sebastian felt his old heart quicken at the look of pure joy that settled on Fury's face. Her eyes were like stars, her smile as radiant as the sun. He wanted to cry when the stars and sun left her features. ''Child, I have no idea what you feel for the Spaniard. What does a man of God know about love between a man and a woman? But I know what I saw in Señor Domingo's face, what I heard in his voice. And I must assume that God, in His infinite wisdom, has given me the insight to interpret his emotions. I believe he is in love with you. What you do with this information is up to you, of course. Now, if you wouldn't mind, I'd like to impose on you for a short nap before I return to the village.''

"Of course, Father," Juli said, holding the door open, her eyes on Fury. She wondered smugly if her own eyes were as star bright as her mistress's. Aldo would arrive, if all went well, after dinner. Her feet literally danced up the long staircase. What was Fury going to do?

"The good Father is tucked in with a cool drink on his night table," she reported on her return to the study. "He'll sleep well; I closed the draperies. Now!"—she regarded Fury narrowly, hands on her ample hips—"what was *that* all about? It's just a letter, it didn't come from your pope. You don't have to obey it if you don't want to. If you have doubts, you shouldn't even *consider* obeying. I heard what Father Sebastian said, and I saw your face, Miss Fury. Does the wind have to blow you over before you wake up to what's in front of your eyes? Do what your heart tells you to do!''

"Juli, in case you haven't noticed, I no longer have a ship in the cove," Fury snapped. "I couldn't do anything even if I wanted to—at this time. Until one of your brothers arrives with information, we have to be patient.''

"You could be making plans," Juli persisted. "Don't you want to see him one more time? That place you're planning on entering, it will be dark and dreary . . . his handsome face could be the sunshine in your thoughts.''

Fury flinched. "I'll be too busy to think about Señor Domingo. Besides, it's unholy to think of a man when I've given myself to God.''

Juli gave her a withering look. "You haven't given yourself yet. You still have two weeks to do whatever you want. Two weeks, Miss Fury!''

"I'll just have to live with that, won't I? The woman posing as my mother probably has knowledge of the diamond consignment and has heard that Señor Domingo is to sail with the diamond merchant. Now that he sails on his own frigate, she won't go after the Dutch ship. She'll probably think it's a trick of some sort and go after Luis . . . I mean Señor Domingo. She'll never get the diamonds, and he—well, he can take care of himself,'' she concluded defiantly.

The silence between the two women grew unbearable. Fury refused to meet Juli's eyes, although she knew the housekeeper was staring at her, waiting. . . .

"You have no guts!" she burst out at last.

Fury was on her feet in a second. "I resent your remark, Juli!''

"And well you should,'' Juli responded. "You were play-acting before, enjoying yourself and the drama you created. Now, when it's time to do what your mother would do, you have no stomach for saving the man you love. You love him, admit it, Miss Fury!''

"I'll admit no such thing. You forget your place. Perhaps my mother allowed you to speak to her in such a manner, but you will not talk to me like this!''

Juli stomped her way out of the study, calling over her shoulder, "Your mother was a woman in every sense of the word. You hide behind a holy facade and mumble prayers that do not come from your heart. You're afraid to become a woman!'' She slammed into the kitchen and began to hack away at a chicken on her table, muttering angrily all the while.

Moments later Fury thrust open the door. "Juli, I'm sorry. I never should have spoken to you as I did. Please, forgive me. You've been a wonderful friend to my mother and myself. I don't know what I would have done without you. Listen to me, I have to make you understand. I'm committed to God. I'm meant to enter the convent. Of course it isn't going to be easy, I know that. There's every possibility I may fail in my vocation, but I have to try. Can't you understand? All my life . . . God is my life.''

Juli sniffed and bent over her chicken without looking up. ''The way I see it, Miss Fury, is you're cheating your God. You'll never convince me you don't have worldly feelings for the Spaniard. If you wish to dupe yourself, that's fine with me. Even those damnable birds haven't touched him. That should tell you something. You say they're attuned to you, so therefore they must know he's . . . good for you.''

''You think I should go after him . . . and do what?'' Fury asked, spreading her hands wide. ''Somehow I don't think Señor Domingo will think kindly of me when I tell him I'm sailing along as an escort to protect him,'' she sniffed.

Juli brought the blade down across the chicken's wing joint with a vicious slam. ''You don't have to tell him *that*. When you catch up to him, tell him you want only to warn him. A man will think kindly of a woman if she tries to apprise him of trouble. All men know we women have a sixth sense.''

''How much of what you've just said is your own insight and how much is my mother's?'' Fury demanded. She laughed bitterly as Juli refused to meet her gaze. The chicken lost its leg with a loud *whack!*

''Cook that,'' Fury said, pointing to the unfortunate fowl, ''and give it to Father Sebastian. I don't want any lunch. Don't ever give me chicken again. I'll be in the garden.''

''Thinking, I hope,'' Juli muttered as the knife severed the remaining leg from the carcass.

Out among the lush greenery, Fury headed for the nearest shade tree to reflect on the events of the past twenty-four hours. What was she to do? How foolish of Juli to assume there were choices for her to draw from. Could she go after Luis Domingo, warn him, and then head back to port and enter the convent? Two weeks wasn't much time. If there was a storm or if another ship accosted her, she could be delayed. If she didn't appear at the convent gates at the appointed time, she might be denied entrance. If she did go to sea and got herself killed or maimed, she could never enter the convent—or anyplace else, for that matter.

Overhead, the branches of the lush breadfruit tree rustled. Fury peered upward into Gaspar's glittering gaze. "I don't know what to do," she whispered. Her eye sought the sun as she tried to calculate how long it would take her to ride horseback into town. If she went by way of the cove, she might make the harbor at high tide.

Juli watched her mistress from the kitchen window. "It's better than nothing," she mumbled as she dropped the pieces of chicken into the boiling water. If Fury's God was on her side, she'd arrive in town with minutes to spare.

Fury gave no mind to her appearance as she spurred Starlight through the trampled jungle path. Within minutes her hair was free of its pins, streaming behind her in damp tendrils. Overhead, the hawks kept pace with her, working the air as they flew directly in her path. The horse's galloping hooves beat to the rhythm of her heart's refrain: Why am I doing this, why? Why? *Why?*

Because I damn well want to! She answered at last. I don't care if he thinks me wanton. He stirred something in me, something I've never felt before.

Juli was right, she could do whatever she pleased until the moment she walked through the gates of the convent. And this damn well pleased her. Telling Luis her thoughts concerning the impostor—even apologizing to him for her mother—was just an excuse. She wanted to see him again. She needed to say good-bye.

An hour later she was within walking distance of the

cove. From there she led Starlight on foot to save her strength for the hard ride along the sandy beach and then back through the jungle to the harbor.

The sound of voices coming from the beach carried to her ears. She noticed then that the hawks had worked their way down and were perched on Starlight's saddle, their dark eyes sparkling in the sun. Fury brought the horse up short and strained to hear what was being said down below. Juli's brothers must have brought her ship back to the cove, she decided. Thank God, the *Rana* was safe—safe, providing Luis Domingo kept his word. She was about to call out when she heard loud cursing in what sounded like Portuguese. Instantly she tethered the horse, then set out, crouching low as she scrambled down the familiar terrain.

The blazing sun was beginning to make her light-headed. The jungle sounds were quiet now, evidence that someone was walking about. Would they recognize the signs of an alien presence? When there was no break in the conversation, Fury sighed in relief, then cautioned herself to move stealthily.

Panting with her efforts to remain unnoticed, she peered below for her first glimpse of the *Rana*—and sucked in her breath at the sight before her eyes. The black ship loomed ahead like a specter, but it wasn't *her* black ship. How . . . ?

Was this the ship Luis Domingo had seen? Or had he sighted the *Rana* herself? It had been scant hours since her frigate had sailed down the river. Suddenly she grew angry. Why should she be so surprised to see the impostor's ship here? she asked herself caustically. If Luis Domingo had figured out her hiding place, certainly the Sea Siren's impersonator could have done the same. After all, it was the perfect—if not the only—sanctuary in the vicinity. So much for thinking herself clever at covering her tracks.

Fury squinted to observe the ship more closely. Armed. A good-size crew if the number of men on deck was any indication. Where was the captain? Below decks, obviously. Should she stay in hiding to observe movement, or . . . She cast a critical eye at the sun. If she wanted to see Luis, she would have to leave now. But if she wanted to discover the identity of the impostor, she would have to remain.

Moments later Fury had reached a decision. She wasn't meant to see Luis again—circumstances dictated but one course of action. She wasn't leaving here until she saw the infamous poseur with her own eyes.

Settling herself behind the dense jungle growth, Fury waited, the sun beating down on her with a vengeance. Her mouth was parched, her wet clothes drying on her back. She brushed at hundreds of insects determined to suck her blood. She was itching from head to toe. If only she could slip into the cool cove water. But no, she had to think, to plan. . . . If the impostor had sailed up the River of Death, she was as apt as the real Sea Siren. And would be equally adept at sailing with the tide, unless . . . unless . . . *The mouth of the river had to be blocked.*

One clenched fist pounded the soft, loamy ground, releasing black specks and bits of greenery. A loud squawk of outrage from a jungle bird permeated the air. Immediately the men below quieted. Fury held her breath.

The voice she was waiting to hear was husky, alluring. Sultry. Fury parted the thick emerald leaves. "A jungle parrot," the woman sneered. "The same kind of jungle bird that gave me this!" She brandished her left arm for all to see.

Fury clamped a hand over her mouth, her eyes widening in surprise. No wonder Luis and the others had mistaken her for the Sea Siren. She wore an identical outfit, had the same long, streaming, dark hair, and had a scar on her

arm that obviously passed for her mother's. With one crucial exception: the impostor's scar was on her *left* arm,
whereas her mother's and her own were on the right.

But she was beautiful, Fury admitted. Achingly, glori-
ously beautiful. With the sun glittering down on the deck
of the black ship, she looked like a golden goddess. Fury
could see the men leering at her, but with one murderous
glance she sent them back to their game of cards. Fury
inched her way backward, grasping at vines and leaves to
prevent herself from sliding forward.

Juli was waiting for her at the stable when she returned.
In a choked voice she told the housekeeper what she'd just
seen. "Did Father Sebastian leave?" she asked.

"Hours ago. Why?"

"I wanted to tell him to alert the Dutch East India Company. The mouth of the river has to be blocked. There's
no other way for the impostor to get her ship out. None
of them would last a day in the jungle on foot. I have to
bathe and go into town. This will finally clear my mother's
name. I can hardly believe it."

"You realize you missed Señor Domingo's departure,
don't you?" Juli demanded as they walked back into the
house.

"What would you have me do, Juli? I did my best. I
thought it more advantageous to find out what I could about
that miserable woman. She's in the *Rana*'s cove, don't you
understand? I must warn the governors about her."

"I suppose so," Juli said reluctantly. "At least we no
longer have to worry about the two men Mynheer Dykstra's had watching the house. They left at midafternoon.
I suppose now that he has no chance of being made governor, Dykstra's lost interest in playing detective and
building up his reputation at your expense."

Fury looked at Juli and grinned. "It's almost too bad, in
a way. I was looking forward to using that balcony. . . ."

* * *

The town was dark when Fury reined in her horse at the parish house. She was on the ground in an instant, straightening her dress and smoothing back stray tendrils of hair that escaped the knot on top of her head. She strode off briskly toward the harbor, hoping against hope that the *Silver Lady* would still be at the wharf. Her heart sank at the sight of the empty slip.

"Looking for someone, little lady?" asked the harbormaster, coming up behind her. Fury whirled to find a kind looking old man with pure white hair staring at her with concern.

"The *Silver Lady*? Did she sail with the tide?"

"Aye, that she did. It was a busy hour this night. The governors left, as did Mynheer Dykstra. Man up and resigned his post—just like that."

Fury bit down on her lower lip. "I suspected he might. Are the offices empty?" she asked.

"Aye, and they'll remain closed until the new manager arrives. That's what the sign in the window says," the harbormaster said jovially.

"A poor way of doing business, if you ask me," Fury said tartly. "When my father was manager of the company, the doors were never closed."

The harbormaster shrugged. "It's getting late, little lady. You best be getting indoors before some of these scurvy seamen mistake you for one of . . . well, before they think Clarice let you out for a stroll. I'll walk with you if you have a destination in mind," he offered.

"The parish house," Fury said, looking about her curiously. Sure enough, she noticed a few seamen here and there, watching her with open interest. The same kind of seamen she'd seen in the cove.

When Fury knocked at the parish house door, Father Sebastian received her with stunned surprise. What young lady traveled about in the darkness doing God only knew what? Furana seemed to make a habit of it.

"What is it, child?" he asked, alarmed. "What's happened?"

Fury babbled then, the way the parrot in the kitchen did the moment his cage cover was removed. "So you see, Father," she concluded, "I can't alert the burghers. They will block the entrance to the river, and while it will seal the impostor's ship in the cove, it means I will never be able to return the *Rana* to her resting place. I don't think my mother would ever forgive me if I allowed that to happen. Oh, I truly don't know what to do. On the way into town I was convinced blocking the mouth of the river was the only sensible thing to do. Now the thought seems ridiculous. What am I to do?"

"Child, I wish I knew," the priest said wearily. "It all seems like a bad dream."

"Father," Fury said softly, her voice tinged with regret, "Luis—Señor Domingo was gone when I finally arrived at the harbor. Do you . . . were you there when he left?"

The old priest nodded. "I gave his ship and two others my blessing before they set out to sea. I don't believe sufficient stores were loaded on any of them. Mynheer Dykstra sailed his own ship. There was a diamond merchant with him, and a fine dandy he was. The governors, too, set sail, with much fanfare. At the last moment there was a delay when a young seaman left Mynheer Dykstra's ship and asked to sign on the *Silver Lady*. Mynheer Dykstra was most upset when the man refused to sail with him. But Señor Domingo was the first to leave." Father Sebastian spread his hands wide. "I'm sorry, Furana, I have nothing else to tell you."

"I'm going around in circles," Fury muttered. "Why is it so hard for me to make a decision? I feel that the impostor is going to attack Señor Domingo's ship . . .

needlessly, Father, because the diamond merchant is now carrying the gems himself, aboard Mynheer Dykstra's ship.'' She shook her head in confusion. ''Oh, it's all happened too quickly.''

''If Luis Domingo doesn't have the diamonds, he can't very well produce them for the impostor. All he has to do is tell her they're on Mynheer Dykstra's ship.'' The priest rubbed his gnarled fingers to ease the pain. ''What do you want me to do?'' he asked.

''Delay my . . . plead my case with the Mother Superior by way of the archbishop. If I sail after Señor Domingo, there is no guarantee I'll be able to return in time to enter the convent. I don't even know where Juli's brothers have hidden the *Rana*. It could take days for them to return and that much time again to set sail. Señor Domingo will have too much of a head start. A spell of bad weather could delay me even more. Will you intervene, Father?'' she pleaded.

''I'll do my best, child,'' Father Sebastian promised.

''That's all I ask,'' Fury said, relieved. ''If things don't work out, if I'm denied entrance to the convent for some reason, then I'll have to take it as a sign from God that I'm not to pursue my vocation.''

''Yes, that sounds reasonable to me.'' He wanted to beg her to stay the night, knowing full well no lady ever traveled alone in darkness—on horseback, no less. But this lady, so like her mother, did not follow the rules of propriety. And she was obviously determined to return to the casa.

''Thank you so much for listening to me, Father,'' Fury said, walking with him to the front door. ''I feel much better now. I'll have Juli or one of the other servants apprise you of whatever I decide to do.''

The night was inky black with a sprinkling of stars overhead. The sultry breeze blowing off the ocean tickled Fury's cheeks and neck. The streets were quiet, the houses dark. For the first time she became aware of the late hour and the long ride looming ahead of her. She'd come to town on a fool's errand, but how was she to know the Dutch East India Companys' manager had sailed on the tide along with Luis Domingo and the governors? Why had they left so soon? she wondered. Her father had told her they sometimes stayed for months at a time. And Dykstra—how strange that he should leave on such short notice. Did he simply plan to abandon his house and his holdings in Batavia? Did he plan to return? Who was to succeed him in the Dutch East India Company's offices? Why had the governors closed the offices?

Fury sat down on the parish steps, her elbows propped on her knees, and tried to fathom the day's events. Dykstra, if he truly did suspect her mother's identity, wouldn't let the matter fade away to nothing. He was an astute business manager, and as such he might have tried to strike a bargain with the governors. Maybe he hadn't really been passed over as governor; maybe it was just meant to look that way.

The moment Fury was secure in the saddle, the horse galloped off, nostrils flaring, mane whipping across her tight hold on the reins.

There was a plan, she was certain of it. All she had to do was puzzle it out. And she would start with Luis Domingo.

What man, she wondered, would give up a handsome commission to return home to Spain with only sandalwood in his hold? Dykstra had first hired him to set a trap for the Sea Siren, and then he'd hired him to guard the diamond merchant on his trip back to Spain. As far as she knew, Luis Domingo was not a rich man, and the commission would have been handsome. But he'd given it up, or so he'd said. He'd also said he was not going to reveal her identity or her mother's. Why? Because of Dykstra? But Dykstra wanted the Sea Siren, badly. How good was Domingo's word?

Then there was Peter Dykstra, who'd been passed over as governor in favor of a younger man, Father Sebastian said. That didn't make sense. The Dutch East India Company favored older, experienced men like her father and Dykstra. In ordering Luis Domingo to capture the Sea Siren, Dykstra could have been acting from personal interest alone. If so, mightn't it have had to do with revenge against her father, her mother, and herself? Yet, her father and Dykstra were the best of friends, and had been for years.

Third, the arrival of the governors was not, by itself, unusual. But the timing of their visit and their abrupt departure were. All details worthy of her attention.

And where did the diamond merchant fit into all of this? Fury wondered. Whose ship was he really sailing on? Or were the diamonds on one ship and the man on another?

So many questions, so few answers. What she had to do now was examine all the details and come up with answers. They, in turn, would lead her to a conclusion.

By the time she reached the casa Fury had a pounding headache. But she also had her answers. Upstairs, she looked longingly at her bed but knew she had to commit to paper her conclusions before she surrendered to sleep.

The diamonds, she wrote, were obviously worth more than she imagined. Possibly a million pesetas if the gems were flawless. Luis Domingo was carrying the diamonds, possibly in his seaman's bag, to throw off suspicion. The board of governors had indeed appointed Dykstra governor, but because of the Sea Siren's "reappearance" they'd come up with the ruse that had been enacted at the von Klausner soiree. Because, she scribbled, the resulting furor would draw attention away from the diamond consignment. Furthermore, the woman posing as the Sea Siren had already accosted Luis Domingo twice and knew he was sailing with only sandalwood in his hold, sandalwood she didn't want. The diamond merchant was sailing on Peter Dykstra's ship, the governors on a third ship. A small convoy, of sorts, but who would be escorting whom?

Fury leaned back in her chair, her temples throbbing. Something niggled at her, something the priest said. A detail, an important one. Fury massaged her temples, knowing the answer would come to her if she could just relax and think about something else for a little while.

She thought of her parents and the games she'd played with her younger bro— The young man who had signed on Luis's ship at the last moment! Father Sebastian had said Mynheer Dykstra had been upset. That little detail had to mean something.

Fury was off her chair in a second, twirling around in a dizzying circle. Of course, he was a member of the impostor's crew! He'd changed ships at the last moment to allow someone at the harbor to inform the impersonator that the diamonds were aboard Luis's ship.

She had it all now. The question was, what should she do? What *could* she do? There was no way to overtake the small convoy at this time. She could sail in a jolly boat down the river and into the cove and attack the impostor. But it was such a foolhardy idea, she felt disgusted with herself for even thinking of it. Her other alternative was to wait for Juli's brothers to return and take her own ship. Somewhere en route she'd lie in wait for the impostor and attack her ship, thereby granting safe conduct for Luis and the convoy.

Fury threw herself on the bed, burying her face in the pillow. "I'll never see him again. He'll never know for certain I am my mother's daughter. Someday," she cried into the pillow, "he might hear a story of this coming battle and remember me."

A stiff breeze ruffled the bedcovers as Gaspar sailed into the room, his talons searching for the bedrail. His wings rustled and fluttered as he inched his way to the pillow Fury lay upon. "I tried to see him again," she whispered brokenly. "I wanted to see him, but it wasn't meant to be. All I can do now is try to make his journey as safe as possible. He . . . I could love him," she sobbed. "Now I . . . I couldn't even say good-bye." She rolled over and sat up, tears streaming down her cheeks. "And what will become of you and Pilar when I go to the convent?" A fresh wave of sobs broke out.

Gaspar moved one talon until he had a corner of the sheet gripped securely. He brought it up gently, offering it to Fury as though it were a prize of great value. She sobbed all the harder.

An angry *swoosh* of air stirred in the room as Pilar took her place next to Gaspar. The hawks stared at the sobbing girl, then Gaspar moved, his wing tips gently wiping the tears from Fury's cheeks. She broke down completely then, throwing herself deeper into the pillow. The startled birds looked at each other, their wings fanning the bed furiously. Pilar lifted her wings until she was satisfied with the draft she created and sailed straight up and out through the open doors, Gaspar in her wake.

Up they flew, into the dark night, high above the jungle trees, and out over open water, their wings flapping together as their jet eyes searched the vast expanse of dark water.

Two days later, as the sun prepared to dip beyond the horizon, Juli's youngest brother arrived at the casa. He was overwrought, wild-eyed. "I saw . . . I couldn't believe my eyes . . . I knew I'd just left your ship and my brothers, but there it was—the black ship sailing from the River of Death. I couldn't see clearly, but the woman at the wheel . . . I swore she was you. I almost killed myself getting here. It was the woman posing as you, Capitana!" the young man said breathlessly.

Fury nodded. "How long ago?"

"A little past first light. It will take us three days to rendezvous with your ship if we leave now."

"Juli, I . . ."

The housekeeper had a sudden vision of her brother returning to the casa with Fury's dead, broken body. She threw her arms around Fury in a fierce hug. "You could encounter the impostor. I have every confidence in your ability, but . . ."

"But what?" Fury asked quietly.

"If she wants the diamonds as badly as we think she does, she'll do anything. Her men are seasoned cutthroats. My brothers are husbands, family men. They can defend themselves, but a fight to the death, if it comes to that . . . They're no match for such men."

Fury nodded. "I've thought of that. I plan to discuss it with them once I board my ship, give them a chance to remain onshore without any loss of face. I'll have Gaspar and Pilar with me."

"In case you haven't noticed, Miss Fury, those evil-looking creatures have been absent for two days."

"They often disappear for days at a time," Fury said lightly.

"Since when?" Juli demanded. "They hover about here like bees at a honey pot. Even at night I hear them."

"I'm not worried, Juli, and I don't want you to worry. I'll be back here before you know it, in plenty of time to . . . to do what I have to do. Now, fetch my things so we can be on our way."

How young this boy was, she thought, and his wife about to give birth to their first child. She smiled at him, seeing the relief in his face at the knowledge he would be returning to his small cottage and his family.

Where were the hawks? Her stomach lurched at the thought of sailing completely alone, something she knew she couldn't do. Everything was wrong; she could feel it in her bones. Every instinct in her warned against this voyage. Give it up, this is a foolhardy thing you're doing. You can't possibly overtake the impostor, do battle, and win . . . not singlehandedly. *Oh, Gaspar, where are you?*

"I hate it when you cry, Juli," Fury said as she prepared to take her leave. "Only weak women cry; women who can't take charge of their destinies. You of all people should know that. Now, when I return I expect to see that handsome houseboy of the von Klausners—what's his name? Aldo?—on your arm proposing marriage. I promise to spend all my time thinking about a suitable wedding present," she teased.

"You take care of her!" Juli growled to her brother as they rode away. "Don't shame me. Tell the others what I've said, too!"

The moment Fury stepped aboard the *Rana*, her confidence returned. "All hands to the quarter deck," she shouted, her eyes on the sky for some sign of the hawks. When her crew was assembled, she made her announcement. The brothers all looked at one another, shuffling their feet.

At last the oldest spoke. "Does the capitana think we aren't capable men?" he asked brusquely.

"Not at all," Fury replied. "I think you're more than capable, and I'm proud to sail with you. It's your families. . . . I don't think I could live with myself if anything happened to you. Juli would never forgive me. There's no telling how much of a fight this impostor will put up, and I've no idea whether I can best her. We might be evenly matched in a fight, but . . . what I mean is, I know you are capable men, but . . .''

The oldest of the brothers grimaced. ''We're with you, Capitana, and I don't think you need concern yourself with our well-being. All of us have been to sea and can defend ourselves as well as one another.''

Fury looked from one to the other, warmed and gratified by the stout confidence, the allegiance, she saw shining in their eyes. At last she smiled and nodded. ''All right, then. We sail a westerly course through the Sunda Strait to open water and then a northwest course. We have a stiff breeze now and can possibly make up some time.''

She brought the glass to her eye to scan the sky overhead. ''Gaspar, where are you?'' she murmured. She'd been watching for hours, the bright sun blinding her, but still she searched. She should never have allowed herself to become so attached to them. ''Please God,'' she prayed, ''let them be safe; they belong to You, as do all creatures great and small. Keep them safe and return them to me this one last time. When I leave this worldly place to join You, I will give them up to You. Until that time . . .'' She sobbed deep in her throat and ran below to her cabin, where she wept in private—great heart-wrenching sobs at her loss. ''Be merciful,'' she pleaded. ''They aren't wild birds any longer, they can't fend for themselves. They need me,'' she wept into her pillow. ''And I need someone to need me, to want me, beside You.''

The *Silver Lady* sliced through the crystal blue water at a speed approaching eleven knots, the Dutch ships trailing in her wake at less than nine. It irritated Luis that Peter Dykstra and the governors of Amsterdam considered the *Silver Lady* an escort, while in truth the Dutch ships were *his* escort.

''Carry the diamonds aboard the *Silver Lady*, and my

lips are sealed regarding the Sea Siren's identity,'' Dykstra had promised. It was his final offer. Luis had argued with Dykstra, called himself every name he could think of, berated himself, cursed himself . . . but in the end he'd agreed to bring the diamonds aboard. At this moment they rested in a velvet-lined cask marked VINEGAR in crude black letters.

All he wanted was to return to Spain in a healthy condition so he could lick his wounds and start over. He didn't want the Dutchman's commission or his damnable diamonds, but he was stuck with both, thanks to his feelings for Fury van der Rhys. He hadn't meant to fall in love, but he had. And now that love would be his undoing.

''Women,'' he snorted, ''should be put together on an island so they could make one another miserable instead of wreaking havoc with men's hearts.''

He should have gone to the casa; he'd had the time to say good-bye. Why hadn't he gone when the priest suggested it? Because, he told himself, he didn't dare gaze upon Fury's beautiful face. He knew he would have begged, like a fool, to . . . to . . .

Luis whipped the glass to his eye, more to drive the thoughts from his head than to scan the waters surrounding him. He felt bruised, battered, and sad of heart at his loss. Would there ever be another woman who could stir him as Fury had done?

''Captain, Captain . . . look! Overhead! What is it? Jesus Christ! It's those devil birds! Captain! Look!''

''I see them. Quiet!'' he roared. He watched, mesmerized at the sight of the black birds in the distance. A chill raced down his arms. Wherever the birds were, Fury was close by. . . . They were closer now, their wings fanning the air, their screeches carrying on the stiff breeze.

Soon the hawks were directly overhead, circling the mainmast at a dizzying speed. Luis's heart began to pound. Why were they here? Where was Fury?

Up, up, up they soared in a straight line until they were almost out of sight. Luis brought the glass to his eye and could see only the brilliant blue sky. Then, suddenly, he saw both birds descend at a speed equal to a cannon shot. He swallowed, his heart in his mouth, when Gaspar checked his descent in midair, his wings flapping to create his own breeze, before he settled on the ship's quarter rail, just inches from where Luis was standing. The moment Pilar took her position nearby, he let his breath out in a long, explosive sigh.

"What . . . what do they want?" Julian asked fearfully.

"How the hell do I know!" Luis muttered. "Bring some meat, they could be hungry." He waited until Julian had returned with a slab of salt pork, then advanced toward them.

"Hawhawhawhaw," the birds chorused.

"And I'm supposed to know what that sound means," Luis grated out.

Their glittering eyes boring into him, Luis advanced with the pail of meat Julian handed him. The birds ignored the food. Gaspar's wing tip feathered out to touch Luis on the shoulder, and Pilar worked hers until she could trace a pattern in the distance. Luis's eyes widened. He turned to face the east, his eyes full of questions. When Gaspar's talon reached out to grasp his arm, he felt no pain and realized the bird's intention was not to hurt him, but to make him turn until he was facing the two Dutch ships sailing in his wake.

In an instant the birds were off the railing and swooping upward, their wings flapping angrily, their screeches keen and shrill. He watched as the birds circled overhead before flying off in an easterly direction.

"We're changing course," Luis ordered. "Turn this

goddamn ship around. Now!'' Overhead, the hawks called their approval before descending to the mizzenmast, where they clung wearily.

"No man touches those birds!" Luis thundered. "Full speed. All hands on deck!" To the Dutch ships he was about to pass, he roared again, "Continue or follow me, it's your choice!"

"What in the goddamn hell do you think you're doing, Domingo?" Dykstra shouted.

"What does it look like I'm doing? I changed course. I have some unfinished business to take care of. If you want your cargo, come alongside. Be quick about it!"

"I'll do better than that. I'm coming aboard," Dykstra roared.

"Suit yourself, but if you miss your footing, I've no time to fish you from the water."

"Where the hell are you going?" Dykstra called a second time.

Luis ignored the question. "What's it to be, Dykstra? Do you want your cargo or not? You can follow me if you want."

Listening to this exchange, Cato almost fell from his position in the rigging. What was he to do? If the Dutchman came aboard, he himself would stay. If the cargo was shifted to the other ship, he would give himself away if he tried to board her. Filled with anxiety, he waited for the Dutchman to make his decision and almost fainted in relief when Dykstra gave the order to change course. The diamonds would remain aboard.

Suddenly he whirled, the hackles on the back of his neck rising. Until this moment he'd thought the devilish birds were high in the mast. If he moved, even slightly, they would be on him in a minute. Christ, he hated them, hated their beady black eyes. It was some kind of omen, he was sure of it.

An hour later Cato was in the same position in the rigging, the hawks only inches away. Luis's eyes narrowed as he watched the birds watching the young man. If they wanted to, they could have toppled him in a second; instead, they chose to keep an eye on him. Why?

Pilar's feathers rustled ominously. Gaspar's head dipped slightly as he prepared to fan out his wings. He was in the air in a second, Pilar working the light breeze he created to follow. "I'll be goddamned!" Luis muttered. They understood what he was saying. Half his brain negated what he'd just observed, but the other half believed implicitly. Cato's white face told him he too was a believer.

Luis watched Cato as he moved off, his head jerking backward with every few steps he took. He looked around sheepishly before he spoke. "If you're as tired as I think you are, then you should rest. I'll keep my eyes on the boy. Your food is on the quarter deck."

"Hawhawhawhaw," Gaspar responded.

"I'll be goddamned," Luis muttered over and over as he strode about the ship. "If I didn't see it with my own eyes, I wouldn't believe it." Craning his neck for one last look at the birds clinging to the mainmast, he wasn't surprised to see their glittering eyes follow his every step.

Now, alone in his cabin, he could think about what the hawks' arrival meant. Fury must be in danger. Either she'd sent the birds after him, or they'd come on their own, which left her without their protection. Luis could feel his stomach start to churn. The hawks seemed content to nest in the mainmast and sail at eleven knots, which had to mean she was in no immediate danger.

The relief Luis felt was so sudden, so overwhelming, he tripped over his own feet, sprawling crossways atop an extra water barrel stored on deck. His curse was ripe and flowery until he saw Gaspar take wing and sail down in his direction. "Son of a bitch!" he muttered, certain the hawk was going to attack him. Instead, Gaspar worked the breeze and seemed to float in the air over his head. When he felt the slight feathering on the back of his neck as he struggled to his feet, he realized the bird was hovering *protectively*.

"I'm all right," he said helplessly. In disbelief he watched the huge bird fan his wings and sail upward in the breeze he created for himself.

A long time later Luis smiled to himself. What was the beautiful, elegant Furana van der Rhys going to say when she found out her goddamn birds were enamored of him? More important, what was his crew thinking about him? He'd seen their sly looks and their fear whenever the birds appeared. They think I'm insane, he thought, and they could be right. What sea captain carrying a fortune in precious diamonds would change course because of two black birds?

One of these days, when the time was right, he'd give his crew a lecture on trust—birds and . . . women. But for now he would content himself with seeking out the newest member of his crew for a . . . chat.

Chapter Twelve

The moment Rego arrived, Amalie set sail for the Sunda Strait, her destination Sumatra, where she would lay in fresh stores and then head for open water. The galleon and brigantine ivory remained behind in the thick gray mist at the mouth of the river, unmanned and ghostly.

Amalie felt paralyzed with fear, an emotion she hated but seemed unable to conquer. She was shaking now, her stomach churning as she contemplated what might happen to her. For some reason she'd always thought she would grow old regally and die in her bed, bedecked with jewels and all her servants in attendance.

The moment Cato left the ship she'd been assailed with doubts of every description. Her instincts told her to give up the diamonds, take what booty she'd salvaged, and return to Saianha. The ivory alone would make her a wealthy woman for the rest of her days. But just when she'd been about to follow through, a vision of the diamonds had appeared before her—a small mountain of them, all shimmery and sparkly. Worthy of a queen and belonging to a kingdom. She couldn't give them up.

Amalie's throat closed at the thought of meeting up with the real Sea Siren, the one her father was so obsessed with, the one who had killed him in the end. *She has no equal*, her father had written. On another page he'd said no man was capable of besting her. He'd died for his efforts, and here she was, foolish enough to think she could succeed where so many others had failed.

For days now she'd been debating with herself about telling the crew what she was after. If they knew of the diamonds, they would fight with her and for her, but when it was all over they would kill her. If the diamonds were divided among her men, they could live in splendor for the rest of their lives.

It was too late for anything now save forging ahead. If she did anything else, she would lose Cato, which would be even worse than losing the diamonds. That particular thought had made her blood run cold. Never, until now, had she believed love would rule her mind and her heart.

Then a second thought struck her, one she'd done her best to ignore for days. If she was caught, she would be turned over to the authorities and either hung or imprisoned for life. Her stomach fluttered warningly at the prospect. Perhaps she should give it all up and return home. Cato knew where she lived. Somehow he would find her.

"Bitch!" she spat out, disgusted with herself. "I want those diamonds, and I mean to have them!"

Seething, Amalie stomped her way from the wheelhouse to the deck. Her crew scattered on sight, busying themselves with the endless task of keeping the frigate seaworthy. She leaned against the quarter deck rail and watched her men go about their duties, lulled by the sounds of water slapping against the hull of the ship. She was calmer now, her breathing deep and regular. Her eyes strayed to the top of the mizzenmast, and she wondered what it would feel like to climb to the top and survey the ocean. Exhilarating, no doubt, but she would not do it. Nothing, she thought morbidly, would drive away this accursed fear. *Too late* . . . it was too late to do anything but stay on course. Whatever was going to happen would happen.

It was dark, she realized suddenly. She'd missed the sun

sinking red-gold behind the horizon. How had she failed to notice the end of a day? She lifted her face to the open sky, relishing the crisp tang of the salt sea as a million stars winked down upon her.

"Mount a square topsail," she shouted. "I want speed, this wind is too favorable to lose. We can make eleven knots easily." Damn their eyes, she hated every one of them. Dirty, filthy drunkards, red-faced from rum and grog.

Amalie's anger drove away her fear as she watched her men mount the topsail. "I could do it faster myself," she shouted.

"Then come up here and do it," came the surly reply.

In a frenzy Amalie scrambled her way up the mast to the insolent seaman. Unsheathing her cutlass, she lashed out at him, slicing the man's arm from shoulder to wrist. He bellowed in pain and fear as he toppled down, down . . . to land on the deck in a crumpled heap.

"Throw him in irons!" Amalie screamed. "I'll have nothing less than respect on his ship. Hear me well, you scurvy lot. The next man goes over the side!" She could hear their muttered curses as they dragged the bleeding man below.

For six days Amalie prowled the decks of her ship like a tiger in search of food. She had not been able to sustain her anger, and her fear was as ripe and rotting as week-old fruit. The need to cry was overwhelming at times. She wished constantly for Cato.

On the seventh day there came a shout from the rigging. "Sail ho!"

"Where away?" Amalie called.

"Dead ahead, thirty knots. She appears to be at anchor. Possibly repairs."

"In the middle of the ocean?" Amalie cried, incredulous.

"She's weighed anchor," came the stubborn reply.

Amalie ran to the bow of the ship and brought the glass to her eye. Damn his eyes, he was right. Only one ship. Where was the Dutchman's escort? Unless the ship didn't belong to the Dutchman, but to someone else, the only person brave enough to weigh anchor in the middle of the sea to . . . lie in wait. She knew in her gut that the ship was black, and the moment the clouds passed across the sun, she would have all the proof she needed.

Now that there was virtually no breeze, her ship's progress slowed. By the time they were within a five-knot range it would be dark. Amalie could feel herself start to tremble.

"Rego, come here," she called softly. "Pass the word, the moment we're within range I want that ship fired on. The shots had damn well better make their mark, or the gunners will be swimming home. Pass the word and do it quietly, voices carry over the water. If we've spotted her, she's spotted us."

"I see her on our stern," Fury called jubilantly. "The wind's dying. One hour, two at the most, and she'll be close enough to fire upon. All we need is two good shots, one on her bow and one broadside. Hoist the anchor. I don't want to make it too easy for her. Quickly now, men. We can't give her the advantage."

"Aye, Capitana. Do you have a mind to play a little game with the black ship?" her first mate inquired in an amused voice.

Fury's soft laughter tinkled across the water. "In a manner of speaking. The cat is always faster than the rat."

Her first mate laughed with her. He had every confidence in this strange young woman with her scanty costume. He listened with interest as she described what she was going to do.

"We'll sail like a bolt of lightning, this way and then that way, a jagged pattern, so to speak. Let her think we're limping and making repairs. She'll think she frightens us. Dawn will provide us with all the light we need to bring about a confrontation. This matter is going to be laid to rest once and for all. She'll never plunder those diamonds in my mother's name,'' Fury vowed. ''If I have to, I'll kill her.''

Amalie watched Fury's zigzag pattern through the glass, the smoke pots creating eerie yellow circles on the water. ''She's playing a game. She's been lying in wait for us. It's to be cat and rat at first light. We'll hold our own, never fear,'' she called to Rego, who passed the word down the line of nervous crewmen.

Amalie cringed when she heard a sound she couldn't identify at first.

''She's laughing at you,'' Rego said. ''I've heard tales of the Sea Siren's laughter, musical as a bell, they say.'' He hunkered into himself.

''You're a gambling man,'' Amalie declared in return. ''Who do you wager will win this . . . confrontation?'' Rego took so long in answering, she lashed out at him with her booted foot. ''I suppose the others are of the same opinion,'' she sneered.

''She's been sailing the seas for over twenty years,'' Rego said hesitantly.

''That makes her an old woman, Rego. Can an old woman best me? Miguel didn't fare too well against me, and I'm a mere woman. What do you have to say to that?''

''I say . . . you will need all the good-luck charms and prayers you have at your disposal. There will be no mutiny on this ship, if that is what you fear. We fear the wrath of the woman on our bow. You would do well to fear the Sea Siren,'' Rego said brazenly, not caring if he upset his captain or not. He wanted to live, and at this moment he didn't give a whit about the cargo she was bent on capturing. Cato, his best friend, had whispered to him that the cargo she was after was a fortune in diamonds and had sworn him to secrecy, promising to appoint him a prince in Amalie's kingdom. He'd just wiped away that promise with his bold, honest opinions. Besides, he didn't believe for one minute that Cato was going to be a king. He didn't believe his captain was going to be a queen either. Kings and queens wore crowns and royal robes. His young face puckered in disgust at his friend's fairy-tale beliefs.

Men were all alike, Amalie thought bitterly. The little skirmishes she'd participated in to prove herself to her crew were nothing in comparison with what would happen shortly. If only she knew for certain that it was the real Siren lying in wait for her, she would . . . do nothing differently than she was doing, she decided.

The thought occurred to her that she could weigh her own anchor or change course, but if she did that, the Siren could come at her from behind or broadside. For the moment she had the advantage—an advantage she intended to keep.

Luis's neck ached with the strain of holding his head steady to peer through the glass. He felt as if he'd been dragged over rough terrain by a runaway horse. For more hours than he could remember he'd done nothing but keep his eye pressed to the glass, and the strain was starting to affect his position with the crew. And now it was almost a new day, he thought tiredly as he accepted a mug of steaming coffee from his first mate.

"If you like, Captain, I'll take the watch," Julian offered. "A wash and a shave will go a long way to easing your tiredness."

Luis nodded and handed the spyglass to his first mate. The moment he closed the wheelhouse door behind him, his shoulders drooped. A wash and shave would feel good. A clean shirt wouldn't hurt, either, he decided.

The faint breeze circling about him felt good. He looked up and noticed the first gray streaks of dawn. A second later he realized the breeze wasn't coming from the ocean, but from the rigging. He arched his neck to see better in the grayish light, and his blood ran cold at the sight of the black birds sailing straight up into the air at a dizzying speed. They continued to circle the topsail, their wings fanning the air furiously. A moment later they were higher than he could see. His eyes burning, he ran from the wheelhouse for his spyglass, all signs of weariness gone.

"Where the hell are they?" he roared minutes later when the gray sky remained clear. He heard them before they came into sight, diving toward the ship faster than a thunderbolt. Gaspar, his wings feathered inward, plunged straight to the bow where Luis was standing. The Spaniard sucked in his breath as the bird fanned his wings and swept outward, away from the railing, just as Pilar rocketed behind him. They worked the breeze to stay aloft at eye level until Luis raised his hand to show he understood. He watched as both birds arrowed a westerly course.

"I'm changing course," Julian shouted before Luis could issue an order.

Luis brought the glass to his eye, straining to see in the early light. There was no sign of the hawks, nor had he expected any. They were on their way to Fury. Their temporary visit was at an end.

He could feel his heart pounding in his chest. Fury was close now. The hawks had come to him for help. If she were in mortal danger, they wouldn't have stayed with him so long. Whatever was about to happen was going to happen soon.

"Tighten sail, full speed!" he roared. He wished then that he, too, could soar and fly to Fury as the hawks had done.

"Now, what the hell are you doing?" Peter Dykstra raged across the water. "You're following those goddamn birds, aren't you?'' He shook his fist in the air. "I want you to turn your ship around and sail a steady course. Stop this foolishness immediately!''

"This is my ship, Dykstra, and if you don't like what I'm doing, fire me,'' Luis called back. "I never wanted your job in the first place. If you want your cargo, I'll lower it in one of the jolly boats. I have no intention of getting myself killed so you can live to be a rich man. The Sea Siren is out there, or maybe I should say both Sea Sirens are out there. One way or another, she's going to come after your cargo. It's my decision to meet her head on. She won't be expecting this kind of maneuver.''

"You're insane,'' Dykstra said hoarsely. Yet in his heart he knew the Spaniard spoke the truth. He lowered his eyes until he was facing the scurvy crew he'd hired at the last minute. To a man, they would cut him down the moment they discovered the true contents of his cargo.

"Follow him,'' the diamond merchant called in a feeble voice. "I'm paying you to take my orders, and I'm *ordering* you to follow Captain Domingo!''

"I'm filing charges against you the moment we reach Spain, Domingo,'' Dykstra blustered. "You won't like languishing in a Spanish prison.''

"Then you'll be right alongside me,'' Luis snarled. "And my countrymen will not be kind to a Dutchman. Think about that, Mynheer.'' He turned to Julian. "Tie the vinegar cask to the jolly boat and lower it.''

"No, no, no!'' the diamond merchant screamed. "I'm paying *you*, not Mynheer Dykstra. I've made no demands on you. I want you to continue!''

Luis was gracious in his acquiescence. "But I want your assurance that our bargain is sealed,'' he called to Dykstra.

Dykstra bristled. "I'm a man of my word!''

"Dykstra, you're a man of *many* words. Just one will do this time. Is it a bargain?"

"*Yes*, damn you!" Dykstra bellowed.

"Sail ho!" came the cry from the rigging.

"I see two sets of sails," came a second cry.

"Where away?" Luis shouted.

"Dead ahead on our bow, Captain. She's sailing at seven knots."

"Man your stations," Luis ordered. "Fire only when I give the command!"

"She's gaining on us, Capitana. We're ready to fire when you give the order," Fury's first mate shouted excitedly. "Capitana, look, to the west!"

Fury whirled, the glass to her eye. "Gaspar!" she cried. "Pilar! You came back!"

Faster than a cannonball, the hawks were on the ship's railing, their talons curled securely on the shiny brass, their glittering eyes fixed on Fury's excited face.

"Where have you been? Oh, I don't care where you've been, only that you're here safe and sound. I knew you'd come, I knew it! It's not time for me to leave you . . . yet." She bent low, her head between the two birds as she stroked their silky backs. "Go up, Gaspar, high in the rigging in case shots are fired," she urged. "Pilar, stay with him."

"Sail ho! On our bow, three ships. I can see the Spaniard on the bow. The frigate on our stern is gaining. What should we do, Capitana?" shouted the youngest of Juli's brothers.

"Those on our bow are . . . friendly. I think," Fury muttered. So *that's* where the hawks had been; they'd gone after Luis! She laughed, a sound of pure joy. Leaping to the stern, she nicked the air in a salute to the birds perched on the mizzenmast.

"Hawhawhawhaw," came the response.

The sudden roar of a cannon shot split the early-morning dawn. "Fire!" Fury shouted. "She's in your sights. Rip her bow to splinters. Broadside now! On the count of three!"

Black smoke spiraled upward on the gentle trade winds, obliterating all view of the pirate ship. Her own ship rocked crazily beneath her feet. "We've been hit, Capitana, our stern!"

"Shore up this ship!" Fury ordered as a second wave of cannon fire thundered through the air. This time the volley of shots came from the Spaniard's ship.

"Try hitting the ship instead of the water, señor!" Fury called to Luis. "You do me no good if you can't knock her guns out."

"Ungrateful bitch!" Luis muttered as he gave a second order to fire. His own ship took a volley of shots then, splintering his bow just beneath his feet. "Fire, goddamn you!" he raged. "Not this black ship, the one on her stern. Drive her into the sea!"

"All hands on deck!" Fury shouted. "Mount the shrouds and yardarms. I'm going to steer this ship directly astern at full speed, and our bow will puncture hers. She won't have time to turn her sail. She's taking on water; one of us got off a good shot. *Fire!*" The impostor was dead ahead, and Fury could see the men scrambling on deck as she shouted orders.

A deafening crash sounded as the cannonball made contact with the enemy ship. As the ram punctured her bow, large splinters of wood flew in the air. Men toppled overboard as other seamen rushed to secure the cannon that was no longer stationary. The crackling and rendering of the ship was ear-splitting.

Fury raced to the bow, her hand on the hilt of the cutlass as several of Amalie's men leapt aboard her frigate. Out of the corner of her eye she saw Juli's brothers defend themselves with an expertise she hadn't known they possessed. Once she risked a glance in the direction of the Spaniard's ship. The entire crew was gathered at the rail, watching *her*, waiting to see if she needed their help.

"I want to see you before I kill you!" she shouted to Amalie, who was standing on what was left of her stern. She was truly magnificent, Fury thought, every bit as beautiful as her mother must have been years ago as she, too, had stood in just such a position, ready to do battle. It never occurred to her that she was equally as magnificent to those watching.

Amalie leapt aboard the *Rana*, landing less than a foot away. "You aren't old at all," she exclaimed, brandishing her cutlass.

Fury laughed. "Why should I be old?" she said. "I'm not real; I'm a legend you refused to let die, and for that *you* will die." She smiled at the rage in the impostor's eyes.

"You're as real as I am!" Amalie snarled. "Blood will spout from your veins just as it will from mine. You're no spirit!" Fury smiled grimly as she unsheathed her cutlass.

"Do something!" Dykstra shrieked to Luis.

"I believe the situation is well in hand, Mynheer Dykstra," the Spaniard called back. "We have only to wait for the outcome. Your cargo is safe."

Dykstra was so upset, he fairly jittered in response. "Look *again*, Captain!"

Luis shaded his eyes to see through the thick black smoke circling upward from the impostor's ship. He'd been so intent on watching Fury and her adversary, he'd ignored the pirate's men, who were now attacking from all directions. Bedlam broke out as Dykstra's crew joined in the battle, followed by the governor's men. Luis and his own crew were the last to leap into the fray.

"Look to your back, Siren!" he shouted over to Fury, who turned with the speed of a cat and slicked her cutlass with a high, wide arch. She watched in horror as her attacker's arm as well as his cutlass rolled across the deck. She whirled back just in time to see Amalie bearing down on her.

All about her the air was filled with shouts and screams as metal clanged against metal. Shots seemed to come from nowhere, and most neither knew nor cared whom they were killing and wounding.

Great black clouds of pungent smoke rolled about the cluster of ships, making visibility almost impossible. Fury rubbed her eyes and backed away to search for firmer footing, all the while intent on the advancing figure of the impostor.

"I want those diamonds," Amalie said hoarsely.

"No," Fury shouted. "Your days of plundering in the Siren's name are over. Give quarter now and I'll spare your life. Prison is better than dying here, with this scurvy lot you call a crew. What's it to be?"

"Never!" Amalie brought up her cutlass.

Slowly Fury raised her own weapon. "So be it," she said, her voice deadly calm. Flexing her knees and lashing out with a sudden thrust, she drove Amalie backward. Amalie recovered quickly, slashing upward at Fury's cutlass. Stunned with the force of the blow, Fury stumbled but recovered quickly and jabbed straight for Amalie's midsection. Daintily she sidestepped, then lashed out again, this time glancing down the side of Amalie's scarred arm to draw blood.

Hatred spewed from Amalie's eyes as she jabbed upward, knocking Fury against the railing. She crouched and with both hands on the cutlass whipped the blade up and down and down again until Fury was bent over the railing, her weapon held crossways in front of her. "I'll kill you for this, you miserable bitch!" Amalie screamed.

Suddenly she sensed a presence behind her and dropped

to her haunches, swiveling as she lashed upward to drive
the weapon from Luis Domingo's hands. Her shrill laughter echoed off the water as the Spaniard stumbled backward, losing his footing. Immediately two of Amalie's
cutthroats were on him as Fury lashed out, slicing close
to her opponent's skull. She feinted to the right and thrust
downward, missing Amalie's back by a hairbreadth. But
the momentum carried her forward, and she slipped and
lost her footing, the cutlass flying from her hands. Frantically she scrambled for her weapon as Amalie bore down
on her.

In a sudden burst of speed, Gaspar swooped downward
from his perch in the rigging, Pilar in his wake. Wild,
shrill screeches ripped from their mouths as Gaspar dove
straight for Amalie's slender back.

Amalie threw up her arms to ward off the deadly attack,
her eyes filled with terror. She shrieked with pain as Gaspar raked her shoulder with his talons. Blood spurted everywhere. Pilar circled around her, her screams more shrill
than Gaspar's. In the blink of an eye she had Fury's cutlass
in her talons, offering it to the young woman as if it were
a precious prize.

With a frenzied shake of his feathers, Gaspar out-
stripped the wind as he plunged upward in preparation of
a killing dive that would render Amalie helpless.

Breathing raggedly, Fury crouched low as she prepared
to leap over the pool of blood. Out of the corner of her
eye she saw Luis fighting for his life. "Pilar!" she
screamed. "Over there!" She jerked her head in the Spaniard's direction.

"This places me in your debt," Luis called as the hawk
distracted his opponent long enough to enable him to heave
his cutlass upward in a mighty thrust.

"They're leaving!" Fury spat angrily as the governors'
ship hoisted anchor. "They value their precious lives more

than they value honor! Dykstra is leaving, too. He wants to live to enjoy his new role as governor. Tell me, señor, whose ship carries the cargo?'' Fury demanded raggedly. ''In case you haven't noticed, we're outnumbered. Give it up before more of your men are killed. These scurve will fight to the death!''

In a makeshift cell in the hold of Luis's ship, Cato worked at his bonds. Amalie's scream of terror was still ringing in his ears. Already his wrists and hands were slippery with his own blood, fingers numb with his efforts to free himself. When the rope slid over his hands at last, he leapt up and raced to the galley for the vinegar cask. Up on deck, no one paid him any mind as he leapt over wounded bodies in search of Amalie. Suddenly he stopped, watching in horror. Gaspar, sleek as an arrow, was hovering over Amalie menacingly as Fury approached, cutlass in hand.

Amalie, one eye on the black bird and the other on Fury, cast away all fear the moment she heard Cato call out to her. Drawing on every ounce of strength left in her body, she lashed out at Fury with her cutlass, knocking the blade from Fury's hand with unbelievable force. She crouched, feinted, and leapt in the air just as Gaspar's talons crunched down on her neck. The force of his descent pulled her backward, and as she groped to remain upright, her blade sliced into Gaspar's chest. The sleek bird dropped to the deck with a cry of pain that pierced Fury to her soul.

The sound carried on the wind to Pilar, who turned in midair, circling the frenzied melee. Up she swirled, higher and higher, screeching her own cry of pain, then she swooped down, ripping and clawing as she raced back and forth across the bloodied decks.

''No, Pilar, she's mine!'' screamed Fury, her eyes

blinded with tears. The hawk halted and dropped to the deck, her wings feathering out to protect her fallen mate.

Every curse, every epithet she'd ever heard, ripped from Fury's snarling mouth. "Kill my bird, will you! I'll run you through till your blood covers these decks. Murdering bitch! I'll slice every inch of flesh from your body, I'll gouge your eyes till you're blind, and while you're dying, I'll laugh! No quarter!" she snarled, her teeth bared in hatred. Luis gawked and moved backward, noticing that the odds of battle had dwindled to his and Fury's benefit, thanks to the avenging black birds.

Luis watched, his heart in his mouth, his eyes filled with admiration as Fury battled with Amalie. To his first mate, Julian, he roared, "Drive these cutthroats over the side. There's to be no interference. No quarter!"

Glazed, hate-filled eyes glittered at Fury as she slashed out again and again. Up and down the cutlass slicked until Amalie's blouse was in shreds, her bare breasts exposed to the men on deck. "Whore!" Amalie shrilled, stumbling backward.

Fury's blade lashed out again, faster than lightning, curling a streak of rushing blood on the impostor's breast. "The *S* is so you'll remember this moment as you die!" Fury cried, laughing maniacally. Amalie's blade sliced upward, but she danced nimbly away. "Now, Pilar! Pin her to the rail!" she screamed as she drove her opponent backward.

Pilar rose on her talons, her wings fluttering dangerously as she sailed upward to obey her mistress's command.

Her breast heaving, Fury brought up her cutlass one last time. Amalie's weapon dropped to the deck, her hand slick with her own blood. Blood streamed down her face as her mouth spewed obscenities, her bare breasts heaving with the effort it cost her to speak. Suddenly her head was jerked backward as Pilar pulled and tugged. She groped for the rail, trying to unleash the deadly talons holding her prisoner.

"No! Leave her be! *No!*" Cato cried as he skidded across the deck, still holding the vinegar cask. He slipped on the blood-slick surface and dropped the cask. Diamonds glittered ruby red as they rolled across the deck.

"Fool!" Amalie snarled—and in that moment Pilar's talons drove her over the side.

Cato's mad, glittering eyes brought Luis to his side in an instant. "Don't even think about picking up her weapon," he snarled.

With a mighty heave, Cato sailed over the railing to land in the water, searching frantically for a sign of his love. Water bubbled all about him from the cannon shot as he reached out and made contact with a pair of flailing arms.

It was over.

Fury was on her knees, her hands cradling Gaspar's head. "Please, Gaspar, don't die," she pleaded. "Not here, like this. I can't let you give up your life for me. . . . Luis, please help me," she cried, looking up. "Please! I don't care about my mother's secret; you can tell the world, if you'll only help me. He can't die. Tell me what to do, please!"

Luis dropped to his knees, his fingers gentle as he probed the bird's bony chest. When he raised his eyes he was smiling. "It's a clean wound, Fury, straight between his ribs. He won't be able to fly for a while, but he'll mend. I can fashion a dressing with some ointment to ward off infection. If we can keep him at rest, he'll live to soar through the heavens again."

Fury dropped her head in her hands and wept, great heartbreaking sobs of relief. "I didn't kill her, the impostor—she was alive when she went over the side!" she cried. Luis smiled at her outburst, knowing she was reacting with her emotions, as a typical female, now that the crisis was past.

Her eyes shimmering with tears, Fury looked up in time to see Pilar's wing tip feather out against Luis's cheek. The sight made her wail, a high keening sound.

"What is it, what's the matter?" Luis asked, touching a lock of her hair.

"They like you. Pilar does that only to me. You've stolen their affection," she moaned.

Luis chuckled. "I guess they know what a sterling person I am. I never meant you harm, I told them that; little did I know that they understood me. I will never forget the day they arrived on my ship. My crew thought me daft for changing course. I knew something was wrong and that they'd come to fetch me. Now, who is to carry this gallant bird to a clean, calm resting place?"

"I want to," Fury said softly. "He'll rest on my bunk until he's better." She bent down to pick up the injured hawk.

How gentle she was, Luis thought, watching her. It was almost impossible for him to reconcile the bloodthirsty, hard-driving combatant with this delicate young woman who would weep over an injured bird. It must be why God chose her to serve Him. His heart shattered with the thought.

"Clear these decks and scrub them till they shine!" he ordered. "Lower all jolly boats!"

"Aye, Cap'n. What's to be done with the diamonds?" Julian asked as he bent down to pick up a sparkling gem.

It was a good question, Luis thought. "What happened to the diamond merchant? Did he sail with the governors or with Dykstra?"

Julian laughed. "Neither, Cap'n. When the fight broke out he went over the side in one of the jolly boats. I saw him paddle off with my own eyes. I've been thinking about those diamonds, Cap'n. I believe they were stolen. He could have taken them with him; he knew they were in the vinegar cask. But he valued his life more than he valued his stones."

Luis nodded. "Sounds right to me, Julian. I myself had serious doubts about our cargo. Mynheer Dykstra pushed my back to the wall, and we struck a bargain. I had no other choice but to carry them on board. I guess they can be considered salvage."

"That's what we thought you'd say, Cap'n," Julian said, reaching into his pocket for a handful of the sparkling gems. "This is your share, and it'll more than make up for your lost cargoes, and your father's cargoes years ago. You could probably live the rest of your life in luxury with the remainder." He drew closer and lowered his voice. "And, Cap'n, I finally remembered what it was about the Sea Siren I wanted to tell you. She didn't kill your father, and she didn't destroy his ship. Aye, she boarded and demanded to see all our hands. But she was satisfied the man she sought was not one of our crew. The shot that was fired and sunk our ship came from a marauder that she went after. Your father toppled over the side. She tried to pull him back on board, but he was a large man, and his weight was too much for her. In my mind and fear, all I could remember was her at the rail with your father. When I saw the lass at the rail, I remembered. It's true, Cap'n, the Siren never killed for the sake of killing. And this lass has that same trait. Her secret is safe with me and this crew. No word of this will ever pass our lips."

"She was magnificent, wasn't she?" Luis said softly.

"Aye, Cap'n, magnificent she is. A man would be a fool to let such a creature escape his clutches. I saw the way she begged you to save that damn bird. There was love in her eyes, Cap'n."

"For the bird, not for me," Luis said gruffly.

"You're a fool if you believe that, beggin' your pardon, Cap'n." Julian grinned. "I know what my eyes saw. The tears were for the bird, the love was for you."

Luis shook his head. "She's going into a convent. I can't . . . she's meant for a life of—"

"The older a man gets, the more foolish he becomes," Julian said tartly. "I think I'll have the crew tidy this ship, shore her up good, and then we'll retire to the *Lady*. Tall tales and rum will be the order of the day, if you've no objection. With us out of your way, you'll have a chance to get to know the young lady before she . . . You understand, Cap'n?"

Luis grinned and winked at his first mate. "Perfectly! Her crew, are they hale and hearty? She'll want to know."

"A few minor wounds that'll be forgotten the moment they receive their pocketful of stones." He saluted smartly and turned on his heel. Luis nicked the air with the tip of his cutlass. "You're a man among men, Julian," he said lightly.

Julian turned. "All I need is a good woman who will know how to spend all my money." His delighted laugh rolled off the decks.

The *Rana* was scrubbed down with holy stones, from bow to stern, and by sundown no trace of the bloody battle remained. A pot of simmering salmagundi stood ready in the galley, compliments of Julian and the crew of the *Silver Lady*. Gaspar was resting comfortably, with Pilar standing guard.

Fury stood on the stern of the *Rana* dressed in a white muslin dress. Luis thought she looked like an angel. It was hard for him to believe she'd fought as valiantly and gallantly as any man he'd ever served with. Now he had questions to ask, questions that required answers. His stomach heaved at the thought of causing this beautiful creature even one moment of discomfort.

When the first star appeared, he fetched two cane chairs and set them side by side. Fury looked up and smiled wanly.

"A diamond for your thoughts," he teased. The rhythm of his voice remained light as he continued. "I—I need to know why you came after me. When the birds came, you weren't in danger. They were content to sail with me in the rigging. I didn't understand then, and I don't understand now."

Fury shrugged. "I can't answer for the birds. I thought they'd deserted me; they were gone so long. They'd never done anything like that before. There are times when they seem to be so attuned to me, it's almost frightening. I came after you because . . . because I wanted to warn you, to see you one last time. I suppose I wanted to say good-bye. You left so abruptly the last time I saw you. . . . I—I should apologize for my behavior when we—"

"You should do no such thing," Luis said harshly. "It's I who should apologize. I acted like an idiot. . . ." His voice softened. "And I'm most heartily sorry, Furana."

The night was coal black, sultry, and sea-scented. Overhead, a silvery moon vied with the diamond-bright stars for illumination. Fury found herself wishing for cloud cover. When the low, swirling fog drifted in from the sea, she knew her prayers had been answered. Soon the only light would come from the smoky yellow lanterns hung about the ship. She smiled in the darkness. "I accept your apology."

"You do!"

"Of course. But I also apologize for lying to you about my mother. I think you . . . deserve to know about her and why I went to the lengths I did to protect—"

"No, I don't want to hear. That's one secret that should remain a secret. I'll carry what I know to my grave," he whispered, laying a gentle finger against her lips.

"In my heart I knew you would say that," Fury murmured. "I have so little time . . . I must sail for Batavia tomorrow. Weather permitting, I shall arrive in time to . . .

'But tonight—tonight is mine. There will be no prayers to ask forgiveness . . . no regrets. I want to . . . I must be certain in my own mind that I'm doing the right thing. It isn't fair to you . . . it's all I can think of to do.''

"Shhh," Luis said, drawing her close. "This is no time to talk."

Fury was aware of him as never before. He was so lean and hard against her, so warm and strong. She felt his hand under her chin, gently turning her face to his as the soft gray fog obliterated the moon. His mouth was on hers, sweet and gentle. She pressed herself against him, her arms circling his broad back, her mouth trembling beneath his. She felt him growl low in his throat and knew she was responsible for the sound of pleasure. It seemed to her a tidal current rivered between them as his warm breath caressed her cheek, her neck. She regretted the fog now, wishing only to see Luis's desire for her in his eyes and for him to see her own. She felt him smile against her cheek as his hands fumbled with the buttons on her dress. Her own hands felt clumsy as she searched for the buttons on his shirt.

"I've never done this before," she murmured.

"I know." Luis chuckled deep in his throat. His voice was thick and husky, her own sounding the same. Suddenly he lost patience and ripped at her camisole. She reveled in his touch, welcomed it, demanded more, and he obeyed, his head dropping to the softness of her breasts. This was no dream, she told herself, this was what she'd dreamed of for so long; what she'd craved. She arched her back, drawing him closer.

She felt beautiful and desirable as Luis murmured her name over and over, his lips trailing down, down, until they reached the flat plane of her stomach.

Their clothes lay next to them, discarded and forgotten. He was against her, the length of him. She writhed with pleasure as she pressed her body against his. He kissed her cheek, her throat, her breasts, his fiery tongue scorching her body. She felt his name escape her lips again and again as his hands reached out, circling her bare back, luxuriating in the satiny warmth of her skin. His mouth was drawn to the place where her neck joined her shoulders, and she was aware of her own shudder of delight and the anticipation that coursed through him. A tear fell from her eye and slipped down her cheek. Seeing it, Luis kissed it away, tasting the salt of it, as though it had come from the sea.

He moved just slightly from her—only far enough for his eyes to focus on her through the soft mist, needing to commit her face to memory so that she would live in him for the rest of his days. How bittersweet this love, he thought as he drew her close again.

Magic spun a web and cloaked them from the world; they were in love this night. His hands caressed down the length of her body, loving her, worshiping her. Their passion, he knew deep in his heart, was a gift from God. A gift for this night only and to be treasured unto eternity.

Fury rolled over, pulling him against her, into every curve, as she fought to keep from losing herself in the fierce, hot joy spreading throughout her body. She felt light, soft nibbles against her lips. The pressure of his lips on hers was increasingly demanding, persuasive. Her breathing became his as he explored her mouth with his probing tongue. His hands on her body were fluid, hypnotic, touching her intimately, spreading fire throughout her entire body. Her arms moved naturally to encircle his broad back. She felt his hands cradle her head as her wealth of ebony hair fell over their faces. She began to moan softly as his hands tantalized her with their gentle, sensuous caresses. The warmth of his body and the rippling muscles beneath her hands so delighted her, she crushed her lips against his, demanding he return her ardor. Her heart pounded as she heard him emit low animal groans of passion.

"I need you," he panted as his mouth came down against hers, crushing her, driving the breath from her body.

His lips were hungry, demanding that he be satisfied by her. She strained toward him, willing him to demand more of her so that she could feed his insatiable appetite. Her lips parted, and she tasted his sweetness as she felt his hands continue to explore her body. She moaned with pleasure when his fingers found the way to the soft, silky place between her thighs.

The searing heat of her desire washed everything else away. Everything was forgotten, all her promises, all her religious longings. All she wanted now was to be near him, to have him be a part of her. He whispered soft endearments that were barely audible as his lips blazed a burning trail from her mouth to her neck to her breasts, his hands tender yet searching. Nothing matters, Fury told herself as she sought his devouring lips and the delicious feel of his body next to hers. Passion rose in her in waves as she felt him stiffen against her.

"Now," he whispered huskily.

Fury gazed at him with passion-filled eyes. He wanted her, needed her as much as she wanted and needed him. God help her, she meant to have him, no matter what the cost. Her eyes flooded with tears as she nuzzled her head into the hollow of his neck.

The prick of pain as he entered her was minuscule as her overriding passions rose and fell to match the rhythm of his thrusts. Suddenly, unexpectedly, the core of her being shattered, flooding her entire body with hot, scorching release.

Spent, they lay in each other's arms. Fury sighed deeply. So this was what it was like to be a total woman, the kind of woman she'd heard whispered about at the convent school. She closed her eyes, reliving each exquisite moment of their lovemaking. How, how was she to give this up? How was she never to think of this again? Her sinful flesh had betrayed her. Could she atone? Tomorrow she would think about atonement. For now she wanted to lie in this man's arms and whisper all the words lovers whispered to one another.

They slept then, their cheeks pressed close together. Fury smiled in her sleep, her dreams sweet and gentle, and when the last tendril of fog lifted to expose the silvery moon and twinkling stars, she woke, her silky lashes fluttering against Luis's cheek.

"It's not morning yet, is it?" he whispered anxiously.

"No. The fog has lifted," Fury murmured. "Perhaps we should wish on a star. Do you think wishes come true?"

"Not this one," Luis said through clenched teeth. How many more hours, he wondered, before he would have to give her up? He didn't want this to end, not ever. How could he give her up? He wasn't made of stone; he loved this beautiful young woman. He'd proved his love, and she'd matched his ardor with her own. What was she thinking, feeling? he wondered.

"My wishes always came true before," Fury said wistfully. "Of course, I never realized as a child that my parents were responsible for making them come true. . . . I'll never forget you, Luis."

"Nor I you," Luis said, stroking her hair. "I want only your happiness, and if I'm not the person to grant you that happiness, I can at least wish you . . . You know what I'm trying to say," he said gruffly.

There was no way she could explain her feelings. She didn't understand them herself. She only knew that she would never be able to drive him from her heart. In her dark cell at night she would think of him and in the morning she would offer prayers, asking forgiveness.

The silence between them seemed more eloquent than words. When Luis reached down to take her hand in his, she sighed with happiness as she felt her body being drawn to his. She was ever aware of his leanness, his maleness. Her flesh tingled with the contact of his. She felt her body move into the circle of his arms as his mouth became a part of hers, and her heart beat in a savage, untamed rhythm. In their yearnings they strained together, mounting obstacles of the flesh to marry spirit and soul, united for eternity.

In the quiet moonlight they devoured each other with searching, hungry lips. At last Luis tore his mouth from hers, his breathing ragged and harsh. But it was Fury whose sensibilities returned first, and she moved away from him, her eyes sleepy, almost content. She moistened her lips, and her bruised mouth tasted sweet to her tongue.

When Luis pulled her to him again, Fury responded by crushing her mouth to his, demanding more. The banked fires burst into flame as she felt his searching hands explore her body. His touch was scorching, searing, as her own hands caressed his high cheekbones and luxuriated in his lustrous raven hair. Moan after moan escaped her as she strained against him, her mouth mingling with his, her tongue darting to conquer his.

Luis drew in his breath at the sight of Fury's body bathed in silvery radiance. His face was inscrutable in the ghostly rays, but his gaze was almost tangible; she felt it reach her, touch her, and she became aware of the all-consuming fire that raged through her. Her body took on a will of its own as Luis caressed and explored every inch of her. She moved to the rhythm he initiated and felt him respond to her in a way she had never dreamed possible. Flames licked her body as she sought to quench the blazing inferno that engulfed her. He kissed her ears, her eyes, her moistened mouth, murmuring tender words of love, his hands traveling down her lithe form, arousing, teasing her, until her breath came in short gasps and her body writhed beneath his touch.

His lips clung to hers as he pressed her down into the coarse blanket on the deck. He buried his hands in her silken hair, twining the thickness, holding her head still as he kissed her savagely. Fury strained against his muscular chest as she responded to his passion with an urgency that demanded release. He caressed her again and again, cherishing her, desiring her, imprisoning her body with his.

He felt her flesh grow warm and taut beneath him; his avid mouth worshiped her, tracing moist patterns on her creamy skin. His dark head moved lower, grazing the firmness of her belly, down to the silky smoothness between her thighs. He parted her legs with his knee and felt her respond to him, arching her back to receive him. Her parted lips were a flame that met his raging, tumultuous mouth. She welcomed him, accepted him, his hardness, his leanness, his very maleness, as he drove into her.

He lay upon her, commanding her response, and she offered it, writhing beneath him, exulting in her own femininity as she caressed his broad back and crushed her lips to his. The unquenchable heat that was soaring through her beat in her veins, threatening to crescendo into a raging inferno. The pounding of her heart thundered in her ears—or was it Luis's that beat and roared about them? Her breathing ragged, she prepared herself for him. And when at last the searing ache erupted within her, she was consumed in the explosion—a soul-shattering cataclysm that carried Luis with her over the brink.

They clung tightly to each other like children fearful of

being separated. "I'll always love you, Luis," Fury whispered.

"And I you," Luis murmured, his lips in her hair.

"It will be light soon, we have to get dressed." For the first time Fury realized that they were lying out in the open on a coarse blanket.

"Who will see us?" Luis teased.

"Those on your ship."

"She's drifted off, a good distance. But you're right, it's time to get dressed. Fury, I . . ."

"Shhh, no words, Luis, please. What we had . . . have . . . will stay with us always. It's time for you to continue with your journey home, and I must . . . continue mine. Please, flag your ship while I see to Gaspar and Pilar. Please, Luis, don't make this more difficult for me than it already is," Fury said through her tears. "Adios, my love. . . ." A moment later she was gone, down below with her protective birds.

Luis never felt so alone in his life.

"How can I live without him?" Fury demanded of Pilar, who was standing guard over her mate. "You must understand what I feel. You battled those in your way to get to Gaspar. You can't bear to be without him, I know you can't. I feel that way about Luis.

"Oh, I'm so selfish," she wept. "I want to have everything, but I can't. I'm promised to God. It's my destiny. There are no choices. Already I've betrayed my God and my faith and will spend the rest of my life atoning for my . . . last night."

Fury washed and brushed her hair, donned clean undergarments and a fresh dress. Tears filled her eyes and streamed down her cheeks. The ship was moving now, no longer drifting, which meant in a matter of minutes Luis would board the *Silver Lady*; Juli's brothers would return, and they'd change course for Batavia. She felt as though her heart had been ripped from her chest.

The moment she heard Juli's brothers on board, she wiped away her tears and ran up onto the deck, racing to the stern. Hair billowing behind her, she waved once, twice . . . and then once again as the man on the stern of the *Silver Lady* saluted her in return.

When the *Rana* was safe in her berth at the cove, Fury, drawn and haggard, issued her last orders. "Clean this ship from top to bottom, see that her repairs are first rate, scour the decks one last time with holy stones, and repaint the ship. Fix her right name on the bow. Last but not least, fashion a litter for Gaspar and I'll carry him to the casa. Adios, my friends. I'll tell Juli you're well."

The brothers banded together and stared at their captain. The eldest spoke, his voice gruff yet gentle. "We know it's not our place, but the Spaniard loves you very much. If you let him go now, he'll never be the man he's destined to be, just as you will never be the woman you are destined to be. Your life will be a world of holy words without meaning." He glanced at the others, then down at his feet. "That's all we have to say, Capitana. . . . Oh, yes, one last thing. Give these to our sister, one from each of us."

Fury accepted the handful of brilliant gems and did her best to smile. "I want the mouth of the river blocked once the ship is secure," she said. "Can you do that for me?"

"Aye, Capitana. We'll send word when it's sealed. Adios."

"Adios," Fury whispered.

It was done.

"You look like death!" Juli grumbled as she ushered Fury up the stairs to her room. "Fetch up the hot water!" she ordered one of the maids.

Fury grimaced. "I know what I look like, Juli. I don't need you to remind me."

"Tomorrow—"

"I know what tomorrow is," Fury snapped. "I'll be ready. Has Father Sebastian been here? Is he going to accompany me?"

Juli nodded. "He doesn't want to, but he will. It's a mistake. Everyone but you knows it's a mistake, and still you persist in this foolishness. You aren't meant to enter that damn convent!" She grumbled as pail after pail of water was poured into the tub.

"I'm committed to God—you can't change that with words!" Fury cried. "Now I don't want to talk about this ever again. Do you hear me?"

"Everyone in the casa can hear you," Juli retorted. "Tell me something, Miss Fury, have you given any thought to the fact that you could be . . . *enceinte*?"

Fury turned slowly to stare at the matronly housekeeper. "What did you say?"

"You heard me. Those things happen when a man and a woman . . . You should think about *that* before you enter the convent, or you will shame everyone—your parents, those good, holy women, and yourself."

Fury sat down in the tub with a loud splash. She cursed then, long and loud.

Juli covered her ears and turned so Fury wouldn't see her smile. "Where did you learn such words? Not from *my* brothers! Although," she added thoughtfully, "I seem to recall your mother using those very same words whenever your father angered her." She chuckled. "Your God will never forgive you."

"As of this minute, Juli, you are no longer in my employ. Take your damn diamonds and go away. Go to Aldo—or go to hell! I don't care. With those jewels you can live in splendor for the rest of your life! . . . What are you waiting for?''

"Your apology and then I'll go. You see, you're upset, and the only reason you're upset is because of Señor Domingo. You know what you're planning is wrong, yet you're still going to go through with it. You lack the courage to admit you made a mistake. You should never have let him go; now you'll never see him again. He could be killed at sea by other marauders, have you given that any thought?''

Fury's eyes filled with tears. "I want to be alone, Juli, please, leave me to my misery. And yes, I'm sorry for what I said. You can stay on here if you like.''

After Juli left, Fury sat in the tub until her skin puckered. Then she crawled into her bed, pulling the light coverlet up to her chin. Through the window she could see Gaspar in his litter in the sun, Pilar perched nearby. A happy ending for everyone but her and Luis.

She beat her fists into the pillows, tears of self-pity drenching the lacy covering. Eventually she slept, but it was a sleep invaded by dark dreams of a squawling baby in her cell at the convent, begging for wholesome food and sunlight. She woke exhausted, with dark shadows under her eyes that no amount of powder could cover.

As she dressed she found herself wondering if she really could be pregnant. It simply wasn't possible, she thought. She was obeying her calling, her destiny was preordained. Her sins of the flesh would be obliterated. God was all-forgiving. She would serve Him for the rest of her life.

Father Sebastian was downstairs; she could hear his voice, subdued yet anxious. Juli would be telling him all the details of her sea voyage, possibly even the intimate details she thought she knew. Fury's face burned as she remembered the things she'd done, the emotions she'd felt. Perhaps she should make a confession before she left for the convent. Her heart thudded at saying the words aloud to the priest. No, she would wait and make her confession at the convent.

"Damn!" she muttered. She should enter the convent free of sin, pure and holy. She was none of those things. "Please, give me some sign that You want me," she whispered. "I will honor my commitment to You, Holy Father, if this is what I'm supposed to do."

She walked out to the balcony to say a last good-bye to the hawks. They were quiet, too quiet, she thought as she stroked them. They know where I'm going. They know they'll never see me again.

"When Gaspar is well, I want you to find Luis and stay with him," she told Pilar. "He'll take care of you, I know he will." She sobbed then, hard sounds of pure grief that neither bird appeared to acknowledge. Pilar's glittering eyes remained on Gaspar, whose own shiny dark eyes remained closed. "Good-bye, my friends," she whispered, and ran from the room, her satchel bobbing against her legs.

Pilar's diamond-bright eyes followed Fury until she was out of sight. Gaspar's eyes snapped open, and he struggled to raise himself but felt Pilar's wings pressing him back down on his bed. She flapped her wings, admonishing her mate to remain where he was, before she spiraled upward and out through the open French doors that led to the balcony. Instead of following the priest's wagon, the hawk flew toward port and then out to sea.

It was hours before Pilar spied the ship she was searching for. She circled in a pattern that only she and Gaspar knew before plunging downward to land next to Luis on the stern. He showed no surprise at her arrival. Pilar watched him intently, waiting for him to speak.

"I can't let her go," he said hoarsely. "I have to try to make her see it's me she needs. I'm not going to ask her to forsake God. I'll beg if I have to. I told her I loved her, but I didn't tell her how much. I had to come back to tell her I can't live without her. Once she walks through the gates, there is no turning back. But I can't make this ship go any faster, and the wind is dying. I need more time, hours at least. There's no way I can make it in time, I know that, but I have no choice. I must try." He looked at Pilar and slowly shook his head. "Why am I telling you all this? You can't possibly understand what I'm thinking and feeling."

Pilar gave a piercing cry as she spiraled straight up over his head. Luis watched until the hawk was out of sight. He cursed at the sea, his ship, and the dying wind. He knew he was torturing himself by continuing, but he couldn't live if he didn't at least try to convince Fury that he could make her happy.

"We're picking up a stiff breeze, Cap'n," Julian called to him. "A storm is following us. If we can outrace it, we'll make ten knots and be in port by sundown."

Luis raised his eyes, convinced he would see Pilar hovering overhead. Instead, a bolt of lightning raced across the sky, followed by thunder that deafened him.

"Thank You," he whispered.

The sun was merciless, Fury reflected as she shifted her parasol to offer shade to the priest at her side. They'd said little to each other, but she knew he was aware that she'd been crying. Now, though, her eyes were dry, all her tears shed. She was resigned to her fate, her destiny. She wouldn't dwell on the fact that this should be the happiest day of her life.

"Oh, no," she exclaimed suddenly as she was jolted from her seat in the priest's wagon. "Father, the wheel's come off!"

"So it has," Father Sebastian muttered. He reined in the horse and offered the reins to Fury while he climbed from the wagon. He lowered his head, his wide pancake hat shielding the smile that tugged at the corners of his mouth.

A moment later he threw up his hands in a helpless gesture. "The wheel's cracked. I suppose it was bound to happen sooner or later."

"Can't you fix it?" Fury asked.

"Child, it's split in two. See for yourself." It hadn't been easy to replace his original wheel; the blacksmith had looked at him suspiciously when he'd insisted on the cracked one.

"We'll have to walk," Fury said firmly.

"In this blistering heat!" the holy man cried incredulously.

"We were riding in this heat; walking will make no difference except to our legs," Fury pointed out. "If you prefer, I can make my way alone. There's no need for you to accompany me."

As stubborn and strong-willed as her mother, Father Sebastian thought. "You won't arrive in time, Furana. The Mother Superior will not open the gates after dark. Even if you ran all the way, I doubt you could arrive in time."

"I'll take the horse, then," Fury said desperately. "If you wait for the sun to set and walk slowly, Father, you can make it back to the casa. But this is my last chance, I must take it. Please, say you understand."

"Oh, I understand," the priest said, nodding. "I hope *you* understand that this is an old horse. There's no speed or adventure left in him."

"I have to try," Fury said through clenched teeth. "I'll leave you the food and water and my parasol."

A moment later she was on the horse's broad back, urging him forward. The animal moved off so slowly, she wanted to scream. An hour later she was convinced she would make better time if she walked. She dismounted and smacked the horse's flanks, watching him clop off in the direction from which he'd come.

Fury trudged on, her rosary in one hand, her satchel in the other. For hours she limped along, every bone in her body protesting the abuse she was inflicting upon it.

Shortly before sundown she saw the imposing convent in the distance. Her heart thudded as she glanced up at the setting sun. She had several miles yet to go, and most, if not all, of her energy was depleted. She dropped her satchel and kept on walking. She'd come into the world with nothing, and she would leave it the same way. She prayed for the energy to continue. The moment she finished her prayer, she felt a sudden burst of energy and ran as fast as her legs would carry her. She would arrive in time. Darkness had not yet cloaked the outside world.

She could see the habits of the nuns as they walked from the convent courtyard toward the gates. In minutes she would be able to see their faces clearly. She ran faster, the heels of her shoes leaving clumps of earth in their wake. On and on she ran, her breathing ragged, her lungs burning. She could see their faces now, so serene and peaceful-looking, their dark habits so protective. One of the nuns carried a lantern, the other a huge brass key. Another minute and she would be there, she thought exultantly. Despite everything, she'd actually arrived in time. It was meant to be.

In the near darkness she heard a sudden rush overhead. She ran faster, her heart thundering in her chest. The nun's lantern light was so close, she could see Pilar clearly as she sailed downward in her own draft to fall at Fury's feet with a soft thump.

Fury heard the key clank into the iron gate's monstrous lock as she dropped to her knees. She stared at the nuns for a moment before her eyes lowered to Pilar. From somewhere far off she thought she heard the sound of hoofbeats. Father Sebastian, she thought; he must have found a way to make the old horse pick up his feet and actually move. They were looking at her. She could feel their eyes on her, but hers were on her faithful friend. "She's hurt, may I bring her inside?" she pleaded.

"No, child, the bird belongs to the outside world," the oldest of the nuns said gently. "Come, it's time."

"I can't leave her, she's hurt. She'll die if I leave her here. Father Sebastian won't know what to do for her. She doesn't know him," Fury pleaded. "Please, just until she's—"

"No, child."

Fury sobbed. "But Pilar is one of God's creatures. How can you turn your back on—" They were closing the gates. She could hear the rusty sound of the old hinges in the darkening night. "Wait!" she screamed.

Luis watched from a distance, his heart in his mouth, waiting for the girl's decision.

"If you can't leave your worldly possessions and . . . friends behind, child, there is no place beyond these gates for you," said the old nun.

"I won't leave her behind. The God I pray to would never forgive me if I . . ." The sound of the key in the lock was so loud in Fury's ears, she thought she would faint. "You're right, Sisters, I don't belong behind these gates," she called to the retreating nuns.

Pilar was on her feet in an instant, strutting about Fury, her wings fluttering softly in the darkness. Fury sank down beside her, stunned. "You tricked me," she said slowly. "You weren't hurt at all. Why, why did you . . . come here, you wonderful friend." She sat cross-legged in front of the convent gates, cradling Pilar, something the hawk had never allowed before. She lost all sense of time as she sat in the moonlight contemplating her future. Luis would be part of it—if she cared to return to Spain. Her heart fluttered at the thought of living without the handsome Spaniard. It might be years before she saw him again. What a fool she'd been. She should have listened to her heart. God in His infinite wisdom had shown her the destiny that was to be hers.

"It's time to go home, Pilar," she murmured. "Gaspar is waiting for you. I'll find my way, have no fear. Somewhere out there in the darkness Father Sebastian is waiting." She clapped her hands, a signal for Pilar to take wing. "Tell Gaspar I'll be along shortly," she called happily as she strode off into the darkness.

"I have this fine steed, Miss van der Rhys. He has a broad back and can carry the both of us with ease, if you have a mind to join me, that is," Luis said huskily.

"Luis!" Fury cried, running to him. "How did you . . . Why . . . Oh, I don't care how it happened. I'm so . . . You must have ridden like the wind . . . did you?"

"Don't you ever finish a sentence?" Luis laughed as he slid from the horse to take her in his arms.

"Only short ones. I love you," she murmured against his broad chest.

"And I love you," he said, stroking her hair. "I told myself I wouldn't interfere, that I would abide by your decision. I thought I would die when I heard those gates creak open. And when they closed I wanted to . . . do what I'm going to do now," he said, and brought his lips down on hers.

Hovering in a circle overhead, outlined by the moon, Pilar voiced her approval before streaking off to her mate. "Hawhawhawhaw!"

Epilogue

Saianha: Two years later

The bone-thin woman swathed in snowy blankets on the veranda stared straight ahead. Her face was heavily scarred, and small patches on her head were shiny where new hair refused to grow. She was ugly now, shriveled and skeletal in appearance. She didn't speak and had to be spoon-fed. She never turned her head to see the splendor of her house, so lovingly restored by Cato with the handful of diamonds he'd taken from the vinegar cask.

Cato was in her line of vision, but Amalie gave no sign that she was aware of him. Soon there would be a fresh vase of flowers next to her chair—flowers she neither saw nor smelled.

Amalie Suub Alvarez existed; she no longer lived.

"You said you were going to open the trunk today, Cato," Clara said anxiously. "You said when the plantation was restored to its original splendor you would open it for Amalie. I had the servants bring it to the veranda. Perhaps the contents will evoke some response in her. Shall we do it now?" she asked as she linked her arm with Cato's.

Clara was heavy with child, his child. His prince or princess, he thought happily. "Yes, let's open it now," he said, helping his wife up the wide veranda steps.

The trunk was old, the makeshift lock older and made to last an eternity, Cato thought as he pounded at it with an iron bar. He looked at Amalie to see if there was any sign of recognition. She continued to stare ahead, her gaze unblinking. It took both Cato and Clara to lift the heavy lid.

"My God!" Cato whispered as he stared down at a king's ransom in jewels and gold coins. He filled his hands and offered them to Amalie. "It was all for nothing, Amalie," he cried. "You were richer than any queen and you didn't know it. You could be wearing these now, dressed in the finest gowns. You would truly be a queen. It was all for nothing." His shoulders slumped when he remembered the back breaking months and years of work it took to bring all the pillaged booty from the caves back to Amalie's kingdom.

Amalie's black eyes glittered malevolently as she stared at Cato's hands. His head was bowed, his eyes downcast, when she brought both of her clenched fists down on his neck. He died instantly.

Stunned, Clara could only stare at her husband's body with fear-filled eyes. She never saw Amalie's foot about to strike her in the throat until it was too late.

Cato's child was born within the hour, a handsome blond-haired male child.

"You will be king," Amalie proclaimed, her mad eyes devouring the child. "All these riches will be yours. I will be your queen!" Her shrill, evil laughter wafted through the trees, carrying to the four corners of her plantation.

There was none who voiced an objection to her proclamation.

"Long live the queen!" she cackled.